How To Kill Gods & Make Friends

B. Berry

ISBN: 979-8-9866182-0-3 (ebook)
ISBN: 979-8-9866182-1-0 (print)

To everyone who wants to believe in magic.

TABLE OF CONTENTS

CHAPTER 1

IN WHICH VIVIENNE MESSES UP

When her psychic best friend tells her *Yes, This Job Must Be Done Tonight, No I Don't Care That You've Been Drinking, It Involves A Minor,* Vivienne knows her night is shot. No amount of pleading can stand in the face of Natalie and her Peace.

It takes two tries for the magic to catch on the boots she'd borrowed—maybe stole, but who cared, everyone was *far* more shitfaced than her and she's too tired for this—but soon enough, she manages to hop up onto a streetlight. There's the silver lining: bounce spells are *fun* while intoxicated. Vivienne rarely gets to use them in her line of work.

She wobbles a few times, but alcohol has banished all remaining sense of self-preservation, so she skips ahead regardless. The night is chill and the fog is straight out of a horror movie. Who knows what else is out and about this late, but it's been a *long* time since Vivienne has feared things that go bump in the night.

She hardly knows what she's looking for. She's used to vague jobs, but Natalie is normally more detail-oriented than *go out into the dark night and save a poor boy who's being haunted.* Vivienne has taken care of a lot of hauntings in her time, but rarely are her targets/victims moving. Or lost entirely. In fact, she'd say an easy ninety-nine percent of all hauntings were stationary (and she would know).

Vivienne wanders in a two-block radius, squinting through fog and avoiding headlights, and debates the merits of calling Natalie back. Her initial orders *had* been vague.

She's more than halfway numb by the time she spots the glowing figure.

Pretty, Vivienne thinks, and lowers herself until she can sit on the streetlight. It takes a longer moment for her alcohol-soaked brain to process the sight. *Wait, glowing?*

Supernatural Hunter Tip #24: Most spirits don't glow.

Ghosts don't, and neither do poltergeists, or any house spirits. Some sprites do, but the figure is a big enough smudge of light to be human-sized. As it nears, Vivienne sees the teenaged boy she is supposed to save next to the golden glow.

Most of his face is visible because he's glued to his phone. His skin is washed out from the light, but he is young, pale, and sort of gangly. His hair is shaggy and brown. He's wearing the shabby high schooler uniform of an unzipped hoodie and jeans, and Vivienne wonders if he's cold, too, on this late April night.

She slides off the streetlight and bounces to an unnatural stop just outside of his immediate sight. When he startles and looks up, she raises a hand and plasters a big grin on her face. "Hey! I'm a li'l lost, and my phone's dead. Wondering if I could get some directions?" At least she doesn't have to try very hard to sound drunk and nonthreatening.

The kid gives her a suspicious squint. He has at least half a foot of height on her, and she knows she doesn't cut a particularly imposing figure. She radiates harmlessness to him as hard as she can.

Vivienne continues smiling but stares hard at the bright form behind him. It's smaller than him, maybe even smaller than *her*, but definitely no sprite. She can see a head, and two arms, and what are probably legs, and no sign of wings or horns or a tail.

"Uh," the kid says and Vivienne turns back to him with rictus smile in place. "Do you need an Uber or something?"

"Nah, I live not too far from here," she lies, "I just want to know which way Cherry Street is?"

The kid grumbles while he pulls up the map on his phone, and Vivienne continues trying to figure out what the hell is stuck to him. Not many spirits haunt humans, mostly just sad ghosts or shades sent after someone. Poltergeists won't stray far from the item they're attached to, so unless he's unlucky enough to be carrying whatever that is on him—and only if this particular poltergeist suddenly developed a case of being a nightlight—she can easily cross that out.

"I think it's that way?" he guesses, pointing to his right.

(Cherry Street is not that way.)

The figure reaches up and brushes its hand over his shoulder, spreading a faint sheen of glittery gold on his sleeve. He doesn't seem to have felt the touch, but he brightens with a laugh. "Oh, wait, wrong way, the arrow thing was messed up. Stupid Google. Looks like it's the next block up that way and to the left."

Vivienne thinks she's catching on to what's going on here, and she *does not* like it. Ghosts are meant to be static beings. She narrows her eyes at the maybe-spirit behind the boy, and it balks once it appears to realize she can see it.

"Thanks," Vivienne replies. The kid shrugs, then blinks when he notices her scowl.

He takes a step back into the thing behind him. He passes through, of course, but it sheds more golden dust like it's going out of style, and who knows what that shit will do to nearby humans.

"What are you *doing*," Vivienne hisses, then makes a grab for it.

Which is also toward Terrified Minor, whoops.

He ducks away from her with a yelped curse and the not-ghost scrambles in the other direction with a squeal. Vivienne catches it by the arm in two steps. The light sloughs off like water with a bright puff at their feet.

Vivienne is left holding the ghost of a Black girl, hardly into her teenaged years and *far* too young to be already dead, who is twice as terrified as Teenaged Boy Now Probably Calling 911—and who is definitely not her first guess at Most Likely To Haunt Teenagers. She's still round-faced with baby fat, hair tied back in two pigtail poofs, only making her seem cuter and more like Vivienne is about to club a baby seal. Her eyes have the wide dryness of a spirit unable to shed tears, and are the brilliant, unnatural gold she'd been cloaked in.

To top it all off, the little ghost is still in the white robes of the newly dead.

Vivienne hesitates.

The not-ghost slips out of her grasp and dives for the Teenaged Boy Now *Definitely* Calling 911.

"Wait," Vivienne tries again, pity for the spirit warring with her need to protect the living. She falters, looking between them with mounting panic. This sort of moral dilemma is *very* bad for an exorcist, but damn it, she hesitates. "You're not supposed to be doing that!"

The boy levels a flat and surprisingly hostile stare at her. "I'm calling the cops if you come at me again, or I'll let you go be a drunk asshole somewhere else. But I *will* deck your ass if you pull anything else."

"No, not you!" Exasperated, Vivienne groans to herself. Then, in direct defiance of his attempted warning, she digs around in her messenger bag. There are *far* too many free glass jars in there—she must reorganize it when she's not drunk or distracted by existential despair—but she pulls out the little envelope she always ensures she carries with her.

Natalie's very own homemade sleep soot, guaranteed ninety-nine percent effective. It beats a *sleep* spell any day. Vivienne tears it open, advances on the boy wielding his smartphone like a brick, and blows it in his face with little remorse.

"You... what did..." he slurs, sways, then staggers.

When he pitches over, the not-ghost *catches* him with another puff of glittery dust.

"The hell did you do..." he tries again. His head lolls, and after a beat in which Vivienne is certain she's swallowed her tongue, he shakes his head and regains his balance.

So he's the one percent, huh?

Vivienne glowers at the little spirit. "You're trying to become a *luck* spirit!" she declares with an accusatory point.

"Am not," the not-ghost squeaks back.

"Are *too*!"

"What kinda shit are you *on*, lady," the boy growls and takes a wild swing at her. He's easy to dodge, but he's going to fall over and crack his head open if he keeps stumbling around. The little not-ghost tries to catch him, following him with much fretting. He steps through her, earning another squeal, and luck flies off her like a blown dandelion.

"You're gonna end up hurting yourself!" Vivienne scolds. She grabs his arm while simultaneously making another try at the wannabe luck spirit. She feels as though she's herding cats or needs an extra ten pairs of hands and some leashes for these two.

In the stupidest and second most intoxicated game of Twister she's ever been in, Vivienne gets a hand on both of them.

"Aha!" she crows, triumphant at last.

Of course, that makes her a stationary target.

The boy's elbow connects with her nose and Vivienne reels back. She trips over the not-ghost and they both go down with another puff of luck. "Oww!" she whines from the bottom of the pile.

"You don't even *feel* pain anymore," Vivienne can't help but snark.

"I'll show *you* pain, psycho drunk mugger lady!" the boy snaps.

Vivienne rolls back to her feet with only a glance at her poor landing pad. The not-ghost has seemingly given up on them both, curling up in her big robes, hands covering her unnatural eyes.

That leaves Vivienne free to face her apparent threat and would-be rescued victim.

"Listen, kid," she starts before he tries to kick out her kneecap. Vivienne drunkenly backpedals with a shriek, so he overbalances, and this is probably one of the most embarrassing fights she's ever been in. (To be fair, she *is* a noncombatant for this very reason.

Hauntings aren't supposed to involve fistfights between drunk exorcists and sleep sooted teenaged boys.)

"Back *off*!" he shouts as soon as he's mostly upright again.

"Why the *hell* is your first instinct here to get into a fight?!" Vivienne demands.

"Why're you a crazy bitch?" he shoots back.

"Okay, I'm getting real tired of your mouth, and I'm *trying* to save your ass from something nasty, you little prick." Vivienne grabs his arm on his next swing and writes the rune down his shirtfront. This has gone on long enough. "*Sleep!*"

Immediately, she knows it had been a mistake.

The drain on her magic is too severe. It shouldn't be this bad, even drunk, even tired—Vivienne scrubs a hand over her face with numbed fingers and tries to blink away the blurriness in her vision. Before her, the kid crumples, finally down for the count.

The little not-ghost catches him before his head hits the sidewalk. She shoots Vivienne another dry-eyed, pained glare, and somehow she remains in contact with him, allowing his head to remain on her lap.

"Go away," she tells Vivienne in a surprisingly steely tone.

Nat's going to kill me, is Vivienne's last thought before she, too, collapses.

· · · ● · ● · · ·

Vivienne wakes when she registers the smell of burnt copper. The cute ceramic teapot, decorated with curling vines and stylized sparrows, sits in front of her nose on the coffee table. She knows that pot. She knows this overstuffed couch. She knows that god-awful smell.

"Mmgh," she intelligently tells the couch cushion.

"You're awake," comes a sing-song voice from where she knows the kitchen is. "Someone doing magic while drunk again, hm?"

She presses her face into the cushion to avoid the guilt and accusations she knows are coming.

Sure enough, not a moment later, a gentle hand touches her shoulder. "Viv, are you feeling alright?"

Vivienne peeks up at Natalie with a guilty expression. "What do you think? Why're we at Mark's?"

"Benji was pretty mad that you took Fi's boots, by the by," Mark says by way of announcement, still in that horrible flippant tone. He plops himself on the far end of the couch, nearly atop her feet, and sets another cute teapot on his coffee table. His eyes flash behind his glasses.

"Sorry, I needed something better than those flats," Vivienne mumbles, "and they weren't too big. S'not like I ruined them."

Natalie sighs. "I know you were intoxicated, and I'm glad you have a working relationship with those two, but *please* try not to piss off rage spirits. Now, drink, and tell us what happened." She pours the steaming not-tea into an ivy-decorated teacup.

Vivienne pretends to gag.

"Look, I got dragged out of a very fun party, *while* I was winning that blood color game, without your help might I add, and am dealing with a very severe hangover right now," Mark sunnily informs her and sips at his own actual-tea. "Natalie's being very kind to us both, making potions to cure us of what ails us."

"Cheap tequila. That's what ails us."

"You're not wrong."

"Mark, please," Natalie says, prim and proper and professional as always. (Or, as she always is around him.) "Please corroborate Viv's story and let's try to solve this mystery. I don't like that it involves a child."

"It's a benign haunting, you said." He squints at her over his mug, not distrustful, but close. Natalie returns his gaze impassively. Mark breaks their staring match and scoffs, "Not that there's such a thing, but I thought this was a mild job."

"It was, but it was also strange. I don't know, which is why I sent Viv instead of anyone else. We need to sort this out."

With tremendous effort, Vivienne pushes herself up into something approaching sitting. Mark at least offers her a pillow to prop herself up, bless his heart. Natalie pushes the teacup toward her, and Vivienne knows she's not getting out of this, no matter how pathetic she acts. She never has.

Natalie is famously one of the most unyielding people she knows. Others could call her cold-hearted—and have—but the thing with Natalie, Vivienne knows, is that beneath her professionalism, she's *horrifically* devoted to people and causes she deems important.

It's only, like, two people or causes. Maybe three.

Vivienne is one of those few.

She takes the teacup and stares at it instead of the two psychics while she mulls over her answer. The drink steams, not from heat. She can practically *taste* the magic in the air.

"I knocked myself out trying to do a sleep spell, of all things," Vivienne explains, "a little basic thing. I was doing bounce spells alright, but I guess that was the last straw. I hadn't noticed the exhaustion. I tried using sleep soot before that, but the kid stayed up. The spirit haunting him was trying to become a luck spirit."

"Drink," Natalie urges.

"And no, you can't chase it with tea," Mark adds with a sip of his own cup.

She scrunches her nose and begins reciting charms in her mind—ingredients to spells and parts of confinement circles and the finer details of tarot readings—anything to distract herself. The liquid is warm on her tongue, thick, coppery, *sweet*. It practically vibrates with energy. It moves down her throat as if it has a life of its own, and she nearly chokes on it, but *like hell* she is drinking this twice.

She throws the rest of it back like the world's worst shot. It's too much to take in one gulp, and she coughs and splutters. She's pretty sure she snorts some out her nose, but she keeps it down. *Somehow.*

Natalie hands her a napkin.

Vivienne sneezes, and if it weren't in her nose before, it is now. She feels the hot slickness of a nosebleed, too, which, *great*. Just what she needs, *more* blood dribbling down her face.

"Here," Natalie gently says and proffers the napkin again. "A luck spirit? You're sure?"

"She's sure," Mark answers for her. Vivienne blows her wet nose into the napkin. "I tried adding mint. Did it help at all?"

"Don't—*urgh*—mess with my recipe, you have no magical talent," Vivienne forces out. Mark rolls his eyes at her. Loudly. A whimper escapes Vivienne when Natalie pours her another cup of that terrible drink. "Oh, come *on*, Nat. I'm fine! It was only because I was drunk. It's not like I'm dying!" She greatly regrets letting Natalie have so much of her research. Some people aren't suited to necromancy.

But Natalie is her friend, and she's a devoted one at that. She could write her own book on the subject. *How To Care For Your Very Own Vivienne Sayre: Second Edition.*

Vivienne massages her cheeks. Her sinuses burn like she'd been snorting purifying salt. *No, don't think that, don't give them any ideas*, she thinks with a suspicious look in Mark's direction. He sips at his tea again in that same infuriatingly smug manner.

"Drink up," Natalie says. "Mark and I will discuss how to track down a... luck spirit."

"Wannabe luck spirit," Mark corrects.

Vivienne nods before downing the second cup. Her eyes prickle and her throat still burns, but at least she's feeling a little better. Not that she would admit it to her horrible, terrible, cruel, aggressively caring friends. Her body feels fever-hot and pin-prickly, eyelids heavier and heavier.

"Sleep it off," Natalie kindly advises with another squeeze of her shoulder.

"We'll be here when you wake up. With normal tea, even." Mark pats her leg, then helps adjust the throw blanket over her lap.

Vivienne smiles for them, though the potion sits like lead in her stomach and, drowsy like this, it's getting harder and harder to ignore the fourth figure in the room. Blessedly, she falls asleep before it can approach.

· · • • · • • · · ·

"Is it still called a canary walk if it's with you?" Vivienne asks with her hands laced behind her head and slyness in her voice. This is more normal. This is a better dynamic, when she's not choking down terrible potions and having to deal with with the experience that is Mark Ito. (Especially not both of those while hungover.)

"You're the only one who calls it that," Natalie replies, as long-suffering as ever.

"Not true! So do most of the other hunters—I know Ramirez does for sure, and so do Rory and Ham."

"Rory uses it because *you* do, and sarcastically at that. Ham is only trying to suck up to Mark."

"He's a Capricorn, you can't blame him for keeping his livelihood secure," Vivienne points out. Hilariously enough, Hammond is one of the few of her friends with a semi-lucrative day job, and probably wouldn't *need* to moonlight as a hunter. That said, when someone throws around money like Mark does, it's hard not to want to mooch.

"Either way, this isn't one of those. I'm not clairvoyant. But considering the fraught situation—"

"Fraught with *what*? It's a kid and a ghost. Even if she turns into a poltergeist, it's nothing to write home about."

"—Vivienne, *please.*"

She remains silent a long moment, light mood plummeting between them. "...Do you think she's in danger of becoming a demon? I don't think the kid was magical, or even aware of her," she finally says. She spares Natalie a sidelong look, trying to gauge her.

But as always, Natalie remains just shy of inscrutable. Her blunt bangs shadow her eyes in the spring sunlight.

"Have you seen these kids before?" Vivienne presses.

"I won't know until I've met them myself. I've seen a lot of strangers, Viv, and it's difficult enough keeping track of those I know already."

"So you *have*." Natalie may win awards for her poker face, but Vivienne can read her voice like no one's business. They're fluent in one another. "You only pay attention to others if you see them more than once, I know, but you were having visions about *me* before we met. Are they going to become important?"

"I don't *know*," Natalie repeats in frustration.

And again, the mood plummets. They walk in silence between the bustle of the midday city and the humidity of mid-spring. A tracker or a clairvoyant would be more suited to this, but Natalie's horrendous commitment is something Vivienne is used to following. She'll tell her the details in due time. As usual.

Still, she can't stand the heavy silence between them. Vivienne's talkative by nature, more so when nervous, and no matter how much she loves her, Natalie is *very* good at unnerving people.

"Why a luck spirit, d'you think? They're not common, not something a kid would normally think of, and it means she had to have been magical before she died. Or got talked into it by someone magical. But she should know about the risks, right? Demons and stuff. So why a *luck* spirit? Where did *that* idea come from?"

Natalie doesn't respond. Vivienne doesn't need her to in order to babble, but Natalie grabs her sleeve in an abrupt iron grip. Vivienne's step and speech falter.

It takes a moment to trace what Natalie's eyes are locked so fiercely onto, but Vivienne soon sees him: a young man on the other side of the street with the shoulder-to-waist ratio of a Dorito, dressed in a cool grey suit, a drink carrier in one hand and a small briefcase in the other. His phone is wedged between his shoulder and his ear and he wears an annoyed scowl. He could be any young businessman, albeit one fresh out of a frat house by the look of him. But Vivienne knows enough not to judge a book by its unassuming cover.

"What's today?" Natalie asks in a tight, stricken voice.

"Er, the twenty-ninth?" As Vivienne checks her phone, Natalie darts off. "Wait—what's so important? Do I need to call for backup? Nat, *wait*!" She runs after her, bag bouncing on her hip. Rare are the times Natalie acts without explanation, but it doesn't take a genius to figure out why.

Someone from a vision.

An important one, or someone who's about to *become* pretty damn important.

He'd appeared human, but that was hardly a reassurance; witches are more dangerous than any single spirit Vivienne has ever fought, and an urban setting only occasionally deters anyone determined enough to cause havoc.

He'd had a lead on them, and Natalie used to be a track star, Vivienne recalls with no small amount of frustration. She holds her bag against herself to stop it from bouncing and fights the foot traffic at the crosswalk. The distance between the three of them grows.

She catches sight of the guy ducking into a sleek office building. Natalie stops outside the doors to look back, but follows him in as soon as Vivienne gives the nod.

By the time she reaches the building, she can't imagine how far inside they've disappeared or how she'll track them down; Vivienne pauses only long enough to see the shiny name plaque outside the shiny glass doors: *L & M Law Offices.*

A lawyer? Vivienne thinks with dread as she pushes the doors open. At least it's not The Peoples Law Firm.

The lobby is just as shiny as the doors would imply; the gleam of polished floors is only broken by the bustle of sharply dressed people. Humans. It doesn't seem like a magical place, but it hardly puts Vivienne at ease.

Vivienne feels severely out of place, dressed in worn jeans and a baggy sweater that's seen better days, but everyone seems too absorbed with their own busy lives to pay her much mind as she slips through them toward the elevators.

There are a *lot* of floors in the building.

Vivienne sighs before slipping into her own elevator. Two others file in after her, one talking on the phone, the other checking his watch for the time every two seconds.

It is with great regret (and a microscopic amount of childish delight) that Vivienne reaches over and smears her hands over the bank of floor buttons.

Scathing does not *begin* to cover the look she receives.

Vivienne flashes them an agonizingly shitty grin. "Going up?"

The secretary gets off the first chance she gets. The poor janitor outside ducks in, looks at the lit wall of buttons, and leaves again without a backward glance. The Last Man Standing with the pathological need to know what time it is stares at his watch to avoid eye contact, until he, too, gets off on the seventh floor.

A few others step into the elevator, but leave just as quickly when they realize what Vivienne has done. She might get security called on her, depending on how stuffy these lawyers are, but no one seems in a hurry to interrupt their own precious time.

She peeks out on each floor, looking for any sign of Natalie, the frat boy lawyer, or any kind of commotion that would point in their direction. Nothing jumps out at her. Few of the suited people glance up at her and everything appears painfully mundane in the sea of desks, office doors, and cubicles.

It isn't until she hits the thirtieth floor that Vivienne finds something.

When she ducks her head out, she catches a whiff of magic. It's faint but unmistakable.

Vivienne stands in the open elevator doors, trying to place what kind it is—familiar, for sure, but hardly more than a tingle on her tongue. The elevator beeps in complaint for keeping the door open so long, so she shuffles out to track down the magic like the world's worst bloodhound.

She finds nothing on the floor beside several paralegals in a mini library, looking at her in puzzlement. Vivienne heads to the stairwell, empty of judgment and buttons to press, and the smell intensifies.

She goes up several more floors, legs protesting with each flight. One floor is only fancy offices and another floor is some sort of gym. The smell intensifies, but she doesn't recognize it until she staggers up to the thirty-seventh floor.

It smells like black magic.

The smell is cloying now, thick in the air, and *painfully* familiar. It's not necromancy, but it reminds her of purge night—before she realizes what *that* means on the thirty-eighth floor.

It means demonic magic.

Vivienne pinches the bridge of her nose, both to massage out the growing strain and to block the pungent, sweet aroma of black magic. All magic has specific smells, but she's always been quickest to identify that. In small doses (and never to admit it), she actually finds it comforting.

But *this* is overwhelming.

"Nat, what the *hell* is this?" Vivienne hisses to herself before pressing onward. Why hadn't she called Foxglove? Normally one doesn't just summon a demon with no one noticing. These sorts of things aren't *surprises*. The covens scry constantly for illegal activities, and it's hard to hide something as blatant as a demon from prying eyes.

Vivienne finds a ward scratched into the paint of the doorframe of the thirty-ninth floor, a basic protection rune up in the corner. One of the most generic things out there. It's the first sign of magic she's found outside of the stench, though, so she'll take it.

She finds another two scrawled on the inside of the door: *unseen* and *quiet*. It wouldn't do much to keep anything big a secret, but it wouldn't hurt, either.

So it was premeditated. Not that anyone summons anything spontaneously—oh, today I'll skip yoga class and summon a demon instead, that sounds like a fun Saturday morning—but Vivienne has never seen layered preparation that looks or feels like this.

She still hasn't found Dorito Guy or Natalie, either.

The magic in the air is thick enough to choke her, like humidity, sitting wetly on her tongue and in her throat. This is definitely the floor, and to her unease, she finds it empty. The lights are all on, and it isn't stuffed full with cubicles like many other floors; it looks like this could be dedicated to storage, largely unused right now. There are no name plaques to signify offices, no large windows to show off meeting rooms.

She finds more runes the further in she ventures. Most are on doorframes and near corners, places where others wouldn't notice, but she knows she's headed in the right direction when the wards get less hidden and more obvious, scrawled across the ceiling and burned into walls.

Protection, quiet, unseen, conceal, confine, deter, and more. Basics, but layered with cleverness. With originality. Someone has done their research here.

Vivienne turns down a smaller hallway, following the scent of magic both familiar and dangerous, when she is abruptly hit with a wall of jarring unease. It is not fear, but something animal and *instinctual* that forces her a step backward.

She shouldn't be here.

She should turn around and leave.

Each step is a fight against unseen forces. Vivienne knows she has to help, to *stop this*, but she cannot go any further in. With shaking hands, Vivienne pulls her silver-edged knife out of her messenger bag.

She opens a cut on the back of her wrist and smears both her hands with blood.

Vivienne puts red handprints on either wall, and instantly, the magic lessens. She still feels the lingering push of the spell to keep her out, but now it's manageable.

She finds the charm scrawled in marker near a door lined with further runes.

She doesn't recognize it, though she reads it as a repellent charm easily enough. She ruins it with another smear of blood, then goes to work identifying the rest of the writing around the door. From within, she hears a faint crackling, but little else. The magic here is so thick she feels as if she could *swim* in it, but reading something helps to keep her mind clear.

Vivienne breaks the locking charm on the door with a line of red. She crouches to pick the physical lock next, but to her shock, it pops free.

It's difficult to tell who is more surprised, her or the guy inside.

It's another young man, but a stranger. He's shorter, maybe Natalie's height, lacking the Dorito figure. He is dressed in an ill-fitted charcoal suit, minus a tie, pant legs rolled up to his knees, jacket tossed haphazardly in the corner. He's barefoot, dark hair tied back in a ponytail at the nape of his neck, with a sprig of sage stuck in it.

Vivienne and the guy blink at each other.

"Ugh," he groans with a great roll of his eyes.

Not what she was expecting, but the pause gives her time to register the fact that he stands in a large summoning circle. An active one, based on the magic shimmering at the edges, but it doesn't look like a conventional one. *Great*. Perfect. Peachy. Just what she wanted for today: a secretive witch with a weird-ass demon summoning scheme.

"Oooookay," Vivienne says in a whoosh of breath, voice somehow *not* shaking apart like she wants to, "okay, okay. So, that's a fuckin' demon summoning mess you're standing in. I can't allow that. What are the chances you'll quit while you're ahead and save us both some pain?"

"I'm not actually trying to summon a demon," says the guy standing in a blatant demon-summoning circle. He averts his eyes and pushes his baggy sleeve back up. "You should go."

"Like hell you aren't!" Vivienne shrills. But in his defense, his circle is *so weird*. She steps closer to examine the runes lining the circle, spotting necromantic sigils along with further protection ones. Summoning demons is bad enough, but doing weird things with them is Infinitely Worse. "What are you even *doing* here?" (She doesn't sound as angry as she probably should.)

"Stop that. Go *away* already!" He punctuates this with a *push* spell. He sends her skidding back out into the hall, but Vivienne shoves her boot through the door before he can slam it shut.

"Stop the ritual, or I'll stop it for you," Vivienne tells him in a shockingly calm voice. Her thoughts have largely ground down to *demondemondemonaaaaaaaaaa*, but she moves forward again, running purely on This Is A Bad Idea That I Should Stop autopilot. (And about ten percent pure curiosity.)

She's a noncombatant, but she has her knife, her bag, and enough desperation to stop a summoning downtown to do *something*. She can't help but be afraid of a witch who's strong enough to hide from both Natalie and the covens, but if *nothing else*, Vivienne knows dead man's blood stops a hell of a lot of things.

He sighs. He half-turns from her, dismissively, and flatly informs her, "You can't stop this. You're not a witch, and you won't be able to break my runes before I'm done without dying. Don't die in my circle."

"Last *chance*, I'm warning you!"

He turns his back on her and raises his arms. Magical light licks up at the edges of the circle, first violet, then it deepens into black. Panic shoots through Vivienne.

She slices her knife across her palm with a hiss that catches the guy's attention. He casts her a suspicious look over his shoulder, but his eyes snap open wide when he sees the fresh blood welling up. "You can't add blood to my circle!" he cries, whirling on her, even as the spell crackles up between them.

"I'm not *adding* it."

He tackles her before she can elaborate on her threat.

Vivienne barely catches herself upright, but her back slams against the wall and her breath leaves her with a wheeze. She drops the knife upon impact, but with catlike reflexes, the witch catches it. By the blade. But he still wrenches it away from Vivienne. Win for him.

Except then they both realize that there is an awful lot of bleeding happening in the middle of a bunch of runes which should *not* come in contact with blood. Rubbing a bit on some outer circle runes is one thing. Actual blood in the actual circle is quite another.

Loss for both of them.

What *would* that do to a summoning circle?

"If you don't stop this, I'll throw the knife into the circle," Vivienne blatantly lies. "I swear to *fuck* I will, don't test me, Ponytail."

"I can't stop it," he replies. He shoves her up harder against the wall, forearm against her throat, and Vivienne claws at him with scarlet fingers. "It's happening, and I promise you, I'm *not* summoning a demon here. Shut up and stay out of my way, and I won't kill you."

She shoves her chin down and manages to bite him. He winces, and lets up enough to let her breathe, but doesn't release her. "I'd like to see you *try*," she hisses at him, then stomps her heavy boot onto his bare foot.

The spell's magic rises around them with a low, crackling hum, audible beneath the yelp he lets out. The witch hops back on one foot, and Vivienne throws herself at him, aiming to grab her knife back.

Instead, she knocks it out of his hands as they both *whump* to the floor.

It is with matching expressions of stunned terror that they watch the knife fall into the middle of the circle.

The circle seems to contemplate this fresh addition.

As it turns out, any kind of blood in a summoning spell does shit to stop it.

With a snap of magic she feels in her *teeth*, the spell ends, and the black magic seeping out of the edge of the summoning circle coalesces in the middle until it resembles a goopy puddle.

It pulls itself up into a longer and longer shape, drips out new limbs, and blinks freshly made eyes. In no time at all, in which both of them can only watch in mute horror, the demon pulls itself onto their plane and plops down in front of them.

Vivienne is normally *so much* better with jobs, too.

There is a man with a broad back and dark hair tied into half a bun standing over wreckage. He is only a silhouette against a bright, blinding light, and he tightens his left hand on a dripping red sword. Buildings lay broken and ravaged around him, and he stands on a charred slab of concrete and rebar like a king surveying his land.

When Natalie comes back to herself, eight days short of fifteen, she finds she's spilled half her ice cream down her shirt.

Hayley tries admirably not to laugh at her. "Another vision?" she asks with a wiggly, suppressed smile.

Natalie sighs and reaches for the napkins. Normally, visions are longer, not flashes of a static scene. Those are rare, though not unheard of. "It wasn't anything important."

Many years pass before she realizes what that vision had been a first glimpse into.

CHAPTER 2

IN WHICH THE SHOP STAFF EXPANDS

Natalie finds them propped against the shut door to the Demon Room.

Vivienne raises her head with a bleary blink, exhausted, and the look Ponytail Witch gives her is twice as tired and three times as baleful. It's pretty close to the expression one would wear when telling someone No, They Don't Want To Discuss Their Newly Discovered Terminal Illness.

(Which wasn't far off.)

"Where's Dorito Guy?" Vivienne tiredly asks.

Natalie covers her nose from the stench of the demonic magic. It must be something if even she can smell it now. "Viv," she says in a tight voice, "what *happened*?"

"Well, a demon happened, and I lost a fight, but then *this* guy lost *big* time. So at least I'm not that bad. He hasn't spoken to me since we locked that thing in there, and he hasn't run off probably because he knows I'll kill it the moment he leaves." Not that Vivienne could kill a demon on her own, but when your life is abruptly tied with another, she supposes a bit of paranoia is to be expected.

Natalie looks as if she may cry. "I'm sorry," she tells him, earnestly, and stares at the door as if it has killed several baby animals in the very recent past.

Ponytail Witch sighs in complete resignation. "Suppose you'll be calling the covens now. This wasn't supposed to happen."

"No, that isn't my intention," Natalie replies. Vivienne's brows raise, but she doesn't contradict her. Yet. "I want to—to help you, if I still can. My name is Natalie Stirling. This is my friend, Vivienne. We could help you."

His expression becomes guarded.

"What's your name?" Vivienne prompts, elbowing him.

"...Mason," he mumbles after a moment too long, "and I was working alone. If you aren't going to turn me in, then—"

"Dude!"

Natalie jumps and the exhausted pair on the floor snap to attention at the exclamation, which is followed by none other than the frat boy lawyer. He looks like he's run up a couple dozen flights of stairs, hair falling out of its gel and suit jacket in his arms.

"Isaac, what the *fuck*," he demands.

Vivienne and Natalie both look expectantly at Not-Mason. Not-Mason, now conveniently known as Isaac, makes a face like he just bit into a lime without having the tequila to make it worthwhile.

"So you're Isaac," comes *another* voice, and Vivienne and Isaac scramble away from the door with much swearing.

But the demon doesn't squeeze out from beneath the crack in the door like spooky smoke. Instead, it boils up out of Isaac's *shadow*, pure black, like the most terrifying Peter Pan shadow in the world. Vivienne dives away from them, staggers to her feet, and digs in her messenger bag as Natalie raises her arms in preparation for casting.

Isaac looks very much like his life is flashing before his eyes.

Frat boy lawyer, on the other hand, just stares down at the scene. "Bruh."

"What does that mean?" the demon asks, winding its way up toward him.

Isaac throws himself at it, clawing at the semi-corporeal, unsettled demon goop with his bare hands like a terrified animal. The demon yelps, out of surprise more than pain, and allows itself to be scooped against his chest. "You need to go," Isaac forces out in a shaking voice, "*right now.*"

"I can't let either of you leave," Natalie says.

"You *did* just summon a demon," Vivienne helpfully reminds him. "Can't exactly let you walk."

"You did what?!" Dorito Guy exclaims.

"I can help you, keep you safe, and we can talk this through. But we ought to go before anyone else notices the black magic you've poured into the building. Not that I know how we're going to get either—*any* of you out of here, with so many people here, and who knows who could be looking for you..."

One hand still tight against the demon, Isaac draws a *pull* spell, hooking his finger for the fire alarm across the hallway. Deafening alarms rip through the ruined hallway, and the demon shrieks, startled.

But it remains, obediently, in Isaac's grip.

· · • • • • • · ·

In the worst case of bad luck yet, the shop is not empty when they return. (Taking the train while keeping an unsettled demon secret is *not* something Vivienne ever wishes to repeat. Another point in her favor concerning the perpetual debate about Natalie charming a broom for her.)

"You're back!" Megan chirps, hopping to their feet by the table. Their gaze fixes on the newcomers. Without judgment or suspicion, they ask, "New friends, or a job?"

Vivienne (wildly unsubtly) looks to Natalie for answers. Natalie gently steers Isaac onto a stool and Dorito Guy plops down next to him. Vivienne likes how well-behaved he is. *He* follows orders and does *not* summon demons. Not to mention the eye candy perk.

"*Vivi,*" Megan suddenly snaps, "you're bleeding! You can't expect to fix all your problems by bleeding on them!"

Vivienne raises her blood-crusted hand. Yeah, that's definitely the problem right now. "Uh. Whoops?"

"Megan, we were not expecting you," Natalie says, "and no one is injured seriously. I will tend to Vivienne myself."

"I can handle a cut once in a while. What good is healing magic if no one lets me use it to *heal*?" Megan retorts and flounces over. Vivienne can't separate from the guys fast enough;

Megan somehow towers over them despite their diminutive height, bright-eyed and too helpful. "You're cut, too, huh?"

Please stay in the shadow, please stay in the shadow, Vivienne prays, but, of course, life is not kind.

The demon winds its way out of Isaac's shadow, up to eye-level with Megan, and cocks its tiny head. "You're new," it remarks.

Megan processes the demon an inch from their nose.

"Would anyone like anything to drink?" Natalie asks before someone screams.

"Vodka," Vivienne says at once.

"Me too," Megan croaks. It beats screaming, and Vivienne ought to know better than to question their healer's spine, but a demon would surprise *anyone.*

Natalie turns to the two men, but Isaac stares at her like she's the head of his firing squad. Dorito Guy has no such qualms. "D'you have any coffee? Black as sin, please—or like this little thing attached to Isy."

"Oh! I'm Megan—not a witch, but I have healing magic, and I'm good friends with Nat and Vivi. I believe in doctor-patient confidentiality, even if I'm still in med school! I don't know a thing about demons, but I can handle cut hands." They look down at Vivienne's hand again, though Isaac hides his.

Natalie smiles fondly before disappearing into the kitchen.

Dorito Guy gestures between them. "I'm Oliver, and this is Isaac, and I dunno who or what the little thing is."

"Vivienne," she adds, because this is becoming A Thing That Requires Introductions. Of course a summoned demon accident does. "First things first: get rid of the sage, *Isy.* It's not helping anyone anymore, and pine will help with the smell better."

Oliver sniffs at his collar, and Megan leans forward to sniff the demon, which reels back with an affronted squeal. Isaac touches the now-useless sprig of sage still in his ponytail. Megan snags a bundle of pine needles off one shelf with a snap of their fingers and a murmur of magic.

Oliver watches with gigantic eyes. "Do I get an answer how you're doin' that stuff yet? Or what the little black talking shadow thing is? Or is this just a prank? Because dude, Isaac, your shadow is *talking*, and I don't see any strings attached to move this shit."

"That's a demon," Megan supplies. "And it was just a well-aimed *pull* spell."

Natalie comes out with a tray and several mugs. (Vivienne wrinkles her nose when she finds peppermint tea instead of vodka in hers.) "I'm glad we can be civilized about this. Isaac, I also brought you tea. Now, let's talk, shall we?"

"Yeah, I'd like that *a lot*," Megan says with a sidelong glance at her.

"I'm sorry to put you in a difficult position, but I'd like to keep this from the covens."

Megan sucks their lips and Vivienne bites back a scowl. She'll trust Natalie's prudence, but she doesn't have to *like* it, or like making Megan lie to their own mother (also known as the head of Foxglove coven, AKA who they should've called an hour ago).

"Covens are witch things, like that horror show, right?" Oliver asks.

"Yes, and they don't take kindly to demons," Megan mumbles and takes Vivienne's hand like it's a distraction. Their healing magic is cool and crisp like water. She's not used to getting it for such a trivial matter.

"I wanted an uncontracted demon," Isaac miserably tells them. He sets his chin on the edge of the table, hunched absurdly, and his new pet curls over him like a perplexed snake.

"Why would you want one of those?" Vivienne asks, with more curiosity than she ought. She flashes Natalie and Megan a preemptively sheepish grin. "Well, it's not standard fare, right? I get to ask that much! If our blood hadn't ended up in the circle, he might've gotten away with it."

"Yes, he would have," the demon agrees.

Oliver looks between them with a growing frown. "I feel like I'm missing a few steps of explanation here, man. You *sure* we're not on a prank show? Isaac, I'll only punch you once if we are. Not even in the face if you fess up now."

"Did you know," Isaac continues in that same miserable, flat tone, "that Oliver had no idea magic existed?"

The others fall into a *very* uncomfortable silence.

"Dude," Oliver breathes, "*what*? Stop it, just tell me if you're in a cult, or if you owe the nice ladies money or something. Hell, I'll drink the koolaid with you if you need someone to watch your back in some bullshit, but this isn't the kinda thing you spring on someone!"

The sound of Megan slapping their forehead is loud in the small shop.

Vivienne downs the rest of her mug like it has become alcoholic to cope with the fact that they just spilled this kind of secret, plus have a questionable witch with a contracted demon right in front of them. And Natalie wants to be cool with all of it.

Isaac sighs, but Vivienne thinks she may see a vindictive gleam in his eyes. "He won't freak out, and he won't tell anyone if I ask him not to. I'd rather know why you bothered dragging us out here anyway, because clearly keeping secrets isn't anyone's forte here."

(Oliver Not Freaking Out means he's devolved into a long, drawn-out "*duuuuuude*".)

Megan and Vivienne also turn to Natalie for her answer to this. It's a Good Question, because normally, Codi would have been called to the scene to put this to a bloody end, or Vivienne would have been asked to call Foxglove to let *them* put this to a bloody end.

Vivienne also wants to know why it was *Oliver* who tripped Natalie's radar, when the star of the show would be *Isaac* in any other circumstance.

"In his defense, he really did want an uncontracted demon," the demon says, surprising them all. It climbs onto the countertop, and Vivienne sees what are definitely limbs this time, though it crawls on a few too many to even pretend to be humanoid.

It also looks larger.

"I only had a brief look at the circle, and I don't understand much human magic," it continues, "but I know that there was no contract written into it. I had to write one when I received that blood. I think it may be a basic one. I don't know many rules here."

"Both our blood went into that circle. Anything could have happened." Isaac finally perks up, attention on Vivienne with desperation. No wonder he hadn't killed her and ran; he still hopes to pin this demon on *her*. (Not that killing her would've helped him in the least.)

"Sorry," she replies.

"Her blood wouldn't work. Did you know that already?" the demon politely asks and sits back on its haunches to regard its summoner. It is definitely larger now. "I think... There are a few rules. Interesting rules."

"A contracted demon cannot lie to its summoner," Natalie recites, and the demon undeniably *pouts*. "And they cannot go far, either, though it can stretch under duress. And if either of them die before the contract is fulfilled, then you both will die."

Isaac must already know this, but Oliver's wide eyes grow wider. They'll fall out at this rate.

"What did you want an uncontracted demon for, precisely? What could you have wanted that you'd risk *this*?" Natalie asks in quiet frustration. Her knuckles are white around her mug. "Even if you're new to the city, there are resources for witches."

"Not resources for summoning," Megan points out.

"Even without joining a coven, there are *options*," Natalie says. "What were you trying to do, that you would risk this sort of danger here?"

Vivienne doesn't want to watch this. Not that Natalie is losing her temper, but it's hard to watch her lose it in this strained way, when she's trying so hard to put vision puzzle pieces together—and moreover, Vivienne does not want to be privy to one of her rare fights with Megan. Coven interference may be inevitable now, no matter Natalie's intentions.

Vivienne slips out into the hallway. She can still hear them, but it's muffled from the noise-dampening wards lining the main room of the shop. She scrolls through her phone, light bright in the dim hallway, and finds Mark's name.

"H'lo?" He sounds tired when he picks up, which, no surprise there. Even if it's late afternoon. Ah, what a life (and sleep schedule) he leads.

"Hi, Mark, just had a quick business question."

His groan is answer enough.

"Have you heard anything from any of the other covens about any demon stuff? Investigations, purges, any suspects?"

"No," he sighs, "and now I'm curious. And paranoid. Are you getting back into blacker magics, Viv?"

"I was *professionally* curious, don't get your panties in a bunch. Go back to sleep. I'll see you this weekend, alright?" she soothes, and she can practically hear him fall back asleep before she hangs up. She supposes it would be too easy to pass this off onto some other coven and not care about the outcome.

"So that's a no, hm?"

Vivienne jumps like a startled cat. In the comparative gloom of the unlit hallway, she takes a moment to register the two pinpricks of light before her.

The demon stands before her, *taller* than her, almost humanoid.

Isaac remains in the other room, and Vivienne can hear the drone of unpanicked conversation. No one had noticed it slip out.

It clamps a clawed hand over her mouth before she can shout.

"Shh, I'm not here to attack you!" She bites its almost-fingers, enough to warn but not enough to make it bleed, but it doesn't even notice. "I'll behave, I promise you. I wished to speak with you for a moment. You're almost like my summoner, too, right?"

Vivienne shakes her head as much as its grip allows. She kicks the wall behind her, but it lifts her effortlessly. It shouldn't be this tangible if it hasn't settled. Vivienne breaks into a cold sweat, but her mind remains clear. She opens her phone again.

The demon grows another hand and plucks it from her grasp. "Really, I should thank you. It sounds as if I dodged a tragedy, due to your blood in that circle. No one wants to get sacrificed. So, thank you."

It sounds oddly earnest. Vivienne's heart thumps in her chest, and slowly, it lowers her back to the floor. She does not immediately shout when it releases her.

"I may not know everything about our situation, but we can find the answers together," the demon offers. "I know that circle would not have held with dead blood in it, so it probably would have exploded. Lucky for me that I got a little of Isaac's blood with that knife. Unlucky for you, I suppose."

"Yeah, great—" And then the exact wording processes, *finally* ringing the alarm bell it should have from the start.

Vivienne narrows her eyes.

Lucky?

No way, no fucking way, but it makes *sense*, in an agonizing kind of way. Getting separated from Natalie, finding a demon, *raising* a demon, having Megan here, and just—*all* of it. No *way*, but it has to be: she's *unlucky*. Literally.

"Are you alright?" the demon asks her.

"Not really," she grits out, "because I think you may be the *worst* byproduct in the history of fuck-all of a certain wannabe luck spirit."

"I'm an alright byproduct. I'm not a threat, at any rate."

"You are a *demon*."

"One with a pact that neither of us can break. If you kill me now, then Isaac will die, too, and you seem like people who don't want further bloodshed. You have enough blood on your hands as it is."

Vivienne blanches, old guilt rearing its ugly head, before she realizes it means that literally. She glances down at the dried blood smeared on her fingers.

Curious, she raises her hand and presses it against the demon's approximate chest.

It draws away with a whine. "I told you that in good faith—you don't have to punish me for it. I would like for us to be friendly."

"Then tell me why you wanted to talk to me alone," she replies, crusty hand raised like a threat.

"I wanted to test something," it answers, vaguely. "And look, look at how far I can go from Isaac already! I'm learning, and that's exciting, even if you are less than thrilled by it, judging from your expression."

"Then why are you still formless? You should be settled already if you're contracted."

"There were a lot of rules broken today, weren't there? I don't know myself, but this is comfortable, for the moment." It shrugs with identifiable shoulders. "This will be a learning experience for us all. All I know—ah, hmm. Well, I do know I'm a bound demon, I like Isaac, and I like you well enough, too. Let's play nice, since it seems like the boss in the other room wants to."

"More than you two deserve, probably, considering that asshole raised a demon beneath everyone's noses." Vivienne massages her temples at the reminder. She wishes Natalie had given her the vodka she'd wanted.

"I haven't even eaten anyone yet," the demon sulks. "Though if you have another troublesome spirit to deal with, maybe I could be of service?"

Vivienne flinches at the thought. She recalls how *young* the spirit had looked, and what a demon could do. "That's none of your business, and I don't want any of your *service*. Nat will decide how to handle you two, and you'll be out of my hair soon enough." Then, she can return to a certain wannabe luck spirit who she is pretty damn certain is *stealing* luck.

"I doubt that," the demon says, "because I am fairly sure she just hired us in the other room."

· · • • • • • • · ·

It's dark in the offices this late, the cleaning staff not scheduled for this floor until tomorrow, and far too early for even the overachieving morning people. The only sound is the rhythmic *krssh-krssh* of their cleaning.

"Scrub harder," Isaac orders.

His demon, still unsettled, still compliant, obeys. It's bound to listen to any of Isaac's commands, in addition to being unable to lie to him. The contract comes with perks like that.

It's what comes afterward that Isaac dreads.

He wipes a sudsy green wrist across his forehead, trying in vain to keep his hair out of his eyes. His fingers hurt from a mixture of harsh cleaning potions and gripping the sponge so hard, but it's already three in the morning. Hardly half the circle is gone.

"Why are you trying so hard to get rid of this?" the demon asks. It curls over another part of the outermost circle. "It's inactive now. Not that all of this was used. What does it say, Isaac?"

"Be quiet and get back to scrubbing," Isaac orders. He'd been lucky that Vivienne had registered nothing beyond the first circle. He yawns and, to his surprise, the demon yawns, too. "...Can you get tired?"

"Seems like it. I'm *fairly* certain I need to sleep. I know humans do. Occasionally."

Isaac squints at it, unsure if it's joking. He knows the basics of demonhood, but most of his research had been related to the default contract rules that came with them. Loyal, powerful servant in exchange for what usually amounted to the witch's life afterward.

He wasn't supposed to end up like this.

"I know what most of these mean," the demon says, conversational, "but some of these are strange. Why is this one crossed out? It looks—"

Isaac scorches it off the carpet with a curt, "*Burn.*"

His demon blinks at him. "Why?"

"Neither of us want to be here, so don't pretend to be friendly. Don't get curious and don't overstep your bounds," Isaac hisses at it.

"It was this or being sacrificed. I'm quite happy here, comparatively." At Isaac's cold look, it coils up onto itself, not unlike a snake. It gestures with not quite human arms. "I can read *that* much, thank you. I wasn't aware it was a secret—that any of this was—until this little midnight jaunt. I thought Natalie was quite welcoming."

Isaac does not trust Natalie with a ten-foot pole. No one in their right mind would let a demon summoner go, would *hire them*, and wouldn't tie him to a post and force answers out of him before killing him. Demons may be hardy, but coven witches are creative in that desperate, cold way of theirs. It is far from impossible to kill a demon.

And with it, Isaac.

He needs to accept that his life is *bound* to this thing, at least until the contract is over. And without knowing when that may be, Isaac is little more than a meal waiting to happen. Even if he didn't die today, he has a countdown.

The demon jumps to attention like an alerted dog. "Someone's here," it whispers, then dives at him.

Isaac doesn't have time to dodge, but it only sinks back into his shadow, safely out of sight. Unless a bloodhound were to walk in, he doubts he would be immediately discovered.

Unfortunately, something worse than a bloodhound appears: Oliver.

He kicks open the door, hands jammed deep into his pockets. He's in sweats and a ratty hoodie and his hair is an ungelled mess, but he's completely awake.

Isaac avoids eye contact and scrubs harder.

"Mom is *pissed* at you," Oliver says by way of greeting.

Isaac remains silent, and his demon peeks out of his shadow, sensing the lack of immediate threat.

"Apparently no one had told her about your resignation letter until tonight, after we both disappeared today. I'm suspended, by the way. The adult version of grounding, I guess, and it sucks ass." He sighs through his teeth, runs his fingers back through his hair, and glares at the ceiling. There are still a few scorch marks from earlier. "And then all this magic shit? What the *hell*, Isaac."

"You've had enough explanations for today." There had been demonstrations of basic spellwork and a tour of Natalie's potion shop. Oliver had been thrilled. It was like a YA fantasy book condensed into one painful afternoon.

"Why didn't you tell me you were in trouble?"

"I'm not in trouble."

"That Natalie lady sure seems to think you are. She's covering for you, right? And demons—that's *bad*, isn't it?" Oliver demands. At Isaac's silence, he presses, "*Isn't* it? Tell me straight, Isy. Is this the bad that's actually bad, or the kind that other people think is bad?"

Isaac looks down at the demon, now in his lap. It cocks its head up at him, waiting on the same answer, and it looks *stupidly* nonthreatening when its claws aren't out and it's only the size of a dog. "I don't know. It was an accident," Isaac admits.

"So what *were* you trying to do?"

"I could explain magical theory to you for the next year, and you still wouldn't understand." Isaac swipes more hair out of his face, sparing his friend a sidelong glance. "...This isn't your average kind of spell, though."

"That is why we're erasing the evidence," the demon helpfully adds.

Oliver has absolutely no frame of reference for *any* of this. Isaac feels bad for dragging him into this mess, yes, but he's also glad he can talk to him with fewer repercussions. Oliver doesn't know that he's standing in layered spell circles. He doesn't ask what certain runes are. He doesn't know any better than anyone else what Isaac had been attempting to do. He doesn't know how to spill these secrets.

Oliver sighs, squats down, and grabs a bucket of soapy, lime green not-water. "So, what's your new friend's name?"

The demon, again, turns to Isaac for his response.

He scrubs a hand over his face with an aggravated sigh. "You're going to make me *name* it?" Naming: the bane of Isaac's existence. It is why half his characters ended up with whatever Oliver suggested, or named after whatever else he'd been playing at the time.

"I have one *hell* of a suggestion—" Oliver begins with a shit-eating grin, but Isaac throws his wet sponge at his face. It hits with a very satisfying *splat*.

"I'm not naming this thing after a manga." A video game, maybe. Probably. But definitely *not* manga.

"You have a very specific kind of opportunity here!"

"No."

"Yes."

"*No.* Get back to cleaning, I'd like to sleep at some point today." And, apparently, so would the demon. Oliver laughs again, but uses the sponge to scrub. The demon slithers fully out of his shadow and obeys again.

It goes faster, with the three of them.

· • ● ●●●● • ·

Proof that humans can get used to anything: it takes only three days for Vivienne to stop jumping whenever the demon in Natalie's shop greets her.

It's friendlier than Isaac, for sure, but it's also sort of nice to come by the shop and find more than Natalie quietly stirring in a corner. The demon still hasn't settled, which is ringing increasingly louder alarm bells, but it's easy enough to monitor. Isaac appears content to spend his days in the shop, under their eye, alternating between struggling through potion-making and teaching his demon.

For her part, Vivienne is content to spend her days finding *fucking nothing* about the haunted teenager. Her actual job right now, not demon-sitting.

She's *very* glad they haven't had coven witches up their asses. On the flip side, however, since they're avoiding the covens, there aren't many available avenues for Vivienne to pursue information.

It's not every day that someone so casually dodges both clairvoyant and precognitive psychics, especially since what *should* have been the only statistically allowable exception is now working for said precog, but this haunted kid and his spirit hanger-on are something else.

So Vivienne is left chasing dead ends. Mark can't find squat, and whenever Natalie puts together a guess, the timing doesn't work out.

There's work to be done in the meantime, training Isaac (read: laughing at), playing teacher for the surprisingly enthusiastic Oliver, and trying to do her own sleuthing about some of the runes she'd seen, plus her normal freelance work shepherding ghosts, but those two haunt her.

The ghost had been so *young*, and it seemed like she had good intentions. (Not that that counts for much in the world of magic.) Vivienne finds her thoughts drifting back to the splash of scarlet on the little spirit's stomach, the way the boy had been so ready to throw down, and that the two of them were out at god knows what hour to begin with.

So her thoughts distract her even on jobs.

Supernatural Hunter Tip #23: Don't get distracted trying to subdue a kelpie. Or anything.

Vivienne can handle herself nine times out of ten—and bullshit her way through the other one—but she's a noncombatant for a *reason*. Monsters aren't her forte; ghosts, poltergeists, and sprites are a walk in the park for her. Escorts, deliveries, and seances are the easiest money in the world.

Wrestling an aquatic horse creature is *not* what she's supposed to be here for.

"You're supposed to be a drowned ghost!" Vivienne wails as the kelpie, again, tries to drag her into the park lake.

How the hell did someone not see the reeds in its hair?! Granted, she hadn't either until she'd gotten close enough to realize it couldn't talk, but she had been here for a *normal* job. She's supposed to be a guide or an exorcist, not a goddamned *cowgirl*.

The kelpie hisses at her and drags her another foot deeper into the mud. That's going to be her death quicker than the actual monster. Vivienne fights to free herself while simultaneously fending off the kelpie's snapping teeth; someone give her the Olympic gold for multitasking.

She frees her foot but not her shoe and unbalances backward. The kelpie dives after her, and Vivienne's focus narrows to the frothy water she chokes on and the fangs and hooves trying to clobber her.

How do you banish kelpies? Vivienne thinks, but she realizes a moment later that she's too used to *banishing* her jobs. Kelpie may be water spirits, and annoying shapeshifters at that, but they were still technically living. No banishing for her.

The kelpie grabs a mouthful of her hair and forces her head underwater. Vivienne flails. The moment her fingers make contact with the cool skin of the kelpie's neck, she casts her *cut* spell.

It rears back with a terrible scream. The drain on her magic is more severe than if she had spoken it, but she doesn't pass out. Vivienne sits upright, gasping for air, and finds the kelpie backpedaling and bleeding badly from the gash in its neck. Its blue blood sits atop the water like oil.

The kelpie gives her a hateful look before it collapses into the shallows.

Heart thundering in her ears, Vivienne stands. Her scalp aches from where it had pulled on her hair, she has water up her nose, her throat burns from the near-drowning, and she's woozy from magic overuse, but she is alive and upright.

She'll call it a tie.

"If you come with me, you can avoid having to answer to a very mean ghost later," she offers. The kelpie does not resurface. She shrugs. "Suit yourself, don't say I didn't warn you!" She rubs at her sore neck, then brushes wet hair behind her ear and out of her face.

The lock swings back free a moment later. Vivienne tries again, and again.

It's too short to tuck behind her ear.

With a screech, she rakes her fingers through her hair, which is *much* shorter on the side the kelpie had been chewing.

Vivienne splashes out as much water as furious *push* spells she can manage before passing out. The kelpie doesn't reemerge despite the fact that she turns the lake into more of a tiny swamp, frigid and muddy and disgusting.

She's stopped shivering by the time she makes it to Mark's. He wraps her in about a dozen blankets, heating pads shoved beneath them, and coos in sympathy as he helps brush out her muddy hair.

"It was a *kelpie*. Not a ghost," she tells him again, just as mad as the first time.

"And I'm sorry for the mixup. But that man thought he saw a drowned ghost. Anyone could make that mistake. At least you're still in one piece."

"My hair," she sniffles. Vivienne hates herself for crying over it and scrubs at her wet cheeks. Anger only fuels her tears. "Mark, it's going to take *years* to grow back out. I h-haven't gotten it cut since the accident."

"I know, I know. I'm sorry."

Vivienne isn't blaming him, and she can only hope he can read that from her in this state. She just wants to throw herself a pity party, because this unlucky streak is getting *ridiculous*. She sniffs and whines and sips at whatever tea he brings her while he evens out her hair for her. Every *snip* hurts anew. She hadn't gotten her hair re-dyed for years now, and he's cutting off most of the color, leaving tufts of soft grey all over his kitchen floor.

He hands her a mirror when he's done. Vivienne turns this way and that, noting her blotchy face and a smear of mud she hadn't washed off earlier.

So short hair. Not the worst thing that's ever happened to her. It makes her face look rounder, but she could work with that. Her hair is just above her shoulders now, only the last two inches or so left grey, the rest of it her natural black. It doesn't look any worse than it had long, but she has a sneaking suspicion that her hair is now going to be *just* too short to tie back out of her eyes.

Mark leans his cheek against the top of her head. He flashes her a smile in the mirror and tells her, "You look cute. Done crying now? You're probably dehydrated."

Vivienne sniffs once more, then sighs, a little snotty. She wipes her nose with her sleeve. "I think it's about time we take care of this luck spirit problem."

The dreaded Before Anything Worse Happens hangs beneath her words. But he didn't need to be a mindreader to get that.

· · • • • • • · · ·

Vivienne and Mark make a competition out of slurping their smoothies. She's a simple gal: hers is pomegranate. Mark, on the other hand, knows no other lifestyle except that of the rich and extra, so he has so many additions and mixes that Vivienne isn't sure *what* flavor his is supposed to be.

It's... pink.

Mostly.

He slurps louder, though.

"For the record," Vivienne says around her straw, "I prefer canary walks with you."

"I've been wondering what you and dear Natalie have gotten up to. You're cagey today."

"Told you. I've been on an unlucky streak." She fluffs up her hair, held back with a pastel blue headband, and spares him a sidelong look. "It's a mess, but I'm figuring it out. As I *always* do, right?"

"Right," he replies, rolling his eyes, but smiling all the same. He takes another obnoxiously loud drink of his pink monstrosity, and she snorts a laugh. "Well, *I've* been quiet lately. Nothing new, nothing noisy, just too many hoarders with poltergeists and kids suddenly into tarot."

(Mark can't even properly read tarot cards. This does not stop him from selling readings by Vivienne, Fiona, or anyone else he can rope into his shady business practices.)

"Anyone else particularly lucky or unlucky lately?" Vivienne asks him.

"I still haven't caught anything you can follow, sorry. I don't have the faintest idea how you can track *luck*, of all things."

The thing about Mark Ito is that he just Does Things. He has friends in high places, low places (Vivienne an excellent example), and weird places (also Vivienne). He has connections to *everything* in the history of ever, fingers in every single pie, knows all that's going on at any given moment.

For him to give Vivienne a shrug is a bit frustrating.

"Giving up already?" she asks, arching a brow, then takes an innocent slurp.

Mark gives her a raised brow in return, eyes sharp behind his glasses. "What will baiting me accomplish?"

"Using your stubbornness for good. *I'm* not lucky enough to catch a lead, but you still could. And you *should*, because you love me and if you want me to keep playing Ghostbuster for you indefinitely, you'd help ease my mind on the subject of little lost spirits."

"You can't save every sad-eyed ghost, Viv," he reminds her.

"When's the last time the city grew a demon, Mark? That's right, it *hasn't*, not in decades, because people like me keep an eye on spirits like that. And, yeah, *maybe* I am worried about her—she's just a kid. They both were, are. We know what unsupervised kids with magic do."

"And who says either of them are any kind of magical threat?"

"The girl had a jumpstart to a luck spirit *somehow*. That doesn't happen naturally." That didn't happen at all, actually, because ghosts were *supposed* to remain static beings. (If they actually did, Vivienne's job would be much quieter and much easier.)

"So let's see if we can't track down that lead, instead," Mark says, at last giving in, though he avoids her triumphant fist pump. "Surely it's easier to find a misbehaving spirit than a couple of particularly lucky kids in the city."

"Well, because you *said it*, now it's not going to be. It's probably a luck spirit, too, of some kind, and it could be around here or in the goblin markets. Or maybe it's a huge stroke of luck or coincidence!" The more she thought about it, the more bullshit luck was; how was she supposed to think *anything* happened naturally in this situation?

"I'll see what I can do. But only because I can't resist your cute little stubborn self," Mark says and pinches her cheek. She bites his finger in retaliation. He draws back with a scandalized gasp, then swats at her for good measure.

She, of course, smacks him back, because that's what friends do: get into slap fights in the middle of the sidewalk. Like adults. Usually, these things end with a couple of bruises and stuck-out tongues, and quickly, since Mark is a tall, gangly nerd who uses his height against poor short girls *mercilessly*.

But Vivienne is particularly unlucky right now.

Thanks to a stray elbow, most of his smoothie gets upended onto her head.

To his credit, he doesn't laugh. Immediately. Handing her the only napkin, he points out, "Seems to me like you may become an expert on luck soon, if only out of necessity."

Vivienne holds her bag out to prevent any pink from dripping onto it, and Mark digs around as carefully as he can—with her as unlucky as she *apparently* is, he can't shove his arm in there without attracting attention. They must pretend it's a totally normal bag full of totally normal things.

Thankfully, he comes up with a pair of cloth napkins with old bloodstains on them. Vivienne scrubs her face and he delicately pats down her hair as best he can.

"I'm headed home," she tells him, muffled, "to shower and find you a book on spirits. I need to stay away from this until we can actually *catch* either of these kids, or their maybe patron. There are worse things I could do to this search than ruin a smoothie."

"That's fair. I'll do what I can." Vague, but he means well, and she'd rather get home before she feels any stickier. "Let's at least try to rinse you off, a little? See if we can't stop any staining."

They're in a cute downtown area, full of family stores and local restaurants and too many coffee shops. Mark drags her—carefully—into the nearest building, a little bookstore with dangling rope lights and colorful book pyramids in the window.

It's aiming to be a cozy, magical place, probably family-owned, or at the very least, someone's beloved small business. One sizeable room, divided into sections by tall bookcases, crammed floor to ceiling with all manner of books. Vivienne knows automatically it's not *actually* magical, but it still has the sense of comfy awe that any bookworm lusts over.

"Hi, could we use your restroom? My friend spilled her drink," Mark calls to the salesperson already approaching.

Vivienne turns to offer to buy something (any mythology section would have a basic compendium of spirits, and it's more the pointed gesture than the maybe-knowledge within), but the words die on her suddenly dry tongue.

The salesperson is *gorgeous*. Saleswoman.

Definitely a beautiful woman, probably a siren knowing her current luck, but *god*, Vivienne would gladly fall into her thrall.

She's nearly as tall as Mark, built like an Amazon, with thick, dark hair piled up in a Pinterest-worthy braid on top of her head. Her smile is practiced but warm. Vivienne feels like she's stepped into a romance novel; she wants to wax poetic about this stranger's gorgeous chocolate brown eyes within moments of meeting her. She would write goddamned sonnets to get her to speak with her.

None of this makes it off her tongue.

And Mark, of course, reads all of this from her loudly amorous brain.

While Vivienne continues privately embarrassing herself, mouth agape all the while, Mark dryly adds, "We'll buy something, but we'd like to get all this stuff off before it gets any stickier. Looks like it's already given her brain freeze."

"Ooh, yeah, that looks messy." The exquisite stranger gives Vivienne the worst look-over in existence. "You do technically have to buy something, please, but you can try to rinse some of that off beforehand."

"You wouldn't want us to get sticky pink smoothie everywhere and ruin any nice books," Mark says, and the woman blinks at him like he'd read her mind. Because he's an asshole sometimes.

She points him in the back's direction, and Mark puts a firm hand on both of Vivienne's shoulders, clearly ready to strong-arm her into behaving something like a functioning human being.

But then, beyond the stunning bookstore lady, Vivienne sees *them*.

She stops dead in her tracks, head craned over, with the type of outrage you only get when you stumble onto something you have been owed for too long. Mark gives her a push, but she digs her heels in.

It's the teenager with the bright gold smudge of a spirit following half a step behind.

He's wearing the same polo and apron combination as the lovely woman, so he probably works there, too, which means they now have a way to corner the spirit and figure out what the hell is up with them.

Still, it's straight bad luck when the first words Vivienne says aloud in front of her abrupt crush are a loud, "Son of a *bitch*!"

The day is chill, but the spring sunlight is bright. Knees in the dirt, Natalie works with delicate and gloved hands to plant her garden. She uses one of the coven community gardens because the myriad of fumes in her shop kills most window boxes she attempts.

Except the mint. The mint will outlast them all.

She dips into her box for another seedling, then finds herself on a different spring day.

Cherry trees surround the area, dripping petals, and a long, white path has been laid out between two groupings of chairs. A tall woman stands at the makeshift altar. Her deep brown hair is up in a crown braid, pinned in place with a wreath of white roses and rosemary. Her bouquet is the same, accented with hemlock. Her ivory dress is sleek, off the shoulder, pooling behind her like a waterfall.

She cannot see many of the guests, but Hayley's ruby hair always stands out in a crowd.

Another woman steps onto the aisle. She holds a matching bouquet and an even brighter smile. Her jet black hair is partially held back by a jeweled comb, the rest of it curling just above her shoulders. Her dress is not white, but silver starlight, glinting in the day like diamond.

Natalie comes back to herself and notices she's already smiling. She has accidentally crushed the pepper seedling in her hand, but for the sake of a happy vision, she doesn't mind. She sets it to the side and resumes her work with new cheer.

CHAPTER 3

IN WHICH EMIL CONTEMPLATES HIS LIFE

Emil has been having a *weird* time lately.

Alright, so the past half-year or so has been something out of a nightmare, but at least it settled into a routine. School and work and work and school. Overbearing neighbors, too-empty apartment, and confusing bills he can't answer for. It's weird, and hellish, but he's adjusted.

And then, things started getting *weirder*, and that's the part he's losing his shit over.

Some jerks at school have laid off, and he's begun getting better grades. Great.

He almost got hit by a car during the last rainstorm, but not only did the driver stop and apologize, it was a nice old man who also insisted on getting him a hot coffee and some food from the nearest shop. Cool, he supposes.

He's found two twenties and a fifty on the ground in the past month, found someone's lost dog (it trotted right up to him) and got a reward of a hundred bucks, and he hasn't been late to work or school in ages. The day he randomly reread his bio notes on the train, they got a pop quiz on exactly what he'd just covered. Neat.

Aside from the bizarre run-in with the drunk Asian lady, his life has been good recently. *Suspiciously* so.

"Too bad you have school, all your shifts have been golden lately," Dana remarks. Emil snaps to attention and opens his mouth, but, just as casually as before, she continues, "No, you can't skip school. But if you think you could make it for another evening shift or two during the week, I'd be happy to let it happen."

"Yeah, I mean, please—?"

She chuckles. "They're yours, but don't make us check your grades." Their store employs a lot of students, mostly college, but some high schoolers. Thanks to the fact that Dana and Nico take the whole family-owned air very seriously—it's not even *their* family, mind—there's a lot of babysitting. The university students claim they appreciate it. Emil has enough mother hens in his life, thank you very much, and most of them are Russian. That's *plenty*.

"Just give me the hours. Please."

So he gets more hours, his grades don't suffer, and everything is great.

Right.

Except he still goes home to an empty apartment, and he can't bear to go into the other room, and every sympathetic look he gets suffocates him. It's been *months*. He's *fine*.

A customer with a stroller nearly knocks over a stand of keychains and bracelets, but he catches it at the last second. Emil didn't know he *had* reflexes that fast.

"Good catch!" Dana exclaims.

"Uh. Thanks." The hairs on the back of his neck stand on end, and it feels like someone's watching him. Unseen. He's felt that *a lot* recently, and he seesaws back and forth on whether or not he wants it to be his mother. It'd be nice. It also sounds like the beginning of a horror movie.

The second biggest, weirdest red flag in his Did My Life Just Become A Horror Movie Backstory list is the recurring figure of the drunk Asian lady who may or may not have drugged him.

All Emil remembers from that night is needing air—at ass o'clock at night and in a maybe questionable neighborhood, sue him—and running into the weird lady with the bad dye job and habit of talking to herself. They'd almost fought, or at least he tried to run for it and maybe punch her, but he could have *sworn* she drugged him with something.

Except he woke in his bed the next morning completely fine. Nothing missing, no injuries, only fuzzy memories.

And now, this is her second time in the bookstore. She's settled into one of the cushy chairs in the reading corner, flipping through the latest Stephen King novel and sipping at a smoothie. Emil has been avoiding her as best he can, but he can *feel* her eyes on him.

So things are weird. He's been having some high points, a lot of little great things stacking up in his favor, but he also has a stalker now. Cool.

"Have you greeted that customer?" Dana asks, leaning across the counter to speak to him. Her face is turned toward him, but her attention is solely on Stalker Customer.

"Uh, yeah," Emil lies. Blatantly. The back of his neck itches again. "She's... just browsing. She's been in here before..."

"Yeah, I remember her. Sweary and blushy." Emil only remembers one of those. Dana misses the squint he shoots her. "You know her?"

Emil shakes his head so much he probably looks like a rabid dog.

"Well, a new regular is nice, but make sure she buys something today." Dana is usually forgiving of the usual people who come in, read something, and meander out; Nico is the hard-ass between them. But even she seems leery of Stalker Customer. "Ask her if she needs help finding anything in the horror section."

If even Dana thinks she's weird, then Emil is in trouble.

He'd once bluffed his way out of an attempted mugging by lapsing into Russian and wildly claiming he had ties to the mafia; he debates the merits of it now.

The woman gives him a sunny smile when he nears. "Hi," Emil bites out, "do you need help finding anything today?"

"What does your mythology section look like?" she asks in return.

Emil stares at her; she's not fifteen feet from it, and both he and Dana had *watched* her struggle with higher shelves for a full ten minutes.

"I mean, how reliable is it all?" she corrects. She closes her book, finger between the pages, making it clear she's not done here yet. "Don't get me wrong, I like books, and I'd love to help a cute little store like this. But in this economy, it's not like I can throw money at *any* old ghost story."

"I'm sure we have several books on, uh, real ghosts," Emil tells her in the dead voice of a retail worker having to talk to That Customer. "Or we can order something for you."

Stalker Customer laughs like he'd told a good joke. "Nevermind then!"

He gets the distinct feeling he'd just been tested. He doesn't like it. "So is there anything else I can help you find? We have a sale on hardcovers right now, if you're looking for more Stephen King."

The woman continues smiling at him, but her eyes find a spot just over his shoulder. Without changing, somehow, her expression becomes a little more *ominous*. (Another checkmark on his Did My Life Just Become A Horror Movie Backstory list.) "I think I'm good for today, but thanks. And don't worry, I'll buy something—please tell your cute manager that she doesn't have to hate me forever."

He'd rather eat his tongue than do whatever *this* is between the two of them, but if it gets her off his back and onto Dana's plate instead, he'll take it.

· · • • · • · • · ·

"Only five more daaa-aaaays," Oliver sings, sprawling across the countertop like it's his new bed.

"Five more days to put up with you here," Isaac mutters. He pulls his pile of herbs away from Oliver's flailing.

"Until what?" Natalie asks, not looking up at either of them, still stirring her pot. She's shockingly dismissive of two strange men doing fuck-all in her potion shop, but Isaac won't be the one to critique her business practices.

"Until he's no longer adult-grounded," the demon supplies.

It flops onto the countertop next to Oliver, making him snicker. "I'm suspended at work. Isaac literally vanished, and I walked off my shift since you guys had kidnapped me."

Natalie only then looks up, and her concern would be touching, if Isaac trusted it. "I'm sorry, it didn't occur to me what sort of trouble you two could get into."

"Just me. Isaac quit, which you *had* to have known, since you shanghaied him here."

"If you're in danger of losing your job, I can do what I can to help you."

Oliver snickers again. "Nah, I'm not in any danger of that." There were perks to his family name being on the building. Isaac could only *imagine* that kind of life security. "But maybe I'll take up potion-making, too? Seems cool."

Isaac spends a horrified moment picturing what it would be like to unleash Oliver Lynch on an unsuspecting magical populace.

"You can't be any worse than Isaac," the demon says, and Oliver smothers his laughter at his friend's expense in the sleeves of his Temporary Unemployment Hoodie. (Isaac doesn't know when they decided to get chummy with each other, but if they keep ganging up on him, there will have to be repercussions.)

The front door bell tinkles and Oliver bounds back to his feet. The demon retracts into Isaac's shadow with a sulk he *feels*.

"It's just me, and you've *got* to work on that smell," Vivienne calls, kicking off her boots as she stomps into the entryway. She runs a hand back through her shorter hair, grimaces, but then smiles tiredly for them. "Hey, Oliver, you're haunting here again? You're gonna make me believe we got a two for one deal."

Oliver spares her a finger gun. "My friend got outed as a witch, ended up with the *coolest* job, and I've got the golden opportunity to teach a demon thing about pop culture."

"I can't get rid of him," Natalie indulgently adds.

Vivienne glances over at the group of them in the store, smile fading. It's gone by the time she's facing Natalie. "Nat, I'm gonna need outside help on this."

Isaac gets the sense that a hell of an unspoken conversation passes between them. Neither look happy, but not angry, either, so he doubts a fight is on the immediate horizon.

"Whatever you think is best," Natalie finally murmurs. "I'll run my errands now, then. Please don't break my shop while I'm gone."

"Thanks," Vivienne tells her, just as quiet, and squeezes her wrist when she passes to leave. She looks at Oliver, but he plays dumb, unmoving in his seat.

"You're going to ask for help disposing of that spirit," Isaac cuts in. With Natalie gone, he unashamedly pushes the dried lavender he'd been sorting aside and rests his forehead against the counter. He wonders if he's running a fever; it feels too deliciously cool to be normal. "Why."

"You're going to have to feed it eventually," she reasons, sitting down beside him, "and some of my jobs are sensitive. Yours included. I plan on bringing back any captured poltergeists, ghouls, and maybe a stupid kelpie, but you can't just feed it pizza rolls and expect this to end happily. Interesting that you think I'm asking about it and not you. "

The demon winds up out of the shadow of Isaac's hood. It wraps itself around her wrist, coiled in her hand, like an overly friendly snake. Vivienne goes so far as to pet it. Her smile returns.

"We're looking into other avenues for this to end without bloodshed. You're a spellwriter, aren't you, Isaac?" she asks.

His head snaps up.

Vivienne smiles sunnily at him, and his demon has put so much of its mass onto her she looks like a snake charmer with a boa constrictor. A very lumpy, top-heavy one. With arms. "No one ratted you out, and there's no scary, intrusive magic on you. I spent a good many years with a spellwriter as my best friend, and I know what they're like, what the magic looks like. You either wrote that circle yourself, or hired someone to do it for you, and considering how closed-off you are, I doubt it was the latter."

"Dude, that was some straight-up Sherlock shit," Oliver stage-whispers at him.

Vivienne laughs. "No, not really! I'm not a detective, and I'm not clairvoyant, though I know them, and *yes*, they're as aggravating as you think. I hope you've noticed that Natalie didn't drag you to him immediately, so, you're welcome."

Isaac will not thank the woman who ruined his spell and dragged him to another woman who basically kidnapped him and his friend for not making his situation *worse*.

To her credit, she must realize how it sounds, because she drops the cheery act and sets the demon back down onto the countertop. "Alright, this sucks for everyone involved, I *get it*. Trust me, I do—I know what it's like to be on the wrong end of the coven morality stick. But you scratch our back, we scratch yours, and we can offer you protection, knowledge, and resources here. Has it occurred to you that you're in a shop *full* of magical ingredients, and you're a spellwriter looking to invent something that's never been done before?"

"...Not in those terms," he admits, and grudgingly, "but I'd fare better on my own. I had this under control already."

"And now you don't," Vivienne points out with zero remorse. But despite Isaac's growing annoyance, she dismisses him and sets her elbows on the countertop, chin in her hands. This puts her nose to maybe-nose with the demon. "So, little demon puddle, how are *you* doing?"

"...Me?"

"Yes, you. We're going to have to get *awful* friendly if we want this shitty plan to work."

"What shitty plan?" Isaac demands.

"Keeping you and your symbiote here safe until whatever Natalie's waiting on kicks in." She has the gall to shrug, too. "You learn to trust precogs, but I understand that it drives you up a wall for a bit. First things first—making you two smell like daisies instead of black magic, and making sure *you* stay fed."

The demon recoils from her, *reproachfully*, enough of its mouth visible to pick out its frown. It does not deny its hunger or defend how well they've stayed hidden together thus far.

It is then that Isaac realizes it can't lie to *her*, either.

Just. Great.

· · • • · • • • · ·

Isaac is, admittedly, skilled at quite a few things. Some marketable, some not, but on the whole, he's content with where his talents lie.

Potion-making is *not* one of those talents.

Natalie appears to be a woman of endless patience, but even she sighs when the third batch of dreamless sleep draught goes up in literal smoke. Isaac keeps waiting for the snap, the anger, the hostility, but so far it hasn't come.

Doesn't stop him from flinching every time something gets set down too hard, though.

"You don't have much experience with potions, do you?" Natalie asks at last.

"I'm self-taught with most of my magic. I've never needed to make anything I couldn't just buy," he mulishly replies.

"There are other places to buy potions?" the demon asks and leans on the counter beside him. The thing still hasn't settled, and he knows that's making Natalie nervous. Something is going to give. Eventually.

"I'm not the only shop in the city. Not the largest, nor the best." Natalie hauls the mixing bowl to the kitchen to dump it out. From there, she calls, "But you shopped elsewhere anyway, didn't you, Isaac? I don't believe you've lived here very long."

"...About two years," he allows. Two years spent with careful prep work and forging a new life in an unfamiliar city, two years of lying and sneaking and hoping—all down the drain, thanks to the happily unsettled demon beside him. Isaac adds, "I appreciate your discretion, but we're not going to be best friends. I don't even know why you're trying to teach me."

"Like cooking, or sewing, or changing a lightbulb, I'm of the opinion that everyone should know the basics."

"Yeah, but..." But Isaac is a semi-employed lying summoner. Natalie doesn't owe him shit just because she and Vivienne were the ones to find him. Keeping them covered and perhaps eventually fed is more than enough.

"Have you thought of a name for the demon yet?" Natalie asks, and Isaac flinches.

The demon turns to him again with what is undeniably hope in its hollow eyes.

"I'll name it when it settles," he deadpans, watching it wilt again. It's getting harder and harder to keep referring to the demon as *it*—spending a solid week with something makes you think of it less as some*thing* and more as some*one*.

Natalie returns, wiping her hands on her apron, and spares them an appraising look. Isaac hates how she makes him feel like he's under a microscope. The other shoe *will* drop—he wishes she'd stop with the waiting game. Isaac has never been strung along like this. He needs to know what she wants from him already.

"I'll clean up here, you can head out a little early tonight," Natalie says.

"Thank you," the demon answers for him.

"Spend the extra time talking over your contract, would you? I'm having to clean the smell every night now, and I'm almost out of charcoal. I don't know when Vivienne will come up with her next latest idea to fix it..."

He nods, mouth a thin line, and shoves his sparse notes into his backpack. The demon goes in with the pile of papers, since Isaac is beginning to *feel* when it goes into his shadow. Not that it's painful, but he doesn't like it.

"And Isaac, you know you can bring your familiar with you, right? Most are smart enough to stay away from the dangerous ingredients, and I've had no accidents with familiars here. Bring her tomorrow?"

Isaac, just a step from the front door (and thus escape), scowls at the wood. Natalie had likely meant to politely imply that with a familiar around, he wouldn't act like he has a stick up his ass. He makes a conscious decision to relax his shoulders before answering. "I don't have one."

He hears her intake of breath from there, and when she speaks, it is with a low, pained tone. "Oh. I'm so sorry."

"No, it's not like that—I've never had one. See you tomorrow." Without waiting for an answer, he heads outside, and slams the door behind him.

The evening air helps to clear the foul taste in his mouth, but he knows that is going to be A Thing to deal with tomorrow. Witches are just so *finicky*. Opinionated, nosy, and generally nightmares to deal with. Himself included, but that's probably why he only has two friends. Two point three, counting the demon.

His apartment is dark and warm when he returns. As always. Isaac does little more than kick off his shoes, pull off his hoodie, turn on the fan, and lay down on the floor in front of it. He groans into the emptiness.

"You're very strange," his demon tells him, as conversational as ever. That's strange, too, but Isaac doesn't have the energy to bother with it. "Why was Natalie concerned that you didn't have a familiar?"

Isaac rolls over onto his back and throws an arm over his eyes. "Natalie is concerned about a lot of things."

"And you aren't?"

"What am I supposed to be concerned with anymore? I'm contracted to a demon. Either an overzealous vigilante will kill us, Natalie is a patient sadist, or I survive to the end of the contract and *you* eat me."

Isaac feels the lightest of touches against his shoulder. "I don't want to eat you."

He doesn't move his arm away. A contracted demon cannot lie to its host, but there is an enormous gap between knowing something to be technically true and *believing* it. There must be a loophole.

Or maybe their rushed contract was so haphazard it *can* lie to him.

"No one wants to get sacrificed," the demon reasons with another feather-soft touch. "Tell me what you were trying to do with your circle, with me, and I'll tell you when the contract ends. Vaguely, at any rate, since it is more of a feeling than a scheduled date."

If it's already asking those kinds of questions, it already knows too much. "You need to settle already. That'd make things a lot easier." Then he wouldn't have to be so paranoid. A settled demon is invisible in a crowd; a talking shadow is decidedly *not*.

When the demon is silent for a beat too long, Isaac peers out from under his wrist.

As it turns out, the old theory that you wouldn't recognize yourself if you were presented with an exact copy is true.

It takes Isaac several seconds to realize he's looking at what is meant to be *himself*.

Hunched over him like it's auditioning for a horror movie monster, dark brown hair falls loose over its shoulders, hazel eyes almost *too* wide as the demon takes in Isaac's every reaction. At least it's not grinning.

He doesn't recognize himself. It's too wrong, although it must be right—it's too *Other*. The demon is naked, back arched subtly like a cat readying its pounce, muscles shifting under brown skin. It even has the same scars as Isaac, from what he can see—the one on the outside of his thigh from where he fell out of a tree as a kid, the one on his hand from a drunk cooking accident with Walker, the one in the crook of his elbow from the time someone tried to find out what witch's blood on a full moon could do.

But it's not *him*. He hates that it's his body, because it's not *his* body, but it is and it *isn't*. He clenches his fists so hard he draws blood.

It's not right, it's not *right*, it's not right at all—

Isaac shoves the demon away. His heart pounds in his ears and his wet hands shake. "No," he croaks and unclenches his fists. He wipes his palms on his sweats, glaring at the carpet instead of the demon.

"I didn't mean to startle you," it says with another touch to his shoulder. This time, it feels like fire, and Isaac flinches as though stung.

"*No*, not—not like me," he tries again. "Not me." He wishes to god his voice would stop shaking. He can't explain the one-two punch of seeing a perfect doppelgänger—already a pretty devastating blow to any human's psyche—mixed with a good old dose of his own body issues.

"I'm sorry," the demon murmurs. It does not touch him again.

Isaac rubs at his arms. He can't *afford* to show any kind of exploitable weakness, no matter how unassuming the demon presents its personality right now.

When Isaac gets his breathing back under control, he finally glances its way again.

It isn't him anymore, at least. Minor miracles. Who knew a demon could create a perfect copy when settling.

Now, it's Vivienne sitting cross-legged before him. Still nude, still watching him with rapt attention. Her hair is loose, gentle waves framing her round face, accentuating her softer curves. Her complexion is far paler, but he's mildly surprised to see just as many scars, if not more. But a woman comfortable in her own skin, no doubt, even if it's a demon wearing it right now, even if she would freak out upon seeing this, too.

"No, not anyone who already exists," Isaac tells it. Calmer now, because this is a stranger in a strange body before him instead of anything else. "You need to—well, be yourself, if you have a self." Why wasn't there a manual for your newly summoned demon? Demons were supposed to arise from human ghosts, and it speaks with a personality, however mild, so that meant *something*. "You *have* a self. Right? Be whatever feels natural for *you*."

"In my defense, following the blood was easy to do," the demon murmurs, before its fake skin sloughs off again like so much ashy-peachy water. It sighs, a puff of air Isaac isn't entirely sure it *needs*, and it rises out of its own not-body with yet another human guise. "I'm not certain anything feels natural," it adds, stretching out new arms, shaking out a shaggy, fluffy crop of sand-colored hair.

Beyond the initial, knee-jerk things to notice—light skin, thin frame—the thing that Isaac first truly registers is that the demon looks *young*. He had been expecting something out of a gritty supernatural television drama, rugged and hard-lined and a touch gothic. Instead, he'd peg the demon at about twenty, *if* that. Fresh-faced and bright-eyed and bushy-tailed.

Actually, very much still tailed, if not bushy.

Isaac leans sideways to squint at the curled black tendril still poking out somewhere behind the demon.

"This feels right, in a way, but no more right than you two. Somehow nostalgic, maybe? As comfortable as any physical form, so if it's allowed, I'll keep with this?" the demon continues. It blinks when it notices Isaac's attention, then twists to look at its own extra limb. "Oh, hmm. Maybe not as good as you'd hoped... This is harder than I'd thought."

"You're a guy?" Isaac asks with narrowed eyes.

The demon looks down at the flaccid cock between its legs.

"No, that's not what decides it. Are you a man?" He cannot bring himself to say *like me* when the image of the demon wearing his image as skin sits behind his eyes. "Or a woman? Something else?"

"I don't understand. Yes?"

"Are you a he. Or a she."

The demon again looks down at itself, but this time, its hands. Its fingers still end in black, sharp points, and Isaac pinches the bridge of his nose in a futile attempt to ward off his coming headache.

"I want to be like you," the demon eventually decides, "but I like this. I don't have many reasons for things yet, I only just got back to this plane."

"...Do you remember your life?"

"Not at all. I wouldn't have thought I came *from* anywhere if you hadn't mentioned it. It was a lot of nothing, nothing I can hardly recall now, and then..." The demon's hands spread wide, slowly fading into healthy pink human skin. "Then you, Isaac. Then me. I don't know how else to think about any of this. You tell me, and I'll follow wherever you will lead me."

Despite himself, that's a pretty tempting silver lining to this mess.

· · · · ● · ● · · ·

"Milya!"

Emil restrains his groan, but he pauses at the top of the stairs for Mrs. Kartashova. "*Dobriy vyecher*, Mrs. Kartashova." It's not worth it to ask her—again—to stop calling him Milya. She ignores his pleas that he's too old for it, and he would rather die than tell her he fights a flinch every time someone Not His Mother uses that name.

"You're getting back so late these days. I hope you're still eating properly—and I *don't* mean sharing your food with that cat."

He remains silent. Guiltily.

"I've seen it hanging around, especially whenever you come home! You do not need a cat on top of everything else right now," she scolds, even waggling her finger at him. He nobly does not roll his eyes.

"I'll stop feeding her," Emil lies.

She bids him goodnight, and he heads up the stairs. He makes it no farther than his landing before his favorite little calico trots right on out, tail held high, eyes bright with anticipation.

Emil smiles when he crouches down to scratch behind her ears. "I like your greeting much better, pretty kitty. But if you keep hanging around here, Mrs. Kartashova is gonna dump water on you."

The cat meows, ears laid back at the very thought. But she keeps arching her back and butting her head against his knee.

"You're going to move in soon, aren't you," he jokes, stepping over her to unlock his door.

Despite his words, the cat remains at his doorstep, tail curled politely over her paws. She really is a handsome cat, and friendly to boot. He wonders why she hasn't been adopted or reclaimed by some long-lost family.

Emil knows he's only a tiny step from admitting defeat. "I'm not naming you," he reminds her as he puts out a plastic lid with some ripped up ham atop it. She purrs as she eats, the rumbling kind with a hint of meow that the internet goes crazy for. Emil, unfortunately, included.

He ends up sitting against his front door, cross-legged with his homework in his lap, the cat munching and then chilling next to him. It's only slightly cold out, now that the sun's set, but thankfully he'd thought ahead to grab a blanket.

He no sooner sets it over his lap than the cat invites herself onto it.

I'm totally gonna end up keeping her, he thinks in despair as he resigns himself to more scratching.

The cat glances up at him, too smug, and Emil scowls back. She *whaps* him in the face with her long tail in a preemptive strike.

"Alright, that's enough." He dumps her off his lap, stands, and gathers his stuff with as much dignity as one can muster while fleeing from a friendly cat. "Brat," he offers before shutting the door in her face.

He gets one plaintive meow, half a whine and maybe half a goodbye, then silence—for approximately three seconds, before he hears heavy boots clomping down the hallway.

Emil opens his door after one knock. He's lucky he doesn't get punched in the face, but it's pretty funny to see Maxim's surprise. (He himself is low-key surprised it's not Mrs. Kartashova again, this time with the proof of a departing well-fed cat.)

Maxim thrusts a tinfoil-covered baking dish at him. "Grandma says this is for you," he says with a bemused blink.

Emil wants to scream. Ms. Yordanova is her own can of worms, twice as terrifying as any of his other well-meaning neighbors, and three times as nosy. "Thanks." He doesn't *need* food and watching over. He's surprised she hasn't tried to move her grandson in with him.

"It's no problem, y'know? You're welcome to have dinner with us anytime, too—"

"It's fine, Max," Emil says with more heat than intended. He avoids eye contact when he takes the dish. "Thanks, and tell her thanks, but I don't need to be babied this much. I still have some homework, so I gotta go. G'night."

Maxim, at least, lets the matter go. Good for him, not being another one of the neighborhood *babushkas* who won't leave him alone but can't help in any way that counts. He'll accept help from the bookstore; more hours means he *works* for more money. He doesn't like the sympathy handouts.

At least the free food tonight is wild rice casserole, one of his favorites.

Emil puts on Netflix, kicks his feet up onto the cracked coffee table, and eats it straight out of the dish. No one's around to judge him, so what does he care.

Even though he feels the eyes on him, anyway.

This vision overtakes Natalie mid-yawn, which is an uncomfortable sensation to say the least.

It's a quiet night scene, overlooking a nearly-empty city park. Two figures sit on the swings. One is an older Vivienne, hair only grey at the tips now, and she kicks her feet idly beneath her.

Her companion is a young Black girl seemingly shining from within. She doesn't move, eyes fixed on her hands in her lap.

Neither speak, but the silence appears companionable. Vivienne shoots the girl several grins, none of which are returned—until the very end, where she peers up from her dejected posture with a shy smile and eyes shining gold.

Despite the calmness of the vision, Natalie comes back to herself coughing. Vivienne today, beside her, thumps her on the back with a concerned look. "A vision? You okay?" she asks.

As soon as she catches her breath, Natalie grumbles, "It ought to be illegal for visions to interrupt a yawn."

CHAPTER 4

IN WHICH MARK GETS INTO TROUBLE

"Emil Zolotarev. Age seventeen, in high school, works part-time at Appleton's Book Corner. The spirit haunting him is or was a human ghost of a young girl, probably near his age, but has progressed at least to the point of being able to manipulate others' luck." Vivienne slides the open notebook across the counter to Natalie.

Isaac, sweeping across the room, conspicuously slows down so he can eavesdrop—a distraction from the inky tendril trying to slither up Vivienne's leg.

She shakes the demon off and gives them both a pointed look. "You'll find out all of this soon enough, since we're probably getting past the point where I can handle this on my own. You're our little insurance plan."

"I'm not little," the demon indignantly replies, and then, just like that, it steps out of its own puddly self and into a settled form. Vivienne reels back from the face suddenly in hers. "Hi," it—he?—adds with a grin a tad too sharp to be human.

He has a shaggy mop of blond hair, grey-green eyes, and faint freckles she can only see because they're so close. But he looks human enough, and even with the teeth, he could pass for a humanoid spirit of any kind.

"Congrats," Vivienne tells him, a little thrown by his sudden proximity. But the moment passes, and she brings up both hands to his cheeks with a resounding *smack*. His *yip* is almost endearing. "You're solid, too!"

"Yes, I am! You are, too!" He also grabs her cheeks, squishing them and pursing her lips.

"Do you have a name yet?" Natalie asks, not at all perturbed by the slap fight in her shop.

"Shouldn't we return to the potential *other* demon?" Isaac retorts, which honestly is answer enough. (Vivienne makes a note to buy him a baby naming book on her next stalking trip.) "If we're being used as exterminators, then I think we need to cover a few basics."

Vivienne stops squishing her new favorite squeeze toy, now worried. "Can you fight? In general, I mean."

The stare Isaac gives her is deader than any ghost she's ever met. "I can. He hasn't been in any fights, though, and I don't like the idea of letting something my life is *tethered* to roam free in some sort of battle royale."

"First off—" Vivienne begins, but Natalie holds up a hand to quiet her.

"Demons are quite sturdy, and we can always help you figure out how to better protect yourselves. But we would never ask you to put yourselves in undue danger without your consent."

"You make coercion and confinement sound so pretty," Isaac says. The demon snickers.

Natalie sighs through her nose, but Vivienne isn't here for this kind of attitude. "You don't get the moral high ground here, *Mason*. Summoning demons good as carries a death sentence in this city, and whether or not you believe it, we're trying to *help* you. Both of you."

Natalie sighs again, but softer, wearier. "...I only want information, Isaac. A bit of help. If you'd like to leave, then leave."

"I'm not sure I want us to leave. But I do want everyone to stop arguing for a bit?" the demon volunteers. Vivienne nearly laughs in her surprise at him, but Isaac glowers like a surly dog. (Natalie, as always: rather blank.)

"Fine! No more arguing. If you two don't want to help, that's fine—"

"I didn't say we wouldn't help," Isaac interrupts, and Vivienne rolls her eyes at him. Loudly. He replies in kind. "But I want certain protections in place. We're not a cleanup crew for your messes, or bait, or collateral."

"No, *we* clean up *your* mess," Vivienne corrects. She boops the demon's nose for good measure. "Granted, you're the nicest demon I've ever met, and I'm still surprised you haven't tried to eat anyone. That we know of."

"None at all," he happily reports.

Supernatural Hunter Tip #42: Everything has to eat—don't judge a spirit by its diet. (Even if it's humans, though that should be avoided.)

"Isaac, why can't you be more like your demon?" Vivienne asks with much glee and irony. She doesn't know how she got so lucky to throw this much shade without said demon trying to munch on her on his master's orders.

Then again, based on that thought, plus the flat look Natalie is drilling into the side of her head, *maybe* she shouldn't push said luck.

So she squishes the demon's cheeks again. "Don't worry, we're not going to throw you into anything nasty. But our hands are sort of tied here, and we *do* need to feed you. Ghosts are easy. But let's figure out exactly what you can do, *and* get you a name."

"Please name him before this situation complicates further," Natalie ominously adds.

· · · · ● · ● · · ·

"I'm fairly certain humans need a thing called sleep," the demon drawls from his spot sprawled out atop the bed. He's the only one in it. Isaac, still hunched on the floor with his back resting against the mattress, squints at the screen. The camera angles in older games are always so shitty.

"Do demons sleep? Regularly, I mean."

"I think so. So far, yes, and I like it." He stretches further, still with a tail, just to be an ass. "You should sleep. Or, at least, please tell me what you're doing. I haven't quite grasped your video games yet."

(Despite *how many times* Isaac has tried to explain.)

After a burst of static, Isaac whips around and headshots the dog monster. "They have different goals, like books or movies."

"Yes, because this one is nothing like the rainbowy driving one you also like. Or the one with the little creatures that breathe fire and lightning."

"This is a horror game. I like those too." Isaac ensures the monster is dead before proceeding. This is something like his fifth playthrough, and rarely do things surprise him in it, but you *always* make sure enemies are dead in horror games. Death scenes can get pretty gruesome, and he doesn't want *more* comments on his time-waster of choice from the demon he's beginning to suspect had been some pearl-clutching conservative housewife in his prior life.

As soon as the final cutscene begins, he sets down the controller and leans back against the bed. Another *Silent Hill* game done. His phone buzzes against his hip, another text from Walker about how she's already beaten her playthrough. The demon looks at him upside-down, eyes shiny with the light from the TV, hair a floppy mess.

Isaac has no idea what to do with him.

"I should name you," he tells him, resigned, "since Natalie doesn't think Demon is a good enough name."

"According to the naming books Vivienne has shared with us, no, it isn't."

"Fine then, *you* pick a name." Isaac tears his gaze from the demon's earnestness and back to the screen.

"That seems dishonest."

"I am dishonest," Isaac says. "Do you *really* want me to name you? I'll probably end up pulling something from a game, or naming you Spot or something."

"I don't have any spots," he replies, but only after a peek down at himself.

"Do you always have to be so literal?"

"I can't lie to you, and I'm still re-approaching life. All of my literalness and politeness make up for how rude and avoidant you are."

Isaac glowers at the game in front of him and hunches his shoulders. The demon pets him with a little chuckle. On the screen, the final boss appears at last, and he switches weapons as soon as he is able. "Alright then, your name will be Sam." His voice is nearly lost in the aged sound of video game shotguns.

"Oh?" Despite his *clear* dedication to the fight, the demon leans off the bed until he is firmly in Isaac's peripherals. He inches ever closer, and Isaac leans further, until he's nearly sideways and his demon is half unsettled in order to loom over him. "Sam. Why Sam? Saaaa-aaaam. Sam? Isaac, why that?"

Isaac can't help but wonder if this, too, is some part of the contract. He's had no prior contact with demons, but he supposes names can have power. "Short for Samael. Congrats. Now let me kill this boss."

(Which is also named Samael. But Sam doesn't need to know this.)

Sam sits back on the bed with a happy sound.

· · · ● · ● · · · ·

Tomorrow's a rest day, but Vivienne already *wants* it. She wants it so bad. Not just because her bad luck has been worsening the few jobs she's been given, but her own thoughts are sabotaging her, too. Pretty soon, that little ghost is going to cross the line of no return—if she hasn't already.

Vivienne's dealt with that kind of sadness before, but the *real* issue with that is that she's going to have to bring Isaac and Sam with her. She's going to have to get used to the idea of utilizing them in the future, too. Magical garbage disposal, how novel.

She trusts Isaac to know his way around a fight, if only because he's so distrustful and standoffish that he *has* to have pissed off enough people to have had to dodge punches or spells before. And demons are pretty hardy. Difficult to kill and physically strong. But they have no magic of their own, and with their lives tethered, would Isaac's paranoia/self-interest outweigh any help he could be?

Vivienne whines to herself and sprawls dramatically over the tabletop.

"Rough day?" Sam asks, pulling the potted thyme out of her way.

It's ten in the morning. Vivienne wonders if he's making a joke, or just repeating the small talk he's heard around the shop.

"How do you think demons do with bad luck?" she muses.

"I'd rather not try. But probably better than you."

"Definitely better than either of us," Isaac says. "Are you going to tell us when you'll use us?"

It's only because she's so close to him, but Vivienne thinks there's something faintly pleased in Sam's expression at the 'us'.

Dangerous.

And cute.

Vivienne's phone rings—her actual phone, not her work phone. It's Mark's ringtone, blaring and poppy and ominous.

The thing about Mark is that he's normally a texter. He'll answer the phone, sure, and he'll call for certain reasons, but he prefers texting, unless it's urgent. And if it's urgent, an emergency, then he ought to call her work number.

"Hiiiii, Vivi!" Mark sings as soon as she picks up.

"Don't call me that," she replies on reflex. Only two people can call her that, and one of them is dead. "Why're you calling? What's up?"

"Well, y'know, this is the number it calls when I ask my phone for you!"

Ah. He's drunk.

Again: ten in the morning. Not that she is one to point fingers about that, and it hasn't been the first time he's stayed out all night *or* started this early. Vivienne settles into a more comfortable sprawl and gets ready for whatever nonsense is about to unfold. "Right, okay. And why did you want me, Marky-poo?"

"My house has been broken into-ooooo," he says, drawing out the last bit into several more syllables.

Vivienne tenses. "Are you alright? What's going on—?" Mark is nosy and threatening, but has no magic and can't fight worth a damn. His house is extremely well-warded, and he has plenty of friends who will play bodyguard for him, however, and there's no way he can have a casual burglar.

He's gotten into trouble.

Again.

"I think it's best to have you come over for this one."

Vivienne is already grabbing her things. She keeps an eye on Isaac while she does, but he pretends to work, no matter how obviously he's eavesdropping. She locks eyes with him.

"I'm leaving," she mouths at him.

"You're leaving us by ourselves?" Sam asks, astonished. When Vivienne turns to shrug on her messenger bag, he follows her, abandoning legs in favor of curling around her like a snake. "Natalie is gone, too."

As if she weren't aware. But even if she could be sure of Mark's safety, bringing him to the shop with those two would be even *worse*.

Mark continues on the phone, "I locked 'em in the bathroom, and I'm in the kitchen with my biggest knife."

"Why was a burglar in your bathroom?"

"Come oooooover!"

She isn't sure how much is Drunk Mark and how much is Evasive Mark. "I'm on my way. I'm at the shop, so it'll take me a bit. *Ugh*, god, I'm gonna need a fucking Uber. Ugh! You and your emergencies! Will you be okay until then?" She tries to think who could be closer to him. Maybe someone else can buy time so she doesn't have to take a car. He certainly doesn't sound like he's screaming death throes.

"I can stab," he replies.

Not reassuring.

She hangs up and turns to their interns/kidnapees. Isaac preempts her. "We won't burn the place down, but how do you know we won't run away?"

Vivienne rolls her eyes at him. "We don't follow you home and hide under your bed. You could have gotten away by now, Isaac. This is an emergency, and I need to go, so you two will be in charge—"

"What if a customer comes in?" Sam nervously asks.

She tries not to roll her eyes at him, too. "Then give them a potion and make sure you get their money. Nat's binder has everything, I mean *everything*, and you can call her if you need anything. I *really* gotta go."

"...Is your friend going to be alright?"

"He's a trouble magnet, but he has a knack for getting out of trouble, too. I'll be back later, I hope, so hold tight."

She barely remembers to text Natalie to tell her she left the other trouble magnets in charge of her shop, but she should be back soon, anyway. Vivienne can't relax, even when she's on the train; she vibrates in her seat, and considers calling Mark back, or maybe seeing where Fiona was, opening and closing the ride-sharing app repeatedly. Maybe she should have chanced it. No matter how much she hates cars.

Two stops down, the train halts, and an accident is announced over the intercom.

Vivienne isn't the only one to sneak off, and not even the only one to use magic. City people have no patience, but she thinks she's in the right in this case.

Car it is. She decides Mark can comp her Uber. It's the least he can do since she's playing knight in shining armor halfway across the city for him. He better appreciate this.

Nearly an hour has passed since she got his call by the time she's breathlessly running up his steps. He had not responded to her texts or called her again. She doesn't know whether her jitters are from panic or being in a moving vehicle.

Vivienne braces herself for the likelihood of finding his corpse in his kitchen and unlocks the door with a rune and a murmur.

Good: there's no immediate smell of blood.

Bad: the door hadn't actually been locked.

Perplexing: Mark is not in the kitchen, dead or otherwise, but is instead sprawled across his couch, snoring.

"Hey, asshole!" Vivienne snaps with a kick to his dangling arm. He jerks awake. "Where is your emergency I had to run across the city for?!"

"Bathroom," he petulantly replies, rubbing his eyes, "I *told* you."

Mark Ito's bathroom is the second best warded residential space in the city. (The rest of his house hovers somewhere in the top ten.) It's not odd that he would use it as a jail cell, but it *is* odd that the burglar was there to begin with.

Or maybe not, since the reason his bathroom is the second best warded residential space in the city is because of his bathtub.

His bathtub is the most beautiful old clawfoot tub, just updated enough to be conveniently modern, but largely antique. Its faucet is on the side so no one has to worry about head or feet knocking it, a gentle curve to help reclining, *and* a detachable showerhead for spice. Hammered copper, deep as sin, and with a cabinet full of bath bombs and oils always within reach, it is a little slice of heaven in the middle of the rest of Mark's gaudy things.

It is the closest Vivienne has ever come to true love.

Bitter wars have been fought over the right to use his bathtub. And when several creatively magical people want to spend time alone with the bathtub, they get creatively defensive. Vivienne herself has layered more wards here than in her own apartment. She will *murder* people if someone has successfully figured out how to steal the bathtub. (She has tried, and thus far failed.)

"How drunk are you?" Vivienne asks and shrugs off her bag so she can dig properly.

"I'm useable," he replies. He clambers upright, swaying only a little, and squints around until he recalls he needs glasses. "More 'portantly, I know what they were trying to steal."

"Good start. Here, take this." She hands him a silver-edged hunting knife. She pulls out a metal bat for herself. "You saw them? Wait, them as in plural, or singular?"

"Probably a woman," he says, shrugging. "Just one. Prob not human, though! You'll see."

"Just *once*, could you not be a drama queen?"

He shrugs again. As they approach his bathroom, he puts a finger to his lips, then opens the hallway closet door. Presumably to find the goal of the break-in.

Inspecting the door, Vivienne finds that shockingly, none of the wards or charms have been broken. She can't even find any sign of stress. She presses her ear to the door and can hear the faint sound of water sloshing.

Vivienne spares him a look over her shoulder. "If you gave me an emergency call because someone is taking a bath in here—"

But the words die in her mouth when she sees what is bundled in his arms.

It's faintly spotted, a gradient of grey, and folded over several times like fabric. It's thicker, though, and has a velvety sheen to what Vivienne recognizes as *fur*.

It's a seal pelt.

One moment Natalie is tensing, rushing forward, perfectly timed and perfectly strong.

The next, she's seeing the inside of a car. A taxi with three people crowded into the backseat. The one in the middle is the largest, which the other two seem to find amusing. He hunches with a feigned scowl. The atmosphere seems happily woozy from both company and alcohol.

The large man in the middle, with a scruff of a beard and hair halfway out of its gel, laughs and tries to hunch down further. He doesn't succeed. Both of the other two laugh and poke at him, teasing mercilessly but not without warmth.

The rightmost, a heavyset Asian woman with dyed grey hair, affectionately reaches over to poke the leftmost man, a Native American man who'd been the most active with his prodding and most vocal with his laughter.

The middle man rolls his eyes at the war zone across his lap.

Turned as she is, the woman does not see the truck coming at them through the car window.

When Natalie snaps back to herself, it's with a screech of metal and blinding pain that is not her own—

And then suddenly it is.

She's sprawled on the ground, knee in agony, having missed her jump's landing. Badly. Natalie doesn't know if her blurry, watery eyes are from her pain or theirs. She lets out a low moan, wordless, before her voice catches. She breaks into her first panicked sob at the same time her first teammate makes it to her.

Natalie's track career ends that day.

CHAPTER 5

IN WHICH MARK GETS INTO FURTHER TROUBLE

"If you don't like it here, we could leave," Sam suggests. The shop is silent with only the two of them; Isaac had long since given up grinding any more charcoal, so there aren't even sounds of work.

With his eyes on his phone, Isaac asks, "And do what?"

"What did you do before?"

"Mostly lie." As if giving up in the face of Sam's earnest questions—Sam may be new to this world, but he's not stupid about how Isaac responds to him—Isaac sets his phone down and faces him with his cheek mushed against his fist. "We'll head out, eventually, if we don't die first. But too many people have seen our faces, know our names, now. It would be easier to lie low here and let them 'protect' us."

He wiggles his fingers in the air.

Sam mimics him, crooking his index and middle fingers. "What does this mean?"

"Air quotes."

"And what are those?"

"For emphasis. I was being sarcastic about their protection."

Sam is coming to understand sarcasm. He absolutely understands Isaac's distaste for everything Natalie or Vivienne do. Or, rather, he understands that Isaac *has* distaste for it. He doesn't understand where it comes from.

"Are we going to fight things for them?"

"If they make us."

"Does someone make you do everything you do?" Sam can't help but ask. Isaac complains about Oliver *making* them come to dinner with him; he complains about Natalie *making* him sort herbs; he complains about Vivienne *making* him hold a conversation. What has Samael made him do?

Isaac wrinkles his nose, mouth twisted in a sneer. "Sometimes, it's easier to go with things than fight against them. Choose your battles."

"What battle are you choosing?"

Isaac doesn't respond.

Sam leans in closer, trying to appear beseeching and open, like how he gets Vivienne to tell him anything. It doesn't work on Isaac. Instead, the witch grabs his jaw, digging his fingers into the hinge to make Sam open his mouth.

"Your gums are still pale," Isaac murmurs, "and your teeth are still too sharp. Are you dehydrated? Are you hungry?"

It's the closest he ever gets to concern. Sam preens with even that. "Humans have canine teeth." It comes out a little garbled thanks to Isaac's iron grip.

"Not *like* canines."

He runs his tongue over his teeth. They don't feel wrong to him, but what does he know? He's content to merely exist here in one piece. In mostly one form.

Isaac shifts his fingers so he's cupping Sam's cheek, his eyes still analyzing. "I've heard demon blood is black... That could account for your pallor."

"I think some humans are just white," Sam points out. Vivienne and Natalie are both lighter than Isaac. Humans come in many colors, and Sam assumes he's a safe shade, despite Isaac's fretting. "But... I'm not certain. You were the one bleeding during the summoning, not me."

Isaac's gaze slides sideways.

There are always tools and ingredients strewn about on any available surface. Natalie's work knife set sits neatly along the far wall.

Sam had somewhat been expecting dissection at some point, although not from Isaac himself. There is likely a term for this—dissection without killing someone, because he doesn't think Isaac is suicidal—but it's all just a distant curiosity to him. He wouldn't die at Isaac's hands, so why worry?

"But," he must ask, "why do you care?"

"Better to find out now than to find out when you get a paper cut in front of the wrong customer."

"You can cut yourself on paper?" Sam asks in alarm. What *can't* humans cut themselves on?! Maybe Isaac needed a demon purely for protection. *Though he didn't exactly want a demon*, he recalls, because a contracted demon would be a better bodyguard than an uncontracted one.

A larger risk, too, though. Isaac doesn't seem the type to particularly like risk-taking.

Instead of delving into paper-related dangers, Isaac narrows his eyes at him again. "Why are you so calmly going with this?"

"It's not as if you'll kill me."

"Most things *don't* want to bleed."

"Fair," Sam reasons. "But I trust you." *Not to kill us both*, he means to add, but to his surprise, he can finish it there. It's not a lie.

Isaac won't kill him, and Sam trusts his need for knowledge. Simple.

But he must remind himself that it's Simple and He Trusts Isaac when the witch advances on him with a knife.

This trust culminates in discovering that demon blood is corrosive.

· · • · • · • · • ·

Vivienne looks at the pelt, then to the bathroom door, then to the pelt again. Mark lets her take her time.

"Is that what I think it is?" she finally asks.

"What do you think it is?" he coyly shoots back.

"You have a *selkie* in your *bathroom*!" Vivienne shrieks. She makes a grab for the pelt, but Mark holds it aloft, out of her reach.

He's glad the woman in his bathtub can't see him; he can't help his grin when he notices how *relieved* she feels. It confirms his theory. There's a reason he called Vivienne instead of Fiona, or even Codi, and it has little to do with the selkie; he needs an expert on obscure magic, and Vivienne knows some of the most obscure shit on the planet.

"Hold on," he says, and unsheathes the borrowed knife. "Bat up, doll."

"Wait, we're—?!" No sooner does she begin then does he throw open the bathroom door.

The woman remains where she had been when he locked her in: in the bathtub. There's an awful lot of water splashed onto the floor, unapologetically, but the tub is still full. He dreads his coming water bill.

Mark keeps half a mental ear on Vivienne's reaction, but most of his focus is on his would-be thief.

Her long black hair floats around her like an oil slick, largely hiding her nudity—soaked clothes long since dumped on the floor—but it does little to hide her marked arms or shoulders. Vivienne hasn't noticed them yet. Then again, not much could hide her physique, muscular as it is. The woman is just shy of a bodybuilder, and she could absolutely break Mark like a toothpick. He pretends not to be intimidated.

The selkie's red eyes narrow at them, but she doesn't lunge or speak.

Both Mark and the selkie register the moment when Vivienne notices the rings of rune tattoos on her thick arms.

"Oh!" Vivienne, bless her heart, is as transparent as ever.

She rushes toward the tub, Research Brain kicking all logic and self-preservation out the window, and Mark senses the jolt of animalistic defense just in time. He grabs Vivienne by the back of the sweater, yanking her precisely out of reach of the clawed swipe from the woman.

Vivienne's eyes track her arm's movement, mind going a mile a minute.

"And I believe that's a wonderful note to leave on." They back toward the door and Vivienne locks it after herself. The selkie did not follow.

Mark herds Vivienne toward the couch. Her bat clatters to the floor when she plops down, and Mark settles in the armchair next to her before pulling out his phone.

'*don't mention psychic thing - not sure she knows*' he types in the notes app and shows Vivienne. She nods.

She digs around in her bag, then pulls out a notebook and a pen. "So," she begins, flipping to a blank sheet, "you have a selkie in your bathtub. Mind explaining more?"

"Like what? It sounds self-explanatory to me."

"How did you come across such a thing?" she asks, eyes narrowed. She absolutely already knows.

"We-eeeell—"

"You found it on purpose, didn't you?"

"Not really? I was looking for a new china cabinet, something in a darker wood, to match the table, you know?"

"Bullshit, you were looking for another cursed mirror."

"This is not a mirror," Mark retorts, poking the pelt.

"It's not a china cabinet, either."

He takes the notebook when she *finally* finds a free page. There are precious few left. '*how much you read off her arms?*' he writes and passes it back.

She purses her lips, then shrugs. '*Lots there.*' She underlines *lots* several times. '*I'd need another look. Stability & Changing runes, lots.*' More underlining.

"Could you get me a list?" he murmurs. She nods.

"You know, you could give it back to her. She'd probably be so grateful she wouldn't kill you."

"No way! I have a pet selkie!"

She smacks him. '*What else do you know about her?*'

'*her mind is weird - some shielding + strange thought processes. mostly feelings from her.*'

"How do you know you could trust her? Just because you have her pelt doesn't mean she wouldn't mix hemlock into your tea the first chance she gets. There aren't happy stories about forced brides in this sort of thing."

"She's not my type," Mark replies, rolling his eyes. "Have you ever dealt with selkies before?"

"No, never. I've only read a bit about them... Are they technically fae?"

Mark *sincerely* hopes not, since anything to do with the fair folk is not worth *any* amount of trouble. "Please find out about that." He would gladly throw the pelt at her face and let her roam free again if that were the case, but he doubts it.

For multiple reasons.

The primary one being that relief.

The doorbell rings before he can debate about sharing his theories.

"...I don't have any appointments until three, and I've already called to cancel," he says.

As he goes for the door, Vivienne scrambles to hide the visible weaponry. Bat under the couch, knife back into her bag, pelt beneath the throw blanket. She grabs the notebook just as Mark opens the door.

With his best Customer Service Smile and warmest tone, he says, "Good morning. May I help you?"

The person standing before him may be one of the most beautiful people he has ever seen. Judging on Vivienne's craning neck and spiraling thought process, she most definitely agrees.

Not handsome, not like Mark himself; not pretty, not like Natalie; not thin, not like Benji; not muscular, not like their new selkie friend. But undeniably attractive in a way he cannot put a finger on.

Their features are classically Asian, probably Japanese, though their skin is slightly darker than Mark's. Their hair is mostly black, with white streaks near their temples (surely not from age, based on their flawless complexion), tied into a short ponytail. Their attire is business formal: a loose, knee-length black skirt, and a crisp white short-sleeved button-up tied at their throat with a black tie.

Most startling of all are the obvious glamor charms on their wrists.

"This is the residence of the—" they glance sideways toward the plaque near his door, thick lashes fluttering, "—famed psychic Mark Ito, correct?"

"Yes, and how fortunate you are. My schedule just cleared up." He has little choice but to let them in with another smile.

Vivienne hastens to sit properly on the couch, and his guest's eyes immediately dart to her. He can read them, but only superficial reactions. It's common with nonhuman guests.

"This is my assistant, Vivienne," Mark introduces.

"Hello!" They don't offer their name, but perch on the armchair. They adjust their skirt around their knees, less for propriety and more for something to do with their fingers. (They're not used to these hands and there's a thin film of uneasiness just barely there, beneath their impassive formality.)

"I can give you a private reading, if that would make you more comfortable...?" Mark prompts.

"I'm not here for a consultation. I wanted to speak of something else?"

Kitchen! Vivienne thinks loudly, almost shouting at him. She bolts to her feet, and with a rigid smile, she asks, "Can I get you anything to drink?"

Their guest blinks, as if the question is strange. "No. I'd rather not have anything you offer."

"Give us just a moment," Mark adds with a smile as she drags him into the kitchen.

The door hardly closes behind them before Vivienne is tugging him down to her level and hissing, "What is this?! What *are* they? Selkies don't need glamors!"

"I am still too drunk to think of a list of nonhuman beings for you," he replies, straight-faced. "They're here for something, and not at ease. But I don't think they realize we can recognize a glamor on sight." Or they believe they have the upper hand. A very common part of being a spirit. "The selkie didn't react, either, and she had to have heard the doorbell. Our guest isn't suspicious of us, either. I'm not sure they're together, Viv."

"Then what the hell is this timing?!"

"I don't know!" Her panic is rubbing off on him, and he wasn't lying; he's definitely still too drunk to handle this sudden situation. "What are our options? What's in your bag that can help?"

"The bag that's out in the living room?"

"You need to put a lock on that thing."

"I have some salt, sleep soot, some holy water. My knife. I can't do anything if I don't know what they are. We could call Ramirez—"

"No, I want this contained, and I'm not letting her ruin my house again." Fiona and Benji could be their emergency plan, but that wouldn't be a quick rescue. Mark chews his lip for a moment, then points out, "I have the pelt. If they're not friends, we could always let them fight it out."

Vivienne pales. A feat for her. "That's the worst idea I've ever heard."

"Great!" And with that, he flounces back into the living room, Vivienne dragging at his heels. "Thank you for waiting."

I'm still unlucky, Vivienne thinks at him as she sits down on the far end of the couch. She scoots her bag over closer to herself. *And I have no idea what this size would need a glamor. Wrong time of month for a werewolf, and fae don't need glamors.*

Mark's smile never wavers, despite her pessimism. "So, what can I do for you, if not a consultation?"

"You purchased a certain object recently."

Mark's poker face remains impeccable.

His guest inclines their head, smiling. Something about it doesn't look right on their face. "I've heard it's illegal here. I'm here to help you get rid of this problem! You're welcome."

"Illegal?" he echoes. "Are you part of some agency?" Certainly not a coven. Mark knows all the patron spirits of the covens in the city.

"...Yes," they reply, after a beat, as if surprised to be questioned on the world's flimsiest cover story.

Do they really think we'd buy this? Vivienne thinks. Wry humor wafts from her like perfume. Or a fart.

"I purchased the skin, and it *is* legal to own here. I did some research last night. Wouldn't want to own any illegal animal skins, right?"

The guest's mouth twitches. The smile, perhaps never there, vanishes.

"Why are you so interested, and how do you know about it?" he presses.

"I wanted it for myself. I'm willing to buy it from you. I can give you a very good price."

"For personal reasons, or for your agency?" Vivienne asks.

They spare her a cool look, then sigh. "Alright, alright, I didn't think this through. I didn't want to lie about anything, either, but humans are so finicky about these things! I only want to save you some trouble with this mess. Get this done bloodlessly."

That was easy, Vivienne thinks at him.

"Alright, so let's cut out the lying. Who are you, and why do you want the seal skin?" Mark demands.

"My name is Mirai," they reply. Vivienne's mental alarm bells begin ringing again. "I'm looking for the seal pelt, but mostly who it belongs to."

"It belongs to *me*," Mark corrects. Vivienne doesn't interject, but she maintains her alarm, which is getting annoying. "What business do you have with her?"

"I'd hoped you would not know what you'd bought," Mirai replies, expression souring. "I wanted this to be a quick errand, wanted to do this professionally, but I'm not used to pretending to be human. Let me start over!"

They unclick each of the glamors from their wrists, and the magic *snaps* off. They stretch out their legs first; their skirt has billowed out further because of the bulk of their feathered thighs, and their legs now end in scaly skin, with talons the size of Mark's hand. Their arms have lengthened and sprouted feathers, bunching up their sleeves, fingers now leathery and clawed like their feet.

Their face and hair have remained largely the same, but their ears are longer and pointed, and feathers creep up over the edge of their collar, up to their chin, mixing with their black hair. Their plumage is black, too, save for wide splotches of white on their wings.

The last detail is the mask they place over their face, despite the fact that Mark and Vivienne have already seen it.

"My name is Mirai," they start again, lacing their claws in their lap, "and I am a magpie tengu of the crow clan, here—pretending to be human—on business. As you can imagine, it must be *fairly* important for me to go to these lengths."

Well, that explains Vivienne's alarm.

A tengu in the human city. They do business in the goblin markets, and Mark has heard about a recent uptick in human-tengu dealings, but they don't *like* humans. It's a minor miracle they didn't stomp in here, ignore Mark and Vivienne, and rip the bathroom door off its hinges to either eat or save the selkie inside.

"What *business* does a tengu have with a selkie?" Mark asks.

Mirai cocks their head, too steeply and too sharply. The mask is creepy. "Someone stole an egg. We've had several thefts in recent months, but this is a theft from someone close to me. I'm here to get it back."

It's only now that the selkie reacts to the conversation she can surely hear. Panic spikes through her, and Mark thinks he hears water sloshing from the bathroom.

"And you believe the selkie stole the egg?"

"I know it was her!"

"So you want to get your friend's baby back. That's understandable."

Vivienne elbows him so savagely he nearly doubles over. Mirai goes rigid, feathers fluffing. "Tengu *sell* their eggs, it's a business! They're not babies!" she hisses at him. "They're *very* protective, don't mix that up!" She grabs him by the back of the neck and forces him to bow, doing the same herself. "I'm very sorry for Mark's ignorance. Please excuse him."

"And you seem to be well-informed," Mirai neutrally replies. "Are you a hunter?" This question is even *more* neutral.

"I'm not, I just perform minor exorcisms and work with witches."

Mirai's posture relaxes. "Human hunters have been bothersome lately. But, as I said before, I'm willing to buy this pelt from you. I am doing you a *favor*!"

"And you'll, what, trap her? Use it as bait?" he asks.

"If I possess the pelt, then I can speak to her to resolve this matter." So that's a yes. Anger runs beneath their words. "I want to get the egg back before anything else happens."

"Well, I have heard nothing about eggs on this side of the city yet, but I will let you know." Mark stands, and Mirai stares at him so hard it's a weight, even beneath the mask. "I'd prefer to keep my legal animal skin for the time being, but we'll keep our ear to the ground about these missing eggs."

Mirai reluctantly stands, too, but they continue to radiate incredulity. It isn't often someone would deny a tengu.

Why not give it to them? We could get rid of this before it worsens. Don't get involved in tengu problems, Vivienne thinks, a mile a minute, staring holes into the back of his head.

"How shall I contact you if I change my mind in the future about this?" Mark asks brightly.

"We, er, have a stall in the goblin market... Ask for me there, if I'm not with one of the vendors."

Mirai allows him to herd them toward the door, and they clip their glamors back on. The sudden magic makes his head swim.

At the door, they whirl on him and whip their mask off again. Their expression is terrifying in its raw desperation. "*Please,* if you find out anything about the eggs, that's the priority. Instead of the thief, if you find an owl egg, let me know immediately. I will pay whatever you want!"

"We will," Vivienne promises from behind Mark.

Mirai barely glances at her. Their lashes spike wetly. "Are you *certain* you won't sell me the pelt?"

"I'll think about it."

"Alright." Then, they rock up onto their toes to whisper in his ear, "Be careful with her. She can break through the locks on that door easily. Don't trust thieves."

With that, they leave. Once the door shuts, Mark sags against it. He presses his palms against his eyes in a vain attempt to ward off his coming headache.

"They *knew*. They knew she was here the entire time."

"And they were a very nice, gracious tengu for not disemboweling us and storming the place themselves."

"You know, that's what I thought, too."

"Tell me what you're planning before I punch you," Vivienne demands and crosses her arms over her chest. "Why not just give it to them? Or sell, if that's what you were worried about, though if it is, *I'm* disemboweling you myself."

"First, I wanted to rush them out before they realized she was here, but that didn't work. But more importantly..." Vivienne leans in for his grand reveal. With a beam, he tells her, "I have a pet selkie now!"

She punches him.

· · • • • • • • · ·

To her annoyance, Mark has lucked out (yet again): selkies are not fae.

They're fairly well-recorded throughout history, and it isn't difficult to dig up the basics. They own a pelt, which allows them to shapeshift into a seal, and appear human otherwise. One of the few spirits that can breed with humans, but most tales of intermarrying are non-consensual. They can swim well no matter their form, they're originally from Scotland, stronger than humans, diet consists mostly of fish and meat, and prone to biting captors.

The last bit is specific, yet incredibly helpful.

Why Mark is obsessed with keeping his new problematic roommate is beyond her. Even without the tengu mess, he's playing with fire. It can't be sexual, and it can't be magical.

And of course he won't tell her.

Yet.

They dodged the fae bullet, but got slapped in the face with *youkai*, of all things. Vivienne scrubs a hand through her hair, trying to ground herself while she racks her brain for a way out of this mess. A way for Mark out of this mess. Won't be the first time she's bailed him out of bullshit, and won't be the last, but he usually knows better than to deal with—

Wait, no he doesn't.

If only Hayley were still around to write her a spell to zap him whenever he thinks about fraternizing with youkai. She could Pavlov him into good behavior.

Well, if he's getting shocked, then that's just punishment, she dryly thinks. He probably needs to be punished from time to time. While Mark is a good guy and one of her best friends, he goes batshit if he doesn't have a finger in every single pie in the entire goddamn city, and his nose for trouble is the worst in existence.

Maybe she can ask Isaac for a spell. She hasn't yet, despite the weird nostalgia she feels every time she sees him mouth runes to himself. It's weird to be nostalgic about a stranger, but it's like torture to just have a spellwriter *near* her again.

She wonders if Natalie feels the same way.

Horribly, she wonders if *that's* why Natalie had wanted to keep him around rather than washing their hands of the demon and turning him loose to the mercy of the coven hunters.

There have been worse decisions made in their little group of friends—see: every entry under Ito, Mark—but it isn't nice to think about. Then again, thinking the worst of her friends has saved her skin more than a couple times, and she's blessed with a circle of friends who somehow always rise to that occasion.

I'm supposed to be worrying about selkies and tengu, she reminds herself. *Maybe the selkie can eat the kelpie for me.* So she may hold a grudge. Sue her.

When she makes it back to the shop, Natalie has hung her Out To Lunch sign in the window, so she must be back, and there is a reassuring lack of burning building. Not that she didn't trust the boys to watch over things—but, well, she didn't trust them to watch over things. Isaac probably spat in a few potions out of spite.

"What did Mark want so urgently?" Natalie asks as she slides a mug of tea across to her.

Vivienne sighs through clenched teeth. "He has a selkie in his bathtub. What else could he possibly want from me?"

"What's a selkie?" Sam stage-whispers.

"A shapeshifter who turns into a seal," Isaac replies at normal volume. "Why was that an emergency?"

"I'm sorry, have *you* dealt with many pissed selkies in your life of law? Do share the secret if you know it."

Vivienne only then notices his bandaged hand. Isaac catches her look, and before she can ask, he answers, "We found out demon blood is corrosive."

She snorts a laugh. "I could've told you that."

"Even I could have," Natalie adds. The corner of her mouth twitches, which for her may very well be a grin. "But I'm glad you two have retained some scientific curiosity. You'll fit right in."

"Great," Isaac says.

"Any other demonic knowledge you could share with us?" Sam asks with a steep cock of his head. "If not for scientific curiosity, then for basic safety. Common knowledge may not be all that common."

It isn't the first time she's noticed, but Vivienne notes a faint accent. Not something he's picked up from them, but she's never heard of a demon reverting to a past life before. Maybe it's something leftover? "Demonic knowledge is pretty sparse, but if we have a willing participant..."

Isaac thrusts his arm between them. "No. No experiments."

"I'm shocked it took this long," Natalie mutters under her breath.

"Listen, I'm an expert on necromancy and exorcism, but there's no one who's an expert on *demons*. At least no one living anymore. We have a rare opportunity here, and if *you* weren't digging around, then why were you deciding to dissect him the moment you two were left alone?"

"We wanted to make sure if he got cut in front of someone—"

"Yes, it'll give it away in a heartbeat, and no, there's no way to mask it. Settled demons are invisible on the outside, but once you get inside, then it's less human."

Sam presses both hands against his stomach. Isaac looks vaguely queasy. "Is a settled form a *body*, or a disguise?"

Vivienne reaches over Isaac's protective arm and pats Sam's cheek. "You're solid, and it's... kind of a body. Probably. I don't know about organs, or anything inside, since it usually looks like mush when it comes out. Everyone's does."

"This is getting macabre. Vivienne, please loan them whatever notes you have on demons, just so we can avoid other simple mistakes. Isaac, Sam, please don't dwell on existential dread. It does little good," Natalie announces.

Sam mouths 'existential' like it's a new word to him. Vivienne thus far has been unsuccessful in making him read a dictionary.

"Let me know when you decide how to handle the luck spirit job," Natalie continues. "And however Mark addresses his new selkie problem."

Vivienne doesn't know much about luck spirits, either, compared to other spirits. "Might need to go on a research binge, between luck spirits and selkies. Would you hate me if I paid a visit to Caoimhe?"

"Vetoed," Natalie replies instantly. "There is no way to subtly ask them anything, much less about demons or black magic, and I would prefer you not to auction yourself off to them anymore."

Vivienne bites her tongue on the fact that she also wants to ask about shapeshifters. She hasn't told Mark about Sam, and she won't tell Natalie about his new roommate's thievery. Yet. She respects that they both like to keep things compartmentalized, even if she's the middle of their Venn diagram of problems, but if need be, she *will* tattle, because the ends (her friends remaining alive and not killed by angry selkies or youkai) justify the means (siccing Natalie and her precognition on what may become of the selkie).

· · • • • • • • · ·

Vivienne is nearly asleep against Natalie's shoulder when she mumbles, "Jus' wish there was somethin' we could do to help her…"

Natalie does not need to ask to whom she is referring. It's certainly not her new selkie problem. It's been weighing on her, too; ghosts and death are delicate topics in certain lights, and Natalie thinks she knows what she's seen of this one in various futures.

The television in front of them flickers nearly mutely, the only light in the living room, and Sunshine is a sleeping, warm lump on their shared laps, purring on every exhale. It's not a bad evening to themselves.

But there is work to be done. There is always work to be done. And the sooner she shares her plan, the better.

"I have an idea, and you will not like it. But it may be the last chance for saving that little ghost," Natalie tells her.

Vivienne snores against her shoulder.

Natalie elbows her, not unkindly, and Vivienne rouses again. Slowly. "Huh?"

"Astral project to speak to the ghost alone, without the boy knowing. You may be able to talk some sense into her, or get more information about the situation," Natalie tells her. Realization dawns gradual and grim on Vivienne's face. Natalie presses on, "I know you wouldn't like it, and I'd prefer to ask Rory and Hammond for help in this. But if the options are this or letting the demon eat the ghost, wouldn't you want to take the chance?"

It may be cruel to play on Vivienne's knack for taking dangerous risks, but at least Vivienne knows that she's doing it. They're both a little too aware of each other.

Vivienne suggests instead, "I could break into his house and catch her while he's sleeping. Or see if she goes elsewhere at night."

"And if you're caught? If he wakes up, or she manages to wake him? You said she caught him when he fell, and that sounds like a poltergeist. Or you could get the police called on you. Again."

Vivienne's face scrunches in displeasure. "Ask Rory, then, if all you want to do is corner the ghost—"

"Viv, we both know that would just pour oil onto the fire, and no one is as good as you at thinking on their feet when it comes to spirits. If it were just a poltergeist, just a ghost, *just* anything, I would ask Rory and Hammond to do it themselves. But it's not *just* anything—who knows what this could become," Natalie exclaims. Her voice has risen more than she intended, and Sunshine cracks open an eye, a single slit of yellow against the thick black of his fur.

She scoops him up and buries her face against him. He's soft, and warm, and still alive. He also tolerates this for exactly five seconds before slithering out of her grasp with a trilling complaint.

"Will you tell me what you've seen?" Vivienne asks. She pulls a knee up onto the couch, so she's facing her sideways, and Sunshine walks along the back until he can sit on the arm nearest her. They stare at her with judgment they don't mean.

Natalie averts her eyes anyway. "I've seen a lot of messy spirits. I've seen things concerning luck spirits, yes, but also more demons and *other* things." Natalie keeps lists of her visions, and Vivienne has access to many of them, but she could never record *all* of them.

This is what their life has become: recording, avoiding, and mitigating tragedy together. It's sad, in a way, but Natalie has only ever been thankful.

"I think we should take the risk to save her," she concludes.

Vivienne, as always, trusts her. Natalie wants to hug her for it. "Alright, we'll do it."

A building falls like a waterfall, tons of concrete and glass and metal coming down with slow-motion grace. Dust and debris fly up ahead of anything else, and in the smoke of the ruined building, a figure stands, radiant and untouched.

It turns its antlered head and reaches for the nearest building, already damaged from the first one's collapse. The figure raises up on too many limbs like stairs. It flows with liquid grace and leaves spears of off-color, cursed body behind to melt.

Anything still moving runs without looking back. The thing climbing the tower like a centipede doesn't turn, but it spears flying spirits and pulls them, screaming, to eat with a mouth too large for its head. There are too many teeth. It hurts to look at it, especially the manner in which it moves and chews and searches for more.

The second building comes down, but beneath the horrible crashing sound comes rumbling laughter, deeper than the earth itself.

The potion explodes in the pot, ruining Natalie's kitchen wall and splattering her face and hair with disgusting goop.

It had been a potion for silencing a neighbor's noisy dog. Natalie supposes this is karma of some sort.

CHAPTER 6

In Which They Astral Project

"Nat, this is a *dumb fucking idea*. And that's me saying that. *Me*. Please give that the weight it deserves, and send them back—oh, hi, you two!" Vivienne turns to Isaac and his demon with a smile already in place. "You know, I think you should actually have the night off—"

She's interrupted by a tug on her hair. "Please excuse us a moment," Natalie says icily, and without remorse, drags her into the relative privacy of her kitchen. "*Vivienne*," she starts, but Vivienne preempts her by grabbing a wooden spoon and pointing it at her.

"No, don't you *Vivienne* me." Natalie removes the spoon from her face with a flick of her fingers. Vivienne keeps pointing anyway. "You just invited an unknown witch and a *demon* into this shop when this is *your* plan. Rory is going to be here! Even if Isaac can't see ghosts, the demon sure as hell can."

"I have a name now, you know that. It's Sam."

Vivienne glares down at the black tendril wound around her leg. He waves up at her with a tiny, clawed hand.

Natalie scrubs a hand over her face with a silent groan. "Alright, it sounds like we have more than one or two things to discuss. Viv, please, I want them here in case the nightgaunt comes for your body. I've already had spirit sight draught, so I can help ensure Rory's safety. Isaac, come in here, too, and I'd thank you not to eavesdrop."

Isaac slinks in, unrepentant, and Sam coils up into his arms like some sort of lap dog/snake hybrid. A moment later, he slithers back out, stepping seamlessly into a settled form. It's unnerving to see him go back and forth, and she can't help but wonder precisely what can of worms they opened to allow a demon to write his own contract.

A matter for another time.

Vivienne crosses her arms over her chest and fixes her best glare on the two of them. "We're going to need your help tonight, but not about what we've discussed earlier. You two *may* have to play very weird guard dog."

"I think we can handle whatever it is," Isaac replies.

"Well, actually, let me reiterate. *Sam* will play guard dog, and you're here to feasibly keep him tethered in the area." Feasibly, because who *knows* what his range is anymore. Who knows anything about demons anymore.

"I also need more herbs chopped, I'm running low on some backstock. I'll keep you busy tonight," Natalie adds, without meanness or smugness, but still, Isaac withers.

"So, a ghost? You had implied you were alright with taking care of ghosts," Sam says with a steep cock of his head.

Vivienne tightens her arms across her chest. "*No*."

"The ghost is a friend of ours. If you do anything to harass, harm, or attempt anything unkind toward him, there *will* be swift and uncompromising consequences. Are we clear?" Natalie adds.

Isaac and Sam remain silent for a long, weighted moment. Sam has yet to be much of a threat in *anything*, but Vivienne is absolutely prepared to fight him to the death if it came to Rory's safety. She'd fight almost anything for him.

"Alright, I'll be the one to ask. Why is an exorcist friends with a ghost? My understanding is that you banish them, or guide them into passing on. Stop them from becoming something nasty," says one of the worst potential Nasty Things that human ghosts could become.

"The world of magic, especially one as densely populated as this city, is full of singularities and exceptions. Rory is a special case, and he's helping us with this job tonight, as are other friends of ours."

"Then what do you need Sam for, precisely?" Isaac asks.

Natalie looks at Vivienne; Vivienne turns from her. She doesn't like to talk about it, and they don't strictly *need* to know. "Hopefully nothing, and nothing he couldn't handle. It couldn't actually hurt either of you." *I think*, Vivienne privately adds, but doesn't voice it, because the last thing anyone needs is more reason for Isaac to be a little bitch. Only half of his attitude is actually warranted. "You're to keep it away from Rory, because, ghost."

"And no other clues than that," Isaac flatly says.

"Ominous," Sam adds.

"You'll know it when you see it," Natalie tells them, "but if it's any consolation, I don't really know what it looks like, either."

"My drawings were *not* that bad!"

"Ominous," Sam repeats, though he seems rather excited. Great. Just what the night needs.

But his enthusiasm beats Isaac's... whatever his deal is, at any rate.

· · · · • · • · · · ·

Isaac has no fucking clue what to expect for the evening. *Ominous* had been right, but when Natalie and Vivienne had begun collecting ingredients and drafting their potion, puzzle pieces slid together.

Ominously.

Natalie stirs a truly frightening amount of linden flowers into her biggest pot, and Vivienne flips through a handwritten spellbook (read: beat-up spiral notebook) while occasionally calling out additional ingredients or steps. Baku fur, lavender dried under a moonless night, chamomile, witch water, holy rope, and, somehow, *more* linden flowers.

He's beginning to suspect they're messing with him when the front door chimes.

"Hellooooo, ladies!" In walks one of the most flamboyantly commanding presences Isaac has ever seen: the man is tall, brown-skinned, and his black hair, tied in a fishtail braid, is even longer than Isaac's. (It may be longer than Natalie's.) No single thing about him is stunningly attractive, but he demands attention with raw confidence, and Isaac can't help but shy from that sort of personality. He doesn't work well with extroverts. Oliver and Walker were bad enough.

Sam watches something else, so Isaac supposes that would be the Rory guy.

"Hi Ham!" Vivienne positively *squeals* and throws herself at him. He spins her around with much laughter and only sets her down after kissing both her cheeks. "Hi Rory!"

She then repeats this with a figure Isaac can't see, so it looks like she does a spin in midair.

He stares at the spectacle, because while he had been expecting a ghost, he had not expected a *tangible* ghost. Those don't exist. And even if they did, they would intersect with the visible spectrum *before* the plane of physicality. Isaac clenches his fists in his sleeves to stop himself from doing something stupid, like touching.

"Hammond, Rory, this is Isaac and Sam, my temporary interns."

"Is that what we are?" Sam asks. Isaac hides his snort in his wrinkled sleeve.

"Yes, that is what you are," Natalie replies without missing a beat. "And this is Hammond and Rory. They're good friends of ours, and also freelance hunters."

"On the side," Hammond slyly corrects, greeting Natalie also with a kiss on each cheek. "Not everyone can skip out on having a day job, and I've seen the sort of trouble being a full-time exorcist can lead to. Exhibit A."

Vivienne bats her lashes at him.

Then, she twists back around to address the unseen Rory. "No, it really was this bad with Hayley, too. You two were just *blissfully* ignorant."

So this Rory is definitely not on the audible spectrum, either. Isaac has never been the only person in the room who can't see ghosts, even during his rare run-ins with other witches. He's never given much thought to ghosts before. But now he's missing a quarter of the conversation, Sam tracks Rory like a cat watching a fly, they're in the presence of a spectacularly perplexing singularity, and their collective familiarity makes his hackles rise.

It is only after the conversation has gone on long enough that they've trotted out inside jokes and the finer details of sleep magic that Isaac realizes Natalie had never introduced Sam as a demon. She hadn't even mentioned Isaac as a witch, much less a spellwriter.

Another arrives not twenty minutes later, the other hunter they'd mentioned, with a tinkle of the bell and much clomping of heavy boots. Isaac snaps into tension at once. Codi Clarkson is a Black woman who possesses the type of beauty only women of a certain age can achieve, with multitudes of braids tied up into a ball atop her head, and eyes sharper than a knife with red eyeliner to match. He's heard of her before, but never met her. Never *wanted* to.

It is not her stature—she easily dwarfs both Natalie and Vivienne, short as they may be—nor her leather jacket and tight leopard print pants that intimidate Isaac.

No, that would be the *shotgun* cradled in the crook of her elbow.

Like Vivienne, she greets Hammond with over-the-top cheer. "*Hammond*, honey, it's been ages! You haven't snapped your legs yet!"

She drops her duffel bag with another heavy *whump*, and Isaac sees what looks like a crossbow handle sticking out of the unzipped side. Codi fawns over Hammond, they kiss each other's cheeks, and Isaac catches sight of a shoulder holster beneath her jacket.

"So, ignorin' the strays Nat's pickin' up again, I'd like to know what we've all been called in for. Mind explainin'?" Codi asks with deceptive silk in her accented voice.

"Especially considering whatever *this* is," Hammond adds, peering into the roiling pot with the Ominous Potion. Sam nods along in agreement.

Vivienne tries to hide under a counter, but Natalie grabs her by the hood and hauls her back up. "Tonight, we're ideally taking care of that luck spirit haunting. Vivienne, Hammond, and Rory, you're going to go track her down. I'm staying behind to maintain the spell, and Codi, Isaac, and Sam will help me ensure the safety of the shop."

"Safety from *what*?" Codi asks.

"Who knows," Hammond hums with the air of someone who Totally Knows. "So, is this potion what I think it is, then?"

"Yeah, I'm astral projecting tonight," Vivienne replies.

Isaac's head whips around to look at her. *Astral projecting?* He's never seen it in person and only knows the basic theory behind it. It's supposed to be pretty dangerous. It explains Vivienne and Natalie butting heads, and it explains why Natalie had only referred to Vivienne's body. So that means they have to ensure the safety of a ghost and a half for the night.

Or the body of one.

"What's coming for her body?" Isaac asks without entirely meaning to—too much attention snaps to him. Too many eyes bear down like physical weight. He presses close to Sam's side as a shield and mulishly adds, "You mentioned something earlier. I'm here to keep Sam here, and the exorcists must be for Vivienne, so Codi would be for us...?"

"Why'm I here for your *kids*, Nat? They don't look like monsters to me."

"I'd thank you not to refer to me as an exorcist."

"Not the time, Ham."

Vivienne successfully manages to hide beneath the counter since Natalie is distracted, massaging her temples. Her sigh, however quiet, cuts through the mounting tension.

With a flick of her wrist and a murmur underneath her breath, the sliding door shuts, and the sounds in the room become muffled from a muting spell. "I'd appreciate your discretion," Natalie tells them all, "but there are *many* delicate topics you've all broached at the same time."

Contrary to her promise of secrecy, Isaac realizes then that she's about to out them. Shit. At least he can stop *waiting* for that other shoe to drop. But Codi Clarkson had been almost at the top of the list of people he'd wanted to avoid in this city.

He grips the back of Sam's shirt and pulls magic into his hands, gauging who the biggest threats could be, whether a shotgun or a witch could do more damage before he can get them out—

"After the second accident, Vivienne has been dealing with unwanted side effects," Natalie says.

Isaac freezes, a deer in the not-headlights of not-attention, but doesn't loosen his grip. *Accident?* Sam cranes his neck to look back at him, but Isaac doesn't meet his eye. He bats away the tendril that tries to pet him.

Vivienne peeks up from her hiding spot, expression pinched, hand held up to measure. "About yay high. Not very friendly. But, thankfully, not *actually* on this plane. Vaguely humanoid. Hostile, but slow and pretty useless. It can't do much to anyone except ghosts, and only when it catches up to us. It's just a not-friendly stalker."

"And as for my interns, Sam isn't human," Natalie concludes.

And everyone nods along to these two explanations like they're totally acceptable. Isaac's hand falls from Sam's shirt, more surprised than letting his guard down, but somehow, he's relieved. *Somehow.* Not that he trusts her, but she could have shared a lot more, and... didn't.

And these strange friends of hers accept that.

Isaac wonders if he's stuck in the Twilight Zone.

He will not let his guard down.

Vivienne pops up like a jack-in-the-box. "No more questions! We have another ghost to deal with and revisiting this for the newbies makes me want to crawl into a blanket fort and sleep for ninety hours. Rory, let's go!"

"Potion first," Natalie deadpans.

Natalie and Vivienne resume their potion-making with little fuss. Hammond helps here and there, familiar with their processes, but also keeping a curious gaze on Sam.

Codi seems totally content to sit in the corner and doze.

Isaac's interest wars with his dissolving caution. He wants, very badly, to see what astral projection is like. Despite everything—he means *everything*, because a demon and getting outed as a witch and getting stuck with this weird lot and did he mention *the demon now contracted to his life*—Isaac rather *likes* magic. He may be shit at potions, but they're useful, and his curiosity mounts against his will.

By the time Vivienne is settling onto a cleaned-off countertop, a branch of elder in the crook of her elbow, Sam has gotten fed up with his indecision. (Isaac didn't know he *could* get fed up. Not a pleasant discovery.)

"If it's so interesting, you can watch from a spot *not* literally over my shoulder." Sam picks him up by the back of his hoodie and plops him back down right by the table.

Hammond snickers from Vivienne's other side, and it turns into a full laugh and a side-long glance at some invisible prompting from Rory. "You know we're going to interrogate Viv as soon as we leave. Want to share any other dirty little secrets now?"

Having a tail or inhuman strength would not identify Sam as a demon. If anything, it would throw suspicious minds off, since whatever Sam is, he isn't a very good settled demon. Isaac glares at Hammond through narrowed eyes, but the man shrugs him off.

"There is very little judgment in our friend circle, Rory's *charming* personality aside. We're all kind of odd ducks. Don't worry," Hammond tells him.

Isaac definitely worries. In fact, now he worries *more*, because of the genuine possibility of a ghost shit-talking him without his knowledge.

"Is he charming? I don't think so," Sam says, which is both Not Reassuring and (slightly) humorous. If they don't die soon, he may have a future as a straight man in comedy.

"Don't worry, Rory. I find you plenty charming," Vivienne tells him with a yawn.

"I do, too, considerin' I never get to see you," Codi adds.

At least Isaac's not the only one out. Some silver lining.

Vivienne downs a mason jar of swirling potion and settles back on the countertop. She closes her eyes, and the room waits with bated breath.

After a moment, she grins and crosses her arms like a vampire in a coffin. Natalie raps her gently on the head before smoothing her bangs back from her face. "Goodnight, Viv."

"See you on the other side!"

And silence again ensues. Natalie writes runes in magic marker along Vivienne's bare arms and on the counter. Vivienne's breathing evens out, and Isaac tries hard to read the runes in the spell, but it's all basic things from this side.

The potion must do the heavy lifting, he thinks, disappointed, and settles into one of the few free chairs, unfortunately by Codi. Her shotgun lays across her spread knees.

After a while, Hammond again talks to spirits, and he and his ghostly ensemble head out. Natalie again pets Vivienne.

It's then that Isaac realizes that astral projections are *boring* if you can't see ghosts.

Codi stretches her arms up over her head, tank top riding up to reveal both frightening abs and the bottom of a tattoo. "Get ready for a long night, and don't eat anythin' except Vivienne's mystery stalker. Anyone up for rummy?"

· · · · ● ● · ● ● · ·

Vivienne floats along on her stomach, trying to remember how to change her robes. They hang off of her, pristine and unmarked, and Rory kicks at her long sleeves every few moments. "Look at you," he coos in a falsetto, lacing his fingers beneath his chin. "A fresh young ghost. Bitch, you are so *cute!*"

Rory, on the other hand, has *long* ago figured out his sense of self and how to adjust his presentation in this plane. Which means he looks like a Ralph Lauren model, and Vivienne looks like a sack of potatoes. He has even managed to do his *hair*, for god's sake; up tonight in an artfully messy bun, beard trimmed neat.

"Suck my dick, Rory."

"Don't threaten me with a good time."

(Supernatural Hunter Tip #34: Ghost sex is best with water-based lube.)

"I hate the fact that I can't talk to you two in public," Hammond hisses at them as they arrive at the train station.

"Oh, pull out your phone and pretend like all the other seers and spirits do."

"*You're* grumpier than usual," Vivienne says with a sidelong glance at him. Rory feigns innocence. Badly. "I've told you everything I know about tonight, and the nightgaunt can't catch up with us that fast. It might stick by my body, anyway."

"Yeah, but you're unlucky right now? And we're about to go mess with another luck spirit, so we'll all be in the red soon enough. But also—*what's* the two you're stuck with?"

Vivienne pretends to clean out her ear and flicks nonexistent earwax at him. "Dunno what you're talking about."

"The grumpy one acts like Natalie killed his dog, and the spirit one has both of you freaked out. Even Codi got called in, and it wasn't for the friggin' nightgaunt. What trouble have you gotten into this time?" Rory demands.

"Nat said they'll be important, so we're running protection. That's all."

Standard fare in their life. Hammond and Rory may be comparatively newer to this magical lifestyle than others in their friend circle, but they've adapted well enough. Being a bonded pair means they're personae non gratae to a lot of the magical community; outsiders stick closer to other outsiders, Vivienne has found. And embraced.

"None of them seemed to know what a nightgaunt was, at least," Rory muses. "Or that you had one."

"*You* don't know what a nightgaunt is."

"I'm the only other one who's ever *seen* it, so you're welcome for helping everyone else believe you're not a crazy bitch."

Vivienne finally changes her robe with a triumphant squawk. Now she's in a sleeveless sundress that gives her bat wings she hates, but it's cute, and that's all that matters in life.

Not that ghost sleeves *can* get caught on many things, but if she's about to get into a brawl with a maybe luck spirit, she'd like to have a full range of arm movement.

They take the better part of an hour to get to the bookstore—Rory is used to moving as a ghost, but Vivienne is stuck in first gear and must be tugged along—but at least he's stopped interrogating her about the shop interns by then.

Of course, it is only then that Hammond asks, "What if the kid isn't working today?"

The ghosts stop short. Vivienne opens her mouth to respond, then closes it again.

Rory turns to her, accusation already written across his face. "You didn't *check*? You're unlucky, Viv! What's our fallback?"

"We're already here, let's just check. If they're not here, we can check the schedule somewhere." It's not a large shop, so there can only be one or two back rooms, and a schedule is likely to be posted *somewhere*. She storms into the shop before Rory can say anything else.

The first thing that catches her eye is not the telltale gold glow they're seeking, but the beautiful woman at the registers.

Vivienne floats dreamily over. Her name tag says *Dana* in big, loopy handwriting, and her hair is up again in a thick bun. Mark had at least given her a basic rundown, not as much as he'd given her on Emil, but it's *so nice* to have a name to put to the beautiful face.

Dana taps a pen against her lip as she reads something on the computer screen. Some invoice-y type page; Vivienne doesn't care enough to snoop when she can gawk in peace. Her shade of lipstick is wonderful. What she wouldn't give to be that pen right now.

Her vision of beauty is interrupted by Rory snapping his fingers in front of her face.

He doesn't seem amused, but Hammond, on the far side of the registers, looks like a kid in a candy store. He can't say anything to them with others around, especially in a small store like this, but she can read him clear as day. Mark must have told them about her first run-in here.

"Focus, please. You can moon hopelessly another time. Seems like *someone* here is lucky enough for this to work." He grabs her chin and turns her head the back corner where the Emil kid is on a ladder to restock taller shelves with the little gold glow by his feet. "Seems like our wayward ghost, unless there are more problems here than we'd thought."

Vivienne casts one last, longing look at how Dana chews the end of her pen before morosely following him. Hammond flounces over to the register to run interference, all part of their plan, except for the part where he begins the conversation with, "Hello! You must be the manager here—you're just as pretty as Vivienne said you were!"

Vivienne whirls back around with a shrieked curse.

"I'm going to *kill him*—grk!" Rory grabs her in a headlock before she can lunge at Hammond (who she can't touch anyway, but by god, *she would try,* she would claw her way back into corporeality to kick his ass) and drags her back through several shelves until they can't see them anymore. "Et tu, Rory? Do you know how completely psychotic this sounds, for a random-ass guy to come in and try to wingman for a girl who isn't here right now?"

"Seems like a good distraction tactic. We'll figure out if she remembers you."

"She does," Vivienne says at once. Because she *does*; she's been in here a handful of times, and every time Dana is on shift, they make awkward eye contact. That definitely means remembrance. Maybe not the best kind, but it's *something*.

Something that must, tragically, come secondary to her Actual Job.

She and Rory float through the last shelf and end up in front of the luck spirit wannabe. She's a blob of brightness again, but her hazy figure jerks up at their approach, and she tries in vain to put Emil between them.

"Hey, hi. Let's not drag anyone else into this today, alright?" Vivienne puts out an arm, stopping Rory beside her. "We won't come any closer. Can we talk?"

"Can you turn off the friggin' brights?" Rory adds.

Surprisingly, after a moment, the little not-ghost dims. She brushes luck off her face like it's dust, and while she's still glowing faintly, her features are once again visible.

"My name is Vivienne, and this is my friend Rory. What's your name?"

Instead of answering that, Miss Luck Spirit Wannabe blinks her big, bright eyes at them and asks, "Are you two *dead*? I'm sorry."

"I am, like you are. Vivienne is doing some magic bullshit so we can talk with you like this," Rory replies.

Vivienne elbows him again for cursing, despite the fact that she has Definitely Sworn In Front Of These Very Minors Before.

"I'm sorry you're a ghost, too. Dying's pretty rough, huh." Vivienne shuffles the tiniest bit closer under the guise of sitting down in the air.

"Yeah."

"What's your name?" Rory tries again.

"...Christine." It's a good starting point. Christine fidgets, sidestepping Emil a bit, and sits down across from them. She *dings* when she plops down; Vivienne spots a thick leather collar around her neck, nearly hidden by her robes. A large, round bell is attached. "Why are you here, again? You don't want me to be here, um, I know, but I'm not hurting anyone."

"Ghosts are static beings. They can't change. If you're trying to change, then you could hurt someone—yourself, or Emil, or anyone around you. Why are you trying to turn into a luck spirit?"

Christine fidgets with her sleeves and avoids their gazes like a guilty child.

Their answer, in the most unhelpful and disastrous method possible, appears before their eyes with a *pop*.

A calico cat floats before them, wearing a matching, tinier collar.

Not just a cat.

A *bakeneko*.

"*Shit*," is all Vivienne has time to say before Emil notices and nearly falls off his ladder with a shout.

"What the—?!" He clings to the shelf, neck craned back to look at the Magical Floating Cat. "Kitty, why are you... Cat. Oh my god. Cat, you're floating."

"Emil, get down before you hurt yourself," the cat tells him.

Magical Floating *Talking* Cat.

"Ham!" Vivienne shouts and Rory hauls ass back through the shelves to get him. The bakeneko hisses at them, long tail bristled, and cat fire bursts into life between them. "*Ham, we have a problem back here!*"

"Leave them alone," the cat spirit hisses. "She's not hurting anyone, and she will not turn into a poltergeist or demon."

Emil presses himself flat against the shelves and tries to edge away from the growing spectacle.

"Oh dear," Christine mumbles, nearly inaudible, and grabs the cat spirit out of the air. The fire poofs out and much of the calico's anger fizzles out, too. "I-I'm sorry—we really are staying safe and taking care of one another. But Kirara, you weren't supposed to talk in front of Emil!"

"No *shit* you're not!" Vivienne exclaims.

Emil books it at the same time Hammond tears around the corner. He catches him around the middle rather easily, and before Emil can kick him, he blows sleep soot into his face. Emil crumples in his arms and Hammond widens his stance to compensate. Rory doesn't return, however.

"You're all together," the cat, Kirara, realizes with her lip curled. Her tail *whaps* into Christine's arm. "State your business, humans."

Vivienne lets out a wild laugh. "*Our* business? What are you doing in the human realm?" The goblin market door is across the city, and youkai are generally something that covens like to stay aware of in their realm.

"I'm protecting the kittens."

Vivienne facepalms.

Hammond, holding the unconscious Emil around the middle, shifts so he's between them. "Nope, sorry, but this is definitely a living human kid and *not* your jurisdiction."

Vivienne can't help but glare at him for hanging Christine out to dry like that. "That's a *human* ghost, too. And human ghosts aren't meant to change."

"Well, I wasn't going to sit around and let her become a demon. Someone had to do something. So now, she's a luck spirit." Kirara punctuates this with much attempted licking of Christine's curly hair. (Judging by her chagrined expression, it happens a lot.)

"She's really not." Vivienne tries to approach them, but the bakeneko throws up another few balls of fire. "Human ghosts can't just... *change* into luck spirits. Ghosts don't work that way, and neither do spirits."

"But look," Christine pipes up and holds out her hand. Luck glitters in her palm. "I can move luck around—I can *see* it—and Kirara says I'm doing a good job..."

These are all True Things About Luck Spirits. Even the feline encouragement, since spirits flock to their own. Vivienne drags her hands down her face; of all the times not to have her bag or her notebooks. "Can you create your own luck?"

Christine looks away.

"Can you jump between points in the same realm? Can you create cat fire, or perform any kind of magic?" she presses. Kirara hisses at her again, so she backs off, hands up in surrender. "Ghosts can't change—if they do, they turn into bad things. But ghosts *can* pass on, and we can help—"

"Stop bullying her!" Kirara exclaims.

"Ghosts need to pass on!"

"Like you two?"

"I'm not dead," Vivienne replies, affronted. "Okay, but tonight is..." A terrible example. She glances around again, but Rory still must be avoiding the angry cat spirit. Not that she blames him, since a ghost could do squat to a higher spirit, but the moral support would be nice.

Who is she kidding, Rory is shit at moral support. Better that he's MIA.

Kirara huffs. "Humans prefer to generate problems out of anything and stick their noses where they don't belong. But I'm taking care of her, and we're both keeping an eye on the boy."

"But why are you here? Higher spirits usually don't interfere with humans like this." Some youkai and fae tend toward mischief or business, and weather spirits can be genuinely benevolent toward the areas they govern, but spirits don't just adopt kittens—*children*.

"There's enough going on that I don't want anyone snatching up an unleashed demon. Can't cats have a heart, too?" Kirara haughtily replies.

"You still can't turn a human ghost into a *cat spirit*. That's not how this works! Any of it!" She has not been an exorcist for so many years just to get shown up by a fluffy cat and a teenager. "Wait, what else is going on...?"

Rory finally makes his grand re-entrance by sticking his head through the shelves. "Viv, we have a problem."

"Tell me about it."

"We won't have a problem, if you'd kindly back off and give me the boy back," Kirara says with a sharp smile. "I won't even burn this place down. It's pleasant, smells like luck and stories. That's how kind-hearted I am."

Hammond steps back, Emil still a dead weight in his arms, and the bakeneko tenses to jump.

Two things happen at once: Christine throws herself forward to keep Kirara from attacking, and the nightgaunt stumbles in through the wall.

All hell breaks loose.

Visions tend to come in moments of relaxation, distraction, or weakness. Natalie is very used to them when falling asleep or waking up, but they can be difficult to differentiate from dreams at times.

She has just laid her head down on her pillow when the room changes to an open warehouse.

Two people are tied up, though only one is conscious; the grey-tipped hair on the one lying prone identifies her as an older Vivienne Sayre. The young man sitting up, cheek resting on his knees, has deep brown hair tied back in a ponytail and sharp eyes. He tracks something unseen.

The unknown man glances down to Vivienne. Blood clings to their clothing, but it seems most of it is Vivienne's, based on the stranger's lack of panic or pain.

Bootsteps draw his attention, and another man strides forward like power incarnate. Something about him seems familiar. "I'm sorry," he says jovially, "but I'm going to kill you both."

"So you said," the first stranger mutters.

"Tell me where you sent the demon."

"And you'll let us go?"

"You've gotten in my way too much, and my employer is pressuring me to leave fewer loose ends."

"Your employer," the stranger scoffs.

"If you won't cooperate." The tall man draws a handgun and pulls the trigger. Vivienne's body jerks and the other jumps as he's splattered with blood. He squeezes those sharp eyes shut, shoulders hunched and shaking around his ears. He dies with another's name on his lips.

Natalie goes to vomit in the bathroom, rinses out her mouth, and slips back to bed. She tries to remember why the man with the gun in his left hand was so familiar.

CHAPTER 7

IN WHICH CATS CAN BE KIND

Emil wakes after having the *weirdest dream*, but as it turns out, it's not a dream at all because the pretty calico cat is staring at him, less than an inch from his face.

He sits up, vision swimming, and scrambles backward until he hits a brick wall. It looks like he's in the alley beside the bookstore, and he had *definitely* just been inside the bookstore. Right?

"What's going on," he croaks, although he's alone here, save for the cat.

"You don't want to go back in there," the cat replies anyway.

Emil stares down at her.

The cat sighs. "Right, humans need explanations about this. My name is Kirara, and this is Christine."

Again: he is alone in the alleyway, except for the cat.

"This is the first time we've formally met, though I've appreciated your company the past few weeks, anyway. You're a very kind human, Emil," the cat continues with a purr.

"You're talking. To me."

"Yes, I am."

"Cats don't talk!"

"My name is Kirara," she repeats. "And I suppose I'm not what you know of as a cat, though I very much am one. I'm a bakeneko. They're quite amazing."

Before Emil could either scream his head off or punch himself to see if he's still dreaming, someone else barrels out of the emergency exit into the alleyway. The man nearly trips over them, despite Kirara's yowl, but catches himself at the last moment.

Emil vaguely recognizes him from his dream: the Native American man with the braid who'd been chatting up Dana.

"Have either of you seen Rory?!" he demands, eyes wide with panic.

Emil shakes his head, but the man doesn't even appear to notice. "Are you bringing that monster out here after you?" Kirara snaps.

"No, it's after Viv, but—she's leading it away, so you three just sit right here and stay out of the way." He doesn't even look at them, distracted with his panic, and darts off without waiting for a response.

"...I suppose so," Kirara says after a beat.

Emil feels like he's missing part of this situation. "Three?" he echoes. (Again again: alleyway featuring him and the weird cat and no one else. Right?)

"It wouldn't hurt for you to know more, at this point." She sighs, and in a beat in which Emil doesn't *see* any change, there goes from a handsome calico cat to a woman crouched in front of him.

Her hair is multi-colored, like a bad dye job or maybe reminiscent of a certain cat, but it's really no mystery at all considering the fact that she *has cat ears*. And a tail. And *claws*.

Emil wishes he could go through the wall behind him to escape this fever dream.

Cat Woman grabs his head and he screws his eyes shut to brace against pain. Instead, he gets a rough lick over each of his eyelids.

When he blinks open again, there is, indeed, a third person there.

Emil finally screams.

The third person, a faintly glowing Black girl, bolts for the bookstore, but Kirara grabs her by the back of the white robe. "No, you're not ruining this introduction, dear. Emil, this is Christine. We both know who you are, but it's refreshing to speak like this—*stop screaming*, would you."

"What's going on," Emil squeaks in a voice a few octaves too high. He blames the abject terror. "Wh-What did you—did you just appear out of *nowhere*?! Are you some sort of ghost?"

"She is."

The revelation that ghosts exist tamps down exactly enough of his fear for him to continue to function in this conversation. Mostly because if ghosts exist, then he could see his mother again.

Holy shit, ghosts exist, and all those stupid paranormal television shows aren't actually stupid. His mom had loved them. Maybe real life has foreshadowing, too.

"This is a rough introduction, but there are worse options, such as that bizarre monster storming in. Still, I'll keep you both safe, and you have each other to help, too. We're away from that group for now, but it seems like they're hunting you. Hunters can be *nasty*." Kirara smooths his hair back from his forehead and checks him over once more. "You look pale. Are you feeling alright? I intervened before they could cast any magic on you, I *thought*..."

"They didn't do anything," Christine pipes up. She's soft-spoken, like the shy girls in his class who blush around the popular kids (not him). "They just wanted to talk. Maybe... help?"

"Humans never help."

"I didn't know cats were friggin' bastions of selflessness," a new voice chimes in, and Emil looks up to find the newcomer literally leaning *out* of the wall behind him. A brunet, bearded man, cozily dressed and sharp-eyed, appearing completely solid aside from the fact that everything below his chest is sitting in brick.

"Kirara, please, see? He's a ghost, too," Christine says with a tug on Kirara's shirt. "That's Rory, he's not mean, and what can a *ghost* do? We can talk a little."

"Right you are. That's all we wanted to do tonight. Talk. Gossip. Shoot the shit." Rory climbs out of the wall and floats nonchalantly beside Emil's head, ignoring him. "Like how a human ghost is trying to become something she's not supposed to be. So, you're guiding her, Miss Kitty?"

Kirara sits back on her haunches, tail swishing, and Rory jumps as though burned. She grins at him with a mouth full of overly sharp teeth. "Jumpy, are we, ghost?"

"I'm looking for my friends."

"He went that way. L-Looking for you," Emil manages, pointing down the alley toward the street.

Rory's surprise is comical. A long, wide-eyed moment passes, then in a flash, he's leaning down so he's level with Emil. Rory waves his hand in front of his face. "You can see me? Since *when*?!"

"Don't worry, it's temporary. It is also none of your business. Go be with your hunter friends again." Kirara makes a shooing motion with her hands and her tail. Emil watches the movement like she's one of those cat metronome clocks.

The thunder of footsteps precedes said hunter friend a moment before he throws himself at the ghost. "*Rory!*" he cries with exuberance belying his stature and age.

But more shocking is the fact that Rory *catches* and holds him, floating off the ground, with the patience of an old dog with a new puppy. "I didn't go very far," he mutters, "but the brat can see me now, and the bakeneko is still around."

"How are you *doing* that?" Emil can't help but ask. "You're floating! And—" On a hunch, he reaches over and flails in Christine's direction. Sure enough, his hand goes right through her. He'd seen Rory go through the wall, too, but just to be sure, Emil tries to touch him. He goes through until he hits the other man's shoe. "Is this still a weird fever dream? Am I sick again?"

"No, and this isn't normal, either," Kirara replies, ears pressed flat against her hair.

"Ghosts aren't supposed to be able to touch anyone or anything," Christine adds faintly. Kirara keeps herself between them and tugs Emil over to them. He barely avoids faceplanting onto the concrete. "How are you—"

"Don't you have an *actual* monster to be hunting?" Kirara cuts in with teeth bared. "Leave the kittens to me. I know what I'm doing."

After a whispered conversation and many sidelong glances, the two back off. The man with the braid waves a little, smiling, but Rory keeps his back to them. As soon as they round the corner, Christine's shoulders drop in relief. Kirara pats her hair sympathetically.

Emil regards the two of them. "Do you actually know what you're doing?"

"Oh, no, I was lying through my teeth. But! What's a luck spirit to do except make it up as she goes and let the world unfold before her?"

"Right. Okay, okay. I'm leaving forever now." Time to be done with this surreal nightmare. Emil stands, hands up in both surrender and defense, and edges around what *must* be two figments of his imagination.

Luckily, the side door is unlocked. It remains as he left it: brightly lit with books to be shelved. Eerily quiet outside of the soft pop playing overhead, and he realizes that there's none of the usual background chatter.

He finds Dana slumped at the front desk, cheek mushed against a register, breathing deep in sleep. His heart stutters a moment to find his boss unconscious, but he'd been knocked out, too, hadn't he?

What are these people capable of? he wonders uneasily. He flops Dana back into a chair, hopefully a little more comfortable, and feels her forehead since he doesn't actually know what kind of pulse is normal. "Dana?" he whispers (though he doesn't know why he's whispering; they're alone now). He pats her cheek. "Dana, c'mon, *please* wake up and tell me I'm batshit."

She doesn't stir. Emil sweats.

He doesn't remember any other customers in the store, and they still had about an hour before another part-timer would show up. He has a decision to make, by himself, completely alone, an actual goddamned Adult Decision.

Do I call the cops? On what, some ghosts and a cat lady? Maybe he could make up a story about a break-in. It'd be easy enough to wreck a couple of shelves—therapeutic, even—and maybe break a window or fuck with the door.

Emil no sooner pulls out his phone than he sees movement in his peripherals and Christine asks, "What are you doing?"

He nearly drops his phone, catching it at the last, fumbling moment, and spares her a suspicious squint over his shoulder. "What's it matter to you? Why are you back in here?"

"I'm..." She quails beneath his gaze, fidgeting with her long sleeves, bright eyes askance. "Um, I've been hanging around you for so long, I guess I..."

Right. Ghost. Near him. "Are you *haunting* me?!" He'd assumed she'd been with Kirara, because surely magicky bullshit flocks together. "Haunting *me*," he repeats before she can answer him. Emil points at himself. "Me. Why *me*?! I don't know you."

"No, we've never *met*," she confirms with a nervous titter. "But right now, it's safer for us both if we stick together. Kirara will make sure that monster doesn't come back in this direction."

He vaguely remembers them talking about some sort of monster—also unseen. Hypothetically never to return, and definitely Not His Problem. His Problem: unconscious coworker, being haunted by the ghost he does not want, and maybe a budding adventure to find the ghost he *does* want. If it's an option.

"Right, so, no thanks." He puts his back to the ghost girl and flicks Dana's ear. "Dana, *c'mon*, wake up. Please!"

"It didn't hurt her, I think they just used sleep soot."

"Right," Emil repeats. He shoots her another faintly annoyed squint. "You, uh, haven't seen any middle-aged lady ghosts around, have you?"

Christine shakes her head, but her expression becomes sadder, and he has the unnerving feeling that she knows which ghost he's looking for. Which is impossible—they definitely don't know each other—and it's not like he's known many other *dead people*.

"Sleep soot?" he mutters, because he can't stand that look on her face.

"It's just a powder that makes the person sleep. It's not actually soot or anything, it's pretty harmless. It'll wear off on its own."

"So why can't I wake her *now*?" He eyes the water bottle behind the counter, but Christine floats between him and it with a cross look. "Listen, kid—"

"You're only a year and a half older than me."

"How do you *know that*?!"

Her scowl deepens. "Do you remember Logan Davies?"

It's like a bucket of ice water down his back.

Emil definitely remembers Logan.

He remembers Logan in that way one remembers other survivors of a tragedy; people bonded by sitting in the same lifeboat, or watching their building go up in flames, or crawling out of the same debris. He remembers awkward cafeteria lunches turning into waiting room naps turning into some strange, strained friendship.

He feels like throwing up.

"You're his little sister," Emil croaks. He wants to go back to before ghosts existed, before he found out about any of this, before *today*.

He turns from Christine, pulls out his phone, and dials 911.

"What are you doing?" she asks. Her voice is neutral, maybe even sympathetic. Not that it matters, since he doesn't want any of *her* sympathy. He owes her the sympathy. He just can't muster it right now.

"Calling the cops," he grits out. "Need to send a message and make sure Dana's alright." And if now he's shaken enough to play the part of the scared kid, well, isn't he lucky.

. . . .

Hammond finds Vivienne sitting on a streetlight. Her feet dangle above the reaching nightgaunt.

He's only seen it once or twice before. He only knows what Vivienne has told him: she managed to bring it back with her, it doesn't exist on any physical plane, and it looks like something out of a horror movie. She, apparently, sees it all the time whenever it catches up with her.

It's only a threat when *she's* not on the physical plane, either.

"Stay back," Hammond says, uselessly, since Rory is already across the street and up a fire escape. He gives him a coy little wave when Hammond looks for him. "Okay, I'll take care of this on my own, then."

"Go team. You can do it," Rory calls back, completely deadpan.

"You're the real MVP today," Vivienne adds.

Hammond rolls his eyes at the both of them, but he smiles all the same. "Yeah, yeah, I don't know what you two would do without me."

"Neither do we," they chorus back.

"Alright, Viv, walk me through what I'm doing here." He circles around the nightgaunt, which pays him little mind. The most response he gets is a lash of its skeletal tail.

"Start with a confinement circle, then we'll build on it." She knows better than to tell him which runes to use, trusting his magic as well as she trusts her own, but still, Hammond appreciates it. He wishes he had a dollar for every time a (white, it's always white) witch told him how to cast.

Vivienne kicks her feet as she casually tells him what to add or change, like they're discussing a picnic menu instead of borderline necromancy. The black magic tingles in his fingertips, but this much, he's used to. Hazard of being friends with Vivienne.

The nightgaunt finally notices his presence beside it. It turns a faceless head toward him, and he thinks he sees a mouth somewhere in there. Unlike a ghost, it's hazy around the edges. But with a bit of magic, a snap of his fingers, and some murmured Lakota, he's done with the circle.

Vivienne slides off the streetlight and floats down to mime hugging him. Rory approaches warily, like a stray dog.

They all jump when the nightgaunt lunges at Vivienne.

It *thunks* against the wall of the confinement circle like a bug against glass.

"I'll never get used to that," Vivienne says with a curled lip. She shakes out her hands, like she touched something nasty, and pretends to throw an arm around Hammond's shoulders.

"Thanks, Ham. I had no idea this little shit would catch up to us so fast, but I guess it got excited. Did you talk to Christine or the bakeneko again?"

The sound of sirens in the direction they came seems to be answer enough.

"What are the chances she didn't mess with my luck, too?" Hammond asks, already afraid` of the answer.

"I think tonight is shot. Good job, team. Let's get back before anyone else tries to eat us, or Natalie kills herself out of worry," Rory tells them, and with a hand on each of their shoulders, he steers them home.

· · · · • · • · · · ·

"Sunny-honey, 'm home," Vivienne calls as she kicks the door shut behind her. Post-projection feels like the worst kind of hangover. She'd spent last night at Natalie's, but she knows this isn't going to wear off soon, and she's due for a rest day, anyway. No one can blame her if her feet drag.

Sunshine trots out, tail held high, already meowing in demand.

"Yes, yes, I'll feed you," she tells him as she slings her messenger bag off onto her ratty old couch. It calls her like a siren.

(Supernatural Hunter Tip #16: Never listen to sirens.)

Vivienne dumps a couple spoonfuls of cat food into his bowl and grabs two handfuls of cereal straight out of the box for herself. She really, *really* should eat more, but exhaustion tugs at her.

Sunshine snarfs down his food like it's been weeks instead of hours since his last meal. Vivienne gives him a quick scratch when she stumbles past him again. She staggers into her bedroom and collapses face-first onto her bed. It takes a true feat of will to pull the quilt over her before she passes out.

It's dark out when she wakes again, and she knows that she has not slept enough.

Sunshine is curled up between her feet, but he's raised his head to sleepily glare at the bright screen of her ringing phone. The cat looks as offended as she feels.

Vivienne quiets her phone, pushes it beneath her pillow, and falls back asleep.

She wakes once more the next morning, stumbling out to the bathroom and then the kitchen to feed the cat, and ends up collapsing again on the couch when she's done. Her sleep is as deep and dreamless as ever; Vivienne spends her lucid time studying the frame of her Door and wondering what to do about Christine and Emil.

· · · · • · • · · · ·

Nico isn't happy about the 'robbery', Dana is more shaken than Emil had expected, and for his part, he is *still* being haunted a day later.

He can just see her now.

She's a little blurrier around the edges than she had been last night, but she's still ever-present at his side. (Well, usually behind him; he's jumped and shrieked more times than he can count.) Christine is apparently quiet—the opposite of her brother—but their shared silence is far from companionable.

"Do you sleep?"

"No."

"Do you eat?"

"No, not yet. I think I will when I become a luck spirit...?"

Emil doesn't know what's so special about luck spirits, and he doesn't really know how to process *luck* being a Real Thing, too. Ghosts were bad enough.

"You talking to yourself again?" Nico calls from the back of the store, where he's still painstakingly going over their inventory. Emil feels bad about it, since he knows nothing was actually stolen.

"No, sir."

Though his back is to him, Emil can feel Nico's stare. "Y'know you could have a day or two off. I know you need the money, but..." Dana had taken the rest of the week off. Even Sabrina, who'd shown up to cop cars and paperwork, had been shaken by the prospect of a break-in at their quiet little shop.

Emil refuses to let the guilt pile up. At least it kept the crazies away.

"I'm fine," Emil replies, throwing a grin back over his shoulder.

"Then why do you keep jumping?" Christine asks from his other side. "And you haven't been sleeping that well..."

Gee, I wonder why, he thinks, unable to say it with Nico's superhuman Manager Hearing. Coming to grips with the fact that he's not only currently being haunted, but that he *has been* haunted for the past couple of months (Christine guesses around two, and it boggles the mind, since how the hell does someone forget when they start *haunting* someone?) has been An Adventure.

An Adventure of trying to remember how many times he's showered, jacked off, sang along to YouTube videos while taking a shit, cried himself to sleep, and so on, and so on. The life of a teenaged boy is not for others' eyes.

Emil shoots Christine another vaguely annoyed look. She's dead. He can't be mad at her, exactly. Except he is. And he isn't? There are a lot of confusing feelings in play.

Mostly, he wonders where Logan is, and why she's not with him instead of a random kid she's never met. Did Logan want her to keep an eye on him?

The store closed half an hour ago, but hey, if he's getting paid to stay, then alright. It's money. It's kind of nice without customers, too; he almost never has the opening shift because of school.

He wonders if the owners even know about tonight. From his understanding (read: workplace gossip), they happily let Nico and Dana run things.

"*Oye*, quit spacing out!"

Emil snaps back to attention. (Definitely not a jump.)

Then, softer and uncharacteristically, Nico tells him, "You can go home, Emil. We're almost done here, and you could use the rest."

Emil swallows down more guilt he *refuses* to have. "I'm fine," he says again, "and it'll go faster if I stay to help."

His manager pretends not to have heard him. "I'll call you an Uber." He makes a big show of pulling out his phone, so Emil is left to drag his feet to the back office. The remains of the donuts Dana had sent over are still in the box on the table, but somehow, half of one of his favorites is still there.

Emil stuffs it in his mouth and pulls off his lanyard. Christine floats around to his other side, watching with those bright, bright eyes.

"You have nice coworkers," she comments.

"Nosy. Busybodies." But nice, too, he supposes. Then, because Nico can't hear him back here, he turns to her. "You're going to follow me home again, aren't you? Don't you get bored, just watching me do homework and sleep?"

"Death is pretty boring overall, actually. But Kirara keeps me company at night, sometimes."

On that note, how does a magical talking cat factor into this mess? Emil pulls on his hoodie with a grumpy noise. He didn't ask for this any more than he asked for all the pity from the neighborhood *babushkas*. "Alright, so go hang out with her, then. Thanks for not destroying my apartment, but I don't need anyone hanging around all the time."

"But you're alone," Christine points out.

Emil huffs at nothing and stomps out of the back room.

There is a poltergeist on Cherry Street that needs to be taken care of, and Natalie has two appointments tomorrow that she hasn't started the potions for. One really ought to steep overnight, but it's four in the morning, and she can't stand the smell of lavender for a single second more. She gives herself one night of irresponsibility and actual sleep—after texting Vivienne to see if she could take care of the poltergeist.

She falls asleep with her phone still in her hand.

She does not wake, but becomes aware of something playing out in her mind's eye. It's a gentler start to a vision than she's used to.

A cat slinks down from the topmost shelf, with gleaming, multicolored fur and an overly long tail. The bell on its collar dings as it lands lightly on the countertop. The cat sits, then puts up one paw in a beckoning gesture. "Do you know how long it's been since I've done this for someone?" the cat asks in a feminine voice laced with humor.

"Maybe if you put the proper paw up," the Natalie in this future replies.

The cat swipes her tail around her hind paws. "You don't want more customers? Maybe I'm inviting a friend in."

"Luck, if you'd please. I'm fully booked on appointments for the moment."

The cat makes one more gesture with her paw, then delicately shakes it, sprinkling golden luck everywhere. "Luck is a funny thing, sometimes."

The bell on the door tinkles as a customer, a teenaged boy with a mop of sandy brown hair and curious eyes, pokes his head in. The cat jumps down to the floor, and just as she disappears between that Natalie's feet, Natalie slides gently back into true dreams.

She dreams of soft touches, softer smiles, and lips against her own.

She wakes the next morning with the thought of luck.

CHAPTER 8

IN WHICH THE MAGIC NEWBIES LEARN A THING OR TWO

Oliver understands Hermione Granger *so much* now.

He wants to soak up every bit of magic like a sponge, even if it's just knowledge, even if it's just indulgent parlor tricks and listening to the *chop-chop-chop* of Natalie working in the kitchen. Her shop always smells nice—*he* doesn't smell any of the demon stuff everyone else is so worried about—and every day she or Vivienne gives Isaac something new to wear in his hair. It's so nice to come back from office hell to this kind of cutesy shit.

"What's this?" Oliver asks, chin in hand, pointing with a wooden spoon to Isaac's ponytail. There are so many little white flowers tied into it he's half a step from a flower crown.

"Chamomile."

"Suits you, dude," Oliver says with a smirk. He prods at it, and Isaac swats his hand away. "Though I thought they were daisies. Is all this flower language stuff part of being a witch?"

"It's more like ingredients than flower language," Vivienne offers from the kitchen. She and Natalie come out with arms full of boxes of jars; Oliver hurries over to help, whereas Isaac watches. "Oh, thanks! At least *someone* is polite around here."

"Are we supposed to be polite?" Sam asks, raising his head. Oliver is still getting used to the whole human body and name deal, and the ladies are still getting used to the fact that the demon can slink back into his shadow whenever he wants, despite being settled or whatever. There are learning curves all around, apparently.

"Would you two help me carry these out to the curb before the car gets here? The last thing I want is someone spending too much time in front of a shop that doesn't need mundane attention," Natalie says. Sam crosses to her in two strides, without an order from Isaac, and she nods in gratitude.

"Aren't there, like, magic Ubers?" Oliver asks.

Vivienne barks out a laugh. "What, like renting out brooms? Can't carry boxes on a broom."

"Brooms can *fly*?!" Oliver gasps with what would be theatrical levels of awe if he weren't being totally genuine. He's getting deeper and deeper into *Harry Potter* and he is *loving it*.

"Only witches can use brooms," Isaac tells him.

"Unless they're specially enchanted," Vivienne adds with a wink.

They stack the boxes right outside the shop, and Natalie ushers them back in with a tired wave. Vivienne goes, so the demon goes, and like hell Oliver is going to be stuck outside alone with the witch. She's pretty nice, but she's also pretty creepy, and he's never liked small talk.

"So, while mom's out running errands, we get the place to ourselves!" Vivienne wastes no time before literally kicking her feet up onto a countertop, leaning back dangerously far on her stool. She rewards the three of them with a shark-like grin. "Let's play twenty questions."

Oliver's arm shoots up into the air before Isaac can even frown. "Yes! I want to go first!"

"Relax, I *love* explaining magical theory, so we're already besties. But I want to ask some questions in return. Maybe more toward Isaac than you? And our new mascot." She rummages around the counter to pull out her rather beat-up bag, then shoves her entire arm in there like she's auditioning for Pornhub. She pulls out a jar with a flourish. "A gift, for starters! Happy birthday."

Sam gives her a suspicious squint. He's *very* easy to read, now that he has a face, but Oliver doesn't think he's a very good liar, either. (Even outside of all those weird contract rules.) "I'm not certain when my birthday is. I'm not certain this counts. What is it?"

"Dinner."

His eyes sparkle, suspicion gone in an instant, and Isaac hastily swipes the jar from him. "That's a piss-poor bribe. What are you interrogating us for?" he demands.

"I still want to ask questions!" Oliver points out with his arm still aloft. Vivienne nods to him. "What's in the jar?"

"Demons, like most spirits and creatures of magic, eat other spirits. Or sources of magic. That is a lower spirit in there, so pretty harmless, and doing us all some good if it becomes his dinner. My question—what were *you* planning on feeding your pet?"

"Some kibble and a grilled cheese," Isaac flatly replies.

"You had mentioned providing for us—for me. We were waiting to see how that panned out," Sam explains, despite Isaac's icy look. (Oliver wonders if demons are like snakes in the fact that they only need to eat every so often.) "Why did you wait until Natalie left to speak to us? You've done that before."

"We'd assumed you were friends," Isaac adds.

Oliver finds it kind of funny how quick they are to play off each other. Isaac would probably curse him or some shit if he were to mention it, so of course he makes plans to bring it up at his earliest possible convenience.

Vivienne, however, doesn't seem at all bothered with the suspicion. "We're excellent friends, and it'll take more than a demon to shake us at this point in our lives. But we have different... moralities, let's say, sometimes. And we're at peace with that—we work together and let each other do what we have to. Dirty business sometimes, but hey, I'm a freelance exorcist. I'm already elbow-deep in questionable morality."

"Speaking of elbow-deep, how does your bag work?" Oliver must ask.

Vivienne brightens, away from her evil interrogator persona and into what Oliver is more used to seeing from her: earnest nerdy interest in discussing magic. "In the easiest terms, it's a portable pocket of empty space! Like a pocket dimension or something, but it's not on another plane."

"*Hammerspace* exists?!" Oliver hisses at Isaac. Isaac shrugs, because literal pocket dimensions somehow *aren't exciting* to him. "Dude, shut up, be excited. What all do you have in there? How much can it fit? Can *you* go in it?"

Vivienne's grin widens further, cementing Oliver's generally positive opinion of her. "One: most everything I need for work, and a hell of a lot of junk I don't. Two: I haven't reached the limits yet, and I don't plan on it. Three: my body could fit, but I would definitely die. Empty space kills humans, even lower or weaker spirits. It's kind of like a vacuum, without all the sucking pressure."

"That's not what a vacuum is," Isaac mutters.

She jumps down from her stool and holds out her bag. She doesn't wait for permission before grabbing Oliver's wrist and pushing him in.

His first impression is that it's cold, in that split-second way you think it's cold before you scald yourself in the shower. It doesn't heat back up, though, just still feels weird-cold, and maybe a little softer. Vivienne guides his hand around, and he feels little compart-ments—*pockets* within the pocket dimension thing. "Yo, Isy, feel this!" He pulls out a stick, maybe a foot and a half long, and brandishes it like a sword. "I got a stick!"

"It's ash, and I've used empty space before," Isaac replies, still all monotone and sour, because he clearly doesn't believe in fun. "That's quite the item to have, though."

"I told you," Vivienne indulgently replies, "I used to be friends with a spellwriter. She made this for me. It's one-of-a-kind, and super kickass. Now gimme the ash back, the last thing I need is another near-drowning experience." She stows it again and sets the old canvas bag across her lap like she's a proud parent.

"If it kills things you put in it, then is this dead?" Sam asks, sadly, holding up his Dinner Jar.

"Not likely, that's a warded jar. We need to transport things live sometimes, so we figured out a way. They're usually good for about a day in there."

"So hypothetically, if we had a space suit—?" Oliver begins, but Isaac yanks him back onto his chair by the back of the shirt.

"My turn," Vivienne says. She crosses one leg over the other and laces her fingers over her knee. Oliver already misses the nerdier version. "I know as a spellwriter you can make spells and charms and manipulate all that stuff. But I saw runes in your circle I've *never* seen before, and I'm pretty well-read. Did you *make* runes for yourself?"

"I'm a creative person."

"Must have some great inspiration."

Isaac doesn't respond.

"I know why people want to summon demons. They're the strongest thing you can summon without a sacrifice, and they can offer a lot of magical augmentation. And you didn't want a contract with one, so clearly you weren't angling to dodge that, although I have no doubt you'll figure out a loophole for yourself in due time. So *what* did you want a demon for?"

Sam's gaze, on the back of Isaac's head, could be *glowing* for all its intensity.

Isaac remains silent, however.

"Isaac, the only bargaining chip you have left is information. If you'd just work with us—"

The shop's door *tinkles*.

Vivienne and Sam go ramrod straight, wearing matching guilty expressions, and Isaac looks like he'd lost a couple years off his life from the fright. Oliver twists around to see a man ducking into the main room of the shop.

"Welcome," Oliver says, before he realizes that A: Natalie is not here to give this dude whatever he's here for, and B: the demon is still standing *right there*.

"You look like you saw a ghost, Vivienne," the man drawls with a dry chuckle. He would hardly stand out in a crowd—average height, black hair tied back in a half-bun, fair complexion, well-dressed but not what Oliver is used to seeing daily at the firm—but his smile is charming and the rare kind of sincere that you can't train yourself into. Too many of his mother's coworkers try too hard to smile like that. They fail.

"No new ones," Vivienne replies.

The man's eyes rove over the other three, and Isaac shifts, almost imperceptibly, to make sure he's between the customer and Sam. "Natalie hired more help? Or you two are picking up more strays?"

"Isaac is our new trainee, and the other two are his hangers-on. Boys, this is Thomas, a kinda regular here. I think Natalie has some of your dreamless sleep draught somewhere, would one of you go grab some?"

Sam scurries off without further prompting. Thomas doesn't seem bothered, at least by him—Oliver can see that there's some weird tension between him and Vivienne, based on the way they both smile but don't *look* at each other.

"Business must be going well, then. Good," Thomas says, awkwardly, pretending to examine a rack of upside-down drying spices. "I mean, to have extra help around here. That's good. I'm just—glad. Jesus. Ignore me."

"It's okay, I know," Vivienne says with a smile closer to a grimace. "Wait—you don't think my potions are up to snuff?"

"Mine certainly aren't," Isaac flatly says, surprising everyone.

Thomas laughs, then relaxes just a tad. "Natalie's talented and a pretty good teacher. Keep your nose clean and she won't steer you too wrong."

"*I* will," Vivienne says.

Thomas' laugh that time is more strained. Oliver can't help but wonder why Vivienne is tormenting a customer like this.

Thomas replies, "Right. Well, you shouldn't, either. I heard you've been behaving lately, though."

"I behave as well as you did at Pride last year."

He scrubs a hand over his face with an embarrassed groan. Oliver and Isaac exchange a sidelong glance. "Thanks, Vivienne. *Thanks.* I know there are worse things you could harass me with in front of strangers, but now I'm going to have to avoid nightmares of that. Again."

Sam slinks back out and passes off the sizable jar like it's a hot potato. He doesn't make eye contact and stays as far from Thomas as possible. Vivienne pours a roiling, misty blue potion into a smaller bottle, then tops it off with a sprig of lavender.

She's all smiles when she hands it over to Thomas. "Here you go. I'll let Nat know you stopped by."

He gives her that pleasant smile again, eyes on the bottle instead of her. "Thanks, Vivienne. I'll see you at next month's meeting?"

"Maybe, provided I'm not dead! I'll see if I can talk Nat into coming again, too."

Thomas' smile strains. "That'd be nice. ...See you around." He spares a glance at Oliver and Isaac out of the corner of his eye. "Nice to meet you all. I look forward to working with you in the future."

They remain in silence until the door's bell chimes again.

Vivienne waits exactly three seconds, then sinks against the countertop with a whine. "On a scale from one to ten, how awkward was that?"

"Twelve," Isaac answers.

"Well, the magical community is both bigger and smaller than you'd think. I'd rather be on weird footing with someone than *bad* footing, but..."

"An ex?" Oliver asks.

Vivienne makes a face like a cat about to puke. "We don't like anything about each other like that. We just have a weird history."

"I'm starting to think you don't have any normal relationships," Isaac says, gesturing to their side of the table.

"Uh, dude, *you* don't, either," Oliver has to point out. Isaac glares at him for this betrayal, but Oliver shrugs back at him, because if he doesn't pester him, who will? "Can we get back to twenty questions? Because now we have a bit of dirt on you, and I'm still curious about all these wonders of magic an' shit."

"I'm immune to dirt," Vivienne retorts. But she props her chin up in her hands and spares them all a tired smile. "Sam, you okay?"

"Is there a reason I shouldn't be?"

"Well, you haven't interacted with many customers, much less Eyebright witches. And Thomas is one of the top ten people you don't want to meet in a dark alley. You seemed scared. You okay?"

He rubs his arm, awkward, and funnily enough, pink rises into his cheeks. Oliver laughs before he can stop himself, and Sam just blushes brighter. "I-I'm *fine*! I wasn't—scared." Based on the hitch, he'd been close to a lie.

Oliver senses weakness, but Isaac shoves his hand in his face and pushes him away. "You're being annoying, Oliver. You're the only one who didn't smell the magic on him."

"You didn't, either," Vivienne dryly corrects, "but he's right. Thomas would probably kill or banish a demon without batting an eye. But so long as you're in this shop, so long as you stay settled, you'll be safe. Both of you."

"Is the magic outside world that scary?" Oliver asks, muffled by Isaac's fingers practically in his mouth. He licks them to be a jackass, but Isaac doesn't budge. "No—I oughta know, too, dude! What if I say something stupid and blow your covers?"

Isaac begrudgingly releases him. "Then just don't talk to anyone. Ever."

"We're not all *you*."

"Don't talk about Sam to anyone and don't mention Isaac's a witch to anyone. There you go, easy fix," Vivienne interjects. "Most customers we get here are regulars, and they're used to Nat and me having weird friends, though not everyone approves. But it makes for an excellent cover!"

"Like the ghost friend you, an exorcist, has?" Isaac peevishly demands.

"Who?" Oliver stage-whispers.

Vivienne's smile becomes strained, but she doesn't balk. "Listen, there are *reasons* we're willing to bend the rules for you, so let's not bite the hand that feeds you, 'kay? Ham and Rory are exceptions to a lot of rules, yes, and not everyone is okay with that. But also, unlike *every other* ghost everywhere, Rory is not in danger of rotting away into a poltergeist or worse."

Oliver's arm shoots back up. "Why the *fuck* do ghosts rot?!" he nearly shouts, because what the fuck. Yeah, he's seen goopy horror movie monsters, but those are *movies*. If there's one thing he's already learned about the supernatural, it's that movies have been very, very wrong.

Vivienne looks at him like she's remembered he exists in the same space as them. Isaac turns from him, less grumpy now, and a little chagrined.

But Sam mimics Oliver's raised hand and says, "I believe I'd like to know, too. I'm realizing that I've been agreeing to things I don't understand. Like what a Samael is."

Vivienne and Oliver both squint at Isaac.

"Ghosts," he defensively reminds them.

She sighs. "Alright, so... Humans are the only things that create ghosts when they die. And they're also the only type of spirit that can pass on. Every single person has their own, unique Door that they can pass on through, and *only* they can pass on through it."

"Passing on like to heaven?"

"No one knows the specifics, but we know it's a good thing. Some positive afterlife." She shrugs, as if disinterested. "Ghosts are static beings, and cannot interact with magic. But, of course, magic is everywhere, so it happens anyway. And that's how you get things like poltergeists, ghouls, sometimes wraiths... Demons, too."

"Demons used to be *people?*"

"I thought I explained this to you," Isaac mutters in a long-suffering sort of way.

"I knew it. Sort of," Sam adds with his own shrug. Like none of this is Cool and Interesting and also really, really Dark. "Not that I remember being a ghost, or a person."

"That's normal. I've never heard of anything remembering its life, except kind of poltergeists, but they're also the closest to ghosts, so. But death is inherently traumatic—"

"What a shock."

"—I *will* launch into a TedTalk of birth and death trauma, so don't tempt me, little witch," Vivienne says and smacks Isaac's hand. He stares at her as if this has never happened to him before (which is patently untrue, since Oliver smacks him all the time, and he definitely smacks back). "But that's it! Magic can mess with ghosts, so that's where exorcists like me come in. We get rid of the nasty stuff, and herd good little ghosties into passing on."

"Which is why this luck spirit ghost is causing so much trouble," Sam concludes. When Vivienne nods, he lights up like he won the lottery. "I know you failed the other night, so does this mean we're getting called in?"

"Haven't decided on the exact details, but I think so. The problem here is that there's a bakeneko involved. So it means we might need *both* of you—Isaac to field the cat, and you to take care of the ghost before she becomes something bad."

"You mean eat her. Right? Sam's gonna eat a little girl?" Oliver asks, and judging on everyone's expressions, that is precisely what they'd been talking around. "That sounds like the *opposite* of what we want him to do! Weren't we all worried he was gonna eat Isaac?"

"Living people are different than ghosts—" Vivienne begins, but Oliver slams his fist on the countertop. Everyone startles.

"So no one cares about dead people?"

Vivienne recoils as if he'd slapped her.

"You like cats," Isaac breaks in with another tug on his sleeve. "So do you feel sorry for the rats?"

"I like mice, dude. Bad metaphor."

"If a couple mice were going to eat all the other mice *and* some cats, would you still feel sorry for them?" Vivienne asks.

"Why do I feel like I'm back in school?" Oliver retorts. He runs a hand back through his loose hair and glares up at the ceiling. *And why do I feel like I'm losing this argument?*

"Look, I *know* what it's like to think of magic as all the flowery, sparkly stuff," Vivienne says, hands up in a gesture of peace. "And it can be. But it can also be nasty, and that's why people like me get jobs. The end. It's the same as the guys who take care of roadkill."

That pulls him up short. With wide eyes and burgeoning horror, he asks, "Are there ghost deer?"

"*Only* humans," Isaac snaps. But at least his dumb question gets a chuckle out of Vivienne.

· · • • • • • · · ·

Emil hasn't seen the cat—Kirara—since the night she revealed the secrets of the universe to him. So he has to get answers from Christine while sidestepping the whole Dead topic as best he can. Considering he has the verbal grace of a newborn giraffe on a *good* day, he's bracing for some awkward times.

"So. Magic," he announces to the air.

Christine continues staring off into space, floating a few inches over the arm of the couch like she's sitting and spending time with him. She does not respond.

He snaps his fingers in front of her. "Hey, Christine. Magic?"

She whips over to him, blinking rapidly, then answers, "Oh, you were talking to me?"

"You think I talk to myself?"

"You *do* sing in the shower, and you do kind of talk to yourself from time to time... Not in the crazy way or anything! I think just to, um, fill the quiet sometimes..."

Emil smothers his face in his hand. Right, she's been privy to *everything*. "Do ghosts not know anything about privacy?"

"I didn't *spy* on you. You're loud."

Emil glares at her, but Christine is already backing off, gnawing on her lip.

"You wanted to know about magic? What about it?" She asks it with the air of someone facing a firing squad: scared and reluctant, but ultimately resigned.

"Not just magic, but like, everything? You're telling me dragons and wizards and shit exist. I'm gonna want a little more to work with here."

She squints at him for a long, thoughtful moment. "...Well, um, first off, they're witches. Wizards don't exist. I think."

"You think?"

"I've never heard of one! But there are a lot of things about magic that others don't know. I really don't think any one person would know *everything*...? It's a lot like having specialties, like college or jobs?"

(Emil immediately wonders if Magic College exists.)

"Dragons exist, but not really in this region, except for the migration. And, um, you don't need to be a witch to do magic, actually. Lots of people have the potential and never figure it out." Christine cocks her head and taps her chin as she thinks. Emil unconsciously mirrors her. "Witches have familiars, but they aren't all black cats. Werewolves exist, and so do vampires, I think—a lot of supposedly mythological creatures from across human cultures exist in some form. I think fairies are meant to be rude."

He goes down his mental list. Maybe he'll need a physical list, because all of this piling on top of the initial Ghosts Are Real and Magic Is Real is beginning to be overwhelming.

"And ghosts exist," she adds, spreading her hands in a gesture at herself.

As if he could forget.

"I know a bit about magic, and stuff like that, but I don't know much about other things... Maybe it'd be best to ask Kirara when she gets back," Christine tells him.

"And when will that be?" Emil asks, scowling.

"Um, I don't know?"

"What a surprise, magic cats come and go as they please, too." He never minded the cute little calico begging for food once in a while—the company was nice and she wasn't a picky eater. But surely she could have expected him to have a few questions.

"I can tell you what I know," Christine mumbles, a touch defensive, "but it's hard to start wherever. Give me a prompt and I can go from there."

"Magic," Emil says again, with appropriate wiggly fingers.

"...And what about it?"

Emil groans and throws himself against the couch cushion. Dramatically. He's entitled to some drama, for sure, because his life is one step from a terrible Hallmark movie, and it *sucks* to be living it, even if it's in its supposedly heartwarming upswing part.

"I told you a bit about witches already. *What* do you want to know?" Christine demands. It's the nearest he's seen her angry, and she doesn't pull it off well.

"If I knew, why would I be asking?"

"What are you curious about, then?!"

"I don't know! This is all new to me, and I know *nothing*, so I can't ask!"

Kirara (Cat Forme) *pops* into being beside them on the back of the couch. Christine jumps with a squeak; Emil flails backward and falls off the couch.

"Are you two already fighting?" Kirara asks with a swish of her tail.

"Warn a guy, would you?" Emil wheezes as he scrambles back to Uprightness and Having Dignity-ness. He doesn't like the look the cat gives him in response. "We aren't fighting, and you can't just teleport in and not expect people to be surprised. ...Oh my god, you can *teleport*?!"

"It's only jumping," she dismisses, "and it sounded a lot like fighting to me. I'd expect you two to be nicer—you're about the same age, both humans, and you have some other things in common. Also, Emil, be nicer to Christine, she's been giving you a lot of luck."

"I'm not being mean," he deadpans, because they would *know* if he were being mean. Luck stirs a vague memory of That Night, but it is with a slow dawn that he realizes that they mean luck *literally*.

Kirara fixes him with a dead stare and shakes one of her paws at him.

To his astonishment, golden dust floats down like the finest snow. He can barely see it, a glittery suggestion more than anything else, but the thought that luck is a *thing* and he *has it* is mind-boggling.

"Where the hell was all this when—" He bites his tongue on his outburst at the very last moment.

But his words still hang in the air between them.

Kirara jumps onto the couch cushions between them with a jingle of her collar. (Which she *certainly* didn't have when she was pretending to be a stray and begging for food.) "Don't humans have a saying about gift horses' mouths? Do that." Then, softer, and with a paw on his knee, she adds, "Luck can't fix everything, and I didn't know either of you existed that long ago. Isn't it enough to be given a future together?"

"Why is it together?" Emil asks. He understands a little of where she's coming from—lump the two kids together, he'd probably do the same if there were two talking cats in front of him—but the fact that Logan's little sister is haunting him makes him want to crawl the walls with unknown emotion.

"Because you're both my kittens now! Think of it as my jurisdiction."

Yeah, he called that.

"It's easier not to argue with her about the kitten thing," Christine advises in a whisper.

"Right, well, I appreciate it. The sentiment is nice, and all this magicky stuff is cool. And mind-boggling. But I don't need to be adopted, 'kay? Or haunted. I'd just like a few more explanations of all this stuff, and then we can all be on our merry ways."

"It's safer for you two to stick close, and this is practically home for you two now, anyway."

"It's *my* home," he points out. "It doesn't need ghosts." Except one, who is not Christine. "Do ghosts need territories, or places to haunt...?"

"She's not a poltergeist," Kirara exclaims with a scandalized gasp.

"He knows nothing about this," Christine murmurs, petting her, then peeks back up at Emil. "Ghosts don't need to haunt anyone, or anything. Most pass on. But poltergeists have places and things they haunt, so that's probably what you're thinking of."

"See, those are answers," Emil says with a gesture even he doesn't understand. He sort of just wants to shake her by the shoulders until information drops out of her like luck, but hey, people can't touch ghosts. Who knew. "What else?"

Christine blinks those big, eerie eyes at him. "What else would you like to know?"

"I don't know! That's why I'm *asking*!"

"Well, you have to *have* something to ask—"

"Alright, cut it out, you two," Kirara butts in. Her tail lashes behind her, and her ears are pinned flat to her head. "You can figure out all these circular questions later, but I will not have you two fighting over it. Understood?"

"We're not really fighting," Christine mutters.

Emil nods. "We're not! It's just... circular, I guess. Like you said. I *guess* I can be patient and figure out, like, a list or something."

"You guess many things, huh?"

"I could. But it'd be easier to do all this with *answers*. That you two can give me?"

Emil's answer comes in the form of Christine popping out of existence.

Kirara continues speaking as if nothing happened, gaze on the now-unseen ghost. "I haven't been around *that* long, except comparatively, yes. But it's wiser for most spirits to steer clear of humanity."

During the lull of Christine's presumed response, Emil thrusts his hand forward into the empty space. Not that he could touch her before, but at least the visual of his body not-touching something usually gave him the heebie-jeebies.

Now, nothing.

"Hey, shh," Kirara says at once, pulling what must be Christine to the side. She spares Emil a pointed look. "Do you mind? That's rude, for several reasons."

"There's nothing there," Emil replies. He waves his hand through empty air again.

"So, it's worn off." She swats at his wrist, tail curled around nothing. "Of course, even if you can't see her, you shouldn't be flailing around. Girls don't like to be grabbed at."

"I'm not—There's nothing *to* grab! Turn it back on."

"I can't. It's only good once, and you should thank us that you were lucky it lasted that long."

Emil wiggles his fingers through the nothing again. Yeah, okay, so he hadn't *wanted* to be haunted, but it is infinitely better to see the ghost than not. Christine is the furthest thing from creepy, appearance-wise, but the thought of *anything* watching him, unseen, sends chills down his spine.

"How do I turn it back on, then? Without you?"

"There *are* ways humans see spirits," Kirara muses, head cocked, "but I only know vague things. Some potion? Something to do with those Doors of yours? You'd be better off asking another human for that one."

Except the only living humans Emil knows of that are supernaturally aware are Those Two. Crazy Lady and Braid Man. Not that he *wants* to speak to either of them, but it's not like he *could*. It's been a hot minute since the woman had been back in the shop.

Kirara seems to follow his line of thinking. "Look for potion shops instead. There are several in the city, so you wouldn't have to go to the markets. Do that thing humans do to search—goggle? Google, that one."

Emil squints at her. "You want me to google magic potion shops."

"Or you could use the phone book, but I was under the assumption that younger humans have phased those out."

Of course you can just *google* magic. That seems trustworthy and totally a great way to keep this kind of shit secret. He's going to make a list for all this magic bull. For when he gets Christine back, or Kirara decides to be uncatlike and answer things straight out.

And maybe to ask these potion shop people.

"Happy birthday, Nat!"

"Happy birthday, dear!"

"And happy new year!"

Natalie blows out the last of the candles and gives her friends a smile. "Thank you for setting all this up," she says, because it is no easy feat to find a party venue on December thirty-first, and means to say more, but she can't.

Natalie is abruptly watching a woman with black hair falling out of a bun, red dress ripped in several places, swinging with inhuman strength at a well-dressed Thomas Novak. There's another incredibly beautiful woman with long white hair and a shocked expression behind him. Thomas intercepts the punch with a hiss of might-strength and saves the blow from his companion.

"You're causing a scene, y'know," Thomas comments, as if disappointed.

"Stay the hell away from Mark!" the unruly woman snarls.

"Why aren't you turning into a dragon this time?"

"Should you be baiting the lady who can turn into a dragon?" the white-haired woman says with a sharp voice.

Thomas swings the other woman around and into the wall behind her, cracking it.

"Stop fighting!" the white-haired woman cries, and both of them freeze with teeth still bared. "Bon sang, you're both causing a scene. This is what you were trying to avoid!" She circles both of them, movements unusually fluid and certainly not human. "Alright, so a shapeshifter. Are those normally spirits? You could save Lucien the trouble of risking his tail for you."

Thomas suddenly slumps, then adjusts his tie as if nothing happened. "I'm not sure she's a spirit, exactly—"

"What do you think you're doing to her?" interrupts another voice, dangerous and low. The speaker does not become apparent until the last moment: a magpie tengu, in full, immaculate formalwear.

Then it's the restaurant again, and Natalie is looking down at a slice of cake on a plate for her. Red velvet, her favorite.

She eats without tasting anything.

CHAPTER 9

IN WHICH EMIL GETS INTO POTIONS

As it turns out, if you google magic potion shops, a *lot* of nonsense comes up.

Emil does not know how to filter this. He'd grown up on the internet, so he normally possesses a finely tuned bullshit radar, but with this? He doesn't know any of the technical jargon, what words to look for and which to avoid, or if there are different *types* of potion shops. He's not looking for vape shops or special bakeries, and he thinks a few of the results are creatively named bars. His dumb grade school computer literacy classes aren't helping him now.

Christine must still be around. Somewhere. Kirara has ditched them (again), but *knowing* Christine is around and being unable to ask her for any advice is a frustration he's shocked by the intensity of. It's like being little and having the cookie jar *just* out of reach.

Not like she offered criticism before, but her silence is infinitely worse. For all he knows, she could be talking up a storm. He just can't hear or see her. Maybe she left entirely.

She stayed with him for months before without being able to speak to him, but maybe meeting him turned off whatever charm haunting him had had. He wouldn't blame her. He isn't sure what the charm *had* been. Surely not his personality and hopefully not his body.

Emil aggressively scrolls through his phone. How hard is it to find a real potion shop? He prays that whoever he ends up finding will answer a few more questions—directly—than what he's had so far, because he doesn't feel like getting fleeced and being given arsenic or LSD or dyed water in a fancy glass jar. *Hey, can you give me a potion that lets me see ghosts? Yeah, this jar full of bubbling green goop seems legit. Here's fifty bucks.*

He grudgingly remembers the woman from the bookstore.

Crazy Lady hasn't returned since he called the cops (in his defense, not exactly *on* her). Which is nice for his general state of mind, but less nice for... well, his general state of mind. Emil doesn't know who else to turn to with Kirara off doing whatever cat things she does. And whenever she *does* pop in, she mostly talks with Christine, and points out to him that she doesn't know much of human shops or technology.

He types in a jumble of every magic word he can think of, just to see what comes up.

And, *somehow*, Emil comes up with something that seems legit.

The Crow's Cup is in one of the quieter sections of the downtown business district, near where those bougie apartment complexes went up, and has a very minimalist, professional website. It lists reasonable business hours, with an Appointments Available button underneath, and features a header with a shelf full of many pretty jars and bottles.

It definitely *looks* like a potion shop.

"Look legit? Heard of it?" Emil asks the empty air, holding up his phone. He waits what he hopes is long enough for his ghostly roommate to look it over. "I don't work tonight, so... You're supposed to be lucky, right? Keep me from getting fleeced."

It's only when he's in the station waiting for the next train that it dawns on him he has no idea how to budget for magic fucking potions.

He doesn't get paid until Friday, and most of what he's been making has gone straight into the rent fund. He's covered until August, but that's looming ever closer. He has enough food for the week, and gets lunch at school, and could always ask the neighborhood *babushkas* for dinner if he's desperate.

(He isn't sure he'll ever be *that* desperate.)

The potion shop isn't a very long trip, and he ends up getting a seat on both trains, despite the crowded hour. He wonders if Christine pretends to sit anywhere, or if she floats along like a balloon. From what he'd seen, he's inclined to think the latter, but he'd been so freaked about people thinking he's talking to himself that he paid little attention to her in public.

"Sorry," he mumbles, for no particular reason.

· · · · ● · ● · · · ·

Mark pinches the bridge of his nose and sighs through his teeth. "You're joking, right, Viv? You're not going to Dante for—for *what* did you say?" There's no way Natalie allowed this, but what could he say to her?

"Secret, for the time being."

"Why is our friendship just trading headaches back and forth?"

"Pretty sure you started that." Vivienne laughs, coming out like static over the phone. "But I'm offering, alright? Even if selkies aren't fae, odds are Caoimhe could tell us *something*."

He will not let her sell her soul for something he knows is a farce. Mark rolls off the couch, ignores his pounding headache, and steps outside. The sunlight doesn't help. Hopefully, his guest's hearing isn't sharp enough to get through this many walls.

"Viv, she's not a selkie," he tells her. Her silence is expectant. "A shapeshifter, yes, but it *relieved* her when you called her a selkie. That's her cover, and I'm trying to figure out what for. Her thoughts are as easy to read as a brick wall."

"Caoimhe could still tell us about other shapeshifting possibilities. There aren't that many that use skins, right?"

"Javi doesn't," he agrees, "and selkies do. And that is the total extent of my knowledge on the subject."

Vivienne's turn to sigh. Maybe it will be her turn for the headache soon. "I'm offering," she repeats. (Apparently that's a no on the headache front.) "We have a lot to bargain, and I wouldn't mind getting more out of them. And I think she'd know more about this than tengu—plus it'd be a hell of a lot less suspicious."

It has been a long time since Vivienne has dealt with Dante and Caoimhe on her own. Mark pretends like he doesn't know what goes on behind those closed doors.

Mark tells her, firmly, "I'm not that desperate, and you shouldn't be on my account, either. I don't know what Nat's currently embroiled in, but I'm sure she's already shot you down, too. Don't get into trouble over this."

Vivienne's silence is telling. "Fine, fine," she relents after her guilty pause. He wonders what *else* she's digging around for besides a luck spirit. "Wouldn't want to take *your* title of Trouble Magnet away."

"We surely wouldn't want that," he dryly allows. With many smooching noises, they hang up, and Mark heads back inside.

He immediately wishes she were still on the phone, however, since the not-selkie stands in his living room. The bathroom door is ajar behind her and she unrepentantly drips bathwater onto his carpet.

"The pelt isn't here," Mark informs her. He has several people on speed dial, but no one is close. He can't fight her. "And the door is right here."

"How do you know I am not a selkie?" the woman demands. That answers the question about her hearing abilities, as well as blatantly confirms his suspicions.

"You're not very good at doing your research, are you?" Mark asks archly.

"I want my skin back. I've no quarrels with you."

She's being chatty—so he would be a fool to pass up this opportunity. He would also be a fool to pick a fight with an unknown shapeshifter, but oh well. He has been accused of worse.

"I told you, it's not here right now. Which you ought to know."

The woman's eyes narrow further, slits of scarlet.

"Let's trade," Mark offers with his best, sunniest Customer Service Smile. "You know where the towels are, so let's sit down and talk this out like civilized people."

The woman shakes off like a dog. Her hair is too long to make this successful, and she splatters water in an even wider circle around herself on his poor carpet. Then, she runs her fingers through her hair and pulls the water out with magic.

Hair now nominally dry, she dumps that water on his carpet, too.

She's still nude and still damp, pale skin pink from the bath. She sits down on the tiniest reasonable edge of his couch. "You have one thing to trade with me. What are your demands?"

"I have more than a sealskin, my dear."

She doesn't react to his tone or his words. Her mind, as usual, broadcasts stubborn static.

So he continues. "Safety, for starters. Clearly, you have been enjoying your time here, away from certain feathered parties, am I right? Mirai seems like a lovely person, and *maybe* I'll just tell them who my houseguest is, after all..."

"You want the First egg?" the woman asks.

It takes every ounce of his considerable willpower not to let his expression chance. *What* had she just called the tengu egg? "I want a lot of things. Your name, what you are, who *sent* you to fetch such a thing."

As predicted, alarm blares through her mind. Her poker face is impressive, however, with not even a twitch giving away her sudden apprehension. "Bryn."

Mark rolls the name over a few times in his head. She hadn't sounded deceitful, so while he doubts it's the full truth, he doesn't think it's an outright lie. Not what he was expecting. It is also very little clue as to *what* she could be. "And the other two?"

"What is to stop me from tearing you apart here and now?"

"You'd never get your seal pelt back. And the next time Mirai tracks you down, I doubt they would be so pleasant."

She remains silent. It's hard to put such a soft name to a woman who could (and likely will) kick his ass six ways to Sunday, but Mark has found that once someone opens up the littlest bit, they will fall the rest of the way soon enough. And he has *so* much to pick at now.

"I thought this was a conversation. A trade. These sound like threats and guesses," Bryn says.

"Even by refusing to answer, you've already told me that your skin is more important than your freedom, you *are* at least somewhat afraid of what the tengu will do to you, and you're definitely working for someone else."

Another little *ding* of alarm. And again attached to the thought of her boss. Interesting.

"Then trade me to the tengu and be done with it. What do you stand to gain by keeping me here?" she demands.

"As you've made it clear by breaking out, I'm not *keeping* you anywhere. And from you, information. Maybe protection if something *else* tries to break into my home, because if something happens to me, you're not getting your pelt back."

Bryn scrunches her nose. "You speak strangely, your house smells like magic but not yours, and you have some form of psychic connection to those around you."

So she is only somewhat aware of his clairvoyance—stranger still that she doesn't know what a psychic human is. Even the fussiest higher spirits in the goblin market know the basics of human skills.

Taking a step toward him, Bryn forces on ahead. "You know not what you are digging into, human, and I suggest you stay out. Give me my skin back and I'll leave you be."

Her mind echoes her: a looming shadow, a threat behind the already intimidating figure in his living room.

"Who are you working for?" Mark tries again.

Her thoughts take shape, no matter how she tries to fight it. She has experience with mental prying, if only for how deftly she hides herself. But it's the pink elephant problem; if he keeps prodding the same sore spot, she can't *help* but think of it.

He gets a flash of a monstrous form, lashing tails, and a voice that *burns*. And all of her thoughts of the figure are drenched in terror.

He isn't aware his nose is bleeding until he tastes the copper.

"Huh," he says, fingers coming away red, and he wipes them on his shirt.

Bryn's eyes have narrowed back to dangerous slits. She can suspect all she wants; it isn't until she acts that Mark will worry. And now he has his own suspicions, anyway. She is probably using his home for safety from more than the tengu, and that puts a new spin on things.

· · • • • • • · · ·

Take two of investigating the properties of demon blood (since Natalie and Vivienne are again out, entrusting the shop to them, and Isaac only feels comfortable experimenting without their eyes on him) is now centered on how to *stop* said demon from bleeding. They don't clot like humans do. Isaac is still trying to bandage Sam's hand without touching him when the door tinkles.

"Go," Sam hisses at him, and shoves his half-bandaged hand back under the running water. It rinses the black into less suspicious clear.

Isaac hates dealing with customers directly, but he'd hate getting killed for having a demon more, so he shuts the kitchen door behind him and tries to seem polite instead of nervous when he greets the customer. "Welcome," he says, a touch above deadpan.

It's a high school kid, gangly and awkward and looking around with the wide-eyed expression of someone very new to magic. At least he shouldn't know a demon on sight.

"Can I help you?" Isaac asks. He realizes his hands are still wet and hastily wipes them off on his jeans.

"Uh, I need a potion? Like... a real one?"

Isaac stares the kid down. *Duh.*

"I'm new to this, and I'm not sure what's right and what's not. This place looks legit."

"It is legit."

"So it's... magic? Like, for witches and things? Not that I'm a witch, or magic, but I need some stuff, and I was told that potions could help!"

God help him if he needs to give the kid a healing draught for an STI or an intellect potion for a test. Isaac can't remember what it's like to have problems so banal; his hand throbs again in reminder of another burn.

"I'm a witch," he flatly informs him, "and I can vouch for the legitimacy of this shop. What, exactly, are you looking for?"

"Oh." For a long beat, the kid stares at him with huge blue eyes. Isaac may be the first witch he's ever met. Should he grab a broom for effect? "Oh! Well. Cool. I need a potion that'll let me see ghosts."

Not what he had been expecting. It could be for a dumb reenactment of whatever latest ghost hunting show is on these days, or it could be a very well-planned Halloween prank. "What kind?" Isaac asks.

"There're different kinds?"

He sighs. Natalie is nothing if not thorough, but the inventory book is in the kitchen. (They'd been looking for something to soothe the burns, then something to seal up a demon's open wound. They hadn't found either.)

Of course, Sam has heard the entire exchange, and comes out of the kitchen with a smile on his face, oven mitts on his hands, and the book in his grasp. "Hello there. Isaac, looking for this? I couldn't flip through it very well by myself, but here you are."

Then he freezes.

Sam's eyes track something to the kid's left, something not visible. If Isaac hadn't gone through this so recently with Natalie's friends, he might not have recognized it so quickly, but as it is, he knows they're not alone here.

A teenager has come into the shop with a ghost haunting him. How about that?

"Why is it you want to see ghosts?" Isaac asks, casually, as he scans through the index for *sight, ghosts/spirits*. There are a lot of options. He doesn't know shit about potions, much less ghosts, and he doesn't have the time or interest to go digging.

"I think I'm being haunted. Benignly! And we have some unfinished conversations to have, so. That. I'm not trying to become a psychic or hold seances or anything," the kid replies.

Isaac wonders when either of his babysitters will be back, and what he should do about who he is pretty damn certain is in the shop. *Vivienne's going to shit a brick*, he thinks. "If you wanted to take care of it, there are plenty of exorcists in the city."

"No! No, I'm good. For now."

To Isaac's displeasure, he knows he's going to have to decide which potion to give the kid, and he knows somehow he'll get judged for it later. "'Kay," he mutters, and flips to the Spirit Sight Draught page. According to Natalie's records, she has it in stock. *Where* in stock is another question entirely.

"Got it," Sam says from where he's reading over his shoulder. "So, what's a benign haunting like? Are you sure that thing behind you is only a ghost?"

"You can see ghosts?" the kid asks. His eyes are going to pop out of his sockets at this rate. "I didn't think—I mean, I guess, sure, but *how* do you see ghosts? My friend wouldn't tell me the secret."

"Er," comes Sam's blatantly guilty and answer-less response.

Isaac is mildly surprised that the kid even knows that people could see ghosts, but at least it means Sam's not suspicious. (He probably doesn't even know demons exist, unless Vivienne had told him.) "It's not an option for most people."

But now Sam is curious too, puppy dog eyes in full effect. "This draught has a host of nasty side effects. Isn't it responsible to discuss options with the customer?" he says pleadingly.

Isaac needs to teach him about the metaphor of digging oneself into a hole.

"Side effects?" the kid asks with a squint.

"Potions, like medicine, have side effects. This one's is…" Isaac drags his finger down the page. Sam was right; these side effects are nasty. "Insomnia, eye strain, dizziness, hallucinations, headaches, migraines, and, in rare cases, hospitalization may be needed. It worsens with continued use."

The kid is even paler now, nearly a sheet, and he swallows audibly. "What about the other option? People can see them without that gunk, right?"

Isaac fixes him with a flat look. "You need a near-death experience. *Very* near-death. I don't recommend it."

It's not an unreasonable thing to happen, and it will work as an easy cover story for Sam going ahead. Vivienne and Hammond must have gone through it to see that Rory friend of theirs. Other witches have, too, plus random people all over the world.

It's just massively dangerous and impossible to do on *purpose*. He's heard from Walker that even some attempting suicide don't get close enough to death to see ghosts afterward.

It's a pity Vivienne isn't here to take care of this right now. Both the magic professor lecture and the exorcism.

"I'll take the potion," the kid meekly replies. "How much?"

Isaac's newest problem in his ever-growing list of problems: Natalie, for all her record-keeping, doesn't have a price list in her inventory book.

He scrubs a hand over his face to stifle the groan that wants to come screaming out of his throat. "Just. Give me ten bucks or something. Then leave your name and number and when the shop owner comes back, I'll let her know."

"I'd rather pay it all up front."

He's frustrated enough that Sam pats his back. "Ten bucks or something," he repeats for Isaac, because he's still getting a grasp on currency terms, "and we'll take care of any difference. But since these side effects are quite strong, we'd like to let the owner know, should any complications arise. Also, the potion's effects only last a few days, so unless this is a temporary curiosity of yours, we will need to see you again, anyway."

The dosage listed in the book is shockingly tiny, but he knows from experience how exact potion-making can be, so he just looks for the smallest bottle they have. Sam beats him to the punch; with a flourish, he holds up such a tiny purple bottle that the lid is an eyedropper, and pours the spirit sight draught in until it nearly overflows. It doesn't take much.

The kid fills out one of the appointment sheets with his contact information. Isaac gives him a halfhearted wave, and Sam is all cheeriness and smiles.

When the shop door tinkles again, Sam flings off his oven mitts and sags against the counter. "My hand hurts," he whines and holds it up for Isaac's inspection. The bleeding has stopped, but black blood is smeared all over his palm, and the cut isn't crusting over like a cut *should*. So demon injuries *will* stop bleeding, but without clotting? Interesting.

Isaac runs his finger down the cut across Sam's palm. Even dried, the black blood burns. Isaac sticks his finger in his mouth in reflex, but ends up with a stinging tongue, too. He holds his mouth open with a frustrated noise, sticking his tongue out, and gestures at Sam until he grabs a bottle of water with an unsettled limb.

Sam snickers as he hands it over, though.

After washing his mouth out, Isaac demands, "Why are you *laughing*? You shouldn't laugh at the person who's going to patch you up."

"It's entertaining to see that you aren't as clever as you seem. And I didn't feel that or your finger, so I know you're fine," he pleasantly points out. He spreads his injured hand in front of Isaac's face, and Isaac reels back to avoid a burnt nose on top of everything else. "Now, what will we do about this?"

"It isn't as if there are books to explain how to take care of pet demons. We'll bandage it up again, and it'll heal on its own." What else would it do?

Before they return to the kitchen to wrestle with bandages and clean up more corrosive blood, Isaac glances over the sheet the kid had filled out.

Name, number, address, email.

He briefly considers keeping it until he needs a bargaining chip with Vivienne, but he has the sneaking suspicion Sam would rat him out. He doesn't yet want to figure out where the grey area in Samael's contract is concerning her, though he knows he must. Eventually.

· · · • · • • · · ·

The second the potion hits his tongue, Emil knows he's Fucked Up.

He'd been prepared for a nasty taste and that intimidating list of side effects, but it stings the inside of his mouth like acid. There's so little of it he probably ends up swallowing half the bottle. He spits what he can back out; the rest burns all the way down.

His stomach revolts and he doubles over. Tears sting at his eyes, but he realizes with a thrill that he can *see* despite the watery vision. It's not exactly Christine, but it's a sharp blur of bright gold, and who else could that possibly be?

He can also see colors that don't exist in the normal human spectrum. Maybe he's becoming a mantis shrimp.

One hell of a potion, then. Emil hopes he remembers to take exactly one dose next time.

His tongue feels swollen, and he can't let go of his cramping stomach long enough to make himself throw the tiny potion back up. It will surely pass—the potion is *working*, so these are just side effects he has to weather. The other people in the train car probably think he's a horribly hungover kid.

When he spits a little of the burning shit into his sleeve, he finds it red.

Hungover kid or the next Ebola case, maybe.

Emil searches for Christine, as far as he can raise his head, but now even the blur of gold is gone. The other passengers have given him a leery distance, but even those ten feet make them hazy silhouettes to him.

But one approaches.

He doesn't realize it's not his swimming vision until there's a hand on his shoulder, and Emil coughs out another wet glob of thick, scarlet saliva. He glances up at the stranger, looking for help—help, call the police, the kid is bleeding out after ingesting unknown substances, yeah *that* will go over well.

But the young do-gooder ignores his gurgling and steers him off just as the train doors open. Another flash of glittering gold slips out behind them.

The stranger shoves his head over a disgusting public trashcan, and with a weird tickle on his back, Emil throws up. They keep rubbing his back through the most sudden and most violent heaving he's ever suffered.

His view of puke and trash still swims in weird, blurry colors, but he feels instantly better. Emil raises his head, but the hand on his back keeps him down.

"Hold on," his savior says, halfway understandable now, voice is soft but firm. "I don't know what you drank, but I'm casting a general purification spell now."

The rubbing on his back isn't the smooth, circular pattern he's used to, more like someone writing on him. His bleary brain takes a few moments to put two and magic two together, and by then he's feeling *far* better.

"There you are!" the stranger chirps with a too-hard pat on his back. "Drink some water with charcoal stirred in tonight, and take it easy, and *don't* drink potions improperly anymore. I don't know if it was a dare or curiosity, but there are better avenues for kids these days to figure out their magic."

Emil stares at his savior. First off, they could be in high school too for how young they look, round-faced and freckled and cute. Second, they're just blurting out all of this magic stuff willy-nilly, like it isn't a secret and like he hasn't had all of it dumped on his lap in the past week.

Third, he doesn't *have* charcoal to stir in water.

"What," he croaks, though he ought to say *thank you* or *please teach me* or *why did that potion try to turn me into a ghost instead of let me see them* instead.

"Here!" His magical savior rummages around in their purse, then thrusts a business card at him. "You look like you're still young enough, so you can ask for help at Foxglove if you need it. It's best to get help from others rather than experimenting."

Foxglove Coven, the business card says. And that's *all* it says.

Emil has enough non-poisoned brain cells left to croak, "Not a witch. Bought a potion from a shop."

"What sort of potion was it?" They don't ask what shop, or how he knew it was legit. Maybe there are so many it's like Starbucks.

"Spirit sight draught."

His savior cocks their head, strawberry blonde curls bouncing with the movement. They could be a model for a shampoo commercial. Or maybe that's magic, too. "Please leave the ghost hunting to the professionals."

Fat chance, he thinks, but aloud, he says, "It didn't work."

They squint at him for a long moment. "You said spirit sight draught, right? You're certain?"

Emil nods and spits into the trashcan again. He needs to track down a vending machine for some water. At least that's an easy step forward, compared to everything else.

"You don't *drink* that—you're lucky I was here! Where did you say you bought that potion?"

The way they say it, it sounds like he shouldn't have had it in the first place. Emil avoids their suspicion and instead looks around for any more gold. Nothing. "It was some shop I found on Google? I'm pretty new to this, and I don't really remember the name. But, uh, thanks. For helping me."

"Oh, no problem! I'm pretty used to cleaning up magical mishaps, and I won't charge you or anything. Just be more careful with potions in the future, okay?" The next train rolls up, and his mystery savior bids him goodbye with a cheery wave.

Is magic insurance a thing? is all Emil wonders.

Well, that and why he can see yellow in his peripherals and nothing else.

· · • • • • • • · ·

"Here you go!" Vivienne sing-songs and dumps a stack of dirty notebooks on the countertop.

Natalie's sigh can be heard all the way from the kitchen.

"There's a lot of overlap of black magic in here, but this is all I have on anything remotely close to demons. You're welcome!"

Sam looks at the pile, over to Isaac, up to Vivienne, then back to the notebooks. "Why is this in front of me?"

"Because *you* are the demon here, and maybe this will coerce Isaac into coming out of his grumpy corner."

(Isaac grinds lavender even harder.)

Sam had put little thought into learning himself. Strange, but he'd assumed in hindsight that Isaac would spoonfeed him whatever he needed to know. He hadn't thought of seeking knowledge *himself*.

Strange, so very strange, that it would not occur to him.

Maybe sad.

Samael picks up the topmost notebook by the corner. It's dusty, yet it's also partially soaked in... *something*. Something long-dried, but something he can smell even now.

Vivienne plucks it from him, opens it, and brushes off what may have been a cobweb. "So they're a little old, so what. I didn't get into necromancy properly until high school. Did you have a necromantic emo phase, Isaac?"

"Necromancy isn't demonic," Isaac says instead.

"But it *is* black magic, and if there's one thing I know about magic, it's how much overlap there is. I don't know much about life or blood magic, and my contract knowledge is pretty specific. But this much, I can tell you *aaaaall* about."

The first legible page is of a chart: *Ghost* is written at the top, followed by a bullet point list. Judging from the different ink colors and handwritings, he surmises that the list wasn't written all at once.

Poltergeist, Wraith?, Ghoul, Demon, Dybbuk, FOOD, Wendigo??, with several crossed out between.

"These are the things human ghosts become. Some easier and more common than others, and some require some time and effort, like you." Vivienne punctuates this with a poke to his nose. "Luck spirit is not on there, as you'll see, and demons are the strongest of the bunch. Hurrah."

"I knew I'd been human," Sam replies, though that thought is strange to him, too. It's one thing to know something, and quite another to *think* about it.

"What about physiology? You told us that demons were a pile of goop inside. Any *useful* knowledge?" Isaac calls from the Grumpy Corner. Sam had assumed that once Natalie and Vivienne returned, he would tell them about their customer, but this is a fascinating distraction.

Vivienne shakes her head. "It was a while before I actually ran into any, and that was only during purges. Unlike *some*, I don't raise demons in my spare time. Try the third or fourth notebook."

"Please keep in mind," Natalie says, coming out of the kitchen with an absolutely massive pot in her arms, "that we're giving you this in the interest of safety and secrecy. Not to encourage anything else."

Isaac's retort is lost to the twin sounds of Sam and Vivienne gagging from the smell.

Isaac cocks his head, apparently unaffected.

"Sorry," Natalie briskly says and plops the pot down on the counter. Vivienne scuttles away, hand clamped over her nose, and Sam is quick to follow her example. "Foxglove wanted a batch of seance juice for a preventative seminar they'd like to run."

"Seance juice?" Sam asks. His eyes water with how bad the potion smells. Witches must be immune, and a new emotion flares through him: jealousy.

"It's what we called it way back when, and Nat's mad it stuck. Even though it's cute! The potion helps with seances when seers aren't available, or if it's a larger group. What it *actually* does is open up your mental barriers and gets you closer to death. That's why it reeks—*lots* of dead things in there," Vivienne explains in a nasally voice.

"Are you going to the goblin market soon? I'm out of hellhound heart," Natalie serenely asks. Totally unbothered.

"And why are you two acting like it's a dead hellhound rotting in front of you?" Isaac demands, suspicious of their reaction and Natalie's lack thereof. (It would be easier to notice things Isaac is *not* suspicious of. Sam makes a mental note to try.)

"It's not the heart that's the smell," Vivienne grumbles.

"It's the death they're smelling. They're closer to it than you or I. Be grateful," Natalie replies.

Sam looks over at Vivienne, more curious than ever.

"Did you know that we had a customer while you two left us in charge?" Isaac asks, cutting across Sam's curiosity.

"It *is* a shop. We need those from time to time," Vivienne replies.

"A specific customer. Since I'm apparently doing your job of tracking him down for you now," Isaac corrects, and Vivienne and Natalie finally look up from the potion.

"*No*," Vivienne says, scandalized.

"Yes," Isaac replies.

"To ensure we're talking about the same thing, it was the teenaged boy with the ghost trying to turn into a luck spirit tailing him," Sam chimes in. "The boy, Emil, wanted a spirit sight draught. Presumably to see her. She seemed rather flustered by that—but more flustered by my attention. Isaac had them fill out a contact sheet for you."

Vivienne dives for the address book, but Natalie lifts it out of the way and holds it over her head. "What will you do with them, Vivienne?" Natalie asks. "We need to come up with a concrete plan."

Vivienne, still halfway folded across the countertop, turns to Sam. "What was she like? On a scale from one to ten, how much luck was she shedding? Any cat spirits haunting her? Teeth, claws, demonic smell?"

"She didn't look dangerous," Sam replies. "Neither of them did, but she didn't smell like a demon. I could see any luck. What does that look like?"

Vivienne makes another grab for the book. She fails again. "If there's a reason I shouldn't exorcise her, tell me now. I won't be able to figure out how far along she is without seeing her, but if she's still a ghost, I can still exorcise her, or talk her into passing on."

"You sold four doses of spirit sight draught to Emil," Natalie says instead, scanning over the sheet Emil had filled out, "so that will give us roughly two weeks before he would need more, considering how lucky he is. Vivienne, would much change in that time frame?"

"Depends if that bakeneko is actively hanging around her. Does he know it's four doses?" Vivienne asks.

Natalie pauses, finger still in her book. "More importantly—does he know how to take it? *Not* to drink it?"

"What sort of potion are you not supposed to drink?" Sam asks, confused, while Isaac remains guiltily silent. Sam, personally, hadn't known that. Isaac hadn't, either. Vivienne facepalms.

Emil must not be very lucky, after all, if it had been *Isaac* who had advised him on potion-taking.

"You're doing it wrong," Vivienne complains, cheek mushed on her fist, and draws an erase rune in the air with her free hand.

The teenaged boy kneeling on the floor in front of her sulks as the circle he'd drawn disappears. "Maybe if you taught me better than trying it fifty billion times."

"You have to be able to write from memory if you want to progress to circles," Vivienne loftily replies.

"How the hell are you supposed to memorize all of those things?"

"You only know what, a dozen runes? Twenty maybe? It's like an alphabet—actually, it pretty much is an alphabet. Wait, aren't you Russian? They use another alphabet!"

The boy snorts and starts drawing on the floor again in magic marker. "You're still a shitty teacher."

"Maybe you're a shitty student," Vivienne snarks back.

There is no animosity in the scene, even when she declares the next circle another flop. The boy sits back on his haunches, swipes his brown hair out of his eyes, and he must be as stubborn as she is to keep going.

Natalie wakes when Sunshine jumps onto her stomach. She wheezes, pushing the cat away until he heavily makes his way over to his witch, then rubs at her eyes. The clock says two in the morning. She finds it difficult to fall back asleep.

CHAPTER 10

IN WHICH VIVIENNE NARROWS DOWN HER OPTIONS

Vivienne tells herself it's for research. Or work. She doesn't care what reason it is, so long as it's not the embarrassing truth.

The bookstore is only nominally crowded—before school or work gets out, but after lunch. Emil isn't here, and neither is his hanger-on. Vivienne still isn't sure how she'll approach That Problem yet, but she remains aware of their ticking clock. It may be worse now that Emil can see ghosts.

Or is dead from drinking potions he shouldn't.

But the kid's probably too lucky to be that dumb. His luck ought to keep him from further dumb decisions. Or maybe that overprotective bakeneko will?

Vivienne rubs the furrow in her brow. *Fucking youkai*, she allows herself, then banishes it from her mind. This is supposed to be a fun shopping trip. Full of innocent book purchasing and no ulterior motives.

She almost walks into an endcap in her distraction.

Supernatural Hunter Tip #46: Luck is bullshit. That's one she has recently added.

Vivienne keeps the stacks from being knocked over completely, with much flailing and an unflattering squeak, but she claims it as a victory.

Until she hears a chuckle behind her.

"Good catch," Hot Manager Dana says, smiling. (The smile is about eighty percent Customer Service and twenty percent Genuine Amusement. Vivienne will take it.) "Is there anything I can help you find today, or would you like to continue wrestling with romance novels?"

Vivienne chews on her tongue. She glances guiltily at the pile of books that have gravely embarrassed her. First smoothies, then smut—will bad luck take *everything* from her?! "Mythology," she blurts.

It is unlikely the most awkward thing Dana has dealt with in the store. "What kind?"

"Shapeshifters? I'm not picky right now."

"We have a few collections of folklore from around the world." With a beckoning gesture, Dana leads her toward where Vivienne already knows the mythology section is. Dana knows she knows. Because Vivienne is half a stalker and simultaneously feels gross and elated by the conversation thus far.

"I'm Vivienne," she says out of nowhere. Because she knows Dana's name from receipts (and a psychic) and she knows *so much else* about this store, and Dana only knows about smoothies and awkwardness. It's not fair. Vivienne wants to make it a little more fair before she shoves her foot deeper down her throat.

Dana glances back over her shoulder, down at her. (Vivienne marvels again at her height.) "I've seen you in here from time to time. I'm glad to put a name to a face, especially for regulars. I'm Dana, a manager here. If you hadn't already figured that out."

"Charitable to call me a regular," Vivienne mutters.

"You've bought a few books and haven't stolen anything. You've only made googly eyes and made all of us sweat every time you brought another smoothie in." Dana winces, and hurriedly faces forward again, just as they arrive at the small mythology section. "Not that you've *spilt* anything in here, but you were... dripping, that one time."

"Sorry, again!"

"No harm done. Is there any kind of shapeshifter in particular you're looking for?"

Vivienne has not had a Normal Job in, well, ever. She's been freelancing since high school, full time since university, and freelance exorcising does not lend itself to much customer interaction. But she knows, from Natalie and Fiona and even Megan, that being *any* sort of feminine in customer service leads to plenty of assholes hitting on you while you're supposed to be in work mode.

Vivienne does not want to be that asshole, no matter how much she'd love to get to know Dana. So she swallows down an offer to get coffee, grins up at her, and chirps, "Just shapeshifters, so I'm good browsing through these. Thanks!"

Dana smiles back, polite but warm.

Vivienne, strong enough to Not Be That Asshole, is not strong enough to resist adding, "And I like your hair today! It's really pretty."

Dana reaches up to her dark brown hair, as if she had forgotten she had it. It's up in another Pinterest-worthy braid, this time pinned with gem-like barrettes, and Vivienne would dearly love to discuss with her which gemstones would be best for accentuating beauty and self-confidence. Maybe another time.

Dana's smile warms further. Totally genuine now, and Vivienne doesn't fight the thrill that gives her. "Thanks. Your hair is cute, too. Let me know if you need any other help today, Vivienne."

Dana leaves, but probably not fast enough to miss the giggle Vivienne can't suppress as she combs through her (tragically) short hair. Pastel purple headband today.

A giggle. Hair-twirling. All she needs is to bat her eyes at her next time and she'll be halfway to a Disney romance.

Vivienne makes a note to ensure perfect eyeliner next time she stops by the bookstore.

Why is the stereotype that girls can't flirt with each other? she wonders as she turns her attention to the shelves. (Books. Yes. That is what she is here for and *no other reason*.) But then, with horror, Vivienne wonders if that *wasn't* flirting. Girls compliment each other's hair all the time. It was what they *did*.

Maybe she should be a little more blatant, anyway, just in case—

Her phone goes off with Natalie's ringtone. She wedges it between ear and shoulder and answers, "Hey, Nat."

"Are you out right now? I'd like to come over." Her voice is thick with tears, but unwavering for the moment. Vivienne's heart seizes anyway.

"You can meet me there, I'll be back soon." Shapeshifting books would have to wait (not as if this cute little hole in the wall would have what she's looking for, anyway).

"I'll wait for you." Natalie is the only other person with a key to her apartment, but she has not used it in nearly three years.

Vivienne tragically doesn't get the chance to wave goodbye to Dana since she's busy with another customer. "Vision?" she asks once outside and vaguely anonymous.

"Yes. Deirdre called about an accident, and I—I hadn't realized at the time what it meant." Visions of the possible future were rarely straightforward. Who knew?

She narrowly beats after-school crowds on her way home. Vivienne finds Natalie sitting by her front door, knees up to her chest, face buried in her arms. When she raises her head, her eyes are dry, however.

Vivienne unlocks the door and Sunshine meets them with much meowing. "You can come in here without me," Vivienne reminds her, "you know Sunny would love it."

Natalie looks around the cramped apartment like it's the first time she's stepped foot inside. Like always. "It was a vision of a young girl in the subway. I only saw her screaming, like in pain, but she didn't have any visible injuries, and it was sudden. And short. I never recognized her, and it's so vague, I never could follow up on it..."

Vivienne takes her hand and tugs her toward the couch. Natalie no sooner sits than Sunshine jumps onto her lap, purring up a storm.

Natalie stares down at the black cat without touching him.

That isn't how this normally goes.

Vivienne pauses in her tea preparations, watching Natalie like one would watch an injured, feral animal. Sunshine is The Best Cat Ever (scientifically proven), and while Natalie's relationship with him is fraught, she has always adored him, and he her.

Sunshine's purring dies down as he, too, ponders this change in routine.

"The girl's familiar bonded to her just before. A rat. And when it tried to get to her, the train killed it," Natalie tells them without inflection. Her hands hover over Sunshine's long fur.

"Oh," is all Vivienne can say.

In this, she is an outsider looking in. Only witches ever gain familiars.

Non-psychic witches.

Vivienne may be outside the house, peering in through the windows, but Natalie is inside, trapped in the closet, unable to touch or look or join.

Sunshine chirps and butts his head against Natalie's hand. The dam breaks, the tears fall, and Natalie can finally touch him again.

Neither of them will ever truly understand what a witch's bond with a familiar is like, but they've seen it in action. And have seen the aftereffects when one loses the other.

· · • • · • · • · ·

Emil sits cross-legged on his couch. Christine politely floats over the opposite end.

She looks like a badly aged photograph. It's like he's viewing her through a glittery yellow lens, and she's still transparent to boot. But he *can* see and hear her. He can interact with her again.

"A coven. A witch thing, right?" He flicks the business card at her and it hits the other arm of the couch.

"Yes." Her voice sounds as if it's filtered through water or they're using those old tin cans with strings. Combined. But the potion *worked*. He got sick in public and still feels wrung-out, but a victory is a victory. "Foxglove is a big one. I'm not—I wasn't a witch, but my brother was in one. ...Two."

"You can be a part of several clubs?"

"He switched after I died," she warbles, sadly, shrinking into herself. "He went into Eyebright, so he could get help with his research on... all of this. Alkanet wouldn't have let him." Christine waves her arms, white sleeves flapping like wings.

There's a lot sailing clear over his head here. He needs to pick his battles—and make a list for later. "Right. Cool. We'll skip witch talk, and circle back to magic talk." And he's not sure he's ever ready for the Oh God She's Actually Dead talk again. (He's not sure she's ready, either.)

"Um, then what did you want to talk about?" She cowers like she's expecting a blow. Not that he could touch her if he wanted, but he definitely doesn't want to hurt her.

"Luck."

"That's something to ask Kirara. I only know the basics."

Emil cannot help his grin. She cringes from that, too. "I'd like to know a few things that mama cat probably shouldn't know about. Like, this luck, it's a *thing*. And you two have been pouring it on me for a while, so I'm *lucky*, right?"

"Yeah. We've told you that."

His grin widens. His cheeks are starting to hurt. "So, say a kid strapped for cash like me happens to be obscenely lucky. Does this stuff affect lottery tickets, gambling, that sort of thing?"

"Oh *nooo*," Christine moans like she's auditioning for the world's quietest horror movie. She hides beneath her sleeves like that'll save her. Or maybe she's hiding from a teenaged boy's morality.

"You've been haunting me for a while, and we both know what kinda situation this is. I'm just saying, if *someone* were to hit it big, don't you think karma owes me this one?"

"There are *laws*!" she hisses at him. "You—You're not even *old enough*—and more importantly, there are guards against that!"

The laws don't faze him; the prospect of guards does. "What kind of guards?" (He is, admittedly, imagining very large witch bouncers standing outside fancy casinos.)

"Do you think you're the first one to think about using luck to gamble?" Christine asks, pitying. Emil scowls. Maybe sulks. "Luck spirits aren't allowed *near* casinos, there's almost always some witch or spirit on staff that prevents it."

"But you're not a luck spirit," he points out.

Christine balks, not hurt, but surprised.

"Not yet," he adds, just in case she has feelings about that. "And judging on, like... *everyone's* reaction, ghosts are super basic."

"They would be on the lookout for cheating."

"We wouldn't have to hang out, and it's not like anyone would suspect we're related. Just float by every so often, do a little shimmy, and next thing you know, we're millionaires."

Christine fiddles with her sleeves. "This is stupid," she pouts, "and you'll get in trouble."

Emil doesn't want to put into words the exact *trouble* he's in if he doesn't magically (ha) pick up another source of income. And if need be, he'll just snort the luck or something and head in on his own. He has a nice suit from the funeral, so he should be able to look eighteen enough to match the fake ID Maxim made for him.

"Scratch cards would be smarter," Christine says instead. "You can buy those anywhere and the guy at the corner store already doesn't card you when you buy beer for your neighbor."

At her initial protest, he had, admittedly, figured she'd be a goody two shoes stick-in-the-mud. This is much, *much* better. Emil holds his hand up for a high five, and, with a shy smile, Christine pokes her fingers through his.

· · · · ● · ● · · · ·

Natalie hates asking for Vivienne's stash when it comes to Codi, but her tastes in music are... limited. Terribly limited. She likes what she likes and has none of the Spotify searching talents that others possess.

"Isaac, Sam, half day today, you can leave at one," Natalie says as soon as Vivienne slinks into the shop. Yesterday had been a rest day; she still looks hungover and half-asleep. Natalie has been doing the math, and the solstice *should* be alright. She'd prefer if Vivienne could join her, but she supposes she's not *vital*. Only preferable.

Vivienne yawns in greeting. Despite it being June, she's in a slouchy turtleneck and leggings. Natalie checks her forehead as soon as she nears, but there's no unusual fever or chill.

"How are you feeling?"

"Tired."

"You look tired," Sam volunteers from Isaac's workstation, grinding charcoal into the admittedly finest powder she's ever had the joy to work with. (Which means Isaac has slunk off to the back room again, where Natalie had discovered a blanket nest where he apparently prefers to play video games while his demon does his work for him. For a demon summoner, Natalie had expected a *little* better work ethic.)

"I am tired," Vivienne agrees and slumps onto the stool nearest Natalie. Her messenger bag drops to the ground. "But it's goblin market day, and that means playing bodyguard and whoring myself out to a gumiho."

When Sam perks up, Natalie quickly cuts his strange, eternal helpfulness off. "I don't think it wise to bring you to the goblin market just yet, Sam. Maybe if Isaac were to help make you some sort of charm or spell to ensure a disguise...?" She raises her voice enough to be heard from the back room.

"You're not missing much. Crowds, weird smells, and pushy fae. But witch potions sell, and there's plenty of stuff you can't exactly go down to the corner store and buy here. I'll bring you back a souvenir," Vivienne says, probably half-asleep, but Sam brightens like a child promised a treat all the same.

Natalie has already made her list for the day, thankfully nothing too heavy or gruesome, and despite Vivienne's dramatics, they won't be bothering Yun-hee overmuch. Codi weighs more on her mind.

Isaac drags Sam out at *exactly* the strike of one, but Natalie doesn't mind. She's mildly surprised he's still with them at all. A spellwriter, even with a contracted demon, surely has many avenues of escape if pressed.

"Viv, I need a song," Natalie says as they pack up. "Have your pennies?"

"Wait, huh?" Vivienne blinks, bleary-eyed. Processing.

"I think we should target the migration during the solstice. With Isaac, we'd have the firepower, and this could be an excellent opportunity. I'd like to hire Codi too, but I need a song. Please."

Codi Clarkson is one of Natalie's good friends, but she is also one of the absolute best hunters in the city, and does not give friend discounts. She is a professional through and through, even if her payment is strange and two-part: money and a song she likes but has not heard before to add to her hunting playlist.

Natalie's tastes run orchestral and classical.

Codi's tastes run technopop, indie rock, and *weird*.

And Vivienne is one of two people Natalie knows that has a *list* of songs to eventually pay Codi with, rather than desperately scrounge each time. It's the anime. Natalie had only watched some of *Sailor Moon* growing up, usually with Hayley and Vivienne, but apparently anime openings and endings are a wealth of the upbeat poppy stuff Codi prefers to shoot things to.

Vivienne finally processes.

"We're hunting dragons?" she asks, eyes wide, mouth ajar in either excitement or horror. It's not as if they have not done this before. "Shit, Nat. What do we need that badly? What made you decide this—it can't just be Isaac. Have you even asked him?"

"I'd like to talk to you, Codi, and Hammond and Rory first. We couldn't do this without Isaac and Sam, but I won't overstep."

"What do we need off a dragon?" Vivienne presses.

"Its heart, for starters. I'm almost out and I can't keep buying new ones."

Vivienne's surprise melts away in favor of guilt, which is why Natalie had preferred not to disclose that part. It is Vivienne's potion that needs the slivers of dragon heart. Not much, and a few other rare potions use it, but it adds up over the years. They haven't brought down a dragon of their own in six or seven years.

Natalie places her hand over Vivienne's. "This isn't just for your sake, Viv. You know that. The liver and fire sac are vital in many potions, too, and even the skin can keep the shop afloat without profits for months. I think this is worth a shot. You'll get hazard pay."

"I'm on board. You know I would be. And I can get you a song for Codi, and Ham... He'll probably be into it, too. He's always up for the adrenaline. But I can't see Isaac willingly throwing himself at a dragon for the sake of teamwork. We might get an in with Sam, but..." Vivienne trails off into thoughtful muttering, putting puzzle pieces together without bothering to share, and all of Natalie's doubts are dispelled. Vivienne has a way with people she will never possess.

They pack up with the chorus of Vivienne's planning as background. The potion jars are heavy, but there aren't many, and this is more of a purchasing trip than selling. Natalie hefts her backpack, Vivienne retrieves her messenger bag, and they head out to the market.

The city is a rarity for having a goblin market door, since there are less than a dozen across the continent. It has definitely informed the higher than average magical population, and the *incredibly* higher than average nonhuman population. Old magic cities in Africa, Europe, and Asia likely have similar populations, but in America, not so many.

The nearest train station is a mere block from the door, undoubtedly not an accident by city planning. It is located down two alleys and through a half-overgrown overhang, wrought iron dripping in foreign ivy, and looks by all accounts to be a regular, if old, wooden door. The only things that set it apart are the not-subtle guard leaning against one brick wall, arms folded and gaze sharp, and the small collection jar next to the door handle.

Vivienne fishes around in her pockets.

Natalie hands her the two pennies she knows she forgot, and Vivienne thanks her with a sheepish laugh.

The toll to any of the goblin markets is exactly two dollars and thirty-seven cents. It makes no change and takes no excess. (Curiously, checks made for the exact amount work.) Natalie drops her toll into the jar, and the door opens itself. Vivienne shoves hers in and shuffles through before it can shut between them.

The goblin market is, as always, bustling. People of all races, magics, species, and cultures mingle freely, as the markets are neutral ground, connecting multiple planes and locations. Vivienne looks marginally more awake at the burst of action around them, and Natalie holds a hand back to her so they don't get separated.

The first stop is, of course, Yun-hee's stall. She is lucky enough to have a permanent position on one of the larger streets, and the gumiho breaks into a wide beam when she spots them. Her tails wag behind her.

"Nat-ah! Vi-yah! I wasn't expecting to see you today, but you're lucky. I just got some new soju we can share!" she chirps, all charm and appeal. Her hanbok-style dress is grey and baby pink, and her butterfly norigae is probably older than half the occupants in the market.

"No thank you, Yun-hee-nim," Natalie replies.

"You're no fun," she pouts, then turns to Vivienne and in the same breath asks, "What about you? We can continue where we left off when you asked for that special bath bomb!"

Vivienne tries to hide her face with her sleeve. "No thanks, Yun-hee-unni. I couldn't handle you or your soju, you know that. But tell us, what do you have today?"

The fox spirit thankfully isn't put out by the rejection. "A new shipment of alkonost blood you'll be interested in, nice and fresh. Oh, I traded for some moonlight-dried fae herbs the other day, you may look at those! I'm out of anything related to melting dragon scales, though, with the migration coming up and humans being terribly stupid, so all of my strong acids are gone. But I have some powdered wyvern bones I could give you a special discount on!"

Yun-hee goes on, listing off her products with unerring accuracy, though there are only three jars and two bundles of ash twigs on her stall. Natalie listens, filing away what she'll need and what she can barter for, but Vivienne fidgets at her side.

She initially had chalked up Vivienne's shyness to the flirting she'd had to do with Yun-hee to get her help enchanting that bath bomb, but it is unlike her to *remain* shy. Vivienne knows little shame and never for long. Her sleeve remains up against her face, shielding it, and she is carefully keeping on Natalie's side.

On the other side of the gumiho stall lies a youkai stall: the tengu.

Natalie, to her amazement, sees one of them trying *very hard* to wave at Vivienne.

Yun-hee realizes she has lost her customers' attention, and looks between them, dipping ever lower over her stall. She cranes her neck to look up into Vivienne's face. "Vi-yah, what's wrong? You're paler than usual and didn't even want to know about my sale on old Italian grave dirt."

"Oh, wait, how old are we talking?" Vivienne asks at once, hand shield faltering in her interest.

"*Vivienne*, I knew that was you! I recognized you!" the tengu exclaims.

Yun-hee startles like a cat, Vivienne freezes like a frightened rabbit, and Natalie continues staring at the prospect of not only a friendly tengu, but one that knows Vivienne enough to *want* to be friendly.

"Does this have to do with what Mark has been doing?" Natalie asks faintly, twisting to stop Vivienne from hiding behind her again.

"*Watashi wa anata o shi*—uh—*shirimasen*," Vivienne calls back, tripping over her Duolingo-fed Japanese, and Natalie hastens to stop her from leaping over Yun-hee's stall to hide. Yun-hee laughs in delight, too many teeth and too much open mouth.

"Excuse us, please," Natalie says, presumably to both spirits, and hauls Vivienne back toward the market door. There is always drama at the market, but there are always prying eyes and perked ears to take advantage of it. The market side door guard seems perplexed to see them leaving again so soon.

Natalie shoves Vivienne through the door. It may be the roughest she has been with her in years.

"Vivienne. What is Mark doing with tengu." She does not ask.

"In any visions, have you seen a ripped woman with super long black hair and rings of rune tattoos on her arms?" Vivienne replies, just as fast.

And Natalie has.

She has seen so many strangers in her visions of myriad futures. Some recurring, most not. Most human. She knows this woman Vivienne describes is not human. She knows more about this woman than she wants, and she knows they are in *trouble* if she is here.

Natalie lets out as calm a sigh as she can manage. "Yes, I do. I don't know her name, and I can only guess at what she is in this realm for, but she's a shapeshifter and—"

"Do you know what kind?" Vivienne eagerly breaks in. "She is using selkie as a cover. She *has* a seal pelt, that's the confusing part, and she must use it to transform, but I'm not sure what else uses a *skin* to transform aside from selkies and some swan maidens—"

"*Vivienne*," Natalie barks.

She falls silent.

"What has she done to Mark?"

"To Mark? Nothing yet. She's living in his bathtub because he's holding the pelt hostage. The tengu showed up to buy it off him, because they claim she stole an egg, and we kind of got recruited to find the egg instead since Mark didn't want to give it up. Their name's Mirai. Apparently a friendly little magpie."

Natalie takes another breath to keep herself calm, present. "She has a First egg already?"

"She has a *what*?" Vivienne asks back with wide eyes.

"Vivienne, please."

"Yes, she has *an* egg... She had this before she crashed his bathroom, apparently. She can't have it on her, we met her naked, and tengu eggs aren't something you can shove up in there to hide."

Natalie had no idea things were already so progressed. She struggles to keep her heart rate steady, to stop herself from hyperventilating. *She can still be stopped*, she reminds herself. *She can still be swayed.*

Supernatural Hunter Tip #38: Precognitive visions don't always come true.

"Nat, what's going on?" Vivienne asks in a small voice.

Natalie recalls flashes of feathers, sharp teeth, dragon wings, and a looming *monster*.

Vivienne makes an alarmed noise, suddenly in her face, cool hands cupping her cheeks. She tilts Natalie's head back. "Your nose is bleeding," she says. They know what this means.

Natalie pinches her nose, but it'll run its course soon. There is no accompanying migraine. "We have to get that egg. And *you* have to play nice with the tengu, Viv. It's rude to ignore your new friend."

· · • • • • • • · ·

A psychic scream rips him from sleep and propels him from bed.

Mark heaves for breath, mind coming online more slowly than his clairvoyance, and can't hear anything over his thundering heart for a long moment. His bedroom is dark and still. The only light comes from the full moon behind his curtains.

He hears muffled speaking from the bathroom's direction.

Mark creeps into the hallway. Bryn's voice is subdued, but not a whisper. He cannot make out any distinct words, but she sounds calm.

Then what woke me? he thinks. His head pounds from unknown pressure.

In a flash, her calm words are buried beneath the atavistic *panic* of her mind. An animal trapped by a predator, age-old, timeless. The hare screaming in the coyote's jaws. The coyote ripping through its own leg in a trap. Mark rarely hears that from humans, but once in a while from a spirit.

Always a spirit as it's getting eaten.

The bathroom door is shut, and it's warded to hell and back, but it is far from soundproof.

"—predisposed for the moment, master. I thought it prudent to avoid further provocation of the tengu, but I'm sorry, I—"

Mark eases open the door. Bryn stands before his mirror, steam thickening the room like fog. She whirls on him, surprised, but not with the shrieking terror of her brain.

He only gets a glimpse of the mirror. Runes in blood have been written through the steam around the edges, and he has a hair's breadth of a second of *something* in the mirror before it cracks, then shatters.

Bryn twists again, watching the shards fall into the sink and across his floor, all of them blackened as if by smoke.

"Who were you talking to?" Mark asks. His head pounds and his face feels hot. The steam sticks to his skin uncomfortably.

Bryn spares him an annoyed, sidelong look.

"Was that your master? How were you checking in?" Seers could scry on mirrored surfaces, but scrying is a waste of time on top of vague confusion, and is never communicative.

"You are a foolishly nosy human. Are you going to give me my pelt back?" Bryn spits.

"You were scared," Mark tells her.

Her expression falls open in the way the discovery of painful secrets produces. Her face had been neutral, her voice even, but no one can hide high emotions in their thoughts, and self-loathing overcomes abating fear.

"No," he automatically replies, and scrubs a hand over his moist face. Instead of sweat, he comes away with blood smeared on his palm. A nosebleed, for a psychic, means many things, all of them bad and all of them strong. "Your—boss. This is bad, and that's okay. I can help you. I don't care how bad of a situation this is—"

"Shut up," Bryn snaps.

"You're afraid of them. They're forcing you to do this, to steal from tengu, to put yourself in danger—"

"Shut *up*. If you cared about my danger, you would give me back my skin!"

"You were calling them because they're not *here*! They're far away from you right now, right?"

Bryn's hands on the sink clench so hard she cracks the porcelain. But Mark has never been one for self-preservation instincts. He presses onward, heedless.

"I have the power to keep you from them, give you safety and shelter. I have already, haven't I? The tengu only want their egg, I can keep you from this boss of yours—"

"*Lloignyth mnahn'* thinks he knows the world!" Bryn snarls. She rips the sink from the wall, half of it crumbling in her grip, and water sprays across them from the broken pipes.

Mark's ears ring, but not from the sound of her destroying his bathroom. Her *words* had burnt. The room sways, his nose gushes more blood, and when he touches the side of his head, he finds red near his ears, too.

His front door crashes open.

A monstrous beast of a dog lunges forward and crosses the living room to his bathroom in two bounds. Bryn throws the sink, either not realizing or not caring that Mark is directly between them, but the inugami shoves him to the wet floor and bats it out of the air like a crumpled piece of paper.

Fiona squeezes in behind Benji, shotgun pointed at Bryn's chest.

"Stop," Mark wheezes. He grapples at Fiona's leg for support, getting back to shaky knees, and at least Bryn has the sense not to continue this fight in cramped quarters. "You two got here fast. Suspiciously fast."

Fiona remains silent. Her aim does not waver.

"Were you sleeping on my lawn again?" Mark asks.

"It's warm this time of year," Benji says, voice a harsh growl in this form, but his tails give a halfhearted wag.

"You're bleeding," Fiona adds. She aims the shotgun one-handed and pulls a handkerchief out of her pocket for Mark. The same one he had given her years ago. He gratefully wipes his face with it.

Bloody nose is an alarm bell, but a vague one. The ears were new; those words were new. An abusive, controlling power with a scared person under their control is a little less new, especially considering present company, but that track record is hit or miss.

This may be a bigger job than he initially expected.

But Mark Ito is not a quitter. He gives Bryn a sunny, bloody smile. "Say hi to my friends, and some of your new friends. Hate me later, but I don't like this boss of yours, and I think I have a bone to pick with them on your behalf. You're welcome in advance."

With their hands laced under the table, Hayley's head resting on Natalie's shoulder despite how she must stoop, and the extra large milkshake with two straws with an obscene amount of toppings before them, they paint a rather cute picture.

"Poster children," Hayley had sighed against Natalie's hair. "We're so fucking cute. Huh, huh, Nat? We're adorable!"

Being on a double date doesn't make this a competition.

Being on a double date with Mark and Vivienne, however, does. *Natalie tries not to get caught up in their weird competitions, especially when other psychics are involved, but one can only say no to Hayley West so many times. Natalie had foolishly wasted her quota on refusing to be the one to bathe Sunshine. The cat bath would have been better.*

But they're probably winning. Mark's eyes narrow a fraction, perhaps gleaning some thought from her head, so Natalie spares him the hint of a smile and sips at her horrifically sugary concoction.

Instead of in a cafe, she finds herself in a familiar bathroom.

The clawed foot tub is overflowing, leaving an inch of water on the floor, and the mirror is fogged up. There is blood in the water. Mark stands in the tub, wet up to his thighs, nose pouring blood and eyes black as pitch. "Shuggoth, this need not end in death. Give me the egg," Mark says, and there are responding hisses of pain to the first word.

"Give him back," comes Vivienne's voice, from off to the side somewhere.

A woman Natalie doesn't recognize, shirtless and tattooed and dripping blood from one hand, steps forward with a smack *of her bare foot. "Give him back," the woman repeats in an animalistic growl. In her other hand, she holds a pelt of scales and claws.*

"Stop this, yhri. Give me the egg and come back to me."

"I sure hope you have a plan," Vivienne says.

The woman pulls on the mass of scales as if pulling on a robe. Her hands turn to claws. Mark drips more blood down his chin, and his coal eyes widen.

Natalie comes back to herself when she pokes herself in the nose with the straw.

She leans back, rubbing her nose, too distracted to be embarrassed, despite the way Hayley and Vivienne both giggle. Mark eyes her coolly over the thick rims of his glasses. She briefly wishes she could read minds; how much of that had he seen, did he understand?

Blood drips from his nose onto the collar of his nice sweater.

CHAPTER 11

IN WHICH VIVIENNE FRIENDSHIPS HARDER

After a knock on the door, Emil opens it to find Crazy Asian Lady on his doorstep.

He slams it in her face.

"What's going on?" Christine asks, peering up over the couch as he presses his back against the door like that woman is a charging elephant.

"Hide," Emil hisses at her. He locks the door and dives for the couch. Christine squeaks and floats out of his way, through the couch, then curiously over toward the door. She leans her entire head outside it.

"It's Vivienne," Christine says as soon as she pulls back. She doesn't seem as apprehensive as she ought to be, in his very informed opinion. "She says the door won't stop her."

See, very informed opinion.

"What does she *want*? How does she know where I live?!" It has to be the potion shop's fault—he wrote down his address and it's the only brush he's had with the magical outside of talking cats and subway saviors.

Chris leans out the door again, but backpedals immediately. The lock slides open and Crazy Lady stands there again on his doorstep in all her short glory.

"Hi," Vivienne says and steps into his house. She has a beat-up messenger bag on one hip and a paper bag in her opposite hand. She sticks out her free hand, although Emil is half a room away. She says, "My name is Vivienne Sayre, and I think we've gotten off on the wrong foot a couple of times now."

Emil doesn't respond, his silence as icy as he can manage.

If I need to run, what can I grab? His laptop is on the table, surrounded by scratch cards, but his wallet is on the kitchen counter and his phone is in his room charging.

"You're Emil Zolotarev," Vivienne says anyway, then turns to Christine. "And it's Christine, right?"

"Yes," she meekly replies.

"You're friends with the potion guy," Emil finally says with narrowed eyes.

"Friends is a loose term, but that is how I know where you live. No finding magic here." She spreads her hands wide to show that they're empty (aside from the bag, which he now sees has LUSH on the side). "Let's talk. Please. I'd like to salvage this situation, if we could."

"We're doing *fine*. What's to salvage?"

"You have two ticking time bombs sitting beneath your nose. Three if you drink dangerous potions."

Christine had already uncomfortably informed him of their conversation in the bookstore when he'd first met her, but that's stretching one. "Two?" he can't help but ask.

"Youkai are fickle, and so are cat spirits. I advise against hanging out with bakeneko, but I'm really just here for her. So, where's your bathroom?"

Vivienne walks into his apartment like she owns the place. Christine all but flees before her, but Emil stands his ground. Vivienne walks right up to him and cocks her head. He's so much taller than she is, and she's round, chubby and soft and pretty about it. Yet he can't help the roil in his stomach when he thinks about how it went down at the bookstore.

"'Scuse me," she says, and makes to step around him.

"*Hey*!" He grabs her wrist. She's cool to the touch, despite how warm it is outside. "What the hell do you think you're doing?"

"Hopefully teaching you both a lesson before something gets worse. Or messier. The finer details involve a very expensive bath bomb and some experimenting with our wannabe luck spirit." She holds up the bag again. "Please tell me this place has one of those shower tubs. A sink will work, but it'll be a lot more disappointing to look at."

"Why are you showing us a bath bomb?" Christine breaks in, quiet as a mouse.

But Vivienne grins at her, anyway. "You, mostly. It's a luck bath bomb! I had to do a *lot* of schmoozing with a gumiho to get this scraped together, for the record, and that's an awkward position to be in."

A luck bath bomb sounds... cool. And pretty. But for all the jokes Kirara has made about coating him in luck, this seems a lot more literal, and something Emil can't pass up after making seven hundred dollars off scratch cards in the space of a single afternoon.

"We're already lucky," he points out.

"Then show me." Vivienne still faces Christine, still pleasant, but Christine quails. "Show me some luck right now. Luck that's not what you've stolen from me or given to him. Which, by the way, I also came back to zero that out. I *really* can't stay this unlucky, someone's going to get killed. Me, probably."

She exudes so much casual knowledge that Emil's head spins. Sure, he holds a grudge, but here is a person who clearly knows a lot about magic, dropped into his lap, trying to make nice. He doesn't have to listen to her judgment. They can pretend to play along and absorb everything she offers. Unless she presses for a promise written in blood, he can play game.

"This way," Emil relents and drops her hand. She follows him into his cramped bathroom. He hasn't taken a bath in probably a decade, but he stops the drain and starts running the water for her.

Two people in the tiny bathroom are pushing it. He's lucky Christine can float halfway through the wall, but then he notices something that makes Christine squeak: Vivienne accidentally bumps *into* her.

Just like her friend, he realizes.

"Sorry," Vivienne murmurs without a thought. She jumps to attention, however, when Emil reaches forward to flick his fingers through Christine's fuzzy hair. She covers her head, but he passes right through, as always. "Okay, I'll head you two off here. No, you can't touch ghosts."

Emil shoves her against Christine. Vivienne falls against her, Christine squeals again at the touch, and her bell collar *dings* with the motion.

"How are you doing that?" she demands, eyes like saucers, and she floats after Vivienne after she backs away.

Vivienne frowns, sad in a way that makes Emil uncomfortable to look at. She cups Christine's cheek, and Christine, despite all of her shyness, leans into her touch like a tame cat. "I'm sorry," she says, and the sorrow there is too personal.

"Why can you do that? Why could your friend?" Emil demands. When he crosses his arms, he nearly elbows her. The bathroom warms with steam, a match to his rising frustration. "You can't say something and then do whatever you want."

Vivienne sighs.

She pulls away from Christine, and the ghost follows her with a whimper. "No, c'mon, I know you're touch-starved, but today's about luck."

"You don't understand!"

"Yeah, I do. Remember Rory? I have more experience with ghosts than you do, little wannabe." Vivienne steers her back with a boop on her nose.

"Explain," Emil nearly growls.

"I'm the exception to a lot of rules. Necromancer, exorcist, expert on many dead things, et cetera—none of which *you* are, kid. And, for the record, my friend is a different kind of exception, and can only touch Rory. It's like a very specific anchor, not for everyone. There's no catch-all to this."

"Except you."

"You can't do what I did, promise."

"Why not?"

"Two people died, for a start."

Emil can't argue with that one.

Vivienne upends her paper bag into the water. A sparkly gold bath bomb *plops* out. "Most of this is glitter, sorry to say, but I know that there is a fair bit of luck in here, too. Not that you or I can see most of it. But you can, right, Christine?"

She nods, edging closer to Vivienne. But now, at least, she looks curious about the bathtub, rather than like a sad dog. Emil leans over both of them to watch.

"Try pulling some luck out. Give it to me." Vivienne cups her hands expectantly.

Christine phases through the shower curtain to hover over the water. Though he can see only the suggestion of a glimmer, it's clear she's pulling *something* from the water. She scoops this maybe-luck into Vivienne's waiting hands.

"Good! Now make some luck of your own."

Christine's face falls. "I-I can't do that yet..."

"Because you're not a luck spirit. Only luck spirits can create luck."

"I'm *working* on it!"

"She is!" Emil adds. Not that he has seen her train or practice or whatever, but how should he know what that looks like? "And ghosts can't move luck around, either, can they?"

"No, and that confused me for a bit, too. But the answer is this." Vivienne reaches forward to *ding* the bell on Christine's collar.

She lights up like a flare.

Both Emil and Vivienne shield their eyes, surprised, and somehow, Vivienne unbalances and splashes into the glittery water with a yelp.

· · · · ● · ● · · ·

Isaac is almost free for the night when Vivienne slinks back into the shop. Her clothes are damp and her hair is a tangled, wet mess. Her headband's soggy bow makes her look like she has sad rabbit ears, too.

Without looking up from her stirring, Natalie asks, "How did it go?"

"She can't make luck, Emil's making the spirit sight draught stretch, and the bakeneko didn't show."

"You took a risk," Natalie tsks. "Sam, please fetch a towel for her? I can't leave the pot."

One of the (many) things Isaac hates about potion-making: it's so *needy*.

"Does this mean we will be needed?" Sam asks.

Vivienne ignores him, though she welcomes the towel. "Nat, you *have* to tell me if you know anything else about these kids. Why are they so important to you?"

"It's not me," Natalie mildly replies.

Vivienne waits a beat. "*Me?*"

And the psychic feminine mystique continues to be a mystery, as Oliver chooses that moment to barge into the shop with a loud, "Yo, Isy! You done yet or what, man?"

"Hello, Oliver. It's not six yet, but so long as everything gets cleaned up, you can have them."

"Am I a piece of meat?" Of course, Isaac's deadpan sarcasm is lost in the whirlwind of Oliver's so-called helping. Granted, by now he knows where most things in the shop go, but Natalie stirs a little harder each time he breaks herb stalks or delicately dried flowers.

Her spoon is scraping the pot's sides by the time Oliver and Sam cheerily scoop most of their work into various tupperware containers.

"What's got you two so excited?" Vivienne asks from beneath her towel.

"We are going to the gym," Sam replies as if it is a great, exotic thing.

Isaac hates ever promising Oliver to be his gym buddy. He hadn't meant it to go on for so long, and he definitely hadn't meant for it to continue plus one. *Are they alike because they're spending too much time together*, he wonders, *or is it because the universe hates me?* Why must he attract peppy people? They're exhausting.

Oliver pumps his fists as they head out the door. Sam mimics him. Isaac drags his feet.

"Are you upset that we missed another one of their arguments?" Sam asks. His curiosity does nothing to dampen his excitement. "Oliver says the gym is a good way of getting rid of stress. You need that."

"It'd be nice to know if there's a reason we're getting tossed into a bakeneko's waiting mouth," he allows, though his heart is not in it. No, he doesn't want to be part of more of their drama. Curse his own curiosity.

Oliver turns so he's walking backwards, although he becomes a massive blind battering ram to the poor passersby. "So, I did some research on that thing? Google mostly gave me fox stuff, kit-soon or whatever—"

"Kitsune," Isaac corrects in a sigh.

"—sure, man! I don't speak Japanese. Which Google told me that those cat things are. And the fox things. But the fox things are the bigger thing? So at least it's not one of those! And anyway, aren't demons like, scary strong or something? Sure scared Nat and Viv shitless, and they seem real cool with other things, or like they're not scared by death or magic or stuff."

Isaac could tear his hair out. "Do not say the d word in public. Remember?"

Oliver stares at him. "Dick."

"*You're* a dick. The gym sucks, and I thought we'd be done with this by now."

Oliver gets that scary stare then, way too intense and way too much like his mother. Way not dumb jock persona enough. "'Cause you'd ditch me after quitting the firm, right? Nope, no way, man. Even without the magic, you're an antisocial nerd, and I'm not letting you hole up and angst about de—magic things 'til the end of the world. Besides, you're a stick! You said you wanted to bulk up, and how *else* are you gonna do it if not at the gym?"

Sam looks between them like they're a tennis match. He is unfairly enthralled.

The metro is still crowded with rush hour masses, but Oliver's battering ram-ness helps. Sam is getting better with crowds, too, though he keeps his fingers firmly tangled in Isaac's hood. The leash imagery is not lost on him. They wedge themselves into a car, Isaac smushed between his unfairly taller escorts, Sam's arm around his shoulders to keep his grip.

Oliver's gym of choice, blessedly, is not a long ride, nor is it as packed as the station. Isaac is familiar enough to scuttle in without getting the New Client speech, and Oliver's infamy is enough to get Sam in with no more trouble than a wave of his membership card. It is largely populated by rich gym rats, pumped up Insta influencers, and the next generation of the one percent.

This is, of course, Oliver's natural habitat.

Sam openly gawks at the muscles and skin on display.

"Don't stare and get changed," Isaac says, elbowing him. Sam is again borrowing some of Oliver's gym clothes, after a hilariously disastrous attempt at putting on a pair of Isaac's sweats.

The borrowed pants end up falling off his hips and they have to cinch it so tight and high at the waist he's left scandalously showing off his ankles. Oliver tries to get the demon to hold back his floppy bangs with a headband while Isaac ties his ponytail higher. They could hold their own fashion show at this rate.

"Why do we have to change at all?" Sam demands as soon as he tires of their chuckling. "My other clothes were comfortable and I had a full range of motion."

"Yeah, go running in jeans, I'm sure you'll still think they're comfortable," Oliver snorts. Then, after a moment of deep thought, he asks, "Dude, *does* he sweat?"

Isaac scowls. "What do you think I do with my life that I would willingly get sweaty?"

"Not even during *alone time*?" Oliver coos and Isaac swipes at him. "I know you ain't social enough to get laid. Pity."

Samael follows them, perplexed as ever, into the main room again.

Isaac had not realized just how bad of an idea this would be until Samael picks up a treadmill.

Oliver's cackling doesn't quite cover the *whump* when he drops it again. Enough people are staring at the combined noises that Isaac can't be certain how many were looking before, but super strength doesn't immediately give away demons. They could very well be escorting a curious spirit.

Sam may not be sweating, but Isaac sure is.

"Match me," he orders, instead of giving Sam any kind of numeric lifting limit.

Sam's next attempt at lifting, a five-pound weight, involves much whining and groaning and heaving. Oliver must lean against a pillar just to stay upright with how hard he's laughing.

Isaac never thought he'd want to be back at the potion shop.

• • • •• • •• • •

"Look at us. Look at how adorably domestic this is." Mark pours a cup of tea for each of them, the steam being lost in the general semi-permanent sauna of his bathroom. But at least she hasn't discovered any bath bombs or oils yet. Mint tea is the only smell aside from sweat and heat.

Bryn glowers at him, almost entirely submerged, only her eyes and bridge of her nose above water. Her hair floats around her like a horror movie mermaid's.

"You have to eat *sometime*," he tells her. "Water, fine, ruin my water bill, but even spirits need to eat. Shapeshifters especially go through a lot of calories."

"I don't have my skin," she burbles.

Interestingly, he gets a flash of spotted sealskin from her thoughts, but also a spread of cold white feathers, more white than Mirai has in their plumage. He wouldn't say she is easier to read, but he is becoming used to her mindscape. Not human, not animal, but a touch wild and more than a touch alien.

"I decided not to print out a paper menu, given all the water you've splashed on me since becoming my houseguest, but I've several meal options for you tonight, my dear."

Bryn continues glowering.

"A fine skirt steak, cooked however you please. Or raw, if you prefer." He sips at his tea, gauging her reaction, but none comes. "I just purchased some Alaskan salmon this morning, if that is more your preference. I have a great recipe for honey garlic salmon, and I don't mean to brag, but I *am* a spectacular cook."

"I am not hungry," Bryn growls. She has eaten nothing since she broke in, and while she has access to water aplenty (and could, hypothetically, leave anytime she wished), Mark is certain she has not done anything. He doesn't want to become her dinner, only her savior.

"You're not a snake, or a reptile at all, as far as I can tell. You want to stay here and stay safe from tengu and your *boss*, right? That means you have to take care of yourself. I'm not going to let you wither away to nothing out of spite, or guilt, or whatever."

Bryn surges out of the bathtub, hanging her muscular arms over the edge, but does not reach for him. Mark stares at the tattoos on her biceps. Concentric rings of runes, only a few of which he and Vivienne have been able to concretely identify. *Seal, change, form, stable, body*—but so many more.

Bryn picks up the teacup and takes a delicate sip.

"I have nothing to give you," she tells him.

"Information. I'm offering you a hand up out of the hole you're stuck in."

She sips again. "I have no information for the human realm."

She doesn't even realize that's information itself, he thinks, amused. *What sort of shapeshifter doesn't live at least part time in the human realm?* The whole point of shapeshifting was to blend in with others, usually human. She *definitely* has a human form.

"You want to help the tengu, but I will not give up the First egg," she adds, "so what is your plan?"

"My plan is to figure out *what* has got you so scared that you'll fight tengu and humans for."

"And the dog."

Mark furrows his brows in confusion.

"The dog spirit, the one like the *ulfhednar*, who tried to set me on fire. He is a rage spirit, yes?" Bryn gives him a level stare and sips at her tea. "I will fight him, too, for this fear of mine."

Mark wonders who (what) she has been speaking to that she so blatantly gives up information without meaning to. She does not know what an inugami is, but knows Benji is a rage spirit. And the word—he doesn't know it, but he recognizes the *u* sound as a Nordic accent of some sort. He knows he's smiling, unable to help it in the face of all this *information*.

"His name is Benji, and the woman with him is Fiona. I know you know they've been staying with me."

"Not right now. I could rip out your throat right now."

"They're at work," he says, ignoring the threat. If she wanted to kill him, she would have done it by now. "Good friends of mine. I helped them, years ago, escape a bad situation, too. I can help you."

"You cannot."

"You don't know what I'm capable of, Bryn."

She empties her cup with a flat look. "You know not what you mess with, human. You don't want to help me."

"I really do. Call it a bleeding heart if you will, but I hate to see those with power shoving others beneath their heels because of it. You're *afraid* of your boss—doesn't that strike you as a bad thing? Don't you want to live unafraid, free of things like masters who send you on suicide missions?"

Bryn stands in the bath, long wet hair plastered to her thick body in a facsimile of clothing. Her red eyes blaze and her fisted hands shake at her sides.

"You know nothing of fear, human, or of bad things or suicide missions. I *got* the egg, no matter the cost to me, and I lived. I will continue living, no matter what my master asks of me. That is how I am, and will be for centuries more. I reached out for help once, and will never do so again."

Mark picks up his half-full tea cup, but leaves the pot and her empty cup. She *does* need more than water, and mint tea is supposed to be calming. Doing his best to seem unperturbed, he tells her, "I'll make the salmon tonight. You're welcome to join me in the dining room."

She glares at him until he leaves. He shuts the door behind himself, but he's long since stopped locking it, and she's never tried locking herself in.

Bryn does not join him for dinner. He leaves a plate outside the bathroom door, and it is empty in the morning. Progress.

Wait until she sees the next step in my plan, he thinks, warm with glee. Sealskins and thoughts of white feathers. He may be onto something wonderful here, if she'd stop being so goddamned stubborn.

· · · · ● · ● · · · ·

Vivienne knows she has to make a decision, and she knows she can't make it alone. She's given both psychics enough time to do their thing. And she could handle one thing, but one thing *each*? She's not paid enough.

At least Mark already knows about Emil and Christine. It's easier to segue into Hey So Nat Has A Pet Demon Now after they sort out the little luck spirit wannabe and discuss options for her. It's easier to admit to a demonic garbage disposal. Mark has seen worse. He possibly has worse in his bathtub.

Mercifully, Emil has warmed up to her enough that they accept her invitation to a diner. (Free food goes a long way with anyone, Vivienne knows, having fallen for the same ploy time and time again. And she will continue to do so.) The pair show up fifteen minutes late, Emil's stomach growling, and Vivienne offers them a sunny smile.

Not that Emil accepts it. "Why are you playing nice now?" he demands as soon as his hands are on a menu. Christine politely reads over his shoulder.

"I've *been* nice. Most exorcists wouldn't let you two play house for so long."

Behind her in the next booth over, Mark pretends to laugh at something Fiona says. His back is to Emil, so there's little chance of recognition. Hopefully. Fiona and Benji, at least, are new to them.

"If we're playing nice, why didn't you want Kirara to come?" Emil asks.

Christine floats a hand over his arm. "She wouldn't exactly blend in…"

"Catgirls stand out without a glamor," Vivienne agrees. Behind her, Benji laughs. (He's had a lifetime of trying to blend in with humans, so she supposes he's allowed to laugh.) "Also, don't pretend like you're here innocently. You wanted this, right?" She slides over a little dropper-filled bottle of spirit sight draught. "Natalie even gave you an eyedropper lid. Don't want you cheating death more than you have to."

The thought of death via potion dampens his teenaged hostility. He smiles for the server and glares into his water instead of Vivienne. Win for her, and better for Mark's flimsy cover.

Vivienne patiently waits for him to order. (He does not order anything for Christine. At least he's not hopeful-slash-delusional about this.) She's glad Mark is footing the bill; she had almost forgotten how much a teenaged boy can eat. Spite may also have something to do with the obscene amount of food.

"You know how much this stuff is actually worth, right? Our intern grossly undercharged you. Pretty lucky, hm?" Vivienne asks, tapping the tiny potion bottle again.

"That wasn't on purpose," Christine meekly points out.

"Oh, I'm aware. And bless Nat's heart, but I'm not here to play debt collector. I'm also authorized to give you a pretty steep discount on this refill." She pushes it across the table, but her finger remains on the lid. "On a few conditions. This is expensive and dangerous, and you are minors. Uneducated minors whose only magical supervision may or may not be a bakeneko. Forgive a couple of caveats here."

"Fine. What do you want?" Emil grouses.

"Check-ins, for starters. Knowledge of your plans."

"Plans?"

"You want to become a luck spirit and seem to have *some* sort of plan for that. Whether or not it works, we can't let two teenagers with that much luck run loose. So, what will you two do then?"

The look they exchange tells Vivienne neither has thought that far out. Entirely unsurprising.

She softens her tone. "Luck spirits are corporeal. Living in the fact that they eat and sleep and breathe, but not human. What would you do with a new life, Christine?"

She blinks her bright gold eyes, suddenly glossy. (Emil looks afraid of the prospect of her tears.) "I... want to go back to school. I want to eat whatever I want. I just want..." And she, of course, begins weeping. Emil appears appropriately mortified.

Vivienne's eyes drift down to the splash of red across Christine's middle on her otherwise spotless robes. She's insanely curious why these two have ended up together when they seem to have only just met. "You don't want to return to any family—?"

Emil makes a chopping motion.

Vivienne quickly changes tack with an awkward clearing of her throat. "You know, ghosts can change their appearance! You don't have to stay in the robes all the time. It's pretty easy once you know the trick."

Their food arrives, their server oblivious to the sniffling ghost she reaches through. Christine flinches. Vivienne pokes at her blackberry pomegranate muffin, and Emil stares at his burger and pasta like it killed his puppy.

Christine sniffs one more time and wipes her nonexistent tears with her sleeve. "Tell me the trick, please. I'm so tired of looking like a ghost."

With that hurdle passed, Emil wolfs down his food, while Vivienne's heart seizes at Christine's words. She remembers Rory saying something almost identical three years ago. How terribly nostalgic. She's such a sap.

So she pastes on extra cheer and chirps, "Being a ghost is all about the ego! The psychological kind. All about your sense of self and the intent behind it. Sort of like a placebo—tell yourself it'll work, and it will. Tell yourself that you are someone who belongs in a dress or whatever. Not exactly *forgetting* you're a ghost, but not attaching so much meaning to your death. Think of it as your default outfit if you were an anime character. Or video game, I don't care."

Mark snorts behind her.

"Attaching... to my death?" she murmurs, hands drifting toward her stomach. Vivienne nods as gently as she can. (Emil seems to be under the impression that if he eats fast enough, he can avoid this topic.)

"Most ghosts don't stick around long enough to get into this, but, well, you've met my friend Rory. It took some therapy and a lot of self-reflection for him to get to that point, of course—"

Christine's floppy sleeves retract and the white warms to a yellow, sunflower-patterned shirt. Straps slither over her shoulders from a deep brown pair of overall shorts. Emil snickers into his spaghetti at Vivienne's outright shock.

Christine looks pleased with herself, and Vivienne thinks it may be the first time she's smiled so genuinely.

Their meal wraps up. Vivienne had barely finished her muffin; Emil needs *multiple* to-go boxes, and he asks for a piece of pie to go. Vivienne hands over Mark's card without remorse, and waves goodbye with a smile and a promise to see them again in a week.

As soon as they're gone, she twists in her seat and puts her arms over the back of it, over Mark's shoulders. "So, verdict?"

"You're cruel, stringing her along like that. There's no chance she'll actually turn into a luck spirit or whatever," Fiona snaps.

Opposite of her glower, Benji beams and reports, "No sign of anything other than ghost or luck. She's in no danger right now of becoming a poltergeist or demon." Vivienne can imagine his tails wagging to match his tone.

"So, it's been independently recorded that there's no demonic threat here." Mark delicately dabs his mouth with his napkin. "Congrats. So *why* are you so invested in this? It's been going on for weeks, Viv."

"If she won't pass on, I'll take care of her for you," Benji eagerly volunteers.

"About that. Already have a Just In Case someone lined up. And Nat says that this pair is gonna become important to me, so may as well see how this plays out. May as well give all this a shot."

"Are you cheating on me?" Benji asks with a puppy dog pout that has never worked on anyone in the history of anything.

"What can I say, I like to keep dangerous friends. Speaking of, Mark, have you let this lovely couple here know about your houseguest?"

To her surprise, Fiona's temper doesn't snap. "We've had the pleasure of meeting her already," she says thinly.

"Well, that makes this easier, then!" Vivienne chirps, though she is surprised Mark hadn't ended up with a bloodbath. "Nat's seen her, you know. I didn't mean to ask specifically, but it's an easy description to match up. But she doesn't know what she is, either."

"...How do you always end up in the middle of the worst shit?" Fiona asks.

"Which one are you asking?" Benji wryly adds.

"Still don't know what she is, no," Mark sighs dramatically, "but she is using a selkie as her cover. I believe she's working for something nasty."

"*Why* is she sticking around? Picking up more strays, huh," Fiona says in disgust. All present know it's only a cover; she was one of Mark's rescued strays, once upon a time.

Mark rolls his eyes. "Yes, I believe she'll be around for a while yet, and *no*, I don't want you two babysitting me until we know what she is. I don't want her pissing Benji off again."

"You think she would?" Benji asks in return, with no hint of offense or annoyance. Vivienne always found it fascinating, how a rage spirit could be so cavalier about his own temper. (When not pissed off, of course.)

"I think she'll lash out at other spirits if she feels cornered. And she does. I think she needs a *lot* more coaxing before she even realizes she could escape her boss thing, much less that I could help."

"If she hates you so much, why is she sticking around?" Fiona repeats.

"Protection from the tengu she stole from," Vivienne innocently informs them.

"Mark, you asshole, stop getting involved with youkai!" Fiona snarls. Benji laughs. "No, this *isn't* funny, you furry shit. He'll get himself killed yet!"

"Yes, because not everyone is as friendly and easy to get along with as you two," Vivienne points out.

"*I'm* a delight. I would also like to make sure our favorite psychic remains safe. What are your plans going forward?" Benji asks.

"Yeah, Mark, what are your plans?" Vivienne parrots, poking the side of his head.

"Ugh, *fine*, the plan is to figure out what she is, who her employer is, and what they want with a First egg. And figure out a way to get said egg back so we all don't get eaten."

Mark attempts to headbutt her in retaliation. Vivienne avoids a bloody nose, which tells her Christine really zeroed her out. Score. "Now, tell me Natalie's trouble. It better be worth *this*. I know you're only dragging this up in front of these two if you need help with something Natalie has going on, too."

He gestures at his dinner guests. Fiona remains grumpy and Benji bats his eyes.

"Oh, you'll have fun with it, rest assured, Marky-Mark."

Natalie enjoys the sunlight coming in through her window. She gets to sleep in today, and she's going to enjoy herself, damn it. The shop doesn't open for another three hours, there are no appointments until the late afternoon, and she hasn't heard of any trouble for anyone to take care of.

She rolls over, to allow the sunlight to fall over the backs of her bare legs, and finds herself in another place.

Two figures are only barely visible in the gloom. "It is no matter to bring life back from death," *an insidious voice croons, coming from everywhere at once.*

"A specific life," *comes a man's voice.* "I want a specific life brought back from the dead. I want her life extended, and protected, and tied into mine."

"This remains no matter if you can truly do what you say you can for me," *the nowhere voice replies.*

One figure shifts, perhaps uncomfortably.

"Your blood will be your contract with me, yhafh'drnn," *it continues,* "and you will pledge your lives to bringing me unto shugg."

"We will figure out the price *specifically," the man replies.* "Swear to us."

"Your lives are nothing to me, and your desires are nothing for me. You will have whatever your price."

Natalie blinks at the clock on her stand. The sunlight doesn't feel so warm anymore.

CHAPTER 12

IN WHICH CHRISTINE HAS PLEASANT AND UNPLEASANT SURPRISES

"Your phone is ringing," Sam says. Isaac has those headphone things on, which means it hypothetically muffles sound, but Sam can hear some, anyway. He squints at the screen. "It says... Maybe: Natalie Stirling. We know her. You shouldn't ignore phone calls, Isaac."

"Walker, can you get those bees before evening?" Isaac says into his headphone things. Sam understands most of it: the private sound (that doesn't muffle as much as Isaac claims), the microphone to talk to someone, and the cat ears on top, Oliver had told him they were the most important part. He had not elaborated.

Samael's hearing is good enough that he can hear game music and a feminine tone on the other side, but cannot hear specific words. He has heard Walker before, but Isaac has never explained, no matter how he asked. He thinks it's a name.

"I'm going to answer Natalie," Sam says, holding the phone out, and as predicted, Isaac swipes it out of his hands without looking away from the screen.

The phone buzzes again, this time with *Oliver* flashing across it. Isaac drops it into his lap without answering, but he makes it stop buzzing with the press of a button. Sam has yet to grasp how one button can do so many things on such a small device. At least Isaac's laptop and game controllers have more than one button.

Questions for later. So many questions for later.

Samael plasters himself against Isaac's back to hook his arms over his shoulders to grab at his phone. Isaac lets out a snarl of outrage, but this close, Sam can hear the other voice in his headset, and that's momentarily more fascinating.

"That your roommate? When are ya gonna tell me about him, Mouse?"

"Is that what I am?" Sam asks while Isaac flails and fights and fusses. The arms restricting his movement are really only a distraction; he curls a tendril out to snag the phone while Isaac keeps his controller safe in one hand and his headphones on his head with his other.

"Ooh, was that him?!" the mystery voice coos.

Then Isaac pushes him away with a hand to the face until he's flat on his back with his summoner perched above him.

Isaac adjusts his headphones, straightens his ever-wrinkled hoodie, and scowls down at him. His hair is loose and messier than usual. Samael reaches up to help him keep it out of his eyes, but Isaac slaps his hand away.

The phone in Sam's now-discovered tiny extra hand buzzes *again*. Maybe: Natalie Stirling.

"You should answer her," Sam tells him.

"It's my day off," Isaac growls back. The voice on his head titters out another exclamation, and Isaac's eyes skew sideways, as if attempting to glare at his headphones. "Walker, it doesn't matter, I told you. He's just a nosy busybody—*no*, it's not like that, trust me. It couldn't be farther from that."

"What's that?" Sam asks. He tries to slide open the phone's call, but evidently, the screen cannot recognize demonic limbs.

He may not be able to make out any words now, but he can definitely make out laughter. Isaac looks more and more irritated.

"Who's Walker?" Sam tries again. Not the first time he's asked, and it won't be the last, until he gets an answer. He ought to know. He's with Isaac.

Even if he won't tell him his plans, or his friends, or what he did at Oliver's job, or why he'd tried raising a demon, or why he's so grumpy when he looks at Sam's still-bandaged hand. The bleeding has stopped, but it has yet to scab over or heal in any regard. It doesn't hurt, and he doesn't think he can get infected, but apparently, that is still cause for worry.

Everything is a cause for worry with Isaac. And no matter how he tries to minimize himself on that list, Sam cannot help but feel he is a perpetual problem.

The phone buzzes, this time a shorter one with the notification of a voicemail.

"She knows you're ignoring her," Sam informs him, and tries to pull the phone toward his settled hand, but Isaac again bats it out of his grip. "Why don't you like her?"

There is more tinny laughter from the headphones. Isaac's expression dips further into irritation.

"She's helped us, I can see that much. If you told me more about this, maybe I could help—"

"Why do you think you can help?" Isaac snaps. He throws the phone across the room and it *bangs* against the wall. The Walker voice chirps in alarm. "You're trouble, even wearing a pleasant face, just like her—no, at least I know you aren't lying to me—*fuck*." He pulls his headphones off, pinches the bridge of his nose, and takes a long, heavy breath.

"I'm not trouble," Sam replies in a small voice. He doesn't *want* to be trouble. He and Isaac both know he cannot lie to him.

"I'm not talking to you—or her—about any of this. It doesn't concern you."

"I'd say it does—" Sam begins, but Isaac shoves him back against the carpet with a forearm against his shoulders.

"You were a mistake that has a delay in biting me in the ass. Natalie is a wolf in sheep's clothing, and I wish you'd stop playing so nice with them. She won't trust you. She won't trust me. She wants a spellwriter, she wants information, and then she'll hang either of us out to dry because that's *both* of us, probably hand us over to the coven she's so friendly with. I need you to keep some goddamned distance so you don't become a liability when we run."

Isaac, satisfied Sam is staying down, retreats off of him and pulls his headphones back on. He settles back down too-close in front of his screen and picks his controller back up.

His voice is softer, *kinder*, when he speaks again. "...Yeah, it's deep shit, Walker. But you don't have to worry about me. Nothing I can't handle, right? Now it's night, shit. Bees tomorrow?"

Sam remains prone on the carpet. Isaac sits in his peripherals, illuminated by the dim glow of his game, but his attention is on the ceiling. His thoughts race. His chest *hurts*. He hardly understands the former, much less the latter.

I didn't ask to be summoned, he thinks. He can't remember anything before that room, seeing Isaac and Vivienne for the first time, settling into the magic circle with whatever tethers he could haphazardly grasp at. He doesn't know why he'd been summoned, or why Isaac hadn't wanted a contract with him, and he *ought* to know that, right? Everyone seems to want to know that, but this is directly concerning him.

But Isaac only seems to care about whatever's directly concerning *himself*.

Sam had thought they had been making progress as the weeks passed. He had thought Vivienne kind, and Natalie polite, if distant. He likes Oliver. He never understood Isaac's general distaste for others, even the annoyance he shows Oliver, and he knows nothing about demonhood other than what they've discovered themselves.

Why am I a problem?

Sam doesn't understand why his eyes are prickling. Not itching, not quite, but he rubs at them. The feeling does not go away.

He sits up and hot moisture runs down his cheeks. He touches it, surprised, then realizes aloud, "Oh, I'm crying."

Isaac turns to him. With the light on half his face, his expression is hard to discern, and Sam doesn't much want to look at him right now, anyway.

"I'm not trouble," he says, and his throat feels oddly constricted. He swallows and tries again. This crying thing is terrible. "I don't want to be trouble, for you or Natalie or Vivienne. I don't want to eat you, Isaac, now or at the end of our contract. I understand you don't like this situation, but... *I* don't like it, either."

He doesn't realize it until he has said it. Sam *doesn't* like this situation: Isaac is annoyed at best and cruel at worst; Vivienne may be smiles and helpful information but she also discusses destroying spirits and banishing problems without batting an eye; Natalie is an enigma that not only frightens Isaac but seems to disregard everything to do with Sam. Does he like them? Yes, probably. But he feels dismissed and an object of, if not fear, then unwarranted caution.

"You were going to sacrifice me. Do you know what that means, for me? You were going to kill me before I could even come here, be *me*. I enjoy being me. Why do all humans jump so quickly to killing anything that doesn't look like them?"

"You—" Isaac jerks his headphones off again, but it's a precious moment that means he does not build enough steam to order Sam to stop.

"You're mean, Isaac," Sam tells him.

Isaac stares at him. This can't be the first time he's been called mean in his life, but there is surprise in his half-shielded expression.

Sam looks away from that face. "I'm going to go into the other room for a while. I'd prefer it if you didn't come in there. I don't want to talk to you while I think."

The room is silent as he crosses it. The game screen flickers, only Walker's character moving, with Isaac's controller lax in his hands. He watches Sam, surprise gone, calculation in its place. He could order Sam to stay, but why would he? He has made it clear that he doesn't *like* him. He only likes Oliver and that Walker person.

Sam wishes he had someone he liked like that. Thinking more on it, he's sure he *wants* to like Isaac and Vivienne.

He also wants to live. Wanted to, in that circle closing in on him like a noose, and wants to now, with a sour contractor and threats he doesn't understand hanging over them.

"You can take the phone," Isaac says, returning to his game, "so you don't get bored."

Sam wonders if it's meant as an apology. He thinks he wants a real one, anyway.

·•·•••◦•••·

Christine runs her fingers over Emil's messy bangs.

He snores in response.

She can touch him, but only sometimes, usually only when he's asleep. She wishes it could just be one way or the other; these teases are worse than being shut out of physicality entirely. Logan had always preached about hope, but this is cruel.

Death is cruel, she supposes.

Christine swipes more of his sandy brown hair out of his eyes, but he rolls over, through her thigh, and ends up with more of his hair in his face than ever. She readjusts so she can pretend she's sitting next to him, and tries again, but her fingertips go through him.

Kirara's entrance is punctuated with a *ding* as she pushes the bedroom door open.

"Oh, here you are," she says at normal volume. Christine hastily puts a finger to her lips, but Kirara just blinks those big cat eyes and replies, "The boy sleeps like the dead, you know that."

"The dead seem to be more restless than that saying implies," she mutters back.

"Luck spirits aren't dead. I wonder when you'll cross that line?" Kirara hums and jumps into the air. She hangs before Christine's face, head cocked, tail swishing beneath her like a pendulum.

"I-I don't know." *How would I know that?* Ghosts don't magically change into luck spirits. This is uncharted territory; all she knows about luck spirits had been from Logan's research and what Kirara had told her herself. Haphazard does not *begin* to describe her knowledge of luck spirits.

"Well, come. Let's take a walk. He'll be fine for a while."

Without waiting, Kirara turns in the air and *pops* out of the room.

Christine sighs and tries once more to move Emil's shaggy hair out of his eyes. Again, she fails.

Kirara waits for her outside the front door. She can't walk through walls, but jumping between planes seems the cooler power, if Christine is honest. It's definitely faster.

But floating isn't bad. It's not like flying, exactly, since she doesn't have much vertical control. But it makes jumping off the balcony pretty fun when she floats to the ground like a dandelion on the breeze. It had scared her the first few times, but heights matter little when she can't touch the ground and can't die again.

"Where are we going?" Christine asks since Kirara seems content on leading the walk.

"You'll see. Something to make you happy again, kitten."

"I'm not unhappy," she replies, delicately, and thinks back on recent days. Emil works at the bookshop and Christine gets to listen to children's books during story time hour. Vivienne may be weird, but she sort of likes her. It's easier to be dead when others can see and hear her.

The night would be warm, she thinks. She can't tell temperature, but it *looks* warm, and it's mid-June. It might be humid. She watches trees for signs of wind and listens hard for night bugs. She may miss touching others the most, but she misses touching the world, too.

They pass by a bank with a clock out front, and she is mildly surprised to find it close to four in the morning. Christine used to be in bed by ten. She decides she misses sleep, too, and not only because nights are boring and lonely by herself.

When Kirara turns them onto Ash Vine Avenue, she knows where they're going.

"I'm surprised you haven't visited her on your own yet," Kirara says, smug, catching Christine's eye.

(She doesn't want to admit she's not good with directions when unable to use a GPS.)

"Have you?" Christine asks instead.

"Not my thing, but the little rat makes you happy, and that is good enough for me." Kirara leads her up toward a tall, bland apartment building. This one has indoor hallways, but they go through a wall and Kirara tugs her up through floors until they arrive on the proper one.

Christine floats through without waiting for her as soon as she spots the right apartment number. She had only been here before once, but it isn't as if she could forget it. Her eyes prickle and she searches through rooms until she finds the child's bedroom, and the large cage within.

"Hey, Sadie," Christine chokes out. (She definitely misses crying, no matter how many times Logan called her a crybaby and how those memories sting now.)

The white ferret snaps out of her hammock and against the bars with a squeal. Christine puts a hand to her mouth to stop weepy noises from escaping, even if the room's only other occupant wouldn't hear.

"Shush, will you, you'll wake everyone," Kirara scolds as soon as she *pops* in, and she fiddles with the lock until it clicks free.

Sadie barrels out at Christine with another shrill squeak. Kirara shushes her again, more aggressively, and opens the window before scooping her up. They all float gently to the ground, several stories below, and once on the ground again, the ferret lets out the loudest squeal of all.

"Hey Sadie-bell," Christine says again, and wants to pet her *so bad*. Kirara lets the squirming ferret loose, and she happily runs circles around them both. "Oh, it's so good to see you, sweetie. I'm glad you're settling in well."

Sadie stands up against Kirara's shin, demanding up again. She wriggles until the bakeneko begrudgingly picks her up and holds her against Christine's face. Sadie tries her best to lick her, and Christine tries her best to weep touched tears of joy.

Sadie wiggles out of her grasp again and circles around them, a white blur of excitement, only pausing sporadically to sniff at concrete. Christine sits as close to the ground as she can manage and contentedly watches. Kirara had been right; this does make her happy.

Not that she had been *un*happy before, she maintains.

She wonders if she could somehow let Sadie meet Emil some time. Not that she'd know who he was, since animals had never been allowed at the hospital, and as far as she knew, that was the only place he and Logan ever hung out. It couldn't be a late-night rendezvous, either, and since Sadie's adoptive family only thinks of her as a regular ferret, it's probably for the best not to raise further questions. Kirara had already done so much to help her get a new home.

"Familiars taste so good," Kirara sighs. She eyes Sadie's zooming with much displeased tail-swishing. "You're lucky, little rat. You're welcome for that. Can't believe you used my own luck against me..."

Christine is in such a good mood she can't help a little cheekiness. "Maybe it was *my* luck?" She touches the collar around her throat, reminder of Kirara's generosity, and somehow, that soothes the bakeneko.

Sadie squeaks again and tries to throw herself at the collar's bell. She sails on through and lands in a wiggly pile behind her.

"I'm glad you're so energetic. And you've gained your weight back," Christine tells the ferret, because at this angle, Sadie looks like more belly than anything else. Fat animals are always the cutest, but Logan had always been careful not to let her get too chubby.

Sadie pretends to chew on a rock for good measure.

"We should bring her food next time!" Christine exclaims, turning to Kirara with too much hope for her to resist. Sadie again hops through her, but sits up on her hind legs just in front of her lap, begging like a dog. "See, she wants snacks!"

"*I* wanted a snack," Kirara replies, rolling her eyes. "Come, let's return her and let her be someone else's problem for a while. It smells like baku around here, and we don't know if nightmares will wake that child up."

Sadie hisses, but Kirara pays her no mind, scooping her up.

"If you bite me, I'll drop you," she advises as soon as they're two stories up.

"No!" Christine gasps.

Cats can't blush, but they can lay their ears flat and twitch the tips of their tails, which she has learned is pretty close. They all know it's a hollow threat. Sadie most of all, because ferrets are smug monsters of chaos and can sense any and all weakness. It's one of the things Christine loves most about her.

She makes kissy faces as farewell and Sadie tries desperately to lick her face. Kirara's smile is fond, then self-righteous when she plops the ferret back in and locks the cage door.

"Start remembering the way on your own, for when you can come steal her yourself," she advises as she tugs Christine through the wall and back out into the maybe-warm night.

She kindly does not ask if Christine *would* take her back. There are too many heavy, terrible memories there, and without her witch, Sadie deserves a pleasant retirement.

Christine takes her hand with her own warm smile. "Thank you, Kirara. This did cheer me up."

· · • • · • · • • · ·

Natalie wakes with Hammond's foot in her back.

She edges away, groaning at the ache already present, and squints toward her clock. She doesn't drink often for good reason, and last night she had only had one wine cooler. Yet she feels hungover. Such is the burden of sharing a bed with one Hammond Two Feather.

Vivienne snores against the carpet below them.

Natalie doesn't know where Rory is, but she can assume he's nearby, laughing at Hammond's contorted sleeping position. She slides out of bed, stretching again, and tiptoes around Vivienne despite the fact that she's the heaviest sleeper Natalie has ever known.

Hammond only drinks rarely, too, but Vivienne partakes frequently and merrily. Last night had been a special case, granted; it isn't often one takes on *dragons*. With Vivienne and Hammond on board, she only needs to confirm Codi and get hold of Isaac. She has the song and the money, but Codi had been unusually cagey when first asked.

But, when finding her phone, she discovers good news: a text back from the woman herself.

'*I'm in*' is all it says, but it's a weight off of Natalie's shoulders. Hammond is no slouch with a rifle, but Codi had been in the military and is good with *everything*. (Probably not because of her military training. Natalie doesn't ask.)

One witch, two fliers, Rory potentially as a lookout, and a walking armory. They have the firepower to take down a dragon, but it would require luck and more worry. It would be easier with a second witch, or a second shot.

The text notification is the only one on her phone. Isaac had not called her back.

She ducks out into the hall, pads down the stairs, and begins making tea for what will undoubtedly be an unholy wakening whenever the troublemakers upstairs get up. She puts the phone on speaker when she dials Isaac again.

It rings and rings, and eventually clicks through to voicemail. Strange that he doesn't screen the call. He is meant to come in later today, and while avoidant, he must know she won't be happy with him.

I can ask Megan, Natalie absently thinks, stirring honey into her tea. In an ideal world, there would be no injuries, but Natalie is a realist. Coven members may be bidding for Megan's attention if they plan on tackling the migration, however, and Natalie does not wish to make waves. She'll ask anyway. No one ever got hurt by asking for help.

She is on her third cup of tea by the time Hammond shuffles downstairs. He rebraids his hair with bleary eyes, but smiles gratefully when he spots his own mug on the counter. "Thank you, angel," he says with a kiss on her cheek. "How'd you sleep?"

"Before, during, or after all of the kicking?" Natalie flatly returns.

"Sorry. How long do you think Viv will be out?"

"For most of the day, I'm afraid. Would you like breakfast?"

He checks his cell phone, and Natalie already knows the answer. "Sorry again, but I'm already running late for practice. Thanks for the offer! Rain check?"

"Anytime, Hammond. Good luck at practice, and bye, Rory."

Once he's gone with his usual whirlwind of energy, Natalie stretches out her back again. She wishes Vivienne had taken the bed with him instead, since she could sleep through an earthquake, much less lumbar realignment. Psychics do not live long lives, but if this is what eighty feels like, perhaps she's not missing much.

It is near noon when Isaac and Sam come in. Vivienne is still asleep upstairs, and she briefly thinks about asking Sam to move her to the bed, but once she sees the boys' expressions, she drops the thought. Isaac always looks surly and ready to bite any hand that feeds him, but Sam is normally cheerier.

"Is everything alright with you two?" Natalie asks, neutral as possible.

Neither answer. Fair enough. She won't pry, because there are bigger priorities to wrest from Isaac's tight lips than a rough night.

"Today I'm replenishing my float potion stock and I'll need both of your help with that. Gloves on, please, and Sam, would you go into the backroom and bring out all of the dried sunflowers I have? And if you see any more basil hanging back there, bring it out. It can dry out here so I know how much I have."

"Alright," Sam mumbles and slinks off.

Natalie is directly between Isaac and the glove drawer, and she remains there. She has dealt with unruly witches before. She has dealt with skittish spellwriters and distrustful outsiders. She has no patience for anyone who won't give her the benefit of the doubt when it comes to having spent *months* together.

"You didn't answer my calls yesterday. Or this morning," Natalie says.

Isaac stares over her shoulder.

"I was going to ask you a question, and I still am going to. But now I'm going to be less polite about it and give you less of a choice, which I'm sure is what you were trying to avoid to begin with."

His eyes flicker toward hers, grimace already growing on his face, but Sam comes back before the tension can mount further. He has a bundle of sunflowers under one arm, and behind Natalie, he fetches two pairs of gloves.

"Here," he says, avoiding eye contact with Isaac, and slides them across the table before gently setting down the sunflowers. "What's a float potion?"

"A potion that makes you float," Isaac all but snaps. He takes the gloves and picks the table furthest from both of them.

"That's correct," Natalie concedes, "and it's used by humans to achieve a mild sort of flight, combined with motion spells."

"Oh. Why don't people use that more often, then?"

"It only lasts an hour and gives you a hangover," Isaac says.

Natalie arches an eyebrow. Isaac has never displayed any talent with potions, and his knowledge is spotty. "Also correct. We'll be using these next week during the dragon migration. *That* is what I was calling about—I'm asking you two to help with our acquisition of a dragon. Actually, I'm really not asking at this point. I can provide a broom for Isaac, but I must admit, I'm not entirely sure if a float potion will work for Sam. We can test that later today—"

"He can be on the broom with me," Isaac interrupts.

Sam's head swivels around like an owl's, and even Natalie must admit her surprise. (Nevermind the fact that a small portion of her wished to learn how effective human potions are on demons.)

"No arguments about helping?" Natalie mildly asks.

"I'm picking my battles. I assume you have a plan to take down a fucking *dragon*, and maybe this will get you off my back for a whole second."

"I have only ever been *on your back* about that summoning spell of yours—"

"Which I won't share. Period. Maybe this will sink it in for you." Isaac adjusts his gloves but keeps an icy eye on Natalie. "I'd rather fight a dragon for you than share any of my spellwriting. Also, you called at an inopportune time. I'm not at your beck and call all day long."

"You were playing video games," Sam says, instead of addressing anything else mounting between them.

Natalie, however, had expected as much.

She has seen much of Isaac, and even Sam, in her visions. In many, he warms to her, to Vivienne, and could appear to be called a friend. In a few, he is cruel and vicious and a foe. In almost all, he is capable of great magical feats and has little remorse in showing that off.

He has never once opened up to her, in *any* future she has glimpsed.

"Alright," Natalie says, and sets her mug down at last.

"Alright?" Sam parrots back, since Isaac is only regarding her with the utmost suspicion and silence. "Are you two done fighting?"

"I'd never like to fight with either of you. I may be a witch, but I've hardly ever dueled and haven't fought many things. I think we could be great allies. But, all in all, I accept your demand for silence, provided you continue to help me in the shop. And with the occasional heavy lifting."

"Like dragons and luck spirits."

"Yes. Who knows what else may come up."

Natalie knows.

She has the sneaking suspicion Isaac knows, too. What else would make such a defensive witch take such an enormous risk?

• • • • ● • ● • • •

Tsukiko rarely pays visits to psychics—their dreams taste acrid—but Mark Ito is a special case. First, she wants to be in the dreamscape as long as possible, to avoid the storm in the human realm. Second, he does nice favors for those he likes. Third, he's really handsome, for a human.

The baku slips into his dreamscape with a content sigh. Lucid dreams are comfortable. It smells sweet tonight, so it's probably a pleasant dream. It's been several moons since she's last visited him, and she is happy to see he is having good dreams without alcohol or more baku interference. Nice humans deserve nice dreams.

She doesn't see or sense him anywhere at first, but that is normal. His dreamscape runs large. Tsukiko can't decide if his dream smells sweet like pastries, or sweet like flowers, but both are pleasant and don't point to the risk of running into any vulgar dreams. She snuffles around a few hazy patches, tasting old memories, using her short trunk to flip over sequin-like stones and pop bubbles of growing nightmares. Her tail wags as she works.

She finally senses him, like one would feel a ripple in a pond, at the far end of his dreamscape. Blue and silver trees sprout up in a growing forest of thoughts, feelings, and desires, and she trims bushes and eats azure butterflies as she goes. Time has little meaning in a realm of dreams, and Tsukiko has never known hurry in her life.

When Mark notices her, he breaks into a wide, warm smile. "Tsu-chan! What a pleasant surprise. I was wondering why I was having such a delightful dream."

"Mark," she happily replies and floats over to nuzzle him. She snuffles over his hair, checking for sleep soot, but he seems fine. "You are being unusually calm tonight. There is hardly any work for me to do!"

A wrought-gold rose bush springs up at their feet, blooming into a dazzling purple mums. Humans and their flowers. She grazes on them anyway, accepting the gift. It tastes like the mildest, blandest of flowers. She wonders if tapirs in the human realm eat such boring food.

The sting of old magic pricks her like a rose thorn. Tsukiko jumps, tail lashing, ears up high. "What was that?"

Mark cocks his head. Dreamers are never very clever, even lucid dreamers. "What was what, dearest?"

The old magic cleaves into the dreamscape. The sensation of ripples turns into churning, frothing waves, and the color drains out of the growing garden. The rose bush heaves and dies, and Tsukiko clamps her paws over her trunk to stifle the foul smell. This isn't a nightmare. She isn't sure *what* it is.

"Tsu-chan, are you okay? What's wrong?" Mark kneels by her like he doesn't notice the dreamscape tearing itself apart around him. It could turn into a nightmare yet, perhaps a night terror, but that isn't the source, and she doesn't know what it'll do to his dream. What it'll do to *her*.

A figure appears opposite of the grove of withering iron trees.

It looks human, but only for a second. Antlers, fur, wings, hooves, tails of all sorts—the forms shift around like a shimmering haze of heat. The figure steps forward, hair black as night hanging like a curtain around itself, like that horror movie girl too many humans have nightmares of.

Tsukiko catches sight of one gleaming red eye, glaring out at her from behind the sheet of night hair. Stars, just as black, twinkle in its hair, and it takes a step forward on what is a human leg with too-long claws, then a hoof, then something furred.

"Bryn?" Mark asks, surprised, but not scared.

Tsukiko squeezes her eyes shut and sucks in as much dream as she can through her trunk. When she reopens them, she sees what Mark is seeing: a human-looking woman with long black hair and a thickly muscled form. Human arms lined with magic runes. No wings, no scales, no antlers, no feathers, no fur, no claws.

That image fades and the ever-changing monstrosity edges closer.

"What are you doing," the figure growls, voice deep as the frigid seas. "You cannot hurt him."

"Bryn, is that actually *you*?" Mark asks.

Tsukiko backs up until she runs into his chest. She could leave the dream, and she prepares herself to jump, but she doesn't want to just *leave* one of her favorite humans with what is surely a monster. A dream-invading monster! She has never heard of anything like *this* before.

"Get away from him!"

"Wait, Bryn—I know her, this is a friend. A baku who checks in on my dreams sometimes. How are *you* here?"

"Mark, you need to wake up!" Tsukiko cries.

She pushes him out of his dream. The dreamscape shatters around them, crumbling into precious metals and dying flowers, and it churns her stomach, but she had no choice. She drops back into the waking realm just as Mark sits up, holding his head. Blood drips from his nose.

"What happened," he grumbles, squinting at the red dotting his sheets. He tilts his head back and pinches his nose. "Tsu-chan, that was a *rude* awakening. That was Bryn. How she got there, I don't have the faintest..."

A shadow shifts in the dim room, and Tsukiko's hackles raise when she realizes there is a figure in the dark doorway.

"So you're a shapeshifter with dreamwalking abilities. Your mystery is turning into a migraine, my dear," Mark calmly tells her. "Tsu-chan, she's a temporary houseguest. She only wanted to keep her meal ticket safe—"

"That wasn't dreamwalking," Tsukiko interrupts. She pastes herself against the wall, tail lashing, fear prickling at her. There are no nearby dreams to jump into.

"Learned talent," the Bryn-monster grunts. Gone are the shifting images, leaving only the human-looking form with the long, wild night hair. But she still smells of old fur and older blood. Of truly bad dreams.

"Can we make peace now? We know everyone. We're friends. Friends with a lot of questions, but no one will hurt each other tonight, right?" Mark tries.

Bryn bares her teeth. Tsukiko jumps out of the room with a *pop*. Mark may be handsome and a nice human, but she remembers the inugami he befriended. She'd been willing to write that off as an accident, victim of a sad human heart, but twice is folly. Living on others' dreams has taught her that she has to come first.

• • • • • • • • • •

Christine hasn't seen Kirara since their jaunt to see Sadie, but with Emil asleep on the couch and the witching hour come and gone, she's feeling brave enough to traverse the night. She could get a phone once she's tangible again, but how would she afford it? Scratch cards and low-key gambling, like Emil? She wants to finish high school and go to university, but how will she afford *that*?

That's a nasty rabbit hole to fall down. She shakes her head to clear the thoughts.

The night is overcast, threatening rain, and definitely windy enough for her to notice the leaves and trash tumbling by. The solstice is coming up, and that always riles the weather spirits, but she hopes it doesn't pour rain. Emil, like most dumb boys his age, doesn't believe in umbrellas. And rain makes Kirara cranky.

When will I be able to feel the rain again? And *smell* it, she definitely misses smelling things. Without hunger, she hasn't missed taste often yet, but with summer in full swing, she knows she's missing flowers and rain and barbecues and her favorite seasonal body sprays.

"Hello, small spirit," comes a voice from behind.

Christine stiffens, shoulders up to her ears, and turns. It isn't often she's addressed by anyone other than Kirara or Emil. Discounting Vivienne, she could count those instances on one hand.

For someone who hangs around a floating calico cat, she's surprised to find a floating *fox*.

Even minus the floating and speaking bit, he's pure black, only the smallest bit of grey on the tip of his tail and his muzzle. He's *beautiful*, and she, again, hangs around with a glittery cat.

"H-Hello," Christine manages, offering a nod, hands clasped tight behind her. It is only his foxiness that disarms her; she is still being approached by a presumably adult male spirit, and human ghosts are definitely tangible to those.

The fox cocks his head. His tail swings beneath him like a lazy pendulum. "You are a very curious case. I'd like to ask you a few questions."

That is a good step away from potential assault or eating. But Christine still looks around, furtive, for avenues of escape. "Um, about what? We don't know each other, and y-you know, not supposed to talk to strangers…"

"*Je suis un matagot.* I have seen you around, small spirit, but I have never seen anything *like* you."

Oh god, that's French, isn't it? He sounds frank and snobby enough to be French. She squeaks out, "Like me?"

"Something caught halfway."

His forward movement smoothly melds into a man stepping out of his fox form. The streetlight casts his skin as tawny and his long hair blacker than his fur, eyes deep-set and nose pointed. Perhaps most surprisingly, he wears a double-breasted suit, black as well, shoes shiny enough to reflect even the yellow light overhead. Like Kirara's human form, he maintains fox ears and his bushy tail, the only things disturbing his immaculate presentation.

He bends, so he is nose to nose with Christine, but stops her shying with a hand on her shoulder. For the first time, she wishes she *couldn't* touch.

He releases her shoulder, but grabs her chin instead, tilting her head gently but firmly up. "Not a ghost, yet not a demon. *This* is the answer, *non*?" the matagot asks.

He reaches for the thick collar at her throat.

Christine throws a forearm sideways to break his grip like Logan had taught her. "Let go of me—don't touch me!" Her chest heaves with nonexistent heart pounding. Kirara had given her that collar, and she is not so naïve about magic or spirits to think it has nothing to do with her luck spirit progress. She hasn't taken it off since she received it, and the only other time someone had touched it, she thought she'd die. Again.

"I offer to take it off your hands. It seems it isn't worth the trouble of dragging a ghost through stasis."

"No!"

He only then retracts his reaching hand. With a flourish, he produces a golden lump. Not like the glittery luck Kirara sheds, but *solid*—actual *gold*. "Do the dead care about money these days?" he muses.

The fox spirit opens his mouth wide, *too* wide, like the hinge of his jaw isn't where it ought to be, and swallows the gold again with a prim lick of his lips.

"Human spirits aren't so bad," he reasons. He again steps toward her, and she again backs up, now in the empty street. Half a block down, the traffic light changes to yellow, as if narrating her life.

"I-I'm a luck spirit," Christine stammers out with trembling fists, "that's wh-what I'm going to be. Leave me alone now."

"Luck spirits are also delicious," he replies. "But they are often on good terms with spirits of fortune. Let's be on good terms."

Does he want to eat me or be my friend? She doesn't know, and she doesn't want either. "I answered your question, a-and refused your offer. I want you to leave me alone now if *you* want to be on such good terms."

"What an odd spirit," he hums.

When he approaches again, Christine dives through the ground.

She falls into an empty subway tunnel and leaps for the far side. She hopes matagot are like bakeneko in the fact that they can't pass through matter and have to do their weird jump thing. She hears the telltale *pop* a moment later, just as she reaches the far wall, and she scrambles up it like she can touch it.

Christine floats up through the concrete again, now on the other sidewalk, and flees through the nearest building. She may not outrun him, but he would have to check every room in the building if he wants to find her, and she mercifully has phased into an office complex.

She claws her way up through two more floors, and down two hallways into the bathroom off a janitorial wing. She floats over the toilet, one hand over her mouth, the other holding the bell on her collar from giving her away.

She doesn't need breath, and she doesn't have a hammering heart, but she shakes with nerves.

She had been lucky, even before going down this road, to have found Kirara first. She has *known* there are less-than-friendly beings out there, spirits and monsters and humans and creatures of all kinds. Ghosts are easy prey. She isn't yet a luck spirit.

Halfway? she recalls, wondering if that ought to give her hope.

Boring grocery runs become significantly less boring when one has a vision in the middle of choosing grapes.

Natalie is dunked without warning into a fight full of flashing claws. There's only a tussle of bodies, snarling and writhing, unable to focus until the two spring apart. One is a black-haired man—no, spirit, based on the dark animal ears and tail lashing behind him—and the other is a teenaged girl with a bell collar around her neck.

Despite the size and age difference, the girl is winning, based on the red blood dripping off her black claws.

The spirit huffs a laugh, holding his bleeding side. When he smiles, his sharp teeth are red, too. "You've grown into your claws, mademoiselle.*"*

"I'll show you how well I have!"

But when she charges forward again, she stumbles, and falls with two crossbow bolts sticking out of her back. The spirit tilts his head back and laughs. He nods to someone unseen, then kneels by her side and places a hand on her back to keep her on the ground. "You're not the only one with friends, small spirit," he says and reaches for the collar she wears.

Natalie jolts back to herself. Seeing action in visions always fills her with adrenaline, and she leans against the display of grapes until her breathing evens back out.

She's seen that girl before, though she's never heard her addressed as spirit. What is she? Natalie wonders.

CHAPTER 13

IN WHICH VIVIENNE GOES SHOPPING

Emil knows enough not to ask a girl if she's on her period. Especially because of a touchy mood. He doubly knows that ghosts don't have periods. (He doesn't think bakeneko do, either. But he is also not stupid to bark up that tree. Ever.)

But he can *think* it.

He's gleaned much of ghosthood from Christine, even if not all of it has been directly so. She doesn't speak much of her death, and he would rather eat his laptop than ask. He's put enough of two and two together to come reasonably close to four.

He understands that ghosthood is lonely. Christine tries to touch him more and more, and leans against Kirara whenever she's around so much they may as well be glued. She'd done the same to Vivienne, a near-stranger with a questionable-at-best agenda.

And he's certain she doesn't mean to, but the way she *watches* him eat makes him... uncomfortable. Very. Incredibly. Dyingly. Starving dog metaphors don't cut it; there is so much more than hunger in her golden gaze when she sits by him during meals. Hunger can mean for more than food, sure, but this goes so far beyond any meaning of it. She is too calm to call it desperation or heartache. Vast hunger for the very state of *being* hungry, of fulfilling a basic living need again.

Zombies probably don't exist, and it isn't as if he fears for the safety of his brain, but she *may* have featured in a nightmare or two with those bright eyes and that more-than-hungry look.

But this is pissy without food around and not the sad she gets when Kirara fucks off to whatever cat things she does.

Day two of ghostly PMS hell leads Emil to ask, "Is everything okay?"

The dead girl floating above his couch like she wants to sit on it turns to him with lamplight eyes.

Emil wishes he could swallow the words back down. But then she'd probably look at him with that not-hungry look. He'd settle for shoving the words up his ass. She hasn't yet gotten sad about horny things, so that should be safe.

Oh god, now he's remembering all the horniness he had exposed her to before he knew he was being haunted.

"Why do you ask?" Christine finally responds. She looks back down at her lap, hands folded delicately.

"Wondering if something happened, I guess. You've been... off." That's still a safe word to use around girls, right? Christine doesn't have a scary bone in her body, and it's not like she *could* hurt him, but he's a little worried about hurting *her*. She's been through enough.

She doesn't need to be exposed to any more teenaged insensitivity than she already willingly endures.

Not that he understands why she does that, either.

Except it is half an answer to the aforementioned loneliness.

"The dragon migration is coming up," she says, all casual-like, fingers playing absently with the hem of her ghostly shorts. "That's why it's been storming. It makes spirits restless... Would you buy that as an answer?"

He plops down onto the couch next to her. The indent from his weight makes her float even higher over it, but she soon settles to compensate. "We both know I don't know enough about magic to question anything you say. But you don't want a convenient excuse. But I don't know if you want to talk about it. Whatever it is. Or maybe it's nothing. Grief is like—I mean, I know our situations are pretty different, but grief comes and goes, so some days are just fucking terrible. I get that."

"We're not that different."

"Christine," Emil gently says, and she looks at him, confused by the softness. "I don't know how to break this to you, but... I'm not dead."

She snorts a surprised laugh.

Relief floods through him. She doesn't completely laugh, she'd been mostly surprised, but the smile remains afterward. That is light years ahead of where they have been. She has a round face, cherubic, and a smile seems to fit best. She also has a dimple. Has he ever noticed that before? Why not?

Right, because the sad ghost doesn't smile a lot.

When does his life get the tragic Hallmark movie it deserves?

"You're terrible," she mutters, clearly not meaning it, and presses a hand to her cheek like *she's* surprised she's smiling, too.

"We can talk about the fact that you know so much about *dragons* if you don't wanna talk about anything heavy. Because I definitely want to talk about dragons. They migrate? From where?"

"I'm actually not sure..."

"Why do you only know little bits of magic? What about the interesting stuff?!"

"If an alien came to Earth, would you know how to answer all of their questions?" she asks. Emil stares at her, because he had never considered that angle, and it seems like a very specific example to trot out at a moment's notice. Christine rubs at her cheek again. "Logan said that a couple times. Explaining things is only for the knowledgeable. Most people only know enough to get them by in life."

"You're more knowledgeable than me."

"But I don't know how to *explain* things. Um, it's like... You know how to use your phone, and you could probably explain how to use most of its apps, right? But what about how it *works*? How to build one, repair it, take it apart? What if an alien asked you *exactly* how electricity or batteries or circuits worked?"

"I'm beginning to think you think I'm an alien."

"To magic..."

Emil pretends to smack her. She grins again and pretends to hide behind raised hands. "Don't jinx us!" he scolds. "The last thing we need on top of everything else is *aliens*, and your luck can bring it down on our heads!"

She wiggles her fingers. "You can be haunted, and then abducted. What other conspiracies can you check off?"

"Ghosts actually exist, though. ...*Do* aliens exist?"

"I don't know! I don't think so...? I think there may have been a couple of coven members trying to research that, but Logan never looked into it. The closest he got to space was buying me a star for my birthday when I was twelve."

"I could see him doing something that sappy," Emil muses.

They both realize at the same moment that they both mentioned him without the usual awkwardness or pain. Emil only feels the guilt a moment later; he has no claim to the guy, barely knew him, and he doesn't want to bring up her dead brother and make her even *sadder*—

"I miss him," Christine whispers. She sighs, nearly mute without actual breath to add to it, then slumps against Emil's shoulder. "But yeah, he did do stuff that sappy," she adds.

Emil, meanwhile, has completely frozen.

Guilt has left—shock remains. Shock has overridden everything else.

Christine only realizes once she flops through him, a full six seconds after contact. (He had been counting.)

They had *touched*.

They stare at each other with wide, open, astounded eyes. Emil doesn't remember being this close to her recently, but is he only thinking that because she is abruptly an actual *presence*? Ghosts can't touch. Vivienne, despite her rule-breaking, had made that clear, and even Kirara agreed with that.

Luck spirit? he wonders, wildly. *Am I going to die soon? Is it because we talked about Logan? Is she finally doing it?*

With trembling hands, Christine reaches up to his face. He waits with bated breath.

Her fingers phase through his cheek.

All the loneliness and sorrow crash back into her expression, and before he can gather his own disappointment into words, she floats through the couch and through the far wall. Christine had been completely silent, but it feels like she slammed a door in his face.

Emil touches his cheek where she hadn't touched him.

· · · • • · • • · ·

Folding magic into viscous liquid is delicate work, so naturally Vivienne's phone blares and jars her into spilling half the bottle across the countertop.

Natalie frowns at her newly bronzed counter.

When Vivienne sees Emil's name on her screen, she spares her cohort a look. *These kids better have a good payoff*, it says, because she is being called on by things not yet happened to babysit and she'd *really* like to know why when she doesn't know the first thing about luck spirits (and too many sad things about ghosts).

Upon answering, Emil tells her, "I need more potion again, and I think Christine wants to talk to you. Like, a girl talk. I work until eight, and tomorrow, but I'm free the day after. She's free, y'know, whenever."

"Yes, Your Highness, whenever you please, Your Highness," Vivienne replies. She holds her phone on speaker with her clean hand and ducks into the kitchen to try to wash off her sparkly fingers. The polish might come off, the magic may *think* about coming off, but glitter is forever.

Emil remains silent for a thoughtful beat. Then, "You told me you're a freelancer. Shouldn't you have some flexibility with your schedule?" He sounds like a kid trying to be an adult and schedule things on his own for the first time, which is precious, and absolutely *not* true since he's had a job and school and weekly check-ins and who knows what else with his absent family situation.

"So, about that—the rest of this week is out for me. Stay inside, too, it's gonna storm something fierce through the migration. I have prep work the next two days, and then I get to fight dragons. Woo. It locks in my schedule pretty tight, so, sorry. Can you put Christine on the phone?"

"...How?"

"Speaker?" Vivienne suggests with a roll of her eyes. "It's a fifty-fifty shot on whether ghosts work on technology these days. Cameras aren't great, but sometimes, microphones work. Haven't you ever watched a ghost hunter show?"

There is a longer silence this time, so Vivienne assumes Christine is there, and that this will not work. Worth a shot either way.

"I can send a delivery for your potion," she relents, because she's a sucker for overly attached kids in over their heads, "but I'm sorry, I *really* can't afford to hop around town right now."

Emil hangs up with a dejected grumble. Vivienne wipes off her nominally clean hand, then digs around the kitchen for wherever Natalie keeps the padded envelopes. (As it turns out, not in the kitchen.)

"Once you're done with that batch of polish, could you run to the goblin market for me?" Natalie asks while Vivienne remorselessly rummages through her entire shop. "And they're in the top-right drawer of the shipping shelf, Viv. Are you going to ask Sam and Isaac to run that to Emil?"

"Uh, no? I'm going to mail it. Like a normal person. Speaking of normal people, *they* can go to the market—"

"This will give you the chance to make nice with that tengu. I've already drawn up a list—" Natalie beckons over a paper list with a curl of her fingers, still stirring her pot, "—and honestly, Viv, I don't think Sam should go to the market yet. Isaac has yet to do any real shielding of him, spell or charm, and I'm not sure cloaking potions work on demons. It won't hurt you to be polite to youkai."

"Yeah, it *could*," she mutters, rebellious.

"I don't believe so. It is statistically unlikely, anyway."

"Ha! So you *have* seen a future where I get viciously mauled by tengu!"

"Not the little black-haired crow one."

"Why are there more tengu in my future?!" Vivienne groans, cursing her not at all inevitable future. Most of Natalie's visions don't come true, not even partially. Maybe befriending Mirai is the way to *avoid* other tengu trying to vore her. "Seriously, though, ask someone from the coven to play errand boy. This batch of polish is almost done, but this is the only batch, and we're covering five people, six if you want to try your luck with Sam, and I haven't even begun to ward Codi's bolts."

"I can ward," Natalie primly informs her.

Vivienne rewards her with a flat look. Natalie can, by technicality, ward things. It is not, however, her strongest suit, or second strongest, or even third. If Vivienne is here and has the magic, as she does two days before the migration, *she* ought to do it.

But fighting with Natalie Stirling is always a lost cause.

So Vivienne traipses to the goblin market, trying to come up with a good wording for *No Mx. Tengu I Have Not Found That Egg My Friend Roped Me Into Finding For You Also Can I Buy Another Egg From You*. It's not great however she cuts it. Alright, she hasn't been trying very hard to find that missing First egg, but she has a lot on her plate and exactly zero leads on the subject.

Well, one lead, and that's a silent shapeshifter with unknown identity and ability. Personally, fuck any boss who tried to get her to stand up to youkai who actually caught her; she doesn't understand why Bryn wouldn't trade the egg for the chance at safety. Mark can be a great shield, but that's for humans and friendly spirits and not *against* youkai. Bryn doesn't even *know* that.

If I were a shapeshifter who didn't belong here, where would I hide a First egg, Vivienne wonders as she drops the toll into the jar and heads into the market. It's even more humid there than in the city, and she wrinkles her nose in disgust.

She has never seen a First egg, but regular tengu eggs aren't small, and it isn't like a random ass Whatever She Is could open up a safety deposit box. She hasn't left Mark's house in weeks to check on it, so it must be secure.

With a partner? She doubts it, especially since Mirai had zeroed in on her so quickly. *Some place that can dampen the smell and magic of it, maybe in a container, but the location itself would have to help...*

Natalie's errand list turns out to be more akin to a grocery list. Pixie dust, bottled maiden sigh from a peri, cinnamon from cinnamon bird nests, parandrus milk, raskovnik, and a goddamned tengu egg. Vivienne crushes the list in her fist.

Fae are hard to speak with but all too happy to sell to humans, especially something as simple as pixie dust, and cinnamon bird cinnamon and parandrus milk are easy to get from Graham Yu, beast master extraordinaire. A wood nymph with a hedgehog on a leash sells her raskovnik. While it takes the better part of two hours, she eventually finds a peri who has a maiden sigh that isn't for a literal arm and a leg.

She puts the tengu off until last. But, surprise of all surprises, Mirai isn't even at the stall.

Yun-hee, beside them, leans over into their space with a hugely unsubtle stage whisper of "It's *that* human!"

Vivienne spares her a flat look.

The tengu manning the stall raises their head from their slump. Whereas Mirai is slight and dark-haired and plumaged, this tengu is tall, willowy, and fair all over. Their hair is an even mix of tan and creamy white, matching their feathers, long and straight and falling over their shoulder in a loose ponytail. They wear the robes Vivienne is more used to seeing youkai in, old-fashioned, sleeveless, and loose to allow room for extra limbs, thick thighs, and long feathers. It's white as well, but patterned with delicate twining vines and flowers.

Their mask is moon-round and far flatter than what she expects of a tengu. (They're pretty well-known for their long, beak-like noses, after all.)

A barn owl, she realizes. Separate from the crow clan entirely.

"You are the human Mirai contracted to find my egg, are you not?" the tengu asks, violently throwing all of Vivienne's hopes for separation out the window.

"You know them? Wait—*your* egg?" she squeaks with a rictus smile. She clutches her bag to her chest. This is probably going to be the tengu that viciously mauls her, then. Good to know. "Mirai is—I mean, they're a *crow*, but I hadn't known the egg was—yours?"

The tengu sighs behind their mask. They slump again, dejected, feathers ruffled and sad-looking, somehow. Which is a shame, because they're so *pretty*.

"I do not know how much Mirai has told you, but this is not human business. There are other missing First eggs, but the daft little magpie is so upset over *mine...*" They cover their head with their arms... wings... arm-wings.

And Vivienne realizes they're *embarrassed*.

She sees the barest hint of pink on the tips of their pointed ears, and she marvels at the rarity of this. She didn't know youkai possessed a sense of shame! Now she's suddenly invested in this tengu drama. It's a spiritual soap opera. She thought *she* and her gang of losers were the drama queens around here.

"Mirai asked me and my colleague to find, er, your egg, yes."

"And what of the thief? What of Mirai's payment to you?"

She had assumed at the time that the payment would be not being eviscerated. But a grateful higher spirit is *something*, and she wonders if the dollar signs are visible in her eyes. "I am the muscle of this venture, tengu-san. My colleague, Mark Ito, is the principal liaison. It just so happened that I came to the market before he did, so when Mirai saw me..."

"It was unbecoming," the tengu miserably says. "I will double their payment if you drop this matter."

Getting paid to do nothing is Vivienne's greatest dream. *Especially* when the other option had been desperate, potentially violent, and with a severe lack of leads.

Supernatural Hunter Tip #2: If it sounds too good to be true, it is.

A bundle of black and white feathers pelting out of the sky dashes her hopes. Thoroughly. Mirai nearly clips Vivienne's head when they swoop in to land atop the other tengu, their mask askew and their robes twisted from their flight.

"Hatsu!" they cheer, nuzzling their cheeks together, further upending their mask. Instead of adjusting it, they pull it off with a relieved breath and offer a sharp-toothed smile to Vivienne. "And Vivienne, it is so nice to see you again! Please ignore my honored senior if they were trying to persuade you not to pursue the egg's location. You should still do that."

"And if I were not doing such a thing?" the other tengu, Hatsu, archly asks.

"Then be happy!" Mirai cries and nuzzles them again. Hatsu sighs beneath their round mask. "But I know you would never try to undermine my business, Hatsu."

"You are not on market duty today, little one. Go back home."

"Perhaps I have business with Vivienne!" Mirai exclaims, then turns to her. She expects the beseeching, imploring googly eyes of one silently asking a favor, but receives a prompting, imperious look that she would more expect from a haughty royal.

But Vivienne has dealt with fussier clients. "Actually, yes," she sighs, "I would like to purchase an egg. A normal one, not a First one."

"First eggs are not for purchase," Hatsu grumbles from beneath the magpie pile of Mirai's enthusiasm.

"Of course! And I'll give you a discount, because you are an excellent human!"

They have met two-point-one times, but Vivienne will take a discount. It's a salve to soothe the lost hope of being able to wash her hands of their eggy woes. "Thank you, Mirai. I'll let Mark know we ran into each other."

"Or you could drop this inane ploy for attention. Humans need not be involved in our affairs," Hatsu says while Mirai rummages beneath the stall for an egg. "Listen to reason, for *once*, Mirai! What can humans offer us?"

(Vivienne stays silent. She is not out of the mauling woods just because she knows Hatsu's name and sense of shame.)

Mirai pops up with an egg the size of a toaster. "Business," they smartly reply, "and thus human money that is good in this market."

Vivienne pauses with her hand in the purse pocket of her bag. "Uh, do you take US dollars? I don't have any yen right now."

In the stall next to them, Yun-hee's many tails wag. Fox spirits, ever masters of markets and wants, would definitely carry several types of modern currency and even more certainly fleece her for them.

"Dollars are fine!" Mirai chirps. "Eight hundred and eighty-eight dollars for this egg."

Not for the first time feeling envious of Natalie's ingredient budget, Vivienne hands over the money and gingerly takes the huge egg under one arm. Rather than set it down, she awkwardly digs in her bag for an extra sweater, then wraps the egg up before placing it in one of the inner pockets. The egg could withstand the weight of both her and Natalie tap dancing on it, but knowing her luck, she would end up with a soggy pocket dimension.

"Do tell Mark that I will drop by to discuss his progress after the migration passes through," Mirai says, still beaming. The fact that their eyes are icy and their teeth are all on display is not lost on Vivienne.

"You shouldn't," Hatsu groans, tugging at Mirai's black feathers.

She hates to pick sides, especially with that mauling still on the future table, but Vivienne smiles as best she can and responds, "I will relay your message. Thanks for doing business with me."

"See you around, Vivienne!" Mirai calls after her. They wave with both arms, flight feathers flapping, and Yun-hee offers her a coy wave as well, just to be a brat.

It is going to be a busy week after the dragon migration.

· · • • • • • · ·

Mark never does things by half-measures, but Bryn wouldn't have the patience for him to hype this up as much as he thinks it deserves. Because it *does* deserve hype. He thinks he's finally gotten more than his foot in the door when it comes to whatever Bryn has going on. Mark Ito has found his in, and that makes him feel back in control, and he knows better than anyone what that does to his already-charming personality.

"Bryn, dear, would you come out here? I think we need to have a little chat," Mark calls.

"No," comes from the bathroom.

"I know about your other pelts," he replies.

Silence falls over his home, thick and dangerous. He keeps himself calm and sips at his tea. He doesn't hear Bryn emerge, but he feels the pressure of anger advancing on him, and when he glances over, he finds her looming behind the couch. As usual, she drips onto his carpet.

"You know nothing, *shuggoth*," she hisses at him like a cat. The word stings at his ears.

"Would you like to take a seat for this?" he offers, but she continues glowering at him. Sighing, he continues. "I know *plenty*, I'll have you know. And you're not very good at hiding your reactions to things, especially things you think are secret. Now, I'll admit that I can't read your mind as well as I can a human's, or even the glimpses I can get from higher spirits, but you're not an impregnable mental wall. More like Swiss cheese, in fact. Which, fine, easily explained by whatever your employer is—you're terrified of it, and it has some sort of psychic impact, and that was easy enough to figure out.

"But *you*. You have been a delicious little mystery since the moment you broke into my home. You used a selkie as a cover story, and you obviously *have* some sort of connection to the seal pelt, which threw me off for some time. Not many things turn into a seal, after all. But you stole a First egg from the tengu, which is no mean feat, and pretending to be a selkie wouldn't have helped you there. They would have seen anything human-looking—or seal-looking—a mile away. And I've seen white feathers in your thoughts. Mirai is a magpie. Most of their plumage is black. So, how would a *seal* shapeshifter infiltrate the tengu realm? And then, an idea hit me: she didn't look like a seal or a human. If you're using a skin to shapeshift, you can probably hold a partial transformation, can't you?"

Bryn looks madder and madder the longer his Sherlockian explanation goes on. Frankly, Mark is pretty proud of himself for it—and yes, it had been wild guessing, but her *reaction* gave her away. Again. He only has to keep guessing and let her answer, and soon enough, he'll have her all figured out.

But this is easier to approach her than her employer.

Mark beams up at her. "If you had got caught out in the human realm without your seal pelt, tell me—what would your cover have been then? Swan maiden?"

"How did you know it was a swan pelt," Bryn growls, clutching the back of his couch. Fabric rips beneath her nails.

"I didn't," he replies, unable to help himself from chuckling, "but it's the only other thing I know of that shapeshifts with a pelt that has *feathers*. So, you have a seal skin, and a swan skin?"

Bryn rips a chunk of his couch out. He wishes she were the type of being who had access to money, so he could possibly blackmail her into replacing it. But alas, she has something even better than money, even if it won't replace his furniture.

"I'd like to propose a deal for you, Bryn," Mark tells her. He crosses one leg over the other and laces his fingers over his knee, ensuring to be the picture of poise. Mark has a flawless poker face, so may as well capitalize, even facing down a very angry mystery being who has already demonstrated enhanced strength and incredible temper. "I want to help you. I do. But I know all of my words mean less than shit to you, because you don't know how to trust anyone else, much less a very handsome and charming human like myself. So I'm going to offer you a way *out* from your boss' thumb—a dragon pelt."

She stares at him. Her posture is still tense, tattooed shoulders up around her ears, but anger leaches out of her blazing red eyes.

"Dragon scales repel magic of any kind. And your boss isn't *here*, are they, Bryn? Whatever connection or hold they have over you, this can cut it. You can turn into a *dragon*, and that's not something to mess with. I'm offering you freedom, though force, which you ought to respect."

"Why," Bryn finally says, her voice hardly more than a whisper. He's heard all manner of growling and shouting and grumbling out of her, so this is new. And promising. Maybe he's peeling back that defensive shield of hers.

"My bleeding heart," Mark replies, but she rips another chunk of wood and padding and fabric off his couch.

"*Why*. What do *you* gain from this?" she demands.

"Information. I want you to tell me why your boss wants a First egg so badly that they would throw away a useful being like yourself. I want to know their plans, I want to know what *your* instructions were, and anything else you'd like to volunteer about the thing that has you so terrified. I have the feeling that that thing isn't exactly a friend-to-be, so I'd rather prevent that kind of monster from making trouble, if I can. And I'd like to think I can."

Mark can tell that he has her on the hook. She *wants* a dragon pelt; she knows what it could mean for her. A concrete way to defend herself and gain some independence, and it isn't reliant on his kindness or her trust of him, since it is an object. He knows what that can mean for someone feeling so trapped. She needs to have something for *herself*.

"How could you get such a thing?" Bryn asks, feigning disinterest, eyes averted. She rubs a hand over her impressive bicep, fingers tracing the bottom-most row of tattooed rings. She'd have to make another set, based on what he assumes about her shapeshifting abilities. (It'd be *way* too much of a coincidence that the woman walks around with tattooed rings of *animal* runes on her for that to be unrelated. Mark doesn't believe in coincidence.)

"I am a very powerful man," Mark happily replies. It's not a boast if it's true. "And I have a lot of friends, a lot of connections, and a lot of information about how to do these sorts of things for *my* friends."

Right when he thinks she may demand proof, or draw out her mistrust longer, Bryn—shockingly—gives in. "...I want the dragon skin, *and* I want what my master has, and only then will I tell you everything." She glances up at him through her long hair. "My master has another one of my skins. I want it back. If you say you are powerful, then prove it."

"...I'm going to have to know a bit more about this boss of yours to do such a thing, you know," he fields, off-guard. So there's at least one more pelt out there, in addition to the swan—where did that go?—and the seal one, in his possession.

"I will tell you where it is located *after* you give me a dragon skin and prove yourself to me." And there's the arrogant, pissed-off Bryn again, the one he's come to know so dearly.

Mark won't argue about the finer points of what information she will have to give up in order for him to try to do this for her; she isn't fae or a ruthless businessman who has to have an ironclad contract. Bryn is ruled by emotion, and Mark can work with that. He has before.

So, to begin building the bricks to prove himself to her, Mark makes a call. "Hello, Codi, darling? I have a rush job for you. Double pay if you can deliver it within the week."

"Truth or dare!" Hammond only narrowly avoids slopping his wine over the rim of his glass. "Since Mark isn't here, there can't be any cheating!"

Their group is smaller this year. Mark had politely ducked out to deal with something about a shapeshifter friend of his.

When it comes to her turn, Natalie sips at her juice, allowing a solemn moment before she answers, "Truth."

There are disappointed groans from the others, but Vivienne's eyes glint. "Have you ever had a vision of one of us jacking off?"

There are whoops from Certain Parties about the prospect of oh so proper Natalie Stirling answering something so lewd, but honestly, she's disappointed. "Sex, no. Masturbation, yes," she replies to an even greater volume of shouts.

The noise dies away suddenly, leaving the quiet, grief-stricken sound of sobbing in its wake. "No, no no no!"

"Fiona, we have to go!"

"No—not him, too, please, no more!"

Hammond suddenly dashes by, shotgun in hand and rifle slung sloppily across his back. In his other hand, he drags Fiona Ramirez. She is in an uncharacteristic state of emotional vulnerability, eyeliner streaked down her cheeks, cutting through grime and caked blood. Her expression is fierce and desperate.

Hammond stumbles over the uneven ground, inadvertently yanking her down, and she raises her rifle to shoot at something unseen.

Natalie comes back to herself when Vivienne dabs at her hand with a napkin. She has spilled her glass, and she hastily sets it down to help her clean up the mess.

"What'd you see?" Codi asks curiously.

Natalie hesitates, just for a moment, and hides it in the patting dry of her dress. Not even Vivienne notices the hitch. "Ham masturbating," Natalie says, and receives a grieved moan of a much different kind.

CHAPTER 14

IN WHICH THEY HUNT DRAGONS (AND GET HUNTED IN TURN)

Natalie presides over dinner like Jesus at the last supper. Except no one will die tomorrow, and there will be no betrayals, and all the kisses will be platonic.

Vivienne thinks she maybe needs better feast imagery.

Much of the dinner is nostalgic: Natalie had thrown these dinner parties every time they went after big projects in the past, and there are some of the same faces and many of the same dishes. The boiled tengu egg sits as the centerpiece, in half of its own shell, the other half already in the back room drying to be ground later. Dinner is only nominally potluck, and Natalie had spent a full day and a half creating everything.

Codi paints her nails as she eats. They still have to talk Isaac into painting his—the polish Vivienne had helped make hooks magic, and she did not work so hard for it not to be used goddamnit—and maybe even Sam. That's how normal slumber parties are supposed to go, aren't they?

"If no one else wants it," Hammond says, "I call dibs on taking the rest of that cikavac."

"Isn't that breakfast?" Codi asks without looking up from her nails.

"We haff bagelff," Vivienne replies, mouth full, "but go nutff."

Sam has hardly touched his food, something which most of the table has not failed to notice. Vivienne is cramming her face with twice as much enthusiasm as usual, hoping to coerce him into eating people food like a mama cat teaching kittens the joys of wet food, but it has yet to work. The way Isaac picks at his food, he expects poison, so he is not helping matters. Baby ducklings imprint. Maybe not-so-baby demons do, too, and maybe they should not have handed theirs over to the grumpiest witch on the planet. If Samael eats someone, it's because Isaac never taught him the power of friendship.

Or maybe because Isaac eats people.

"Here, say ahh," Vivienne says. She holds up a spoon of tengu egg yolk. It isn't magical, but it contains tremendous amounts of magic like a battery, and maybe that will make it more appetizing to him.

Sam stares at the spoon, mouth only slightly parted.

Rory floats over his shoulder and opens his mouth wide. "Ahh," he dutifully says, and Vivienne rolls her eyes at him. "You should count your friggin' blessings. Not everyone has a cute girl trying to feed them."

"Are you cute?" Sam asks Vivienne.

Rory snorts a laugh. "Yeah, Viv, are you?"

Vivienne rolls her eyes again. Loudly.

"She is the cutest," Natalie says, completely straightfaced, and her deadpan proclamation makes Rory and Hammond howl with laughter. Even Isaac hides a smirk.

Vivienne shoves the spoon back into the egg and hides her flaming face with her sleeves. "Assholes. Of course I'm the cutest." Teasing from Rory is nothing new. Technically, compliments from Natalie are also nothing new, but they always get to her. Natalie is earnest in her simplicity. No one can stand up to her blank-faced praise. Vivienne is a weak, gay soul.

"Sure you are, sugar," Codi agrees, and it's the final nail in the coffin of gay pain. She coolly blows on her nails like she didn't just wreck the last shred of Vivienne's dignity. "Ignore her. Eat up, we got a big day ahead of us tomorrow, boys. Not entirely sure yet what your deal is, but I know you're doing the heavy lifting with me, and I don't abide laziness. Even spirits have to eat to keep their strength up, and that goes double for skinny little witches who think they're hot shit."

At least now Vivienne isn't the only one blushing, even if Isaac's rosy cheeks are of indignation.

Sam looks to him, guileless. "Are we lifting the dragons?"

"Someone must carry them out of the storm and to a butcher," Hammond points out. "There is only so much me and Vivienne can do ourselves, and it is going to be *pouring* rain tomorrow. But no, sweet pea, that is not as literal as it sounds. Mostly."

"Sweet pea?"

This one is Isaac's question, not Sam's.

Hammond and Rory look over with eyebrows raised and threatening amusement matching in their eyes. "Jealous?" Rory asks with too much bite in his tone. Vivienne flaps a hand at him, trying to call him off, but he ducks her and puts himself between Sam and Isaac. Isaac can't see him, but Sam tracks him like a cat with a fly.

"Ham likes sweet nothings. He'll respect your preference if you don't like them, but it comes with his lovely character," Natalie advises. She cuts through Hammond's curiosity like a hot knife through butter, but Rory is only slightly blunted in his approach. She can temporarily see him, thanks to a potion taken as a polite hostess, but it does not mean she is used to dealing with him.

Vivienne catches Sam's chin in her fingers, tugging him toward her, then cups his cheek. He blinks at her, long lashes and big green doe eyes, and she pats him once. "People talk shit because they don't understand how attached some people can get to each other. *Some* people talk shit because they think all attachments come with illegal magic and it's a fun sore spot to poke at."

"I'm not wrong, bitch," Rory retorts. "There is something between them."

"Is there something between us?" asks Sam.

"And I'm takin' *that* as my cue to leave," Codi announces. She points to Vivienne and Rory with a wet nail, though she can't see him, either. "Don't poke hornet nests. I'm gonna go say goodnight to my girls. When I get back, I expect y'all to be playin' nice again, because the last thing we need before tomorrow is drama."

"Is that what we're doing, Viv? Drama?" Rory asks. "I'm only asking what kind of friend you've made this time. That I'm expected to trust with Hammond's life tomorrow."

"We're trusting them, Rory. Isn't that enough?" Natalie asks.

Isaac scowls. "I don't like the ghost shit-talking us. I also don't like inquiries into our private affairs from nosy busybodies. We're doing you a huge favor, and I don't need to see or hear the ghost to banish him."

"You even *think* about banishing him and I will cut you open, sew your pet inside you, and watch as he eats his way out when—"

"Vivienne, *please*, we are trying to have dinner," Natalie cuts in with an aggrieved sigh.

"Evisceration isn't dinner talk?" Hammond asks. For the one who is in many ways the cause of this butting of heads, he is awfully calm as he continues to vacuum up roasted cikavac. "Come now, Natalie, what's a few threats between friends? Especially burgeoning friendships. Rory talks shit, we're all very curious about your interns, Viv reminds us why we love her, and Isaac eventually comes around and wants to hold your hand. Sam, he already seems okay. I'm sure he'll warm up to humanity yet."

"If this is how dinner talk between friends goes, I'm not certain I want to," Sam replies. He casts a suspicious look at Vivienne, so it is her turn to sigh. She won't apologize to Isaac, and he likely will never apologize for anything up to and beyond the day he dies. But she hadn't expected to intimidate the *demon* of all things.

· · · · ● · ● · · ·

Rain lashes like razors and the whipping wind makes it so there is no single direction to face to avoid the worst of it. Isaac is glad for his jacket, but feels bad whenever he catches sight of Sam's face. He looks like a child psyching himself up for a shot. Except the shot is an entire storm, and it isn't going away soon.

The rain isn't bitingly cold, which is its only mercy. It's late June, and no amount of dragons in the sky can drop the temperature that much.

Isaac clutches the wet broom with one hand, his other a fist in his pocket. Their little group is in a knot on a rooftop, sopping wet and already miserable, waiting like a taut bowstring for the first break in the cloud cover. The sky remains stubbornly grey. Thunder crashes around them—Samael jumps every time—and lightning forks overhead.

Vivienne looks paler than usual, already shivering from the rain. Isaac doesn't pity her, but he hopes she can do her job without undue discomfort. She, Codi, and Hammond have already downed their flight potions, and those last only an hour.

"Those dragons had better hurry the hell up," she grumbles, and Hammond nods emphatically.

Finally, after what felt like an eternity in the storm, the first sign appears: the clouds part, just a sliver, and a great, shining body wends downward.

It looks like a white Eastern dragon, long like a snake and slithering through the sky. Its whiskers trail after it like streamers. The mane and tail look green, or maybe blue; the storm makes colors at a distance difficult, and he doesn't *care* what color these (beautiful, incredible) things are so long as they can kill one and be done with it.

"Up," Natalie says and mounts her broom.

Isaac swings a leg over his, but Sam remains transfixed beside him. His hat has all but fallen off in the wind, so there is nothing to shield the look of raw wonder on his wet face.

Isaac grabs his arm, and when that doesn't sufficiently get his attention, he seizes him around the waist and tugs him against the broom. "Sam, we have to get going. Get on the broom and put your arms around me."

Vivienne climbs into the air like ice skating up a steep hill, Hammond on her heels, somehow with the grace of an actual figure skater. Sam watches him, but then the order *finally* gets him moving. Blinking at Isaac as if leaving a trance, Samael carefully winds his arms around his stomach. Isaac doesn't ask if he's ready before he kicks off of the roof, because he has a grip on him and Isaac knows how to keep a broom steady.

His mistake.

Sam's arms vise around his midsection, knocking the wind out of him with a wheeze. They nearly tumble over the edge of the roof, barely ten feet in the air, but then suddenly five stories up with wind buffeting them from every side. Isaac struggles to keep a hand on the broom while elbowing Sam off of him, unable to form a word, much less a coherent command, and they do a somersault he never wishes to repeat. Sam may break ribs soon.

A firm grip rights them. They hang over the alley, wind whipping around them, but stationary and upright and stable enough that Isaac jams an elbow into Sam's midsection. "Off," he hisses. He doesn't know how he is heard over the storm, but Sam releases him, and Isaac sucks in the biggest breath he ever has. The most grateful breath, too.

"Are you alright?" Natalie asks. Isaac turns to find her wide-eyed behind her goggles, one hand still on Sam's shoulder. She doesn't wait for an answer. She glances upward, where more dragons breach the cloud cover and her other staff are above, approaching that danger, then returns her attention to them. "I have to go," she tells them, with an abortive gesture with her rod. "I need to be higher than them. Be safe."

Codi hangs lower than Vivienne and Hammond, rifle at rest, but obviously watching the exchange. Natalie offers her a small wave as she shoots upward, past her, and Isaac ignores her. Natalie may have been concerned, but Codi's interest was professional at best. So long as he can breathe again, Isaac can work a broom.

"I've discovered I am afraid of heights," Samael informs him with a hysterical edge to his voice.

"Really," Isaac growls. "Oh my god. Thanks. Great. Don't grab me like that again, I'm *steering*, and I promise you we won't fall."

He idly wonders how promises function in conjunction with orders, while Sam's grasp relaxes from I Am Trying To Snap You In Half Like A Twig to something appropriate for a passenger on a fast motorcycle. Who needs a binder crushing his ribs when a demon would do?

Overhead, the mass of dragons in the sea of clouds cluster and writhe like fish in a pond with someone holding food out. They wind and burst and slither and swoop in and out of each other's way, splashing clouds about and catching lightning between them. Different types snap at each other, similar types bray at each other, young ones play together, and enormous, ancient dragons fly so sedately amongst the chaos they may very well be sleeping.

Natalie has reached the highest point of their group, not fifty feet beneath the migration. One arm raised with her rod extended, she perches, empty jars dangling from her broom, their very own personal lightning rod. They may have to worry about a dragon chomping on them, but at least they won't get electrocuted.

Vivienne and Hammond are next highest. Hammond has a crossbow, and Vivienne has... nothing, as far as Isaac can tell. She has a backpack—not her messenger bag from hell—and he knows there is at least a specialized net in there, but he doesn't know what weaponry she holds. Hammond's crossbow is warded enough to punch through a dragon's scales, and Isaac personally would have charmed them as well, but that isn't his job. He did not volunteer.

Codi had not joked about being the firepower of the group, despite her nonmagical status. She is familiar enough with flight potions to brace herself against the wind and use empty sky as a cushion while she aims her rifle.

Isaac waits for her to pick her shot. She's too far into the storm for him to accurately guess which she is aiming at, but his job is to help take out whatever she chooses. As far as he knows, all dragonhide is the same, but the insides vary depending on the type. (All he knows is he is *not* helping them mess with any fire sacs.)

Between the storm and the dragons churning the clouds, the sky is busy. Isaac circles halfway between Natalie and the rooftops below, monitoring their group, but the constant movement of the dragons is distracting. An unusually large, brilliant orange wyvern ducks close enough to Natalie that he almost fears for her safety, but she remains in place with her rod held high. The dragon winds once around her, then moves on.

"They're big," Sam says in his ear.

"Duh," Isaac replies. "They're *dragons*."

"It's not as if I've ever seen one before. Have you?"

"Not a live one." Only the strong and stupid hunt dragons. He has never needed ingredients for potions like Natalie, either. "Are you okay? With the flying now?" He takes care to maintain a steady, even speed, but at least with everything going on overhead, he doesn't have to tell Sam not to look down.

"I'm trying not to think about it. Do you think someone will get hurt?"

"We won't fall, I told you."

"From the dragons, or from the other hunters. Humans don't play nice together."

"The what?"

Sam tugs on his shirt on one side. Isaac whips around, heedless of prior safety concerns, and Sam's arms snap shut around him again. Isaac wheezes out a *grk* noise, but it doesn't break him in half or send them careening to their deaths. He bends over his broom, panting, and finds the silhouettes on the rooftop half a block down.

They would never be the only ones out here today, no matter how suicidal it can be to hunt dragons. They'd passed another knot of people on brooms two miles south of them, and there are spectators on roofs all around the city, he knows. You don't just *skip* a dragon migration, if you can see them. (Unless you're him. He slept through the last one and has no remorse.)

But these silhouettes are armed, and too close to the bubble they've claimed as theirs. *Poachers*, Isaac thinks with gritted teeth. "Let go," he gasps out, and Sam's arms loosen at once. "Don't do that again." It doesn't matter if Sam's afraid. Why hadn't he ordered him to do that to begin with? "Those two down there, they're going to steal our kill."

It makes sense. It's easier to kill humans than it is to kill a dragon. There are only two of them—that he can see—but one clearly has a rifle, and he thinks the other is holding a crossbow. There are probably brooms, probably wards, probably backup plans.

But Isaac doesn't have any qualms over killing humans in the name of self-interest, either, if they get in his way, and he'd rather nip this in the bud than have Natalie sigh over him after the fact. He is being proactive for once. She should thank him.

"Shouldn't we stay near the others? They said they needed our help," Sam says as soon as they float down. The other pair are four buildings down, one standing (crossbow) and the other kneeling (rifle) by the rooftop's low wall. The rifle is propped up on it, pointed upward. "Do we know them? Are they dangerous?"

"You're asking too many questions." The gun looks wrong. As he watches, the stranger goes from kneeling to laying, looking through the scope.

No, the gun isn't wrong; the angle is wrong. It's pointed upward, using the wall and its stand to keep up the sheer angle, but it's too far forward. Only the frontmost dragons are there, sparser and thinner and more in the cloud cover than the bulk of the herd. The better shot would be farther to the person's left. Unless they're waiting for the migration to pass overhead, but the person would lie on cold, wet concrete in a storm for several extra minutes.

Isaac is a building and a half away from them when the stranger calmly shoots Codi out of the sky.

The report of the rifle is loud enough to hear over the storm, and Sam's arms tense around him, shaking but not clamping down against the order. Isaac doesn't realize the shot had been true until he hears a scream from behind them.

He and Sam twist on the broom to see Codi falling out of the sky, Hammond diving after her.

Isaac gives up on stability and his demon's comfort and shoots forward toward the other hunters. The standing one with the crossbow notices them first, and they're clearly a professional for how fast they aim, but brooms are fast.

Sam leaps from the broom at the same time the stranger fires the crossbow.

Isaac jerks back from the force of Sam's jump, only half expecting it. Samael lands on their assailant, both of them flailing for a moment, before they go down with the demon atop. With the hood down and now closer, Isaac registers enough to see it's a young white man. Maybe just a teen. Who the fuck cares, he's shooting at them.

Isaac twists the broom to go after the rifle person, but pain lances through him.

Oh, he hadn't been shooting *at* them. He'd shot them.

Isaac stares at the end of the crossbow bolt sticking out of his jacket. He can see only two inches, which realistically, means the rest of it is in him and potentially *through* him. Emotionally, he's pissed his jacket has a hole in it.

He has a hole in him.

"*Isaac!*" Sam's shout is so full of anguish and terror that Isaac almost forgets about his clothing. He finds him crouched over the crossbow hunter, one fist bloody, eyes so wide he can see a clear ring of white around the edges.

The bolt had struck Isaac in the side, just below the ribs, so it missed the lungs and his heart. Unless it nicked his liver or spleen, he will be fine. Or if they charmed it, then he'd also be fucked.

It is hard to explain this in mere moments to a panicking demon who does not know much about human anatomy.

Isaac flips his broom up just as the rifle person comes into play.

He's played enough *Counter-Strike* to know that sniper rifles suck in close proximity and quick scope doesn't exist in real life, so the person's shot goes wide, but it is even louder up close. Isaac steers the broom with his thighs, somersaulting instead of barrel-rolling, and writes runes in the air—*light-magic-sharp-form*—and draws back his arm like pulling a bowstring.

Isaac shoots the hunter in the forehead with a magic arrow.

He lands on the edge of the roof a moment later.

The second poacher is also a man, but older. Tinted goggles and black hair and practical, borderline tactical clothing. He groans and sits up, rubbing his bleeding forehead, rifle by his feet.

Isaac would have gone for the gun, or at least used a *push* spell to toss it over the edge of the roof, but crossbow guy isn't down for the count, either.

Isaac *feels* it when the bolt goes up through the bottom of Sam's jaw into his head.

Sam rears back with a snarl, clutching at his face, and the poor kid below him screams when he discovers that he has just doused himself with corrosive black blood. Isaac holds his throat, feeling like his own jaw has been slashed open, pain pounding behind his eyes. But Sam is still moving; Sam is still alive. That means Isaac will be, too.

Isaac pulls his arm back with another magic arrow. The unspoken magic burns at him, draining energy he didn't have to waste, but now these people know he has a demon with him. He can't allow that to get out.

Before he can layer on anything to make the arrow more lethal, he hears the scrape of metal against concrete. He snaps over to the rifle guy and looses the bolt before he can lever his gun back up into shooting position.

But the asshole jerks to the side, just in time, and it surely had to have nicked his ear it was so close. Isaac bares his teeth in a silent snarl and swipes his hand with a *cut* spell. Concrete rends at the man's feet instead of at his throat.

Buffer shield, basic, didn't stop the arrow, Isaac thinks, a mile a minute, *not immune to physical damage but need to get the gun away from him, need to get Sam out of here—*

He aims a *push* spell at the rifle, and the force is enough to knock it out of the man's hands, though not send it flying very far. It clatters to the ground just behind him, near a shelving unit filled with jars that Isaac kicks himself for only *just* noticing.

The man returns his *push* spell with one of his own. Isaac tumbles over the edge of the roof, which would have been fine, if not for the fact that his broom didn't come with him.

Isaac finds himself in one *long* moment of freefall that isn't long or actual freefall. Terror not his own shoots through him, seizing his heart, and he swears he even sees himself fall over the edge from another view. His mouth still hurts. His side still hurts.

Isaac catches himself two floors down on the fire escape. His shoulders scream at the abrupt grab and his hands slide on the slick metal, but he halts his fall. His feet dangle. His side protests the strain, and he feels hot blood sticking and spreading from around the bolt still in him. He shouldn't have skipped arm day.

Isaac musters more adrenaline than muscle and pulls himself up the fire escape. He isn't dead, which means Sam hadn't been immediately slaughtered above him, so that's nice. That's better to think about. He's not dead yet. Such a great thought. He grits his teeth until his jaw aches.

He would have made it, he thinks, if the sky had not opened up above them.

So much magic floods the air, he chokes on it. The overcast sky shimmers with it as the clouds evaporate around a *tear*, jagged and huge and wrong and alien.

A hand descends out of the hole in their plane. Isaac's grip slackens as the foreign magic drowns them. Like in slow motion, he falls, face still tilted toward the being overhead.

It dwarfs any of the dragons—enormous, clawed, terrible, and it grabs a fistful of them like a child with so many wriggling worms. Dragons scream just as well as any prey animal. They scatter like rabbits in the face of something bigger and stronger and more dangerous.

The claws pull whole dragons through the rip that should not be, and just like that, it is gone again.

Isaac is still falling.

This is it, he thinks, only now able to shut his stinging eyes. *This is the end of the world.*

· · · · ● · ● · · · ·

Hammond catches Codi twenty yards up from the roof. It must jar her shoulder, arresting her fall with the catch of one hand—that's something the movies never show, the dislocations or sprains or torn muscles.

Hammond splays his legs out behind him to balance her weight. They hang in the air, and the feeling of *nothing* holding him up is a queasy one, but he knows to trust magic in life-or-death situations. He's had too many to do otherwise.

"*Codi*!" Vivienne screams from above, shrill against the lashing storm and rumbling dragons.

Codi rips the dart out of her arm with a snarl. "Fucking." It is a complete sentence, one he readily agrees with. He wishes she didn't immediately toss it, but before he can protest, she swings from his grip into something a little better. The impact, the shock, maybe whatever is now pumping through her system; he isn't certain what punched the flight potion out of priority in her body, but she can't support herself anymore.

"Hold on," Hammond says, and she tries, kicking uselessly beneath her. Her boots catch and slip again, like trying to climb gravel. She won't give him her other arm, despite all her weight in their connected grip. "Come back up here—stop *squirming*, please!"

"Fuckin'," she repeats, noticeably more slurred. The dart was tranquilizer or poison, neither of which are combated hanging from air nine stories up. She swings as she digs around a bulging pocket on her cargo pants.

Hammond twists to see where Vivienne is—she's better at talking sense into reckless hunters like Codi, despite not following her own suggestions—and finds her halfway between them and Natalie. Flight potions are not as fast or flexible as brooms, and the wind fights them, but she skates her way down toward them like she rides the gusts.

"Viv will know what to do," Hammond says, half a lie. Vivienne is not experienced with poisons or drugs. But neither is he.

Codi scoffs. Fair.

She pulls a tube out of her pocket and bites the cap off. It looks like a thick pen inside, and how she doesn't slide it out of the tube into the city abyss below, he will never know. But he doesn't recognize it for what it is until Codi shoves the autoinjector against her thigh.

"What the *shit* is that?!" Hammond screeches and tries to haul her up toward him. She cooperates like a lead balloon. "What did you just do to yourself—were you *expecting* to get shot at today?!"

"Atropine and adrenaline," Codi slurs. She smacks her lips a couple times. "If it was a tranq, I'll be good for another few. If it was somethin' to kill, well, I'm dead either way."

With great strength and greater patience, he somehow yanks her up enough that he can get an arm underneath her armpits. Her chest heaves, breath coming in worrying pants, but her expression remains placid. Hammond wishes he could face maybe-death with as much dignity, but maybe-death sucks.

"You're crazy, and Megan's going to kill you," he informs her. She nods, a jerk of a motion, too-fast like a bird. "Now what? Your potion's still shot, sunshine."

She points with one boot at the roof beneath them. "My rifle, if you'd please."

"We don't know who shot you—"

"*Someone* still has to bag a dragon. Technically, two, and I haven't failed a job in over a year. I'm not willin' to give that streak up just yet, Ham."

Hammond sends out a quick prayer. "Two. Codi, sweetheart, you've just been shot with an unknown substance, injected yourself with *more* drugs, and you want to shoot at dragons. Of which we are supposed to catch *one*."

"Took another job. Nat knows, and you know me. Friendly overachiever. Now drop me or escort me on down."

Of course Natalie would know. Of course he wouldn't. Hammond sighs through his teeth and starts dropping them back out of the stormy sky. He only has a crossbow, useless at any significant range, and he and Vivienne were *supposed* to be on body duty. He can catch a falling body (demonstrably).

He doesn't spot Isaac after a quick scan around them. Not that he was entirely certain what he would do to a dragon; Codi and her beloved sniper rifle are tangible, known quantities, and if she wants to go out shooting at dragons, far be it from him to stop her.

Codi waves Vivienne back as they descend. She is close enough that Hammond can see her confused expression, but she follows orders from pretty bossy ladies.

Codi's boots touch down on the roof, and the sky opens up over them.

His back is to it, at first, but he sees the bright light reflected in the puddles, and magic rolls over them like a wave. Hammond tumbles onto her, suddenly glad they hadn't been hundreds of feet in the air, but pushes himself back off the wounded woman a moment later. "Are you okay?" he asks on reflex.

Codi stares up past his shoulder, her brown eyes rimmed with blood like her usual eyeliner. Her gaze is glassy and her expression gradually turns to dread.

"*TuŋwÁŋ*," Hammond murmurs and puts a hand up to shield his eyes.

Even with the simple spell, his eyes *burn* when he sees the rip in the sky. Clouds churn and dragons flee with shrieks and roars. Light pours out like water. Hammond blinks through his stinging eyes, only to find a giant *hand* reaching through the tear.

He rips his gaze away and covers Codi's eyes with both his hands. "Don't!" he cries with more authority than he means. He doesn't know what it is. He doesn't know what it's there for.

He knows it's huge and terrifying, however, and he knows above all that it is *wrong*. It shouldn't be there, regardless of size or danger level or the magic it's pouring out. It does not belong here. It is an invader of the most horrifying kind, and he knows that so deep in his bones it shocks him he doesn't explode with the knowledge.

Dragons scream. He hears human screams beneath their reptilian noise. Codi's breath is rapid on his wrists and the magic presses over them like a weighted blanket, heavier and heavier. The storm seems an afterthought.

All at once, the magic is gone.

The atmosphere lightens, like fresh, over-saturated daylight after a storm, but they're still pelted with rain, whipped by wind, and lightning still forks overhead. But Hammond sucks in a deep, grateful breath like he'd been drowning.

Codi gropes blindly by her side for her rifle and draws it to her with a screech of metal. "We still alive?" she asks.

Hammond peeks over his shoulder before releasing her face. The migration is in an uproar, and clouds roil like boiling soup, but there is no sign of the claws or the rip or the foul *wrongness*.

"Looks like we're not walking on just yet," Hammond replies. When he lowers his hands, she still has blood on her lashes and her eyes are bloodshot, but no longer glassy, and no longer bleeding. He gets a smear on the back of his hand when he checks his own. *What causes that much optic damage so quickly?* He has no idea; so few things can cause eye damage to begin with.

"Great. Hold still darlin'," Codi says, and uses his damn shoulder as a brace for her rifle, because that's how his day is going. "Let's not break that streak now. I'll give ya a cut of the secondary pay for being such a hero today."

Hammond squeezes his eyes shut and covers the ear closest to the barrel. "Just shoot your damn dragon, woman."

• • • •• •• • • •

"*Isaac!*" Sam shouts as the witch falls. He doesn't even notice the chaos in the sky until he registers the bright reflection in the water at his feet.

He can't help but look up at it, to behold it, just as the other hunters do, yet it *hurts* to look directly at it. The claws drag half a dozen dragons back to where it came, and just like that, the hole in the sky vanishes. The clouds roll back over the spot with a fork of lightning.

"N-No," the one below him croaks. "Fuck this—no, that wasn't supposed to—!" He rolls onto his side, still halfway beneath Sam, and vomits. It ends up tinged red from the bloody burns on his face where Sam's own blood had splattered him.

Sam lets him scramble away in favor of spitting out the rest of the crossbow bolt and trying to find Isaac. He didn't come back up—his eyes land on the broom, sitting innocuously on the low concrete wall.

Sam almost trips over the edge with how fast he rushes over.

Two things happen at once, and only one of them can be attributed to the poor decision of turning his back on a hostile witch.

The blade rips through his stomach through his back, and a feathered form streaks up from the alley.

Sam coughs, stumbling forward, and stares down at the blade protruding from him. It's not metal. It's red, like blood, now sponging the black from his wound.

"Oh, shit," the older hunter says from directly behind him.

Sam elbows him, getting him to release the blade, but he thinks the man would have released it anyway when he finds that it is a large, feathered person now floating before them.

They smell of magic, *old* magic, and primal danger, but Sam doesn't care a whit about either of those things when he sees Isaac clutched in their talons.

"Oh, *shit*," the hunter says again. He scrambles backward, somehow not tripping. Sam doesn't bother with caring if the guy has a gun or another red sword or anything else and rushes toward the feathered person with his witch.

The feathered person throws said witch at him, and Sam catches him only in the sense that his arms are in contact with him and his fall is mostly broken—by his body. They both *whump* onto the wet concrete.

Isaac is breathing and bleeding from his wound and his nose, but his eyes are only slitted open, and that breathing is shallow. Sam thinks he's unconscious. He thinks that is what humans are when they are unresponsive but not asleep, and it doesn't stop him from shaking Isaac. His head lolls, and the black blood from his own injury drips onto him.

The stinging is enough to get a small moan from him.

"You're not dead," the man says behind him. "Oh, shit. You're a demon."

"And you are a repetitive human who chose the wrong fight," the feathered person snaps and lunges at him. Their talons clip Sam's head.

He crouches over Isaac, and it reminds him so much of the time when he tried settling that he wants to laugh. He does laugh, in fact, and doesn't recognize his own voice; he sounds wild and upset and not at all how people sound when they laugh.

"Sam," Isaac breathes. He raises a hand to his wet face, fingers twitching away from the corrosive blood, but staying enough to tilt his head to the side. Lucidity slowly comes back into his hazel eyes. Blood spikes in his lashes. Sam keeps staring into them, registering when more and more of Isaac comes back online. "We never even... fixed your hand. How are we going to...?"

"That man knows I am a demon, there is another spirit here, and I don't know if you're dying. If I'm dying, too," Sam replies. He leans into Isaac's palm. "What do we do?"

"It'll take more than that," Isaac grunts. He sits up, spits off to the side, and immediately tumbles onto Sam. He braces himself against his shoulder to get upright. "Sam, why is there a tengu here?"

"They were with *you*."

Isaac scrubs a hand over his face, then hisses when he smears black blood along his nose. "We're out of here. We need... a broom, and to find a place to..." He pitches over again after just a step, and Sam barely catches him in time to stop him from faceplanting. Isaac's face hovers inches from the concrete, hair mostly loose from its ponytail and hat, hanging like a wet sheet to conceal his expression—and state of consciousness—from Sam.

With shaking, jerky movements, Isaac catches his own weight on his arms. He tilts to the side, and Sam tries to catch him again, but the witch braces himself on one elbow in order to gesture with his free hand.

"*Strength-pull-gravity-force,*" he grinds out. Sam isn't even certain he's writing the runes, much less properly, but he is still a witch and even a semi-conscious bleeding witch has enough magic to speak spells into being.

The hunter hits the concrete with a sickening *crunch*.

But he, too, must be a witch; in a position mirroring Isaac's metaphorical last stand, he rolls onto one elbow, and throws an empty hand toward them. The man has more magic or more presence of mind not to telegraph his magic, but it sends them both skidding across the roof. Sam's nails dig into the concrete, but Isaac rolls into him.

The force ends as soon as the tengu person smashes their taloned foot into the hunter's head.

The man snarls, and the mystery of the red blade is solved when Sam sees him pull his own blood into a shining dagger the length of his forearm. He slashes the feathered thigh pinning him, and more blood splatters into the air, only to be pulled into the red knife, now mixing it into burnt orange. Literal blood magic.

Sam launches himself at him, but Isaac catches his ankle. He scrambles a moment, for balance and momentum, but Isaac's grip is as good as steel. "Stay," he orders, and Sam freezes, laying on the cold, wet concrete. "We need to go."

The hunter shoves off the gravity spell and tengu both and leaps to his feet. He slashes at the tengu again as they careen backward, favoring their uninjured leg, and feathers fly from one of their wings. As soon as they're off balance, protecting their wing, he drops the blade, splashing it into the puddles below, and dashes for his corner of the roof.

The hunter does not retrieve his rifle or any of the jars on the shelving unit. He grabs only his broom and vaults off the roof with it.

Isaac pulls another shimmering arrow into being, but the hunter doesn't make the mistake of flying high enough to become a target again. Smart, probably, which is going to make Isaac even unhappier. The witch's anger is enough to make Sam believe they're not dying, however, at least not in the immediate future.

"Actual blood magic. I thought humans grew out of that centuries ago," the tengu grumbles from their position being an irritated, feathered pile in a puddle.

Isaac turns his arrow on them.

Then promptly passes out.

Alarm shoots through Sam, but the stay order doesn't rescind. He wiggles against the ground, whining, slowly growing into full panic. "Isaac? Isaac!"

"I do not think he's dead," the tengu replies.

"Help me up! Please! I need to get us—out of this rain, at least, he's injured!" Sam begs. His nails dig deep furrows into the concrete, and several have broken.

He only barely knows what a tengu is. He doesn't know who either of those hunters had been. He doesn't know what happened to Codi or anyone else from their group, though he can vaguely feel that Vivienne is still around in some capacity. But he's hurt, *Isaac* is hurt, and for the moment, Sam is stuck staying put.

But whatever a tengu is, they clamber to their feet, limp over to them, and tug Samael to his feet.

"Thank you," Sam says, and barely resists throwing his arms around them in a hug. He knows others rarely enjoy hugging. He doesn't know why.

His movements feel sluggish, exhausted, but he gets Isaac in his arms. The witch seems so much smaller like this. He knows that Isaac is smaller than him and appears to be underfed, of course. But he has so much presence, he has never felt *small*.

"You caught him," Sam says, casting a sidelong glance at the feathered stranger, "why? I'm grateful, mind, but... I don't know you." There is a steel door leading to a stairwell at the far corner of the roof, and he staggers toward it.

"I don't think it very kind of a guest in this realm to watch someone splatter against the ground if a kind, flying passerby is there, hm?" the tengu replies. They limp after him. "It wouldn't be a matter if he turned out to be an enemy. Witches aren't hard to dispatch."

"That other man got away."

The tengu bristles, black and white feathers on end, sharp teeth bared. "Tengu are masters of the sky, and I am a *great* flier, but this storm is dragon-brought and I'm in no shape to chase a scared witch on a broom! Not over something like... a guess."

"A guess to what?"

They reach the door and Sam kicks at it. It dents, but that isn't the open door he needs. He shifts Isaac, but the witch groans in pain, and Sam freezes up again as if ordered.

The tengu reaches past him and kicks the steel door in like it was made of paper.

"I am trying to track down an egg thief," the tengu replies and nudges him inside. They shake the rain out of their feathers with a shudder, then examine the cut on their leg. It bleeds orange. "Well, another one. There have been several, but supposedly one of them had been by a human. I assume a witch, because they're the only strong-seeming humans. You're wearing cheap fabric. Rip some off for me?"

Sam stares at them, nonplussed.

They scoff and toss their head to the side, then wring out water from their black and white hair. "Bandages. Humans can still make cloth good for *something*. There is a lot of bleeding to be stopped here."

"I'm Sam. And this is Isaac." And he isn't human, but he is wearing human clothing, so that counts. He gently sets Isaac against the wall, then covers him with his jacket. Coldness will set in soon. Sam has no way of contacting Vivienne or Natalie short of standing on the roof and waving his arms.

But tengu, as they said, can fly, up among those with flight potions and brooms.

Sam peels off his shirt and tears it into strips. He passes a couple to the tengu, careful not to let his blood-covered hand touch their claws—then quickly colors and realizes that black blood is a giveaway to *anyone*. He turns to hide his bloodied face and snatches his hand back as though burned. The rain washed away a lot, but he is still bleeding, too, and on that note, how is he supposed to bandage Isaac when any touch could hurt him? He knows the basics, cover wound and apply pressure, but there is still a crossbow bolt sticking out of his summoner and *a lot* of blood they're both losing.

Sam kneels by Isaac and hovers over him with trembling hands.

Then he twists to give the tengu a pleading look. "Help us. *Please*. You already helped me on the roof and I—I don't know what I'm doing."

"Why should I help you?" they ask in return, not with malice, but genuine curiosity.

"Because—because I asked? Because it would be decent? You saved Isaac from falling, you helped me move again on the roof, you helped fight that man, so we have some common ground, right?"

"Do not mistake me deigning to help as generosity to be repeated," the tengu says with narrowed eyes. They tie a strip of Sam's shirt around their leg, feathers sticking up every which way around it.

"I helped you!" Sam blurts and points at the makeshift bandage. "You helped us, I helped you, your turn again! That's what friends do, and I heard that the enemy of your enemy is your friend, so. *Please*."

To his amazement, the tengu does not offer another retort, nor balk at the suggestion of helping further. Instead, they *blush*. Full-faced, up to the roots of their hair, their tawny complexion turns nearly as red as the human blood surrounding them. "Y-You—! You are *asking*, to. To be friends?!" they splutter. Their feathers puff up more and more, like an angry cat's fur.

"I helped you!" Sam stubbornly repeats. He tilts Isaac's head back and the witch's eyes flutter. He appears to be coming to again, but slowly, and his face is ashen. "Why not ask? I've achieved a lot by asking strange people for help, and I *need* help right now! So, please, tengu person. ...I don't know what else to do."

They cover their face in their clawed hands. "You are really just *asking* to be friends," the tengu mutters into their nails. "F-Fine! I respect displays of boldness, and you said you would continue to help me! I have more to do in this realm, and I will need a guide that isn't so timid as psychics and humans are."

Isaac's eyes crack open. His head lolls against Sam's careful touch. There is still blood on his cheek, and Sam realizes a moment too late that this is the palm with the old cut from their experimenting. Isaac hisses out a breath at the touch of the black blood.

But the red blood—*Isaac's* blood, his summoner's blood, eases the ache in the old wound. Isaac blinks, blearily, and stares at Sam's bare chest. "Your stomach..."

From carrying Isaac, holding his bleeding side against his own stab wound, there is half-dried scarlet smeared over his pale skin.

And no more stab wound.

"Isaac, I think I know how we heal me," Sam says in wonder.

"Great. I still have an arrow in me." Isaac takes a deep breath, but unlike before, he does not seem in a hurry to get back to the action. He has registered that he is out of the rain, out of the fight, and momentarily safe. With his eyes still closed and head tilted back against the wall, Isaac tells him, "We will use my injury to fix your face and any other injuries I can't see. Then, you will go back into the rain and wash all the blood off. *Then*, you will help me extract the bolt and stop me from passing out while I cauterize it."

"That will hurt. I thought there were human medics," the tengu comments, and Isaac jumps back to attention.

"Who are you? Sam—why are we—don't come any closer!" Isaac all but snarls, grabbing for Sam, reaching for magic he shouldn't be using. Sam grabs his wrists and keeps him from writing runes. "*Sam*, what are we doing here with—them?"

"Mirai," the tengu supplies with a sharp-toothed smile. "Sam has already introduced the two of you. I saved you! And he did me a favor in exchange. We are going to exchange help from now on, because we're... f-friends now."

Isaac stares. The defensive anger leaches out of him, fight-or-flight abating, but the shock remains. Sam looks between them a few times. He knows humans and spirits do not get along, but there is no need to restart a fight, and with Isaac so exhausted and hurt, he does not like their chances in round two. Sam just wants to go *home*.

"Sam," Isaac says slowly. He turns to Sam, but his eyes remain fixed on Mirai. "Are you friends with a tengu?"

Mirai flusters again, but somehow, they seem pleased.

"Yes?" Sam replies.

"You have no idea what a tengu friend is, do you."

"No?"

"Oh," Mirai realizes aloud. Isaac buries his face in his hands with a groan.

Natalie listens to Hayley practice guitar with a smile. She's played since high school, so even her picking idly at it is skillful, pleasant. It matches the mood of the sunlight streaming through the window and the cat curled up on her lap.

She think she's drifting off into a doze, until the vision clarifies itself around her.

Hayley, older here, ruby hair up in a ponytail, gestures to a white board filled with scribbled notes. Vivienne, on the other side of the white board, smacks her side too. Natalie recognizes the room from a rec center owned by Foxglove.

"Listen up!" Hayley declares with a fierce expression. "We don't know when this shit could be coming, so we have to iron out all the kinks now, yeah? And we need to actually share information amongst ourselves! Can we handle that much?"

"There's a first time for everything," Vivienne adds, "so let's start now. Here's what we know—"

Natalie comes back to herself and tries to remember what all she had seen on that white board. She rolls off the couch, despite Sunshine's meowed complaint, and flails over the coffee table until she can find her journal.

Sphinx heart, First egg, unicorn blood, powdered dragon teeth, pixie dust—the part she remembers clearest had looked like a list of ingredients. But higher spirit and lower spirit had been there, too.

Spirits as spell ingredients? Natalie wonders worriedly, placid mood gone.

CHAPTER 15

In Which There's A Lot To Clean Up

Mark sips at his tea and pretends there aren't a bunch of knives, cymbals, nails, and rusty spurs dancing between his temples. Bryn huddles beneath a quilt opposite him. She trembles hard enough to make the fabric quake, and her breath comes out in little animal, hitching whines.

Good news: he has apparently appealed enough to Bryn as a potential benefactor that she has *some* sort of protective instinct toward him. It had taken almost a year before Benji had given him the same courtesy, and that'd been when he had been an impressionable, eager to please puppy.

Bad news: *something* gave him a fucking seizure and scared the wits out of Bryn.

Mark takes another sip. *Breathe*, he reminds himself. Deep, even breaths. It had not been his first seizure, and he doubts it will be his last. While still scary, at least they are a known concept to him. But this is the first time he had one without an obvious trigger to it.

Well, clearly there *had* been a trigger, something Bryn had picked up on. Animal instinct, perhaps, or maybe another annoying case of her knowing more than she let on. Most likely, a mixture of both.

The water on the floor is cold. He thinks the old bathwater in the tub is also cold, and there is no steam to warm the bathroom. She may be shivering instead of shaking soon.

What is known: something spooked Bryn, Bryn doesn't know how to handle someone having a seizure (moving them is *not* advised), that same something knocked him on his ass so it had to have a psychic component, *and* he is wearing soggy socks. And he's developing a migraine. What a terrible fucking day.

Mark sips. "What do you know? And please, speak quietly."

Bryn trembles beneath the quilt, an old, cozy thing made by Hayley's mother years ago. He thinks it had been in his hall closet; she must have grabbed it when he crawled to the kitchen for tea. His memory is fuzzy, the mental equivalent of ringing ears.

Her face isn't visible, just her chin and the wet, hanging ropes of her thick hair. He doesn't think she is going to respond when she surprises him. "That was not mine."

It is more of an admittance than she's made yet. Mark checks off a few mental boxes. "Multiple cases of... something large and terrible. Peachy. You know this one?"

"No," she croaks. Maybe that is where her fear stems from. "It should not have happened. They can't have enough yet."

"Enough what?" (First eggs, he's guessing.)

"Magic. Ingredients. *Knowledge.*" She peers out from the veil of the quilt, crimson eyes huge and bright. "It had taken me twenty-eight years to leave and make it to the tengu to take an egg."

Mark roughly swallows tea in order not to choke. She doesn't look her age—whatever ridiculous number that may be, spirits age weirdly, and who knows what the hell she *is*—but that is a long con if he's ever heard one. "Leave? From where? The tengu have doors in more than one goblin market."

Bryn's expression hardens, shutters.

"Please, come on now. I just had a seizure from *something* and you were kind enough to incorrectly drag me from the living room into my bathroom. I appreciate your intent, I really do, but I'd appreciate some goddamned answers more. *Where* did you come from? *Who* are you serving? And what the hell just tried to take me out?"

"I fled. I fled my home, to *Norðreyjar*. I tried to find Hel, or *Fólkvangr*, but I was so terrified of being tricked by the wild folk there that I fell into something... worse."

She only hides her face then, though her tremors have subsided. Mark hastily categorizes the Nordic terms, tries to place them, but he also can't help but wonder if sharing is some burden lessened.

"There are old gods, older than me or fae or any realm, but they want *this* realm. My master has called it a return. It is not the only one, but I do not know who else is so foolish as to try to break realm borders to loose such horrors."

Mark swallows down another choking feeling. "Old gods. Right." There are certainly beings, spirits or monsters or otherwise, that have been construed as deities by others. But *gods*? Actual gods? Mark is a realist, and probably an atheist.

But *something* fried his brain. *Something* scared a strong shapeshifter enough to steal from youkai powerful enough to carve out their own realm.

And she is confessing to aiding one. He meant to help her—he wants to—but he likes to know more before fighting powerful beings. For the first time, Mark does not want to step on someone's toes. He fears more information.

· · · ● ● ● ● · · ·

Megan pulls on a fresh pair of gloves after slathering ointment on Vivienne and Natalie's burns. Codi remains unconscious. They only know half of what's in her—at least she had the sense to relay to Hammond what *atrocious cocktail* she'd injected herself with—but it doesn't help with combating whatever had been in the dart. They've stabilized her heart rate and breathing, and don't know what else to do. At least burns are straightforward.

They aren't the traditional vein-like burns from actual lightning, but they aren't minor either. Natalie had hardly reacted at the initial application; at least Vivienne had flinched away, alert, normal.

Seizure, Megan thinks, watching the psychic out of the corner of her eye. Natalie has had them before, and Megan had helped with two directly, and half a dozen more afterward. No medication or potion has ever helped, but they have only been in response to excessive mental stimuli. *Is this what mom was freaking out about?*

"No, there's only *one*, and it's a miracle we got *one*. What part of hazardous circumstances don't you understand—*yes*, I know it was the fucking dragon migration!" Hammond all but snarls into the phone. Rare are the times he raises his voice or loses his temper. Megan can see why this is a special circumstance. "Graham—no, Codi took it down, but it's *Natalie's*, and we had a deal!"

"Downed a dragon in one shot while drugged out of her mind," Vivienne mutters with a queasy laugh. "Only you, Codi."

"That gun of hers could take out anything she points it at," Megan sniffs. They don't much approve of guns, legal, or appropriate for hunting monsters, or otherwise. They've dug too many bullets out of coven members to like them much.

"Graham, *please*, who knows if it already got poached. I'm telling you, there is a blue dragon on the roof of some building on Rosewood, it's ours, but we *really* can't deliver it ourselves right now! There were casualties, alright? And I know you and Natalie have a deal, so can't you *please* pick it up—no, she's fine, she just can't come to the phone right now," Hammond says with a sidelong glance at Natalie. She doesn't appear to notice.

Megan waves their fingers in front of Natalie's eyes. She doesn't track it until the third pass. "Nat, come back now. It sounds like Ham needs help with your butcher." *And you're scaring me,* they don't add. Scaring doesn't cover it. Terrify, perhaps. Grogginess and confusion are expected after a seizure, but it had happened almost an hour ago. Seizure, fall off broom, death-defying midair catch, jarred lightning smash, burns, call medic, wait at potion shop until medic could race across the city in a storm. "Vivi, *what* was it? What happened, exactly?"

"Fuck if I know," she murmurs, dark eyes also fixed on their resident precog. "But I think she might." She sighs, then heaves herself off the counter. She's pulling on her soaked jacket before Megan can catch her arm. "C'mon, Meggy, let me go, we still have men on the frontlines or whatever. We're missing our two interns, and they're not the type that ought to be left alone, *and* I think they might've gotten a good look at who Codi's latest friend had been. I'm going out looking."

"Looking for a witch on a broom in a raging storm?" Megan asks.

"Best case, he's sitting on the dragon after he saw it go down," Hammond says, phone away from his mouth. But then he winces, and continues, "No, we have *no* guarantee of our guys on the dragon! That's why I'm asking *you.* Consider it a personal favor—"

"Let me talk to Graham," Natalie says.

Megan could faint with relief. Natalie swipes damp bangs out of her eyes, but does not move from her spot on the counter. She sways where she remains. Hammond looks just as relieved as he hands the phone over to their de facto boss.

"Hello, Graham. Thank you for speaking with Hammond while I regained my bearings. Yes, I contracted you only as the butcher, but I know you can fetch the dragon, and that is what I'm asking you to do now."

Natalie could talk the skin off a snake, no matter her lack of charm or general distaste for wielding her somewhat political power. The dragon will be taken care of, one way or another, though Megan doesn't like to think of the bloody details. The good news is that they will all be paid. And they're all in one piece.

Though one is still unconscious and two are missing.

The demon, they think, heart thudding in their chest. They check over Codi again to distract themselves. If Isaac were going to do anything, he would have already; Natalie has given him quite the range, despite vowing to monitor them both. *Codi, Codi, we need to focus on her! Think—what else can we do against an unknown sedative?* If it were swallowed, charcoal and a pumped stomach could have headed off the worst. But an unknown drug injected in an unknown amount?

Codi's breathing remains even and terribly slow. Her braids drip onto the floor, her face is slack with not-sleep, and the only other injury she sustained is evidenced by the crusted blood sticking to her lashes.

When Vivienne tries to slip past, Megan grabs her arm again. "Hold it. What, exactly, did you say you saw?"

"Fuck if I know," she repeats. Megan tugs her closer to examine her eyes, but there's no dried blood and no ruptured vessels. "When something breaks reality, I know better than to stare. Also, Nat was about to fall off her broom, so I was getting to her."

Natalie signs '*thank you*' from her perch on the counter.

"It was a hand," Hammond says, as before. "Huge hand, colored like... Not colored, but colorful like an oil slick. I don't know what kind of thing can cause eye damage that quickly, but it was big, so maybe that had an impact. We were also reasonably close, considering its scale."

"We were, like, a hundred yards away. That's not close."

Hammond rolls his eyes. He unties his ruined braid, and flatly replies, "Darling, learn how to tell distance already. It was at least two hundred, and I'm talking about the *scale* of it. If the hand was that big, the entire thing could probably span that distance."

"Maybe it had yaoi hands."

Megan smothers a laugh despite themselves. Vivienne looks pleased with herself, which she shouldn't, since that mental image ought to be illegal.

Natalie signs '*no*', as much as scolding as anything else.

The momentary levity is broken by the front door banging open with a gentle tinkle and a howl of wind. Megan and Hammond both jump at the sound.

Isaac limps in, completely drenched, dragging a stick behind him. Sam slinks in after him, similarly sodden, looking twice as sorry for himself.

"Oh thank god," Hammond groans. "You're both still alive—and covered in blood, holy shit."

Megan's eyes widen at the realization, too, but it's all *red*. Sam appears to be missing his shirt underneath his jacket, but even that is waterlogged and reddish in places. At least they were smart enough to wipe off any obvious evidence before traipsing back to the potion shop.

It is not a broom that Isaac had been dragging. He dumps a rifle onto the table beside Codi. "Dragon tranquilizer of some sort," he tonelessly informs them. His complexion, normally darker, is ashen, and Sam is white as a sheet.

"*Dragon tranquilizer*?!" Megan shrieks. Screw their hatred of guns—they fumble with the rifle until they can check the chamber and find a dart still in it. It doesn't look like what they've seen used in animal documentaries, but it is close enough. "*Strength*," they murmur, drawing on their jeans, and snap the dart in half to look at the liquid inside. Five CCs about, tinged bluish, which means it is most likely pesanta blood as the driving force. They can work with that.

They bustle around the potion shop, knowing it as well as any coven house they've worked in, and definitely better than their dorm room. The Crow's Cup has been as much a home as the main Foxglove house to them, and never has Megan been so thankful for that familiarity before.

"So, no broom?" Vivienne asks, somehow the calmest of the group.

"Broke."

"Long way to walk."

"Try walking it freezing and bleeding," Isaac snaps back, teeth bared.

Megan couldn't care less how they got from point A to point B, so long as they were currently still alive. "How are you hurt?" they ask as they mix dried thyme and cinquefoil.

"It's taken care of."

While he is covered in blood—and the crimson covering Sam had to have come from somewhere—Isaac is speaking, aware, and upright, so Megan lets the matter lie. For the ten minutes it'll take to push Codi into a true sleep and out of the woods, anyway.

They lift her head to drip the mixture into her mouth. Some dribbles out, and she almost coughs once, but with a bit of magic against her throat, Megan gets it down.

Natalie hangs up the phone at last. Isaac flinches like she'd cocked a gun. "The dragon is taken care of, and I will speak to Codi about figuring out a way to cover for her second job when she wakes. Thank you, Megan, for your help to put us back together."

"It's what I'm here for!" they chirp. Codi's breathing finally deepens, and they lower her head back to their jacket-pillow.

"Isaac, thank you for whatever intervention you did, apparently at cost to your own health—"

"After," Megan interrupts.

The room freezes; few interrupt Natalie, least of all Megan, and they will gladly use that surprise to their advantage. They whirl on Isaac before he and Natalie can get into it, and he is appropriately (and unfortunately) the first to react.

"Already taken care of," Isaac says, hands up, backing away as they advance. Sam looks between the two in confusion. "The wound's been closed and I'm just tired. I wasn't shot with any drugs, neither was Sam, and I can let Natalie know who we fought, and then I'd like to *sleep*. I don't need babied."

"You're *covered* in blood," Megan retorts.

He is closer to the hallway than she is, however. "Scratch that. I'm going to sleep first." He all but runs out of the room, and Megan draws up short. He doesn't go to the stairs, so he isn't commandeering Natalie's bedroom, which is nice and possibly the most polite they've seen him.

"He has a bed nest thing set up in the backroom," Vivienne wryly explains. "Sam, how are *you* feeling?"

Megan initially balks at the prospect of working with a demon, but the Hippocratic oath doesn't care about corrosive blood or a diet of humans. They hope their reluctance isn't obvious.

Sam looks toward the back, then to Vivienne, frowning and confused. "I'm tired, too, but not sleepy tired. I think Isaac should get checked out. The bird person helped burn the wound closed—cauterized?—but that looked painful, too. And there were, er, other minor burns..." He looks guiltily at his feet.

"*Cauterized*?" Megan wheezes.

"Bird person?" Vivienne squeaks.

"But I feel better!" Sam hastily adds. He holds up two unblemished hands as if that is all the proof he needs. "We figured out how to close my wounds!"

"Do tell," Hammond says.

"Shove it, Ham. Sam, not a word right now—"

"Viv, *rude*, don't I deserve to know after all this shit today—"

Megan pushes past the demon and tunes out Vivienne and Hammond's bickering. The backroom is closed, locked, but familiarity with the lock itself is half as good as the magic they use to unlock it.

Isaac's nest largely seems to be just that. There is a comforter pushed into the corner, several pillows, a surge protector with a pair of chargers plugged in, plus one irate witch already curled into all of this.

"Do you *live* here?" Megan asks in sudden worry. They've seen this angrily self-sufficient behavior in runaways in the coven, and it may answer some questions as to why Natalie is going so far to offer a haven.

Isaac's eyes narrow further, furious slits they are impervious to. "Sam helps more in the shop than I can, and your boss has never complained. I told you, I don't *need* any help. I'm fine."

"No, I don't think you are," Sam says, over Megan's shoulder. They jump and squeak, but he blinks down at them with all the guile of a puppy. "You're a healer, right? You offered to help, and you know what I am. His blood fixed me, but we used a lot, and he's exhausted."

"Samael, shut *up*," Isaac snaps. Sam's jaw shuts with an audible *click*. "I'd be more worried about the woman shot with dragon tranq, personally, but that's just me."

"Codi will be alright after she sleeps it off. You—you've lost blood, you look terrible, you have visible wounds, and your—uh, friend here, he said you *cauterized* the wound yourself. What wound?"

Sam nods, mute. Isaac's glare could peel paint, but Megan is the only child of a coven leader. They've seen worse. They close the distance in the small room in two big steps, falling to their knees, watching his reactions as he backs up. He doesn't move one arm as far up as the other; likely injury to that shoulder or side. Limping earlier, too, same side.

"Don't make me bind you," Megan threatens and wrestles for the hem of his shirt. He kicks well enough, shoving one knee out from under them, but Megan growls right back at him and sits on that leg. He is active, but it's likely another bout of adrenaline, and they categorize each of his defenses like they have a microscope. Their knee presses into his hip; Isaac flinches and bites back a groan. He struggles to uncurl one set of fingers to grab their hair in a petty attempt to pull them back.

"Get *off* of me!"

"Let me look at you!"

"You're crazy and I don't need your help, I'm *fine*!"

That he hasn't used magic yet to push them off is also telling. Megan ends up pinning Isaac to the corner, though they may be missing a chunk of hair for their troubles. They're certain they see strands of strawberry blonde in his grip.

But when they finally wrest his shirt up, they freeze.

The burn is severe, angry red with white and deeper red spots. It could be third degree in places. It was certainly not done with heated metal. The area is perhaps the size of a spread hand, so the original would not have been large, but this damage seems almost *worse*.

And just above his ribs, Megan sees the blood-drenched hem of a binder.

"I'm sorry," they blurt, though they're still holding his shirt against his chin and are sitting on his thighs. "I didn't realize—"

"So you'd manhandle anyone else, aggravate injuries, and piss people off?" Isaac snarls.

Megan presses one open palm against the top edge of his burn, and the other against his face. They push soothing, healing magic into both, one to hopefully calm him, and the other to *try* to begin undoing the damage he did to himself.

"You knew Natalie would've called me here," Megan replies, quietly. The tension eases out of Isaac's shoulders, gradually, as their magic combats his raised heartbeat. "You knew she'd have a healer on standby. So... what, you didn't trust me? You didn't want to get outed? I'm sorry, but I won't tell anyone. That's not my place."

"It wasn't your place to find out," he half-heartedly snarks back. Isaac pushes at the hand covering his eyes, and they move, so they can carefully cup his side.

"You're right. But this is not something you can just *do* to yourself! Sam was worried sick, and you know Natalie would have..."

"She doesn't worry about me. Not like that."

"Vivi would."

"They just want to know what happened," Isaac replies. His words are slurring, but his hazel eyes remain clear. They're not trying to put him to sleep, only shove as much numbing magic into his burn as they can manage. The drain throbs at the back of their head.

"So, what happened?"

Isaac manages a weary glare.

"If you tell me, I'll tell Natalie and Vivi and Ham, and you can sleep in here. I'll only tell them about how you got hurt." Megan glances back over their shoulder, to where Sam is obediently and silently sitting cross-legged in the other corner of the room. "How you both got hurt. It was a fight, right? Against whoever shot Codi?"

"Two men, probably professional hunters, both were witches. One was younger, maybe your age. He had a crossbow. Dark hair, undercut, kind of skinny, pale as Sam."

"You can't be much older than me," they scoff.

Isaac doesn't argue that part. "The man with the rifle was probably mid-thirties. Black hair, goggles, well-dressed. He used blood magic."

Megan freezes again. There are very few witches who practice blood magic, and only one fits the vague description Isaac had just given. Megan's hands suddenly feel clammy, and it is not from magic usage. They remember fixing another bullet hole he had put in a friend.

"Ugh, thought so," Isaac sighs. He allows his head to loll against the wall. "Sam, you can speak again. Did your guy have any distinguishing features? I don't know about inter-coven drama, I don't *want* to, but all the research I've done makes it seem like that guy works alone."

"I don't know who either of them were. The witch I was fighting had hair that was longer on top, shorter on the back. I think he had an eyebrow piercing? He vomited on me and fled after the hand appeared," Sam dutifully supplies. Megan hardly hears him. Their hands shake, vision tunneling, and with great regret, they pull away from Isaac.

"That's all I can do today."

"It already feels better. Thanks," Isaac replies, deadpan. "Get off and leave me alone."

"Tomorrow, I can—"

"You've done *enough*," he snaps.

When he tugs his shirt back down to cover the wound, his skin doesn't look so raw, and his movements are easier. Megan wipes their sweaty brow and gives him a smile. "It's what I'm here for. Let me help you again."

"Go back and report to your boss. That's how you can help."

"Yeah, I-I will." Megan wipes their hands on their jeans and stands. Their vision is fuzzy, but they aren't dizzy. They pretend it's comfort when they put a hand on Sam's shoulder. "Sam, how are you feeling? I'm not sure... I mean, I've never exactly *treated* someone like you."

"My wounds have all closed and you look tired."

"Sam will stay here and make sure I don't die after your *stellar* care," Isaac snipes. He burritos himself in the comforter, then, reluctantly, raises a corner for the demon. Sam's expression lights up and he zips into the opening. "See? Guard demon."

Samael looks more like a child tucked in after a bedtime story than a fearsome guard demon. "Cozy," Megan allows, smiling again. They ease the door close behind themselves, though Isaac will sleep through the apocalypse with that much healing magic in his system.

In the main room, Natalie has moved from the counter to a proper chair, and everyone has mugs of tea. Mint wafts strongly in the air. Another mug on the table waits for them.

"How is he?" Vivienne asks.

Megan checks Codi's breathing and heart rate again. She seems to be improving, so Megan heaves a sigh of relief and retrieves their tea. "Worse than he said, of course, but not life-threatening. Sam seems... fine, I think. They're going to rest in the backroom for a while."

"Did either say anything about the 'bird person'?"

"No? What bird person?"

Vivienne grumbles into her mug, "Nevermind."

"Did he explain what happened to them?" Natalie asks.

"Yeah, it's..." Megan's not sure how to share this. "Two other hunters, one with that rifle and another with a crossbow, both male and seemed professional, but..."

"We suspected it was other hunters."

"But why shoot *Codi*? It's one thing to snipe a kill, but we hadn't gotten anything done at that point. It's another thing entirely to piss *her* off."

"To prevent her from doing her job?"

"Why does anyone care about our dragon status? Why can't we be temporarily rich?"

Megan sips at the tea, letting Vivienne and Hammond deduce/bicker. They hadn't thought about motive; they rarely do. People get hurt, and it's their job to fix that. Nothing more. "Isaac said they were both witches. He said... one used blood magic."

The room goes dead silent. Megan glances at Vivienne, then watches Natalie for her reaction.

And she doesn't seem surprised.

"So it was Thomas," she says, then sips at her tea. There is only one male witch hunter who uses blood magic, and he just so happens to be the strongest witch in generations, and the Eyebright golden child. "I suppose I will have to ask him a few questions if he has the gall to return for his usual potion, then."

· · · · ● · ● · · ·

Thomas pulls off his goggles and tosses them onto the hotel bed. They hardly bounce. He's sopping wet and shivering, his eyes sting something fierce, his ears are still ringing too, and the only good thing is that Avery is already there, dabbing ointment onto his face.

Thomas balks when Avery's familiar flaps into his face with a caw. "*Gah*, why is she inside again?" he asks, more harshly than he means, just to cover his jump.

"It's fucking storming out and there may be people following us," Avery replies. He leans closer to the stained mirror and cranes his neck.

"People or tengu?" Thomas mutters. He strips off his coat and soaked sweater and shakes out his hair.

"Tengu?"

"Nevermind. Later." He passes him, aiming to claim a hot shower first, but pauses. Thomas tilts Avery's chin back to inspect his cheek. The burns appear mild. Actual demon, who knew? How had none of the covens cottoned on to *that*? "Glad you're okay, kid. Sorry about the surprise."

Avery scowls at him and jerks his chin away. "*Which* surprise? The boss thing trying to fuck us over, or the fucking *demon* trying to fuck us over?"

"There are more words in the English language than 'fuck'."

"Thanks, mom. When you find another one that covers the emotion of 'I shot someone in the face and they kept attacking me and dripped *acid blood* on me because they're a fucking demon', let me know, I'll be *so* hype."

Avery Gunvaldsen may be one of the most talented and ambitious young witches Thomas has ever met. He is also, unfortunately, nineteen years old in every sense. He had only taken him on with this because of his insatiable need to be better, stronger, learn more, get more; Thomas literally needs him in that regard. He had certainly not chosen him for his oh so charming personality. Or the large crow familiar that seems keen on being inside a tiny hotel room as much as possible.

"I'm showering first, we can debrief after," Thomas tells him.

"About which surprise?"

"Our employer. I'm in the dark as much as you are on the other front."

He retreats into the bathroom and turns the shower on as hot as it'll go. While it steams the mirror, he grabs the nearly empty bottle of saline solution and rinses out his eyes. He'd barely caught a glimpse, and he'd had charmed goggles to boot, but he's not risking damage or another infection. This is the biggest bottle Amazon sold, and it's his third one. This isn't his first rodeo.

First one the thing had tried to crash, however.

Thomas pushes all thoughts from his mind as soon as he steps into the scalding water. He's a talented man in many regards, but he especially prides himself on his compartmental-ization. He probably couldn't keep going without it. As it stands, he only has to operate on muscle memory: rinse off blood, scrub until raw, lather, shampoo, done. The tiny bathroom feels like a sauna even after the quick shower, and what he wouldn't give to spend another hour under the hot spray.

Avery is starfished on the bed, dozing, when he reappears. He slits open an eye to regard him. "Do you think," he asks, quiet and uncharacteristically docile, "that that *was* the boss thing trying to fuck us over? Like, genuinely? Is this safe anymore?"

It was never safe, Thomas wants to say, but knows better. Summoning a Great Old One isn't a safe job. Avery knows that. But there is a difference between holding a winning poker hand and the other player trying to play fifty-two pickup.

Thomas knows he's being used; that's why he's using it just as much. But he *needs* this to play by the rules, inasmuch as gods do. There'd always been a risk of... worse.

"I'll ask, if I can," he says instead of anything else. He sits on the edge of the bed, toweling off his hair, and avoids looking at the teenager or the bird. He's not a sentimental man, not anymore, but hey, even he has morals, and using kids in an apocalyptic plot pricks at them. "But if nothing else, this proves it *needs* us. We just need to run with that."

"Why'd it care about someone else getting a dragon? It got plenty of dragons."

"Politics. Even deities aren't immune to interpersonal drama."

Avery scoffs, and Kasa lets out a little caw, like a laugh.

"Even that much dragonskin can't thin the borders between realms for something to brute strength it. That's nice to know, huh?" Thomas asks, nudging Avery's ankle. He scoffs again. "Anything else you want me to ask the big boss before you get going?"

"When are you gonna let me talk to it?"

"When you're older." Thomas will *never* let Avery talk to it if he has any say in the matter. And since he is literally the only person in the entire human realm to have spoken to a god and lived in the last few centuries, he thinks what he says goes. "It's not pleasant, I told you. And your brain is still developing until you're twenty-five. Who knows what that'd scramble."

"Oh my *god*. You're raising a fucking evil god thing, and you are the fucking biggest mother hen on the face of the *planet*. You're horrible."

"And you know all of one word. Go on, get out of here. If anyone was tailing us, they would've busted down the door by now." And they'd have to clean up another body. At least Avery isn't squeamish, but a teenager being so cavalier about killing doesn't make for the best partner in crime. (Well, it does, but not to Thomas' conscience.)

"Call me if we're fired or anything. I can probably make it to the next state before it finds a way to rat us out."

"I don't think an ancient deity has the presence of mind to tattle on us to witch covens, but I will call you in that case," Thomas flatly replies.

Avery pulls on his coat, beanie pulled low over his dark hair, scowl in place to prevent anyone from stopping him on his way home. Kasa perches on his shoulder until he's out the door. The storm is still going strong, would be for the rest of the day and into tomorrow, but with the bulk of the migration past the city, it isn't as windy. Sheeting rain is easier to deal with when it's coming from above, not horizontally.

Thomas continues toweling off his hair until he feels the slight tug of Avery passing the furthest perimeter wards.

Then, he tosses the towel, takes a deep breath, and gets to work.

Visions come to her like locusts in a plague. She lets Deirdre know only two months after it starts. Despite having formally left the coven, Natalie still relies on them; they had been her family. They still are.

Visions are valuable. Natalie sells them when they're useful, but the lines between useful and uselessly ominous are blurring. Usually she can pick out the rotten apples, but she's noticing growing trends in what she can see. Her friends are beginning to resemble who she sees in her visions. She wonders how many years they have left until... whatever this is.

Natalie turns the corner into the kitchen of the main coven house, brushing elbows with the guests from other covens, and instead comes out on the rooftop of a building.

She herself is not in this vision, it seems. Natalie is relieved. The ones where she is present feel unnatural.

Icy wind whips at Codi Clarkson's braided hair. Her scarf stands out behind her like a flag, and she looks down the scope of her rifle, finger on the guard. The building is tall enough to dwarf the surrounding buildings, though not the tallest in the area. It's a good vantage point.

Codi lies on the cold concrete and rests her sniper rifle on the edge of the building for stability. Even with that pixie spell of hers, Codi cannot work miracles, and it's clear that she would need a miracle to hit anything in this weather.

A hideously wrong thing made of radiance and many branching, antler-like limbs boils up over the edge of the building. Codi scrambles back, mouth open, and the monster rears up like a snake aiming to strike.

Codi shoots it anyway. It writhes and curls away from her, bullet wound sizzling in the frigid air, and Codi makes a mad dash for the edge of the building. She throws herself off instead of facing whatever horror pursues her.

Natalie collides with a kitchen counter.

A strong hand catches her arm before she can bump into anything else, and Natalie blinks a few times to reorient herself. Many witches mill around, guests from other covens here for the meeting, but few seem to have noticed her daze.

Natalie looks up at the man who caught her, unused to seeing men in Foxglove spaces, and she realizes she recognizes his tall, imposing figure. "Are you alright?" Thomas Novak asks in a voice that has become as familiar to her as her own.

Natalie nods. She doesn't know what else to do.

CHAPTER 16

IN WHICH BRYNJA GIVES IN TO HOPE

Vivienne is due one hell of a rest day, but Emil had left her three voicemails and more texts than she cared to count, so here she is, making a house call. Lucky them.

She shines her penlight into each of Christine's eyes. Of course, her pupils don't contract, but she winces away. (Supernatural Hunter Tip #9: Most ghostly reactions come from mental muscle memory, not current need.) "Remind me, how long have you been dead?"

"Um, a few months...?"

"Is that like two months, or nine? Hold on—I'm going to put my ear to your chest, nothing kinky, promise." Despite the warning and disclaimer, Christine freezes when Vivienne presses against her chest. No heartbeat. Also of course. "Breathe in." Not that she needs to. "And out." Her chest expands beneath Vivienne's temple, and there is no sound of lungs from within.

"Seven months," Christine mumbles, eyes askance in Emil's direction. It's late June now, so that puts her in December as a date of death. "Um... I don't really breathe, you know."

"But you still told your ghostly body to do it, huh?" Vivienne replies. She's been through all of this existential angst before. If the person thinks it, a ghost can do it. Just unnecessarily. "Is it okay if I touch your hair?"

"Oh, okay." She meekly bows her head, and Vivienne carefully rubs at her scalp.

Her hair is in two cute little poofy pigtails—she hasn't seen her change it at all—and she doesn't know how she'll help retie them if she tugs something loose. The less ghost physics are thought about, the better. Vivienne pulls her fingers away, squinting at the pads against the light.

"Thank you," Christine says, quietest yet. Vivienne has to lean in to make sure she'd spoken. "For, um, asking. Kirara... doesn't really ask. It's annoying."

Vivienne winces, rubbing her fingers together. "Ooh, yeah. Spirits have a *really* different sense of personal space and autonomy than most humans, and add in the fact that she's a youkai—Japanese spirit? I can't imagine she's very used to... uh..." Vivienne isn't very used to this, either. She would never dare touch Codi's hair without permission (or even with permission, as she has been privy to some of the wards she weaves into her braids). "Historically charged racial sensitivities?" Vivienne awkwardly guesses.

Christine smiles, as awkward as she feels. "I've noticed."

"On the upside, your cat babysitter definitely seems fond enough of you by now that she won't set you on fire if you ask her not to touch your hair, or overstep any other bounds!"

"Why did *you* ask to touch my hair? Is it oily or something?" she asks, squinting.

"Oh—look here!" She splays her fingers in front of Christine's face, making her reel back, but she can probably see it better than Vivienne can, anyway. "Luck! Luck spirits like bakeneko produce it like a coating, and with your dark hair, it was easier to see the shine. I'm not certain how much of this is yours just yet, but if by some miracle this messy experiment works out, you're gonna have permanent glitter hair. Maybe skin. Who knows, this type of thing has never happened before, because it doesn't."

Christine touches her own roots with wide-eyed, bright-eyed wonder. (Vivienne wonders what color her eyes had been originally.)

The little ghost seems as much as she has been in their few meetings: quiet and shy, but friendly enough. Not anything that Emil would've been freaking out about. And despite his strong implications that it could be a Girl Problem, Vivienne knows with one thousand percent certainty that ghosts *definitely* do not have periods.

Vivienne casts a sly smile in the kid's direction. He's been hovering this entire time, trying to seem like he wasn't (and failing miserably). He jumps to attention as if he'd been spotted reaching into the cookie jar. "Emil, want to go down to the corner store and fetch me some pomegranate juice? I can stay here with Christine for a bit."

"But. Uh. Is everything okay with her?" he asks, in that Trying Hard Not To Sound Concerned voice that all teenaged boys possess.

"I'm fine," Christine says, automatically, and her entire expression shutters.

That's new.

Vivienne looks between them a few times, calculating. Boy problems? One does not haunt a random boy for several months for shits and giggles, and existential angst compounded by unrequited love would be a *hell* of a funk to be in.

But Emil had been present—annoyingly so—for the duration of their check-up so far, and Christine had not seemed bothered.

"Juice, please."

"Pomegranate? That's specific. What if they don't have it?" Emil asks with a nervous glance toward his ghostly roommate.

Vivienne is *highly tempted* to tell him to try different stores until he finds one. She is also *highly tempted* to point out that with his luck saturation, finding a strange fruit drink is the least of his concerns. "Emil. Come on. Give us girls some privacy already. I'll text you when you're not kicked out anymore."

Emil slinks out with such a surly grumble that Vivienne nearly laughs. That Christine matches his grumpy expression is priceless. Vivienne valiantly does not laugh in the face of such teenaged angst, because she was a teenager in over her head with magic once, and because she doesn't think that would endear her to Christine, plus she would like to leave sooner rather than later.

Silence rings for a terse period before Vivienne heaves a sigh. (It somehow does not come out as a giggle.)

"He's really worried about you, you know? I know you don't want to talk about certain topics with certain guys, but he was getting panicked, and he's a clueless boy."

"Stop right there. This isn't any kind of boy drama," Christine orders, firmly, so out of character that Vivienne drops the subject.

"Okay, wow. Then what is it? If it's death stuff, you can talk to me about it, trust me. Or, I keep meaning to introduce you to my ghost friend, Rory, properly. You two could... talk. About heavy shit."

"No, that sounds... sad."

"You gotta give me something. What happened? Why is Emil worried, but your cat babysitter isn't?"

"Well, she hasn't been here for a week," she mutters. "She probably didn't notice."

Abandonment issues, fun. Vivienne maintains a patient smile. "Again, spirits are... different from humans. Really different. *Especially* cat spirits, good god, put a regular standoffish cat in a human-ish body with fire magic and no morals."

"I wish she didn't leave without explaining herself, but I understand she's not actually my babysitter." Christine peers up at her, another glittery squint, lips twisted into a pout. "And I'm sixteen. I don't actually need a babysitter, it's not like I'm in much danger anymore..."

Something flickers in her expression, some dulling of the gold in her gaze or the abrupt droop to her shoulders. And Vivienne *realizes.*

"Oh. Oh, okay, I see." She holds out an arm, and Christine gives her another suspicious look, but she keeps the embrace offer on the table. "You ran into another spirit, didn't you?"

"...How'd you know?"

"Ghosts are the bottom of the spiritual food chain, even lower than living people. Kirara's presence will act as a nice buffer, and I don't know your specific timeline, but I'm guessing this is your first run-in with someone less friendly. A lot of spirits will treat human ghosts as a snack, and if anyone sees you as particularly lucky... Am I getting it?"

"The broad strokes." Christine shuffles into the crook of her arm with a sad sound. Vivienne waits her out, mindful not to stroke her hair, but provides something she so rarely gets: physical comfort. "...My big brother *always* gave me so many talks about strange men, and guys, and strangers, and. You know. Trafficking and kidnapping and assault and stuff. For a while, when I first... died. I wandered around, kicking old guys' heads and feeling ignored differently than a Black girl usually is. I wasn't there to be *seen* by men. But there was this spirit. A fox spirit. He wanted the collar Kirara gave me, and he could *touch* me, and I felt so *stupid*. Logan gave me so many cheesy speeches about stranger danger, and I wasn't used to being seen for so long, and he just... I ran away."

Vivienne teeters on the tightrope of pressing for more information and trying to be blandly comforting. She can't imagine what it's like to be one kind of vulnerable in life and having it come back to bite her in the ass in such a way in death, but she's never been a dead teenager with a bakeneko's collar around her neck.

"Taking care of problematic spirits is kind of a specialty of mine, you know," she replies, lightly. "Perk of my friendship. You said fox spirit, any other identifying features? How many tails? He say anything to you?"

Christine sniffs and wipes at her dry eyes. "He was French, with one tail, said he was something like a mata-something. Started with an M."

"Good, workable start. No friendly introduction with his full name and address?"

That earns a brittle little laugh. "No, but at least he doesn't have mine, either. Or, um, Emil's."

"Also good. I'll see if I can't track something down for you, make it clear to behave or else."

If Christine feels some kinda way about the threat, she doesn't vocalize it now. It can be a problem for Future Them, then. Easier to face down hard morality choices when they're impossible to ignore any longer—and not a moment sooner.

"Alright, keep an eye out for a French fox, keep an eye on how sparkly you get, and let's both keep Emil from freaking out."

Christine nods, though she looks far from pleased with her new waiting game life. Or maybe it's another babysitter that's rubbing her the wrong way. That Vivienne can commiserate with; she's been babysat and watched and tailed and side-eyed ever since she animated her first corpse.

"Anything else?" Vivienne asks as she texts Emil it's safe again.

"Not much new. Emil keeps asking me questions, though... I think he should ask you. You seem to know a lot more about this stuff."

"Death and ghosts and the academic side of magic, yeah, for sure. Luck spirits? Not so much, but I could ask around. That collar probably has more secrets than I could ever find out, though." Vivienne reaches over and *dings* the bell, expecting the way Christine lights up this time. "How long were you a ghost before you got that?" *And what would prompt a bakeneko to give up a collar?*

"Not very long. Just over two months, I think? It was a week after..."

She doesn't remember the date of her death, but something else is a concrete marker in her mind. This won't be a pleasant conversation, but the more information Vivienne knows, the better equipped she is to help them navigate whatever this mess turns out to be.

"After what, Christine?" she presses.

"After my brother died," she mumbles.

Vivienne had suspected at least some portion of dead family. "Can I ask you about him?"

"Surprised you haven't yet," she mutters, even quieter. "He was a witch."

"Were you magical before you died?"

"No, not really. But Logan was a witch, and it was his plan to..." Christine wraps her arms around her middle, where the red splash had been on her robes. "We knew I was dying. It was his plan to give me a new life. He worked *so hard* to avoid anything that could turn me into a demon..."

"Jesus," Vivienne hisses under her breath. Death has a habit of making mad scientists out of anyone, she knows from personal experience, but this is a new angle. "And I'm guessing you're not with him because that backfired."

She nods and wipes at her dry eyes. "He died. He d-didn't become a ghost. I was left alone, and I *can't* talk about this with Emil, and Kirara doesn't understand."

"So, she found you after your brother died?" Vivienne asks as gently as she can. She can dig into Logan the witch on her own time, so there's no need to make Christine relive any more painful memories.

"A week after. She appeared because she wanted to eat my brother's familiar, but, um, I think she felt sorry for us. She looked at the luck he'd collected, and I told her I was trying to become a luck spirit, and she gave me this..." She touches the bell collar at her throat. "I know it's valuable, but I'd give it back in a heartbeat to have my brother back. I didn't want his plan to *kill* him! He swore he wasn't trying to trade his life for mine, b-but I couldn't read all of his research, so what if he *was*—?!"

Vivienne pulls her against her chest to quiet her racking, dry sobs. So much for avoiding painful memories. "Shh, it's okay. I can look into his research, but I'm sure he didn't... lie to you, or anything." How can she say that about a stranger? This was clearly a brother who dearly loved his sister, and Vivienne knows what people will do for love in the face of death. "I'll look into it. I'll see if I can find out what he was doing, and I'm sure you're fine, and maybe it'll help you now? Shh, c'mon, you're breaking my heart with your sad ghosty crying. And Emil will be terrified if he comes back to this."

She gives a snotty, watery laugh.

And Vivienne realizes why Natalie had said that these kids would become important to her. *Damn it.* She's gotten goddamn attached to them and their sad little story. She *wants* to give them a happy ending.

By the time Emil scoots back in, Christine has composed herself and Vivienne has layered several more wards onto his apartment. (Kirara may be pissed when she discovers them, but if there is a fox spirit out hunting, Vivienne thinks she's in the right.) He has a plastic bag with a sweating pomegranate juice cocktail and several winning scratchcards in it, the latter of which he tries to hide.

"I'm not going to judge you, you know that, right?" Vivienne asks as she takes the juice. She downs half of it in one go, cherishing the sugar flooding her system. Anything to keep her awake long enough to make it back home. "I have a memory charm on my landlord to make him forget about my rent. I'm *not* here to judge."

"Except the magic eye drops, and the dangers of luck spirits, and hanging out with cat spirits," Emil deadpans.

"Mmhmm," Vivienne agrees and chugs the rest. "All with known side effects. Using magic to get some extra money is the least of your problems right now. Thanks for the juice, you two keep inside until the storm passes, and don't text or call me for at least twenty-four hours because I'm going to go pass *out*."

It's two in the afternoon, but Christine offers a smile and a, "Uh, goodnight, Vivienne."

"Thanks for coming over. I guess," Emil adds.

"You're lucky I'm cheap enough to be bought with some juice. Next time, smoothies from that nice place by your work."

Outside, the storm pours buckets, but the wind and lightning are gone. There might be some flooding in some bad areas, but it should be done by tomorrow, and she plans on sleeping through the rest of it. Her umbrella keeps her mercifully dry to the train station.

She takes her first train, but gets off before her transfer because she remembers that, besides sleep, she needs a thing called food. She ducks into a convenience store across the street, shakes out her umbrella, and tries to remember how much wet food she has for Sunshine, too. Cat food is more expensive here, but she is too damn tired to pinch pennies when she could sleep instead.

She grabs a bag of tortilla chips, cheese spray, two ramen cups, and lingers in front of the refrigerated booze. Alcohol always makes her sleep well, and doesn't she deserve something for *hunting dragons* mostly successfully?

She grabs a six-pack of Mike's Hard and a bottle of Grey Goose. She can treat herself. And a couple cans of wet cat food, just in case.

Vivienne shuffles into line, careful with her basket and umbrella, and almost ends up dropping everything because none other than *Dana* is the person in front of her.

Vivienne stares at the back of her jacket. Dana is turned just enough that Vivienne can see her profile, her strong nose and the thick loops of today's braided hairstyle, her attention on her phone.

I must be lucky, Vivienne thinks. Oh god, she touched the luck in Christine's hair. Was that enough? Is she finally zeroed out and into something more positive? There is no customer barrier now, they're just two people, ran into each other, totally normal ladies who can have a totally normal conversation outside of the confines of a bookstore.

Vivienne's umbrella clatters to the floor, hands just slack enough.

She jumps, and almost drops her basket, too. Dana jumps at the noise as well, turning around. She stares at Vivienne for a long moment.

Vivienne's face flames as she stoops to pick up her umbrella.

"Oh gosh, Vivienne! Hi! What a coincidence," Dana says, breaking into a real, not Customer Service smile.

"H-Hi," she wheezes. Her arms feel too full and too uncooperative. She may melt. "Hi, Dana. What a coincidence, yeah."

"You live near here?"

"No, on my way home."

"Oh, me too. Even weirder coincidence," Dana says with a full grin. She has such a nice smile. Vivienne hopes this line never moves. "I'm on my way home from dog-sitting for a friend, but one of them chewed through my phone charger, so I'm getting a new one." She holds up the small box, glancing down at Vivienne's basket. "Party tonight?"

"Just—no, uh, just restocking," Vivienne says with an awkward laugh. *Thank god I didn't get the Burnett's*, she thinks with horror. Alcohol and shitty food is one thing, but *cheap* alcohol? Or, well, any cheaper.

"You have a cat?" Dana asks. Prompts. Like she wants to keep the conversation going.

"Oh, yeah!" Good god, how had she never played the cat card before? Easiest conversation fodder in the world! "His name is Sunshine—here, let me fish out my phone, I have a billion pictures."

"Let me hold something for you," Dana says, stowing her phone, and reaches for the sad basket. Their hands brush. Vivienne's heart stutters.

"H-Here," Vivienne says as soon as her phone is out. Sunshine is her lockscreen, curled up into a black blob of a ball. She unlocks it and opens up her photos. She has nothing to fear since a solid ninety-six percent of her pictures are of the cat.

"Oh, so precious! Sunshine, for a black cat? That's cute."

He used to be yellow is on the tip of her tongue, but that's hardly something she can say right now. "He came with the name. I sort of inherited him. He's a Maine Coon, also known as the *hugest* cat in the world, and he's a big baby."

"He looks it," Dana says, smiling fondly, scrolling through photo upon photo of indistinguishable black fur. "Oh, you're so lucky, I wish I could have a pet! I've never had a cat, but I had a dog growing up, who was about as fluffy as yours. But I got to spend two days with dogs, so—here, let me show you pictures, too."

Dana carefully hands the basket back to Vivienne so she's now in no danger of dropping anything else. Their hands don't brush, but they're definitely standing closer now, and Dana rummages around in her coat pocket.

She shows Vivienne a picture of a German Shepherd with its tongue lolling out in a big doggy smile. "Here, the chewy culprit herself. There's another dog, but she never sits still long enough for pictures. My friend Leti has them both trained *so well*, and they like me, but a babysitter is nothing compared to mom, right?"

"Oh right, I definitely know what it's like to have pets play favorites. She's so cute! At least you get to go play with your friend's dogs. I have a friend with a German Shepherd, too, and they're just the *biggest* ball of energy."

Dana laughs and shows her another picture, the same dog now rolling around with her belly up. "Trust me, I know. Which is why I can't have a dog right now. My apartment is microscopic and doesn't allow pets."

"If you ever wanted to come over and see Sunshine, you totally could," Vivienne blurts. Then, processes.

It almost sounds like an invitation to hang out, or maybe half a date, but all of her smooth ideas about coffee dates or dinners or movies is trumped by a *cat* visit.

But it goddamn works.

"Maybe, that sounds great! I'd love to meet a black cat named Sunshine."

Vivienne lets out an embarrassingly girlish giggle. "Great! We should exchange numbers. You know, for sending more pet pictures back and forth, and, well, chatting. Coordinating hangouts. And things."

"And things," Dana agrees with amusement.

After they exchange numbers, the cashier pointedly clears his throat, and Dana steps to the counter with a sheepish laugh. Vivienne cradles her basket's handle and grins to herself. She got Dana's number. She got her to smile, and talk about something that isn't books, and for once, joy outweighs her fatigue.

She doesn't even need the booze to fall asleep easily that afternoon. Sunshine curls up next to her, fed and purring, and Vivienne drifts off with a smile on her face.

· · · ● ● · ● ● · · ·

The moment they're off duty, Mirai shoots off for home. They strip armor off as they fly, used to that by now, though it means awkwardly hooking spaulders on one talon to stop them from dropping several stories below.

Their home is dark and cool and empty. Mirai throws their guard uniform onto their bed without bothering about things such as cleaning or folding or anything remotely proper. *They* don't care for propriety. That's the job of every other tengu in the realm. They wrestle sleeves on over their feathers, and in record time, they zip back out of their tiny home and speed toward the market door.

Hatsu should be on market duty today.

They nearly trip over a swan tengu in the doorway connecting their realms, both masks askew, and Mirai gets smacked for their trouble. "Sorry!" they call, wriggling out from beneath white feathers, and dart off into the market.

Hatsu reclines on a cushion at the stall, chatting with the neighboring gumiho, and Mirai's heart swells at the casual slouch of their robe and their relaxed posture. They don't know *they* could keep that calm if their First egg were missing. Hatsu truly is a wonderful role model.

(Better prospective mate, but it may be a few years yet before Mirai convinces the elders of both their clans that they're suitable for one another.)

"Hatsu!" Mirai cries and crashes into them instead of a proper landing.

Hatsu, of course, had expected this, and Mirai ends up on their lap with only ruffled feathers to show for their rough landing. "Mirai," Hatsu deadpans, one arm around their waist, only for stability. But Mirai leans against them happily. "I see you are off duty now."

"How cute, the haste with which you two visit one another," Yun-hee coos, her tails waving behind her.

"Do *you* ever possess haste?" Mirai asks with amusement.

Hatsu's expression must be as blank as their mask. "What brings you to the markets today?" they ask as if they're unaware of the answer.

"You!" Hatsu holds them at wing's length before Mirai can claim an embrace. "Fine, I am going to the human realm again. But I wished to see you, Hatsu."

Their long ears dip low, pink on the edge. Their pale skin and plumage always show blushing so easily. "You needn't contort yourself into this busy mess to get my egg back."

"Of course I do! It's your *First* egg, and you and I both know there are more missing eggs than yours. I thought I had a lead on a missing one from the crow clan—a *human*, can you believe it? But that's not *yours*."

"You are doing too much for someone too young," Hatsu says, cupping their jaw beneath their mask.

Mirai leans away from the touch, no matter how they crave it. "It is my *duty*—!"

"Your duty is as a guard. My duty is as a merchant. You need not hunt through two realms, one of which you hardly know. Tengu don't belong in the human realm."

"Haven't for a few hundred years, anyway," Yun-hee agrees, broadcasting her eavesdropping.

"It was on *my* duty that the thief took your egg," Mirai growls, feathers raising despite themselves. They smooth down their flight feathers with an angry huff. Hatsu nudges them off their lap, and Mirai regretfully gets to their feet. They could spend time with them, man the stall and watch the different beings, but they take their duty seriously. (Sometimes.)

"I have heard nothing about any eggs," Yun-hee says, "and no one has tried to sell any."

If anyone were to go to all of the trouble of breaking into another *realm* to steal from youkai, it would not be for money's sake. Mirai spares the gumiho a look down their nose. "What do you know of the humans Vivienne and Mark?"

"The humans you *should not* have asked for aid. What are you paying them with?" Hatsu groans.

But Yun-hee ignores the collective tengu grumpiness with tails wagging and furry ears perked. "Every spirit here worth a damn knows of Mark, he is a clairvoyant human. *And* Japanese. He has an inugami friend! Shouldn't you have already known of him?"

"He doesn't come here himself very often," Hatsu replies on Mirai's behalf. Their heart soars again. "Always sending others to fetch his goods. Clairvoyant humans cannot deal with goblin markets well. It is understandable that no one aside from merchant class tengu would know of him."

"But *I've* heard the crow clan have separate dealings with humans," Yun-hee says with vicious glee. "I would expect a guard magpie to know about that."

Hatsu gives them a pointed, sidelong look, but at least the masks make it easy to pretend to avoid such attention.

"Ah, Lucien!" Typical of foxes, Yun-hee's attention snaps away, and she leans over her stall to wave into the crowd of passersby. "Lucien, here, we have a question for you!"

To Mirai's disappointment, another fox spirit wanders over, a siren on his arm. Not a gumiho, not with only one tail. Mirai is more interested in the siren accompanying him; her feathers are pretty, soft white, just like the underside of Hatsu's plumage.

"Excuse me a moment," Lucien murmurs and kisses the back of the siren's hand. "*Mademoiselle* Yun-hee, what a pleasure to have caught your attention. To what do I owe the surprise?"

"Have you heard anything about tengu eggs in the human realm? You spend *so* much time there, I thought you would have heard something useful."

"See, *this* is what happens when you drag others into our affairs," Hatsu hisses at Mirai. They droop, embarrassed.

Lucien cocks his head to the side. His skin is brown, but the rest of him is black—black hair, black fox ears, black fox tail, black human clothing. The siren at his side titters a pretty giggle. She tucks a lock of long white hair behind her round ear and gives him a playful elbow. "Yes, Lucien, you *do* spend so much time in the human realm."

"Where else am I to eat? Where else am I to bait humans with gold?"

Ah, a wealth spirit, Mirai realizes with displeasure. The ego ought to have given it away. Mirai may not have given thought to paying the humans yet, but a spirit of fortune is a *terrible* thing to pay. "No, thank you! I'm taking care of tengu business."

"Is that so," Lucien replies, noncommittal. "What of a trade, then? I am also looking for something in the human realm."

"We do not need to do business with you," Hatsu cuts in with a protective wing in front of Mirai. "Yun-hee, stop gossiping. You two, purchase or move along."

"How rude," the siren says with another tinkling laugh.

"I'll do business with you!" Yun-hee declares with a full grin and wagging tails. "What is it you need? I can procure *anything*, you know this."

"Luck."

"Ah, you're looking for the *other* gold, right? I just had a human purchase a luck-filled bath bomb a few weeks ago! It seems to be growing in popularity."

"A bomb?" Lucien asks in alarm, ears flat against his hair.

"No, no, a *bath* bomb. A human thing! A sphere you put into bathwater to add color and smell and charms to it. I've already tried one, and they're lovely!" Yun-hee gushes, complete with a dreamy sigh. Her hair cascades over her shoulder as she melts onto her stall, heedless of her wares. "I helped her put luck into one. I may begin selling those."

"I'm looking for other sorts of luck," Lucien replies, not sold on the idea. Mirai doesn't blame him. He touches the knot of the tie at his throat (another disgusting human thing). "A maneki-neko's collar."

"You want to kill a cat spirit?" Yun-hee asks dubiously. Mirai scoffs.

"No. There is one that has been given away in the human realm. I'd adore your help with obtaining it, or another like it, *Mademoiselle* Yun-hee."

Mirai scoffs again. They will *never* understand the need of fox spirits to act so amorously.

"If you find me that collar, I would be more than happy to hunt the human realm for missing eggs," Lucien pointedly adds.

"We do not need outside help," Hatsu replies.

For once, Mirai agrees. "I can handle these personal matters on my own. Do your fox business with your own kind!"

"Rude," Yun-hee says with glee. But there is a sharp gleam in her eyes, and a heaviness to the surrounding air.

Mirai does not know Lucien or his siren, but they know gumiho, and they can easily curse even tengu. Their displeasure remains, but they will hold their tongue slightly better in the future. "I will be off to conduct my *own* business in the human realm! Bye, Hatsu!"

They lean in for a quick cheek nuzzle, heedless of the onlookers and Hatsu's embarrassed growl. Mirai wings back into the air, unable to help a smile at the siren's friendly wave, because those with feathers generally have more sense.

When they duck through the door and breathe in bright human air, they find the storm has broken. Excellent sign and easier flying. It is with high spirits Mirai again traverses the alien realm.

·· • • • • • • • ··

Vivienne wakes after twenty-two hours asleep. A new personal best. She thanks god for auto-feeders, though she'd left out several dishes of wet cat food for her needy boy. One day, she'll probably fall asleep forever, and Sunshine will eat her. She is resigned to that fate.

Vivienne stretches, muscles still loose with rest, and her needy boy jumps to attention at the foot of the bed. Sunshine meows at her. "Yes, yes, papa hears you, Sunny. Give me five minutes to actually become *awake*."

She takes seven to slither out of bed to the bathroom to attend to her equally needy bladder. She's dehydrated, and she fills a cup from the tap before staggering out to the kitchen. Sunshine sits by his food bowl(s), ears perked, tail folded primly over his paws.

"So polite," she jokes, and gives him an entire can of wet food for not waking her earlier. They have an agreement, and he happily snarfs down his bribe.

Vivienne sucks down more water while she checks her dying phone. She sits at the tiny kitchen counter to let it charge at her sole kitchen outlet. She likes this apartment and doesn't want to move, but the microscopic kitchen had *not* been a selling point.

Several missed calls from Mark, one from Hammond, a dozen texts from Emil, and two from Dana. Vivienne throws all the others into a mental dumpster and holds her phone aloft with a beaming smile. Numbers exchanged, yes, and number *used*.

One text is a picture of a black cat in a flower crown, probably from Pinterest, the other asking, '*does yours ever dress up?*' Tame and neutral and absolutely splendid.

She allows herself to bask for another few minutes. Sunshine did dress up with Hayley, but not so much anymore. But like all good cat parents, she still has ancient pictures on her phone.

Too bad they're of a yellow cat.

Vivienne grimaces at a years-old picture of Sunshine dressed as a bumblebee. She glances down at the current, very black Sunshine, then asks him, "Any chance you'd become a bee again for me?"

He flicks an ear back and continues snarfing down his food.

Supernatural Hunter Tip #8: You can't force a familiar to do anything they don't want to do.

"Didn't think so, Sunny-honey."

Vivienne waffles on what to text back—this is a first text impression, she doesn't want to disappoint, so does she send the bee picture and pretend it's another cat, or does she claim Sunshine is boring and naked all the time—and looks through her other messages.

Emil asked, not subtly, about Christine's mood, but that's for *them* to discuss. Mark didn't leave any ominous messages, so Vivienne calls Hammond back first. It almost goes to voicemail before he answers, out of breath. "Hello, Viv? How's my favorite sleeping beauty?"

Hearing music, she asks, "Did I interrupt practice?"

"We needed a water break, anyway." The background music fades. Hammond catches his breath, then says, "So, Rory and I were talking, and now that Codi's alive and well again, we should go out. Even Nat's already agreed."

"Oh, she woke up? Thank god. *And* you got Nat to agree to a social event? You must be a miracle worker, Ham."

"Well, the catch was that she wanted to invite Isaac and Sam, and would only go if *they* go..." He trails off meaningfully.

Vivienne sighs. "So she's actually a no."

"But Sam likes *you*! You should talk them all into going out with us. Codi still has an in with the club downtown, the one with the good bar, *and* if Nat agrees to go, you know she'll pay for the night."

"She'd just give me her card, anyway."

"But she deserves a relaxing, fun night, too!"

"I *agree* with you, Ham! I'll see if I can get her interns to agree, but it might be a longshot. Did she agree to a date?"

"Saturday." Which, great, only gives her a couple of days to bat her eyes at a demon. "C'mon, we believe in you! We *deserve* a night out after finding out that Thomas Novak of all people wants to fuck with Codi. That's going to be a war."

Natalie doesn't drink much, but even one beer is enough to loosen her tongue. Maybe she can get some more information about Thomas' sudden hostility, and what sort of visions she has seen about Christine.

"Sounds like a fun night out, Ham. I'll see what I can do," Vivienne tells him with a growing grin.

· · · · ● · ● · · ·

Brynja has been tempted by the thought of escape before. How could she not? She has lost track of the centuries, especially with the time difference between realms, but it has been *so long*. So much of her life dominated by fear and pain.

She admits this may be the closest she has gotten to an actual chance, however. She has not been in the human realm for so long—it has changed tremendously—and she cannot feel the pull of her master here. A dragon pelt is a tempting bribe. She has done worse for less.

She stands in the bedroom's doorway and contemplates the sleeping figures within.

Mark lays with all his limbs spread, open and vulnerable, face different without his glasses. It doesn't look like him when he is not scheming. Beside him, the rage spirit sleeps, smaller now. Shaped like a domestic dog, albeit a large one, pressed up against Mark's leg with a tail curled over his foot.

Another rage spirit. Who would have guessed. She didn't think any humans were so foolish as to care for them, much less spend extended periods of time with one. Humans have been ruled by fear for too long; that much, she still has in common with them.

The barrel of a gun presses against the back of her skull.

Brynja had heard her coming, had smelled the human sweat and metal of the gun. "You're up late," Fiona whispers.

"You're protective of him," she dryly observes.

"He said you were getting there, too. It's his charm," she deadpans.

"If you are unwilling, why are you—"

"I'm not unwilling to help Mark. I'm not unwilling to fight monsters. I'm not unwilling to splatter brains inside his bedroom to clean up later."

"You're angry, too. For a human," Brynja observes, tilting her head toward the barrel to shoot Fiona a look over her shoulder. "Is it your blood? I smell the rage spirit on you, *in* you, but I don't understand it. Mark Ito has strange friends."

"My emotions are my own and have nothing to do with Benji," she hisses.

"I am going to go back to the bathtub now. Don't shoot me for that," Brynja tells her. Fiona lowers the shotgun.

Brynja slips back into the bathroom. Cold water sloshes in the tub, her sealskin folded over the edge. She thumbs it before tugging it on. Mark had given it back to her so easily, under the guise of earning trust. Becoming a seal again is a comfort she had considered lost. Becoming *anything* again had been thought of as out of her reach; Mark had called it a suicide mission, and she is only now inclined to agree. She had never thought about how much she had prepared to give up for the sake of that egg. Her master had always asked much of her, but never so much so fast.

It was going to toss me aside, too. It was done with me. This was my purpose, she bitterly realizes. She ducks under the surface and listens to the distorted sound of water against the edge of the tub. Unlike waves, but still calming.

It'd offered her hope, so many years ago, and gave her a purpose she had lost. It had given her the one chance at life again. All for this moment, all in preparation for coming back to the human realm.

Brynja slows her breathing, concentrates on the soft rocking of the water, and slips into the human dreamscape.

It's different here. It is an echo of what she knows, an imperfect mirror, a jagged offshoot of what it once was. But it still fills her with terror and loathing to step foot here.

It is not the Dreamlands, she tells herself with every step forward. *My master is not here anymore.*

She finds Mark amongst a greenhouse of jewels, not with the little trunked monster. She ducks under thick branches and fights off creeping vines to get closer to him. She is almost on top of him by the time he notices her.

"Oh, Bryn," he says, turning to her with a vacant smile and glassy eyes. He is not wearing his glasses here, either. She hates how human dreamers look; the only redeeming quality about humanity is its vibrancy, and dreams sap even that. "You're back again. Not just a one-time special then, hm?"

"I was called *Brynja in mikla, Brynja hvalmaga*. Then, I was called *Brynja in óða*. Then, I became *Sleitu-Brynja in draumspaka*. I was plucked from the hatred of humans by my master, the Great Old One Yaehathal. I will not tell you about my past or the magics that made me."

Mark blinks up at her, slowly, uncomprehendingly. This may have been a poor decision to make in a dream, but it lifts a weight off her heart all the same.

"But I want to work with you, Mark Ito. I want to be free of the grip that has been crushing me all these years," Brynja says. Traitorously, her throat threatens to close, and she swallows thickly. She does not deserve to cry. "I will help you keep the human realm safe from my master's reach to the best of my ability. In return, I want my freedom back. I want safety and an escape. I want my *self* back. You gave me my seal pelt, but I want my *selves* back. Only with your agreement will I give you the egg back and my cooperation."

"Of course I'll help you, Bryn—" Mark begins, but she cuts him off with a shake of her head.

"No. Bryn is a human name, and I am no longer human. I've no wish to return. I am Brynja. Only Brynja."

Mark smiles. He seems a bit less like an empty doll, a bit more like the thinking, nosy, scheming, terrible human he is. Brynja releases a shaky breath, emptying herself of centuries of fear and pain and dread.

She wants to believe in hope again. Maybe this human, who is surrounded by other monsters and still offers his hand, can help her.

Natalie jolts awake in bed, pouring sweat, blood gushing from her nose.

Already, the vision fades from her mind—her mind hurries to hide it from herself. She can normally recall visions with clarity, stronger than most memories, but this one is fading like a dream. But it couldn't have been a dream, not if she has a nosebleed, not to mention the rising headache.

She recalls a woman, a tall and muscular white woman with wild black hair and tattooed arms. There had been someone else with her... But there, Natalie's memory fuzzes out. Not someone, but something, and it's something her brain staunchly refuses to recall. She can only remember pieces.

The setting—a lush tangle of impossible trees and colorful sky. The woman—hands extended, as if receiving something. Receiving... what? And from what?

More blood drips onto her sheets.

The last thing she remembers from her forgotten vision is that she had only woken up when the other thing *had turned and* looked *at her.*

CHAPTER 17

IN WHICH THERE'S A LOT OF TROUBLE TO BE HAD

Emil carefully drips two drops of potion into each eye. Not the first time he's done it, and it won't be the last, but it *is* the first time that he *bumps into* Christine when he stretches to put the tiny bottle back on the table.

They stare at each other.

Christine reaches for him, through his shoulder, and her face falls again.

"We should keep a tally," he blurts, and those golden eyes peek back up at him. "Because it's going to only happen more often, right? You're on an uphill climb, and that's two touches now."

"Uh, more than that. Sometimes, when you're sleeping... I-It isn't as bad as that sounds!" Christine backpedals, hands up in front of her, until she accidentally phases through his fridge. She ducks back out with a sheepish, imploring look. "Kirara mentioned it could be easier without human preconceptions. So, um, sometimes I tuck you back in at night...? A-And when we first met Vivienne, and she blew sleep soot on you, I caught you when you fell. It's been more than twice, I mean. That's all."

Emil maintains a smile, even when inwardly screaming. Right, being haunted, and all the creepiness that entails. "Okay. Boundaries. When I'm in bed—my bedroom is off limits!" He is terribly reminded of morning wood frequency, wet dreams, and alone time in what should have been his own home. His face feels traitorously hot.

"It was platonic!" Christine cries in dismay. She can't blush, but she sheds the hint of glitter like a substitute. She looks ready to hide in the fridge again.

"I know it was! I'm not calling you a creeper, but you understand that it *is* creepy, right? Being haunted is creepy!"

"It wasn't like that, I don't like you like that, I'm trying *not* to haunt you!" Christine wails through her fingers.

And ouch, his ego. He isn't sure why he's suddenly offended at the *like you like that*, but it stings all the same. "Bedroom, off limits. We can start a tally now."

There is an old whiteboard on the fridge, back when there was more than one person living here and things like grocery lists mattered. He writes the date and makes two tally marks beneath it.

"And one day, you'll make your own tally. ...Will you be able to touch things before people, or people before things?"

"Touching things is a poltergeist thing, so I haven't tried very much," she admits.

"Fair enough. We'll get some more marks on here before you make your own, but *eventually*, it can be your job. When you're comfortable and stuff." Vivienne had asked what their plan was, and that sounds like a good first step. Not to mention some evidence to show her in case she gets judgy again. She hasn't gotten back to him yet, but playing teacher would be a far sight better than playing bully.

• • • • • • • • • •

The first day the shop is reopened, and Isaac is back to work, Vivienne pounces. She sidles up to Sam in a way that is lost on him, bats her eyes, and paws at his shoulder to get his attention. "With everything going on before, I didn't get the chance to thank you two. You did a good job, jumping into the fray. Thanks."

Sam blinks down at her, but Isaac is immediately suspicious and sets down his pestle with a *clack*. "What are you on?"

"Nothing! I actually got a good amount of sleep yesterday, I'm glad we're all in one piece, and I'm thanking the newbies for going above and beyond. What's wrong with a friend complimenting another friend's good job?"

"Are we friends?" Sam asks.

"I think we can be, yeah."

"He's getting into the bad habit of going around asking *anyone* to be his friend because of you," Isaac mutters.

"So long as he's settled, most people can't tell what he is. What's wrong with being friends, Isaac?" Vivienne coos. She drapes her arms over Sam's shoulders, just for the way Isaac's eye twitches.

He lets out a breath, releasing the tension in his shoulders, and musters a smile. "Nothing, of course. Sam can be *friends* with whoever he chooses."

She is *definitely* missing something there, something she will not like if Isaac is being a prick about it. They didn't make friends with Thomas or his accomplice. So who could that be?

But she has to choose her battles, and she wants fun drunk social time instead of self-preservation right now.

"You know what else friends do? Hang out together outside of work hours."

"We do that with Oliver," Sam says with a nod.

"I'd like to do it, too!" Vivienne agrees. She rubs her cheek against his fluffy, sandy hair. "So, Sam, how about you do me the honor of accompanying me to a Hooray We Survived Dragon Hunting party on Saturday?"

"A party?" Sam whispers in awe.

Vivienne knows she's hooked him, but he was always going to be the easy one. She gives Isaac a sly smile over the top of the demon's head. *You wouldn't want to break his heart, now would you?*

She gives it seven in ten odds that Isaac tells her to fuck off, anyway. Yet he does not *immediately* shoot down the idea, which is truly shocking. "You want to see what a drunk demon is like, don't you?"

"Absolutely!" If he wants to blame this on her experimental nature, who cares! Yes, she would gladly party with a demon and who knows what else if it got Natalie to let her hair down for five whole minutes. "You don't?"

"It would be entertaining," Isaac allows, "but not in a public setting."

"It's the Chaos Club, downtown? It's magic-friendly, plenty of nonhumans dance and drink there, too. Maybe if *someone* would get him a charm that keeps him smelling rosy, and if demons don't turn into puddles when drunk, I think it'd be worth the risk!"

"Not your head on the line," Isaac deadpans.

"Fair, but consider me your personal bodyguard for the evening. I make a very good meat shield."

"Is there a risk to a party?" Sam asks him.

"...So long as you don't turn into a puddle," he allows. "I've been working on an amulet that suppresses smell and stabilizes form. I could have it done by Saturday."

This is going better than she'd ever hoped.

"Is Oliver invited?"

"Uh, I don't think so? He didn't fight dragons with us. Do you *want* him to be?"

Isaac glares into the mortar of thyme. "No. Never party with Oliver Lynch if you want to be alive the next morning."

"Did he try to kill you?" Sam whispers, aghast. Vivienne snickers against his hair, then slithers off of him. "Why are so many people friends with so many other violent people?"

"The city attracts weird people. I'm sure they're fine, Sam. Are you excited to go to your very first club? Isaac, what are you dressing him in?"

"Oliver gave him some clothes."

"Clothes suitable for a club?" Vivienne prompts. Isaac thinks, then shakes his head. "And how are you going to *ask* for clothes for a club without getting Oliver all hyped and inviting himself along?"

"I don't understand why humans care so much about what *kind* of clothes you wear. If something is comfortable and gives you a full range of movement, why does the material or the color matter?" Sam asks.

Vivienne pats his shoulder. "Smarter people than you or I have grappled with that very question, and the answer is always quashed by the monolith of the fashion industry. Welcome to being human."

Sam lets out an adorably aggrieved sigh. "Same," Isaac agrees.

Natalie finally pads downstairs, steam-pink and damp, hair a frizzy mess. She yawns as greeting.

"How's the moonshine potion going?" Vivienne asks with no small amount of cheekiness. Natalie's bathtub is, naturally, larger than her largest pot. And some orders require higher volumes than others. It may also be a semi-legal order, which makes it all the sweeter.

"Should be done next week. My bathroom will smell like rosehip for *months*," Natalie admits and slumps onto a stool. Isaac and Sam seem taken aback by seeing her so out of it, but summer is usually a quieter time for big orders. It'll only ramp up now that they're past the equinox.

"Well," Vivienne sweetly informs her, "then I am very pleased to let you know that you'll be coming with us on Saturday to unwind. The boys agreed."

Natalie raises her head, confused. She furrows her brow at Isaac. "Oh. You were supposed to say no."

"Sam wanted to go," Isaac replies.

"I do," the demon happily agrees.

Isaac shrugs. "And he gets one free Do What He Wants. Plus, Vivienne looks excited to see what a drunk demon looks like. ...I kind of am, too."

"Oh," Natalie repeats. She settles her head back into the cushion of her folded arms. "Then I suppose I'm booked for Saturday."

Supernatural Hunter Tip #28: Don't drink with spirits.

But in this rare case, Vivienne looks forward to breaking her own rule.

• • • • • • • • • •

Getting people together for anything short of a dragon migration is no easy feat. Herding cats would be easier. Hammond had a last-minute lesson, so he will meet them at the club. Megan is finishing up helping their mother with coven things, so they will arrive Whenever. Codi is on the way back from the goblin market from a meeting with Graham, so she'll meet them downtown, halfway there. Isaac says he and Sam will meet them at the club, but Vivienne has doubts.

But Natalie's already with her, so no take-backs.

Natalie's home above her shop is not large, but not tiny, but she *is* lucky enough to have a walk-in closet. That it is packed full is the only vice Vivienne is aware she possesses. Vivienne had had to help her choose between four little black dresses—without entirely understanding the differences—before they could get to makeup. Vivienne appreciates the dedication to going out, however; Natalie never does things by half-measures.

So Natalie looks resplendent in a high-low black wrap midi dress. It hugs her curves like a second skin, mesh for the collar and shoulders, asymmetrically high up one thigh. The only jewelry she wears are dangly silver earrings, a waterfall of miniscule chains. She looks gorgeous. Vivienne makes a note to make a bet with Hammond to count how many times she gets hit on tonight.

Her love of nice clothes does not include shoes. Natalie wears one of two pairs of heels she owns, a basic, strappy low heel whose only embellishment is a silver buckle at the ankle.

While Natalie is sexy and classic, Vivienne loves attention and glitz when going out. (She may not have as many clothing options as her friend, but she does well for herself.) She wears a two-piece set, shimmery with itchy (but Worth It) sequins on the top and skirt hem, all of it soft grey. The top has three-quarter sleeves and a v-neck, deep more due to her chest size than the cut, but she's not complaining. She can hide so much booze in her cleavage.

Since they're meeting Codi downtown, which *happens* to be just two blocks from the smoothie place Vivienne has fallen in love with, it is easy to talk Natalie into making a stop there. It is also just a block from The Bookstore, but Vivienne is still weighing the pros and cons.

Pros: she probably gets to see Dana, Dana could see her smoking hot outfit, and she could get a compliment from Dana.

Cons: it's awkward to visit stores when dressy, Dana might not be working, and she would have to deal with Natalie's brand of quiet smugness about her crush.

They step outside, smoothies in hand, and Vivienne reaches down her shirt to pull out the half bottle of wine she'd stashed. She drinks down enough smoothie to dump some in.

Natalie looks at her in quiet, disconcerted horror.

Vivienne stirs her drink. Blueberry pomegranate and white wine. Maybe she's onto something new. "Pre-gaming? Want some?" she asks with a sip.

"I'm not sure it would go with mine," Natalie replies and protectively switches her mango smoothie to her other hand.

"I also have some vodka in there."

"Vivienne," Natalie sighs.

"Everyone does it! It's not like I *won't* order drinks there." Turns out, her concoction isn't half-bad. She sucks it down and adds a bit more wine. "Where are we meeting Codi, exactly?" Vivienne is going to put her money on Codi showing up in something bright red, so she scans the evening crowds.

Natalie checks her phone, straw in her mouth. "She says she's in a store nearby," she murmurs. Then, eyes askance, she demurely asks, "Could I get some wine, too, please?"

Vivienne shoots her a triumphant grin. Between the two of them, they finish the half bottle. Vivienne's bra thanks her for lessening its load.

They wander, sipping, noses in their phones. Hammond has texted that he just finished up his lesson, so he needs to run home and shower and change before meeting them there. He's another with a ridiculous amount of clothes, and Rory can change into literally anything, so she wonders what kind of fashion show they'll bring her tonight.

Natalie huffs and ends up calling Codi, frustrated with the spotty texts. "Yes, Codi? Where are you? We're wandering on West Elder Street... Yes, there was a smoothie shop. *Where* are you? Oh. Alright. See you in a moment."

"Nearby?"

"Still in the store," Natalie replies. She stashes her phone in her tiny purse—accessories are also not something she's a fan of—and heads down the sidewalk. Thankfully in the direction of the train station. Vivienne's ankles will thank her for a seat soon, nevermind the fact that the night has yet to begin.

But Vivienne pulls up short when Natalie leads her to Appleton's Book Corner.

"Uhh," she says.

With a hand on the door, Natalie gives her a confused frown over her shoulder. She looks at Vivienne, then at the sign, then back to her, then back to the bookstore. The windows are filled with book towers and new release posters, but she can see Codi inside by the registers.

By Dana.

Talking to Dana.

Laughing with Dana.

Oh my god I'll kill her, Vivienne thinks suicidally. Codi is hot enough and confident enough to get *anyone* she wants, so it is not fair that she is hitting on the one girl Vivienne has gotten a phone number from in the past five years. Codi usually prefers men, anyway! (Vivienne had tried barking up that tree long, long ago.)

"Codi?" Natalie calls as she pushes open the door. Vivienne has no chance but to follow her inside.

Codi leans onto the counter, ass out, shockingly *not* in red. She's in a high-necked mesh top with a purple corset overtop, multiple necklaces hanging down. She also has on black short shorts and knee-high boots with buckles up the side. Her hair is up in its usual million tiny braids, with a messy, low bun. In a true twist, she has on purple eyeliner instead of her usual red.

"Oh, hi, Vivienne!" Dana says brightly, already rosy-cheeked from laughing with her new boo. She falters when seeing that she came in with a stranger. "Er, I mean, welcome! Anything I can help you ladies with tonight?"

"Not precisely dressed for book shoppin', I'm afraid," Codi says, pushing off of the counter. "Hey, girls. I was just chattin' with an old friend, thankin' her for doing me a favor."

"You know Leti?" Dana asks.

Natalie and Vivienne stare at her. Codi(?) pinches the bridge of her nose. "Oh, right," she mutters to herself.

"I mean, Leticia," Dana corrects.

"No," Natalie replies blankly. "Well, yes. But we know this mysterious woman as Codi Clarkson."

Dana swivels her attention to Codi(?).

"I go by that now, Haddad. You know how these things are."

And Dana somehow takes this in stride. "Might take me some time to get used to. But this doesn't seem *new*."

Codi shrugs. "Haddad, this is Natalie and Vivienne. Whom you seem to know already."

Dana grins, sheepish, and that rosy tint comes back into her cheeks. "She's been a regular here for the bookstore, so we've struck up a friendship. Of a sort."

"Oh, of a sort?" Codi teases, eyes flashing.

"Excuse me," Natalie breaks in, "I am still confused by this mysterious past and how you two know each other?"

"We served together," Codi chirps.

Like she doesn't completely derail Vivienne's mental shrine to her crush in the process. *Uniform*, she thinks. On loop. Dana in a uniform. She'd known Codi had served for several years, and sure Dana is built like an Amazon, but uniforms were worn. By her. This must be added to the crush shrine at once.

"A Black gal and a brown gal, surrounded by a bunch of white boys with their heads up their asses, we stuck pretty close after we met. Wasn't easy. Took her under my wing," Codi continues.

"And you used my dorm to crash at when you'd been out too late so you wouldn't get caught," Dana wryly adds.

"It was a give-and-take arrangement that turned into true, lastin' friendship."

Codi is friends with Dana. Has been for years. They've all been aware of the large parts of her past that Codi doesn't share with others, and many hunters and witches have changed names. But it is *awkward* to find this out all at once from someone Vivienne is trying to woo.

Is she aware of magic, then? Vivienne warily thinks, preemptively embarrassed. She knows Dana can't see ghosts—the astral projection incident would have been *humiliating*—and she'd never mentioned anything when Vivienne had put out feelers. One does not simply ask Hey Do You Know About Magic. Maybe she should have?

Codi catches her eye and gives a small shake of her head.

That solves that.

How the hell does she know Codi and not know about magic, she then thinks, somewhat irritably. Codi may not have any magical talent herself, but she hunts magical creatures for a *living*.

Then Vivienne remembers the dog photo.

"Oh my god, that was Princess!" Vivienne exclaims.

Dana cocks her head and Codi arches a perfect eyebrow. "Oh, the dogs I was babysitting? Yeah, they were hers."

"I didn't recognize her without that stupid collar," she groans.

"It ain't stupid," Codi retorts. Her two dogs, Princess and Queenie, have literal diamond collars. Because they are spoiled rotten and Vivienne supposes Codi must spend her ridiculous hunter fees *somewhere*. "But yeah, someone had to watch my girls while I was out last week. Couldn't just leave them alone."

"This has been enlightening. Codi, we will of course respect your privacy with your past. Dana, it has been a pleasure meeting you. But we do, unfortunately, have plans tonight, and I'm afraid Isaac and Sam will ditch us if we leave them waiting at the club," Natalie says.

"Fine, don't get your panties in a bunch."

"I'm not able to wear any in this dress."

Dana's eyes widen at her bluntness and Vivienne gapes at Natalie for her betrayal. "Good to know," Codi replies, rolling her eyes, and puts a hand on her hip. "Say, Haddad, why don't you come with us?"

Dana's cheeks darken. "You ass, I'm not dressed for going out like you are."

Vivienne thrills at the prospect of hanging out with Dana, but they are about to celebrate a successful dragon hunting, and Dana doesn't know a thing about the supernatural world. That might get awkward. Oliver had been bad enough to introduce to the world of magic.

"You get off in half an hour. I can get you something to wear. Think about it and call me," Codi says, smooth as sin, and sashays away from the counter.

Dana scowls at her back, but then meets Vivienne's eyes. Her lips part and she looks momentarily torn. Vivienne's heart *thuds* in her chest at the thought that *she* may be a draw for Dana. She may want to spend the night with her just as much as Vivienne might.

But the whole magic thing.

Vivienne opens her mouth to suggest another night.

"Wait," Dana says.

Codi spares her a look over one shoulder, smiling like a cat with a canary. "Yes, sugar?"

"If you're offering, not just to be nice..."

"You know I'd never *just be nice* with you, Haddad. Any offer to party from me is an earnest one. You're fun, and you'll be on me, as thanks for watchin' my girls."

Vivienne inwardly groans. This is a dream and a nightmare rolled into one. How is she supposed to talk with Rory? What if Sam *does* melt into a puddle? The Chaos Club is magically friendly, so who knows what *else* she might see there?

The only choice is to get her so drunk she can't see straight. Clearly.

Or let the secret slip and blame it all on Codi.

Natalie waits by the door, politely lost.

"Do you think your interns would wait half an hour?" Codi asks her.

"I could text him," she replies, flat as a board. It would be impolite to retract the invitation now, but Vivienne can't help but wonder if it annoys Natalie that their celebration is being crashed. She knows she'll like Dana, and Vivienne wants so bad to spend more time with her and find out more about her—like wow, really, serving in the military at the same time as Codi, what else will she discover tonight—but she had already mentioned to Isaac that Oliver wasn't explicitly invited.

It's not her party to plan, but she cannot help the anxiety. She just wants everything to go well, everyone to be friends, and to have a fun night with zero worries.

Vivienne wishes there were a way to surreptitiously fish out the vodka hidden in her cleavage to start pre-gaming harder. She needs more wine smoothie. She needs to be numbed to her own worries, because this isn't her circus or her monkeys. Natalie is paying; Codi is inviting someone else. Vivienne is a bystander and faultless.

They wait until Dana is off.

The replacement manager, a man with curly brown hair and who is clearly trying to avoid the attention of the gaggle of girls, shoots Dana a Look but does not comment. Dana throws her lanyard at him.

"Give me just a moment, please," she says and rushes to the back (after politely retrieving her lanyard).

"Has Isaac responded?" Vivienne asks Natalie.

"No. I'm not surprised."

"Think he'll show?"

"I wouldn't bet either way. Codi, I appreciate your social nature and all of the help you've given us through the years, but do you think it best to invite someone along who knows nothing about... this?"

"She thinks I'm a mercenary, or maybe an assassin," Codi muses, "and she's never asked questions. She's a wonderful gal. Oblivious as all hell. Why, is there a reason she shouldn't be around your interns?"

"You know Sam isn't human," Natalie replies in a low voice.

"Yes, and I don't know much else about him."

"He'll behave," Vivienne cuts in. Now is *not* the time to be discussing demons. "I'll keep an eye on the boys. But what about the club? What about anything *else*?"

"She may not look it, but Haddad is a lightweight. She ain't used to drinkin', and after a magic margarita or two she won't notice anything that ain't sparkly and right under her nose."

"I'm not against playing distraction for her," Vivienne replies. "But I was also supposed to be on Sam duty. I'm only one girl, tragically out of her element here."

"We'll manage. Like I said, she's on me. I'll take responsibility."

"If you're sure," Natalie murmurs. She checks her phone again, with still a lack of response from Isaac. At least if the boys don't show, it's one less risk. (Even if Vivienne *had* been looking forward to a drunken demon.)

Dana comes back, bright-eyed and bushy-tailed, with her polo shirt untucked and unbuttoned in her best attempt to appear less retail worker chic. Her obvious excitement derails any further misgivings. Whatever happens will happen. Oliver found out, and that had yet to bite them in the ass, so Dana couldn't possibly be worse.

The train is too crowded for any of them to sit, but Vivienne makes sure to squish in next to Dana. It may not be a solo date, but they're about to hang out on purpose outside of the bookstore. There will be dancing and drinking and talking about things other than books and dogs. She wonders what kind of drunk Dana will be. She wonders how bad she herself will get. She planned to get sloppy drunk, because this is a celebration and Megan is her (tied) favorite to party with and she has nowhere to be tomorrow, but maybe not the best first impression.

But Vivienne has *never* turned down semi-unlimited free booze before.

The biggest surprise of the evening is not the revelation of Codi's past or Dana's brush with the supernatural community, but that Isaac and Sam are, in fact, waiting outside the club for them.

Oliver had clearly donated to Sam's wardrobe again, and just as clearly, Isaac put all of his own effort into dressing him and none into dressing himself. Isaac, attention solely on his phone, is probably only passably dressy enough for the club in black jeans and a black button-up. His hair is up in a twisted bun instead of his usual ponytail, but he has not forgone his habit of greenery. A black hellebore (for protection) is pinned into his bun.

Sam tears his attention away from Isaac's phone and waves excitedly when he spots them. He has a black leather bomber jacket on overtop a sage button-up, and skinny black pants with high boots. His sandy hair has been artfully swept back. If he's hot in the summer night, he doesn't show it. The only thing not model-worthy about his loaned outfit is the large sodalite amulet around his neck.

"Sam, Isaac!" Vivienne enthusiastically greets, because neither Natalie nor Codi will. She trots over to them, beaming, and shoves Sam's new amulet under his shirt with the pretense of straightening his collar. "Let's not show off unduly, shall we?"

"But Isaac made it for me," Sam pouts. He tugs the necklace back out of his shirt, thumbing the blue stone.

"Anyone as nosy as you would only think it's for self-confidence and pick up lines," Isaac adds. He does not raise his eyes from the video on his phone.

"I thought you two would have cut and run already. I'm glad you waited for us."

"He wouldn't let us leave," Isaac replies, like he is the one bound to follow orders. Vivienne chuckles at that. She is finally discovering a soft spot. Or maybe Isaac is finally developing one?

"Thank you both for coming tonight," Natalie says, nodding in greeting. "Isaac, Sam, this is Dana, a friend of Codi's. And Viv's. She will be joining us tonight. Hammond and Megan are on the way."

Isaac peeks up at Dana, dismisses her, then returns to his video. Vivienne hears gunshots and chatter, so she's guessing more video games.

"It's nice to meet you both. I'm sure I'll forget everyone's names again in an hour or two," Dana says with a pleasant smile.

"You're not dressed right," Sam tells her with a suspicious squint. Vivienne smacks him, but he isn't fazed. "Isaac, you said we had to dress specially for tonight. And even you did it, so I know you weren't teasing me again."

"Ah, I'm just coming off work. This wasn't planned," Dana says, grimacing. Vivienne tries to smack him again, but he catches her wrist, and then her other when she tries again. "Hey now, it's okay. Leti—uh, Codi? You said I could change?"

"Yeah, you ain't getting in without something nicer. Thankfully, I'm a VIP here, and I got plenty of perks, like borrowin' a closet or two."

"I thought I was borrowing something of *yours*!"

"You think I keep a wardrobe at a club? C'mon now. Let's get you appropriate before Ham shows up and steals the show."

Vivienne and Natalie exchange a glance at the thought of a dedicated club wardrobe. Smart. Probably highly exclusive. Vivienne wishes she could try on a few pieces, just to pretend to be a celebrity for the night. Maybe she could find more sequins.

They approach the short line to the entrance, but Codi sidesteps it and waves the bouncer over. She murmurs something in his ear and produces a matte red card.

They're swiftly welcomed in. Dana does not bat an eye at the glamor charm around the bouncer's throat, but to be fair, it's easy to get swept up in the entrance of the Chaos Club. Mirrors and small, twinkling lights—some of them miniature witch lights—line the corridor, creating an endless, sparkly photo-op most influencers would die for. Codi leads the way with confidence and a dazzling smile.

They get to coat check, and only *then* does the music roll over them.

Bass thumps hard enough to make Vivienne's teeth rattle, which makes her wonder if there are fae here tonight. Sam winces at the sudden noise, but Isaac tugs his hand away when he tries to cover his ears.

"You boys go be good and grab our table and some drinks. Should be on the left wall, look for the Dragon Lounge sign," Codi says and seizes Dana by the shoulders. "I'll take a Sazerac, Haddad will have a Long Island Iced Tea, and get a round of afterburners for the table."

Natalie's shoulders droop in a sigh lost to the thumping music. "I'll go with you, it's under my name. Don't forget to give Megan and Hammond's names to the doorman so they can get in."

"Already done! Let's go, let's go!"

Codi manhandles Dana down the tiny hallway, and Vivienne has no choice but to follow. Because she *really* wants to see the club closet.

It looks exactly like coat check, but with full outfits, and not even spaced out to show them off like a celebrity's walk-in. Most hangers have dresses; only about a quarter of the closet is menswear. Vivienne thumbs through sequin-adorned prom-esque dresses. Most, if not all, are not her size. A pity.

"Let's see, you're tall, so that'll be tricky…" Codi whirls through different options, and Dana idly picks through a corner. "You look good in warm tones, but those *legs*—you ain't gonna let me put you in a miniskirt, are you?"

"Not a chance," Dana drawls and examines a long-sleeved crop top. "Are you *sure* I can borrow something here—?"

"What part of VIP status of a special club did you misunderstand?"

"Just go with it. You can't argue with her," Vivienne advises.

"Don't I know it," Dana agrees and lets Codi work.

The first try involves a midi skirt she can't get up her hips. The second try is a navy dress that earns a flat rejection. The third try turns out to be the charm, as it usually is: a black jumpsuit with a wide keyhole cutout and a faux belt with a bow. It's short on Dana, coming well above the ankle, and she doesn't have heels or jewelry to dress up the plain black, but it fits well and Vivienne happily stares at the uncovered chest.

"Well, it works for a night. I don't want to know what the price tag is, so I'll have to punch anyone who spills a drink on me," Dana says, twisting in the mirror on the door. She flashes them both a smile, and Vivienne could swoon. "Thanks. Mostly Codi, but you too, Vivienne. For letting me come along."

"No sweat, sugar!" Codi crows, cutting across whatever sweetness Vivienne could return. She throws an arm around Dana and steers her out into the club proper.

Vivienne had only been in Club Chaos twice before, and she only remembers once. (Mark's twenty-sixth birthday remains a blur.) It is all shiny black, polished walls and floor, with plenty of red and purple neon. The dance floor's low lights pulse with the beat, and shafts of white light visible in the smoke and haze create the only walls. The DJ booth is set in a high corner against the ceiling, windows mirrored, which is good because Vivienne knows half their DJs aren't human. Glamors are *supposedly* enforced here, but it's usually not worth it trying to reprimand drunk spirits.

Their table is enormous, set into the floor, ringed by plush booth seating. Vivienne all but dives in after Dana to ensure a spot next to her, ignoring Codi's laugh. The faux leather will stick to her legs in no time flat, but she's glad not to be tottering around in heels for a moment.

"Sangria," Natalie says, pointing to one pitcher, "and pomegranate margarita. We ended up ordering two rounds of shots because of Isaac. The rest of the drinks are coming."

"Oh, you're actually going to party? I thought you'd be watching your phone all night," Vivienne says, only half teasing.

"A friend of mine is streaming," Isaac says. He glances up from his phone, the light casting his skin sickly pale, and he grins. Ironic, but for a moment, *he* looks like the demonic one. "And Sam wanted to try Fireball. I thought we could all do shots."

"Oh, gross!" Dana says, and Vivienne pretends to gag. "Sorry, I know we just met, but I'm judging you. A little."

"Sam's never drank before," Natalie serenely explains. "He wants to try new things."

"That's mean, Isaac," Vivienne says, and he scowls, more darkly than she deserves. "Sam, lots of drinks have fun names. Ask us for a description first."

"He heard cinnamon and wanted to try it," Natalie replies.

"I haven't drank much either. I never did until I enlisted. But Sam, I can promise you, you are going to try this and regret it for all your life," Dana tells him, solemn as a grave, and puts a hand on his.

Sam blinks at her. This is one of the few people he has interacted with at face value; she is not a customer, she does not know he is a demon, and they are not talking about magic. He looks to Isaac for help, but why he expects help in a social situation from Isaac, Vivienne could never guess.

"I like cinnamon. I think," he finally decides on replying. He pulls his hand away from Dana, still confused, but she merely chuckles.

A server, who may or may not be a love spirit based on his sheer beauty, arrives with a platter full of tiny glasses. Half are smoky red, the other opalescent. Vivienne and Natalie, the ones on the ends of the circular booth, help pass them around.

"Bottom's up!"

"*Saude*!" Codi cheers. They raise their glasses, and she's the first to toss hers back. Vivienne gets the Fireball over with, burning all the way down in a way she knows she'll be feeling the rest of the night, and gleefully watches Sam choke his down. There are several impolite chuckles.

"Does all alcohol taste like this?" Sam asks. His hands hover over the next tiny glass, searching for something to wash the taste out, but his trust of partying has been broken forever. What a pity.

"Not the taste. The burn may be similar, depending on its strength," Natalie replies. She pours him a glass from the sangria. "This will be sweeter, but still strong."

"I love booze newbies," Codi sighs happily, "they're so impressionable. So *fun*."

"I remember," Dana mutters. She glances at the two pitchers, hesitant, so Vivienne pours her a glass, too. "Oh, thanks."

"Better get over the shyness quick if you want to last with this bunch," she replies.

The beautiful server arrives once more with their actual drink orders, and more passing glasses and calling out whose is whose ensues. The chaos of bar nights is fun, if only for the Tetris-like table planning they require.

"Second shots first!" Codi reminds them.

Sam glares at the shiny shot glass like it may bite him, and Natalie, with the foresight of getting water already, sips with a queasy look. Depending on demon physiology, Sam is either going to drink them under the table or be in the running for the biggest lightweight. His competition: Dana (supposedly), Natalie (psychics and alcohol do not mix well), and Vivienne (sort of). Hammond somehow possesses the innate ability of knowing *exactly* when to stop drinking, Codi is a skilled questionably Southern lady, and Megan can speed up their liver's detox rate just to be a brat.

(It's funny to see a tiny, cute enby out-drink an entire bar when Vivienne is not part of the crew trying to do it.)

Hammond arrives just after the afterburners go down and Beautiful Server arrives with a pitcher of water and a notepad to take his order too. (He's definitely some sort of spirit, since he also nods to Rory in greeting.)

"Hammond!" Vivienne squeals and scrambles out of the booth to hug him. He kisses her on both cheeks. She wants to hug Rory, too, but Dana is not drunk yet and, of course, paying polite attention to the newcomer. She settles on a quiet, "Hey."

Hammond bends to kiss Natalie on both cheeks, too, and Sam shies away like he expects the same. "Oh, the shocking guests themselves. Thanks for coming, you two."

"I'm counting an extra head, unless Megan suddenly grew two feet and became Middle Eastern," Rory says, reclining in the air. He is dressed in his usual Ralph Lauren model way, enjoying the lack of price tags and physical clothes.

Hammond, just as sparkly as Vivienne in a rhinestone-studded black dance vest overtop a white long-sleeved dress shirt, turns to Dana with a wicked grin. "Ah, the manager of the bookstore," he says, like he hasn't met her (and knocked her out) before. "Vivienne has told us *so much* about you."

"How'd she get roped into this?" Rory adds.

"As it turns out, Dana and Codi are old friends. Unplanned socializing followed," Natalie answers. "Dana, this is Hammond Two Feather."

"How many people do I get to be ignored by tonight? Unless your crush is suddenly cool with magic," Rory remarks.

Vivienne gives him a small shake of her head. Potions and alcohol don't mix, so it's just her, Hammond, and Sam. (Unless Codi's run-in with the dragon tranq counted as a near-death experience. Doesn't look like it, though.)

Hammond slides into the booth next to Vivienne and Rory hangs over the edge behind them, leaning on her shoulder, just to be annoying. He rubs his cheek against her carefully coiffed hair. "Oh my *god*, I'm going to be so *neglected* tonight! Pay attention to me, bitch. I'm feeling extra needy."

"Shush, you," Hammond says and shoves him into the booth behind them.

Dana cocks her head, and he hastily pretends to brush something off his vest.

"So as far as I understand, drinking in loud places like this is meant to be fun. Alcohol loosens inhibitions, and then that's... fun," Sam says.

"Oh, how far in are you all? This is going to be fun indeed!" Hammond laughs.

"There's dancing, too!" Vivienne exclaims. "Ham, you're gonna regret sitting by me, I am going to need to pee *constantly* and I'm gonna go dance!"

"Not yet, you aren't, you couldn't have had that many without me," Rory replies, hooking his chin over Vivienne's shoulder again.

Vivienne knows he's trying to get a rise out of her. She also knows it will work—later, after more fun and more alcohol. It wouldn't be the worst thing in the world to talk to ghosts, but she'd still rather not look crazy in Dana's eyes. For as long as possible.

"Megan's on the way," Natalie announces after checking her phone. She's already swaying in her seat.

"That's the last of this lot, unless there are more old friends popping up tonight," Codi informs Dana.

"This seems like quite the occasion," Dana says expectantly.

Codi shrugs and stretches. "Just a celebration with some coworkers, sugar! And for you, a thank you, like I said."

Dana scans the crowded table. Vivienne knows she's wondering, *especially* if she thinks Codi is a goddamned assassin, but she still retains enough reservations to not ask outright.

"How long do you think before she asks about something?" Hammond mutters in her ear.

"Inside an hour," Vivienne whisper-yells back. Hopefully Dana isn't turned off by the supernatural and the prospect of dating an exorcist. "Hey, Dana, ever tried pomegranate martinis? Try a glass!" She pours her one without waiting for an answer. "It's one of my favorites. Add a splash of cranberry like this place, too, and it's just." She kisses her fingers like a chef.

"I'll try anything once," Dana gamely replies, and takes a big gulp.

"We should do shots!" Hammond exclaims.

"Shots shots shots!" Rory echoes in tune.

"Rory, shut *up*," Vivienne hisses.

"We already did two rounds. No more shots for a while," Natalie says.

"I'll do some! I want tequila and ginjinha!" Codi says and reaches around both Dana and Vivienne to high-five Hammond. "Here's to survivin' another day together, Ham!"

"It is too early for tequila," Natalie groans. Isaac nods, attention still otherwise on his phone. He has taken his two shots without protest, but otherwise appears unconcerned with the festivities. That won't do at all.

"Isaac," Vivienne coos, leaning over the sticky table, "Isy, drink more with us. What do you want?" He is either going to be the grumpiest or the most fun drunk, and she cannot wait to find out which.

"Sangria is fine for now," he absently replies.

"You can't hear your phone over the music," Sam points out. Isaac shoots him an irritable scowl. "Are all clubs this loud?"

"It's louder over on the dance floor. They have some wards set up to support the sound system," Vivienne replies automatically, then freezes. She glances at Dana out of the corner of her eye; she doesn't seem to have noticed the term ward, or cared about much other than stealthily trying to obtain more pomegranate martini.

Megan finally arrives, flanked by Beautiful Server, and Vivienne wonders what kind of charm he has on the table to know exactly when to appear. More service industry workers should be allowed to use magic.

Megan throws their arms wide and cries, "I have arrived! The party is here!"

Contrary to their usual cutesy style, tonight they're in a sleeveless rainbow crop top and shiny gunmetal shorts. A white tie hangs loosely around their neck and their hair is straightened and slicked back. Vivienne would think them better dressed for a rave, but she's dressed in more sequins than fabric, so she will not judge.

"That Portuguese stuff that Codi always orders!" Megan excitedly tells the server and slides into the booth next to Natalie. They're packed in tight, but amicably so. They lay their head on Natalie's shoulder with a pleased smile.

"Ginjinha," Codi supplies, then, to Hammond, "Told you we should order it."

Isaac looks less than thrilled with Megan's arrival, which Vivienne only happened to notice and also finds interesting. If anything, having a healer around on a drinking night is a good thing.

Megan blinks twice when she registers Dana's presence. "Oh, hello. Vivi, who's your friend?"

"How d'you know she's mine?"

"I thought you two were holding hands under the table."

They most certainly were *not*, and both Vivienne and Dana pull their hands up and into plain view. Vivienne's face flames.

Megan beams at them both. "I'm Megan, nice to meet you!"

"Dana," she mutters, looking anywhere but at Vivienne. "And Codi invited me, actually."

Meggy, how could you, Vivienne privately whines, wishing they would spontaneously develop mindreading powers. Dana has yet to fully relax, surrounded by near-strangers, alcohol not quite knocking them on their asses yet. Soon, hopefully. Vivienne's head does swim a tad when she moves too quickly, though.

More drinks arrive. Vivienne has already lost count of who's ordered what and what number she is on, especially since she's happier to moon at Beautiful Server, but she has a seemingly endless supply of pomegranate martinis. Natalie pointedly orders another pitcher of water.

Megan does shots with Codi and Hammond, Rory cheering them on, and Vivienne cajoles Sam into trying the fruity martini and a tequila shot. The salt perplexes him. She wishes there were more room at the table; she'd love to sidle over and become even more of an enabler.

"Isaac, what're you so busy watching? You should order mimosas with me!" Megan says, flapping their arm across Natalie and Sam's chests to bother him. Isaac scowls harder. "Want straight champagne instead? We can share a bottle! Oh, let's get a bottle for the table!"

"You're peppy tonight," Sam remarks.

"We're celebrating! Any job you come back from alive is a great one!"

Dana stares into her glass, chewing on her bottom lip. Vivienne catches Natalie whisper something in Megan's ear, but right now, Vivienne's enthralled with the thought of chewing on Dana's lip *for* her. She should not have joined in the tequila shots. Did she? It's usually only vodka and tequila that put her straight into horny drunk.

With a gasp, Vivienne remembers her illicit accessory. She shoves her hand into her cleavage—Dana unabashedly stares—and comes up with the half bottle of vodka.

"That's some magic trick," Dana says. Vivienne grins at her. Her grin widens when she notices that Dana's eyes are not on her face. "Oh, um, sorry! That's just—wow. I mean, I could never fit a bottle of anything in my boobs. It's impressive. That. Not the size. That is too. But I just meant the. Um. You know."

"Oh my god you're drunk," Vivienne realizes with glee.

"Getting there," Dana admits. "Probably there. I haven't drank with Codi in years, I forgot what a monster she can be."

"And if you're still creatin' compound sentences, you should have more tequila!" Codi advises and pushes over her own glass. Dana pushes it right back with her tongue stuck out.

"Should we not be able to create compound sentences?" Sam asks.

"No! Definitely not!" Megan cheers. Beautiful Server comes back with a bottle of champagne and a tray of flutes, neither of which Vivienne remembers actually being *ordered*, but Megan lights up and claims it all the same. Natalie looks faintly apprehensive. "C'mon, Sam, you'll like champagne, I bet. Everyone likes champagne!"

"Because it gets you drunk faster with the carbonation in it," Isaac drawls. *Finally*, he turns off his phone, and stows it away. He faces the table for perhaps the first time that night. "Her stream's over," he says with a shrug.

"Oh, who was streaming? Who do you follow?" Megan asks.

Isaac's annoyed expression returns. "A friend. What's it matter."

"Alice was streaming *Overwatch* tonight! I know she's a big deal in gaming. I know her, she's a healer, too. You like gaming, right, Isaac? Have you heard of her?" they press.

Vivienne tries to catch their eye, but Megan ignores her. They're not *that* drunk yet; why are they trying so hard to be friendly toward Isaac? If anything, Sam is the one to tease tonight. Vivienne hopes no one is catching feelings, because Megan deserves *way* better than Isaac.

Isaac grabs his champagne before any toast could be made and downs half of it.

"*Saude!*" Codi cheers, and it starts a late round of cheers. "C'mon Haddad, you too."

"I'm sitting out a few rounds," Dana sheepishly replies.

"Spoilsport!"

"Drinking water between rounds keeps the hangovers away," Hammond wisely advises, and pours Dana a glass. "Always keep hydrated."

"Take a fucking sip, babes," Rory adds just as Vivienne goes to do just that.

She ends up snorting a laugh into her drink. "God—Rory! Stop it!"

Dana looks at her curiously. Vivienne's face heats again. Hammond recovers smoothly and refills Vivienne's half-spilt cup. "Old nickname. Ham, Rory, they're the same, right?"

"Ham and Rory?" Dana laughs, almost snorting herself, which is *adorable*. Illegally adorable, surely. "Ham-Rory. That sure rolls off the tongue."

"Haha, yeah," Vivienne nervously agrees. She glares at Rory out of the corner of her eye.

"Oh, wait, like *hamrammr*! Ham-Ro-Ree, Ham-Ram-Errrrr," Dana says, delighted at her own discovery. She laughs again, then looks down at her water. "I should absolutely drink more water if I'm laughing this stupid."

"I don't think you're stupid," Vivienne says at once.

"What's a *hamrammr*?" Rory asks. "Sounds like some kinda accent, but definitely not... whatever she is. Ain't her last name Haddad?"

"What was that word? Might be my new stage name," Hammond asks, sipping at his champagne like he doesn't have the world's most annoying ghost in his ear. Vivienne surely would've gotten into a wrestling match with him by now if there weren't spectators.

"Oh, it's, uh. Sure, you can have it? My mom used to tell me bedtime stories about it. It's like an old shapeshifter thing, like a Norwegian version of the big bad wolf."

"I don't think I can pass for Scandinavian," Hammond replies with a wry smile.

Dana nods with her own awkward attempt at a smile. It comes out crooked. Another adorable point for her. "I think I definitely need to sit out the next round of drinks. Sorry for being weird about your nickname."

"Come on, let's go dance, then! We can let them finish the bottle while we take a breather," Vivienne suggests, pushing at Hammond to let her out. He graciously slides over. Vivienne scoots free and grabs Dana's hand to tug her out, too.

Once upright, Vivienne has The Moment. The moment where you realize *exactly* how drunk you are. She wobbles a terrifying moment, but Dana grabs her hip and keeps her from yelling timber. Probably best she sits out the next round, too.

"Careful there," Dana says. She keeps her warm hand on Vivienne's waist as she slides out of the booth, too. Her fingers are on her bare skin above the hem of her skirt. Vivienne stares up into her eyes, lost in that small point of warmth, marveling again at their height difference.

"Wanna move again anytime soon, or make googly eyes at each other the entire night?" Rory flatly interjects. Hammond clears his throat.

"Oh, sorry," Dana says and steers Vivienne away with that hand. The music from the dance floor grows louder with every step, a thumping bass to mirror Vivienne's suddenly fast heart. "I'm so glad I wore flats today, even if it's ugly as sin with this outfit. Did you actually want to dance, or were you giving me an out?"

"Both," Vivienne replies with a smile. She grabs Dana's hand again, now leading them. The lights are strobing and neon, adding to the electric atmosphere, and even at the edge of the dance floor, it's crowded. The Chaos Club on a Saturday night—Vivienne steels herself and braves the throng.

The press of bodies is hot and humid, a writhing, living mass swaying to the near-deafening music. Vivienne takes care with each step, since tripping now would surely lead her to being trampled to death, but she already feels more confident and less wasted with Dana's hand in hers.

"Is this Sting?" Dana shouts in her ear.

"What?"

"This song. Isn't it a remix of an old Sting song?"

Vivienne has literally zero idea. Male vocals are about all she can make out.

Dana frowns, adorably, and leans down to tell her, "I had the biggest crush on him when I was in middle school. I'd recognize him. Stop looking at me like that and take my word for it."

"Of course!" Dancing at a magic-friendly club with a pretty lady to a remix of a Sting song. There were worse ways to spend a night.

Vivienne puts Dana's hand back on her hip, and grabs her other to mirror it on the other side. Unfortunately, Vivienne isn't tall enough to comfortably put her arms around Dana's neck, or even reach her shoulders with more than her wrists. Dana laughs at her scowling and switches their positions. Vivienne's hands tremble on Dana's hips. The fabric of the borrowed jumpsuit is irresistibly soft.

They sway for a few moments, finding their rhythm and each other's, beat thumping loud in their ears. Vivienne can hardly tear her eyes from Dana's. She knows her eyes are a beautiful shade of brown, but in the darkness, they look like the warmest black.

Vivienne falls into a merengue step out of habit. Hammond would be proud. Dana mirrors her, even when Vivienne adds more sway to her hips, and soon, she finds herself in the lead. She's only ever taken dance lessons as the follower, so this is a novel thrill.

Or, she *thinks* she is the leader, until Dana takes her hand and spins her. Vivienne finds herself pressed to Dana's front, momentarily frozen in gleeful shock, but a firm grip on her waist gets her moving again in a nasty grind.

More gleeful shock. Vivienne doesn't entirely know how to handle this. She knows how to dance, and she knows how to be filthy about it, but she still feels off-kilter by *this* side of Dana. Do girls do it this way? Whenever she gets Natalie to dance drunk with her, Vivienne usually can't remember it the next morning.

Dana leans down so she's level with Vivienne's ear. She feels her breath, warm and moist. Vivienne wonders if she should turn, capture those lips with her own, figure out once and for all how nasty Dana wants to get on this dance floor.

"I didn't get the chance to say this earlier, but I like your outfit tonight," Dana tells her.

"Oh, thanks!"

"It's really cute on you."

Cute is not what Vivienne is getting from this right now. Cute and pretty are things Dana has called her, and those are Splendid Things to be called. But they are also things girls call each other (and others) all the time. Cute and pretty from a woman's lips are pleasant, but tame. Hell, Vivienne has called Sam *adorable*, and that's a lot less girly platonic.

Vivienne cranes her neck so she's nose-to-nose with Dana. "Just cute?" she prompts.

"More than cute. Sparkly, attention-grabbing, very sexy," Dana amends.

Vivienne smiles so hard her cheeks hurt. "That's better," she says, and thinks of purple prose to return the favor, but her eye catches on *antlers* in the crowd behind Dana's head.

A faun tosses his head off time to the beat. A flower nymph dances next to him, her hair dripping daffodils and peach blossoms. Vivienne is certain she spots the lustrous flash of wings of a fae, too, as the crowd shifts around them.

She *knew* glamors wouldn't be enforced. Who knows what else is dancing around them. Fae can blend in at a glance, but the flower nymph sheds more foliage, and if the faun has antlers out, he probably has furry legs and hooves to match. Vivienne doesn't want this moment to be ruined with the Oh My God What Is *That* conversation.

Dana notices her attention wandering and turns to look.

Vivienne catches her cheeks with both hands, not a thought in her brain aside from vague panic. If Dana has to find out about magic, she wants it to be, well, *magical*, not from sweaty fauns and nymphs dancing near them while not complimenting Vivienne enough.

She blames the alcohol in her system when her distraction tactic turns out to be capturing Dana's mouth in an abrupt, bruising kiss.

Instead of drifting off to sleep, she drifts into a vision. It's not uncommon, but it can be unpleasant, and Natalie wishes instead she could get a full night's rest for once.

The scenery is disjointed, confusingly so; she doesn't understand what she's looking at for a long moment. There is magic in the air, but it's alien. Strange. The ground appears crystalline but ashy, and something pounds at her ears, below audible range.

"Kadishtu n'ghaog, lloignyth," she hears behind her, then a wet sound.

Vivienne's severed head rolls into view.

Natalie rips herself from the vision with tears in her eyes and a scream burning her throat.

CHAPTER 18

IN WHICH EMIL PUNCHES SOMEONE

"And then I kissed her. I didn't want to kiss her like *that*! I mean, I did, but not like *that*," Vivienne groans into the pillow. The icepack on her head does little to dampen her headache. She is certain she is still drunk.

"I really don't have much sympathy for you right now. You ignored my calls and only came over to complain," Mark *tsks*.

"You didn't leave any voicemails! Or text."

"Your inbox is full, idiot. And I didn't text you because I wanted to speak with you in *person*. This is delicate information!"

"So text me that. A 'hey, come over, wanna talk about something important'."

"Then it sounds like we're breaking up."

"But you *could've*."

"And would you have come over?" Mark asks, eyebrow arched.

Vivienne grumbles into the pillow. "Probably not quickly... Had to check on Emil and Christine, and we had a celebration night on Saturday... And Dana came along! Mark, what am I going to *do*?"

"Well, it's Monday, you're still trashed, and if she hasn't called or texted you, then you're fucked."

Vivienne throws the pillow at him with a wounded noise. "Asshole! You're supposed to be comforting me!"

"I'm stating facts, dearest. With as much sympathy as you gave me during *my* time of need. Brynja could've eaten me alive and you wouldn't know!"

"...Brynja?" Vivienne repeats, confused.

Mark smiles wanly.

"I don't eat things while they are still alive," Bryn(ja?) calls from the bathtub. The door is open, which Vivienne thought odd, but if Mark is suddenly buddy-buddy with her, it's one less thing trying to kill him. Good for him. *Of course* he'd be able to befriend a mysterious shapeshifter in no time. He already has a pet rage spirit.

"Well. We're together now. Comfort me and I'll hear you out," Vivienne tells him, more civil now that there may be Actual Developments she may have missed (and not just Mark's usual flair for drama).

Mark rolls his eyes. Loudly. "Well, after you kissed her, what did she do? Push you away and run screaming in the other direction?"

"No, she... I think she kissed back? That's the problem, I can barely remember! I remember we danced, and then Megan joined us, and that had to have happened afterward. Dana hasn't texted me any questions about magic, so I don't think she saw the faun or anyone else."

"And now you're having a gay crisis. How perfectly you, Vivienne. What is your plan of action?"

Vivienne pathetically peeks at him from beneath the ice pack. She doesn't know why she's still humoring him with it. She's cold enough. "Die alone."

"So long as you have a plan. Now, as to what *I* have been up to—"

"You're just mad we didn't invite you along!"

"Well, yes, because *apparently* others got invited, anyway. And I love that club. But Vivienne, please, I'm trying to segue into something important here! Did Natalie explain to you why Codi had another job?"

"No," she grumpily admits, "but Ham mentioned something about that. Nat never told us much, other than she knew about it and okayed it for Codi."

"Well, the other job was for me."

Vivienne grumps at him. She'll grump at him forever. It'll be even worse when the hangover begins in earnest.

"Brynja, dear, would you come out here? This directly involves you."

"No," Brynja calls, also in the Grumpy Club.

"So, her name is Brynja now?" Vivienne asks. Grumpily.

"It has been, and we're going to respect that and the trust she's given us. Me. Now Brynja, dearest, *please* come out here."

"*No*," she calls out, still in the Grumpy Club.

"I know about your other pelts," Mark calmly says.

The silence that follows is weighted and tense. Like the electric calm before a storm.

Vivienne wonders about other pelts—obviously, the seal pelt is hers, and she's supposedly *not* a selkie, but what else uses animal skins? For demanding her help, Mark seems to be several steps ahead of her. *Why* had he demanded she come over if he's this far ahead?

Brynja walks out, and for someone sopping wet and built thick, Vivienne does not hear her approach. She's too woozy to startle properly when she notices the curtain of black hair and the muscular shoulders suddenly leaning over the back of the couch.

Vivienne traces the tattoos on her arms, again. Counting the runes she's already mentally catalogued and always seeking new ones she recognizes. It surprises her how many she *doesn't* recognize. *Seal, elk, fur, stable, form, change,* yet so many more.

Skins, plural, huh?

"What do you mean," Brynja asks, teeth bared. Her nails dig into the couch cushion and her long hair drips onto Vivienne.

"I'd been wondering since we met how you managed to steal a First egg from the tengu. They never bring them out of their realm, and it is easy to spot a human—or anyone human-looking—even at a distance in a crowd of feathered folk. Originally, I had assumed a glamor, or even some sort of shapeshifting potion. Or partners in crime."

Brynja's nails rip into the couch's fabric. Vivienne wishes she weren't directly underneath her, and somewhat between them, but she can't help but be fascinated by her straining biceps as she struggles to keep calm. Somewhat calm. She seems to be failing.

There—Vivienne recognizes a rune that looks a lot like *wing*.

"You *can* change animals," she gasps before she can censor herself.

Brynja's crimson glare snaps down to her.

Supernatural Hunter Tip #50: Shapeshifters have red eyes, but are not the only things that do.

A concern niggles at the back of her mind, unformed, vague, and impossible to pin down.

"I want a decision from you, Brynja. You stay and help us fight what your boss is doing. Or you finally leave our hair and take your issues with you. Either way, I've given you your pelt back, and I have no further ties to keep you here."

What is her boss doing, Vivienne thinks at Mark. *I think we should have discussed this boss and what the hell you think you're doing prior to luring out the angry, beefy shapeshifter. And why the hell did you return the one thing you had keeping her tame?!* And had he said *First* egg? Her brain is way too mushy to be dealing with this shit right now.

"You never speak plainly. What are you doing?" Brynja demands.

"I told you. I want your choice—are you staying or are you leaving? I am not forcing you to stay."

She flinches and rips a fistful of foam and fabric off the couch.

Mark smiles in triumph. Vivienne dearly wants to get out of the crossfire zone, but her alarm with the situation is worsening her headache and she fears she may throw up if she makes any sudden movements. (Plus, she is increasingly worried Brynja will snap into predator mode at said sudden movement.)

"Vivienne, Brynja and I have had a *marvelous* few weeks together. We've learned a lot about each other, haven't we? For example, besides these other skins, I've learned a bit of this boss of hers—"

"Don't speak of it!" Brynja snarls.

"I don't know its name, but I know its goal, and I know it has her scared shitless. And it has something over you—another skin. It kept collateral and turned you loose on the tengu. You wouldn't get it back if you didn't do what it said—"

"You don't know what it's *like*—!"

"I know enough from you!"

Stomach be damned, Vivienne takes her ice pack and slithers over the arm of the couch. She processes what Mark has been up to without telling her; she is not his full-time babysitter, and while she could have checked in earlier, he is causing this scene for the drama of it. She'd thought he had enough of these kinds of theatrics after Benji had almost killed him.

"I'm getting you a dragon pelt," Mark tells her.

Brynja's face falls open into vulnerable, delicate hope, with eyes wide and all tension gone from her frame.

"You're *what*?!" Vivienne screeches.

Mark shares a conspiratorial smile with her, like she's been in on this mad plan all along. Which she *hasn't*. Things would be going better and with less ruined couches if she'd been privy to his machinations. "Nat and I made a deal over the dragon Codi brought down for her. Not ideal, but workable. I didn't need a whole dragon, really, just the skin."

Brynja settles onto the couch Vivienne vacated, cross-legged. Her hair sticks to her like a shield. "You think I can be bought with fresh skin?"

Okay, they're just *going* with the different skins then. That's confirmed. And more confusing than ever. Vivienne has no clue what uses *multiple* skins to transform.

"Dragonskin repels magic. Dragons are huge and powerful and terrifying. You have little to fear if you're a dragon when you want to be."

And this is something we want to be giving away to an unknown woman who pissed off the tengu? Vivienne loudly demands in her brain.

"That god touched this realm and it still almost killed you. What makes you think a dragon would protect me?" Brynja asks.

God, Vivienne thinks. Blankly.

All other muddled thoughts vanish before that simple term.

There are plenty of powerful spirits out there. Angels are closer to biblical horrors than their cherubic pop culture representations. Tricksters can bend reality (or perception, many academics are torn, but what is reality but someone's perception of it?) to their whims. Gumiho, kitsune, and huli jing can cast curses with a flick of their multiple tails. Spirits can control the weather, fairy queens can spend years in a matter of days, and phoenixes defy death. Many of those and more have been called deities throughout history.

But there must be a higher tier to magical beings. There is always another rung up the ladder.

And it sure as hell explains that *thing* that grabbed dragons and knocked out several city blocks.

"You work for a god?" Vivienne croaks.

"See, if you had come when I called, we could've discussed this. When that thing happened in your neck of the woods, I felt it even here, and so did Brynja. She explained a few things then. I figured out a few more things on my own."

"So you are bribing me for further information?" Brynja asks with a hollow laugh. "Information on what, human? Yes, a god is going to break into your realm and take it over. Several are vying. The one during the dragon migration wasn't my master, but I can tell you it must have had allies on this side. Other humans would be easier to sway than I."

"Wait, there's *more* of these things—?!"

"Viv, dear, try to keep up. Maybe keep in better contact with me—"

"I will *throttle* you, Mark Ito! You think this didn't qualify as an emergency?!"

"Nothing is happening quickly. A tengu First egg is a necessary ingredient to get enough magic and spellwork together to get something as enormous as a deity through realm borders. It hasn't been done for millennia. Which means in order to stop this huge magical feat, we just need to monitor who has the rarest ingredients."

"Mirai mentioned other missing eggs," Vivienne agrees, "but we weren't asked to do anything about them. And no one mentioned that this was a *First* egg! And we don't have any leads as to what the *fuck* else is going on here."

Except, they sort of do. Multiple missing tengu eggs all around the same time is a big, flashing arrow pointing in that direction. A god(?) ripping into their realm when a bunch of dragonskin is concentrated in one area is another huge one.

But the *other* finding from the dragon migration is a third, terrible lead.

With a growing queasy feeling, Vivienne asks, "These other angry deities looking to munch on the human realm. Do they know you're here?"

"Likely," Brynja warily replies.

"And they know what you are? With the other skins, that shapeshifting stuff?"

"Likely," she repeats.

Vivienne holds her roiling stomach. "I'm gonna throw up."

"What's wrong, Viv?" Mark asks, only *now* concerned about the emotional fallout of his dramatic reveal.

"Tequila shots is what's wrong," she groans. "But Thomas Novak was the one who tried to kill Codi to prevent her from doing her job. *Your* job. Your job to get a dragon pelt for your new shapeshifting friend. Who else would want to stop her from something we only found out about?"

"Thomas?" Mark repeats. He pales and adjusts his glasses to cover his sudden unbalance. "That is... a lead. Thomas Novak may be in league with someone working against Brynja, and thus us. Oh, that's perfect. *Peachy* perfect. Fucking perfect!"

"Since when are we 'us'?" Brynja deadpans. "Who is this human you are so worried about?"

"The greatest witch in generations, who has the strongest coven in the city at his beck and call. Master of blood magic, huge green thumb, once shot—"

"The point is," Vivienne interrupts, scowling, "we know him. He knows us. And if he knows Codi was in league with Mark, they know about you. This is a mess, we're several steps behind, and *what* are we going to tell Mirai?"

"Oh, well, for starters, Brynja dear, we're going to need that egg back."

"No," she retorts.

"Then I will give you to Mirai. I'm sure being a seal will protect you from six-inch talons."

"Nothing protects you from that," Brynja mutters.

"So, here is what I propose—you give the egg back to us, and we broker a deal about getting your other skin back."

Brynja's eyes narrow to crimson slits and her lip curls. Her canine teeth could give Sam's a run for his money. "What. Skin."

"You snuck into the tengu realm somehow, and you can't stop thinking about white feathers. Mirai certainly didn't have much white on them. So, I was thinking to myself, what would Brynja's cover be if she didn't have a sealskin with her? There aren't many other shapeshifters that use pelts—except, of course, swan maidens. And, not going to lie, the big angry bird image *really* fits with you."

Brynja stays stubbornly silent.

Vivienne could throttle him. "Mark, your extrapolation skills need to come with footnotes. I thought you were getting her a goddamned dragon skin, not swan."

"She already had it. Didn't you, dear?" Mark asks with a sunny smile.

She remains silent.

"One your boss is holding over you as collateral, as you've mentioned. One to get into the tengu realm as a disguise, that had to be a bird obviously, so what? Some sort of half-worn transformation? Frankenstein's swan maiden? Your sealskin, here, as transport? Or disguise once you escaped through the goblin market. You're going to need a disguise to keep nosy humans off your back. But that's not all, right? Look at you, you're clearly a fighter, so I think there's more than an egg stashed somewhere. Something in case you had to fight your way back home, hm?"

"That's not my home. And you are very good at guessing and stealing from other's minds."

"Agreed," Vivienne mutters under her breath.

"So, you don't want us to get the egg because of whatever else you have there. Fine. *You* get it, you return it to us, we negotiate with Mirai. Were you going to give that up as a loss?"

"Better a skin than my life."

"But I'm giving you a dragon pelt on top of freedom!" Mark exclaims, frowning.

"Freedom you cannot guarantee. Not from a god older and stronger than anything you can fathom. I want more insurance than your *words*, human."

"But it's there, and you're here. And *you* hold the key to keeping it that way. If you don't return, don't play fetch for your horrible boss, then everything stays okay."

"Until something bigger and more terrible enters your realm and tears it apart."

"Okay, cutting in before I run off to puke at the horrors Mark is casually describing," Vivienne butts in, arms around her middle, but for the moment, calm enough to speak properly. "These things are in other *realms*. Not ones connected to ours, not connected to the goblin markets. The tengu realm is *only* connected there—they made it themselves that way. If these monstrosities are stuck elsewhere, how did *you* get here? And how are you getting back?"

"It is much easier to slip a being of my size and strength through a crack between realms than something like a god," Brynja primly replies.

"So a matter of scale, fine. What is your plan to return?" Vivienne demands.

"Does it have to do with your dreamwalking?" Mark asks.

"Her *what*."

"Oh, all those calls you missed from me? I may have had a run-in with Tsukiko, that cute baku, but Brynja chased her out of my dreamscape."

"Shapeshifters don't dreamwalk. Period. I don't care what she is, they don't! Spirits only get one!"

"A learned talent," Brynja dryly corrects. "One of the many my master has impressed upon me through the years. Years spent planning this, creating a way for something as small as I to get to your realm."

"No, you don't *learn* that, not in the human realm! Humans dream, and their dreamscapes aren't connected—"

Vivienne's throat closes up in her jarring, abrupt panic.

"Not anymore," Brynja says, shrugging, offhand and dismissive and not at all caring that Vivienne may be the singular person alive who fucking *knows* exactly where she is from.

"I'm going to throw up," Vivienne announces and dashes for the bathroom.

· · · ● · ● · · · ·

Emil shifts from foot to foot while he waits for Nico to finish locking up. The night is unusually cool for July, but he is fine in a thin hoodie overtop his polo; he only fidgets because he wants to get home and eat already. He feels like he's hungry enough for both himself *and* Christine.

"Oh," Christine murmurs, the only warning before a hand comes down on Emil's shoulder.

He must jump a foot in the air. He whirls around to see Javier, who he really only knows as Nico's boyfriend and as the one who bribes the staff with baked goods to let him in the back to surprise said boyfriend.

Javier puts a finger to his lips. Emil scowls, face hot from his embarrassment, and steps aside for the guy to scare his boyfriend.

"I've seen him at the store a few times. He's with your other manager, right?" Christine asks.

Emil nods. Javier throws an arm around Nico's waist, causing him to jump too, so at least Emil feels a *little* vindicated. Guy can tiptoe like no one's business.

Nico chews Javier out for scaring him in front of an employee, like Emil and the others haven't seen this exact scenario play out a dozen times before. Emil tunes them out, because *he hungers*, but he's not so rude as to cut and run before he's officially dismissed from his shift. Even though technically he's pretty sure the shift ends when the door locks.

"They're cute," Christine remarks. Because of course she does. It's one of the girliest things she's ever said. "Um, really weird question, but what color are his eyes?"

Emil gives her a strange look. First was girl comment, then was bizarre comment. But the other two are still right there, so he pulls out his phone and opens up a note app. '*brown i think*' he types and angles it so she can read over his shoulder. '*why??*'

"Just curious!" replies the one who was clearly more than curious.

Javier whispers something into Nico's ear, punctuating it with a nip to the shell of his ear, and Emil rolls his eyes as loud as he can. "I'm still *here*. Can I go home if you two are gonna make out against the front door?"

"Now there's a plan," Javier says, eyebrows waggling, but Nico shoves him away. The store has a family atmosphere they strictly enforce, which means no PDA, especially for the managers. (Vivienne is in for a rude awakening, if *that* mess ever gets sorted out.) No one would ever tattle on their manager for brazenly flirting at work, but Emil is under the impression the old couple who *actually* own the place would be less than thrilled. Especially about the gay thing.

"Get home, Emil. See you tomorrow," Nico tells him.

"Oh, that's not a no to his suggestion, babe."

"Don't *babe* me. You're a menace."

Emil imagines ever being able to call someone babe. It kind of sounds wrong, from a guy to a girl. Normal pet names make him sick, but Russian ones are too hard to explain. And he *still* flinches whenever someone calls him Milya.

Emil ducks out from lovey dovey manager hour because the door is locked and he got permission from the manager, after all. Christine floats after him. It's not late, but it is dark out, and in the middle of the week there aren't so many people out and about. He can risk a conversation.

"What's your deal with Javi?" he asks. Christine has never said anything about Vivienne's blatant flirting with Dana, so he doesn't think she has an issue with the gay thing.

"No, nothing, it was just weird. I thought we locked eyes for a moment? Some people can see ghosts, um, obviously, but I've never run into someone random before."

"He works at a bakery, so I don't think he's the magicky type. Can you bake with luck? Would lucky cupcakes be a thing?"

"I've never tried. This luck thing is new to me, too, and I haven't been able to touch an oven for several months now," she deadpans.

"Oh, you can," comes another voice, smooth as sin.

For the second time that night, Emil jumps. He whirls around and Christine backs away with a frightened squeak.

He doesn't recognize the man in front of him. He's tall and thin, dressed head to toe in a finely fitted charcoal suit, with a pointed nose and eyes squinted in an insincere smile. Emil doesn't register much more than those broad strokes before he notices the *fox ears* and bushy tail wagging behind him.

"Can I help you?" Emil demands. Christine puts him between them.

"I answered your question. You *can* bake with luck, and ingest it in noticeable quantities, although I do not know how that would affect the human digestive system. It's very fragile," the man says. He has a French accent. A French fox spirit, who knew?

The man leans down so he is nose-to-nose with Emil. His smile widens further, past the realm of what human mouths are capable of. Emil cranes his neck to look for Nico or Javier, but they leave in the opposite direction, and the surrounding street is empty.

"So you have a friend, small spirit?" the man asks Christine.

"You know this guy?"

She shakes her head wildly.

"Back off. We're spoken for, by a bakeneko," Emil snaps.

"And she is not here right now," the man points out.

"I have witch friends." He recalls that business card his subway savior gave him. "The Foxglove coven watches out for us."

"They do not. A coven would sooner dissect something halfway than bother with it. And, *mon cher garçon*, the Foxglove coven is women only. You have a lot of bravado for a young human, though, I will give you that. But you are in over your head. You both are."

"G-Go away," Christine stammers out.

"I am not here to eat you. I'd like that collar of yours. I am willing to pay, isn't that generous of me?" The man holds out a gloved hand, and to Emil's amazement, solid chunks of gold bubble up out of the black leather. In moments, the man is holding a trio of gold nuggets.

"Is that gold? *Actual* gold?" he can't help but ask. Kirara only makes little fire balls and luck dust. Why the hell couldn't he have gotten a spirit that makes *money*?

The man chuckles. "It certainly isn't solid luck. Humans still like gold. I think they always will. How about it, little human? Would you trade your friend for this price?"

Emil shuts his wonder down *hard*. He backs up a step, teeth bared, and is about to snap back at this presumptuous asshole, but when he backs up, he backs *into* Christine. Emil falters, she squeaks, and he twists around to stare at her. She stares back, lamplight eyes huge, mouth agape.

"Watch out!" she cries and Emil snaps back to attention.

The fox man reaches for them, and with only half a thought, Emil punches him in the face. His nose gives way with a *crunch* and Emil reels his aching hand back with a hiss of pain.

The gold nuggets *clunk* to the ground, and the man scrambles back, clutching his bleeding nose. "You little *shit*!" he snarls.

"Run!" Emil shouts. Christine can't run, but she can float, and it's faster than nothing. But it is *not* a sprint. She can go through walls, but he doesn't want to shove her into a building and split up. He'd only end up by himself.

Emil grabs at her hand, fingers sliding through fingers, and looks for some way they can beat a hasty retreat. Nothing jumps out at him.

But the man only snarls at them again, a full animalistic growl, and turns into a black fox. He curls in the air, paws over his snout, and glowers at them from his spot half a block down.

"My kindness has run out," he growls, then vanishes with a *pop*.

Emil stands on the corner with his chest heaving. "He... didn't chase us."

"You broke his nose," Christine points out. Her voice wavers like she's out of breath, too. "He chased me, but only a little ways, last time..."

"So you *do* know him."

"Only once! He was a jerk. He wants this collar," she replies, hands on the leather collar. The bell *dings* at her touch, as if on cue. "It must be valuable. Maybe it's the thing making the luck, not me..."

"Luck is valuable, I guess? But you're doing it, too, didn't Vivienne say it was in your hair now? And you can manipulate luck. Cat collars can't do that."

She peers up at him, hands still at her throat, bottom lip wobbling. "I suppose. Um, thank you. For defending me. I-I wasn't expecting you to."

"Why wouldn't I?"

"Uh, that was an adult spirit, and the only other spirit we know likes to set things on fire and has big claws?"

"I'm not sure that guy was much of a fighter. Seems like the type to buy his way out of trouble," Emil says, glancing back at where the asshole fox had disappeared.

The earlier amazement returns in full force: the gold nuggets are still there, glinting on the sidewalk.

"Holy shit. What are the chances those things are cursed?"

"I think only multi-tailed fox spirits can cast curses? Wait—Emil, we shouldn't!"

"We shouldn't what, steal from the guy who tried to mug you? Maybe eat you? He can make this stuff, I doubt his wallet will miss it." Emil dashes over and scoops up the nearest. It's heavy for its size. That means it's actual gold, right? "Oh my shit. No, Christine, we're keeping this. We deserve a windfall!"

"You've made how much off scratch cards?" she asks in return, voice arch.

"For a luck spirit, you don't like to get lucky, do you?"

"I'll work on it."

· · • • • • • • · ·

Natalie sings her aunt's old lullaby to the love potion. For some reason, lullabies work well, usually better than love songs. She stirs evenly, never allowing it to splash, voice tired but still going strong. It'll be another hour yet before she's done.

Isaac has already retreated to his cozy corner in the backroom, but Sam nominally helps her out front. There has only been one customer today, an old regular for a plant care potion, and Natalie doesn't expect anyone else. It has been two weeks since the migration, and Thomas has not shown his face again. He'll be running out of his dreamless sleep draught soon.

So many futures where he hasn't done this, she thinks with a mental sigh. Natalie has done all she could to monitor any bad players. She thought she'd avoided them.

But there have always been so many futures where he *did* do this. There are still a wide variety of paths this can take, and some are more pleasant than others. He can still be stopped. Up until the end, he can be stopped. Natalie plans on it.

"What does friendship mean?" Sam asks, apropos of nothing.

Natalie glances at him. She is still singing, he knows this, and she's discovered he does not understand sign language. She tilts her head at him to continue. She can at least hear him out while he navigates having emotions and relationships. (A friendly ear often does more to ease pain than any potion she sells.)

"Oliver says he and Isaac are friends, but he seems annoyed by him. Isaac says he and this Walker voice are friends, but he never spends time with her in person. Vivienne said we could be friends. She said you two are friends. Why is friendship so *broad*?" Sam sighs with all the angst of a middle-schooler facing his first school dance.

Natalie shrugs. She wishes she could offer more to him. She wishes she knew the answer herself. '*I don't know*' she signs. '*Friendship is difficult, but it's important to have.*'

Sam squints at her hands, uncomprehending. Natalie wonders if Isaac knows any ASL, and if she could offer to teach either of them. Isaac seems he'd rather eat his hands than accept help from her, however.

He knew about the apocalypse, she thinks, *and that is why he wanted a demon for something. I wish he would tell me what that spell was.* She thinks she knows, but gleaning information from visions of the future is far from a perfect science. And with magic that strong, you don't want to guess.

"What's a tengu friend?" Sam asks, and Natalie hiccups her song.

The potion hisses and spits at her, and she tries to regain the tune, but the potion has decided it's had enough. It churns in the pot and splashes out, turning from a rosy pink to frigid, rotten white.

Natalie hastens back, dropping her spoon, and looks for something to cover the pot with. Sam throws one of her kitchen towels over it before she can ask.

The potion burps once more, then quiets, ruined but not likely to explode. "Thank you," she says, a touch raspy. That will be a pain to recreate, but she can wait another day.

"Did I do that? I'm sorry," he replies like a guilty child.

"It's fine. No one got hurt. Where did you hear about tengu friends? Has Vivienne dealt more with that magpie tengu?"

"Mirai?" Sam asks, cocking his head.

The name sounds right, though how *he* knows, she doesn't have the faintest idea. But she has a bad feeling about this. And psychics know to trust their bad feelings. "Have you run into Mirai, the magpie tengu? Has Vivienne asked for your help finding an egg?" Natalie asks.

"They *were* looking for an egg. I guess it makes sense that Vivienne is looking, too. I think Mirai mentioned asking humans for help."

"Sam, *when* did you meet Mirai? Has Isaac taken you to any of the goblin markets? Does your amulet work?"

He thumbs the blue stone hanging from his neck, breaking into a pleased grin. "I haven't been anywhere new aside from that club, but it works, like he said it would. I can't even stretch my limbs with it on. I'm perfectly settled."

"You should have been within hours of being summoned."

"Oh, well."

"Sam. How do you know Mirai?"

"The bird person who helped us during the migration? The one who burned Isaac to make him stop bleeding."

Natalie screams inwardly, but she has always been able to maintain her poker face. She hardly remembers the fallout from the dragon migration, not much at all after her seizure. Megan had informed her of most of the damage done and nowhere had tengu cauterization been mentioned.

"And did they mention anyone being tengu friend?" Natalie calmly asks.

"Me? But I haven't seen them since. I'm not sure what their friendship is going to be like, since I don't want to get annoyed with them. Isaac didn't seem happy about it, then he seemed *too* happy, and I can't read him at all. Being friends with nonhumans is different than with humans, right?"

Oh my god, the demon became tengu friend, Natalie thinks, still screaming inside her brain. Of course Isaac didn't mention this to anyone. That could be his escape route. From Natalie or an apocalypse, she doesn't know.

Natalie believes in honesty, but she also believes in harmless lies and omissions of truth in the name of peace. She will not coerce Isaac into playing at friends longer than he likes, she will not obstruct his movements out of spite, and she will not tattle on him unless he becomes a direct danger to her or her loved ones.

But if he doesn't want to play at friends, then she doesn't see the need to be overly friendly, either. She only wants one thing from him. The rest is his business.

"Yes, nonhuman friendship can be very different," Natalie tells Sam. "It can lead to some cultural clashing, miscommunication, and other issues. But that is the same as with any friendship. They are still someone who wants to be your friend. Do your best, Sam."

"What *is* my best? Friendliness annoys Isaac."

"It doesn't annoy Vivienne or myself. Isaac has a thick shell, but he is only scared and protecting himself."

Sam shoots her a suspicious squint. "Scared of that big hand, you mean? Scared enough to start some spell with me?"

"Yes."

"How did he know that it was coming to be scared of it?"

"I would also like to know that. I can see possible futures, and I—"

"*You* saw that thing coming? Why didn't you warn anyone?" Sam hotly interrupts. "People got hurt at that migration job! Isaac got really hurt and Codi got really hurt. Shouldn't friends warn each other about danger?"

"I see *possible* futures," Natalie icily replies. She has heard these accusations before, but not in many years. Most of the magical community knows about her abilities and their limitations by now. "I have seen two futures where you have eaten Isaac. Do you want me to discuss those?"

Sam stays silent, anger gone, replaced by confused fear.

Natalie sighs. She keeps the towel on top of her pot and uses it to protect her hands as she carries it toward the sink. "Bring me the powdered charcoal and the dried alkanet, please. I'll need the alkanet ground and mixed into the water before we can pour this down the drain."

Sam fetches the items for her. He slinks around her shop like a kicked dog; she has not seen him act like this since he'd been summoned, and even then, the behavior had been tempered by his curiosity at the world.

"I have seen many, *many* futures. I've been precognitive all my life, and began recording my visions to the best of my ability when I was in the second grade. I have notebooks upon notebooks filled with things that will never happen. I've developed a slight skill to determine which futures are likelier than others, but it is not and never will be perfect. I am doing the best I can with the conflicting information I have."

"Okay," Sam quietly replies. He stays as far as possible from her while remaining at the counter to grind the herbs for her.

"I have seen two visions of that atrocity attacking the dragon migration, one of which ended in everyone's death. The other incited coven involvement and led to wide-spread—more widespread—panic. I have seen many visions with Isaac, and he has been singularly the most contradictory person I've had the displeasure of sorting through.

"I have foreseen tragedy, and accidents, and chaos, and pain, and death, all more times than I can count. I have also seen joy, and weddings, and births, and friendship, and accomplishments, and genuine happiness. I have been in therapy for the cognitive dissonance since I was nine. I do not share everything, not half, not even a quarter. Vivienne can read some of my records, and others I trust can as well. Because they're my friends. But I am also protecting my friends by *not* sharing every possible future, because that would drive them mad. Ignorance can be bliss, and sometimes, Sam, protection is *not* sharing everything."

"Okay," he repeats and slides across a bowl of ground alkanet. "I understand. Sorry."

"I don't need an apology from you. I only ask for understanding."

"Okay. ...So Isaac knew about one of these bad futures, and I was going to stop it for him?"

Natalie shrugs. "I highly doubt that. A demon is stronger than a human, and can overpower a witch, too. But a skilled witch or any number of higher spirits can also kill them. I believe the fact that demons are the strongest thing one can summon without a sacrifice was more key to Isaac's plan for you."

She has more pieces to the puzzle of Isaac's plan than that, but the demon does not need to know them. Educated guesses, based on what she has seen of various futures. She didn't see Sam becoming tengu friend, but it is always harder to pay attention to strangers (even spirits), and there are larger, worse things she had never seen coming.

Natalie pulls her wet hair over her shoulder and turns her face into the spray. She's indulging in an extra hot and extra long shower tonight.

So it shouldn't be a surprise that her relaxed state leads her to slip into a vision.

She recognizes the setting immediately: it's the Old Moon Ball. She can't be certain which year it may be, since visions rarely come with a calendar in sight, and formalwear does not lend itself to dating as well as casual fashion can.

The vision settles on Mark and Vivienne, who are in perfect dance frame, finishing up a waltz. Smooth dances don't suit their height difference, but they've had years of dancing practice together, cajoled into lessons by Hammond. It's nice to see that some things remain constant, no matter the future.

What's shocking is that Hammond is here, however. He claps and whoops from the sidelines, dressed immaculately in a full black tuxedo, hair pinned up for the night. Vivienne flounces over to him—her midnight blue dress is very poofy, so flounce is the right word for it—and beams and preens and accepts all his compliments with her usual pride. Both of them wear the flower crowns they'd been gifted for the evening. Rosemary and snapdragon for Hammond, larkspur and forget-me-nots for Vivienne.

When Natalie comes back to the hot water, she finds herself puzzling over those flower choices for each of them. Perhaps she'll be able to get a date for this vision, after all.

CHAPTER 19

IN WHICH A FEW THINGS ARE EXPLAINED

"What did you call us both here for, my dear?" Mark asks with a sidelong glance at Natalie. "It's been some time since I've seen either of you requisition a coven house for anything."

"*Technically*, this is a rec center, with all the normal routes to use its facilities that that entails. That it has muting charms and privacy wards is a bonus," Vivienne primly points out. (She'd refreshed several of the wards on her way in. This is not something to be sharing around just yet, if at all.)

"Does this have anything to do with the shapeshifter Mark is harboring?" Natalie asks without judgment.

Of course, Mark hardly takes it neutrally. "Don't put this on me, miss psychic. I may not be able to read your mind, but I *know* you've known about some of this prior to this."

"That's true," she blandly replies.

Supernatural Hunter Tip #39: Clairvoyance can be stopped with the proper mental shielding. Always practice mental shielding (because clairvoyants are annoying).

"Okay, this isn't pointing fingers. We all know how psychics operate here," Vivienne interrupts, flat as a board. She pats the whiteboard behind her. "*My* meeting time! You both know things, but different puzzle pieces, and I've realized *I* know some uncomfortable puzzle pieces too. So let's be friends and put it all together and stop something nasty from happening."

"There is an apocalypse coming. Probably," Natalie says at once. She sips at her tea like this is a normal remark to make. Even for them, that's pushing it to hell and back.

"Some sort of horrible old god is trying to break realm borders to get into the human realm, presumably to eat us all, wreak havoc, and destroy the world. But it's still in whatever other realm, one that is not connected to anything we're already connected to, and moving something so massive and powerful is not easy. Brynja has agreed to help us stop her old boss."

"There are others," Natalie points out.

"I don't remember her *agreeing* to your bribe," Vivienne adds. Still, she turns to write on the whiteboard: 'Brynja' and 'old god' and 'other realm'.

"She *did* agree, mostly, but with a few catches. Like getting her other skins back for her, which includes from that nasty old boss of hers. And Mirai. But if we can get the egg back, we could trade."

"You two need to secure tengu friend status for you both in that deal," Natalie pipes up. Mark scowls at her, but Vivienne shoots her a confused look. "Sam has tengu friend status."

"Sam?" Mark asks.

"The demon," Vivienne groans. "You're telling me—that *bird person* he mentioned—dear fucking god. And of course, Isaac didn't want to share all of this with us."

"Isaac knew about a coming apocalypse, too," Natalie replies, "and I believe tengu friend status could be an escape route if he needs to cut town. I will not stop him, but I need that spell from him."

"You've seen it?"

"Wait, you two, *who* are these people? Demons?"

"Okay, remember, I told you Nat had her own dirty laundry and pet demon? That's Sam, and Isaac is his summoner, and really Marky-poo, keep up here! Sam is a nice little bean, but apparently a tengu friend now, so a little scarier. You know what kind of spell Isaac wrote that he was going to feed Sam to?"

"*Wrote*?" Mark asks. He scrunches his nose in confused displeasure, then demands, "You two, explain more properly! Is he working with Adam?"

"No, the little shit *is* a spellwriter. That's how no one saw him raising a demon beneath our noses, and why his created spell is so interesting. Keep up! Spellwriter with a demon who's friendly to youkai. We need him to give us that spell, apparently?"

"I don't entirely know what it does," Natalie admits, "but he knew about the apocalypse, and he had confidence in this spell regarding that. So I would like to keep him closer rather than farther, even if that means harboring him from the covens. Megan unfortunately knows about them, but they've kept it quiet from Deirdre so far."

"Well, if we're infodumping vital information, then Brynja has confirmed that there are at least two others trying concurrently to take over our realm. Some sort of ancient deity arms race. One of them was the thing that fucked with the dragon migration and short-circuited all the psychics in the city—yeah, I talked to Alex, he had a seizure too—and apparently didn't want Brynja to get that dragon pelt I purchased from you. So that's onto her and Yaehathal's plan, and it has a way to fuck with us here and now, via Thomas Novak. Yay for us. She didn't know that one's name, only that it's in yet *another* other realm."

"Oh, my turn!" Vivienne exclaims. She finishes writing these additions to the whiteboard; the relations and ordering can come after everyone is honest with one another for five minutes.

"I know you've been an accidental liaison between us, Viv," Natalie begins, but Vivienne finishes her writing with a flourish and turns to them with a wide grin.

"More than that! *I* know where Brynja came from. You figure out what she is yet, either? That definitely sounds Scandinavian or something."

"Oh, she's definitely Nordic. She had these super long Viking-sounding titles, but I couldn't remember any of them, since this friendship happened in a dream. That I needed reminded of after the fact. Natalie, dear, do *you* know what kind of shapeshifter can dreamwalk?"

"I have only seen this woman in visions. I know little about her except what future potential actions could be."

Vivienne interjects. "No, the dreamwalking has nothing to do with her! I still don't know what she is, but I do know she was human—especially if she had old human names—and I know how *she* got from the human realm to the hell place where her god-boss is. She wasn't lying when she said it was a learned skill."

"Well?" Mark prompts with an unimpressed look. "Do tell, Viv. I cannot wait for what arcane bullshit you give me this time."

She *wishes* it were arcane bullshit. Well, it technically is, but nothing she learned through weird research this time. It had been learned through unfortunate experience instead. "Sooooo. You remember my accident? And I got my stalker? The place was called the Dreamlands. It *used* to be a giant shared dreamscape where human dreamers could travel to, but it got cut off from the human realm *centuries* ago. I think that's how Brynja got from Point A to Point B. Then it got sealed with that thing in it, and she got banished along with it. Now it's trying to get that access back."

"A centuries-old shapeshifter? Most are restricted to somewhat human lifespans. You said she was... Nordic? Like Norwegian?" Natalie asks.

"Good a guess as any," Mark says with a shrug.

"Vivienne, could you ask Dana if she knows anything like that?"

Vivienne nearly drops the marker as she fumbles in her surprise. "D-Dana? Why would I do that? She's not magic."

"She said her mother was Norwegian. She mentioned that wolf thing on our celebration night."

Vivienne avoids eye contact, because she's guilty as hell, and clicks and unclicks the marker cap. "I still don't think that's a good idea. She's not magic, and old lore is usually so far removed from what present-day spirits are—"

"But this one is old, too. It is a start."

"Viv," Mark begins, and she avoids eye contact even harder. The whiteboard is suddenly quite interesting. "Vivienne. Darling. Doll. Dearest. Have you not talked to Dana since that night?"

"I haven't needed to go to the store, I have Emil's number now..."

"Vivienne," Natalie preemptively scolds. "You like her, and that's—"

"She hasn't texted me, either! This is a two-way street!" Vivienne defensively exclaims. "I'm pretty sure we kissed, I was sloppy drunk, who knows *what else* happened, and now she's not talking to me."

"And you're not talking to her. Maybe she believes you're avoiding *her*," Natalie replies. With judgment this time. Unfair judgment. Vivienne doesn't deserve this.

"When you and Hayley were flirting, before you were together, didn't you have any will-she-won't-she angst? Flirting is *hard*. Pre-dating is hard. Getting drunk around someone you like is hard."

"Hayley asked me to hold hands the second time we met. She should not be held as a standard of flirting. And look at this from Dana's point of view—she was invited along to a celebration with a friend group, she only knew two people, and now one of them isn't talking to her. Don't you think *she* thinks she may have messed up?"

Vivienne sulks. "I hate it when you're reasonable in the face of my worry. But that's still a thin lead to follow—shouldn't we probe Brynja for more information?"

"I think this situation is one that is best to cast a wide net with. And I also personally think that you two should speak again. You're cute together."

"Aw, I only saw the beginning of this gay debacle. I want to see them again now," Mark pouts.

"The apocalypse. We were talking about that? The impending end of days, destroyer of worlds, bringer of death? I think that's more important than my love life!" Vivienne exclaims and slaps the whiteboard again.

"It is, but your love life is also potentially involving Norse story time, which we may need. I know nothing else about Old Norse lore or history outside of watching the *Thor* movies. Somehow, I don't think those are something we ought to rely on," Mark replies with a falsely thoughtful air.

"Show them to your new roommate. Maybe it'll get her talking, if only to correct everything. She's talkative when arguing with you."

"Noted and already taken advantage of. That said, I'll handle her. I'm working on getting her used to Fiona and Benji, while letting her warm up to the idea of not killing us all. You know, friendship baby steps," Mark says.

"Be very careful with her, Mark. I have not seen many pleasant things from her," Natalie advises with another sip of her tea, calm as can be.

"Is fraternizing with her the reason I get mauled by a tengu?" Vivienne asks.

"I don't know. They're certainly no fans of her, if she did successfully steal a First egg."

Mark shrugs. "She's never denied having one, and Mirai said there were witnesses. We're just lucky getting that egg back trumps any retaliation they want. If she doesn't actually have the egg, there would be a lot of angry feathers flying, and we'd probably have a dead shapeshifter on our hands. And speaking of eggs! That seems to be a key ingredient in powering whatever dimensional rift they're trying to sneak through. So we can follow those other missing egg leads that Mirai mentioned. Volunteer to help."

"Speaking of, *I'm* still the one doing the groundwork for that. You haven't even gotten the egg back from the *known* thief," Vivienne retorts.

"Thomas Novak does not have a First egg yet," Natalie serenely points out, "so we need to prevent him from obtaining one at all costs."

"Wait, if *he* doesn't have it, then who the hell has stolen other eggs? Fearing a god-thing that can horrifically eat you and stuff is one motivator, but what the hell else would do it? Mirai seems unusually sweet for a tengu, *especially* a crow. If anyone else decides to go hunting in the human realm, there will be swift and wide bloodshed, and I can't think of many reasons to risk that."

"Unless they weren't in the human realm."

"The tengu practically live in the goblin markets. Plus plenty of other spirits who'd love to schmooze. *Also*, there are only so many realms you can access! Hence the whole stealing hugely powerful magical artifacts from hugely powerful scary spirits to try to make new doorways!" Vivienne exclaims.

"I don't have all the answers, Vivienne. I feel as if I barely have any," Natalie replies, with as much frustration as she ever shows. "But we've come up with joint leads. Mark, continue befriending your... Continue getting to know Brynja. Please, *please* try to get on her good side—she is not someone we wish to have as an enemy. Viv, please talk to Dana about what she could be."

"If we're friendshipping, what's it matter what she is, exactly? We know she's a shapeshifter and we know she uses animal pelts."

"Because the last thing we need when facing a potential apocalypse is surprises," Natalie reminds them.

• • • • • • • • • •

Isaac knows the sound of Natalie turning her Open sign to Closed. He looks up hopefully, but she rewards that hope with a disappointed look. Of course he couldn't get out early. "The shop is closing because I need to run some errands."

"We've watched the store without you before," Sam points out.

Isaac does not point out that they also sold a horribly expensive, horribly dangerous potion to a minor for ten dollars. Natalie, kindly, also does not point this out.

"You two are coming with me on these errands. Now that you have an amulet to keep your form more stable, I'd like your help with goblin market runs."

"And if I said that it wasn't worth the risk?" Isaac asks in response.

Natalie spares him another cool look. "First, I doubt you have so little confidence in a charm you yourself made. Second, I was not asking. Third, there is already such a broad mixture of loosely defined people in the market, I doubt anyone would notice him. Even if they do, other spirits are not the ones to spurn demon summoning. And even if, all this aside, someone accosts you, you have my full permission and my full help to fight back."

This isn't worth the fight. Isaac sighs in defeat. "Fine, we will be your pack mules. What's so important or heavy you need us to come along?"

"Graham has finished processing the dragon. We're to pick up the hide and many of the organs today, and I'd rather not haul such valuable material with only one set of eyes on it."

"I'm not a bodyguard."

"No. As you said, you are a pack mule," Natalie replies. "The weather should be similar to here, so you don't need jackets, and I will cover your fare. You're welcome to do any shopping of your own, but I'd like for us to stick together."

"No thanks. Don't need anything." Isaac has rarely been to the goblin market. He understands the value of a huge melting pot of goods and services and beings, but he's a spellwriter. If he needs something, he makes it.

Sam already looks *so* excited to go, however. Isaac bites back the rest of his complaints. It's been some time since their maybe-fight and Sam had called him mean. Isaac has definitely been called worse, but not by someone he lives full-time with, and for some annoying reason, the remark still sits with him. Sam may have been an unwanted accident, but he's still nominally living and nominally a person. Isaac isn't a nice person, but he can at least be neutral to him instead of cruel.

They take a car there, which is another new experience for Sam. He may vibrate out of the amulet and out of his own human skin at this rate. Isaac understands that spirits regard regular human activities with wonder, but he's had Sam for four months. It has to wear off *sometime*.

"Why doesn't Vivienne like cars?" Sam asks as soon as they arrive. "That was so fast, and clean, and better than the trains!"

Natalie turns to him in open surprise.

Sam cocks his head, guileless as ever. "When she had to run to that other friend's for that emergency, and she left us in charge, and we sold that potion to Emil? She was swearing about whether or not to take an Uber. I know those are cars."

"Oh. Well, no, she doesn't like cars. She was in an accident a few years ago." Natalie guides them to the market door, and hands them each their fare, but pauses before Sam's open palm. "You're very observant, Sam."

"Thank you," he replies, nonplussed.

Natalie spares Isaac another look, as if blaming him for his demon's memory. "Let's go. Stay close, if you'd please. I'd rather not have to force anyone to hold hands in the crowd."

Sam grabs Isaac's hand, anyway. Isaac gives a halfhearted yank, but as soon as they're through the door, he lets it be. Evidently, today is a busy day at the market. Great.

Natalie leads them, but every three steps she looks back to ensure they're still together, and Isaac *almost* wants to submit to holding her, too, if only so she'd stop. Then again, if they get separated, he's uncertain how to find her again. Cell phones don't work in other realms, Isaac doesn't have finding magic, and short of seeing if Sam has developed bloodhound senses, it may be a messy game of Marco Polo.

Graham Yu's stall is thankfully off of the biggest street. Isaac knows he's one of the few humans to have a permanent stall here, and it immediately becomes apparent why: he has half a farm behind his table. There is a pair of fenghuang preening, a barghest with a wagging tail beside him, a jackalope in a pen, and a mare and foal *unicorn* duo tethered behind him.

"Hello, Graham. I see you're as busy as usual," Natalie greets with a nod.

Isaac knows of him, but it's his first time meeting the man, and he is not what he expected. He wears a tailored vest over a white button-down, glasses pushed back into close-cropped hair, but his immaculate dress is ruined by his enormous, stained leather work gloves.

Graham breaks into a perfect smile. "Natalie! My troublesome psychic friend. Thank you for picking up your parts on such short notice. And I'm glad you've brought helpers, because I've already had a qilin try to buy the dragon heart off of me. It's only a matter of time before the fae hear about it."

The pile of scales behind his chair that Isaac had *assumed* was the dragon pelt uncoils and slithers into a stretch. It reveals itself to be a basilisk, a blindfold knotted securely in its feathery mane. It sits as tall as Isaac, and when it yawns, it shows off teeth as long as his forearm.

"What is ready today?" Natalie asks, completely ignoring the massive snake. "I know you mentioned the pelt, and I assume the heart?"

"Most of the organs, the hide, and I've pulled the teeth. The fire sac almost ruptured, so it's in stasis, and I'll be discounting the services for that, but as of right now it's still in one piece. Just be careful with it."

"Thank you, Graham."

"Not entirely sure why you asked for the hide not to be treated or preserved, though. It's still pretty messy," he says expectantly.

"I'm not keeping it myself, so I'm not entirely sure. But I will be careful with the mess, too," she replies. Isaac can respect her polite sense of privacy. "Sam, I'm giving you the potentially smelly job of carrying that hide. I'm sorry in advance, but please, be careful with it."

Isaac can also respect her sense for taking advantage of an opportunity. Sam will have a cover in case the amulet isn't up to snuff, and should they get mugged for dragon parts, anyone who targets Sam is in for a nasty surprise. (Aside from his demonic hardiness, however, Isaac privately thinks he may be the least threat among the three of them.)

"Part of my payment will be a favor. A minor job. I have what I want in mind, but I have to work out a few more details before committing," Graham says while shifting things beneath his stall to look for the dragon parts, "so I'll call you whenever I set that up. Probably the next new moon."

"I'll keep that in mind. Thank you for your help and fair pricing with all of this, despite how little it went to plan," she replies. Graham beams at her when he pops back up with a pile of things.

They divvy up the goods. Isaac and Natalie end up with unwieldy coolers and they give Sam a canvas duffel bag stuffed round. It crinkles when it moves. Isaac keeps a wary eye on the blindfolded basilisk, but it doesn't have any interest in the market at large, much less the strangers in front of the stall. Graham Yu must be incredibly brave or incredibly crazy to keep such a menagerie out in the open; Isaac must wonder what he keeps *secret*.

Marching through crowds with a heavy cooler in his arms reminds him of helping Oliver set up for office parties (that he ducked out of as soon as feasible). He could cut and run and end up with several thousand dollars' worth of goods, six digits easy if he has the heart, but that would require more effort and antagonism than he ever wishes. Natalie, for all her nosiness and control, is a safe umbrella to wait under.

"This way, please," Natalie calls, though they're only two steps behind. No more holding hands, though Sam shifts closer and closer until Isaac's afraid he'll get stepped on.

They take another route back toward the door—or so Isaac thinks, until it becomes apparent that Natalie wants to go *shopping*. They meander down another major road of the market, more crowded than ever, and Isaac thinks his fingers may break with how hard he grips the cooler. He doesn't do well with crowds. Maybe he'll chuck it into the throng and run for it.

"Couldn't we have done this *before* hauling around all the expensive things?" Isaac grouses while Natalie looks over a rack of jewelry with a mermaid in a tank smiling behind the stall.

"Why would I want to bring these things *twice* through the market? I'm using several as bartering tools today."

Isaac shouldn't have skipped arm day. (He's regretting skipping so many gym sessions with Oliver more and more in very specific circumstances, and he hates all of them.) The cooler is too large to shift to carry under an arm. He shouldn't have accepted pack mule status with no complaint. Alas, alas, alas.

"Do you want to swap?" Sam whispers.

"Tempting. We'll see how long our shopping trip lasts."

Natalie appears to be a window shopper; they pass several more stalls of various goods without making purchases. Isaac is completely lost, never having been blessed with a sense of direction on a good day, so he can't gauge how close they are to the door back home yet. He glares at anyone who looks twice at any of them. He catches a pair of fae whispering to each other while peeking at the packed bag in Sam's arms. Surely there is iron to be bought *somewhere* in the market.

Natalie trades three dragon teeth for two bundles of raskovnik and moly from a wood nymph. An eye goes to a fae jeweler who gives her a large jar of pixie dust. (It regrettably goes into Isaac's cooler.) A lung goes to an alkonost, who Sam stares at so hard she threatens to put him in a thrall.

"There are plenty of feathered beings who aren't tengu," Natalie dryly advises as soon as that business is concluded. "Although, I would like to stop at their stall as well."

Sam had already informed Isaac that he told Natalie about his tengu friend status. Isaac sighs, resigned to seeing this play out in real time.

Luckily or unluckily, it is not Mirai who is manning the stall, but a barn owl tengu slumped onto the table like they're napping. Isaac isn't sure how he would feel, seeing Mirai again; the memories of heated claws searing his flesh shut are not pleasant ones, but Sam had simply *asked* to become a tengu friend and they had allowed it, and that is objectively *hilarious*. The status will probably be rescinded in due time. All the more reason to milk its hilarity while they can do so without being disemboweled.

Natalie stands an expectant moment in front of the stall without getting greeted. "Excuse me," she finally says.

The owl tengu hardly raises their head, but at least their shifting means they're awake. No one would be foolish enough to steal from a tengu, but it's still not the wisest idea to leave unattended goods in the goblin markets.

"We are closed right now," the owl says and slumps back to the table. They sound miserable.

"Are you alright?" Sam asks, because of course he does, not having grasped the concept of customer distance or to let sleeping spirits lie.

"They're depressed because of personal reasons, but they are still here because they're waiting for a certain magpie to return," the neighboring gumiho advises with the glee of a known gossip.

Magpie, so probably Mirai, Isaac notes, because the chances of any *other* magpie tengu running around the human realm are slim to none. Tengu friend works on all clans, but if Mirai hasn't been back, they likely have not been reprimanded—or let others know about their new best friend the demon.

"I'm open, though!" the gumiho cheerily adds.

"Thank you, we will be there in a moment, Yun-hee-nim," Natalie replies.

"Unless you have any information on a missing egg or the little magpie tengu, you will only bother them. I wouldn't suggest doing that," she says.

"Oh, we know a magpie tengu. Are they missing?" Sam asks.

The owl tengu raises their head. It is impossible to read an expression with their (crooked) mask on, but their body language screams grudging, depressed worry. "Are you others that Mirai has dragged into this debacle?"

"They have not been formally asked to find that egg. That would be my associates, Mark Ito and Vivienne Sayre," Natalie replies. "They only met Mirai briefly several weeks ago."

"You're another human who knows our business," the tengu moans and slumps once more. "This is mortifying and unnecessary. Is Vivienne the round human woman? I will triple her payment if she ceases this. Mirai need not drag so many *others* into this—it has happened and it's *over*."

"I will relay your generous offer, tengu-san," Natalie says and inclines her head.

"What happened? Is it your egg that's missing?" Sam asks. A kind soul who still has no notion of keeping out of others' business. This is going to start a fight. It'll teach him not to be so damn nice, at least.

Isaac shuffles off to the side, because at least Sam can take one hit before keeling over. He can use the space to cast his own retaliation.

"What nosiness," the tengu laments, "but yes, why not tell the world! My First egg has been stolen and it appears everyone in the human realm is now aware of it."

"No, I know Vivienne too, and Mirai chatted with us for a bit. I am an intersection," Sam proudly points out.

"Sam, let's not pry," Natalie says, hushed, but Sam's attention remains fixed on his new friend.

"Mirai said there were more than one stolen, and they suspected one to be by a witch. Is that the one with your egg?" he asks.

"No, mine was... We saw her. There were witnesses to the crime."

"Oh, so you know who it is. Then it ought to be easy."

"Mirai thought so, too," the owl moans, "and look what this has turned into! If no one has recovered it by now, we ought to move on to the proper mourning."

"Mirai's working really hard to help you!" Sam scolds, because of course he *scolds* a tengu. If they don't rip his head off, he should still survive that first blow. Isaac supposes space will be key, so a big *push* spell and then perhaps a gravity spell to keep them pinned for the moment it takes to grab his demon. He could throw the cooler and cause some chaos as a cover while they run.

Isaac has never before faced the prospect of death with such humor.

"I know they are," the owl tengu replies with equal parts affection and despair. "But Mirai is doing too much. It is not their duty, and they should not leave our realm so often. They're a guard, not one of those human hunters."

"If you are someone's friend, then you *want* to help them. And we're friends with Mirai, so we can help them look! They mentioned needing a guide to the human city, though we haven't seen them again."

"You're... friends?"

And there it is.

"Just him," Isaac mutters. He backs up a few more steps so he is squarely in front of the gumiho stall.

"Mirai and *you* are friends? You're a tengu friend?" the owl clarifies.

"It appears that way. Sam is not known to lie," Natalie replies.

"What has that young fool done *now*...! I'll pluck them myself! What could you have possibly done to garner such attentions, such privilege?!"

"I helped them bandage some wounds. They helped us, we helped them, and that's what friends do," Sam replies, still confused by the exact definition of tengu friend.

(Isaac only knows the vague details of it: the equivalent of a VVIP foreign diplomat, and very rarely handed out. A coveted position.)

The owl tengu's angrily puffed plumage droops with obvious worry. "Wounds? Mirai was injured?"

"Yes, we fought a pair of witches? There was a crossbow, and a rifle, and blood magic, and they were hurt. Not as bad as me or Isaac, which is why we needed help, but we helped *each other*. They were pretty nice, if stuffy," Sam replies.

"Mirai fought *what*?"

"It is not our place to share information if Mirai has not," Natalie breaks in. A surprising move, coming from her. "But they did my associates here a great favor, and they did their best to return that. Any personal friendship that resulted is their private business, is it not?"

"Yes, that is true..." the owl murmurs, but the depression has set back in, replacing their momentary alarm. "Oh, I'd rather have *them* alive and whole and returned to me than any egg of mine. I never wanted them to risk their safety, I only thought they were *searching* for that thief."

"I'm sure Nat-ah will relay the message to her other associates. This egg mess will be cleared up," the gumiho says soothingly.

Isaac glances at her table when she speaks, having already dismissed her gossip and wares and knowing enough not to piss off yokwe just as little as youkai, but his attention catches on the two jars she has near her elbow.

One is full of pitch black, seeming to glow with its own darkness. Isaac has never seen it in that quantity, but he now knows demon blood by sight.

The other jar is full of roiling, pearlescent white, also glowing. That jar is smaller than the other one, as if holding a rarer material but still wanting to look full, and is closer to the gumiho like it needs to be guarded extra.

If that one is demon blood, then the white one must be—

"We are sorry for any distress we've caused you today, tengu-san, but I will relay our conversation to Vivienne and Mark," Natalie says. She not-so-subtly pushes Sam away from them and toward Isaac and the gumiho. "Thank you for your patience and willingness to speak with us."

She must mean to beat a hasty retreat, but Sam halts when he lays eyes on the jar of black. His brow furrows, his nose scrunches, and his mouth twists into something unpleasant.

"Don't say a word," Isaac orders. Sam's reaction proves that that must be demon blood, however.

Which makes the white one *angel* blood.

Isaac's heart stutters in his chest at a foreign feeling: hope.

If he has angel blood, he doesn't need a demon. He doesn't need to recreate his circle or even go through with that spell. He can use its power to skip to the second half. He can actually *do this* again.

He had given up hope, and Isaac had not realized until this moment how bad that felt. He'd tossed whatever future he'd cared for toward Natalie and her precognition, not out of trust, but apathy at having his life leashed to another. Sam had been a final nail in his coffin; his spell had failed, and so he would fail, too. The apocalypse would come and he'd die. It didn't matter what the cause or exact timing was. May as well let someone else worry about it since his only plan had backfired so spectacularly.

But with that, he could do it again.

Inspiration strikes him, new spellwork laying itself out in his mind's eye, a missing puzzle piece to something he'd feared lost. Sure, he still has Sam to contend with, but that isn't a death blow now.

He could do this. He could *do this*. He could still come out on top, against all odds, against a literal apocalypse.

"How much for the white jar?" Natalie asks the gumiho.

Isaac freezes, so tense it's painful.

He'd been staring. Of course she noticed. Of course she would take advantage of an opportunity. Of course this was being taken away, too, dangled in front of him like a carrot on a stick.

"What a discerning eye," the gumiho purrs, "but it is very rare, very expensive, even for you, Nat-ah. This is pure angel blood. I'm not certain it should fall into human hands. What are you offering?"

"A dragon liver," Natalie says without hesitation. The gumiho's eyes widen like saucers. "The entire liver, treated only for preservation, otherwise raw. I can even give it to you today."

The gumiho sucks her sudden salivation off her painted lip. Her eyes find the cooler in Isaac's grip. "Oh, that *is* an offer... But I know you, Nat-ah, and I know you aren't coven anymore. This is still a dangerous item to sell to a human."

"I retain clearance to purchase Class A materials in the goblin market, authorized by the Foxglove coven. Do we have a deal?"

Isaac's heart still thunders in his ears, and his knuckles are white from his grip on the cooler. He couldn't afford it, and he couldn't steal it. A higher spirit would have no use for a spell written for them so he can't barter with this fox spirit. He doesn't know how else he could get it, but the fact that Natalie has seen his interest and is buying it rankles him.

"Mm, that is alright, but. This is *such* a rare and valuable item, Nat-ah. And I do adore liver, and dragon liver is also rare, but not *that* rare."

"The liver, an eye, two canine teeth, and a horn," Natalie adds without missing a beat.

The gumiho's eyes sparkle. "How could I resist! You have a deal."

With trepidation, Isaac watches as they trade dragon parts and the jar. He won't be using the same spell if he has that as an ingredient, but he still cannot in good conscience share his spellwork. He trusts Natalie not to toss him to the coven guard dogs by this point, but he wouldn't trust *anyone* with a spell of that magnitude. She knows more than she shares, too, and that raises more than one red flag in his book.

They stow the blood in Natalie's cooler. Surely calculated, even if hers does have more space. It is the last stop before they leave the market behind. Isaac wonders if that, somehow, was calculated, too.

"You know, you're observant, too," Sam remarks as they head back through the door.

Natalie regards him, silent for a moment. Then, she replies, "Thank you. It is my job to be."

• • • • • • • • • •

Hammond shifts his smoothie to his other hand and pulls open the door. He pretends to hold it open for Rory, too.

Christine is the easiest to spot, of course, even at midday with summer sunlight coming in bright through the windows and rope lights decorating the walls. No artificial glow comes close to magic. (Sunlight is a tossup.) Rory wishes *he* could glow, but ghosts don't do that. Ghosts don't do a lot of things.

Three months left.

"Target spotted," he says, hands mimicking binoculars. He shoves darker thoughts aside in favor of embarrassing the living. "Oh and look. Two-fer today with Dana."

Hammond inclines his head, half a nod, and ambles around the front table of new releases. He waits patiently for whoever will notice him first.

"Oh," Christine's voice floats over.

Rory glances up in time to see her *tug* on Emil's shirt and point over to them. That's new. He taps Hammond's head and jerks his chin toward them. Hammond glances up to him, then to the kids, then back to the table. He's had three years to perfect the art of not looking at ghosts in public.

Emil has not had the same skill. With one furtive look toward the registers, where Dana remains, he marches over and hisses, "What are you doing here?"

"Worried someone will see me? It happens. People see ghosts. Like you're doing right now," Rory points out. "Also, way to be friggin' obvious! What if this place wasn't totally deserted and you started talking to empty air?"

"We're working on that," Christine replies in a quailing voice. Rory rarely has sympathy for others, much less unprompted, but everything about her delicate demeanor cries out for him to be protective and not bitchy. He wants to cheer her on. Too bad he's not cut out for that kind of optimism.

"Earbuds and your phone in your hand," Hammond advises.

"Oh. That's actually a good idea," Emil replies, taken aback.

"We have those sometimes," Rory deadpans. "Maybe listen to your elders for once instead of prancing around, snorting luck and slipping closer and closer to—"

"Oh, play nice," Hammond interrupts with all the fondness in the world. "You kids have fun now, I'm going to go see if I can talk a woman who hardly remembers me into texting someone."

"Good luck. Be nice for Viv's sake," Rory says and mockingly smooches Hammond's cheek.

Hammond rolls his eyes, then turns to the manager with a hand up. "Excuse me, I have a couple questions." He strides over with as much confidence as he ever does anything. (A very small, almost kind part of Rory genuinely wishes Hammond well with his wingman tightrope routine he decided to take on for Vivienne.)

Which leaves Rory alone with the children. He tries not to grin evilly about it; he's supposed to be *playing nice*. Informative and pleasant and genteel. "Now it's time for our talk," he tells them.

Emil's guard goes up, but Christine bats those big gold doe eyes. No wonder everyone is bending over backwards to help her.

"Anywhere you can pretend to stock books for a few minutes and be left alone? Otherwise you're left nodding and shaking your head. Doable, but annoying as fuck, and *apparently* you're an active party in this catastrophe."

Emil leads them to a corner, complete with book cart, and helpfully out of direct sight of the front registers and the door. Obviously, this place had been built years before Emil was even a figment of his parents' imaginations, but how *lucky* for him that such a spot exists in the store.

"Vivienne said she was going to help us avoid trouble. Aren't you going to do the same?" Christine asks.

"Yes and no. I'm a walking hazard warning, and Ham and I think it's high time we give you the dirty details on that. I know Emil already noticed the whole touching thing."

"Hammond can touch you, and I'm guessing so can Vivienne. Because Vivienne can touch Christine, too. But like most adults, she's already trotted out the Do As I Say Not As I Do commandment," Emil replies and crosses his arms over his chest.

Rory fondly remembers being a surly teenager. (Hammond would argue he never grew out of it.) He reaches over and flicks his hand through Emil's cheek. The boy jumps, but there is no contact, of course. That's what's *supposed* to happen.

"I saw you grab his shirt when we came in," Rory tells Christine. She hesitantly nods. "That's not a good thing, you know. Ghosts are static beings. They don't touch living beings, only other spirits." He holds his hand out again, and Christine touches him, a soft brush on the back of his hand.

"Luck spirits are corporeal," she replies. "Vivienne already gave us this talk. What makes you and her such exceptions?"

"Not me. *Him*," Rory says and jerks his thumb over his shoulder to point at Hammond. "A friend of ours wrote a spell to keep me here, as a ghost, without the decay risk. The spell is in turn anchored onto a living human body. It was a one-time use, and now that spell is dying too, and we have no way of renewing it."

"Why not do the spell again?" Emil asks, like a total magic novice.

Rory heaves an empty sigh. "Because, kid, the person who cast it is *dead*. No ghost there. Vivienne got hamstrung, too, so she doesn't have the magic to cast it even *if* she knew how to solo. No one knows how it was done, and no one knows how to renew it. It was also dangerous and sketchy as fuck, and I would not recommend it. Ham almost died."

"What about Vivienne, then? Her deal?"

Rory restrains a bitter laugh. "Viv is a special case. Always has been and always will be. You can't replicate that, either. We're singularities, and so are you, but none of us are getting happy endings. I've had a few years to come to terms with that."

"I *know* I died," Christine replies, almost mulish, but her fidgeting fingers give her away. "I've... come to terms with that. I had a lot of time to come to terms with the fact that I was dying."

"Yet hope is a hell of a drug. You think you're going to come out of this rosy, don't you? Sneak your way back into a way of living, be able to eat and sleep and shit and fuck again, and there will be no repercussions whatsoever. Beat the odds. Get *lucky*."

"Kirara is helping me! I have this—this collar here, and it's special!" she cries, touching the bell collar at her throat. It *dings* gently, as if in agreement.

Rory nods, indulgently. "And if you actually thought of it as *yours* instead of hers, you'd already be a poltergeist. Smart of you to ditch your old attachments to avoid that fate. But that's not the only thing waiting. Give me your hand."

"Wh-What? Why?" Christine shies away from him like he'd grabbed her.

Emil's eyes narrow, and he steps halfway between them. "What is your angle, man? We know this is a longshot. Kirara is helping. Vivienne changed her tune, too, so why aren't you?"

"Hand. Now."

Christine extends a shaking hand.

Her skin is a warm medium brown, palm lighter, nails unpainted. "If you were a white girl, someone would've already noticed. Have your fingernails grown since you got that collar?"

"I-I don't know? Ghosts don't... grow. I haven't paid attention. Not like I could trim them, anyway..."

Rory turns her small hand over in his own larger ones. Then, he grabs her index finger and holds it up for both of them. The very tip is a subtly darker shade than the rest of her skin.

"Bet your toes'll turn, too, but I don't wanna touch your feet. The extremities go first. It's like frostbite."

"What is that?" Christine asks with huge, terrified eyes.

"I don't see anything," Emil adds.

"Human ghosts are singularities in the spirit community in a lot of ways. We're the only things that can summon Doors—that *have* Doors—and we're one of the few spirits that can turn into other things. 'Ghosts are *supposed* to be static beings' should be the repeated phrase. We definitely aren't. Unless you're in a convoluted stasis spell like me. Don't recommend it, again. The magic smells like shit."

"Y-You said so yourself, I'm not going to become a poltergeist. My brother and I avoided that," Christine replies and snatches her hand back to her chest. She looks so affronted he could laugh.

"Glad to see you weren't headed into this completely clueless!"

"We did *research*! There was a plan!"

"So then why are ya becoming a demon?" Rory asks, unable to help his cruel glee. The cutest things are always the most fun to kick.

She stares at him.

Rory continues, "Magical decay only happens to a select subset of spirits. Besides being delicious to about damn near everything out there, ghosts *rot*. We're not meant to stay. If you have earthly attachments, bam, poltergeist. If you tried to eat people, boom, probably wendigo, or more likely ghoul. Definitely some sort of nasty hunger spirit. But if you just try to hang on as long as possible, and *if* there is sufficient magic around you, then you get the special privilege of becoming a demon."

"Logan always told me to leave when he was doing magic," Christine whispers, a distant realization. She holds her hands tighter against herself. "He knew... But he was always careful."

"I don't know how to do magic. I'm not casting any abracadabra spells anywhere. And Kirara's hardly around, so she doesn't count, either," Emil butts in.

"You're lucky there—other magic wouldn't do it. Only human stuff," Rory concedes. "But this is a pretty heavily magically populated city. There's stuff in the air all around us, all the time. And who knows who's done stuff near you. I know Vivienne stopped by to give your place some wards, right? Not that she was doing anything on purpose. Warding is pretty low on the magical ladder. But that shit adds up over time, minute bit by even tinier iota, like radiation."

"I'm not becoming a demon!" Christine exclaims with watery eyes. It makes the gold in them even shinier.

"No. You're still months, years away. But you're not in the clear. That's a lot more likely than becoming a luck spirit. And you know what? Demons are corporeal, too."

"I don't *want* to become a demon! I'm becoming a luck spirit!"

"Hey—stop being mean to her!" Emil snaps like this is a playground fight, not the facts of the afterlife. Rory shrugs and spreads his hands in mock surrender.

"Just saying it like it is, kiddo. Best to be prepared. It's avoidable, if you know what to look for, and who the fuck *knows* what the luck is doing to your system. That's new ground for sure. *Buuuuut*."

"But what?" Emil growls.

"That was the news for her," Rory says with a boop of Christine's nose. His finger goes through Emil's when he tries the same on him. "I come bearing a message for you, too. And I was nice enough to deliver this information in *that* order. I'm actually a really kind guy."

"What do you *want*? What is it?"

"Vivienne's offering to teach you magic."

Emil stares at him. The defensive anger is gone, replaced not by shock, but of some sort of childish awe. Like being told magic is real, probably. Rory wishes he'd been able to learn magic when he was still alive, but he only learned about this stuff afterward. Oh well.

"Get you tested to see your general ability level, see if you have any natural talents, then offer you some basics in protection stuff. Basics, unless you turn out to be some sort of wunderkind. There was a bad run-in with another spirit, right? Something to deter anyone getting too friendly when they see a tasty ghostly snack *or* all the luck you two are collecting. Either could make you big walking targets."

"I could learn magic?" Emil whispers.

"Statistically, yes. Most people have a bit of ability."

Rory guesses that something bigger than a single run-in with another spirit has happened, based on Emil's thoughtful expression. Christine stays meekly silent. She's probably the type to cave to whatever he decides, but learning magic when there is a magic sponge around waiting to turn into an unwanted monstrosity is a very specific situation to be in. And it should be something they both talk about.

But when have teenagers ever talked responsibly?

"Wait," Emil says, putting together only *then* what Rory had already told them. Rory rolls his eyes. Emil looks to Christine with fear and embarrassment overcoming his earnest curiosity. "Wait, that'd be bad for you."

"Over time, yes. A lot of time. And only if you two stick together."

"Why wouldn't we?" Emil asks and they both blink up at Rory, completely guileless, like the thought of leaving each other's side had never crossed their mind. These dumb kids are going to be the death of *someone*. Rory hopes it isn't Vivienne.

"Well, for starters, if you start casting fireball hourly, it *might* have an unwanted side effect on the ghost you're cohabiting with? Like I just explained?"

"Is there actually a fireball—"

"*But* if you're smart about it, and try not to hug her while shitting dumb magic spells, then it would only be marginally more dangerous than the ambient magic in the city. This is basically an offer of self-defense classes. Turning into a poltergeist, or ghoul, or demon is pretty bad, but so is getting eaten. Especially because getting eaten alive still applies to ghosts, so to speak. Personally, I'd rather turn into a monster, because there's no suiciding your way out of being eaten as a ghost, and I *don't* want to know what that feels like, or what the precise moment of second death is like. No way. Top ten ways to die to fucking *avoid*."

Christine claps her hands over her mouth like she may puke. Her bell *dings* again with the movement.

"Never thought about it in those terms, huh?" Rory asks.

"You're kind of disgusting, you know that?" Emil asks in return.

"Yeah, well, the messenger need not be all sparkles and rainbows. I wish half this stuff had been explained to me," he finishes with a mutter. Rory doesn't mean to sound bitter, but, well, there's been a few years to fester. Always look at the fine print of spells when signing up for shit. "Think about it, you two. It's a group effort. Know that Viv is a brilliant teacher, I mean it, seriously. She's not going to put either of you in danger. I think it'd be worth the risk, but hey, that's just me and my three years of avoiding being eaten."

"We'll think about it," Emil uneasily replies with a sidelong glance at Christine. Rory does not envy him *that* conversation.

He gives them a sarcastic salute and leaves them to their existential angst. He floats back through several shelves, long since having embraced the lack of need to go around obstacles, and finds Hammond being talked into buying a set of audiobooks for the ten-year anniversary of some high fantasy series. Total swords and sorcery type deal. Rory does not recognize the title, but he has heard enough of Dana's gushing explanation to get the gist.

Hammond glances at him out of the corner of his eye with a strained smile that screams *help me*.

"Don't know what you want me to do. At least this seems to be going well. If these are for me, I can't guarantee I won't rip them to shreds," Rory observes, leaning over Hammond's shoulder to examine the minimalistic covers. "I know you *aren't* supposed to judge books by their covers, but these are boring as shit. How'd it go with Dana?"

Hammond's eye twitches. Rory loves annoying him when he can't respond.

"It's a great deal, I mean, I'm not trying to badger you into this, but these are *steeply* discounted. It's definitely the audiobooks I'd recommend right now, and it's a whole trilogy!" Dana brightly explains.

"Aw, babe, did you get sucked into sales because you were looking at new books for me?" Rory coos. He floats around to Hammond's other side and sets his chin atop his head. "Viv's gonna be *jeaaaaaaalous*," he croons, right into Hammond's ear.

Hammond maintains his Hey I'm Not Talking To Thin Air And Looking Totally Crazy facade all the way through the end of the transaction. Emil and Christine remain out of sight, too, probably mulling over the prospect of introducing the magical to the spiritual.

A lot of the terms are used fairly interchangeably, but if being dead for several years has taught him anything, it's that there *is* nuance. Annoying, specific nuance. Like the whole Magic And Ghosts Don't Mix thing.

Hammond waves goodbye to Dana, juggling smoothie and bag, and they're finally back out into the warm summer air. "How did yours go?" Hammond asks.

"Kids were spooked, Emil seems interested, and Christine is a huge sad puppy. The gold eye thing is creepy, but in a cute way. If she *does* turn into something we have to put down, no one's gonna pull that trigger. It'd be like shooting Bambi."

"I think we've handled worse. I miss the days when I could pass you things to hold. Wait a moment." Hammond chugs the rest of his drink to free up a hand to hold his phone as a cover for the conversation. "Okay, so, no answer right away. Probably a good thing. The last thing anyone needs is a gung-ho teenager who's probably lucky enough to... I don't know. I'm failing in a metaphor. All the luck I've ever thought about was that time you possessed that guy holding Natalie at gunpoint for not selling it."

Rory shudders. "Don't remind me. Possession is *disgusting*." Another supposed perk of ghosthood. True possession is rare among spiritual skills, and it feels like wearing someone else's poorly fitted, very moist skin while wading through foreign and confusing memories. He's only done it twice. Disgusting is an understatement.

"I wonder if they're smart or dumb enough to try selling luck," Hammond muses.

"The kid didn't know random people could do magic. I don't think he's going to stumble onto the idea of a magic black market anytime soon. Now, enough about the darling children—how are we passing judgment on Dana? Is she good enough for Viv? Or is she gonna be smart enough to run for the friggin' hills once she gets a closer look at *aaaaall* that baggage?"

"I think she'll stick around, and I'm good with feeling people out," Hammond replies with the sort of smile that means he knows something more than Rory doesn't.

Megan is weeping in this vision, but their expression is overjoyed. (And embarrassed for all of the weeping.) In a black graduation gown with a hat still pinned to their curly hair, they throw their arms around a unicorn foal.

"M-Mom, I can't believe you—you got me a-a unicorn!" they bawl and hide their face in the unicorn's fluffy mane.

Deirdre looks on, wiping away her own tear. "You're a college graduate now. Off to med school—I can hardly believe it, sweetheart. But you're going to be a doctor, and a healer, and you're going to do so many wonderful things, that I wanted to make sure you had every possible opportunity at your fingertips."

Megan cries harder into her unicorn's mane.

Natalie slips back into her present, already smiling. It had been a private moment—she had seen no coven members around—but it had been a joy to witness. And she even has a sense of when to expect this one. She'll have to get Megan unicorn-themed cupcakes.

CHAPTER 20

In Which Vivienne Plays Teacher

"Thank you for helping us with this," Natalie murmurs, unable to help her warm smile, and tries to hide her affection under the guise of straightening Megan's collar.

"No problem! I understand wanting to step away from coven reach sometimes," they chirp. "Plus, I wanted to see Vivi's powerpoint, too. It's been a while since I've seen her in research mode."

They preen a moment longer under Natalie's attention, then flounce back to help Vivienne wrestle with setting up the smart board. Megan had kindly requisitioned a room in one of their campus buildings, conveniently one that already had muffling and dampening wards written into the space thanks to decades of stressed students struggling to find a quiet place to study.

"Why're *we* here again? I don't think a witch—or a spellwriter—needs magic lessons," Isaac complains. The room did not come with individual desks, but it came with tables and chairs and an old, particularly finicky smart board.

"Because he's here," Vivienne replies and flaps a dismissive hand at Oliver, who sits with rapt attention beside Isaac.

"I haven't been at a college in years. This is kinda bringing back memories! Isn't it for you?" Oliver asks brightly.

"I never went to college."

"You worked at a law firm, dude."

Isaac levels a disbelieving stare over the edge of his phone. "I *lied*, Oliver."

"Dude."

"Anyway," Natalie politely interrupts, checking her watch, "I asked you to be here since the shop is closed today. You could help with demonstrations."

"No thanks."

Oh, if Natalie were an eye-roller, the *workout* she would give her eyes when dealing with Isaac. "Then maybe you can learn, too. Everyone should always be learning. I'm sure Sam will benefit from this, too, if only for the sake of understanding what we're doing."

Sam sits ramrod straight on Isaac's other side. Another too-eager learner. "I would like to learn!" he immediately agrees, hand in the air.

"Today I'm afraid it is only gauging your magical abilities. Not yours, Sam, but Oliver and Emil's." She checks her watch again; Emil and Christine still are not here.

Vivienne crows in triumph at the smart board. "Okay, think I got it! Where are the kidlings?"

On cue, Emil slinks in, ruffled and out of breath. Natalie goes to the table of their supplies and fetches the spirit sight draught.

"You could've said *which* brick building it was," Emil grumbles between sucking in breaths. "And this place doesn't have an elevator! We're on the fourth floor! And—" He freezes, eyes wide, staring at Megan.

"Oh, that makes sense," Megan says with a cock of their head.

"You. You—know them?"

"This saves time on introductions. My name is Megan, and I'm friends with Nat and Vivi, and I saved his life when he tried *drinking* the potion you illegally sold him," Megan says with a sidelong glance at Natalie.

One she doesn't deserve. Without batting an eye, she passes the buck. "Isaac was the one who sold it to him. This is why a bit of knowledge can go a long way. Emil, it is nice to finally meet you. My name is Natalie, and I'm the owner of the potion shop that Isaac and Vivienne help out at."

They go around in the circle, formalizing names, with Megan taking over, though they've only just met Oliver themselves. Natalie puts just one drop of the potion into each of her eyes.

She'd heard physical descriptions of Christine, of course, but it is still sad to see a teenaged Black girl as a nervous-looking ghost. She seems outwardly fine, at least, which is a relief. Vivienne has been known to fudge the truth about danger conditions.

Emil is likewise as described: a teenaged boy with light brown hair and too gangly for his own body. She knows his last name is Zolotarev, and he certainly *looks* Russian. He is also trying very hard *not* to seem excited to be in a magic class.

"Oliver, Isaac, I'm going to give you a half dose of spirit sight draught so you can interact with Christine."

"No thanks," Isaac says at once.

"May I ask why not?"

"I know what ghosts look like. Not to be rude, but I don't care enough about these baby magic lessons to be invested enough to take more potions than I have to."

"If you write a spell to let you see ghosts, let me know," Natalie wryly replies. "Oliver?"

"Hell yeah!"

She tilts his head back and administers a drop into each eye. His gelled hair smushes against her blouse with a *crunch*. Based on Isaac's remarks, Oliver is likely the only person present who could actually *afford* this potion, but Natalie lets him pass for now.

"Woah, hi, ghost girl! Chris, right?"

"Oh, um, sure."

"Christine," Natalie gently corrects. Christine wilts with appreciation.

"Cool, ghost time! Now, magic time! Dude, I'm mad you kept this magic thing from me for so long."

"You've interacted with other witches long before you ever met me," Isaac replies without looking up from his phone.

"Yeah? Are there lawyer witches?"

Natalie, Vivienne, and Megan blanch at the very abrupt and very jarring realization that Oliver Lynch *would* have likely met the one and only Dante Peoples, owner of the Peoples Law Firm and one of the most infamous witches in the city. Oliver Lynch is one of the *last* people who should be in contact with that kind of temptation.

Christine chews on her lip, then breaks into a wobbly smile. "I-I know there are witches and people who can use magic all around, statistically, anyone can bump into them."

Right, Vivienne had said Christine's brother had been a witch, too. And as another Black witch, there is no way he would *not* have heard of Dante.

"Most people have some magical ability," Vivienne says, eager to segue, and she taps the board to pull up her literal powerpoint presentation. "Today, we'll be testing you two for that, and explaining some magic basics. Unfortunately, we'll have to wait until the full moon to see if you have any natural aptitudes, but we can at least see if you have the capability today."

"Aptitudes!" Oliver cheers. Natalie can see he will remain *very* enthusiastic about today. She wishes she could spare them a bit of time and simply announce what he was skilled at. Emil, too, she has seen use magic in various visions, so he seems a safe bet.

"I'll need to prick both your fingers for a bit of blood. Hold this thread until it soaks up enough to turn red," Natalie says and passes each of them a small bit of string. She holds up a needle and Oliver scrunches his nose. Even Christine looks faintly queasy. "I see we're dealing with babies today. Please grin and bear it."

"So magic is in the blood?" Emil asks when it's his turn.

"It's in all parts of the body. Did you want us to cut off a piece of flesh?"

"That's called a *vivi*section," Vivienne stage-whispers, winking and holding up her knife.

"No, it's called a biopsy," Megan corrects.

"Magic is everywhere in a living thing, like on a cellular level. No one's ever looked at it in a lab. It's just there. You both probably have *some*," Isaac says, bored enough at last to join in.

"This is true. And for spirits, it is both in higher concentrations, and more prominent. It's possible to see magic if it is in high enough concentration."

Vivienne clicks over to her next slide, one Natalie knows is her favorite: it is a picture of a giant cartoon rainbow. Each side ends with a fluffy white cloud and underneath is a pure black shadow.

"Supernatural Hunter Tip #6: Black and white magic are just colors. All magic can loosely be color-coded. Some of it makes sense along the lines of pop culture, and a lot of it does not. Black magic and white magic are not any more special than any other type of magic, and it is only because of a *long* history of racism by European colonizers misunderstanding African and Afro-Caribbean magic systems such as hoodoo, and later conflating that with voodoo, that there is such a stigma attached to it in America. And I would like to go on record as saying that I have *not* added this because Christine is in the room, but because if magic grad school were a thing, I'd do my thesis on this shit."

Silence reigns in the room. Natalie and Vivienne are both used to that reaction; Natalie is used to people being awkward around Vivienne's open practicing of necromancy, and Vivienne is used to blank stares whenever she infodumps.

"And this is why she's the teacher today instead of the witch," Megan wryly jokes.

"I knew about the color system," Christine mumbles and sinks low into the chair she's floating over.

"Sorry for singling you out."

"Is that why I bleed bla—" Sam's question is cut short by Isaac clapping his hand over his mouth with a furious growl. "Mmph!"

"To answer your question, yes. To answer Isaac's retort, don't ask any more questions if you want to be let go anytime soon," Vivienne smoothly replies.

Emil raises his hand next. Natalie finds it amusing how quickly they have returned to grade school habits. "Is magical undergrad a thing?"

"Not really," Megan says with a giggle, "but I have gotten some tutoring on how to apply healing magic covertly in a hospital setting. There are few institutions that semi-publicly recognize magic, but plenty of stuff goes on under the table."

"Why is this all a secret? Why not just have magic be a thing everyone knows about?"

"Good question!" Vivienne says. She hastily scrolls through several of her slides, ending up on a big Venn diagram with too many words inside each of the circles. "So, this stuff *does* pop up naturally. Anyone can see ghosts if they have a near-death experience, so that's why they're so widely recognized across cultures, even if a large portion of the population doesn't publicly believe in them. Likewise, there have been studies done on the theory that hysterical strength is a form of magic. People lifting cars, punching bears, that kind of thing. Anyone want to guess what color force magic—that'd be stuff including strength augmentation—is? Isaac, put your hand down."

"But I know the answer," he drawls.

"I thought you didn't want to take part in class," Natalie remarks and Isaac scowls.

In the world's most obvious note passing, Isaac types something on his phone and slides it over to Oliver. Oliver's arm shoots up.

"Cheater," Emil grunts.

"It's purple!" Oliver exclaims. "So like, the opposite of the Hulk."

"Both are true. I guess. Anyway, magic has probably always been a part of humanity, and it manifests in different ways, but not all of them are available or visible to everyone. Some cultures *do* openly—within their own ranks—embrace magic as a part of everyday life. There are a lot of cities that are full of old magic—whole *arrondissements* in Paris, the big souq in Damascus, three districts in Beijing, and so on. America's old cities were Native American, and the Europeans didn't like those, so we don't have the same old age, only concentration of population. New Orleans and New York are probably the closest we have to the same urban concept of magical acknowledgement. Here just has the concentration, thanks to the goblin market door."

"The *what*—?"

"Is this a history lesson?" Natalie prompts as soon as Vivienne pauses to take a breath. "We had a rough lesson plan for today."

"I'm answering my students' questions," Vivienne primly replies. She clicks back through her presentation to the rainbow graphic. "But, alright, yeah. Basics. Most people tend to be stronger in one or two types of magic, and worse in another or two. But anyone can use any kind, provided they know what they're doing. Baby steps first. You two done bleeding on your thread yet?"

"Oh, yeah," Emil realizes aloud. Oliver holds his out, too. "What are these for? Besides the blood. I mean, how does the moon come into play?"

Natalie pulls on a pair of latex gloves and takes Emil's thread first. They've already set out two disposable trays filled shallowly with witch water. Natalie murmurs a simple identification spell, lights the thread on fire with a lighter, then drops it into the water.

"Timer, please," Natalie calls as soon as it hits the surface. Megan taps their phone. "How long the thread burns indicates your magical ability. Under the moonlight, we should hypothetically see the reflection of your magic in the water. Did you ever use litmus paper in science class? Same principle."

"Time! I call dibs on the math!" Megan exclaims. They jump up and down next to Vivienne until she pulls up a blank drawing screen on the smart board.

"I don't think anyone would argue *for* doing math," Vivienne says.

"That didn't seem very long. Am I going to be bad at magic?" Emil asks.

"That was twenty-six seconds. That should be good," Christine says. Natalie arches an eyebrow at her, and she ducks down in her seat again. "I did this twice with my brother. Um, he liked the math magic stuff, too..."

"I'm gonna get, like, a *minute*, dude. I'm gonna be a witch, or the next best thing," Oliver declares, because of course he does.

Natalie takes his thread and uses her phone as a timer while Megan writes out the equation. (She'd rather avoid the math, too, if given the choice.) "Eighteen seconds, Oliver."

"So *close* to a minute, too," Isaac snarks. Oliver smacks him, and Isaac slaps back, and Sam scoots his chair away from them both like he fears a war. "You *have* magic, so stop complaining! That's all you wanted, right?"

"Uh, no? I need runes and stuff! I see all those magic writing things you use all the time, I know that's how you power it! I'm super good at memorization, man, so I'm just gonna out-nerd even Viv and learn *aaaall* the loopholes in this."

"Fat chance!" Vivienne declares.

"We will get into *how* to cast, including the writing of runes, next time. Vivienne will be your teacher, so I don't think I'll be needed. Isaac, I still recommend you take part, if only for Sam and Oliver's sakes."

"Firstly—Supernatural Hunter Tip #1: Intent is a solid 80% of magic. What you *mean* to do is arguably more important than how you cast the magic, what runes you use, what order, verbal command, et cetera."

"Do you have a whole *list* of these things?" Isaac asks.

"Of course I do. I've shown you my research notebooks. We've known each other for months now, Isy. You can't be surprised at my stunning brainpower *now*."

"Don't call me that!" he snaps while Oliver cackles at his misfortune.

"Now, onto the demonstrations!" Vivienne cheers with her own excited hop. She shuts down the smart board and dashes to the table of supplies. Megan vibrates beside her, just as excited. Natalie sighs. She loves Vivienne—and Megan—but she doesn't particularly *like* the idea of what's about to happen.

Megan digs into the bag and pulls out a scalpel. "Rainbow order! Red magic is up first! Again, these are visible colors, just an organizational system. However, this one is one of the ones that makes the most sense and will be super duper easy to remember."

"Are we going to be *quizzed* on this?" Emil asks in alarm.

"If you want to take future lessons, yes!" Vivienne gleefully answers.

Natalie looks away as Megan digs the scalpel into the back of their forearm. Christine squeals and Oliver sucks in a gasp. "Also, if you have to use blood for any magic casting, don't cut open your palm like in all the movies," Megan advises. "Hurts way too much and can affect your hand movements. Alright, Nat, you can look again."

Megan holds up a healed arm with only a smear of blood and a faint pink line to show for the injury.

"For the record, I'd also used a numbing spell on the area, so please don't think I'm a masochist. Healing magic is life magic, which falls under the red category. Red like blood, so easy, right?"

"Is blood magic also red magic?" Sam asks with a hand in the air.

"Yes, it is. Blood falls into the life category. Most things having to do with a living body do," Natalie replies. Megan nods in confirmation.

"For orange magic, we can't really cast anything in here, but we do have a super easy example to show you! Oliver, this one's for you," Vivienne says and puts Natalie's broom onto the table. "Flight magic is orange, along with moon magic and sight magic. This doesn't make as much sense as red, huh?"

"Oh, and just to be clear, there's more red stuff than just healing magic. And blood magic. This is not an all-inclusive lesson," Megan hastens to add. "Now, Nat, if you'd please?"

Natalie takes the broom off the table and sits on it, perched in midair. "Only witches can use brooms, unless augmented with a specific spell tailored to a specific person. Technically, utilizing a broom takes magic, but it is such a miniscule amount that no one would notice, even after hours of flying. It is a passive kind of magic use."

"Onto yellow! If we could get a lovely volunteer from the audience?" Vivienne says while Natalie dismounts. Vivienne holds her hand out to Christine, who points at herself with a confused frown. "Yes, you."

"Why me—oh, right." She floats around their table and waits next to Vivienne.

"Yellow magic does, in fact, include luck. Of course, luck *can* be visible to the human eye, and it appears gold. Lovely assistant, if you'd please?"

Christine sucks in a breath she doesn't need and makes a pulling motion. She gathers a little sphere of the *suggestion* of glitter in her palm. She could see it clearly, and Sam probably can as well, but that is the best they can do for human eyes.

"Question, *sensei*!" Oliver calls. "What happens if you snort luck?"

Emil's expression reveals he is also wondering this.

"Don't snort anything ever. And for the record, I don't know, but it would not affect you any more than licking it or rubbing it on your skin. Actually, no, don't eat luck, either. Don't eat anything we don't tell you to. And to wrap up, yellow magic also involves fire magic, which, against Natalie's better judgment, is a spell we'll be teaching you next time. I personally think having a lighter anywhere you go is handy."

Both Oliver and Emil pump their fists in pyromanic victory. Natalie hopes her store will not burn down as a direct result of these lessons.

"Okay, next up is green. I'm operating under the assumption that everyone knows the colors of the rainbow. Nat, your turn again. Everyone else, get out of your seats and stand along the far wall."

"I don't like this," Natalie reminds her, but Vivienne shrugs. Too late now. Except it's *not*, they could figure out another way to demonstrate this without the shock and awe. Natalie personally is skilled with green magics.

"Here, you three with this one, and Emil, I'll be with you. You two." Megan passes out the floor mats they'd taken from the shop.

"Are you doing what I think you're doing?" Isaac asks, dread clear in his expression.

"Yep! Don't worry, these are lined with rubber, and it's only a precaution. Plus, I'm here! I haven't lost anyone yet," Megan chirps.

Vivienne stands near the door with a lightning rod in hand. Natalie is about twenty paces from her, most of the length of the classroom, and cannot believe she talked her into casting a lightning bolt at her.

"*Lightning-line*," Natalie murmurs and draws the runes in the air.

It is small compared to real lightning, and they are in a semi-controlled environment, so at least they are not deafened by any following thunder. Everyone is still standing as the flash fades. Vivienne looks like her fine hair has been rubbed with a balloon, and she quickly drops the lightning rod with a hiss, but she is still upright and still conscious. Natalie lets out a sigh of relief.

"Green magic involves lightning and other weather effects. It also involves natural magic, such as helping plants grow, and the sun," Natalie flatly explains while Megan looks over Vivienne's mildly burnt hand. "Don't try this at home. We will *not* be teaching you how to do that."

"Thankfully," Vivienne says as Megan holds her healing hand, "blue magic is another easier one, and totally safer. Emil, I actually tried casting some on you when we first met. Isaac, are you *sure* you don't want to participate in this one?"

"Can I cast it on Oliver?"

"He has to learn, so no."

"Then no."

"Dude, what," Oliver hisses at him.

"Meggy, do you mind?" Vivienne asks with her best puppy dog eyes.

"No, not at all. And there, your hand is good as new. Not that bad. Probably wouldn't have even blistered. Don't forget to catch me!"

They arrange themselves. Vivienne writes down Megan's chest, then mumbles, "*Sleep.*" Megan slumps into her arms with little fanfare.

"I remember that," Christine says.

"I don't. Is that why I don't?" Emil asks with a frown.

"I also dumped sleep soot on you, so mixing the two probably could've addled the memory a bit. Who knows? None of this shit is exact science, no matter how informative I sound. C'mon Meggy, awake time again now."

It takes a few minutes to rouse Megan again; Natalie steps in to help because Vivienne should not be wasting magic.

"Anything to do with sleep or dreams is automatically blue magic. Also water! Another easy one," Vivienne explains while Megan blearily readjusts to teaching time. "Purple, as mentioned before, has to do with force magic. This also includes gravity and earth magic. Basically, if it's a hard science, it's probably purple. Next up is the fun one!"

Natalie looks away again. There isn't much to clean up, and she doesn't want to seem disinterested in front of others, so she stays carefully off to the side.

Vivienne dumps a duffel bag onto the table with a *whump*. "Black magic is *my* specialty. Some of it is the stereotypical stuff you'd expect, but it also involves physical and touch magics. Now, you all are aware I call myself an exorcist and an expert in necromancy, right?"

Natalie is fairly certain this is when their students realize what is about to happen and what is inside the duffel bag. Isaac pulls his shirt up over his nose as a preemptive measure.

With professional glee, Vivienne unzips the bag to release a rather foul smell. Christine whimpers and she can't even smell. Carefully, Vivienne takes out a dead rat and lays it on parchment paper.

"Oh, gross!"

"Dude, *what?*"

Emil and Oliver cover their noses, muffling only some of their complaints. Sam cocks his head. "How did it die?"

"Cat got it this morning. Fresh bodies obviously have the most flesh to them, and are the most complicated to reanimate, but also the sturdiest and, depending on time and method of death, can be used for the most things. Wait a moment while I write this out. Full necromancy requires a circle."

Vivienne scrawls on the paper beneath the rat. It's a mammal, but a small one, so it does not take her long to complete the circle. She presses her hand to the ring of runes and with a flash of dark light, the rat twitches and sits up.

"This is what most people would call a zombie. It does not hunger, especially not for brains, and does not thirst. Magic is the only thing animating it, and when that runs out, it's over. You can't reanimate the same corpse twice. Also, if, for whatever reason the magic keeps going, the spell would fall apart when the body decays or is broken into so many pieces it can't function anymore. It can follow simple commands, either written into the circle, or commanded with fresh magic. The suffix -mancy *technically* refers to the concept of obtaining information from them, like talking to the dead, but reanimated corpses are incapable of speech or higher thoughts. This isn't alive. There are no thoughts, no soul. It is a puppet that makes most people gag."

Vivienne looks up from her rat to meet Christine's wide eyes. This is half the reason for this show, after all.

"There is *no way* to bring someone back from the dead as they are. You can move a body again and you can communicate with ghosts. Necromancy does not bring the dead back."

"I-I know that," Christine whispers through her fingers.

"Okay, good! Now then, thanks for the help, little guy." Vivienne pets the rat with one finger before ending the spell. It *plops* back to the table. Oliver gags. "Next one!"

"Wait, there's *more*?" Emil croaks.

"This one has less flesh. How else do I get to show off my rare and specific talents?" Vivienne puts the dead rat in a plastic bag and seals it shut. Natalie purifies the air to get rid of the smell. "I might pass out casting this one, but I want everyone to know: worth it. Step back. Sam and Christine, you take extra steps back, just in case."

Megan helps Vivienne lay out more parchment paper on the floor. This circle is bigger and more intricate. It also doesn't smell, except to Sam, who wrinkles his nose.

"You good, Vivi?" Megan asks as Vivienne pops the cap back on the magic marker.

"Of course. This is also a special treat, and I'd like to see how it plays out. Alright kids, who knows what a wraith is?"

Isaac groans. Natalie could live without their theatrics, too, but at least this one isn't freshly dead.

Vivienne casts the spell. She wobbles on her knees, Megan putting a quick hand on her shoulder, but remains aware as her magic coalesces inside the circle. The edges peel inward, flaking like rust, until it all bubbles together into a goopy, dark grey, vaguely skeletal creature.

It immediately lunges at Christine.

Vivienne grabs it by a goopy maybe-rib and slaps it back down to the floor. "Down, boy. No. Stay."

It sits by her like an obedient dog, dripping.

"Wraiths were not human souls, but we *think* they were parts of one. This isn't and never was a full person. It does not need to eat or breathe or do anything, but it is corporeal and has its own reactions. I wouldn't say thoughts, but it can operate independently, and use basic problem solving to follow commands. I also might pass out before the end of this lesson."

"C'mon, deep breaths, Vivi," Megan says with a spread palm against her back. Everyone is wasting so much magic today on show. (At least with Christine's lucky presence, they're unlikely to run into an emergency.)

"I-If it wasn't hungry, why did it lunge at me?" Christine squeaks. She is still behind Emil, peeking over the top of his head at it.

"I summoned this one with the most basic spell I could think of. I'm guessing it saw the only thing lower on the ladder than it. Like I said, these don't have *thoughts*, but instinct. Lots of spirits have an instinct to eat human ghosts."

"Looks like CGI," Oliver observes. He has remained where he stands, but bent forward at the waist, chin in hand and squinting suspiciously at it.

"You get used to looking at different things. Like how little kids are in awe of zoo visits?" Megan replies.

"Alright Sam, your turn. Num-nums," Vivienne says, and with a point, the wraith wriggles toward Sam and Isaac.

"What? What do you want me to do?" he asks in alarm. Isaac narrows his eyes, but this was part of today, too; they won't out Sam as a demon, but they have to admit he's not human.

"Eat it. Dinner time! I can't say it'll taste the best, but it's mostly magic and leftover spirit matter, so it should be plenty nutritious. I think."

"You eat these things?" Emil asks queasily.

"Sam can. Here's another excellent lesson for you—not everything that looks human *is* human. Not every spirit is a catgirl. 'Spirit' itself is an incredibly broad and vaguely defined term. I'm definitely not saying that anything inhuman is a monster not to be trusted, but keep in mind that they'll have different morals, thought processes, magical ability, and diets. Many would be quite happy to snack on Christine. Some would be happy to snack on you both."

"Do you have a to-go box for this?" Isaac flatly asks. He nudges the wraith with the toe of his shoe.

"I brought a warded jar for you," Natalie says, because she knew Isaac wouldn't want anything that could incriminate Sam. She has only seen a demon eat once before, and it was messy.

"Yummy," Oliver sarcastically remarks while Vivienne scoops the wraith into the jar. "Don't envy you that diet, man. And I thought protein shakes were gross."

"I thought borscht looked gross," Emil agrees. He shoots a wary, sidelong look at Christine. "Are *you* going to eat things like that?"

"No! I mean... I don't *want* to, but..."

"We really don't know what is going to happen with her, but there is a high possibility. Bakeneko are perfectly happy to eat a diet pretty similar to cats—not wet food, but lots of meat with some green veggies from time to time. But even if you become some kind of luck thing, you're not going to become a cat."

"I am fine with that," Christine mutters.

"Let me know the *moment* you get hungry again for the first time. Might be kinda scary, so let's not have you eating Emil or chewing on your cat babysitter. I don't think her kindness toward you would extend that far," Vivienne tells her. She tosses the jar to Sam, who fumbles it, but thankfully does not drop it. Warded glass shards are a pain to clean up.

"Thank you all for coming today. Megan, Vivienne, thank you again for your help. Vivienne will be in charge from here on out, and I'll relay the findings of your magical aptitude to her," Natalie says.

Oliver brightens into a blinding grin. "Thanks for having us! This was super cool. I can't wait for more lessons and I'm totally gonna become a stronger not-witch than Isaac. This beats *any* law course ever."

"Uh, yeah. Thanks for this," Emil adds. Christine nods in shy agreement.

Natalie considers the first lesson to be a success. She hopes future ones play out so well.

· · · ●· ●· · · ·

Vivienne is still tired from the magic lesson the day before, but she doesn't have any (scheduled) jobs for another two days. She can take it easy.

She's cocooned on her couch in two quilts, Sunshine nestled in by her feet, book half forgotten on her lap. She's warm and drowsy, a pleasant feeling.

Vivienne pulls out her phone and opens up her messages with Dana.

'hey, sorry I've been quiet, busy life! hope you've been okay and I didn't scare you off with that party we dragged you to' she texts. She'd rather explain herself in more than pixels on a screen, but it'd be even weirder and even more nerve-wracking to call her out of the blue. Vivienne believes in minor victories.

Dana texts back quick. Vivienne cannot help the smile stretching her cheeks. *'Nice to hear from you! Sorry I was quiet, too. I thought I was saying stupid things in front of your friends and I was embarrassed.'*

Vivienne has heard *far* stupider shit out of far drunker people. She can't even remember Dana saying anything weird.

'can I call? faster to get all the embarrassment out that way' Vivienne replies.

Dana's response comes as a call notification. Vivienne grins wider. Sunshine spares her a reproachful look for the interruption of his nap.

"Hi," Vivienne says, voice and cheeks warm.

"Hi," Dana replies. She doesn't sound annoyed or wary or regretful. "I'm, uh, glad to hear from you. I think we were not talking for some silly reasons."

"I thought so, too. Truce over embarrassing drunk escapades?"

"Truce," Dana says with clear relief. "So how have you been, these past couple of weeks? Clearly not dressing up your cat to send pictures."

Sunshine sends her another reproachful look, this time with added warning.

"No, I don't think he's in the mood. Too hot this time of year. But I've been good, just busy with weird little odd jobs."

"You, uh, work with Codi, right?" Dana asks, suddenly hesitant.

Vivienne remembers that Dana apparently thinks Codi is some sort of fancy assassin and bites her tongue to stop from laughing. It's a cover story she'd love to take in other circumstances; not very many questions asked, so she wouldn't have to come up with feasible lies as her day job.

But she doesn't want Dana to think of her as a killer for hire. The things she banishes are already dead, so she's not *killing* anything. Dealing with a lot of dead people and sometimes dead bodies, sure, but she didn't do the deed.

"Kind of adjacent. Definitely nothing so messy or dangerous, I'm not brave enough for that kind of stuff. My friend Natalie, the quiet one at the celebration, she runs this little... indie shop, selling things she makes. I help there a lot."

"Oh, like jewelry, or clothing? I wasn't really sure how to do the polite smalltalk with so many people that night, so I didn't get a lot of details about anyone. Not that I don't want to get to know your friends! But it was a lot."

"No, that's fine! It was probably really overwhelming," Vivienne says with an internal groan. She's lucky Dana didn't head for the hills after meeting so many of her weirdo friends. "No, Nat makes like..." She cannot say potions. Synonyms are failing her. "Drink mixes? Some tea stuff? Then stuff like body scrubs and, uh, skin stuff..." All *technically* items Natalie offers in her potion shop.

"That sounds really cute. I love little shops like that. Obviously, since I work at a tiny little bookstore, but you know. Support local businesses, fight big capitalism, all of that."

"Yeah! All of that. I could bring you something from there, next time I'm at the bookshop? What kind of tea do you like?" Tea is safe. Tea is normal. Tea will not cause sudden unexplainable side effects.

"I don't know enough about tea to say. Surprise me. Another manager's friend works at a bakery, and he drops stuff off sometimes. We could have muffins and tea sometime, with a bit of planning."

Vivienne's heart soars in her chest. It dances a happy, almost fast beat. "Or we could skip the bookshop altogether and go somewhere else for muffins and tea. Like, lunch at a cafe? Or dinner together?"

"I'm glad we're not locking ourselves into a muffin date."

"I'm fine with any kind of first date with you. Just so long as it's just the two of us and sans a loud, crowded, boozy club. Let's go sober next time."

"Deal," Dana says with a smile in her voice.

After the call ends, Vivienne happily screams into a pillow. Sunshine abandons her and her noise once and for all.

Natalie presses her fingers to her mouth, hard, trying to keep further sobs from escaping. She has cried so much. Her entire body aches, both with the raw, physical pain of grief, and the tatters her heart is in. They're both dead. They're dead—it's not fair, she had seen them in visions—

Natalie takes a shuddering breath. Her throat constricts painfully, but she does not let out any noise.

Rarely has she tried to induce visions. It can be done, though she herself has only managed it once before, and it had been with half a coven at her back. So many other times, she has failed, but now, she needs to try again. She had seen them. She had seen Hayley. Visions both light and dark, frivolous and serious, heartwarming and never, ever heartrending.

Visions come more frequently to her when she knows a person. She has been having visions of Hayley for over a decade. Natalie has seen so much of her future, her future that must exist. It cannot be gone, cold and still and dead. Hayley cannot be gone. Natalie had never, in all those years, seen a single hint as to what had transpired in that apartment.

With shaking fingers, she lights the candles, and tries her best to calm her breathing again. She has already had so much eyebright tea in the past ten hours that she cannot stomach anything else. Her magic forcibly calms her, and Natalie closes her eyes.

She sits in the circle of candles and waits. She sits for many hours, for a vision of the future she wants to still believe in.

When it comes, it comes not as the storm of many others, but a whisper of a breeze.

The room is drenched in sunlight so strong it's nearly tangible. Red and orange leaves, damp and over-bright in the way that means it has just rained, are plastered on the ground outside the open window, with a few stuck to the glass.

Megan Della Vecchia leans halfway out the window, bracing themselves on the sill. Their hair and dress flutter in the autumn breeze. They duck back inside after a moment, and their smile is blindingly bright, warm and sincere and naïve to any evil in the world. "It doesn't look like it will rain again today," they say happily, "so we can go for a walk later!"

A hand comes to cup their jaw, brushing over the softness of their cheek. "I'd love to," comes a voice both alien and terrifyingly familiar.

Megan's smile dips into something more private. Smaller now, but more intimate. It is the smile of a person in love and unafraid of it. "I'm glad we can finally get you out of the shop once in a while. With everything that's going on—"

Natalie, in a cold sweat, reopens her eyes to the dimly lit room that smells too strongly of rosemary.

But she—with Megan—with all of that warmth and joy surrounding them—

Natalie curls into herself, wracked with fresh sobs.

CHAPTER 21

IN WHICH ISAAC WANTS SOMETHING

July slips into August, and Vivienne still hasn't gone on a date with Dana. She is going to kill Christine herself if this is a luck issue.

First, work schedules didn't match up. Then, Sunshine ate something bad and Vivienne had to take him to the vet. Then, Dana's motorcycle broke down, and Vivienne is left with the image of Dana *riding a motorcycle* and a cancelled reservation. It isn't fair. Dana is too much for her to handle and she hasn't even gotten the chance to handle her yet.

The basic magic safety lessons go well, at least, which is probably the only reason Vivienne doesn't explode.

She stops by the bookstore from time to time, gets to see Dana then, and bothers Emil while he's in Customer Service mode. (Christine, at least, is on Vivienne's side and admits it's funny.) Unfortunately, her frequent visits backfire spectacularly.

"Do you two know each other?" Dana asks while she wipes down dust from bookshelves, conveniently near the armchair Vivienne has sequestered for the morning.

Vivienne freezes. "Huh?" she squeaks in surprise.

"You and Emil, that part-time boy over there. I've seen you talking with him a few times, more than getting help finding something. You know this store pretty well by now." Dana pauses, registering Vivienne's blatantly suspicious behavior. "I think he's a little young for you, if your thing is hitting on bookshop workers, Vivienne."

"No, it's not like that!" Vivienne exclaims.

Luckily, Christine has noticed the conversation, and she floats over with her own mild alarm. Vivienne can hardly talk to her in front of Dana, but maybe she'll think quick on her (floating) feet.

"Just curious," Dana says with a shrug.

"No, it's, well... For the new school year. When he starts up school again? I'm in this program, uh, like a tutoring program, like a Big Brother Big Sister thing?" She could sell the lie if she didn't make everything sound like a question. "It's new to me, not sure about all the details yet. But, haha, you know, as luck would have it, looks like he might be my kid."

Christine nods, following along, and zips off to relay their new cover story to Emil. He wanders over with Christine at his elbow, still whispering in his ear. "Hey, Vivienne," he says without preamble. "Are you still flirting with my boss, who is still on the clock?"

"I was just asking how you two know each other, don't turn this around on me," Dana scolds.

"I'm tutoring him," Vivienne repeats. She finally finds her footing again. "Call me Viv-noona, Emil. When's school starting again?"

"Noona?" he asks instead.

"Big sister in Korean. Like that *program*?" she blatantly prompts.

"I thought you were Japanese," he says, frowning in confusion.

Vivienne gives him an epic eye roll. Both for refusing to play along and drag the subject away, and because *what the hell*. "I'm Korean, thanks."

"Wait, not like that, I only thought that because I've *heard* you speak Japanese when asking about new releases."

"That's my love of manga and the glory of free learning apps."

"Okay, you two, I know you're *apparently* siblings now, but no fighting in the store, if you'd please," Dana breaks in with her own eye roll.

"Sorry," Emil mutters.

Vivienne is not sorry, and she refuses to even say it, but she nods along.

"Wow, sheesh, sorry I even brought it up. Okay, there's no fraternization rules here, but don't bother him too much at work."

"Like I bother you?" Vivienne asks and bats her eyes.

Dana flushes, but her expression remains stern. "I have an excellent work-life balance and level of professionalism I have *never* seen in teenagers. Emil, you're a hard worker, and your shifts have been stellar lately. But you two together are probably just a couple of goofballs who will mess around with any little thing. Not on the clock, please?"

"Yes ma'am," Emil and Vivienne chorus.

• • • • • • • • • •

"If Thomas Novak is doing big, illegal magic, then there are ways to track that. Ingredients. A location. Maybe he wrote the plans in his diary," Vivienne says, mostly to herself, glowering down at her scribbles in her notebook.

"It's not that hard to hide large magical acts if you know how to do it," Isaac points out with smugness. Vivienne wishes she had an extra pen to throw at him.

"Ingredients will still be the way to track him," Natalie says before Vivienne can find any other projectile options. "But he had the opportunity to obtain a dragon from the migration, and as far as we know, he didn't."

"He left his rifle on the roof and his associate fled with only a crossbow," Sam says.

"There were four documented dragon kills. He has no connection to any of them," Natalie agrees, "so it is unlikely his method has anything to do with using dragon parts. Or it is only one or two parts, and he will purchase them at a later point. That's still trackable if we lay inquiries out now."

"Lots of rich people buy dragon parts. And what if he uses Eyebright to purchase it? We can't go snooping in their records," Vivienne irritably points out. "He didn't seem to know why he was contracted to stop Mark from getting a dragon skin. Didn't even realize he only wanted the skin—so he probably doesn't know you sold yours to him, right?"

"A safe assumption to make for the short term," Natalie agrees. "Has Mark spoken to his friend anymore about what methods her employer is using to accomplish the same means?"

"Tengu First egg seems to be non-negotiable. But the tengu have mentioned several missing eggs, so that might already be a lost cause. What else would you use if you were trying to summon a big, angry, old god into another realm?"

"Are you actually summoning it?" Isaac asks. Vivienne raises her head to look at him, brow furrowed, both confused and annoyed because *yes*, they are operating under the assumption that Thomas Novak is summoning a big nasty god to wreck their lives. It's a pretty big and pretty important assumption to make. "Is it a *summoning* of the being across realms, or is it a weakening of the realm borders to allow a temporary break? Are you making a tunnel or a door?"

Vivienne processes for a beat.

Then she groans into her folded arms. "Ugh, Isaac, I could kiss you. You're right! I've missed working with a spellwriter."

He scowls at the offer. "That's what the dragon migration was, wasn't it? That wasn't a summoning, and definitely not by that Thomas guy. With all that dragon skin in one area, it could've weakened the realm border in that specific area. Hard to plan for, but hypothetically possible. It just didn't work. There are more to realm borders than magic."

"Okay, okay, you're right. Still operating under the assumption that that one was Thomas', not Brynja's—"

"Vivienne, are you sure you want to be sharing names with everyone?" Natalie gently interrupts.

Isaac's expression sours further, Vivienne notices. But she only shrugs. "How else are we going to figure out how he's doing this? Isaac can at least give us options. Is there some reason we should keep secrets now? I think Mark can take care of himself at this point."

"You've mentioned those names before. Was it supposed to be a secret?" Sam asks.

"Apparently not."

"You wanted to enlist them, so I'm using them," Vivienne retorts.

"*I* wanted other information," Natalie maintains.

"He can multitask."

"Don't I get a say in this?" Isaac asks. After a shared glance, both women nod. "I want payment if I'm being used as a sounding board. Even if I'm not writing a spell for you, I'm offering a service you apparently can't get elsewhere."

"I would've figured it out eventually," Vivienne mutters.

"What do you want as payment, Isaac?"

"You know what I want."

"No, that is a separate transaction," Natalie easily replies. "We can work out another arrangement instead."

"You two doing under the table deals without me?" Vivienne asks, equal parts curious and grateful for the distraction from her frustration. (Sam ducks to peek under the table with literal curiosity.)

"No, we're not," Isaac replies and yanks Sam back up. His head *thunks* against the table and he yelps. A shadow of concern passes over Isaac's face, and Sam leans against him in a sad bid for some sympathy. To Vivienne's delight, Isaac pets him. "If you figure out *what* kind of spell he's supposedly trying to build, then we can talk again. But otherwise you're blindly guessing."

"Yeah, welcome to fighting the future, Isy."

"Stop calling me that. It's Oliver's."

"A cute nickname for a cute demon summoner," Vivienne reasons. Isaac immediately stops petting the demon. "Aw, sorry, Sam. And here I thought we were bonding, Isaac."

"Over my dead body."

(Supernatural Hunter Tip #3: Don't tease anyone who can set you on fire.)

"You know, apocalypses tend to leave a lot of those. Isn't that good enough reason for helping us?"

"We'll see if it is."

•••••••••••

Benji's tails have not stopped wagging since he spotted the car. It better be impressive; Mark paid extra for a driver who'd turn a blind eye to an obvious spirit, and whatever Uber Lux entails. The car looks nice. Fiona rolls her eyes at his opulence and tosses her Actually Styled For Once auburn hair over her shoulder.

"I know the car would crumple before you would, but seatbelt, please," Mark reminds him while Benji pastes himself against the tinted window.

"Behave," Fiona mutters, "and don't start any fights. This is my only pair of dress pants."

"We'll see," Benji replies, still glued to the passing scenery.

"Is it smart to have such a grand entrance into Eyebright territory?" she asks Mark instead of pushing for a promise of good behavior.

"It's *always* a wise idea to have a grand entrance. Haven't you heard that saying, always dress like you may run into your worst enemy?" he replies.

"Are we admitting to having Eyebright enemies?"

"No, though Thomas remains on my shit list. Today will be more cordial. I hope. The twins *technically* aren't Eyebright witches anymore, remember?" Being one of three psychics in the city earns Mark a baseline of respect from anyone who knows who he is, but it doesn't mean it is a carte blanche to do whatever he pleases, wherever he pleases. He's never allied himself with a coven, not like Natalie or Alex had.

Then again, he's not a witch.

Adam and Alex McAllister *had* been the co-heads of Eyebright coven, once upon a time. They were formally stripped of the title, but never formally kicked out, so they remain a wary pair at the edge of the peripherals, like wolves circling prey.

It also unfortunately means they are quite content to live and work deeply entrenched in coven territory.

The car pulls up to the curb, smooth as silk, and if Mark wanted to bother with flashy cars, he may have asked the driver more about it. As it stands, the woman doesn't bat an eye at the backseat conversation or the man with the dog tails and ears pawing all over it.

Of course, it is not as if they are laying siege to a castle. Mark had texted Adam earlier about meeting him. He's not as close to him as he is his brother, but the powerful players in the city all endeavor to know each other. They walk up the short sidewalk and press the doorbell to be buzzed in. Not everyone lives in the semi-suburbs like Mark and actually owns houses, but the twins' penthouse apartment is nothing to sneeze at.

Adam greets them as soon as they step off the elevator. His eyes dart immediately to Fiona and Benji, flanking Mark, but his smile does not dim. Unfortunately—for multiple reasons—he is identical to his brother, and Mark can only tell them apart by the subtle differences in how their mental shielding functions. No one here is dumb enough to let him read thoughts openly. Or to let Alex.

"What a surprise to see you here. And you brought your friends," Adam says, and leads them to his front door. Though Mark has been here before, there is always something to say for grand entrances, and grand places to enter.

"Had some earlier trouble with some Eyebright witches. Can't blame a man for being too cautious these days," Mark replies.

Adam shows them to the home office. It is plushly decorated and quite inviting, which is great, considering he and his brother run a small therapy business for the magically aware.

Benji throws himself onto a chaise lounge and makes himself comfortable. Adam's eyebrows raise, but he waves them all in. Fiona perches by the inugami's feet.

Mark sits opposite Adam's armchair and crosses one ankle over the other knee with a beam. "Do you want smalltalk, or do you want the reason I came to you instead of Alex?"

"Well, you two in the same room is a migraine-inducing echo chamber, so I'm guessing *that* has something to do with why you never meet in person. As for me, well, I can only assume you want a spell written," Adam says with as much ease as Mark strives to exude.

Truthfully, he is anything but calm. Spellwriters are nothing to mess with, and Mark is here to gauge whether or not he is working with Thomas. If he is, this could get very messy, very fast. If he isn't, best-case scenario is walking out in one piece without raising a coven alarm bell on him.

Most likely: Adam refuses to tell anything.

"Where's your familiar? I smell her," Benji asks and Mark could smack him.

"Having breakfast, most likely. It is nine in the morning, and I see no reason to disrupt her meal time for the sake of a rage spirit's poorly concealed hunger," Adam replies.

"Well, it *is* breakfast time," Benji points out.

"Shut up. You're not eating anyone's familiar," Fiona snaps. "McAllister, you know what we're here for. Work with Mark. Otherwise, I don't want to ruin these dress pants, and the nicest thing I can do is promise you I won't let Benji eat your familiar in front of you."

Mark could smack *her*. "Would you two *please* shut up?! Some of us are trying to be civil."

"What do you expect, working with—*them*?" Adam asks with the thinnest of covers on his disgust.

"He expects help. I think you should help him, too," Benji replies.

"*Down*, boy," Mark hisses. "Adam, I must apologize for their characteristic rude behavior. But I didn't bring them for their charming personalities."

"No, you brought them for protection and a show of force, because you make grand gestures and you're expecting to do something today. I still don't have the faintest clue what that could be. I seriously don't know," Adam says with a pointed look at Fiona. She glares right back. "You *don't* want a spell written? That's what I do these days, you know that."

"I'm good on unknowable magic spells right now. I just want information."

"I don't sell out customers."

"But you could confirm something for me. This is bigger than patient confidentiality, Adam."

"I'm listening. And that's all I'll agree to do without more information," Adam says and leans back in his chair with the air of a royal awaiting a briefing. That much hasn't changed about him.

"Did you write a spell to either create a realm door, or to break down, erode, or weaken realm barriers?"

Adam waits a beat, then realizes Mark is done. "What, one impossible spell isn't enough? Why the hell would I do that? *How* the hell could I do that? That's something that'd take years of work, and it's the first I'm hearing of it, so no, I definitely don't have something like that up my sleeve."

Mark cannot read his mind, but he can glean vague emotions and impressions of thoughts. From that slim information, he *thinks* Adam is telling the truth. And, of course, he does not trust that slim information.

"Isn't Eyebright's whole deal limitless magical research? You said so yourself—you already created one impossible spell," Mark loftily points out.

"Alex did most of that, remember?"

"And now Alex isn't the spellwriter anymore. You are. Someone is trying to break something else into our realm. There are likely different avenues of trying, but *someone* has to have written a spell for something like that."

"It wasn't me," Adam maintains and crosses his arms. "How did you come across this information, exactly?"

"You're the only spellwriter in the city right now." (As far as Adam is aware, anyway. Vivienne has sworn up and down that Isaac remains a secret.)

"And I didn't do it. I wouldn't know *how*. The goblin markets are the only direct doors to another realm on this *continent*, and I haven't spent my free time figuring out how they work. Now, your turn. *Who* is doing this, *how* did you find out, and *what* is going on?"

Mark shrugs. "I only have the vaguest of leads to follow. You were one, and you were apparently a dead end, but at least that's information, too. Have you heard anything about missing tengu First eggs?"

"I've heard something to that effect."

"A lovely magpie tengu from the crow clan contracted me to find at least one, though there are more. I think these are related to this issue of mine. Know anything about it?"

Adam's eyes narrow, but he nods. "I heard that one came through the goblin market. Caused a lot of chaos and the youkai version of a car chase. That's the extent of my knowledge, outside of hearing that the songbird clan has been asking around, too. This isn't just the crows."

"I thought as much." Brynja could have been that one in the goblin market; she caused an obvious stir and Mirai said there were witnesses. Still not a new lead.

Adam inclines his head toward Benji. "One youkai isn't enough for you to mess with, Mark? You're going to bite off more than you can chew."

"I'll wiggle my way through, somehow. I always do."

"And what about this realm breaking of yours? Something like that could start an apocalypse, depending on what was doing the breaking and entering."

"Hence my talk with you today. You remember that incident during the dragon migration that knocked Alex on his ass? I believe that was related. How, I don't entirely know yet, except maybe an attempt that backfired. Imagine that on a wider scale and one that doesn't disappear in a minute."

Adam nods, solemn, still seated. Mark rises, pats imaginary dust off his pants, and grins at him. Fiona snaps up to her feet and Benji rolls off the chaise lounge with a long sigh and a longer stretch.

"Thanks for having us, Adam. Give my regards to your brother. Hopefully, I won't have to shake you down for any more terrifying information anytime soon."

Adam does not see them to the elevator, but they still wait until they are outside the building to speak.

"Do you think he was telling the truth?" Fiona asks with a suspicious look backward.

"Likely, but his mind is a locked door to me. Not like I can rummage around in *everyone's* brains. But if a spellwriter wasn't consulted, that means that other avenues are being used for this."

Fiona calls a car while Mark mulls this over. Brynja's master's plan was to brute force its way through. Which is all very well and good for a *god*. But there still must be agents on the human side; Brynja, gradually and regretfully, had shared bits and pieces. Even she did not know all the details, but it looked to be like a spell that simply had so much magic poured into it, it did not need to be compressed.

Even a witch as talented as Thomas couldn't handle that. He probably couldn't even handle a written spell of that magnitude. He must have accomplices, and possibly outside help with the spell. And was it to do directly with the realm borders, like Yaehathal? Or was there another way to approach the terrible issue of getting a massive deity from point A to point B?

Mark has far too many magical questions for someone with no magical ability. He sighs and resigns himself to dumping all this onto Vivienne.

Vivienne shrieks and leaps back from the spilled bowl of demon blood. She pats down her jeans, then shakes out her hands, dancing from foot to foot while she figures out how to clean something she can't touch.

A young man with a mop of blond hair watches with a pout. "Are you alright?" he asks with clear concern.

"That's what you two get for experimenting with demonic magic," comes another voice, speaker unseen in another room.

"What do I get?" the blond one asks, confused. "I don't care if she spills it."

"She'll have to get new blood from you now. She's going to bleed you like a pig."

"I can't believe you have a demon and you don't want to learn anything about him!" Vivienne irately calls back. She then sighs. "Sam, can you help me clean this up? I would like more blood, though..." She puts on a puppy dog pout, batting her eyes at him.

He doesn't fluster or become annoyed, but cocks his head to the side. "You can have more. But you shouldn't keep spilling it everywhere, since you're already complaining about the smell."

"Trust me, I have years of practice getting the smell of black magic out of my clothes and hair. But you'd have to be a fool to pass up this kind of opportunity, so let's take advantage! I'll teach you both to have some scientific curiosity yet!"

Natalie comes back to herself already sighing at this potential future of Vivienne's. She's no fan of her preference for black magic, even if she is skilled at it—she does not need to be working with demonic magic on top of that. She'll end up killed by a coven yet.

Not that Natalie will ever let that happen.

CHAPTER 22

IN WHICH AUGUST 19TH COMES

The Day dawns bright and full of sunshine. August nineteenth. The three-year anniversary.

The shop is closed and her phone is off for the day. Natalie will mourn in her own way, away from outside eyes and judgment. Vivienne, she knows, will do the same. This is how they spend The Day: more apart than they have ever been.

Megan comes over. Their presence only started last year, and Natalie still has conflicted feelings about it, but she knows it is for the best. She hopes Vivienne isn't alone, either, but this is one day she allows herself *not* to care. One day she allows herself to be *angry*.

Natalie drinks a concoction of rosemary, eyebright, and orange liqueur. It will help tamp down her powers, because on top of every other feeling she allows herself to remember today, she *cannot* deal with a vision too. Megan brings pot brownies and a bottle of old, dark whiskey. They never offer anything outright, only place them where Natalie can partake if she wishes; she can never tell how anything will deal with her mental state until she's already there.

"Thank you," Natalie tells Megan, again and again, until she's certain it's the only thing she can recall how to say anymore. Natalie drowns herself in her grief. She *languishes* in it.

Megan only offers their presence. Natalie can hardly recall anything; she naps, she drinks, she tries to cook, she loses herself in Netflix. Most of this is spent leaning literally on Megan for support. She isn't truly drunk, she isn't truly high, but she is some mixture of everything. It's too much. Pretending to be okay for the rest of the year is too much.

Vivienne wears her heart on her sleeve and Natalie allows her own resentment of it. Vivienne was allowed to feel the guilt and sorrow and panic and grief. Natalie was treated like a delicate widow, lost and confused and not to be treated with anything less than the lightest of touches. Vivienne was raw in her reaction to the accident; Natalie was forced to be the pillar of support when it was the one time *she* wished to crumble.

"I was glad," Natalie sobs into Megan's lap. Megan only brushes her hair out of her face, a tender, repetitive motion. "I was *glad* when she died—I can't stand that I was glad!"

She doesn't even know how much Megan knows. Being the immediate family of a coven head means there is a certain amount of information shared, but Megan has also been a coddled, insulated only child. Deirdre would gladly hide dirty details. She has before.

So Natalie doesn't know how Megan takes these annual breakdowns. She doesn't know why Megan came to her last year, and why they willingly did it again this year.

When Natalie throws up, Megan holds her hair back. When Natalie sleeps, Megan is a pillow. When Natalie drinks, Megan joins her. When Natalie finally thinks she can stomach food, Megan orders dinner.

"You really are a healer," Natalie murmurs, dazed, while they wait for pizza. She thinks it's pizza. She wants pizza. "You are the best of us, Megan."

"I do try to be a healer," they lightly joke.

"Why aren't you with Vivienne? You're closer," Natalie says, half an accusation, half a deep-rooted fear. *Everyone* is closer to Vivienne. Vivienne is friendly and personable and funny. Natalie has too many sad memories and too many future neuroses.

"You need me more. And maybe I want a day where I can be angry at Vivi and Hayley, too. I need to be apart from her for that," Megan replies.

"I don't want to need you," Natalie croaks, and the tears come again, abrupt and overwhelming. "I don't want to be this broken thing t-to protect, or put together, or shield. I don't want to have to need you. I don't want to have to need anyone a-anymore."

"Shh," Megan soothes, and Natalie collapses into their lap once more, exactly the broken thing she fears.

Just for The Day can she be a broken thing, a grieving not-widow, a bystander to an accident that never concerned her. Tomorrow, she'll put herself together again, thank Megan again (more soberly), and do what must be done to stop an apocalypse.

Without Hayley by her side, despite the numerous visions she'd been looking forward to of their future.

· · • • · • · · ·

Vivienne arrives at Mark's door on the twentieth, swaddled in two quilts, a robe, and fuzzy socks. She'd hardly registered the weird looks she'd gotten on the train; city folk have *always* seen worse. She is certain she is still drunk. She is certain she still wants to die.

A headache pounds behind her eyes and she squints up at Mark when he opens the door. "Wow, you look terrible," he remarks and lets her in.

Vivienne shuffles two steps in, then registers the naked, muscular woman on his couch.

"Oh. Right. You're still a thing," Vivienne grumbles. She isn't certain she can handle this today. The day after The Day is supposed to be detox with cuddling and a mind-numbing marathon of Ghibli movies.

"This is who you were expecting?" Brynja asks with eyebrows raised.

"Yes, and I'm demanding the couch back. For today, she's more important than you," Mark replies.

"I'm always more important," Vivienne mumbles. She staggers to the couch and falls over the arm, onto Brynja's legs. She runs hot and Vivienne nuzzles toward the warmth.

"I thought there were more important things to deal with than... this," Brynja snaps. She yanks her legs back and skulks away like a suspicious dog.

"We're only human, my dear. We all need days to ourselves. Haven't you heard of the term 'rest day'? If you work out forever, you'll overtax your muscles and burn out, or do harm to your own body. You have to rest once in a while," Mark replies. "Now shoo. You can have the bathroom or the bedroom—"

"I want a bath," Vivienne sniffles. "Later. I want a bath. I haven't had one in *so long*."

Brynja's eyes narrow to angry slits. "I do not understand how you humans operate, but this is pathetic. I will allow you use of the bathtub for the afternoon."

"So kind of you two to politely divvy up *my* bathroom," Mark snarks.

"Maaaark," Vivienne whines from beneath the quilt pile.

"Fine, fine." He sits down and they arrange themselves into their usual cuddle puddle. The couch isn't large, but neither have any sense of personal space. "*Spirited Away* first?"

"Uh-huh."

Vivienne settles in, draped over his chest, listening to the steady *thump* of his heartbeat. He's warm, too. Warm and whole and alive. Still here for her. Despite everything, still here for her.

Vivienne lets her eyes lull, not quite shut, relaxing into a drowsy state of nothing. The movie is familiar and comforting. Her place in Mark's home is the same. Not even the nightgaunt, leaning toward her over the couch, can dampen her mood. It's another reminder of how things went wrong, and today, she can almost accept it as her new normal.

Three years, Vivienne thinks to herself. It feels so far away, and yet so raw. She thought she'd gotten used to the way grief comes and goes after Rory's death, but as it turns out, no one can get *used* to grief. *Two months left*, she remembers, painfully. They have a spellwriter again in the form of Isaac, but they're hardly friends. She doesn't think she can entrust Rory to him.

She doesn't think she can entrust Rory to herself, either.

She doesn't know what to do.

Natalie sighs in utter bliss. Deirdre has let her stay over in one of the coven houses, and she likes a good bath. The tub here is spacious enough to allow her to recline comfortably and stretch out her legs. She has to heat the water herself, since target practice gone wrong blew up the water heater last month, but she'll gladly spare some magic. It's a rare treat, this kind of relaxation.

Naturally, it cannot last.

Natalie is still herself; it's the uncomfortable sensation of trying on wet clothes that should fit, but don't. She's seated with her back against cold concrete. Her right leg is bloody and badly broken, but Natalie does not register pain as she stares at the wreckage of her leg.

Megan kneels at her side, tears dripping down their cheeks, and tries to mend flesh and bone. "J-Just hold still, I can... manage something..." Their voice is frail, but as determined as ever. Their entire frame trembles.

As a passenger in her own body, Natalie can only watch as someone steps up behind Megan and presses a gun against their strawberry blonde hair.

Natalie wishes she could scream. No sound escapes her, even when the trigger is pulled.

Blood and worse splatter all over Natalie. Megan's body slumps forward over her broken leg, expression erased by the exit wound and the delicate way their curly hair falls over their face.

The gun turns on her. She sees the empty black eyes of the possessed, and bruise-like curses curving up over the exposed face of the black-haired man. He pulls the trigger again.

Natalie finds herself in the bath again and jerks upward, splashing excess water from the tub. This is her first time experiencing her own death. She's never seen Megan's death before. Bile rises in her throat, and she fights it back down long enough to make it to the toilet.

She heaves over the toilet bowl as the air grows cold around her.

CHAPTER 23

IN WHICH A BET IS LOST AND A FAVOR IS CALLED IN

It is the beginning of September and three things still have not happened: Vivienne still has not gone on a proper first date with Dana, they have not figured out if Oliver has any kind of magical aptitude that could *prevent* him from doing basic spells, and no one has asked what she had *assumed* was an obvious question.

"Come *on*!" Oliver groans. His focus could burn a hole through the table.

Emil shoots him a grin, smug little shit, with his own tiny *fire* spell flickering over the tip of his finger. He has so far performed that, *light*, and a *pull* spell he has yet to replicate.

Oliver has not been able to perform a single bit of magic.

"You *have* to have some gimmick," Vivienne reasons, sitting cross-legged on the table next to him. "There's an initial hump, yes, but Emil's caught on and he's distracted by school now."

"I *do* have a full-time job," Oliver retorts.

"And you also *do* have some level of magical ability. So why can't it catch?" Vivienne hums and rubs her chin. "All magic users should be able to use all kinds of magic, *somewhat*, though there could be some difficulty..."

But they've tried an assortment. Even some runes that Emil had not been allowed to look at, just to see if Oliver was some sort of really weird outlier.

And nothing.

"Calm down, you'll break your own fingers," Megan advises and carefully pries his white-knuckled grip apart. "It can be hard, but you'll get there."

"I can handle hardness!" Oliver exclaims. Emil snickers, and Christine covers her mouth to prevent the same. "Dude, not helping! I like a dick joke as much as the next guy, but this is *serious*! How can I look Isy in the eye if I get actual goddamned magic lessons and it *never works*?!"

"Well, um, Isaac stopped coming, so at least he doesn't know," Christine reasons.

"That's because Nat stopped coming, and with school back in session, the potion shop is busier. He *does* technically work there. We're not a charity running witness protection."

"I still don't get how he's such a big deal," Emil says.

"That means we're doing our jobs," Vivienne replies. The kids may be somewhat stable now—Christine has shown no signs of being anything other than a golden ghost—but like *hell* she is going to let them get cozy to a demon, even one as nice as Sam. That contract is going to run out eventually, and she fears he may have some true colors underneath the sweet exterior. She'd rather he eat Isaac than Christine.

"Anyway, back to my problem? Fuck Isy and his weirdness," Oliver says, and Vivienne is grateful for his... Oliver-ness. Blunt and dudebro and privy to *far* too many supernatural secrets. "Isn't there *something* else I can try? Give me something like Sam to work with!"

"We tried the wraith thing, and that didn't work out. Healing is a no-go, and we are *not* letting you try to cast thunderbolt."

"I could be Pikachu," he complains, "and we'll never know. Ain't there anything *else* I could try?! Wait, what about... Hey, wait. You never showed us white magic," Oliver realizes. He finally releases his death grip on his own hand and sits up, puzzled, searching his memories. He counts off on his fingers.

Megan bursts out laughing. "I win! I won the bet!"

"Oh my *god*," Vivienne groans.

"Wait, what? What bet?" Emil asks. "Why'd we have a bet going and we weren't part of it?"

"The luck thing, man," Oliver points out.

"Oh my god!" Vivienne repeats. She slides off the desk and retrieves her phone from her bag. "I'm texting Nat. That took *forever*—I can't believe you two!"

"I won! I told you it'd take longer than a month!" Megan continues to cheer.

"That was way longer. That's *unfair*. Where's your scientific curiosity?!"

"Well, we got sidetracked when you summoned a wraith. That was a big distraction. Then you tried to get Sam to eat it, and then we were a little scared of him, and you didn't do it on *purpose*? I thought we ran out of time or something," Emil says.

"I forgot about it," Christine admits with a shrug.

'*they finally asked about white magic. meggy won the bet*' Vivienne texts Natalie. She'd thought that'd be easy money, too. Kids these days. "Okay, well, thanks for eating into my anime merch fund, you two. Very rude."

"I can't believe I won it! *And* you didn't prompt them into it! You behaved so well, Vivi," Megan says, still laughing like the little brat they are. Underneath the kind and nurturing exterior lies a *monster* who insists on winning any and all bets they partake in.

"I *tried*," she confesses, despairing.

"Uh, anyway, white magic? What if I can do that?" Oliver prompts with his hand in the air.

"Well, then, you're shit outta luck, because no one can do white magic," Vivienne replies without looking up from her phone. Natalie hasn't responded yet, so she's probably busy. A pity. Vivienne could use an ally in loss.

"But what *is* white magic? Usually that's healing and stuff in video games."

"Definitely not healing," Megan snorts. "White magic falls under two big, scary umbrellas—time magic and angelic magic."

Silence reigns in the room. Vivienne pockets her phone.

"Angels exist?" Emil whispers. His expression is unreadable, but overwhelming. Vivienne realizes in hindsight this conversation *could* have been more diplomatically approached. Even raised Catholic, it has been a *long* time since she has thought about angels as most of the world does: kind heavenly beings.

"Wait, no, hold on—*time magic*?!" Oliver whisper-yells. "Time travel is real?!"

Yeah, both topics should have had more thought put into them. Whoops. Vivienne takes a deep breath and debates which one to start with.

"Okay, so, time magic. It is, theoretically, real. We have no concrete proof of it, and only *suggestions* as to a few higher spirits capable of it. There have been no documented cases of successful time magic ever cast, either by humans or recorded spirits. Think of it as the magical equivalent of quantum physics. *All* theory. Hence, no example given. No one wants to get eaten by a hound of Tindalos today," Vivienne explains.

"A *lot* of magic just exists in theory, and most documentation as we understand it only started in the past century or so," Megan helpfully adds.

"As for angels... Yes, they exist, again theoretically. A little more than theoretically, since there have been documented cases, but not exactly something you can just run into. They live on another plane, not exactly heaven, but maybe that's where some religious stuff came from. They're not religious, not these. I'm not getting into religion talk here. But I will say these are a lot closer to the biblical description of angels than the Renaissance ones."

"What's that mean? I didn't really grow up Christian or whatever has angels, so I just know 'em as the pretty winged things," Oliver asks.

"Angels in the Bible greeted humans with the phrase 'be not afraid' for good reason—there are a lot of different descriptions, but a lot aren't even humanoid. Multi-eyed, winged, lion heads, bull horns, ring of fire, goat hooves, draconic, you name it. Lots of wings and lots of eyes seem to be recurring features. Theologically, there is no consensus, except that there are multiple types of angels and they all looked pretty freaky."

"Magically, we don't know much about them, either. They could look like that. All we know is that they have their own type of magic and are beings of *extreme* power. Because of all the aforementioned magic," Vivienne concludes with a shrug. "So again, no examples will be given. If you can find something capable of doing white magic in a quantifiable amount, call me first, 'kay?"

"I could," Oliver says.

"No, you couldn't," Megan replies with a chuckle. "Humans can't handle that much. You know how if you actually used the full power of your musculature you'd break your bones? It's like that. We'd pop like popcorn."

"Um, if angels exist, and ghosts can, uh, decay into demons, then...?" Christine begins hopefully, but Vivienne shakes her head. She wilts again.

"Sorry, it doesn't work that way. Angels and demons aren't like what a lot of Western religions say. Or Christian religions, whichever. But I *do* know about the supernatural, and ghosts don't turn into angels. Angels don't pass on. Wherever they live, it may or may not be heaven, but it's not where ghosts pass on to."

Megan cuts through the heavier mood. "Anyway, enough talk of impossible magic. Let's talk about how Vivi owes me a hundred bucks and let's figure out what Oliver can do!"

· · • •• • • · · ·

Emil hadn't looked forward to going back to school. It is his senior year, and senioritis hits different when haunted and orphaned.

Christine, on the other hand, had been vibrating with poorly concealed excitement for the last month.

Two weeks into the semester and her enthusiasm still hasn't waned. Emil would find it cute if she wasn't *his* ghostly shadow in all of his classes. Or he'd find it funny if he didn't loathe school so much. School means pitying looks from teachers and fewer hours on his paycheck. School means *homework*.

He also can't pretend to be on the phone to talk with Christine. He's already figured out that scribbling in his notebook works, but it's slow and distracts him.

'Weren't you a year behind me? You said you were sixteen' he writes.

"Yes, but I was in some AP courses. Also, aside from math, a lot of courses aren't progressive. Like this," Christine says. They're in World History now, which, okay, history isn't changing anytime soon. "Also, it's nice to get out of the house! I miss school. I went a few times with you in the spring, but this is better when you can hear and see me."

And more distracting, he thinks. He's okay with history. It isn't his favorite subject, but it isn't his worst. That said, two weeks into the semester is not the time to be allowing himself to slide. If he wants to stand *any* chance at getting a scholarship, that means good grades.

College seems a far-off, expensive dream, however.

Still, good grades never hurt anyone.

But he's pretty sure he has covered ancient Egyptian history in *every* non-American-centric history class he's ever been in, so excuse him if he can't get excited to learn about the Nile for the nth time.

"Ibises are really pretty," Christine sighs as the teacher goes to the next slide. "What do you think Kirara would think of the fact that the Egyptians used to worship cats?"

'They worshiped a cat goddess - not cats themselves' he writes back.

"Okay, they *revered* them, mister pedantic. Along with ibises, and crocodiles, and that breed of dog they made. But what do you think a Japanese cat spirit would think?"

Emil is pretty sure the Japanese like cats, too. Probably not as much as the ancient Egyptians. He doesn't think anyone likes cats as much as they do, except perhaps the modern internet.

Does Christine like animals? He wonders if she'd like a visit to the zoo while the weather is still nice. It's not like they could touch the animals anyway, so looking would be a perfect trip for her.

Right when he's about to ask, Emil sees something plop out of the ceiling.

It drops out of the corner and lands on the tile with a wet *smack*. It's not large, but it's a *thing*, and no one else reacted to it, so he's guessing it's absolutely a spirit thing.

"Oh my gosh, what *is* that?" Christine whispers.

The gnarled little creature crawls to its feet and surveys the room. There are ten minutes left of class, and there is a monster in the room with his teacher, all his classmates, and his apparently very edible ghost friend. Emil sweats bullets.

The thing looks like the dirty lovechild of Yoda and a Shar Pei, maybe about two feet tall, the color and texture of tree bark. Emil has barely gotten the hang of the most basic of basic magic; he doesn't have any banishment charms or whatever fancy circle stuff Vivienne does. He doesn't even know how to put it to sleep.

It toddles closer to his teacher.

Can he get Vivienne here somehow? Not quickly, and not without causing a scene or sending Christine on a very slow fetch quest. He doesn't know of any magical teachers or other kids. Whose jurisdiction is this usually? Did this happen often, and this is only the first time he's experiencing it?

The thing is now close enough to bat at his teacher's pants. Emil sees a definite movement of the fabric, but she just shifts her weight to the other leg, unnoticing. Does that mean it can or can't harm people?

He could set it on fire. That's a bad, bad idea, but he *could* do it.

"What do we do?" Christine whispers through her fingers.

'*You need to get out of here. What if it wants to eat you?*' he writes as fast as he can. He's between her and the thing, and it does not appear fast, but he is not taking chances. Shouldn't they be lucky enough for this to be a harmless thing?

"It seems more interested in your teacher. Do you think it's dangerous?" Christine replies. She floats higher, a hand on his shoulder to boost herself, craning her neck to look at it. "I've never seen anything like it, but I'm not an expert or anything."

Emil doesn't know what he should do. Christine, for the moment, is not listening to him or the chance of danger. His teacher could be in danger. His classmates could be. He can't do anything, even if he was willing to stand up and cause a scene, which is the *really* frustrating part.

If all else fails, he'll grab it and punt it out the window, he supposes.

The fire alarm suddenly goes off.

The classroom processes this for a moment; students had been awaiting the bell, but not that one. The teacher lets out a long-suffering sigh and steps over to her desk, away from the thing. "Okay, class seems to be over either way. You're supposed to leave your stuff here, remember, and file out of the room. I'm sure it's just a drill."

A few boys laugh at the timing of it and several girls grab their little fashion backpacks, regardless of the order otherwise. Many check their phones. Emil jumps to his feet, staring at the confused gremlin thing, but there are still people here, so his hands remain tied.

Students file out, not in any hurry, but the thing doesn't go after any of them. It watches raptly.

A moment later, the regular class bell tries to cut through the fire alarm, and there is another smattering of laughter.

Christine covers her ears with her hands. "Does that actually work?" Emil asks, risking a question in all the noise.

"I guess not..."

"Come on, the rest of you, too," the teacher calls. "Wait, do *not* go to your locker! I see you!" She ducks into the hallway with an irate shout. The last couple classmates duck out after her, which leaves Emil conveniently alone.

He darts over to shut the door. He hasn't learned locking spells yet, either, but the only window into the classroom from the hallway is on the door, so it shouldn't be impossible not to get caught. Not for someone lucky, right?

When he turns back around, a calico cat is sitting on the teacher's desk.

Kirara raises a single paw in greeting, gold eyes sparkling with mischief. "It's quite easy to get a teenaged boy to pull a fire alarm, did you know?" She leans down and bats at the creature. "Seems like you two are having an exciting day at school."

"What *is* that thing? What is it doing here?" Emil demands.

"It looks to be a bogle. They're little domestic spirits, usually harmless or even beneficial. I've never heard of one appearing at a school, however. It might've been attracted to the luck," she says conversationally and smacks it again.

"Oh no," Christine says, drooping in the air.

"Oh, that's not your fault. Emil is also covered in it. This could be a good thing, really. Aren't you practicing magic now?"

"Trying to learn. I wouldn't say *practicing* yet," he replies. "Not like I can banish it, or put it in a confinement circle."

"Look at you and all of your newfound terminology," Kirara proudly says. She stops batting at the bogle. "Well then, Christine, would you like it?"

"M-Me? Why would I?" she squeaks.

"Haven't you gotten hungry yet?"

Christine shakes her head fast enough she shakes off luck. "No! I'm not—I'm not becoming anything!"

"You're becoming a luck spirit, remember? We eat. Eating is one joy spirits share with humans."

"I am not yet—I don't. Not yet," she says, relenting, and wraps her arms around her stomach. She floats low enough her feet drag through the floor. "Not yet," she repeats.

"That's fine. Eventually, you will have to eat, however. Keep that in mind."

"Hold up. You wanted her to eat *that*?" Emil says and points at the bogle. It opens its gummy mouth at him and shuts it again without a sound.

"Oh, no! That's disgusting! Kirara, I *couldn't*!" Christine moans and hides her face in her hands. "I can't do that, not as a spirit, not things like *that*."

"Emil could cook it for you. I'll teach you fire magic."

"I know fire magic!" He knows how to make a half-inch flame on his index finger, which isn't all that impressive, but it is fire out of nowhere, and it *is* successful magic use. "But I'm no cook. I'm definitely not a butcher. And that thing..."

Is disgusting, but still somewhat alive, and Kirara had called it harmless. The most Emil wants to do is punt it out the window.

"I'm not certain how much cooking it would need, but a nice char helps anything taste better. Are you two sure you don't want it?" Kirara asks. Both of them shake their heads. "Suit yourselves. I'll take this one. And you better get back to your classmates—best not be seen with me at school, right?"

"Oh, right. Thanks, Kirara."

"Of course, kitten." Kirara gives them a cat smile, eyes flashing, then stoops to pick up the bogle with her teeth. It squeals silently and kicks, but she vanishes with it and a muted *pop*.

"How much do you think she *actually* watches over us?" Emil asks. Christine shrugs. "How much do you think is luck, and how much do you think is her selectively deciding to drop in?"

"If I wondered how much of this life is luck, I'd go crazy," she replies. "Let's just... content ourselves with the fact that she is looking out for us. A little. When she wants."

"When she wants," he agrees. Because, right, cat spirit.

•••••••••

Natalie hangs up with a sigh. Isaac looks up like a gun had gone off. She dislikes how jumpy he has become; she thinks she deserves more trust by this point. But flies and honey and all that.

"Two things," she says, and that grabs Sam and Vivienne's attention, because like normal people, they respond to verbal address, instead of every small sound. "Graham is done with the rest of the dragon processing. I'm selling most of it through him, but I need the spine, ribs, and the claws from him."

"Oh, another fetch quest. That's what they're called, right, Isaac?" Sam asks.

"I can handle this on my own. I don't need your help with this, but thank you for the offer," Natalie replies. "The other thing—part of this deal with him involved him asking for a favor, and he is calling that in now. Vivienne, he asked for you."

"Me? He's not getting Sunshine as a stud."

"He does not want to breed the cat, Viv," Natalie deadpans.

"I know he breeds familiars on the side," she mutters, defensive.

"No, this is what I believe Isaac would call an escort quest."

Sam looks to Isaac like he is supposed to be excited at the terminology usage. It would've been funny if he would, but mostly, Natalie said it to reinforce his notion that she doesn't know a thing about video games or technology. She can't be much older than him, but it *is* fun to pretend to be the oblivious un-hip person from time to time. (Megan once refused to speak with her for a week after Natalie had incorrectly-on-purpose explained to Deirdre what 'lit' meant.)

Isaac is not amused.

"Ugh, what does he want me to babysit?"

"No, it actually is to escort—you get to herd two unicorns across town tomorrow morning. They will be picked up at the goblin market door and will need to be delivered to a pen on West Elm. The route has already been plotted for you. It isn't far."

"Anywhere with two unicorns is *too far*. Tomorrow, really? Do I want to know what time?"

"Pickup is at four."

Vivienne's groan is long and well-deserved. She is not a morning person. She is barely an awake person on a good day. "I thought you loved me, Nat! This is cruel and unusual punishment for crimes I'm sure I haven't committed!"

"This is a favor on behalf of myself, so I'll pay you triple your usual hazard rate."

"Um, why is Vivienne the one doing this and not you, if it's *your* favor?" Sam asks, confused and curious.

"She is better suited," Natalie replies.

"Psychics taste good, regardless of whether or not they're a virgin," Vivienne adds. "And I probably don't taste good! I'm also disposable in ways others aren't."

"Don't say it like that," Natalie scolds, frowning, but Vivienne merely shrugs. "Yes, he asked for you, but more because of the... taste thing. Unicorns are known to be picky eaters, and the less they chew on people, the better."

"I thought unicorns were like horses," Sam says, looking to Isaac.

"They look like them. They prefer to eat virgin flesh and blood, though. The Middle Ages had that much right."

"Tomorrow at four in the morning... Ugh," Vivienne says and slumps back to the table. "It'll be easier to stay up all night. Do *me* a favor and don't call me tomorrow afternoon, I'll be sleeping. Maybe nursing a unicorn bite."

"I'm sure it will be fine," Natalie soothes, "and I'll even send a delivery of cupcakes over. You ought to teach Sunshine to open the door. He's big enough."

"Just what I need, a *more* independent cat."

"I'll trade you pets," Isaac flatly offers.

Sam appears thoughtful for a moment, processing, then gasps. "Wait, me? I'm not a pet!"

"Sam is easier to handle than Sunshine. Don't make deals you don't intend to keep, Isy," Vivienne teases.

Natalie smiles to herself, relieved that Vivienne (for all her moaning and groaning) will take the job. She opens up a delivery app and starts browsing for cupcakes. She wonders if she can find anything unicorn-themed.

· · • • • • • · ·

Isaac paces. The sun has long set, but he hasn't turned on the light yet, so the only light in the room comes from his television screen. He's used to such setups. When his eyes go, they go, and he will not regret it.

Sam hasn't appeared to realize yet that this isn't usual human behavior, or at least does not complain about the constant darkness in the apartment.

Sam's contributions to Isaac's thought processes are to sprawl on the bed and play with his amulet like a cat with a toy. He's hardly taken it off since Isaac gave it to him, and when he has, it remains in his grip as he turns it over, chews on it, tosses it around, examines it, and so on. Isaac would feel better about his attention to the charm if it hadn't been such a basic job.

"You're thinking. A lot," Sam observes.

Isaac switches the controller to his other hand. The game sits, paused, and he has done nothing else except *think* about it. He wishes he had someone to soundboard this out with. He and Walker had written a spell together, years ago, to create an HRT alternative with magic. They had gone back and forth, late into so many nights, working on tiny details with shared magic. It'd been a wonderful bonding experience.

(They had later discovered that the spell would *only* work for her, created specifically with her body as a pattern, so they couldn't mass market it as expected. Oh well. For a healer, she doesn't like pills or needles much, so she gladly uses it herself.)

Isaac has *always* had to work alone on his spells; that single exception had spoiled him. He doesn't strictly need someone to talk this through.

But he kind of wants someone.

I did it the first time alone. I can do it again, he thinks, irritated with himself, and tosses the controller to the other hand again.

But the first time, he'd had a year to puzzle it out, and the spell itself is a pattern, so he had only had to change details rather than construct multiple layers from nothing.

With the angel blood, he's looking at a new spell entirely. It will give the same end result, sure, but it would be built completely differently to handle that much power at the start, and he wouldn't need the repeating buildup, either. Instead of wading in, he'd jump straight into the deep end. *Technically* less spell to write, but more complicated, and more dangerous, and with fewer precautions on the front end.

He can do this. He's written complicated spells before. They're only complicated until that *click*, the moment when it all comes together, then he can write it out and compress it into a workable, castable form.

But until then, he's left with this.

Isaac glares at the TV.

He unpauses the game and moves around the map.

"That doesn't look like your usual playing," Sam remarks.

"It's not," he agrees in a grunt. "Creative mode in *Minecraft*. It's an open world thing, not really a game. I'm using it to design."

"It's a game that isn't a game?" Sam asks, confused.

"I'm just using it as a tool right now. I'm not *playing* it," he says, and is unsure how else to explain it. Sam has grasped a lot about video games, if only through exposure, but that's normal games that are played with plotlines and characters and goals. "It's like drawing," he adds.

"Oh. I do see the different colors."

"I'm using each color to represent a different rune." Oh no, is Isaac really considering using a *demon* as a sounding board?

But Sam already saw his original circle. He was *part* of it. He doubts Sam figured out all the nuance, but he read more than Isaac had originally liked, and he must've understood a little of it. Isaac can order his silence. If he dies, they both go down, so Sam has a vested interest not to let Isaac die via dangerous spellwork. Or die via blabbing about dangerous spellwork.

Isaac groans and gives in. This is possibly the stupidest idea he's ever had, but it could make the difference of *months* in his creative process timeline. Considering he's not precisely sure when this apocalypse could happen, or when the contract between them is up, he does not have the luxury of more time.

"Okay, so there are different colors and textures in these blocks. Each one is a perfect cube and they're all the same size, but each has its own material. I know all of them by sight and I've assigned a specific rune to each one."

It would be nonsense to anyone else looking at it, and it's his own private local map, anyway. There is no written key, and while some could be guessed because of their common usage, like breaking a cypher by figuring out which letters mean the vowels, it cannot ever be broken completely because Isaac has written his *own* runes.

Writing runes is not like writing spells. Anyone, technically, can write their own spell. They'll probably die while casting it unless a spellwriter compresses it for them, but it can be done with enough knowledge of what they are intending to do.

Creating runes, however.

That is *inventing* magic. That is creating completely new things, which is rare when it comes to magic. Some higher spirits may do it—Isaac doesn't know. He only knows human magic, and he knows that only he has created these runes.

"Oh, it looks like a circle, I think. A square circle," Sam says, head cocked, as Isaac runs around his setup in the game. "It's like building blocks, right?"

"Yeah, pretty much. These white wool ones are shielding parts of the spell. I'm working on something new, but I cannibalized enough of the first spell that I have the basic framework." The *very* basic framework.

"The first spell... As in, me?" Sam asks with a point at himself.

"Yes, you. You and your *interruption*."

"That wasn't my fault. You were the one who put the blood in the circle. I told you, I don't want to die, either, so what else was I supposed to do?"

"You could've gone for the greater good."

"My good is staying here, with you, and learning about colorful video game blocks."

Isaac sighs. He doesn't want to get into an argument over this when he's almost at peace with being leashed to a demon he didn't want. A demon he didn't want who is now tied to his life. He is going to have to think about his spellwork, making it powerful enough for more than one person.

But what about Oliver?

Isaac shakes his head, loose hair flying. He swipes it out of his face with an annoyed growl. "I used what I could from *that* spell, but I'm building from the ground up this time. But the key is that white jar that Natalie bought. She hasn't offered it to me yet, and it's driving me up a wall. I don't know if she's expecting me to cave, or if she's waiting for something *else* to happen, and I don't know which is more frustrating."

"Why wouldn't she want it for herself?"

"You saw that she only bought it because of my reaction." A fact Isaac still curses himself for. He needs to work on his poker face. "But if she wanted it as a bribe, or a trade, why hasn't she said anything yet? That's the part I don't get."

"She could be waiting on you. She seems to like to wait for you to do things. I think she prefers to react instead of act," Sam remarks. He tosses the amulet once more into the air, but he misses the catch and it smacks him in the forehead. "Ow. Well, she's like you, in that regard."

"I'm not like her," Isaac retorts.

"You wait for others to do things, then you react to them. You're also reticent with people you don't know, and you prefer to hold your tongue unless you're upset. These are all things you have in common. You're also both witches without familiars."

"She's a psychic, they don't have them."

"And you?"

Isaac scoffs. "I understand why *she's* upset I don't have one, but why are you? I don't need one. I've never had one."

"Vivienne said it's healthy for witches to have a familiar. Even she has one."

"Yeah, her dead friend's. It's not hers," Isaac mutters. He thinks it's macabre to keep someone else's familiar like a pet.

"I think you should be healthier, Isaac," Sam replies.

Isaac regrets the direction this conversation has gone. "The spell? That I am working on? *That* is what we were talking about, Sam."

"What is the spell supposed to do? That seems different from the one you wrote for me."

"It wasn't *for* you. It was for me. And I want to work on *this* spell right now, not what you call yours, and you're *supposed* to be helping me talk this out," Isaac grinds out with a gesture at the TV. White and purple blocks sit in front of his character.

"I can't talk you through writing a spell. *You're* the spellwriter, not me," Sam replies with a wrinkled nose.

Isaac clenches his fists and imagines Sam's neck between his fingers. "I need. A sounding board. *I'm* the one writing this, but I work better if I can talk through my problems. I don't actually need your help! Just a body to talk to."

"That's a metaphor. Vivienne taught me what those are," Sam proudly says. Then he frowns, realizing what Isaac said. "Also, that was mean of you, again."

"I'm not trying to be mean! I am trying to work out a way to save our lives!"

"Oh, well, I'd protect you. You said so yourself, I'm hardier than humans."

"Not to a god you're not. Not to a higher spirit you're not. Not to a particularly skilled or dedicated hunter you're not."

"How did you even know to prepare for something big? Natalie is only now making references to it, and she's supposed to be precognitive," Sam points out, changing tack. Isaac wonders if he's being stubborn about his power—or his odds against witches.

Still, Natalie was right; Sam is observant. Annoyingly so, when it's turned on him.

Isaac figures he has to let the other person sharing his life know *some* things. "...I might've known, a little, that something is coming. Something big and bad. Something I *was* working to avoid."

"How? You summoned me in the spring. That was a long time before Natalie got that white jar and you started playing that building game. So how did you know before she started acting different?"

"Well, if you're trying to break the rules of reality with a lot of magic you can't control, who *else* would you contact but a spellwriter?" Isaac sarcastically replies. "It was an anonymous posting, and I was an anonymous witch, but I can put two and two together. And I'd rather our realm stay in one piece, thanks."

"I'd like that too. ...Is that why you're scared of Natalie? Because she'll think you helped?"

"If she thought that, she would've turned us over to the covens by now. She must have seen something about me in a future vision. Not that that helps *me* at all."

Sam grins like he's figured it all out. "You two could help each other! She can give you that white jar you really want, and you can give her information about that spell they wanted written!"

Oh, to live in Sam's world, where everything can be solved by making friends and there's no nuance to anything. Nothing like paranoia or suspicion or the threat of betrayal. "I'm not giving her anything, but especially not something she already suspects from me. She's wasting her time if she's after my spell."

"She could be a body to talk to," Sam suggests, "since she likes to be quiet and listen to others. She seems smart. And Vivienne knows all about those necromantic runes you wrote into my summoning circle."

Isaac bares his teeth at him, restraining a snarl, irked at the reminder that Sam saw too much of that first circle. Vivienne, thankfully, never noticed or never remembered the necromantic runes. They were *not* standard in a demon summoning circle. They would probably give too much away. Vivienne is not as smart as he is, but she could talk her way into figuring him out, given enough time.

That friend of hers had been a spellwriter. She knows how they operate. They must have been close, for a long time, for her to pick that much out from a single nonstandard circle.

Natalie must have known that spellwriter, too. Shit, he hadn't thought of that, not in the same way as he had with Vivienne. A precognitive psychic, familiar with how spellwriting works, who *knows* he has a spell and possibly what it does. She has all the cards in this game.

So why the hell hasn't she offered that angel blood to trade yet? And if she *does* know, then why does she need Isaac at all? Just to *write* the spell for her?

"I don't trust her," he mutters, annoyed and angry and distrustful and a little scared. Everything Sam isn't. "She's planning something. With me. I'm *not* ever working with her on a spell. I'm barely working with *you*, and we live together."

"I can be helpful!"

"You were, before this conversation meandered so damn much. I liked it better when you had questions about video games and nothing else."

"Too bad. Vivienne says to question the world around you, and I've enjoyed doing that thus far. I'm going to keep asking about you, Isaac, and why you don't like anybody else, and what you wanted to do with me. I'm allowed to have a curiosity of my own."

"Yours and everyone else's is *annoying*."

"I'll stop being annoying if you answer me!"

"No, you won't."

"Will too," Sam maintains, scandalized at the notion.

"No, you won't."

"I will too!"

Isaac huffs a small, still-annoyed laugh. "I hate you, you're as childish as Oliver."

"You're lying," Sam says, eyes glinting, leaning toward Isaac. Sitting on the bed, he's shorter than Isaac, but he still seems too large the closer he gets. "It's not fair, how you can lie to me, but I can't lie to you. But I'm beginning to be able to *tell*. You don't hate me."

"It was mostly sarcasm," Isaac allows, "but don't read too much into it. You're here as the result of an accident, and now as a potential sounding board, and nothing else. Except maybe to annoy me. Which I hate."

"Yeah, but you don't hate me!"

"Fine. I don't hate you. Can we return to talking about *Minecraft* now?" Isaac relents. Sam beams, pleased, and nods.

Natalie all but begs Deirdre to listen to her. She has no sway with Eyebright Coven, but Deirdre does as the leader of Foxglove. Someone must listen to her about this concerning vision. But Deirdre doesn't believe her. Neither does Vivienne.

"You can't just swap fates. Fate doesn't exist! Not in any quantifiable way," Vivienne says, trying for reassuring, but she comes off cross.

"But the twins..."

Natalie's sight fades, and she slumps in Vivienne's arms.

The place feels odd. Incomplete. Unstable. It is a beautiful forest, with colors too vivid to be real, trees dripping gemstones off copper branches. A baku snuffles along opalescent rosebushes.

She stops every so often to sniff out growing bad dreams, happily munching on them as she works her way across what must be a dreamscape. She feels like the only whole thing in the scene.

The baku pauses, withered rose in her mouth, ears perked and tail high. The dream warps before her, crumbling into dust, and the baku rears back with a surprised squeal.

A hulking, monstrous thing *as expansive as the night sky rips through the forest like wet tissue. Its many tails lash behind it, collapsing the dream, absorbing it. The baku looks about wildly, searching for the dreamer, but even that momentary pause is too much.*

The beast with too many limbs crunches her in too-long jaws. Blue blood splatters over the dead rosebushes.

The night-colored monstrosity turns its pinprick eyes on Natalie just as she comes to again.

She finds herself shaking in Vivienne's arms, nose pouring blood, headache pounding behind her eyes. Had that been a dream? If it were a baku, then surely, but she didn't know she could have a vision of a dream.

"But the twins," Natalie starts again with a raspy voice. "They're doing something..."

"And did that vision have anything to do with what they may or may not do?" Deirdre asks.

Natalie shakes her head, and so her warning is ignored.

CHAPTER 24

IN WHICH DANA IS NOT PREPARED

"Four o'clock my frigid ass," Vivienne growls. Her breath puffs in the chill morning air. Dawn is only an hour away, pinkening the sky, and more and more of the city is waking up. Graham is *late*.

She pulls up the map Natalie had sent her on her phone. A little over two miles, walking, a good chunk of it through Westwood Park. It should take her just under an hour, and she *could* do it before dawn if Graham would just hurry the hell up. Unicorns can't wear glamors, but they can pass them off as horses at a distance in the dark.

He *finally* ducks through the market door, heaving for breath, a rope in his hand.

Vivienne crosses her arms and taps her foot.

"Sorry, sorry! There was an incident with the mama and a drunk leprechaun. C'mere, girl, you're okay. We're back home now," Graham says, soothing, and pulls the unicorn through the doorway.

"Nat didn't mention the other unicorn was a foal," Vivienne says, suspiciously. A mother and foal are different than two adults.

"Oh, he's a sweetheart! Just a little baby, total mama's boy. You get her along, and he'll follow just fine. Here's the lead. The mare's name is Sparkle, and the foal is Giggle."

Vivienne hates that she loves those names so much. Both unicorns are a soft dove grey, pearlescent, and Giggle is indeed a baby. Sparkle has a matching grey mane, but the foal has a white mane. Only Sparkle has a full horn, glowing faintly in the dim morning; Giggle just has a tiny, rounded nub on his forehead. It's cute. Both of them have the biggest, prettiest doe eyes in the history of anything that ever ate humans.

Vivienne pretends to maintain her annoyance in the face of such cuteness. "Okay, okay, let's get going. Do you have a cover set up in case someone sees? Since, you know, it'll be light soon and we'll be dealing with early joggers or garbage trucks or people coming off night shifts?"

Graham groans and shoves a gloved hand back through his short hair in aggravation. "No, nothing set up so far, but the buyer is a witch and I can only assume they'll handle any required memory magic. Come on, sweetheart, you're going with Vivienne now. There's a good girl."

He pats Sparkle on the flank and she chuffs. She noses at him a moment, like goodbye, then obediently follows the lead in Vivienne's hand. If she really is as docile as Graham claims, this could be easy. Maybe.

Horse hooves are loud on sidewalk. She doesn't know if they have horseshoes, if they need them, but they're loud in the predawn dimness. Vivienne jumps every time she sees headlights down the road. The chosen route is all quiet alleys, abandoned lots, and through a large park, but this is still ten kinds of stupid, in Vivienne's professional opinion.

She fishes a carrot out of her coat pocket and Sparkle's ears prick forward. "Yeah, that's what I thought. Got plenty of bribes for well-behaved unicorns today," she says and gives it over. The unicorn thoughtfully takes it, careful of her teeth, but snuffles at Vivienne's bare skin a moment too long. "Trust me, you don't want anything I got. Except these nice carrots. And you didn't hear this from me, but I *might* have some sugar cubes, too."

Sparkle keeps pace *very* well, sticking close to Vivienne, following the lead without stubbornness or excitement. Giggle follows at his mother's side, albeit with more curiosity at the surrounding city. Vivienne knows little about horses and less about unicorns, but these two seem incredibly well-behaved.

She gives them each another carrot.

They make it to the park without incident. Vivienne debates leaving the path and cutting through, but she doesn't trust her sense of direction or the ease of the terrain. It may be a city park, but it still has ponds, a lake, dips, hills, and thickets. The path is dirt, anyway, so quieter, and the sparse trees make good coverage from the neighboring streets. Just a woman and her horses taking an early morning walk. No big deal.

Unfortunately, with the park comes foliage. Unicorns are not entirely carnivorous, so Sparkle stops every so often to nibble on a bush or munch on some grass. Whatever good time they were making rapidly evaporates. Giggle sniffs at everything his mother does, with twice as much wariness and twice as much enthusiasm when he discovers it's edible.

"Come *on*, Sparkle!" Vivienne hisses, tugging on the lead. Why would a grown man name a unicorn Sparkle and *god why does she love it so much*. It likely fits in the daylight. In the predawn light, her coat looks soft and dewy, like crisp snow.

There are very few lamps in the park—part of the reason they chose the route—but it's still dark enough Vivienne has been using her phone as a light to lead them. It shines whenever it catches either unicorn's coat.

"Come on, it's just a bush," Vivienne says. She shakes the lead again, but Sparkle only flicks an ear. "Come on, pretty pony. I have a nice carrot for whoever behaves."

Giggle takes the bait, understanding what the human word 'carrot' is and that he likes them. Sparkle, however, remains by the bush, chewing, a careful eye on her foal. They have not gone over ten feet from each other, and Vivienne does not want to be the person who tries to separate them.

She gets them moving, but at even more of a glacial pace than before. They still have the rest of the park to get through, and down another two streets. The sky continues to lighten with the coming dawn. Vivienne hears the distant hum of morning traffic. Early morning commuters will probably be out soon, as well as too-enthusiastic joggers, and they're going to have a problem if anyone runs into two unicorns.

Giggle tugs on the connected lead, suddenly alert, ears perked. A car rumbles by on the far side of the park, headlights flashing through the trees. Vivienne weighs the merits of ditching the path. If anyone else comes in the park, that's where they'd be, and she'd prefer to put distance between the unicorns and any potential virgin blood.

(Supernatural Hunter Tip #18: Virginity means something different in magic.)

She thinks she spies a jogger on the bridge across the pond, and Vivienne urges the unicorns to hurry again. "Come on, come on, nice carrots for nice magic horsies! Look, sugar cubes!"

That gets them moving again. There is still too much lip and tongue action on her fingers when they lick the sugar up, but if they're happy, she's happy. They look so sweet and tame now, but Vivienne does *not* want to fight a unicorn.

Then she sees the ghost.

"Oh, you've gotta be shitting me," she breathes, rubbing at her eyes, but yep, she'd know those white robes anywhere. "Hey! You there!"

The ghost startles and whirls around. It looks like an old man, hair almost as light as his ghostly robes, hands curled into arthritic claws beneath his sleeves. "Oh, my!" he gasps, astonished.

Vivienne trots toward him, tugging on the lead. The unicorns seem perplexed by the ghost, but not scared or hungry. She counts it as a win.

"Oh, my," he repeats, "you really can see me, can't you."

"Yes, I can. What are you doing here? Are you lost?"

"Yes, I'm afraid I am. I can't seem to find... where I was? Where I was going."

"Sir, are you aware you're dead?" Vivienne bluntly asks.

The old man stares at her owlishly. "Is that what happened? I saw something, I thought it looked like me, why, wearing the same clothes and everything. I thought some kids were playing a prank."

"No, I'm afraid not. Can you show me where you found your body?"

He leads them just down the path, not a hundred feet from where they were. Vivienne finds the sad sight of an old man in his pajamas sprawled over the dirt with a halo of blood around his head. One slippered foot is still caught in a tree root. It's not uncommon for older ghosts to be more lucid than they had been at the end of their lives, so Vivienne has seen cases like this before.

"Alright, sir, it appears you're dead. I'll call the police to make sure they notify your family. But I'd like to help *you* right now, okay?"

"Help me with what?" he asks with another perplexed blink.

"Can you summon your Door for me? It's time for you to pass on, sir. It'll feel like going home."

"Oh, hm. Why, I don't see why I can't try. That sounds nice."

Sure enough, the old man calls forth his Door. Its outline shimmers with light, momentarily blinding Vivienne, a beacon in the dark park. The old man smiles when he puts a hand on the knob.

Unfortunately, while Doors are great for ghosts, they're not so great for anything else.

Sparkle neighs and rears, yanking the lead out of an unsuspecting Vivienne's grip. She hardly sees the man pass on as she whirls around on the panicked unicorns. Giggle whinnies, feeding off his mother's alarm, tugging on the rope tying him to her. Vivienne's heart clenches when their connecting lead snaps.

No no nononono, she shrieks in her mind and tears off after the bolting Sparkle. She's not fast on a good day, much less in the dark trying to race a *horse*, but at least the unicorn stands out in the darkness. The dawn lightens the sky, but it shoots her depth perception to hell.

Vivienne *definitely* sees a jogger on the other side of the pond.

She sprints faster.

Please don't let us get any kind souls who want to help, Vivienne pleads. Knives fill her lungs. Headlights shine through the trees, and morning songbirds squawk in a panic at the unicorns dashing through.

Good news: Sparkle finally slows, first to a trot, then to an irritated walk, ears flicking, nostrils flared.

Better news: Giggle has stayed with his mother, although even more spooked than she is.

Bad news: That is definitely a person coming down the path toward them.

"It's okay, they're mine! The horses are mine, keep a distance please!" Vivienne hoarsely shouts, praying she makes it to the unicorns before the maybe-Samaritan might.

Worse news: The unicorns turn to face the approaching stranger with hungry interest.

Even worse news: It means Vivienne is now approaching from *behind* the spooked, unruly unicorns.

Sparkle senses her approach and gives a warning neigh. She doesn't outright kick, but she prances away with too-high steps, threatening it. Giggle jumps like a frightened rabbit. The stranger shouts a warning, scared, and Vivienne registers it as a woman and nothing else.

"Shh, shh, it's okay!" Vivienne says. She digs in her bag for sleep soot and triumphantly pulls a packet out right as Sparkle decides that Vivienne is the cause of her foal's panic. She lowers her horn and lunges, and Vivienne screams and dives out of the way—unfortunately *toward* said foal.

She holds her breath and rips open the packet with her teeth.

She avoids getting impaled with a horn and dumps most of the sleep soot in Sparkle's face. Sparkle stumbles with her own forward momentum, and Vivienne twists, trying not to get them both ramming into Giggle, but Sparkle has enough energy left to see that as a threat, too. Of course. Forget mother bears, mother *unicorns* should be the new terror.

Sparkle headbutts her, and it is sheer luck that her horn goes underneath Vivienne's armpit instead of through her chest. Vivienne wraps an arm around Sparkle's neck to keep her still, but Sparkle sways her weight against her, and Vivienne staggers.

The full weight of an adult unicorn comes down in hoof form onto Vivienne's foot.

Well, that's broken, she thinks, distantly, because the pain is a few moments behind. Sparkle tosses her head again, and with her last bit of balance and momentum, Vivienne throws herself onto Sparkle's back.

She lays there folded for a moment, foot throbbing and building into agony, and the drugged unicorn seems to contemplate whether or not she can hold Vivienne's weight. In her second stroke of luck so far, Sparkle stays upright.

Sparkle snuffles drowsily and nuzzles at her foal. Giggle whinnies, nervous.

Vivienne catches her breath for a precious moment. She grits her teeth against the pain in her foot. Broken foot, great. Docile unicorn, for the moment, but now slow and stupid. They're still in the park, the sun is about up, and Vivienne can't walk.

She pushes herself off of Sparkle's back and looks at her foot. She can see ripped fabric and ruined boot, blood dripping onto the grass below. Still attached, however, so she considers that a win. She'll take what she can get right now.

Vivienne slides off of the unicorn onto her good foot. She pulls out her last carrot and gives it to the sleepy Sparkle.

"I want to ask if you're okay, but can you help me with this?" comes another voice.

Vivienne had forgotten about the stranger. She whips around to find Giggle chewing on the jogger's sleeve and panic rolls through her anew.

Wait, that's not a stranger.

Dana grimaces at the foal chewing on her arm.

Vivienne probably stops breathing, but she's always been good at panicked action. She must intervene before the foal hits skin and flesh.

"Oh god, no, you're a virgin," Vivienne realizes aloud. With a pained grunt, she limps over, digging in her pockets for half-crumbled sugar cubes. "Giggle, c'mere, come on, get over here. Get away from her."

"I thought it was you," Dana says. She remains still, naïvely allowing Giggle to chew and sniff, dressed in track pants and an unzipped windbreaker. Her hair is slicked back into an adorably messy bun. She's about to get eaten alive by a baby unicorn. Vivienne could cry. "Is it okay if I get, uh, Giggle off of me? I won't hurt him, but you shouldn't be—*ow*! Why does your horse have *fangs*?!"

"Oh shit, has he broken the skin? Hold still, and for the love of everything, don't let him tear at you. Don't move. Give me your hand, slowly." Vivienne puts her weight on Sparkle, a risk she must take, and takes Dana's proffered hand.

Dana winces again. Then, her eyes widen when Vivienne pulls a knife out of her bag. "What are you—*ow*!"

Vivienne digs the point into the pad of Dana's thumb. A bead of blood wells up. Giggle lets go of her other arm, sniffing the air like an adorable baby shark. Vivienne fends him off with her injured foot and draws runes as best she can on Dana's palm. She ought to get an award for painful multitasking.

She still hasn't processed that it's *Dana*, of all the joggers in the city, standing before her. She has to stay in job mode. Just a bit longer, just to get her to safety, to prevent anything from happening. Nothing can happen to Dana.

Vivienne completes the sloppy marks and presses magic into Dana's hand. Sparkle nuzzles at Vivienne's hair, breath hot against her neck, trying to sniff out the blood. Vivienne casts a basic purification spell, the fastest thing she could think of involving blood with a hungry unicorn advancing on them.

Dana rips her hand away with a scowl. Giggle sniffles at her once more, then, no longer smelling virgin blood, loses interest. Vivienne could melt in relief. One crisis averted, only a thousand left to go.

Without the adrenaline of making sure Hot Manager Dana doesn't get eaten (or licked and nibbled on, since a unicorn the size of Giggle *might* not be able to kill anyone yet), Vivienne is left with the crushing realization of how fucked up everything just got. Still can't walk, Sparkle still drugged, Giggle still not attached, and now, Dana.

"Uh. I can explain," Vivienne announces.

"Yeah, that'd be great," Dana says, staring down at her bloody palm.

"So, well, you're not a virgin anymore?" Vivienne says with an awful grin.

Dana raises her eyes only enough to glare at her, too dumbfounded to be truly annoyed, but the resulting mixture is *hilarious*. Vivienne cannot help but burst out laughing. She sinks against Sparkle, despite how the unicorn sways, then down to her feet. She'll probably never stand on her own power again, not without Megan magically swooping in from the sky, but Dana's expression is just so *much*. The entire situation is so much. If she doesn't laugh, she may cry.

Dana waits out Vivienne's near-hysterics with her arms folded over her chest. (She looks good in a sports bra.) She is at least kind enough to have grabbed Giggle's lead to prevent him from wandering off, but like before, he seems content to remain near his mother.

"O-Okay, okay, I'm good. I'm good."

"Are you," Dana flatly says.

"Probably. I have to be! Just, give me a moment, your *face*..."

"You don't want to know what I'm going to do to your face if I don't get some explanations real quick about these horses and your knife. Also, your foot, it's hurt. We need to get that looked at. Don't make me worry about you when I deserve to be angry."

"You definitely deserve to be pissed! And confused."

"I'm definitely that, too." Dana side-eyes Sparkle, gaze lingering on the horn, but she doesn't outright question it. Yet. "Okay, can you walk? Should I call an ambulance? Or, uh, animal control?"

"No, but can you help me up onto Sparkle? I guess she's my ride now."

"Sunshine, Sparkle, and Giggle. I'm sensing some theme naming." Dana hoists her up onto Sparkle's back. The unicorn is still too drowsy to complain much, and Vivienne's punishment is riding without a saddle. Her thighs already protest the stretch.

"I didn't name these two. I'm escorting them as a favor for a friend of a friend."

"Walking horses around at six in the morning through the city. Yeah, okay."

"Just... give me a bit. I'll explain," Vivienne wearily tells her. Adrenaline and hysterics over with, now she's just *exhausted*.

She directs Dana where to lead them. The rest of the park is easy and empty, both unicorns docile, though they have to wait for a garbage truck to roll past before exiting. The hooves are loud on the sidewalk, but they're almost there. They don't see anyone else close enough to question them.

They meet the pickup almost two hours later than was originally planned on. It's a woman, a brunette witch Vivienne has seen around Foxglove events, and she's furious at Sparkle's drugged state until she sees Vivienne's foot.

"Well, at least they wouldn't have tried to eat you," the woman relents with a sigh.

"Uh, it's... Giselle, right?" Vivienne guesses. She's fallen out of touch with most of the coven members after Natalie left.

"Yeah, but these sweeties aren't for me. I'm picking them up for Deirdre."

"Why the *hell* does Deirdre want unicorns," Vivienne grumbles.

"One is for the coven, and the foal is Megan's graduation present. But shh, it's still a secret! I had no idea Graham would ask *you* to help with this..." Giselle pats Sparkle affectionately.

Vivienne groans into Sparkle's mane. Megan is getting a unicorn. The same one that tried to eat Dana. So much for never seeing these horrible, *beautiful* monsters ever again.

"You actually said unicorns," Dana slowly says, still staring hard at Sparkle's horn. She passes over Giggle's lead without taking her eyes off it. "I thought this was a costume."

Giselle shakes her head. "Uh, no? I guess it's too dark still to see the shine, but these are definitely unicorns. Haven't you ever seen one in person before?"

Dana shakes her head, eyes *still* glued onto the horn.

"Well, sorry about the foot, I'll let Graham know you died nobly in the line of duty. Thanks again!"

Dana is kind enough to help keep Vivienne's weight off her injured foot with an arm around her shoulders. So this happened. It all *Happened*. Dana found out about magic, and in a way worse way than seeing a faun party it up. Natalie will skin her alive if this supernatural secret thing keeps slipping out on her watch. She may deserve it if anyone gets a worse introduction than getting chewed on by unicorns.

"So. I think the nearest hospital is downtown? I don't know this area very well," Dana says. "Can you stand while I check my phone?"

"No, no, I don't need a hospital."

"Vivienne, your foot is pretty messy. I'm certain it's at least broken," she replies, disapproving.

"I have someone I can call."

Dana snorts. "Like what, a black market doctor? Tell me you're going to get this looked at *properly*. I was hoping this wasn't going to turn into something shady."

"I have some bad news for you on that front."

"Seriously?"

She winces at the alarm in Dana's voice. "It's not... *bad*, just different. I'll explain when we're not in an alley and I'm bleeding broken bones. My apartment. I'll explain everything there, I promise, and you can finally meet Sunshine."

"Sunshine, Sparkle, and Giggle. The whole trio in one day. What joy of joys."

"I told you, I didn't name the other two! Wait—I didn't name Sunshine, either!"

Dana keeps a firm arm beneath Vivienne's armpits and Vivienne cherishes the arm she wraps around Dana's waist. It's not so chilly now, and the pain may have something to do with that, but the press of body heat is nice.

"Are you sure you can walk to the station? We should really call a car," Dana says, dubious, but Vivienne is quick to shake her head.

"Nope! I'm good." That's a lie, but she is *not* getting in a car right now. She can't handle that on top of everything else this morning. "The station is what, another three blocks? I can handle that. My apartment isn't too far, and there will only be one transfer, I think."

"I don't think you should walk on that. Or hobble. And there's the matter of potentially bleeding in a train car..."

"If you're so worried, then carry me?" she jokes.

Dana pauses, thoughtful, then releases Vivienne. She wobbles on her good foot.

"No, that was a joke! I'm not serious! I'm too heavy for you!" she hastily backpedals, but Dana bends in front of her, offering her back.

"Come on, hop up. You're not too heavy for me, trust me."

"I'll get blood on your clothes," she pathetically points out.

"I've had blood on my clothes before, Vivienne. You asked, now suffer the consequences. I'll feel better if you put less weight on that foot until it's looked at."

"Oh my god," she groans, but clambers up onto Dana's back. She hauls her up with ease and tucks an arm beneath each of Vivienne's knees. She has little choice but to wrap her arms around Dana's neck, as loose as she can manage, but she hasn't gotten a piggyback ride in years, and it's a little disorienting.

But Dana is warm, and even with sweat cooling on her, she smells nice. Clean sweat and the leftover fruity scent of her shampoo.

"Are you sniffing me?" Dana deadpans.

"No! Getting comfortable with all of this hair in my face."

"Sorry, I know I'm gross from my run, but, well, I wasn't expecting to run into anyone. Much less... *this*. I don't suppose I could take a quick rinse off at your place, please?"

"Of course!" Vivienne will not think of Dana naked in her apartment. But she will think of the domesticity of picking out a towel for her.

The train station is empty this time of day, and so is the train car. Dana carefully lowers Vivienne to a seat, then sprawls beside her. They take a moment to breathe together.

Vivienne can't imagine what is going through Dana's head right now. She barely keeps up with what's going through *her* head. She successfully transported the unicorns, she helped that old man ghost, and Dana didn't get eaten. But now Dana knows about said unicorns, and Vivienne has a broken foot, and she's about to be exposed to healing magic, if nothing else.

And she's going to see Vivienne's apartment for the first time.

Oh no it's still a mess, she realizes with an inner groan. It's always a little messy, but she's been going through old reference books trying to pick out Brynja's rune tattoos, and she hasn't taken out the trash in over a week, and who *knows* what Sunshine has been doing. He always knocks over something when least opportune.

Today is just going to be A Day.

They change trains, Vivienne mercifully being spared the embarrassment of another piggyback ride for the twenty feet across the platform, and this train only has a smattering of people. They get seats and a wide berth when the other passengers see the blood.

Vivienne extends her leg and looks at her foot in proper light. Her jeans have a six-inch tear, but her boots might not be totaled. There's definitely *some* kind of mess going on inside the shoe, however, and with the throbbing, sharp pain and the fact that there even *is* blood tells her it won't be pretty. She hopes her foot doesn't pour out of the boot like soup.

"Okay, this is my stop," Vivienne says with a tug of Dana's sleeve. There isn't an elevator or escalator, and she refuses to let her carry her up stairs, so they hobble their way upward. Not the fastest or the least painful, but Vivienne has bled at this station before, and she probably will again.

It's almost seven in the morning, sun fully up and city awake, when Vivienne staggers through her apartment door. She kicks some notebooks under her couch before Dana can get a good look.

Sunshine trots out, tail held high, but he freezes when he sees the stranger in his presence.

"Oh, wow, he *is* a big boy," Dana says. She crouches and sticks her hand out to him.

"He might smell the unicorn on you," Vivienne warns, but the cat trots right up to her and butts his head against her fingers with an immediate purr. At least someone here can be charming.

Vivienne limps to the couch and flops herself upon it with a relieved sigh. "Sorry about the mess. Wasn't expecting such pretty company, or to do anything other than come back and crash."

"Still not a morning person, huh?" Dana asks.

"No. Never will be. I'll die before I become one of *those*," she returns, fully aware that Dana is a proud morning person. Oh well, no one's perfect. "Okay, I already texted Megan. They should be here soon."

"Megan, the little peppy one from your party?"

"That's the one."

"And they're in on this shady business, too?"

"They're the back-alley doctor, of a sort. You'll see."

"I'm getting a little tired of the 'you'll see', Vivienne. We're here, you have your weight off that foot, and I'm going to get you some ice before stealing your shower. Then we're *talking*."

"Don't think I have any ice," she mutters while Dana takes in her tiny kitchen. "Please don't judge me on the state of my fridge or freezer. I might have some frozen tater tots?"

Dana sighs, but as requested, does not voice judgment at the bareness. Vivienne gets a lot of her meals from Natalie, Mark, or takeout. She doesn't cook much herself and rarely leaves leftovers very long. It creates a sad image, however.

"The bathroom is the door on the right, it should be open. If Sunny just used the litter box, I apologize in advance, because he is a nasty, disgusting man. The linen closet is behind the door, you can grab the blue towel. Sorry I can't give you a tour myself."

"I can figure out a bathroom by myself," Dana replies, halfway amused. "Thanks for letting me steal the shower. Now, time to be alone with my thoughts."

Vivienne waves her off and concentrates on the coldness of the tots against her ankle. She's glad Dana hadn't volunteered to look her over. As soon as she hears the door click shut, Vivienne sits up with a groan, and looks down at her feet.

The good foot's boot comes off as easily as ever. Her fingers hover over the laces of the bad boot. One had broken, loosening it, but she doesn't want to risk pulling it off. She unties her laces with as little jostling as possible, but every minute movement stings anew. She isn't sure if the sharp pain is better or worse for her prognosis than the dull, achy pain.

Her sock is revealed, a wet, bloody mess. Vivienne folds up her jeans and looks at her foot. A lot of the blood comes from a scrape from the hoof, not a pulped ankle, so that's good news. (Not the first or last time she'll bleed on the couch, either.) But she doesn't quite have the courage to peel the sock off completely, not when she sees the gleam of bone sticking out amongst the red.

Dana gets out of the shower in under five minutes. Vivienne can't help but be impressed, since even her rinse off showers are half an hour or longer. She likes a hot shower, sue her.

Dana comes out, towel over her shoulders, just in her track pants and sports bra. Vivienne nobly manages not to stare. Her hair is still up and dry. "I know you live in a small city apartment, but your hot water heater leaves *a lot* to be desired. How do you handle that in the winter?"

"Oh, shit, sorry, I forgot. I mostly use magic to heat the water."

"Magic," Dana repeats. She pats herself dry and sits on the far end of the couch, now eyeing the bloody mess. "So..."

"So," Vivienne prompts.

"So where would you like me to leave the wet towel?"

"The bathroom's fine, like, over the shower rod or anything. Laundry is low on my mental task list right now."

"Fair enough." Dana ditches the towel, but does not return to her sliver of the couch. Vivienne misses even that proximity. "So. You're iced and I'm not so sweaty. No more putting off whatever *this* is."

Yet a knock on the door puts off the conversation at least a moment longer. Vivienne isn't sure if she's grateful; this waiting and dancing around is only building the dread that Dana will take this badly.

"I'm coming in!" Megan calls before they burst through the door. They're in chick-printed pajamas with a thin hoodie thrown overtop, hair wild, cheeks rosy from a rush. "Vivi, *what* happened?! Oh, hi, Dana. It's nice to see you again."

Dana nods in surprised greeting. Vivienne rolls her eyes. "It's like I texted you. A unicorn stepped on me, so something like fifteen hundred pounds of magic horse put its weight on my delicate foot bones."

Megan eyes Dana as they near the injury. "And Dana, you were... there?"

"Yeah, and then I helped her get back home. And now here we are, eagerly awaiting explanations."

"Vivi," Megan preemptively scolds, but she shrugs and throws her hands in the air.

"What was I supposed to do? I wasn't in any position to steal any memories, and I don't even know her favorite food! But the job was successful, and now you're here to rescue me, Meggy."

"And now *you're* going to explain yourself," they order, then settle in to get to work. They pull Vivienne's feet into their lap and peel off the sock without preamble.

Vivienne winces at the sight and quickly turns away. Dana remains standing on the other side of the couch, dubious and suspicious and worried. Sunshine presses against her calf.

Here we go, Vivienne supposes. Can't be worse than Oliver discovering demons on his first day, right?

There are no chairs in her small living room, but Dana doesn't let Vivienne try for an excuse and plops right down on the floor. Sunshine invites himself into her lap. She's overjoyed to see her cat take to Dana so happily, but it comes secondary to the awkwardness suffocating her.

"Alright, *so*! Magic is real. Things like unicorns are real. It's not shady, it's just secret from the population at large," Vivienne starts.

"Uh-huh," Dana says.

"You just *saw* a unicorn, Dana. You're going to have to believe me."

"I saw you get stepped on by a horse with a horn."

"And what do you think a unicorn is?" Megan chimes in with a grin.

"I thought the tail would be different," Dana primly replies. "Like a lion's tail? More heraldic."

"Maybe some kinds, but most look a lot like horses these days."

"I'm curious how you're going to handle this introductory lesson, but Vivi, *what* were you doing with unicorns in the first place? A lot of the meat is pulped, but it looks like you only actually broke two bones, maybe another. You got lucky, but this is a mess!"

"It was just a job for Graham," Vivienne fields. It would be unfair to Megan to give up the secret. They *love* surprises and it's not their fault their new pet tried to eat Dana.

"So you're a doctor?" Dana asks them.

"Well, premed for another semester, then full-on med school! Yay. I'm so excited. Can't you hear how excited I am," they reply, totally dead inside, but crack another grin after a moment. "But your *actual* question is whether or not I'm a healer, right? I do have healing magic."

"That... wasn't really my question. A *healer*? Is this safe?" Dana asks.

"I'd rather be able to walk again next week instead of two months from now. Megan is the best healer I know. And yes, with *magic*. I know you don't believe that yet, but you will," Vivienne tells her.

"Got a marker, Vivi?"

"Messenger bag."

Dana's eyes widen when Megan shoves their arm in the bag up to their shoulder. They pull out a magic marker with a flourish. "Pants are gonna have to come off, Vivi. I think they're ruined, anyway. I can cut this leg open so you don't have to pull them off over your foot."

Vivienne glances at Dana, gauging her reaction, but she doesn't seem to process until Vivienne is unbuttoning her jeans and Megan is pulling out scissors. "Oh! Wait, I'll get you, uh, a towel or something."

By the time Dana comes back with a towel, avoiding eye contact, Megan has cut Vivienne free of her jeans and they've rolled them down the other leg. Vivienne really wishes she wore better panties today. She modestly drapes the towel over her lap, and only then does an awkward Dana peek their way again.

"How gentlemanly, thank you," Vivienne jokes.

"Now's not the time for you to be cute about this. You say magic is real, but I'm about to watch a *premed* student operate on you with scissors and a marker. On a couch. There's cat fur *everywhere*."

"Have you *seen* Sunny? His fur is almost as long as my hand. He's a big shedding machine."

Sunshine, ever fluffy and ever huge, gives Dana a big cat smile and another loud purr.

"You're going to get an infection," Dana weakly adds. She sits back down and the shedding machine crawls back into her lap. She pets him automatically.

"Infection is easier to fight, potions and poultices can do that. I'm sure Nat has tons. I rolled out of bed and ran right here, so I don't have anything with me, but you already called Nat, right?"

Vivienne stays innocently silent.

"Vivi, *right*? You called Nat to tell her you got hurt?" Megan presses.

Vivienne remains silent. It's her right.

"Oh my gosh, *Vivi*! You have to tell her, too! Not only is she going to be supplying you potions for fighting infections, she's your *friend*! And your boss! She deserves to know, especially if there were." Megan's eyes flick over to Dana. "Complications."

"I will, after my foot stops screaming in agony and Dana and I have a chat. I can put it off for an hour."

"Ugh, fine. Let's get started, then. Hold as still as you can. Do you need something to bite on?"

"No, and I'll be talking, anyway, remember? Nice chat time with Dana."

"Do you *need* something to bite on? Does that mean what I think it does? Are you doing this without anesthetic?" Dana asks with wide, worried eyes.

"I have numbing magic, but I'm using most of my magic today to heal the bone and mend the flesh. I won't have enough for much numbing. This ice will help, but I'm not a witch. I can't do everything," Megan replies, with the same sad, defensive tone they always get whenever someone asks too much of them.

"Meggy, you're fine. It's fine. I hardly feel it anymore."

"Fine, fine. Let's go. Deep breaths."

Vivienne settles in, gets comfortable, and looks at Dana upside-down. She giggles when Megan begins writing on her leg. She manages a smile for her. She refuses to show any pain she may or may not experience.

"If you're not squeamish, you could watch the mending part. It might convince you better than anything I can say," Vivienne suggests, but Dana shakes her head. "Alright, just talking for the moment. Magic and the supernatural are real. Witches, unicorns, dragons, familiars, so on and so forth. My job is freelance exorcist. Megan has healing magic. Natalie, our friend, is a witch. Sunshine is a familiar."

Dana nods along, but spares the cat in her lap a suspicious look. He purrs even harder.

"I do odd jobs here and there, like escorting unicorns. But mostly, I shepherd ghosts into passing on, and deal with things like unruly house spirits and poltergeists. Codi isn't a gun for hire or whatever you thought she was. Or, well, she is, but she shoots things like rabid werewolves, not political heads of state. Or *whatever* you think she was doing."

"I tried to never ask. I knew she was doing... *stuff*, ever since we served. But some things are better not asked about," Dana admits. "I was suspicious, but she was my friend and a good mentor. She never did wrong by me. I trusted her—I still do, I mean."

"Any other details of her life, you get to ask her about. I'm not going to out everything about everyone." She is definitely *not* going to mention Emil, perhaps not even if Dana explicitly asks. "How much are you following so far?"

"I'm following everything. It's overwhelming, but followable. Believable?" Dana laughs and shakes her head.

"Meggy, can I do any magic right now?"

"Keep still and don't pass out," they mutter around the marker now in their mouth.

Vivienne scans the room, eyes landing on her bookshelf. She writes in the air and says, "*Pull.*"

The book flops out of the shelf and lands in her outstretched hand.

Dana stares.

Vivienne risks one more simple spell. She draws in the air and murmurs, "*Light,*" creating a witch light over her finger. The orb glows softly, swaying, and Vivienne flicks it in Dana's direction.

She scrambles out of the way with a yelp. Sunshine meows in complaint as he's dumped to the floor. Dana ducks under the light, making grabby hands at Sunshine, crouched in fight-or-flight mode.

"Told you. Magic. Believe it yet?" Vivienne asks. Megan snickers.

"Getting there," Dana shakily replies. Sunshine paws at her until she sits again. He's a better calming agent than Vivienne could ever be. "Okay, *ooookay*. That was... magic. Huh."

"Told you," she repeats. The light blinks out. "Those are basic little things, but all I want to do right now. I'm not a witch, either, so I have very finite reserves."

Dana stares down at the black cat in her lap, stroking him once more, processing. She looks so lost: workout gear, hair falling out of her bun, bewildered expression on her face.

"Alright Vivi, bone time. Grit your teeth and stay still," Megan announces and does not wait for compliance.

The pain is sharp and needle-like in its specificity. Vivienne claws at the couch cushion, spine rigid, jaw clenched, but she does not let out a peep. The pain is brief. Her breath *whooshes* back out as soon as Megan finishes with the first bone.

Megan wipes their sweaty forehead with the back of their hand. "Almost halfway done, that was the bigger one. Deep breath, then we're going again."

The second one is less pain, but more dread, because Vivienne knows exactly what is coming. Sunshine meows, abandoning Dana's lap, and bumps his head against Vivienne's clawed fingers. He licks her until the pain recedes again.

"Aw, Sunny-honey, thanks," Vivienne pants. "What a good nurse cat."

Despite her prior misgivings, Dana scoots around to peer at the foot not-surgery. Megan finishes up with the bone work, then moves onto mending the torn flesh, which is more obvious. Dana appears to hold her breath for all her attention on the red muscle fusing back together.

That part doesn't hurt so bad, just a dull ache, distant and cold. And moist. Vivienne forgot how *wet* it feels and does not like the reminder.

But soon enough, Megan is onto the skin, then done. They throw a hand back through their sweaty curls and heave a great sigh of relief. "And done! Whew. The skin just under the ankle may still scar, and it'll be tender for two or three days. I recommend not putting weight on it for another week, if you could. But you're in one whole piece again!"

"Thanks, Meggy! I feel good as new," Vivienne queasily lies. Both she and Megan look like they're about to pass out, but that's just how healing magic works. "You can crash here for a nap, if you want."

"Nah. I'd rather get back to my own bed, and I'd hate to interrupt whatever talk *this* is going to turn into."

"Well, Dana? Is this going to turn into more of a *talk*? You already believe in magic now, don't you?" Vivienne asks, expectant. Dana slowly nods, eyes fixed on the healed foot.

"Still. I'll be headed off. You crazy kids can have fun without me," Megan replies with much (unneeded) eyebrow wiggling. They are careful when slithering out from beneath Vivienne's feet, but are their usual flouncy self when saying goodbye to Sunshine and slamming the door behind them.

Which leaves Vivienne and Dana alone with the cat and the weight of a freshly revealed secret.

Vivienne averts her eyes and wipes her sweaty hands on her lap towel. "I found out in grade school. My friend Hayley accidentally cast a spell on me, and she assumed I was a coven kid since I was near their territory, so she just starting blabbering on and on about what kind of spell she was *trying* to do and why the magic must have backfired and why it wasn't really her fault but it was an accident and she was sorry. And I was just sitting there, with a skinned knee, staring at her. The start of a beautiful friendship.

"Everyone takes it differently when they find out, as opposed to growing up with it. People who grow up with magic will always approach it differently. And there're all kinds of cultural differences, different relationships with magic and its history, and with a big American melting pot, you get a whole lot of confusion and new experiences.

"You're the third person in the past year I've had to introduce to the world of the supernatural. You'd think I'd have a speech written out by this point, but believe it or not, it never happened to me before this. I mostly deal with dead people. Things matter differently to the dead. Ghosts are real, too, in case that wasn't already said. Most people can't see them, but some can, including yours truly. And yes, I will keep talking to myself until you interrupt me with questions or just even to tell me to shut up."

"Alright, shut up, Viv," Dana says.

Vivienne's mouth shuts at once. Good, her mouth is dry, and she still hasn't been able to gauge Dana's reaction to any of this.

"This is a lot to take in," Dana allows, "and I'm not sure what to make of all of it. Am I going to get flashed by the Men in Black soon? Do I have to swear an oath to secrecy? While I process this, what *will* happen?"

"No one's going to come after you. No one's going to be mad, except maybe at me. It's a secret because it has to be, not because it's going to get you in trouble. Your life will still go on. I'd bet you've already had brushes with magic and the supernatural and you didn't even know it."

"I doubt that."

"I think you'd be surprised," Vivienne fields, amused, thinking of Emil and Christine. And their little escapade at Club Chaos. "Oh, and that ham-thing shapeshifter you mentioned? I don't know a thing about those, but Rory isn't actually Ham's nickname. He's a friend of ours. A ghost."

"You're friends with a ghost?" Dana whispers, eyes wide.

"More than one, but yeah. I knew him while he was alive—we were roommates in college. Everyone dies. I'm lucky enough to get to hang out with him for a bit afterward," she replies. She'll get to hang out with him for another few months or so, at any rate, unless they come up with something to do. But that is something else, heavier and longer, that weighs on her; today is about Dana.

"This is a lot to take in," Dana admits, tentative, and a little sad. As if she's somehow disappointing Vivienne with her reluctance to believe in all of this extraordinary bullshit.

"I know it is. There's no rush on that. I'd prefer if you didn't run off screaming into the hills, though. I can answer any questions you have, any time."

"I appreciate that offer. But this is a lot to take in. ...I bet you've been laughing behind my back about how much I've been oblivious to. Not meanly!" Dana hastily adds, hands up. Sunshine hooks a paw around one of her wrists to tug it back down to resume petting. "I just mean, like, I didn't get the joke for so long. There must have been some fun made at that, right? Especially once you found out I knew Codi."

"It might've come up. A little. Not fun, necessarily, but... Amused confusion? You're far from the only oblivious person in the world, and we all miss obvious signs in our lives. Like, I have no gaydar. I know that's just a check on stereotypes, but so many of my friends are queer! You think I'd notice the signs!"

"Is there gaydar for magic?"

"Surely, statistically, there has to be. But I figure people either know about it or don't, so I suppose it'd only work once, maybe twice," Vivienne admits. "But funny to think about. Either way, I'm sorry for keeping it from you, but it was never in bad faith or to be mean."

"I know, I get that. But I'm still sort of frustrated with this whole thing. We've known each other for a few months now, Viv, and I've known Codi for... *years*. At what point do you tell someone?" Dana looks up from Sunshine, brow furrowed, but her expression beseeching. "What if our lives didn't interfere constantly, and we'd actually went on a date together? What if we went on five, ten, fifty? What if we were dating? *When* would you tell someone that?"

"That's a personal decision everyone has to make for themselves. Me, personally, I... I don't know."

Vivienne had never dealt with the prospect of dating outside the magical community before, and she's never known anyone who had.

She's wanted to date Dana. She still does. (She isn't sure that feeling will be returned after this processes.) But there were a lot of talks Vivienne could imagine having with her before this one, and that's extra funny, because the Hey Magic Is Real talk should happen before any of the others.

"It's been such a part of my life for so long, I've forgotten it's new to others. I was room-mates with Rory for a year, and I never told him until he died. I did have some shenanigans keeping it a secret, but it wasn't out of cruelty, only habitual secrecy. I've never *thought* about introducing someone, it has only ever just happened," she explains and finishes with a shrug. "In that way, this is new to me, too. I hope that comes across."

"Believe me, it comes across that you're not practiced at this," Dana replies with wry amusement.

"Thanks! A learning experience all around."

Their silence is not so uncomfortable this time around, but Vivienne would not call it pleasant. Even Sunshine's purr seems muted. There is no healer to interrupt this time, no more ice to fetch, no more showers to take. Vivienne isn't sure what else Dana would like to know, or have confirmation of, or have an example of. She doesn't wish to overwhelm her any more than she has been.

Mercifully, Dana breaks the silence. "Maybe now we can go out. Now the universe has decided that we can acknowledge this big elephant in the room, and you don't have to tiptoe around me."

"I was really only tiptoeing that drunk night at the club! I only kissed you to stop you from seeing some nonhuman folk. I mean, I *wanted* to kiss you, but it was a distraction tactic, and not a very tiptoe-y one," Vivienne babbles, cheeks heating, grinning in preemptive embarrassment.

But Dana just blinks at her. Stares, and then another blink.

"What kiss?" she finally asks.

Vivienne wishes the unicorn had eaten her instead.

Natalie sits in on the hearing for Adam and Alex McAllister. Vindication tastes like ash in her mouth. She had visions about the twins, had warned Deirdre about them, and for what? For this future to come true.

Witches from the major covens whisper in the fearful way that unknown magic feeds. The prevailing rumor is that they'll be stripped of their rank and excommunicated from Eyebright.

In one blink, Natalie watches the twin witches stand unrepentantly, and in the next, she's listening to screaming.

The screaming is familiar. Huge talons rip into Vivienne's back, shredding clothing and flesh with the same ease. She clings to the pavement, trying to drag herself away, but the spirit on top of her forces their claws further into her back. The spirit, a tengu, has a mix of cream and white feathers, but they're coated in red blood on both feet and wings.

The tengu's mask is gone, revealing their face: beautiful, round-featured, and with sharp teeth bared in a savage snarl. Vivienne's screaming dies off in a wet wheeze.

When Natalie comes back to the present, once again looking at a future that came true while witches whisper anxiously, she hopes this one is avoidable.

CHAPTER 25

IN WHICH THERE ARE IMPOSSIBLE DREAMS

He lays on the ground, face up, hardly able to see the grey sky overhead. It's wet. He's drenched, and *so* cold, but he doesn't hurt anymore. The cold feels like ice in him. Sharp and hard and foreign, but it does not hurt, either.

He can't move his head to get away from the wetness. Water, rain, he thinks. It's always raining. He coughs through the cold wet, and there's hot wet, too, in his mouth.

He's afraid.

The field is quiet like he's been layered in cotton. There ought to be sounds. It'd been so *loud* before, deafening, terrifying, men soiling themselves in fear at the thunderous sound—

He gasps through wetness once more, then wakes up.

Sam jolts back into awareness. His chest feels tight, entire body tense, and he wants to run but he doesn't know why or where. The room is dark. He is on something soft, warm, and so foreign to the dream that's already slipping from memory.

He doesn't know when or why he crawled into bed with Isaac, or how he didn't wake him. Isaac's back is to him, but he remains asleep, chest moving with deep, even breaths. Sam watches that movement for a long moment.

I was dreaming? he wonders, calmer, unconsciously syncing his breathing with his summoner's. Isaac feels tranquil in sleep, not prickly or annoyed or defensive like when he's awake. Sam prefers this peace.

But demons don't dream. He thinks.

"What're you doing?" comes Isaac's raspy sleep voice.

Sam startles again, but this time only surprise, not the tense terror from before. "You're awake?"

"Hard to sleep when a demonic furnace slips into bed with you." Yet Isaac remains placid. He rolls onto his back, one hazel eye slitted open, dark hair a mess all over the pillow. "Did you have a nightmare?"

"Why did you let me into bed with you?" Sam asks instead of answering. He isn't sure *why* he doesn't want to answer, but something feels too vulnerable. He wants to protect that strange, old fear, *not* have it be prodded at by his prickly witch.

"I'm not sure if demons get bad backs from sleeping on the floor, but I'm only human. I could only look at your sad lump on the floor so many mornings." Isaac yawns, not bothering to cover his mouth, and Sam stares at his even, human teeth. "Now we can share the blankets instead of having to divvy them up."

"This is okay now?" Sam asks, tentative. He hadn't meant to be in the bed, but he likes it. He doesn't want it taken away again.

"I guess. Gonna tell me what scared you awake? If demons have sleep paralysis demons, I'm going to laugh," he drowsily warns. He yawns again, then rolls onto his other side, eyes slipping closed again. He looks smaller when he's not glaring with those piercing eyes.

Sam slowly settles back into his side of the small bed. "I think it was a nightmare," he quietly confesses.

"What about? If you have nightmares about monsters, it falls under the laugh umbrella. You don't get to have those."

"Why don't I get to?"

"Because you're a monster, too."

"I don't think I am."

Sam doesn't mean for it to come out so wounded, so raw, but he feels too tender still. Isaac's eyes remain closed, posture lax, breathing even; Sam questions if he fell back asleep.

But after that thoughtful pause, Isaac quietly tells him, "I have nightmares, too."

Sam props himself up on an elbow. "You do? What about? I've never heard you in distress—"

"Because I'm *quiet*. You sleep heavily for a spirit, you know. They're nothing new, but recurring."

"What about?" Sam repeats.

Isaac sighs through his nose. "There's a reason I don't like many other people. I've been hurt by others before—a *lot* of others, okay? Sometimes they're about that. Attacks and threats and stuff. Sometimes they're about being on the streets. Spellwriters get taken advantage of, but homeless kids do more. Sometimes it's just about my parents. Different things, and they all suck."

"Oh," he replies in a small voice, processing. "I'm sorry."

"What was your nightmare about, Sam?" Isaac asks. Topic firmly changed now.

"I don't know, really. It's fading away. It was cold, and wet, and I was alone and scared."

Isaac slits open an eye again. "Could that have been a memory, not a nightmare?"

"I think that's an even scarier prospect," he admits with a frown. "I don't want that as a memory. Here I'm warm and dry and not alone. I'm not afraid anymore. I very much prefer that."

"That's fair. Most people would prefer that. I do. It's nice to wake up to a safe place."

"There, see!"

"What?"

"You said I was a person. I am part of people. Not a monster."

Isaac groans. "Ugh. Too late for these talks. You can be both, so long as you go back to sleep. And as a warning, the first time you kick me, you're out of the bed."

"Alright," Sam says, and does not ask what happens if Isaac is the kicker. He has slept heavily until this point. If it means he can stay in the warm, dry, shared bed, he'll accept a kick or two. The touch wouldn't be terrible, either.

• • • • • • • • •

Christine pulls herself through the walls like it's painful. It's never been this hard or slow before. Never been such an *endeavor*. She has to actually *pull* herself through, hands braced on the wall, dragging herself forward room by room.

Emil sleeps soundly in his bed. He always sleeps through the night, and she's always awake through the night, alone. She doesn't blame him. Or, Christine doesn't *want* to blame him, but as she stands over his bed and she is so painfully aware of her solitude, she blames him for living when she cannot.

Her stomach turns over in her belly.

She is used to the pain in her stomach, from years of cancer eating away at her, rotting her insides to filth. This is the same, but different. It's familiar.

It's hunger.

Christine reaches down with sharp nails and too-dark skin, mouth opening in preparation. She grabs Emil.

And then jerks back into awareness.

Into awakeness?

Christine looks around wildly. She is in the living room, not in the bedroom and not with Emil. Pink dawn light filters through the curtains.

Was I sleeping? she wonders, amazed and scared, hands to her cheeks. She feels awake and aware. She doesn't feel *sleepy*. But what else could that have been? She knows, if this plan actually *works*, she will slip into another life of sleeping and eating and breathing again. It has to happen *sometime*. Maybe in parts, like sleeping just now.

But she doesn't feel tired. She'd assumed she would feel tired first, like staying up too late at night, then curl up somewhere to sleep. Maybe a quick nap. Maybe she'd be tangible enough to lie on the couch by then. Maybe an entire night slept away. Maybe fewer hours to think, alone, or float through the dark city with Kirara.

So, she doesn't feel tired, but Christine wraps her arms around her middle when she realizes she feels something *else*. Something worse.

She feels *hungry*.

She checks her hands. They're still her normal brown skin. She isn't turning into anything else, this is a normal part of the process, and she has nothing to worry about.

Christine pretends not to notice that her nails are sharper. The hunger is frightening enough.

• • • • • • • • • •

"Okay, you definitely should be getting *something* by now. I don't get it! There's got to be a catch somewhere, but we've tried everything," Vivienne exclaims.

"Dude, I'm just as lost as you are!" Oliver replies, just as frustrated. He *has* magic potential. Somewhere. Emil is still a kid, and he's figured out like half a dozen simple spells, and seems to be hitting his stride. Oliver hasn't even gotten to *one* yet.

"Probably for the best," Isaac flatly calls without looking up from his phone.

"Yo, Isy, shut the fuck up! If you get magic, I deserve magic, too!"

That earns him an annoyed scowl. "I *meant* that if you've exhausted the basics, then your talent may lie in something rare or unique, in which case it's dangerous to experiment. People can die from magic accidents. Don't die, dumbass."

"Well, magical experiments *can* be dangerous," Vivienne allows, grimacing, "but there should still be a baseline of basic magical aptitude somewhere in there. I swear, it'll get easier once you get used to it."

"It does," Emil chimes in, and Oliver can't help but glare at him. He'd been one-upped by younger kids enough in law school.

"What about blood magic, have we tried that? He can do that without being able to do healing magic," Megan suggests. They seem twice as exhausted as Oliver feels about his magic, and he feels bad dragging them away from studying, though they've stolen a table to fill with books, anyway.

"Okay, hand out," Vivienne says and pulls out a knife.

It's a testament to how used to this magic shit he's gotten that Oliver extends his hand without a second thought to the woman brandishing a blade.

"Oh my god, don't give him *blood* magic," Isaac hisses.

"Why not? It seemed useful," Sam replies, but Isaac kicks his chair. Sam wobbles with a squawk.

"I'm not *giving* him anything! This is figuring out what the hell he *does* have. What other fringe skills are there? Finding, summoning, blood, healing, thralls—have we checked to see if he can talk to animals or plants yet?"

"Every office plant he's ever touched died," Isaac says.

"That's because I was watering them without knowing the receptionist was, too!"

"If the soil is already wet, *don't* add more water," Megan advises and returns to their books. If it's September, there'll be midterms soon, he supposes.

"Why don't we try all those things you listed? That seems like a good start," Oliver suggests, patient as he can be, despite the fact that Emil is effortlessly making one of Megan's heavy textbooks float. "C'mon, Viv, cut me!"

"Well, we can't try *all* of them. You've already tried healing magic with Meggy's help, and we're guessing at blood magic here."

"So *don't* try it with him," Isaac complains.

Vivienne rolls her eyes. "But with some magic skills, you either have them, or you don't. I can't teach you what *I* can't do. Still, that shouldn't preclude you from the basics..."

"Um, could it be psychological? If he thinks of magic as something witches like Isaac do, maybe he is unintentionally blocking himself from the first step," comes a soft voice.

Oliver's head snaps up, confused, and even more confused to see Christine floating cross-legged over Emil's table. Isaac looks up from his phone and Megan raises their head from behind their textbook.

"That's what I was thinking, but look at him. He's a big, excited, super enthusiastic puppy," Vivienne replies. "He could be super specialized, like I am, but everyone can make a witch light. Hey, Olly, what're you looking at?"

Oliver points at Christine. She looks around, turning to the far wall, also curious. Her bell collar *dings* with the movement.

"You can see her too?" Megan asks. They rub at their eyes. "I thought I'd been staring at these books too long! Vivi, Christine is visible to normal human eye."

"Wait, what?" Vivienne and Christine squeal in unison, Vivienne starry-eyed, Christine watery-eyed. "I-I am?" the ghost adds with obvious hope.

"I can see her, too. This just happened," Isaac confirms. He doesn't seem as excited as everyone else, but Oliver is used to that from him.

"Maybe it's a sign!" Emil happily exclaims, turning to her, bright as the sun. "That's a good step, right?"

"I mean, it might not be *great* to have a girl floating around. That might raise some eyebrows," Megan points out.

Vivienne's enthusiasm fades quickly, however, and she cocks her head with a thoughtful squint. She leaves the knife and Oliver's table and circles Christine. To his surprise, she *grabs* her, raising her arm, turning her over in her examination.

"Yeah, she does that. No, it's not something you can learn," Megan says before Oliver can ask.

"I wanna touch ghosts," he mutters.

"Same," Emil sighs.

"Sorry to burst your bubble, but I think I know the culprit of your sudden shift in corporealness. Corporeality? Whatever. Duck down a moment for me? I'm going to touch your hair again, okay?"

"Um, okay. What is it?" Christine meekly asks.

Vivienne pets her a few times, squinting at her fingertips, and Oliver wonders if ghost lice are a thing. That'd suck on top of everything else to do with dying. "You're still producing luck, or at least able to maintain it. But I think you've been around too much magic. Fingers, please?"

Christine's face goes ashen, and she holds out a trembling hand. Her nails are shiny and pointed, less like a manicure and more like wannabe claws. It looks like the tips of her fingers are darker, too.

"It's okay, this isn't the end of the world. All things happen in stages. I'd even say this is reversible," Vivienne starts with the air of someone giving bad news.

"I don't see what's wrong with being a demon," Sam rebelliously mutters, slouching in his chair. Beside him, Isaac watches with unusually rapt attention.

"I don't want to become a demon!" Christine exclaims in a high, panicked squeak.

"You're okay! That's still a ways off." Vivienne soothes. She tugs her down, rubbing her arms, her voice even and calming. "It's important to keep an eye on whatever progress you're making. We don't know how this is going to work, what phases it'll have, and what signs you'll show. You're visible to others now, and they can hear you, isn't that a good sign? You won't turn into a goopy demon in five minutes."

"I was only goopy for a little while," Sam says with a worsening scowl.

His pouting child act is kinda funny, but Oliver feels awkward watching poor Christine have a near panic attack. Oliver's had those, and they are *not* fun.

But just as he's regretting this voyeuristic lesson, Christine pops back out of sight, like a light turning off.

"She's gone again," Megan points out. "There may be some phase changing if she's doing... whatever she's doing. Have you figured out *how* she's doing any of that yet?"

Vivienne half-turns, still holding the invisible ghost in her arms. She could make a killing as a mime. "I've got some guesses? Ninety percent of them have to do with the maneki-neko collar. I think it's acting as a grounding agent, and a magnet for luck, and then she's luck-bullshitting her way through the rest of whatever progress this is. But these magic lessons might be doing more harm than good. Christine, it may be better for you to sit them out from now on. Emil, keep a lid on practicing at home."

"Oh, okay, yeah," he says, slumping in his seat. "Sorry."

"It's not your fault, Emil. We all knew these were magic lessons and that's what you were here to do."

"Yeah, but..."

"Dude, hey, it's okay. Viv said it's reversible or whatever, right? And we've agreed she's an expert in this shit, yeah? So things suck, but you gotta have faith it'll turn out alright in the end," Oliver tells him, and Emil nods in gratitude.

"Y'know, that's a good life lesson all around, too. Things suck but you have to have faith it'll turn out alright in the end. It's true. I like that," Vivienne adds. She again pats the unseen ghost. "And if anyone can beat the odds, I think it should be Little Miss Luck over here."

The magic lesson concludes with no more magic usage and on a sour, sad note. He almost misses the exuberant frustration it'd began with.

• • • • • • • • • •

Mirai peers into the window of the human house. Their glass is very thin, but all the better to search through. There are no lights on inside and they've yet to see or hear movement. It's probably empty.

"Another lost lead," they grumble to themselves. They crouch down on the branch they're perched on, wings folded against themselves, glaring at nothing.

They're *used* to being in the human realm now, and what do they have to show for it? Nothing! The nights are pleasant, the air is sweet, and there are plenty of food sources (human food and other spirits), but it isn't home and it isn't the familiar chaos of the market. It's just human chaos.

Human chaos that is annoying and deeply unhelpful.

I need to see Mark Ito again, they think, pursing their lips, then chewing on one. *I know he is meant to be an important human, but this is taking too long! I can take her in a fight. I don't have to hurt him.*

They've tried the polite route. They have been diplomatic. But while leads on other missing eggs are lost, they *know* who stole Hatsu's. And they are fairly certain Mark remains in contact with the thief. They don't believe it is in bad faith, only another case of human delicacy about doing what must be done when someone commits a crime.

But they need the egg back more than they need to punish the thief. She could die before giving it up. She had seemed willing, once.

Mirai hunches over and ruffles their feathers with another angry groan. The branch cracks beneath their talons. "Even the trees here are weak!" they exclaim, indignant, and wing back into the air.

They haven't seen Sam since, or that other fox spirit Yun-hee knows. Must they seek further help in this realm? Maybe Hatsu is right; they're dragging too many *others* into this inane quest of theirs. It is so frustrating to know it is *just* out of their reach. It isn't fair to

Hatsu. They deserve better than to lose their First egg! (Mirai believes Hatsu deserves the world and then some.)

Mirai knows nothing about lucky collars and doesn't care to get involved in cat affairs. They never formally agreed to help Lucien.

Sam, however, is a lead not yet followed up on.

And I made him a tengu friend! they recall with dismay. Mirai somersaults through the air with embarrassment. *He didn't even understand what a great endowment that was. Hatsu is right—I am too young for this!* They're going to *eat* them if they ever find out about Sam. Mirai can't rescind the title, but perhaps they could politely ask Sam to never use it? He could be solely Mirai's friend. That could work.

They fly back into the city proper, leaving trees for concrete. The streetlights are nice here, convenient perches and warm light, but all the concrete and asphalt and tar make their nose itch. They wish they were old enough to remember living in the human realm, but hardly any tengu are left that do.

It is late at night, the air crisp, streets mostly empty. So it is very easy to spot the bright smudge of gold from several stories up.

Mirai curiously flies down to investigate. To their amazement, it *looks* like a human girl, but she is coated in more luck than they've ever seen. And a bakeneko, of all things, is curled around her shoulders.

The cat spirit notices them first, of course. "Hey, bird, stop hovering suspiciously. Following ladies in the dark gets frowned upon in the human realm, you know!"

"I wasn't following you," Mirai replies, miffed, and lands on the nearest streetlight. The metal and glass are uncomfortable on their feet, but at least it is convenient.

The little human turns and stares, wide-eyed, up at them. Probably her first time seeing a tengu. Which is fair, because this is Mirai's first time seeing such a lucky human.

Though on closer inspection, Mirai isn't certain *what* they are. Human, yes, but not exactly living, and not fully. They cock their head to one side. "What a strange sight you two make."

Their eyes alight on the golden bell collar at the girl's throat.

"Oh!" Mirai crows and flaps excitedly. "I know you, I've heard about you!"

"How?" the cat suspiciously demands.

"There is a fox spirit looking for a collar that has been given away by a lucky cat. That's you, isn't it? It must be! Can I have that?"

"No!" the cat hisses. Cat fire bursts up around them, little hovering balls of hot warning, but even a prickly, proud cat knows better than to attack without more justification.

"You said fox spirit?" the girl asks with a sad sort of frown. She touches the bell, making it *ding*, and luck brightens her silhouette further. She's very pretty, as far as humans go.

"*What* fox spirit?" the cat demands.

"Kirara, I think that he's, um, h-hunting me."

"I'll kill him myself!"

"Well, he's not multi-tailed, so I think you could win," Mirai reasons. The bakeneko glares, ears flat, fire still haloing them both. "I have no stake in this. I just wanted the collar to trade him to get a guide in this human realm. He offered, but I did not formally accept. I don't care either way!"

"This collar would be worth more than any *guide*. Don't you have a thing in your head besides feathers?"

"Don't be rude, little cat. I can eat you in one bite."

"I can sear my way out of your hollow bones just as easily as I can your stomach. Try it."

"C-Can you two *not* fight? Please? They said they didn't care about the collar or the fox spirit!" the girl pleads. She puts a hand on the bakeneko curled around her shoulders, unusually forward for a human, but the cat relents and drops her fire.

They are close, Mirai notes. How strange that Lucien would want to interfere so badly. "Well, then we have no quarrel here. If anything, you should thank me for this information on your foe. So, you're welcome!"

"Thanks," the girl replies, smiling uneasily.

"What is a tengu doing in the human realm, anyway? It may be late at night, but humans can see you, and you're not bothering with a glamor, I see. You could get chased out by angry witches if you disturb the peace," the bakeneko asks with an annoyed lash of her tail. The girl keeps petting her to tamp down that irritation.

Mirai opens their mouth to respond, then recalls how many others they've already dragged into their business. So instead, they primly respond, "I am here on official tengu business. That is all."

"Stuffy bird."

"Nosy cat."

"Well, if you ever need help finding anything, maybe not *me*, but I am... human, I suppose. I know how the city works. I have other friends who could help you, who are smarter about spirits," the girl offers, quelling the cat with further petting. Mirai thinks all cat spirits should have a kind human petting them.

"I don't need more *human* help," Mirai replies with their nose in the air. "Or whatever you are."

"I'm human," she repeats.

"I don't believe you are. I am not certain *what* you are, but you don't smell human. You barely look it, with all that luck."

"She's a luck spirit," the bakeneko proudly declares.

"Alright, could be. I won't pry into your business. So don't pry further into mine. Enjoy your night, luck spirits!" Mirai bobs their head in farewell, then takes back to the sky.

How strange, to run into another youkai in the middle of the human city. Cat spirits are unusually suited to stay here, unlike most others, but Mirai isn't exactly jealous. The human realm makes for a pleasant location to search and little else.

How foolish that Lucien had been, if he is targeting the little luck spirit with a bakeneko so fond of her. He'd be better off giving up on getting that collar. It is a fool's errand.

Unlike Mirai's reason for trawling the human realm, of course.

· • • • • • • • ·

Christine stops going to school with Emil.

School would be safe, no magic and no other spirits there, but perhaps that is only a false sense of security. That bogle had appeared.

His meetings with Vivienne and the others are also out. She feels so *stupid*—Rory had warned her about the magic plus ghosts equals problems thing. She had gotten too used to hanging out with people who can see and talk with her.

Nights are also spent alone, unless Kirara stops by, and Christine does not risk visiting Sadie on her own anymore. She doesn't want to leave the apartment without Kirara near. Knowing that that fox spirit is still out there, is *enlisting* others to hunt her, Christine doesn't feel safe anymore.

She doesn't know what to do.

She has maybe-napped twice more now, and she and Emil have run out of room on their tally board of touches. She'd been apprehensive, but *had* thought of these as positive changes.

But she's a target. And being near Emil and his budding magic use is dangerous—for her and for him.

If I become a demon, she thinks, and stops the thought there. She can't bear to think of it. Her brother had partook in only two purges and came back both times injured. Demons are dangerous, and *eat people*, and eat ghosts like her. She doesn't want to eat anything except cheesecake and barbequed chicken and spring rolls and waffles and chocolate chip mint ice cream. And other *human* food. Dairy had been the first thing to cut out of her diet when sick, and she *misses* it. So bad.

Her stomach rumbles again.

Christine wraps her arms around herself with a whimper. Thinking of food has made her hungry. Again. She'd been used to it when alive, but now, it's a terrifying prospect. She won't *die* if she won't eat, so she's doing her best to ignore it, and so far, no one has heard her stomach. It isn't like she wants to gnaw on anyone.

But she had years of stomach pain, and the thought of returning to it is a terror she has not felt since Logan's death.

Christine can't go through that again. *Any* other pain, but not a repeat of her last few years of life.

She looks down at her hands. In the dark, she can hardly tell, but that only makes her think of all of her skin turning black. Truly black, not Black, not the warm brown she's always loved.

I don't want to become a monster, she privately weeps. She still can't shed tears. She'll probably return to her crybaby ways when she develops that ability again. If only that were her only problem.

What can she eat, to sate the hunger, to stave off anything worse? She still has waking nightmares about that dream of hers. The thought of eating Emil—the thought of hurting him—the thought of hurting *anyone*! It fills her with revulsion and horror.

She presses her sharp-nailed fingers to her own wrist.

Kirara had called humans squishy before. They really are. Their skin is thin. They don't have fur or scales or armor to protect themselves. Their flesh is soft and warm.

No wonder other monsters eat them.

Us! she reminds herself. *I'm still human. I'm still human.*

But what would she become if she took the bell collar off? Is that really the only reason she has gotten this far? What if her attachment to it turns her into a poltergeist faster than any luck spirit stuff can happen?

Christine thought she'd be free of fear when she died.

"You have a very specific type of magic," the calico cat purrs, curling around a man with broad shoulders. "I haven't ever seen it in humans personally. I've only heard of it. You must be quite lucky on your own, aren't you?"

The small bell collar at the cat's neck chimes when she slithers around to the man's other shoulder. He cranes his head to look at her, but the vision only features his broad back and gelled hair, no face. "Why's it matter? I just wanna do normal magic stuff!"

"You lack imagination, then. Want me to teach you?" she says and butts her head against his temple.

"Teach me what?"

"To use your lucky streak."

Natalie comes back to herself when the kitchen timer goes off. Her pot has boiled over, but at least dinner is easier to fix than a picky potion.

She's seen that calico with the long tail and bell collar before, but the tall man she'd been with remains a mystery. One for another day, Natalie supposes, since she has potatoes to mash. Life needs to be about more than potential futures, and a good meal is the thing she's focusing on today.

CHAPTER 26

In Which Isaac Offers To Help

Dana looks down at her planner in revulsion. Then she turns her glare on Nico. She can't actually forbid him from taking time off, of course. (She herself has time off planned in December.) But it's still a dick move.

"You *sure* you can't reschedule?" she asks again.

"Yeah, I'll get right on rescheduling an international trip," he sarcastically replies. "Dana, I'm sorry, but this has been in the works for half a year."

"We *need* another manager." There are only three of them, and it's two per day with shifts overlapping for lunch hour. She's happy to take opener shifts, as a morning person and all, but it means no late evenings out if she wants to survive getting up at six or earlier.

"Working on it," Nico sighs.

"Can't we put up another ad on Craigslist? LinkedIn?"

"We *can*, but it doesn't guarantee good hits. Sorry, Dana. You're in hell for a week."

"I just want to go on a date, Nico. Like a normal person with a normal work schedule. You and Javi go out *plenty*. How do you manage it?"

He pretends to think. "Flexible schedules and soothing of annoyances with baked goods. Also, the aforementioned international trip to look forward to."

"Yeah, yeah, meeting the grandparents and uncles and aunties and everyone in existence. I know how it is. How's your Spanish?"

Nico glowers at the schedule hanging on the wall instead of at Dana. How polite. "Working on it. His mom already loves me, and they swear up and down they'll translate with no embarrassing pranks, but I'm not holding my breath. I can introduce myself and ask some basic questions, but I'm more worried about trying to listen and translate. Duolingo only goes so far."

"And it's Mexican Spanish, not European Spanish," Dana reminds him. As if he could forget. "You'll have a blast. And I'll be up here, suffering through *running Halloween* without you, you jerk. I hope you get sunburnt."

"It's no different from the little cons we used to host. You'll do fine."

"Fine and single."

"Oh my god, you two make enough googly eyes at each other in the store! I don't see how you two have had such fuckin' difficulties figuring out a time to go make out."

Dana glares down at her planner again. Work is only half of it, truthfully; Vivienne's work schedule is haphazard, too. They've spent hours on the phone together, especially after Vivienne's little revelation, and text several times a day. They've grabbed unplanned, quick meals twice.

But it's not a *date*.

It's not a set time where they can sit down and *talk* with each other. About the magic stuff, about Vivienne's actual work, about Dana's upcoming stresses at basically running the bookshop (more than she already is), about friends, about Sunshine, about anything. About where they stand with one another.

Vivienne hadn't been *lying* to her, she knows. Dana sort of understands keeping an enormous secret like that. She understands she had found out via an accident. They've talked about that much, but only ever over the phone, or through scarily long texts.

Dana *needs* to look at her. Dana needs to see how Vivienne reacts to her hesitance about magic and the supernatural. She needs to hear, face-to-face, what *exactly* Vivienne does for work, how dangerous it is, how violent.

She *wants* to spend time with her. She wants to ask about magic, and other creatures, and ask for more pictures of Sunshine. She wants the lightheartedness back between them. She wants to see Vivienne all dolled up, and in pajamas, and sweats, and whatever her work uniform could be, and never again bleeding on her couch.

Dana opens up her messages with Vivienne. '*Have any Halloween plans yet?*' she texts.

The response comes before she even sets the phone back down. '*sry, no halloween plans for me. 2 spooky 4 me*'

If ghosts are real, maybe there is genuine horror to Halloween. Maybe she'll be staking vampires or exorcising banshees all night. Dana frowns at her phone; she'd gotten an invitation to a party where she hardly knows anyone other than Codi. It would've been nice to go with Vivienne.

They could've had a couples costume.

If only they were a couple.

'*Saturday?*' Dana tries.

'*sorry! meeting with markimoo. sunday?*'

She could weep. '*No can do, have a meeting with a client I'm editing for & he's super needy.*' She considers canceling anyway, even if he's a repeat client and pays well.

"For being so lucky, I'm surprised you two haven't worked out yet. Not to be Debbie Downer, but have you considered that you two aren't meant to be together? Maybe the stars aren't aligning for a reason," Nico suggests, seeing more pouting.

"Don't feel lucky," Dana mutters.

"Oh, right. Of *course* you're not lucky," Nico replies, all too innocently, and checks his own phone. "Halloween will be fine. You have the morning shift, anyway, so you won't be dealing with the drunks or the troublemakers."

"We'll hold down the fort without you. Somehow. Traitor."

"You'll survive. Maybe you'll get lucky eventually. It has to work itself out *somehow*."

"Everything does," she halfheartedly agrees.

· · · · ● · ● · · ·

Natalie *whumps* the rented cauldron onto the countertop. Isaac stares at it with suspicion. Sam leans over to peer inside. "Are these potatoes? That's an awful lot."

"Yes. I'll need these peeled, if you'd please, and with some haste."

"What sort of potion uses *potatoes*?"

"Potion? Well, they are nightshades, but no. I don't think there are any potions that use them. I'm making mashed potatoes."

Isaac's stare is baleful.

"You're getting out an hour early today, unless you'd like to accompany us. If Vivienne hasn't invited you already."

"To what? We weren't invited anywhere," Sam replies.

The front door tinkles, announcing Vivienne's arrival. She adds to it with an exuberant, "I'm here to eat potatoes! Oh, wait. You haven't started yet."

"What perfect timing. You can help."

"Why are we *cooking*?" Isaac asks, nose scrunched. Sam has already grabbed a peeler and is done with his first potato. Isaac, of course, has not touched his.

"Technically, cooking as a verb can be attributed to many potions as well. But to answer your question more directly, I must have mashed potatoes done by this evening for the potluck. You may come if you like. Viv, I'm surprised you haven't invited either of them along yet, if only to embarrass them."

"I've been up to my eyeballs in runes trying to figure out some tattoos. *And* trying to schedule a date like a normal person. Excuse me if my lackluster social life hasn't added a demon and a surly witch to the mix just yet."

"We went to the club with you. That was a social event you invited us to," Sam points out. He's on potato five now. He may have a knack for this, or else Isaac has surreptitiously commanded him to do his share of the work. Natalie isn't certain how demonic orders function.

"Tonight is the monthly meeting of QAFPICC!"

"Kwaff-pic?"

"It's QPICC," Natalie wearily corrects.

"It sounds like Q-Tip, whatever it is. Is this a language I can't understand?" Sam asks, looking between Vivienne and Isaac for answers.

Vivienne laughs and flops onto the stool next to him. She, too, does not deign to grab a peeler. "Queer As Fuck People Inter-Coven Coalition. It's like a gay pride group, half-meant to help foster inter-coven relations. It's open to non-witches, too, of course, and allies and stuff. A few spirits show up from time to time. It's a pretty casual affair, but super fun. We're both part of it, and so is Meggy!"

"It's Queer People Inter-Coven Coalition. Stop adding letters."

"More importantly," Vivienne says, ignoring Natalie, "it's potluck, so there's food, *and* you know who *else* is part of it? One Thomas Novak."

"Ooh," Sam says. The pile of potatoes beside him is impressive. "So you're going to go fight him, then eat afterward?"

"Or before, I'm not picky."

"We're not *fighting* anyone. I'd like to speak with Thomas. That's all."

"So we shouldn't poison the potatoes?" Sam asks.

"No. Nat's mashed potatoes are *amazing*, and I'd rather not die by potato, anyway. There are cooler ways to go. Case in point, starting a public brawl with Thomas!" Vivienne exclaims.

"*No*," Natalie repeats. She shoots Vivienne a disappointed look and scoops Sam's peeled potatoes into a bowl. "Please save those peels, too, Sam. Viv, if you're so into violence right now, work off that energy by cutting up these potatoes. If you want to eat, you're helping."

"So, why would you invite us?" Isaac asks. He picks up a single potato and examines it. Sam must be a quarter of the way through the cauldron by now. "You know nothing about us. About me, anyway. I don't think demons have sexualities or much gender identity."

"You asked if I was a boy, and I said yes. Isn't that how humans do it?"

"He's got you there, Isy."

"Don't call me that."

Vivienne flips her paring knife between her hands instead of doing any actual work. Natalie sighs and grabs another bowl for the peels. At least no one can say demons aren't efficient.

"Like I said, it's for allies, too. I assume you're not a huge homophobe or transphobe, because if nothing else, Megan would've sniffed you out and eviscerated you by now. *Probably* only verbally. But like you said, I know little about you. This isn't prying into your jealously guarded personal affairs. It's just an invitation for free food and a front row ticket to beating Thomas' ass for what he did to you and Codi."

"Oh, that's sweet," Sam says with a warm, pleased smile. "See, Isaac, others can care about you, too."

"That's nice," Isaac flatly agrees. "I'd rather not."

"Think Oliver would like it? You know what way he swings? You ever barked up that tall, beefy tree?"

"Vivienne, leave them alone. If they don't want to go, they don't have to, and for the last time, we are not *fighting* Thomas. I will not watch him shoot you again!" Natalie finally exclaims.

Vivienne's leery persona drops at once and she half-hides behind the cauldron, equal parts surprised and cowed. Natalie sighs through her teeth, annoyed at herself for the outburst, and for saying unnecessary things. There are some things they don't talk about. There are some (a lot) things that should not be brought up in front of others.

"Sorry," Vivienne mumbles.

"No, I'm sorry, too. I didn't mean to say that," Natalie says and rubs her eyes. "It was a long night. Please, help with cooking, since I know you'll eat at least half of this."

"This is a lot of potatoes," Sam says, peering into the half-full cauldron.

"Everyone should bring a meal to a potluck. That's how they function. I bring an extra large portion because Vivienne should not be trusted to cook anything by herself."

Vivienne doesn't respond to the gentle quip. She mutely chops potatoes. Sam slides over the peel bowl for her to put the pieces in, but Natalie gently pushes him back and supplies Vivienne with her own bowl. The assembly line works at last.

"Sorry, Viv. I didn't mean to say it like that. I didn't want to bring up anything negative when you were already so annoyed with Thomas," Natalie quietly tells her.

But Vivienne shakes her head. "*I'm* not the one who's still upset about that. You and Thomas—you two still act like kicked dogs about it. It's hilarious coming from him, y'know, but you... That wasn't your fault, Nat. I'm over it."

"I'm not sure you should be," Natalie sighs.

They fall into silence again, just the *chop-chop-chop* of knives on cutting boards, and the occasional *crunch* of a stolen potato piece. (Sam watches with fascination as Vivienne shamelessly snacks on raw potatoes. When he tries a bite for himself, however, his expression is so disgusted that even Natalie chuckles.)

Sam finishes with his peeling job in record time. Isaac has only peeled two potatoes in all of that time, but Natalie was expecting it to take longer, so she can't complain. She takes the empty cauldron back to fill with water to prepare for boiling.

"So, you have a history with this Thomas Novak man? If the dragon migration wasn't the first incident, why wouldn't you have suspected him to begin with?" Sam asks. It must have been at Isaac's prompting—such pointed nosiness is unlike him—but Natalie hadn't seen them communicate. They're getting closer.

"In the supernatural hunter community, a lot of people shoot at a lot of other people. It's usually pretty professional. Grudges don't last when magic and guns are involved," Vivienne absently explains. "Thomas was apparently stopping Codi from completing another job. It's rare, but it happens."

"But you gave the dragon skin to the other person, anyway," Sam clarifies with a sidelong glance at Natalie. "So he failed, and Codi succeeded."

"Correct."

"Shouldn't he be mad about that?"

"Nothing he can do now. Like I said, grudges don't last, and Thomas *is* pretty professional."

"So he shot Codi, and he shot you, and you go to fun little meetings with him and eat dinner together," Isaac surmises.

Vivienne shrugs.

"Isaac," Natalie begins, and his expression darkens into a near-glare preemptively, which she does *not* deserve, "I don't know you very well, or anything about your past. But I can make educated guesses. Have *you* killed or assaulted *everyone* who has ever wronged you? Or is it better to let matters lie?"

"What if Thomas had killed someone?" Sam asks. "Would we be upset with him then?"

"Yes, of course we would be! This isn't about not being *mad* at him," Vivienne exclaims, though Natalie privately disagrees. There has been bad blood between them for years. It has just been quiet, simmering, easy to ignore in public. "This is about whether or not he is working to bring an *apocalypse* down on top of us. We need concrete evidence of that before we can actually act against him."

"I thought you were respected for your psychic abilities."

"I am. But no future is guaranteed. They are leads, not the concrete evidence we need."

"That someone hired him to shoot Codi isn't enough?"

"No, plenty of people wouldn't want Mark to have a successful job, if they somehow heard it was for him. Respected doesn't mean liked. Everyone powerful has enemies. And like I said, Thomas is known for being pretty professional. It wasn't *his* motive, but his boss', and we don't have evidence of who that was, either."

"So you need a confession? I know you make truth potions, Natalie. Use one of those in the potatoes," Sam suggests.

Vivienne snorts. "First off, that would ruin the godliness that is those potatoes. Seriously, you're both trying them. Second, truth potions are *bullshit*. Shouldn't a demon who's contractually obligated to tell the truth realize what the *truth* does and doesn't mean?"

"I've had to be careful with what I say, at times, but I still can't lie to Isaac."

Vivienne shoots him a finger gun. "Or me. See, that was a lie by omission right there, but you were still telling the truth. You'd have more luck with a polygraph machine than a truth potion. They're usually just sold to desperate housewives trying to uncover affairs."

"And lawyers who don't mind bending the rules," Natalie adds.

Isaac shrugs. "I knew that. Don't care, but I knew it. Don't tell Oliver, though. He'll freak out and get paranoid about his mother and the other lawyers at the firm."

"He still can't cast *light*. I'm not going to tell him anything about potions he hasn't gleaned from his visits. He doesn't need to be excited or frustrated in two directions." Vivienne sighs, flicking the knife back and forth again instead of doing her chopping job. "I think I'm gonna quit the magic lesson thing. It's not working with Oliver, and the only other thing I think Emil needs to know is how to write a confinement circle. Think he'll be heartbroken?"

Isaac grimaces. "He's going to be *insufferable*."

"Good thing he has a witch friend to bug with all of his magic questions. Have fun with that!"

"I thought you enjoyed the socializing," Sam says, "I mean, it was fun. Wasn't it? Is Christine really at such risk to turn into a demon?"

"No, not soon. But it freaked her out to have a sign of it. And you, Sam."

"Me?"

Vivienne reaches over and taps him on the head with the flat of the knife. "I know it can't be easy, hearing someone else go on and on about how bad you are. She doesn't know what you are, and I didn't want to out you, but normal people are terrified of demons. I can't imagine what it's like for a ghost. You're a good bean, and you haven't eaten anyone yet, so you have a pass in my book. But it's not fun to hear someone say shitty stuff about what you are."

"Oh, that's... Thank you, Vivienne," Sam says, slowly, face warming to red.

Natalie can't help but notice that Isaac's expression has soured further.

Is he jealous, she marvels. She, too, has been envious of Vivienne's natural friendliness, and she has *definitely* gotten the idea that Isaac has difficulty with interpersonal relationships. But she's surprised at how at ease Isaac has become around Sam. (She's surprised she has, too, to be fair.)

"Anyway, Viv-*sensei* is done for the time being. It was nice while it lasted, even if I didn't get a paycheck for it. Emil can take care of himself, he hopefully won't burn down his building, and Oliver apparently can't cause any chaos with *whatever* he could do. He's gonna be heartbroken. Should I get him a bottle of wine as apology?"

"He prefers champagne."

"Oh, I knew I liked him for a reason! Such a class act."

"Champagne was the bubbly one, right? I like that one the best," Sam informs them.

"Okay, I'll get you a bottle, too, for not eating anyone. And because I can't really remember a drunk demon doing too much."

"I didn't unsettle or anything," he proudly agrees.

"A pity I can't remember more. But *apparently*, at least I remember that kiss, and most of the dancing."

Isaac snorts a laugh, and Vivienne's mouth falls open. Isaac's face flushes and he claps a hand over his mouth.

"Isaac Whatever Your Last Name Is, was that a *laugh*?"

"At your expense," he mutters. "You were wasted and all over that other woman, and she didn't remember? I think that counts as karma."

"Karma for *what*? I am a fun dancer! I am a fun partier! Right, Nat, I'm fun, right?"

"You're very fun, Viv," she indulges.

"Karma for getting me leashed to a demon and involving Oliver in magic? And now he's found out he can't cast anything. *I* think it's karma," Isaac retorts.

"Yeah, but I can fix mine. I can go smooch Dana *so hard* and *so much*, and you're still stuck with Sam and Olly. I may not have won that night, but at least I didn't lose like *that*."

"I hate you," Isaac growls.

"Hey, you didn't mean it that time, either," Sam says, delighted, and Isaac blushes harder. He buries his face in his folded arms with a groan. "I think this is what friendship is like. And I understand that truth is subjective now, too."

Natalie decides to cut Isaac's misery short. She stands and scoops what chopped potatoes there are into her cauldron. "A good day for life lessons, it seems. Viv, keep chopping those. Maybe all of this good morality will keep with us until we see Thomas tonight."

• • • ❡ • • • • •

"No, Chris Pine, for sure."

"First, Quinto is *way* hotter. Second, young Shatner could *get it*. Third, you just like his eyes."

"They're Jolly Rancher blue! Of course I like his eyes. But he was also an English major and I like a well-spoken man."

"Uh, you like any man who'll actually *talk* to you," Alex says, rolling his own (blue) eyes.

"Not as many of those as you'd think," Thomas mutters and sips at his poorly spiked punch. And who has time for romance when there's old gods to appease? He's not putting *that* on his dating profile, that's for sure.

"It's funny how you of all people aren't getting any," Alex snickers.

"Gee, thanks."

"Did you see Alice actually made it tonight? I haven't seen her at one of these things in what, four, five months? I know she's a hotshot streamer, but *surely* one Friday a month can't be all bad. We need her to keep this place from being a rainbow-colored morgue."

"I haven't seen her yet. You know she's busy." Thomas cranes his head, nominally looking for her, but he knows he'll hear her long before he ever catches sight of her. Alice Henderson is not a quiet person.

"Almost as busy as you, these days," Alex neutrally remarks and sips his punch. His eyes drill into the side of Thomas' head.

"Yeah, well, what else is new."

"Adam says there's a rumor going around about a witch getting into some problematic things."

"What *else* is new," Thomas repeats. He scans the throng of people, recognizing most, though hardly caring to search out Alice. He just doesn't like Alex's probing. The mind-reading is also offputting.

But all thoughts fly out the mental window when he picks a new face out of the crowd.

The guy must be a model, for starters. He has a long, pointed nose, high and terribly sharp cheekbones, and the nicest, most even, slyest smirk Thomas has *ever* seen. His skin is a cool olive brown. His jet hair is pulled back into a low ponytail, curling around the equally black fox ears, and from what he can see at this distance, the man's impeccable suit is also full black.

"Who's *that*?" Thomas asks.

"The one giving you a mental boner?" Alex deadpans, then cranes his head to look. "The fox spirit? No idea. Count the tails before making a move, hotshot."

"He doesn't look Asian, man. What's a fox spirit doing at a QAFPICC meeting?"

"It doesn't have the AF in there and you know it."

"But it's funnier that way. And I think the 'Fuck' is appropriate here."

Alex pinches his nose and sighs through his teeth. "You need to work on your mental shielding again. I don't know what you've been up to, but it's leaking, and I don't like your current train of thought."

Shit. Attraction at first sight completely dismissed, Thomas drags his mental shielding back up. Breathe in, breathe out, calm the thoughts. It comes easily with years of practice. *The fucking thing must've been chewing on my brain again.* He'd realized early on that every meeting with his employer eroded his mental state, but he had also thought that he'd been fixing it as he went.

That could be a problem for Future Thomas.

It *will* be a problem for Future Thomas.

"Heeeeey, boys!"

Alice flounces up and throws both arms around Alex's neck. Megan DellaVecchia trails in her wake, at least two cups of punch into the evening, based on the flush on their freckled cheeks.

Megan's expression immediately shutters when they register Thomas.

"Long time no see!" Alice gushes and smacks a kiss onto Alex's cheek. "Which one are you?" she jokes.

"You are *seriously* not wearing headphones right now."

Alice primps the pastel pink, white, and blue headphones around her neck like one would a fur muffler. "I have a brand to maintain, you know. It's practically an accessory these days."

"On YouTube," Megan giggles into their cup.

"And Twitch! It's so I can tune out the haters when the drama inevitably starts," Alice declares. "Anyway, it's so good to see you both! Alex, what's the good word?"

"I'm not giving you more gossip fodder," he replies, long-suffering.

"You're totally no fun."

"And you look like a pastel tool."

"You're no fun *and* you wouldn't know cute fashion if it bit you in the ass. Did you see who else came back after an extended hiatus?"

"No, who?"

"Is it that foxy fox over there?" Thomas adds.

"Nat and Vivi are here tonight," Megan replies. Their giggles are gone and their stare is piercing.

Thomas cocks his head to one side. They have nothing on him and they never will. "Is that so? I haven't seen either of them in a little while. I guess I need to stop by the shop again sometime soon." He's been chugging baku juice to keep the nightmares away. It rarely works—the things seem like they can smell *something* otherworldly on him—but it serves to knock him out.

But, well, no more being a regular at the potion shop for him. Natalie makes very good potions, but if Megan is openly hostile, then they have certainly figured out that he was the one who ruined Codi's job. He's fairly glad she survived, which is why he didn't use a bullet. But he also hadn't been expecting them there so early, which is why he had nothing *else* to use.

Oh well. Shit happens.

"What did you do *now*?" Alice asks, frowning.

"What makes you think this is my fault?"

"Because my darling Megan here would *never* accuse someone without reason!"

"They haven't accused me of anything," Thomas points out, bewildered, but he's been maintaining a clueless facade for a year and a half now. It will not be this pipsqueak healer who catches him off guard.

"Maybe they already had dibs on your new boy-toy," Alex snickers.

"Ooh, omigosh, who's that?" Alice asks, and even Megan looks curious now. If there is one thing Thomas knows about this community, it's that gossip trumps all.

"The 'foxy fox' over there. Either of you know him or who he came with?" Alex gestures with his cup toward the small knot surrounding the fox spirit.

And Alice's social butterfly persona saves the day. "Oh, him! He's not actually here *with* anyone, that's the crazy thing! He showed up, like, half an hour ago and asked if he could come in because it smelled nice. I think he just wants to talk to different people. Weird, but nice, and his accent is, like, to *die* for."

"You get a name?"

"No, I've barely spoken to him."

"Most of us have just been trying to figure out *why* he's here," Megan adds. "He doesn't strike me as lonely, or one of those curious spirits who've never been to the human realm. He definitely understands humanity."

"He might be looking for someone? I'm just trying to figure out what he *is*. He smells like blood," Alice says and wrinkles her nose.

"That's not blood, that's metal. I smelled it too," Megan replies.

"And he's not a terrorist going to eat or curse us?" Alex dubiously asks.

"I doubt it. Someone would've been tipped off to a hostile spirit in the city by now. And one having the gall to waltz into a big group of witches and hunters? Not gonna happen."

"Now that you said it, it's gonna happen," Alice gravely says. Megan shrugs.

"You're *bleeding* curiosity. Among other things," Alex comments with a sidelong look at Thomas. "Shall we go introduce ourselves, or are you content to stare all night?"

Thomas is about to answer Yes Of Course He Wants To Go Say Hi To The Nice Fox Gentleman, but who else does he spot near him but Natalie and Vivienne. Of fucking course. He makes a face like he bit a lemon and weighs his choices.

He'd much rather avoid them, though he doubts he'll be successful. More important would be preserving good first impression potential to the fox spirit and picking where and when he'd like to have his public drama with those nosy ladies. He has to admit, he's curious what Natalie could have seen.

But that is not for certain others to hear, especially the twins and the foxy stranger whom he *must have*.

First: Neutralize hostile ladies. Second: Inquire about new face. Third: Drink more punch.

Scratch that, move the punch up to first. He downs the rest of his cup and passes it to an annoyed Alex. Thomas hasn't gotten to where he is by failing to pick his battles; the most important part is picking where and when to have those.

He waits until the pair are nominally away from the spirit, Vivienne no doubt stealing more of Natalie's famous mashed potatoes before the meeting starts, and sidles on up along the food table.

"Long time no see, strangers. Thought you two had ditched these meetings for good," Thomas says in greeting.

Vivienne looks up at him, plate piled high with potatoes, and Thomas quickly looks away from her eyes. He fears very few things, and he would not say he *fears* Vivienne Sayre, but she sure as shit unnerves him.

"Good evening, Thomas. Fancy seeing you here," Natalie replies, as if they hadn't intended on ambushing him from the start. "What did you bring tonight?"

"Plates and cups." He cannot cook to save his life, and he would rather help in a support role. In this one thing, at any rate. This is standard. Thomas brings utensils, and Natalie brings her potatoes, and Vivienne leeches.

"So helpful," Vivienne coos around a mouthful of food. "Heard you're helping yourself to some trouble, too. How about that?"

"Is that why we haven't seen you at the shop for your usual order?" Natalie adds, cool as a cucumber. These two are nothing like what they were with Hayley in tow, but Thomas finds himself annoyed by their tag-team.

"Been busy, and I figured after shooting Codi with a dragon tranq, you two wouldn't be so pleased to see me. Was I wrong?"

"A job's a job. Would've had to hunt you for sport if you'd killed her, you know, but she survived and she hasn't called down any smiting on you, so we'll let it lie." Vivienne has always been more pragmatic and straightforward about these things. Thomas tamps his annoyance back down and tries to focus on her. (Without making direct eye contact.)

"Good to know. Thanks."

"Real curious why *someone* didn't want Marky-Mark to have a dragon, though. Not the first time he's asked for the stars and the moon and got it."

"That, I honestly can't say," Thomas replies, actually truthful, and shrugs. There are any number of reasons someone wouldn't want Mark Ito to have a dragon's body parts at his disposal, even if he's not magical himself; however, he doesn't know a single one of those reasons. He doesn't even know how his employer knows about Mark. "I didn't ask too many details. I'd assumed he was getting into trouble himself again."

"Isn't he always?" Vivienne agrees. "What time is it? Left my phone at home. How long until the meeting starts?"

"Still have about fifteen minutes," he supplies, puzzled, because he was expecting more of a fight. He can and will own up to doing his job, but he truly knows nothing about the motive behind it, and they have no way of knowing about anything else going on.

"It's another fight with the South Ash school board about the bathrooms," Natalie dryly adds, "so don't expect a very exciting meeting, Viv."

"I heard there are also some complaints from Alkanet about dues, too," Thomas volunteers.

"If they don't want to pay so much, then they shouldn't have so many members. They're collecting more coven dues than anyone else, so why complain? Now c'mon, Thomas, let's get you some food. I wanna sit together for the meeting," Vivienne chirps and nudges him with her hip toward the plates.

"Oh, uh." *That* he was not expecting. They're in public, which is their advantage, but also an excellent cover for him should they have started an argument. He'd been planning on that. He'd also been planning on continuing this passive aggressive bullshit.

He had not been planning on Vivienne playing painfully nice.

"I'm sitting with Alex, I thought?" Thomas lamely adds.

"*Not* with that handsome fox you were eying?" Vivienne asks, sharp as a knife, and out of the corner of his eye, he sees her expression dip into something a little meaner.

That, too, bewilders him. "I mean—c'mon, Vivienne, he's like ten ways my type. But I've never met the man before in my life. Why, do *you* know him? Weren't you talking to him earlier? Did he say anything about me?"

"You're not friends with him?" she suspiciously asks.

"Haven't had the pleasure yet."

"Oh. Hm." Her shoulders relax and she shoves another forkful of potatoes into her mouth with a thoughtful hum. "Okay then. I'd stay away from him if I were you. He's trying to sniff out trouble in the human realm, and I think he's two seconds from finding some. You wouldn't want any *trouble* on that spotless, golden record of yours, would you, Thomas?"

"Ha. Ha. So hilarious," he deadpans, rolling his eyes. She is the only one who can needle him with such precision. He hates it. He doesn't regret very much in his life, but he certainly regrets what he did to Vivienne. If *only* because of the consequences he now lives with.

"All that aside. Thomas, I'd like to see you at my shop again. I can make an appointment whenever you'd like," Natalie says.

"No thanks. I'm trying to wean myself off of the dreamless sleep draughts. Too many potions can really fuck with your health, you know?"

"That is one of the more harmless ones, addictive properties aside. So, won't you join me for lunch, then? Sometime this week?"

"No, I'd really rather not, Natalie. Thanks for the offer."

Her expression does not change, but her voice takes on an icy edge. "You really won't talk this out with me? We can avoid this, Thomas. You don't have to go down this path."

"I don't know what you're talking about, Natalie."

"It doesn't have to go this way."

"Nothing's going any way. I'm still working through life, same as I ever was. Nothing is different, no matter what weird future visions you've seen. Those don't always come true, you know? Better not put too much stock in something out of character you've seen."

"I don't think it's all that out of character," Vivienne adds, innocent as a lamb, and Thomas grits his teeth so hard his jaw hurts. "We're trying to place nice here, Thomas. Do you want us to play dirty?"

"I really don't know *what* you two are talking about. I think you've mixed up plots. You just said Mark was sticking his nose into trouble, and now you're after me? Try barking up his tree first."

"Oh, I am. You know us, like two peas in a pod. I'll worry about Mark's pretty little head, and whether or not he deserves his jobs sabotaged, but I'd like it if you were one less thing to worry about."

"I *really* don't know what you two are on about," Thomas repeats. He picks up a paper plate with as much force as he can muster and pointedly steps away to another part of the food table. "I'll see you around, but not for lunch, not by the shop, and not sitting together tonight if all I'm going to do is be grilled about my personal life. You two have a pleasant evening."

"Fine, fine, we'll let it lie. So long as you do, too," Vivienne says. She remains planted defensively in front of Natalie's mashed potatoes. "But no potatoes for you."

Thomas glares at her and picks his meal around her territory. Petty bitch.

He sulks back to one of the farther tables where Alex has already claimed a corner. He plops down and scowls at his lap.

"You have *such* a way with women," Alex drawls.

"They're just pissy because Codi Clarkson and I butted heads on competing jobs. No one died."

"You're about the only one who can say you *butted heads* with her and it didn't result in casualties. If it'll cheer you up, though, Alice and Megan talked to that fox spirit. He's French."

"That would be a nice accent," he grudgingly agrees.

"Only one tail, too. You're in the clear, but I'd still be careful if I were you."

"And why's that?" Honestly, the handsome spirit is the furthest thing from his mind. As he'd suspected, Natalie doesn't have any evidence beyond visions, but *what* she's seen is still a mystery to him. The only surprising part was that Vivienne thought he was already in bed (so to speak) with the fox spirit.

"Looks like he's a spirit of fortune. He pointed out someone's diamond earrings were fake and has a hell of a party trick—he made a lump of gold, then ate it again before someone got the *stupid* idea to try to separate a wealth spirit from his wealth."

Wait, rewind.

Did he hear that correctly? Wealth spirit. Holy shit.

Thomas goes rigid, straining to keep his mental walls up as high as they go, all while his mind churns.

A wealth spirit is a higher spirit, usually not great at combat, *and* known for literally insatiable greed. There is a higher spirit wandering around the human realm, not one with huge claws or fangs, and he has waltzed himself into Thomas' sights.

A wealth spirit would be perfect. He mentally kicks himself for never thinking of that angle sooner, but he never thought he'd just *meet* one.

"Groups make people stupid, and who knows if anyone would try to pick a fight with him, but I'm glad he isn't flaunting his gold too much. The last thing we need is to prove that humans really are greedy monsters. Also, I know you're trying to shut me out, but you're practically drooling over him. Disgusting," Alex adds.

"I *must* have him," Thomas announces in a reverent whisper. A true pity he means it differently now.

• • • • • • • • • •

Mirai yawns and ducks through the door to the tengu realm. Home smells nice, but *especially* after another long stint with the humans. They may be getting used to eating there, but sleeping there remains out of the question.

The furor they find inside, however, banishes most thoughts of slumber.

Guards dart this way and that, a multicolored barrage of different plumages denoting different clans. They're still in the common area, granted, but they could have sworn it was the owls' turn today to guard the entrance.

Have I been gone longer than I thought? they wonder in a sudden panic. They've ensured they aren't missing any of their shifts, but if they're a day off—

"Mirai! There you are!" Another crow tengu, Rei, wings down out of the unusual crowd with a wide grin stretching their face. "Did you hear, did you hear? The sparrow Yuki found one of the missing eggs!"

"Really? Which one?!" All exhaustion vanishes in the face of sudden joy.

"The songbird one! But come on, emergency duty for all guards!" Rei tugs at their wing with their foot, dragging them into the air, their own armor only halfway on. "Oh, you'll never *guess* where they found it—what happened—it's a shock for everyone, but I don't yet know how we'll handle this going forward!"

"Breathe, Rei! Tell me what happened!"

A returned First egg is cause for celebration. Never have there been so many missing at once, especially not from multiple clans, but Mirai recalls guiltily that *they* haven't yet succeeded in their own mission. Hatsu's egg is still not recovered. They have a lead, and they have squandered it in the name of diplomacy.

They would rather have the egg than revenge, because Hatsu's happiness is more important than Mirai's pride. But perhaps more force could be used.

"Yuki recovered the egg from the *fae*. A fairy queen had gotten it! Now no one knows if we're to go to war over this or not—I've heard that the egg was given willingly but in secret, or that the queen enthralled someone to steal it, or that they were lovers! No one knows what is going on."

"A sparrow fought the *fae?*" Mirai gasps.

"I don't believe they fought? It only *just* happened—I don't know! Come, come, in case we're needed, go get your armor!"

Rei all but tosses Mirai toward their home and wings off toward theirs. Hopefully to fix that atrocious armor.

But Mirai hardly stumbles through the door before halting.

Hatsu is perched in a nest of cushions, relaxed, one leg folded over the other like humans do. They're just in robes—that makes sense, they're not a guard, they're a merchant—but there is none of the outside alarm in their placid expression.

"Mirai, welcome home," Hatsu warmly tells them.

Mirai stumbles in, near drunk on that much affection in their voice, and mutters, "I'm home. Hatsu, what are you doing here? Outside, there's..."

"Quite the alarm. It's difficult to ignore. But it won't be war, or a panic, or anything more than a lot of ruffled feathers. Come, sit. You needn't get your armor."

Mirai dutifully sits, sinking into the plush cushions, glancing sideways at Hatsu every few moments. To make sure this is real. Hatsu has only been to their home once before, and under far graver circumstances. But here, now, they seem calm, and so comfortable and *at home* that Mirai never wants the moment to end.

"The owls were on guard when Yuki returned with the egg, so I'd gotten the entire story before all the chaos and excitement happened," Hatsu explains with wry amusement. "It was indeed a fairy queen, but it was a shameful secret, not a true theft. There will be more to deal with in the songbird ranks than with the fae."

"Oh, that's... That's good. I'm glad." No war, then. Just a tizzy of excited tengu. *That's* nothing new. "Thank you for explaining, Hatsu, before I was caught up in the excitement."

"You do like to get carried away."

Mirai peeks up at them through their loosened hair. "I'll get *your* egg back yet, I swear—!"

"Mirai, please. That is what I'd like to discuss with you today. I'd like you to let the matter lie."

"No, I can't! It's *your* egg, Hatsu, and it was on *my* duty—"

"Mirai," Hatsu sternly interrupts, and they fall silent. "Mirai, these constant trips to the human realm are weighing on you. They sully your reputation and waste your time. I am at peace with my loss. I'd rather not lose you, too."

Mirai shakes their head, more hair flying loose. They must look a mess, at utter odds to Hatsu's composed image. "I cannot let it lie! I don't care about my reputation, I care about getting your First egg back!"

"You'll care yet about your reputation when it comes to being promoted. When it comes to selecting a mate."

"I want *you* as a mate!" they exclaim.

Hatsu sighs. This breaks Mirai's heart, but then they reach over, and tuck some of their black hair behind their long ear. "I am too old for a young chick like you. And I hate how you've taken my burden onto yourself. I feel *guilty*, Mirai, can't you understand? You are doing too much for my sake."

"Then call it courting! I'll win your attentions and your affection, and get your egg back—"

"Mirai, *please*. For me. It is into October now, and I do *not* want you in the human realm for the human *Danse*. I would pay a dozen eggs if it meant keeping you out of this danger on my behalf. Let it go."

Hatsu cups their cheek and Mirai leans into it greedily. They've never been so open with their affection before, and they *know* it is meant as a bribe to get them to agree to Hatsu's plea. They will happily reject it, however.

"Your happiness means more to me than your affection," Mirai replies, though it pains them. "But I'll avoid the *Danse* for you. Even I am not that reckless, Hatsu."

"You make me worry, young one."

"I'll make you happy, too, soon enough," Mirai vows with a smile.

· · · • • · • • · ·

Emil's eyes sting, but he'd rather eat his foot than admit it aloud. He only vaguely remembers the scary list of side effects, but he knows eye strain had been one of them.

At least he hasn't been getting the migraines.

But *maybe* time to pursue other options. He also wants to ask Vivienne if there's some way to make sure Christine doesn't turn any more into a demon (though he can't see any difference at all). He's stopped practicing magic at home, and she has been spending more time away from home. Both rub him the wrong way.

Of course, Christine is following along at his elbow right *now*, so he has yet to figure out a stealthy way of asking Vivienne such things. He just wants Christine to calm down for all of two seconds; it's been *weeks, and* she's still jumpy and more of a not-crybaby than ever. And while the increased tangibility is nice, it seems to depress her further.

The door to The Crow's Cup swings open, but Emil doesn't see Vivienne anywhere. Or Natalie. Or even Megan.

It's just Isaac, feet propped up on the counter, playing his 3DS. Sam, at least, offers them a smile. "Oh, hello, you two! It's been a little while since we've seen you. How have you been?"

"Busy with school, mostly."

"What's that like?"

Emil is momentarily taken aback. Christine floats forward with a tilt of her head. "Vivienne said you weren't human. So you've never seen a school, or know what it's like?" she asks.

"I've seen them in the anime shows that Oliver likes to watch. And I've read about them online. But no, I've never attended one."

"Self-taught is a valid approach to life," Isaac flatly says. He scans the potion shop, missing Christine entirely, but aware she's there. "What are you here for?"

"Vivienne, but she's not here...? More potion, too, please?"

"She and Natalie are running errands in the market. How are those side-effects treating you?"

Emil bites back a frown. He refuses to rub at his stinging eyes. "Why do you care? I'm still alive and still in one piece. Better than the alternative, right?"

"No need to get snippy. I was asking on Vivienne's behalf. She's worried about you two."

"Oh. We're fine," Christine murmurs with downcast eyes. She fools no one. Then, with a shy peek upward, she asks, "Sam, um, is it rude if I... ask what you *are*? If you're not human. And, um, if that wraith you ate... Did you eat it? What did it taste like?"

"Why, are you hungry?" Sam asks without cruelty, but Christine still flinches.

Emil has seen the way she looks at food lately; he's privately worried, too, that she's *hungry*. He doesn't know what to do with that information. He's left out sandwiches and made extra food, but she won't touch it, and he won't broach the subject. That's Kirara or Vivienne's job. His is to make sure nothing nasty eats Christine.

"You haven't figured it out? I thought his theatrics gave it away," Isaac asks with a half-smug, half-confused twist to his mouth.

"Oh, I thought you knew, too. Recalling, I suppose no one actually *said*?" Sam adds.

"Poorly kept secret," Emil points out. "Sort of like the magic thing. I also kinda wanna know... What did the wraith taste like? Or feel like? Was it as goopy as it looked?"

Sam thinks a moment, hand on his chin. "It mostly tasted of death and magic. Not pleasant. More solid than it looked. The poltergeists Vivienne has given me have been better, but human food is best yet."

Christine looks queasy, arms wrapped around her stomach, but nods like someone calling for the shot at a firing range. It worsens Emil's suspicions.

"So, you two are still afraid of her becoming a demon? Luck spirits eat, too, probably. Don't know much about them." Isaac shrugs. He closes his game, though, setting it on the counter and fixing them both with a weightier look. Emil is taller than him and Isaac can't be *too* much older, but he seems so serious all the time, he could easily be a seventy-year-old in a twenty-something's body.

Emil doesn't like the weight of that attention. He feels like he's under a micro-scope—completely different from Vivienne's research mode.

"I don't want to become a demon," Christine mumbles, quietly angry at the prospect.

"What's so wrong with being a demon?" Sam asks.

"They eat people!"

"So do bakeneko. Or did yours not tell you that minor fact?" Isaac asks.

"Kirara wouldn't—she doesn't *eat* people. She obviously goes around adopting human kids and calling them kittens. Yeah, I've seen her eat some gross spirits, but..." Emil trails off, because Christine isn't arguing. He turns to her in growing dread. Was this another super obvious magic cat fact that no one thought to inform him of?

"I'm not becoming a bakeneko, either. Or any kind of cat spirit. I-I think," she replies, instead, still with that muted, angry determination. It narrowly beats the depression. "No, I don't know the exact process here, but I'm becoming a luck spirit. A-A generic one, or something, but not a cat, and not a demon."

"But you're wearing a lucky cat's collar and you're so spooked about magic that you won't let him practice it. Vivienne mentioned other spirits noticing you two, going after you—*hunting* you. Don't you think a witch-bolt to the face would stop such inquiring minds?"

"Why do you suddenly care?! You barely wanted to go to the magic lessons, and you ditched half of them!" Christine bursts out. (Emil wonders what a witch-bolt is. It sounds like it'd stop nosy fox spirits in their tracks.)

Isaac rolls his eyes. "I care because you're annoying. Demons *aren't* the end of the world."

"I don't want to *become* one! They're evil, a-and eat people, and *ghosts like me*! I'm doing what my brother—what *I* want and I'm becoming a luck spirit as planned!"

"What is your plan? Did he have a spell? More magic wouldn't help your case. You seem to be flying blind here."

"Why are you being so *mean*?" Christine asks in a quavering voice.

Emil steps in. When he extends an arm between them, his elbow brushes Christine's shoulder. "You *are* kind of being a dick. We were only looking for Vivienne and some more potion. Why do you care about demons, and what we do? We're staying out of your way here. I haven't even egged Oliver on with whatever he's doing."

"Sleuths you are not," Sam says. He shoots Isaac a sidelong, questioning look, and the witch nods. "*I* am a demon, you know. And I don't like all that mean talk about what I am. I haven't eaten any humans or ghosts, I'll have you know."

"You're... what?" Christine asks, faintly.

"You don't *look* like a demon," Emil adds with a squint.

"What are they supposed to look like?" Sam returns, sounding genuinely curious.

"Like a... demon. Horns? Pointed tail? Maybe goat hooves?"

Isaac snorts a laugh. "You're very wrong there. Only archdemons have horns, for a start. That's one of the *real* dangers of demons—they settle into a human form. Invisible to the naked eye. Now, would you say Sam is evil, and monstrous, and everything else you listed off?"

"Why are you being so bitchy about this?!" Emil demands with a panicked look back at Christine. "Sorry I—*we*—didn't know that Sam was a demon. Sorry we have some bad preconceptions. But aren't those things true, too?"

"There are worse things than becoming a demon," Isaac says with a shrug. "Not that I plan on pursuing any of the options, but personally, I think becoming a ghoul would be worse. None of the handsome perks of being a demon, but all the eating of people."

"I'm not a monster," Sam adds. "Do you think I am?"

Christine shakes her head with a closed-mouth squeak. Then, after a panic-stricken look to Emil, she turns and dashes out through the wall with a puff of golden dust and a ding from her bell.

"Why are you such a dick?!" Emil demands.

"Testing," Isaac replies, shrugging. "I could see and hear her for half that conversation. She didn't seem surprised. I think she's becoming used to being seen by others. Has that happened more?"

"Testing *what*?!"

"*I* can answer magical questions, too, you know."

"At least Vivienne was apologetic when she tried to banish her."

Isaac spreads his hands in mock surrender. (Emphasis on the *mock* part.) "And I haven't even tried to do that. Like I said, I was testing, gauging her reaction. She *really* doesn't want to become a demon, does she?"

Emil casts another wary look at Sam, not sure how to take *that* revelation just yet. Demons eat people. (So do cat spirits, apparently.) But Sam has been nothing but polite in all of their meetings. "No, she doesn't. I'm sorry if we came off as magic racist or something, but I'm still learning this crap, and Christine is going through a lot right now."

Sam sticks his nose in the air with a huff. "I'm not a monster, and I haven't eaten anyone yet. I want those to go on record."

"Okay, noted."

"Also, most people hate demons. More than you, I'd say," Isaac replies. "There's more or less a standing order to execute them on sight in the city. No doubt your ghost friend is also not keen on that detail."

"Then *why* did you tell us about him? We didn't know anything—you can't tell him from a human! If Vivienne hadn't said anything..." A good lesson on human-looking beings indeed. Emil irritably rubs at his eyes. His vision blurs from a moment; he blinks to clear it again. Isaac watches him intently. "Is this some sort of reverse psychology blackmail?"

Isaac snorts, which is the closest he comes to laughing, apparently. "No. You wouldn't know who to tattle to, even if you wanted to. And look, Sam is a perfectly likeable young man, isn't he?"

"I am," the demon proudly agrees.

"But, yes, I suppose that was mean. I guess I can apologize later, because I know how she can avoid the demon thing."

"What? How?!" Emil asks, animosity and stinging eyes momentarily forgotten.

Isaac shrugs again, like he hasn't just upended most of Emil's assumptions about the sad trajectory of Christine's second life. "An anchoring spell. I can make one for you. It would keep her in stasis. I can give you the details later, after you've talked to her about it. Informed consent and all that."

"A... spell? Isn't that bad? I mean, I've been avoiding magic use around her because of it."

"It would take a lot more magic than what you've been casting to turn her into a demon anytime soon. She spooks easily, doesn't she?"

Emil fidgets, because he doesn't want to agree with the dick, but he sort of has a point. "Vivienne did something like that, right? With her ghost friend?" Granted, Vivienne doesn't seem like a bastion of excellent decisions, but she *does* seem like a bastion of magical knowledge, especially pertaining to ghosts.

"Rory, right?" Sam asks, turning to Isaac.

Isaac regards them both for a long moment. Emil wonders if he got it wrong, but he could have sworn she'd called it anchoring, too.

"...You're smarter than you look," Isaac finally says. Emil cannot help his relief. "Yes, I could write something similar."

"Oh, okay! That sounds... good, I think. I'll talk to Christine and Vivienne—"

"No. Not Vivienne. Talk it over with your ghost friend, but not Vivienne or Natalie. They've been too nosy about my magic," Isaac flatly interrupts, eyes narrowed.

"O... kay..." Emil doesn't like that, either. "I'll talk it over with Christine, then. Can I get more of my potion so I can go track her down before she runs into traffic?"

"Or gets eaten by something nasty like a demon," Sam pointedly adds.

"Sorry, okay? I'm new to this!" Emil exclaims in exasperation.

"And you're already absorbing stereotypes. Didn't Vivienne teach you that black magic is just a color? I'm *made* of black magic."

"Okay, okay. Potion now, talk later, answer later. Okay?"

"Okay," Isaac repeats. He flicks his fingers and a tiny eye-dropper bottle floats off the shelf. "Don't burn your eyes out with this stuff just yet. Good luck, Emil."

Vivienne runs full-pelt through the decrepit mall, messenger bag bouncing on her hip, hair held back with a bowed headband. Behind her, a white boy with light brown hair and a crossbow and a Black girl with tears in her bright gold eyes sprint for their lives. The boy laughs wildly. Vivienne answers in kind. The poor girl wails.

Hooves thunder after them.

Vivienne hops over a Danger sign roping off an ancient escalator and scrambles up the rusted steps. The boy behind her vaults cleanly over it, and the girl simply goes through *it as if it were not there at all.*

Vivienne, in the lead, is three-quarters of the way up when the monster chasing them makes it to the base. The teenaged pair are halfway up.

The bipedal horse spirit roars and clambers up after them, heedless of the screeching, unstable metal.

The girl floats into the air with a frightened squeal. Vivienne dashes upward, nearly tripping in her haste, and dives for the second floor. The boy races up after her, but the escalator gives way, dipping with a loud crunch.

The girl grabs the boy just as the escalator separates from the second floor. He clings to the railing, and she clings to him, but as it slowly crashes, she lifts him into the air and tosses him bodily toward Vivienne's outstretched arms. She catches him and hauls him onto stable ground.

The two of them pant for breath, savoring the stability, and the younger girl floats over to where the escalator had just been. She spares them both a disapproving frown. "Is that enough action for you two? That was dangerous!"

"That was a tikbalang," Vivienne corrects with a finger in the air.

Natalie wakes. She recalls the wild joy Vivienne had shown with a small smile.

CHAPTER 27

IN WHICH MARK FUCKS UP

Mark runs his hands down the smooth direction of the dragon pelt. Against the scales would shred his palm. He may not have any magical ability, but it is difficult not to feel reverent for something like the hide of a *dragon* before him.

Brynja watches him like a cat studying a mouse. She still hasn't touched it.

"When would you like to try? Or can we finally get the egg from you, and make a move against stopping your boss? *Or* are you having second thoughts?" Mark prompts.

Brynja scowls, lip curled, baring sharp teeth. "I have not given my master the egg, have I? That is prevention."

"So give *me* the egg."

She averts her red gaze with a scowl. Mark sighs. He shifts the dragon pelt on his lap, accidentally cutting his finger, and sticks it in his mouth to stop the bleeding.

"Would your boss somehow *know* if you gave up the egg? Is that your hesitance, becoming known as a traitor?" he tries. He needs to *understand* her hesitance, since badgering her only raises her hackles.

"Every night, I dream of it. Do you know how powerful dreams are? How powerful my master is?"

"What, is this thing spying on you?"

Brynja huffs, fists clenched in her lap. "I doubt it, but I can never be certain. *You* have done nothing yet to help me. You have such grand, pretty words, but you are reactionary. What if Yaehathal hears of an egg returning to the tengu? What if it comes to me in my dreams and pulls me back to it?"

"Can that *happen*?" Mark presses.

"You don't understand that this is a god, do you? It can do things you cannot fathom."

"Okay, so... No, I can't fathom that. Humans can only fathom so much power before it turns into eldritch unknowable things. But I do know that it's over there, and we're both here, and we're going to keep it that way. We can give you a potion for dreamless sleep. We could ask Mirai to return the egg in secret."

"Birds don't stop cawing if asked *nicely*."

"We have to give the First egg back, Brynja. Mirai's patience is thinning. What if it tips the point where they care less about the egg and more about their anger at a thief?"

She tosses her head with a scoff. "Then that would solve many of my problems."

Mark frowns. "Do you want to die, Brynja?"

"No. I do not. But it would be much simpler," she frankly replies. "What are you doing about these *other* gods trying to do what my master plans?"

"Working on that. It'd be faster work if we knew how *you* were going to do it, so we could follow those bread crumbs."

She shrugs. "A lot of magic to break realm barriers. But my master is closer than these others. I needed a considerable amount of power to cross the realm border, but not as much as they would. A First egg is a good source, but there are other sources here. Can't you track a witch hoarding magical power?"

"No, they *all* tend to do that," Mark deadpans.

"I see. Humans have not changed much."

"No, I suppose they haven't. And *you're* still being unimaginably stubborn, so you haven't changed much in this time we've known each other," Mark replies with a bright smile. She glares at him. "Let's start with baby steps. I will supply you with dreamless sleep draught. The dragon pelt—"

"I want to prep it," Brynja cuts in. "If my master knows my movements here, then I want to be able to hide in the skin immediately."

"What does this prep entail?" Mark asks, because she has not *touched* the damn thing despite her ravenous looks toward it.

"Studying it. Learning about it. Preparing my body for it."

"Can you do it under supervision?"

"If I must," she relents with a weary sigh. "You know, Mark Ito, if I wanted to steal it from you, you could not stop me."

"No, and then *you* couldn't stop your boss, and I don't think distance from me would erase your hesitance over this. This is a classic and frustrating stalemate. It's your move. Please make it soon in the form of giving the egg back."

"I will make my move. On my terms. In my time. Soon, however, rest assured."

Mark rolls his eyes. "Somehow, I am not assured. But I have played this horrible waiting game with you for this long, so I suppose a little while longer won't hurt." Provided Mirai can also keep up the waiting game.

That earns a smile out of her, even if it's sharp as a razor and not at all flattering. He is going to have to teach her how to control her expressions better. After saving the world. Probably.

· · • • • • • · ·

Halloween is a whole-ass ritual for Vivienne.

And by ritual, she means she locks herself in her apartment and tries to sleep through it. Usually with copious amounts of booze.

Hammond will be busy, as will all other exorcists in the city, but this is one day Vivienne must sit out. She's heartbroken she has to miss all the fun parties—especially the one Dana had invited her to—but she'll live. She has so far.

But morning of, Vivienne's still fine. She'll be fine until moonrise, if a little twitchy. *And* she knows her lovely friend she'd like to smooch is working at the bookshop that morning, so it won't hurt anyone to swing by.

She doesn't bother looking for Emil as she ducks into the store. Christine is probably all kinds of twitchy, too, and that would keep his fretting hands full.

Wait.

Vivienne pauses mid-step, processing her own memories of the past several weeks. Halloween is a day she sits out, so she has never paid much attention to others' schedules.

Did I tell them about the Danse? Vivienne wonders with hysterical horror. Did she not tell the *actual ghost* and newly magical teenager about the *Danse Macabre*? She's been a part of the supernatural community for so long, she just *assumes* it's as big a part of everyone else's lives as it is hers.

"Hey, Vivienne," Dana calls, warm as the sun, and Vivienne turns to her with a rictus smile. "Woah, hey. You okay there?"

"I'm fine! Did Emil happen to mention anything about a *Danse* to you? Is he working today at all?"

"No, he's off. Does his school have a dance or something?"

Vivienne shakes her head to clear the Bad Thoughts. She'll simply swing by afterward and explain it all to them. Simple fix. No harm done.

And, to her delight, it is easy to be distracted when she sees Dana's Halloween costume: the khaki jumpsuit of a Ghostbuster.

Vivienne has to lean on the counter for how hard she laughs.

Dana gestures for her to carry on, arms folded. "Yeah, okay, laugh it up. Us managers are matching, and it was easiest for the part-timers to all be ghosts. We have a sale on horror. You could at least help our conversion today for laughing at me."

"I'm not—not *at* you—it's just so *cute*!" Vivienne gasps out. "You're a-a ghost—ghost hunter—!"

"You're telling me this *isn't* what they all look like?" Dana gasps in fake scandal. "I could've sworn I've seen *you* in this uniform!"

Vivienne shakes her head, hair flying free of her cat-eared headband (her one concession to dressing up before becoming a hermit for the night). "No, but that's—c'mon, Dana, did you choose it on *purpose*? Please tell me you did. Please tell me you wanna be a Ghostbuster!"

"No, I was outvoted. I will say, the jumpsuit is pretty comfortable, though. I have the backpack with the proton wand thing behind the counter."

"Is that what you're wearing to the party tonight?"

"Yeah. Why bother changing? Any chance you have a last-minute change of plans and can tag along?"

Vivienne shakes her head. "No, sorry. You'll have to enjoy busting ghosts without me."

"I'll try to manage. Any expert tips for me?"

"Supernatural Hunter Tip #27: Don't challenge the spirits to eat your ass."

"Oh, a number, huh? You have a lot of those?" Dana asks with a smirk.

"You have no idea."

"You should write them out sometime. Maybe on our hypothetical date."

"I can think of a few better first dates than writing out *lists*. I know you're supposed to be a bookworm, but come on, Dana. Wait, I know. Do you like animals? Besides Sunny."

"And Sparkle and Giggle? Who doesn't?"

Vivienne grins. "How about a zoo date?"

"Oh, sure. I've heard the city zoo is fantastic, but I've never gone. But an idea was only half the battle. We need to figure out a *date* for our date."

"I'll work on that." Vivienne will go off call if need be; Mark and Natalie can deal for a day without her. The city won't explode. "Promise. I'll figure out a time, and I've already figured out a place, so you just figure out the cutest outfit you have and wear that."

"Charming *and* bossy. What a catch."

"I do what I can for the ladies. But I just wanted to stop by and say hi, and see if you were in costume. Have fun tonight, okay? You'll be hanging out with Codi, right?"

"I never told you I was going out with Codi," Dana suspiciously replies.

Vivienne shrugs and tries to maintain her smile. "Word travels fast, and if there's a good party, Codi would get an invite. Plus she's the only friend of yours I know by name."

Dana rolls her eyes. Fondly. "You're a regular Sherlock. It was nice to see you. Thanks for stopping by and wildly guessing at my evening plans."

"Bust some ghosts for me tonight, 'kay?" Vivienne says with a wink. Dana's cheeks flush, but she smiles, which is a win in her book.

Now to deal with the kids before hermit life beckons.

· · · · ● · · ● · · ·

Vivienne finds Emil and Christine at his apartment, clutching at each other and screaming. More or less what she'd expected.

"You really need to remember to lock your door," Vivienne says, drowned out, as she shuts the door behind her. She toes off her shoes. The pair continue grasping each other's forearms, nose-to-nose, vibrating in cute little excited hops. "Mmkay, so, doesn't look like anyone explained tonight to you two. Fun."

"Y-You know what's going on?! I-I'm not turning into something?" Christine asks in a squeaky shriek. Her expression is a perfect mixture of stricken and hopeful.

Vivienne pries them off of each other. "Surprised you don't know, at least. It's Halloween today. All Hallows' Eve? Night of the *Danse Macabre*?"

Christine pauses, processing, then deflates with a long, "Ohhhhh."

"You know what this is?! Why I can suddenly touch her—like, more than a bit, more than a brush or by accident?" Emil asks. Vivienne guesses he'd been firmly in the excited camp until Christine had thought she'd been about to transform into Frankenstein's monster.

"Long story short, because I don't have time for my usual TedTalk and I think you two will have more fun things to contemplate, Halloween syncs up nicely with the beginning of Samhain, All Hallows' Eve, et cetera et cetera—most importantly to us, the *Danse Macabre*. Big spiritual party. Simply put, all ghosts get bumped up a level of evidence. Or, well, it'd be more correct to say that living humans get bumped *down* a level..."

"And what does that *mean*?" Emil asks, half suspicious, half annoyed. Somehow, this combines to make him all excited (again). He cautiously reaches out and grabs Christine's wrist again.

"It means normal people can see ghosts tonight," Christine explains, "and since you can *already* see ghosts..."

Vivienne rewards her with a wink and fixes a finger gun on Emil. "Bingo! You get an extra bump. Why do you think Halloween inspired so many ghost stories? Most ghosts will be visible, audible, and tangible to you tonight. I'm surprised it's started already, but I think Christine might be the special case, not you. Usually, it's from moonrise to moonset, same time as the *Danse*."

"But what is this dance thing?"

"I don't know much about the *Danse*, either, just that it... exists?"

"Big spooky party, as I said! I don't know how it'll affect you, Christine, but go with the flow. The biggest cemetery in the city is the focal point for this area. Big light show, a lot of ghosts come back from the beyond, lots of hauntings and reunions and—"

"Wait, wait wait wait, come *back*?" Emil interrupts. Christine winces at his tightened grip.

Vivienne pries them apart again. "It's the one night a year where ghosts who've passed on can come back for a visit. That's what the Day of the Dead celebrates, in a way. That's how we know that passing on is a positive thing—we get to chat with those ghosts, once in a while. Not everyone comes back, but those with unfinished business probably will."

Emil's expression fills with hope.

So it hurts her to shoot him down. "Yes and no, before you ask, Emil. Yes, that would likely include close family members looking to say hi to loved ones. For both of you. *But*—I don't advise you going. Christine, you'll probably be okay, and like I said, I don't know if you'll even be affected. It's like a compulsion for normal spirits? But you're not normal... But Emil, you're now tangible to *all* ghosts. Well, at moonrise. But a lot of spirits will not be as calm as two screaming teenagers when they find out they can touch a living soul again. You'd get mobbed. At best."

"But..." Emil wilts, torn between voicing all that sorrow wrapped up in him and biting it back like Vivienne has always seen him do. Boys. Gotta be manly and emotionally constipated. But he's probably pretty sick and tired of his own grief, too, Vivienne guesses; she has experience with that facet of loss.

"You two should stay in. Have some cuddle time, watch a movie marathon, laugh while Christine rubs herself against every blanket you own," Vivienne suggests.

"Wh-Why would I do that?" she indignantly demands.

Vivienne isn't sure if it's a trick of the light, but her cheeks look a little rosy in that indignation, too. She smirks. "Remember when we first met—properly—and you were acting like a needy pet? Imagine that with a fleece blanket. Laugh or deny it now, but you'll be doing it inside an hour."

And with that vague time reminder, Vivienne checks her phone.

"Moonrise is just after seven this year, and it'll last until about one in the morning. There will be plenty of spirits causing mischief and that'll last until sunrise, but the *Danse* starts and ends with the moon. But remember, just because you can touch and one of you's dead doesn't mean you can't hurt each other. I've heard water-based lube is the best bet, and I still recommend condoms because tangibility is—"

Christine buries her face in her hands with a wail. Emil forcibly shuts Vivienne's mouth with a hand clapped over. She laughs against his palm.

"Do not. Give us a goddamn sex talk. About *ghost sex*," he growls, face beet red.

"I-It's not l-li-like that—!" Christine bawls. Tearlessly, as usual, but Vivienne is more certain she sees some rosiness to the tips of her ears. Very interesting.

Vivienne licks Emil's hand to get him off. "It's better safe than sorry! Don't knock it 'til you've tried it. Well, it's better not to try it, not until you two get to know each other better, and have the chance to talk out boundaries and preferences—"

Emil makes another swipe for her, and Vivienne ducks out of his reach with another laugh at the skittishness of teenagers. She puts her hands up in surrender and backs up toward the door.

"Fine, fine! I'm out, then. Be careful, don't look for trouble, and remind me to teach you locking wards later. Physical locks will always trump magical ones, though. Oh, that should be a rule, too. Add that."

(Supernatural Hunter Tip #...to be decided: Physical locks will always trump magical ones.)

• • • • • • • • • •

Seeing Sam in his N7 hoodie is doing weird things to Isaac. It's the only hoodie of his (not Oliver's) that fits him properly, but it's a cherished gift that Isaac's kept despite the bad sizing, and sort of looks like a half-assed Halloween costume to boot. It makes him want to replay *Mass Effect*, but his last Shepard had been a full Renegade run and *happened* to be blond and white, too, so Isaac is stuck imagining his own demon making out with an asari.

It is uncomfortably distracting.

He *really* wants to replay *Mass Effect* now, too.

Sam doesn't even *act* Renegade.

"Sam," Isaac calls, both to catch his attention and remind himself that he has shit to do tonight. The demon cranes his head up at him, eyes innocent and questioning, hood drawn low over his bangs. "On a scale from one to ten, how hungry are you today?"

"Is that really what we're doing tonight?"

"There are thousands of ghosts around, so, yeah. I want you to load up." He has a couple of warded mason jars in his backpack, but he's never tried *catching* a ghost before. First time for everything.

"Why?" Sam asks.

"Why... do I want you to eat, and not starve to death, thus killing me too?" Isaac asks, squinting at him.

"Why do you want me to gorge myself? And you're going to try catching more, aren't you?"

"How do I order you to stop being so nosy?"

"Natalie called it perceptive." Sam jumps the rest of the way down the fire escape and gives Isaac another guileless look. He trusts it both more and less with each passing day.

"We can't rely on others to supply your food. It's best for you to practice hunting when there's so much prey around, isn't there?" Isaac points out. Already, he's seeing flickers in the corner of his eye, and he'll probably be able to see any old ghost soon enough.

"Are we leaving soon?"

"...What makes you ask that?" Isaac has been very careful with his movements, but he supposes he isn't used to living with someone full-time. Even *he* can't remain that guarded.

"You want that blood Natalie has."

Isaac can't help his scowl. "I'm not trading my magic. She doesn't deserve it, and it's too dangerous."

"What *is* that magic, Isaac? I saw bits of that circle. I've come to know and understand you. And with the blood of an angel piquing your interest so..." He peeks up at him under his hood again, then innocently scuffs his boot on the sidewalk.

Isaac remains stubbornly on the fire escape. Distance makes him feel more confident.

"That mark you burned off the circle, the night we helped you clean up the evidence of it. That was a rune you made, wasn't it?" Sam asks.

Isaac feels cold, and it has little to do with the chill October night. "You have a sharp memory. And the nosiness from the potion shop is rubbing off on you. What are you trying to get at, Samael?"

"It looked like the human mark for *demon*, but it was changed."

"You want to know about my spell so badly?"

"If we're leaving this comfortable life for it, then yes. Please."

Isaac barks a laugh at his politeness. His demon is all but threatening him for information, and of course he throws in a *please*. "I was going to tell you anyway, you know! Which is the only reason I'm rewarding this badgering."

He swings down from the fire escape and lands beside Sam. More ghostly flickers are visible to him now, and he *does* want him to capitalize on the feast tonight. Best to get the talking out of the way.

"I made that rune myself. It was an *angel* rune. My spell was to sacrifice you to summon an angel so I could steal its grace."

"It *was* about an angel?" Sam asks with wide eyes, like he's surprised at his own correct guess.

"You can't summon an angel normally without at least a dozen witches, an eclipse, and a live sacrifice equivalent to eight humans or greater. But I figured that demons are a magical mirror to angels—sort of an inverse, sort of a parallel running on another magical line. So you share a functional relationship, or at least enough of one I could use it to backdoor my way into an angel summoning. Really, you *are* functionally similar, so I simply had to isolate those factors from the *demon* aspects of the circle."

Isaac finishes with a shrug.

Sam continues to stare at him.

It feels good to get it off his chest. It *is* genius magic, and Isaac is not a humble witch. He did something no one else had ever thought to do, had never understood enough about magic to attempt, and he would have gotten away with it, too. No casualties. No outside help. One single summoner.

"You and Vivienne should talk together more. You are nerds," Sam tells him. There goes his jovial mood. "No, really! That sounds very impressive, Isaac. It would also impress Vivienne. So why would Natalie want that spell from you?"

"A human capable of using an angel's grace would be *dangerous*, idiot. More than any witch or hunter, more than higher spirits. You'd have to use most of it immediately to avoid burning out and dying. And that's all theoretical, anyway..."

"It's still nice to know what I was angel bait for. Thank you for telling me, Isaac."

"Don't tell Natalie or Vivienne. That's an actual order."

"I wouldn't. So, if you had the blood of an angel...? You could, what, circumvent needing a demon?"

"Correct. Mostly. Theoretically, as well. It would be a power source and another, different hook. I'd have to rewrite more than half of the spell, though, and I would need that blood before I could start so I could analyze it. But with how Natalie is guarding it like a hawk, I don't think it's worth the risk."

"Risk? Of what? *Are* we leaving soon?"

"I like to keep my options open," he hedges. Yes, Natalie makes for a convenient shield, and yes, Vivienne has helped in the demonic research area. The paycheck is only so-so.

But with no actual idea of *when* the apocalypse may or may not happen, Isaac will not bet on them.

Isaac continues, "Anyway, I have a backup plan already in motion. It will be a safer bet and doesn't have Natalie looming over it."

"You *really* don't like her, huh?"

"I don't like nosy people. I like magical thieves even less. I like controlling, nosy, would-be polite thieves least of all. If she can see the future, she can figure out how to avoid this, so that's on *her*. Now enough talk for the night. I want you stuffed full. Let's go, Commander."

"Huh?" Sam chirps, confused, but Isaac grabs his arm and tugs him along into the night.

·········

Brynja has hardly been a prisoner during her stay at Mark's home. She knows this, and he knows this, though she doubts he realizes how *much* she utilizes her current freedom under the guise of his protection.

Case in point: Twice she has been out to check on the First egg, touching it again to think *what if*, then carefully stowing it again. She keeps her other skin there, too, because if she does not trust Mark enough to return the egg to him (and thus the tengu) without her plan, then she does not deserve to reward herself with the thought of added security.

It wouldn't help, anyway.

It has been *tempting*, however. She can admit that.

During the witching hour, most nights, Brynja prowls the perimeter of his house, sniffing out scents of various visitors. The tengu has been there more than Mark knows, more than even Brynja knows, and she hates that. They're not supposed to be stealthy.

What are they waiting for? she wonders, again and again, and if Mark can read that much from her mind, he doesn't answer her. Frustrating.

The tengu Mirai had claimed to prioritize getting the egg back than punishing Brynja, and she mostly believes that. But there is still some force they could have used in that regard.

Do they prioritize relations with the human realm to that degree? It is the only logical answer she reaches. An odd one to ponder, too, considering how many centuries she has spent at the side of a god who would love to destroy those human relations.

No, love is too strong of a word. Yaehathal simply does not wish to let humanity live without fear of it any longer than it must. Human feelings on the matter and the state of the realm are incidental.

Brynja carefully paints the runes on Mark's newest mirror. She'd broken it the last time she'd tried communicating with her master; that canine rage spirit had broken it another time when he had gotten overly friendly with her sealskin. (Perhaps that is on her, too.)

Brynja regards herself in the reflective surface. Her eyes match the blood she paints with.

Humans are foolish, and her kind died out long ago. There is no reason to think either Mark or Vivienne or Fiona would know what she is, but with that canine around, she worries. Mark has befriended him, supposedly, but she cannot expect the same for herself.

He is helping you as a matter of convenience. I am using him for the same, she reminds herself and resumes writing. He wants the egg back, to pacify the tengu, and to stop the human realm from being overrun. Brynja couldn't care less about Mirai or the egg, but she wants the human realm preserved, at least. It has been... nostalgic, to live here once more. Calming in a way she did not realize she needed.

Even if her roommate is a nosy mindreader with a pet rage spirit and a human woman who seems even angrier.

Brynja does not understand any of them. Fiona smells like the canine, but she is human, and tends toward human firepower. Vivienne tends toward magic, many small kinds of it, but she smells of death in a way that Brynja finds both horrifying and wistful. Strangest yet that Mark is the least powerful, the most humane human, but he is the oddest in personality of them all.

Greed, she understands—and that it comes in forms more than that for wealth. He's greedy for power and knowledge. Many humans are. But he has no sense of self-preservation to accompany that. Neither do the two women she has most frequently seen him with.

But dwelling too long on the humans in her life is distracting. She shakes her head to clear her thoughts of them.

She finishes the runes on the mirror. Still water would be best, but that sort of magical spot is rarer to find these days, and she knows how to make this work. This will be a brief conversation. One way or the other.

It disgusts Brynja to find that her hands are shaking.

She clutches the porcelain sink hard enough to turn her knuckles white and prevent such visible weakness. Tonight, calling her master ought to be easier, with the *Danse Macabre* soon underway.

Not my master, she reminds herself. She doubts she will be able to voice it.

She takes a deep lungful of normal, human air to steel herself.

"*'Aiagl uln. Nog ynw Yaehathalnyth. Yftaghuog 'ai sll'ha shuggyar.*" The words burn her tongue, but it is an old, dulled pain, merely an ache from old age and repeated use.

The ambient magic of the night makes the connection too easy. Yaehathal's presence, not image, fills the mirror before her, and Brynja reflexively lowers her eyes. She tastes metal. The bathroom suddenly feels oppressive, weighty air instead of steam around her, foreign yet familiar magic probing every inch of her.

"*Ylyri,*" Yaehathal hums, vibrating her bones. "*You have been gone from me so long. What keeps you from me?*"

Brynja clenches her teeth to stop them from chattering.

Modern humanity has a phrase: now or never. It is succinct, apt, and terrifying. Brynja must lance this wound before infection takes her any further—she *must* act now and cut what ties she can if she has any hope of stopping Yaehathal from crossing over into this calm, kind, strange, nostalgic world.

"*Yþrt*," the image in the mirror rumbles, sighs, screeches.

There is no affection in its voice, not as humans or Brynja know it, but the term has been the closest thing she has known to that foreign feeling for years. She stares at the cracked sink beneath her shaking hands and swallows back more metal taste.

"*Yaehāthalnythog*," it says again, and fear so potent it feels like pain sears down her spine. She breaks the sink beneath her grip.

Brynja raises her head, sucks in a breath, prepares for what surely will be worse than death—and then Mark sticks his head into the tiny room suffocating with magic too powerful and too old to be contained.

"Brynja?" he asks, then locks eyes with the mirror.

The ambient magic of the night makes the connection too easy.

The witch with sage in his ponytail and ice in his eyes checks over the circle beneath his bare feet. The suit he wears is ill-fitting and unflattering, with sleeves and pant legs both rolled up, and tie hanging loose from his neck. Candles flicker with every bit of magic in the room.

The circle beneath him has several layers, all convoluted, and all strange. The mishmash of runes and styles indicates he is a spellwriter.

The candles gutter with a stronger wave of magic, and the witch steps back as the spell begins. The limited light in the room dims further, and all the shadows coalesce into the middle, pooling until a figure emerges. It blinks a few times, bright spots for eyes the only contrast in its black form.

"There's no contract here," the demon croaks, confused.

"Because I don't need one."

The demon shrieks as the secondary circle lights up. Black blood splatters against the invisible wall of the confinement circle. It claws at the circle walls, screeching, until it's eaten by the magic beneath it.

All the light blooms into another figure.

An angel.

Its eyes are dark as pitch, and it doesn't blink as it regards the witch. Instead of speaking, it reaches up with one long limb, and places its claws against the confinement circle.

The magic begins to crack.

The witch startles, but with a gesture, he activates more magic. Magic and fire drip off of the angel when it pushes further, and again the circle cracks. The witch activates even more magic, but now he's at his limit. His face is ashen and the sweat on his skin gives him a sickly sheen in the colorless light of the angel. For the first time, he appears scared.

While the last spell cracks between them, the angel can't break through. It presses, inches from the witch, claws scratching fruitlessly.

The witch and angel stare at one another, and the witch almost smiles.

Natalie wakes with a pounding headache and a too-sharp memory of the strange circles the unknown witch had used.

CHAPTER 28

In Which Dana Tries To Be Social

Dana has already texted her a picture of her and Codi (in matching costumes) from the Halloween party. Vivienne is only partially jealous—by and large, she's happy to receive a selfie, and saves it without remorse. The night itches at her, but she's almost home, and while the nightgaunt has been stubbornly on her tail for most of the day, it isn't affected by Halloween rules.

Emil has already texted her, too, in adorable all caps: '*CHRIS CAN TOUCH OTHER THINGS TOO IS THIS NORMAL*'

'*told u so*' she texts back, smiling to herself. She pictures Christine bundled up in half a dozen blankets (like Rory's first Halloween post-death). He had been an exception, and so is she, but it's gratifying to know she guessed right. *Guess she's closer to a luck spirit than a ghost. How recursive is her luck gonna get?* she wonders.

Her neighborhood is surprisingly quiet for Halloween—at least of human revelers. Spirits zip by overhead and dash down sidewalks, loud and happy and unaware she can see them. Her nightgaunt stalker shuffles ever onward about two blocks back, a straight shot, so she can see its ugly mug. At least her apartment wards keep it out of there.

Her phone lights up, not with a text from Dana or Emil, but a call. From Mark. Vivienne rolls her eyes, dreading what trouble he's gotten himself into this time, and debates ignoring the call. She doesn't do jobs on Halloween. In the end, however, she takes it. "Hello?"

"Vivienne, I need your help."

It is not Mark's voice. She stops dead. Female, husky, and strained. "Who—Brynja? Is that you? What are you doing with Mark's phone?!"

She *knew* that shapeshifter was trouble. But she shouldn't be affected by Halloween and its weird rules, no matter *what* she is, and Mark generally knows better than to poke sleeping bears on this night. She prays she somehow imagined the tension in her voice.

"I need you to come over. Right now," Brynja says. It sounds like she's on speaker; there is a crackling hum in the background.

Vivienne grips her phone tight. "I can't. Not tonight. What *happened*?" She bites back the threats until she can ascertain who she should direct them to.

The nightgaunt shuffles closer, half a block back now, and Vivienne shoos it away.

"There is a situation. You are a hunter, yes? I'll hire you. I will pay whatever Mark pays you. But I need your help. *Urgently.*"

"What. Happened."

The nightgaunt flaps closer, faceless head craning like a hound scenting, tail curled like a scorpion. Vivienne shoos harder. She has a physical form right now, so it's nothing more than a spooky nuisance, but she does *not* need even that distraction when she's going down a mental list of Every Stupid Thing Mark Has Ever Done And How It Could Bite Him In The Ass. It's a very long list.

Brynja is speaking, explaining, but Vivienne doesn't hear a goddamn thing, because the nightgaunt thrusts its gnarled head at her and *says*, "*Ya ah grah'n.*"

In three years, it has never spoken before. She didn't know it *could* speak. It doesn't have a mouth.

Brynja drones on in her ear. Vivienne's attention remains fixated on the bony figure before her.

It speaks again in the same rasping, dry tone. "*Ya ah shuggoth.*"

"I'm gonna... have to call you back," Vivienne mumbles.

"Didn't you hear me? He has gotten himself possessed! I need your help!" Brynja snarls.

"He *what*?!"

· · · · ● · ● · · ·

Brynja waits with her head between her knees for what feels like hours. The magic in the house is old and familiar and oppressive. Like a wet, warm skin freshly flayed off a body.

The dark teal of the dragonskin is draped across the hallway, one leg reaching toward her, scales glittering in the fluorescent light.

A new skin had not been worth this. Hope had not been worth this. Mark's promises feel hollow and distant; she had not meant to trade one employer for another, only to end up with one killing the other. Mark Ito will probably not survive the night. Brynja probably won't, either.

Vivienne staggers in through the door, out of breath, eyes bright with panic. She takes two steps in and vomits into a vase.

"The magic is foul, but it won't hurt you in these quantities," Brynja dryly informs her.

Vivienne points a shaky finger back at her. "I took a-a goddamn *car* to get here. Start talking."

"I was communicating with my ma—...employer. Mark decided to say hello. Tonight was a bad night to do it. He seems susceptible, or, *is*, and now he's possessed by the very god he was striving to stop."

Vivienne wipes her mouth with the back of her hand, then straightens, all business. "How long has he been in this state? What sort of possession is it?"

"There are types?" Brynja asks, baffled.

She rolls her eyes. "Okay then, I'll try everything. Length of time?"

"I called you as soon as I was certain."

"Where is he?"

"I confined him to the bathroom. I bound his body to prevent Yaehathal from harming him."

"Alright then." Vivienne strides forward with purpose, messenger bag open at her hip.

But she pauses when she sees the scales splayed across the floor. Brynja half-glares up at her through her hair, daring her to comment on this trust Mark gifted her with. On what she's bet everything on.

Instead, Vivienne only asks, "Is that ready?"

"No."

"Alright then," she repeats.

Brynja carefully folds the dragonskin into a pile on the couch and Vivienne grabs a broom. It seems a comical parallel to Brynja's introduction to her.

Mark remains where Brynja had put him: bound and gagged in the drained bathtub. Blood from his nose wets the sock in his mouth, and his fully black eyes, glassy and unfocused, flutter when they enter.

"Yep, that's a possession," Vivienne announces in a queasy voice. She pokes him once with the bristle end of the broom, eliciting a grunt, then lets it clatter to the floor. She pulls a clear vial out of her messenger bag. "Hold still, Mark."

She grabs his jaw, digs her fingers into the hinge, pops out the makeshift gag, and rips the cork from the vial with her teeth, all in one practiced motion. Mark has no more time than to suck in a wet breath before she dumps the vial's contents down his throat.

He sputters for a moment, eyes screwed shut, but the moment passes. He slits a black eye back open. His voice is not his own when he growls, *"Are you trying to exorcise me? I am older than your religions, shuggoth."*

Brynja cringes at the voice and Vivienne drops the vial in her haste to clap her hands over her ears. "Oh, so you can talk," she says, grimacing, and does a quick once-over on his bindings. "That makes things easier."

"Does it?" Brynja hisses.

"Just to let you know, whatever you are, I am fully prepared to kill Mark rather than loose you on the city tonight. If you harm him in any way, I'd rather do that than risk the alternative. Am I clear?"

Yaehathal laughs. It is bone-dry and echoed. Too layered. *"You are not good at persuasion. All I am here to do is talk, since yhri has not yet returned to me. All I want is the egg you hold here."*

"Why do you want a tengu egg?" Vivienne asks while she pulls out a large, silver-edged hunting knife from her bag.

Mark fixes that black gaze on Brynja instead. *"Give me the egg, or I burn your skin tonight, yhri."*

"If we give you the egg, will you leave? Leave the body intact and unharmed?" Vivienne asks. Brynja cannot hide her surprise; she is not yet sure if she's trying to bluff or appease her master.

"I am surprised at how quickly you roll to show your belly in the name of protecting this one." Its voice dips ever deeper, into registers more like tremors than words, and Vivienne again flinches at the voice. She covers an ear with her free hand. Mark's head tips back and his laugh screeches like a grating bird. *"Shuggoth is a psychic, yes? What a pleasant and comfortable mind to reside in."*

Quick as a flash, Vivienne throws a handful of purifying salt at Mark's face. It, unsurprisingly, does nothing.

"What amusements this realm offers. What amusements shuggothh are. It has been so long."

"It's only for tonight. You won't be able to hold the body past sunrise. This isn't helping whatever your plan is," Vivienne says, digging around again in her bag. She ends up dumping much of it out onto the damp tile, and Brynja's eyebrows shoot up when she registers *how much* that bag had been holding. She only spots two weapons, one of them the knife in her other hand, but she knows what magics can be done with the right ingredients. She hopes Vivienne has a plan.

Mark's head lolls against the edge of the tub, lips stretched wide enough to crack. Another drop of blood rolls down from his nose. His black, empty eyes remain on Brynja while he licks it off with a satisfied *smack*.

It's going to burn through him too soon, she realizes. *It won't wait until sunrise—we can't wait until then.* She doesn't even think Yaehathal is doing it on purpose. It has not been in the human realm for millennia, and it's entirely possible it has forgotten how fragile humans are. If it ever cared at all. *We need to hurry this.*

She leaves the bathroom while Vivienne paints a circle around the bathtub in a dark red paste. Brynja hopes hers is a hell of a plan, because hers is very, very stupid.

She grabs the dragon pelt and bundles it up in her arms. Magic thrums within it, loose and unfocused and raw, waiting beneath the hard shield of the scales. But there is no time for any more prep work. It will have to work.

"Please, work with me," she murmurs against the scales and pricks her finger on an edge. She draws the necessary runes on her arms, burning the marks into her skin, hands shakier than she'd otherwise like. She has never had so little time to bond with a pelt before. She has never done it under duress.

She soon has dragon runes around both biceps. It has to be enough.

Brynja throws the dragon pelt over her shoulders, and as she thought, it fights her. It fights against her form like it is still a living, writhing thing, refusing to mesh with her body like it ought to. She doesn't bother trying to fully transform. When she reenters the bathroom, Brynja knows she must look monstrous, but the important thing is that she has dragon scales from shoulder to claw tip.

Vivienne gapes at her. "What are you *doing*?"

"*Is that what shuggoth promised you? What I scented from you? Are you so hungry for new you forsake the old and familiar?*" Mark asks in a voice like lightning too close to hear the thunder.

Scales creep over her shoulders. Anger burns bright within her. *That* is familiar, more familiar than the pelt, more familiar than anything the god can offer her. The anger has been part of her longer than *it* has.

"Dragon scales nullify magic in this realm," Brynja says and raises her claws over Mark's bound body. He could survive this. It is better than the alternative.

"Wait!" Vivienne yelps, but Mark's black eyes widen with *fear*. That is what Brynja focuses on: a crack of weakness. This could work.

But Vivienne throws herself around Brynja's waist and tugs her back. Brynja hardly moves, easily ignoring a human's strength, fury at being stopped feeding into her desire to *hurt* Yaehathal. It may not even hurt it. It certainly would not wound or destroy it. You can't kill a god. But she finally has that single sliver of weakness, that moment of actual *fear*, the one genuine opportunity she has ever gotten to fight back against what she has been put through by that thing.

Vivienne yanks on her tail. Brynja, not used to having this particular tail and having gotten unused to having a tail anyway, falters and stumbles backward.

"Hold on!" Vivienne cries. Brynja cranes her neck back with a furious glare and finds Vivienne holding her knife against the scales spotting her hip. "You're Plan B! I'm almost done, you haven't ruined my circle, let me try mine before you start throwing claws at our beloved friend!"

Brynja bares her teeth and almost goes for it anyway, but then Vivienne's grip and panic falter. She stares up at Brynja with realization visibly rolling over her.

"You're a *rage* spirit. Holy shit," Vivienne breathes.

Yaehathal lets out another laugh like broken glass. Brynja snarls at nothing and rips her tail free from the ever-nosy woman. "Hurry and cast!" she demands.

Vivienne scrambles back to her circle. The linework appears complete, her fingers coated in the mixture, and she hastens to write the last outlining runes. Brynja clenches and unclenches her fists as she waits. Every moment is a moment too long.

"Hurry it up!"

"Maybe if a half-draconic goddamned *rage spirit* didn't march into my workspace!" Vivienne growls and Brynja almost snaps back. Her sharper teeth ache in her clenched jaw.

"*Why kill this body, yhri? Why betray me now?*" Mark plaintively asks.

Vivienne winces at the voice but does not lift her hands away from her work. Brynja finds her tail lashing in impatience.

"*A new skin cannot replace lost ones. A new life cannot replace death,*" the deity warns, voice more a feeling than anything truly audible anymore. Brynja swipes wet hair away from her ears; her claws come away with more blood. "*Why have you gone from me, yhri?*"

"*Ya naflah hri!*" Brynja snarls and Mark recoils from her.

"You two are literally making my ears bleed, and if I drip any more blood into this circle, our plan is shot," Vivienne complains and leans away from her completed circle. "Step back."

"*What will you—*" Yaehathal is cut off with its own shrill scream when Vivienne activates the magic. Brynja steps back, claws covering her nose from the smell of burnt blood.

Mark thrashes in the tub. He fights against his bonds, muscles bulging and eyes rolling. The screaming climbs higher and higher through the octaves, and both of them clamp their hands over their ears with unheard shouts of pain.

With a flash of light, the sound stops, or at least drops enough that the ringing in her ears drowns it out.

Brynja cracks open an eye and finds a beastly shape of emptiness standing on the tub. Its tail is held high, too many limbs not-balancing on the copper edge, what skin it has is *nothing*. It isn't black; it isn't white; it isn't any color, only nothing, save for distant motes of light twinkling in itself.

Yaehathal's vestige turns empty nothing eyes on Brynja.

"*Lloignyth-hri. Naehye. Hai ftaghu fm'latgh,*" it rumbles and she nods. She accepts. She knew it would happen.

Calmness washes over her even before it blinks out of their realm of existence. Her fury drains away, replaced by exhaustion, weariness, and very distant sorrow. All of these are too many years old within her.

Vivienne pokes her head over the edge of the tub. Eyelashes spiked with red, she's paler than ever, and she is smeared with the remains of her magic work. But when Mark stirs, her face brightens like the sun.

"Wha..." he slurs, fighting to raise his head. He cracks open an eye, and it's blessedly human. White and black and bloodshot—full of human color and life.

Brynja cannot help her smile. Relief. She hasn't felt that in so long. "You're alive," she says in surprise.

"I don't *feel* alive. What happened?" Mark asks. His speech is thick and muzzy, but coherent enough, and he raises his head after a few deep breaths. His mouth and chin are still coated with blood, nose crusted over, and she thinks his glasses got broken in the initial scuffle. He looks odd without them. "I feel like I've been gargling glass."

"You were almost gargling dragon scales because *you* stuck your nose into trouble again!" Vivienne exclaims and throws herself at him. He groans in pain but she latches on like a leech, checking him over like a dog sniffing out another's injury. "Okay, looks good, normal pallor, nosebleed stopped, heart rate slow but steady—"

"If he's not dead yet, he won't be," Brynja interrupts. She lets out a breath with all the tension in her body. The dragon scales slough off like water. The skin still feels strange and alien, but it had worked with her, and for that, she is grateful.

"Oh, you got the skin to work?" Mark blearily asks.

"Just once. Just enough. But there is no time for that. The egg is—"

"Why isn't there time? It won't be using Mark again," Vivienne says, hunched protectively over him.

"There isn't! You didn't kill Yaehathal, you cannot *kill* a god. You didn't even banish it. You only purged Mark of its weak and distant control. But it *will* try again, and it *will* succeed, if more proactive steps aren't taken," Brynja snarls at them. Vivienne's glare darkens, but Mark seems surprised at her tone.

"So, is this a proactive step now? Are we moving forward—?"

"Shut *up* and listen, you nosy humans! The tengu First egg is at the bottom of White Lake in a protected container. Yaehathal is the closest of the gods vying for the human realm, so it needs less, but I believe it *needs* the power that the egg can provide, else it—"

"Why are you suddenly rushing this? What changed?" Mark demands as alarm brightens his expression. It makes him look less half-dead, at least.

"You'll find the list of everything it tasked me to find. The egg is the easiest to track, since the tengu are so noisy about its loss. There are others, I know little about them, but I want—you need to stop *everything*."

Brynja looks at Mark, really *looks* at him, cataloging all of his little human quirks and flaws. He is wet, smeared with blood, disheveled, and still bound, but he is alive and painfully human. Something she thought she'd lost all knowledge of.

"Thank you, Mark Ito. For giving me hope again," Brynja says. "It was nice, I suppose. While it lasted."

Even several dimensions apart, she feels the exact moment her skin burns.

· · · · ● · ● · · ·

Dana is glad she used a backpack for her proton pack. It's bulky, sure, but it has a CamelBak built in and it means she's guaranteed a good drink that *isn't* whatever Codi just handed her. It tastes like sugar and the cheapest alcohol in the world.

She downs it, to be polite and to stand the noise of the house party, then sneaks the nozzle into her mouth and sucks down the refreshing tang of a homemade screwdriver. Codi gives her a grin, privy to her weird plan, but also gives her another red solo cup of alcoholic koolaid shit.

Dana is only sometimes an extrovert—she's certain there's a word for those half people—and the only person she knows here is Codi. She's still disappointed Vivienne couldn't come.

"Omigosh, Codi, you made it!" Someone violently pink throws themselves between Dana and Codi with the air of a perfect Drunk Girl. (Drunk Girls are the best and a very specific thing, Dana has found.)

"Ohh, hey, Alice! Long time no see, honey!" Codi says and hauls her new friend off her with one arm. "Dana, this is Alice. Alice, this is Dana. Be nice."

"I'm always nice," she pouts, then bounces back with a winning smile. Dana's initial impression of *pink* remains correct: Alice's costume is a pink Power Ranger, but she also has pink *hair* tied back in two high pigtails. "It's nice to meet you, Dana! Any friend of Codi's is a good friend to have. You wanna play *Guitar Hero* with us?"

"You already got it set up?!" Codi excitedly asks. Dana could swear her eyes are sparkling.

Dana, from years of experience, knows Codi plus alcohol plus anything remotely musical is a bad idea. She manages a smile. "I'll pass, thanks."

"Suit yourself!"

"Behave, Haddad. Don't do anythin' I wouldn't do," Codi says with a wink before departing in the presumed direction of the poor living room and its poor inhabitants.

Dana makes a point to head upstairs, away from the coming cacophony.

She finds a room with a deck of cards being shuffled and gratefully gets roped in. She can do this; she can be social. The other players are a black-haired guy with thick gloves who definitely pulled his wannabe steampunk costume out of his closet, a brunette woman in a cowboy hat and a plaid dress (Dana sees her matching boots sitting by the bookshelf behind them), a man with furry pants and an antler headband and rather fetching freckles, a stunning woman with long, white hair who also seems to forgo any real costume in favor of a slinky barely-there dress, and an unimpressed auburn-haired woman with whiskers painted on her cheeks, her own cat-eared headband lying in her lap.

"What're we playing?" Dana asks while she sits down. She sets the proton wand down, but sneaks another sip from her nozzle.

The white-haired woman watches with wide eyes. "Oh, is that a drink? Are you a scuba diver?"

"She's a Ghostbuster. Watch a movie, get some culture," the Cat Lady replies with an epic eye roll. "And we can't decide on a game, because *some people* are being ridiculous. You have any suggestions?"

"I'm *not* playing poker with them," Cowgirl replies, nose in the air, arms crossed. "Yiannis only plays strip poker!"

"That's how you play the game," Fuzzy Legs replies. Dana gives up on learning names after hearing the perhaps-Greek one. She sips more screwdriver.

"Yes, but you're too horny to play with normal humans," White Hair points out.

"What about rummy?" Dana suggests around the nozzle in her mouth.

"What are the stakes?" Closet Costume asks at once.

"Oh my *god*, Graham, you don't have to make everything a bet!"

"Let's be nice and let the new lady decide on that," Fuzzy Legs graciously says.

Dana just shrugs. "Bets are fine. Penny points, or...?"

"It's whatever. I'm betting some Ægir ale," Cowgirl replies, shrugging, and with a flick of her wrist, Dana only *just* notices the massive, furry dog behind her. She'd assumed it was a weirdly fuzzy beanbag. The dog nudges aside the boots and retrieves a bottle of what looks like alcohol. Dana could swear it was glowing. It looks so pricey.

"Ohh, when I win, I want your very nice scuba backpack," White Hair says, leaning forward, showing off generous cleavage.

"Uh," Dana intelligently replies. She fixes her eyes on the ceiling. Penny points means losing a dollar if you *really* lose. A costume backpack and expensive booze are making her worry.

"Relax, Penelope's shit at cards when she can't cheat. And I'm only betting this protective amulet," Closet Costume replies and pulls a *hideous* crystal necklace out from under his shirt.

As it turns out, they're *all* shit at cards. Dana wins handily and ends up with a pile of prizes in her lap: nice booze, ugly necklace, pretty bracelet, handmade scarf, and a bag of herbs (that isn't weed, so Dana doesn't want to think too hard about what she has in her possession).

Downstairs, the music they're *supposed* to be listening to competes valiantly with the music Codi and Alice are *supposed* to be making. She's certain she hears Portuguese. With a jerk of her head, Cowgirl sends her dog over to nudge the door closed, and it becomes blessedly quieter.

Dana wins the second game, and the third. She's a little surprised no one suggests changing games, especially with how upset Closet Costume and White Hair seem to get. Even distracted by the knowledge that there is an un-petted dog in her vicinity, Dana is queen here.

She's probably going to give most of her winnings back, she reasons. She feels *bad* for taking these things—alcohol aside. She's out of screwdriver, already downed the second sugary hell drink Codi foisted upon her, and sets down her cards so she can crack open the fancy alcohol. Some part of her knows she's drinking too much. But she didn't drive, and she's still *winning*, so she ignores that part.

"Surprised you haven't lost your temper yet, Fiona," Cowgirl says, too light for it to be innocent teasing. Maybe they've *all* had too much to drink.

"Not my deal," Cat Lady grunts.

"Oh, aren't we bonding tonight? No bickering with your petty drama," White Hair declares, and Dana chances a small nod.

"Well, at least we aren't dragged into another terrible strip poker marathon," Cowgirl reasons, backing off, and looks longingly to the fancy alcohol Dana has opened.

When she takes a swig—it's sweet, and light, and tastes like how she imagines clouds would taste—attention is back on her.

"Did you just *chug* Ægir ale?" Fuzzy Legs asks in awe.

Dana would not consider two swallows *chugging*, but with the way the room spins, maybe she'll grant him that one. Fuzzy Legs laughs, kicking his legs, and Dana doesn't understand how his shoes work. They look like stubby hooves. This stuff must work fast.

Cowgirl claps in delight. "Now it's a party! I like you, Ghostbuster! Come on, maybe now we can beat her!"

"I'm out of anything I can reasonably bet. Can't we switch to the stupid poker? All I have left are body parts and a jackalope."

"What's that?" Dana asks. Her tongue feels thick. She wonders what the proof of that stuff was, but the fancy bottle has no label. She dizzily wonders if it's a homemade concoction.

"Like a... rabbit, yes?" White Hair says, sticking up her fingers on her head like ears. "Please, let's play more games that don't have us getting naked! Yiannis is too much even for me."

"If I win," Dana says, maybe slurs, swaying on her butt, "I want the dog."

The room freezes.

"I wanna pet the dog," Dana says. She wants to pet the dog. Is that so wrong?

All eyes are on Cowgirl for a tense moment Dana is largely unaware of. "You can... pet him. If you win while plastered," Cowgirl says, haltingly, eyes narrowed and mouth twisted. "Jeez, you're turning into a rude drunk. I take back the party bit."

"'mnot rude!" Dana insists. She feels like she may fall over. Why is the room still spinning?

Even totally sloshed, Dana wins another game.

"It's good luck to catch a bat on Samhain!" Hayley insists, fists on her hips, expression twisted with stubbornness. "Vivi can ride with me, right, right? I just want you along since this is a good bonding experience!"

"Am I going to be third-wheeling again?" Vivienne asks, ducking under Hayley's arm.

"No, you're gonna help me catch a bat!"

The vision fades out, and thankfully, Natalie does not come back to a ruined potion this time. It remains placidly blue in her bowl, inert. Even her visions are getting into the Halloween spirit, she notes with amusement; it's only a week away and Hayley and Vivienne are getting into it with their usual exuberance.

But when Halloween rolls around, and Hayley approaches her with her fists on her hips to demand that they catch a bat, Natalie can only laugh. She's never had a vision come true so quickly *before.*

CHAPTER 29

In Which Christine And Emil Go To A Party

Christine makes this annoyed whine that almost sounds like a *growl* whenever Emil tries to move. It sounds like a grumpy cat. It was cute the first few times, exactly like a grumpy cat, but now, he *really* has to pee and she needs to move. Some people still had working bladders.

He valiantly holds out until the credits roll. Christine wiggles, pressing further into the fleece blanket thrown across them both, and he takes that moment of weakness to bolt for the bathroom.

When he returns, Christine is burrito'd in the blanket and spread across the entire couch. She peeks up at him. "It's odd," she says, unapologetic about taking up space, "but I can't feel any warmth. The blanket isn't too hot, and even leaning on you, nothing."

Leaning on is a polite way to describe her sudden cuddly attack. Emil wisely holds his tongue on that. "Uh, well, I dunno if you'll get that back? I'm not sure how much... tangibility all this has. Or creates. Or anything. I'm talking out my ass even for that single sentence, which should give you an idea of what I think is going on."

"Yeah... Me too. Kind of." She sits up, still a little caterpillar, a poof of hair sticking up from the static of the blanket. Emil stares at it, because it looks *glittery*. "I'm glad, though. I think I needed this. It's nice."

"Do you wanna go to that dance thing?"

"Huh? Why?"

"Because Vivienne said it was a compulsion, right? For ghosts and stuff. If you want to go, you can. We can."

She frowns, reproachful. "Vivienne said that'd be a bad idea for you."

"Not for you. Aren't you curious about a big ghostly dance party?"

"Sounds like you are."

Emil can only shrug. "Well, *yeah*. Maybe I'd learn more about ghosts, then? And... You know. Mom." It feels good *and* bad to voice that. So much death has remained unspoken between them.

"Vivienne said it'd be a bad idea..." Christine repeats.

"For me, not for you," he replies in kind. "I'm curious, you're maybe curious, and it'd be safer if we go together, right? Or we can stay in, I think I have *Hocus Pocus* bookmarked somewhere. No pressure. Honest."

She remains silent in her blanket burrito. He thinks she'll remain a goody-goody, or perhaps is too scared to face another facet of her death, and he tells himself he won't blame either.

"We could take a peek. As a living person, you'd probably get us kicked out," Christine finally says. She shoots him a suspicious, bright-eyed look. "Can you even dance?"

"Like the white boy I am. You'll have to bear with it for a night."

"We're getting kicked out," she says, like it's her decision to make, and stands up, blanket and all.

So they end up going.

Emil wishes he'd grabbed gloves, or maybe a thicker hoodie, especially since Christine is not sharing the blanket. It drags on the ground behind her, but it'd been a cheap thing from Target. It's a pity *she* doesn't give off any heat; it's *weird* to be next to someone who is perfectly ambient temperature. Creepy if he thinks about it for too long.

They're several blocks from his apartment when he realizes Emil has *no idea* where this dance thing actually is.

Christine takes over as navigator with a tug on his sleeve, thankfully. The blanket has fallen from its makeshift hood. Her hair *definitely* sparkles. She hardly looks in his direction, floating on with determination, and right, it was kind of a drive. A compulsion, Vivienne had called it. Also creepy.

Emil spots other ghosts, who he only knows as ghosts because it's a bunch of floating people in white robes wandering around. He sees why people could get freaked out; without the natural movement of a living body, humans are *freaky*.

The sky abruptly brightens. A huge shaft of light touches down somewhere east of them, and just a *hunch*, but Emil thinks that's where they're headed. The clouds reflect it like a dark ceiling, casting everything in a soft glow.

He turns to find Christine glassy-eyed and stock-still, however.

"Christine?" He waves a hand in front of her face.

It takes much poking and prodding before she blinks back to attention. She rubs at her eyes, shedding sparkly luck he can absolutely see now, and focuses on him like she's waking up. "Emil...? I don't... I don't think that's a good... We should go home."

But she's already floating onward.

Emil is torn between curiosity and worry. Mostly worry. "Okay, fine, you win. Vivienne was right. Let's go home and watch more movies."

Christine doesn't reply, and Emil tugs on the blanket, but she lets it fall to the ground. Alarm spikes up his spine. He scoops it up with a panicked whine. He has little choice but to grab her arm, but that doesn't work; he throws his weight at her, but she remains upright. *He* ends up the one being dragged.

Around them, others shamble onward, starkly standing out against the occasional drunk teenager or costumed trick-or-treater. The ghosts all appear fixated on the light, like so many glassy-eyed moths.

Emil has seen enough zombie movies to be okay with *none of this*.

He swings around and plants himself firmly between Christine and the light. She may follow only a few laws of physics, but he is still bigger than her. More mass equals winning the fight.

But Christine's eyes aren't just glassy now. They're *darker*.

He has gotten so used to the lamplight gold that he finds a normal human color odd. They're medium brown, probably lighter than they had been while she was alive, but nothing like they *should* be.

"Christine? Chris, come on, we should go home. Let's go back."

"We should…" Christine falls against him, limp, but after a moment, she reaches for the fleecy blanket again. "We should go to the *Danse Macabre*," she hisses, then ducks under his arm and *bolts*. She's running now, only sometimes touching the ground, but going through the very human movement of wanting to go faster.

All around him, other ghosts whoop and break into jogs and dashes and skips. The animation is nice, compared to the zombie apocalypse he'd faced moments ago, but they're all racing to the light with enthusiasm that frightens him.

Emil has no choice but to follow her.

He pulls out his phone and opens up a text to Vivienne. '*are you SURE this dance thing is okay for her???*' he sends. Maybe she'd recommended against him going because of the freakiness.

They turn down a street, and Emil sees the cemetery fully. It's lit up like a concert, packed with ghosts, and he swears he hears actual goddamned *music* echoing between the buildings. Ghosts rush toward the light, toward each other, hugging and yelling and calling for each other.

It *is* a party. It's a reunion.

(Better than the ghost prom he'd imagined, he supposes.)

Christine is nearly there, pulling ahead while he marveled, and with a curse, Emil tears after her again. If this is actually *bad*, he can throw the blanket over her like a net and haul her home. But if it is happy and chill and just had a moth-y effect to draw the ghosts in, then he will reserve judgment.

He glances at his phone before entering the cemetery gates. Vivienne hasn't responded.

He types another message, but hands clamp down on his shoulders, and he lets out an embarrassing yelp.

An older woman peers down at him. Her expression is faintly unfocused, but nothing like before. "You're not dead," she says. She sounds lucid.

"Uh, no," he says, backing away, but he steps right onto another ghost. The old man growls and whacks him with a ghostly cane.

Emil shies away again, toward the gates, but being this close to the light makes his chest hurt. But he'd feel terrible cajoling Christine into coming out just to drag her away. Should he *leave* her?

There is definitely music now, mostly singing, and more voices calling out happily for one another. It isn't sad or creepy, despite how the hairs on the back of his neck raise.

"Are you lost?" the older woman asks.

"You're still alive?" another ghost asks, shocked, and her call brings another gaggle of glassy-eyed onlookers. Emil begins to sweat, despite the chill in the air. He hugs the bundled blanket to his chest like a shield.

Too many hands reach for him. One goes *into* him. It feels like an electric shock and he scrambles into a dead sprint.

"*Chris!*" Okay, running screaming through the night in a cemetery full of clingy dead people is not the smartest decision of the night, but it's not the dumbest, either. (That would be dragging Christine out in the first place. God, they should have stayed on the fucking couch all night.) "Chris, I'm sorry, let's go *home!*" he shouts as he runs, trying to stay on the path, but the crowds are getting so thick that he has to branch off several times.

More and more spirits grab at him, touching him, going *through* him, and he's worried he's going to end up having a heart attack one of these times. He's never felt it when he and Christine interacted, but he has to say, he's not a huge fan.

Someone snags his hood and effectively clotheslines him. Emil goes down with a strangled wheeze.

"Why are *you* still alive?" his assailant asks and leans down into his personal space. The ghost's breath smells like sour milk and Emil rolls out from under him, tripping over himself to get moving again.

Many of the surrounding spirits are dressed in white robes, some of them splattered with red in various places. But not all. Some look like they really are dressed for a party. The noise of the *Danse* grows louder. Emil can pick out specific names from others, and more than a few childlike cries of *Mama* or *Daddy*.

He's getting weirdly good at dodging the ghosts, since most of them are pretty slow, but the chilly night air hurts his dry throat. He spots the nearest tree, and with a running start, he hauls himself up onto a lower branch to catch his breath.

So now he's stuck up a tree.

Curious and suspicious spirits circle around the trunk, reaching for him, a couple even jumping. Emil coughs as he gets his breathing back to normal. He scans the crowd and really wishes Christine were still glowing her usual gold.

Instead, he finds his mother staring up at him near the edge of the crowd.

His breath catches. His heart stutters.

Her hair is up in its usual loose bun, and she's wearing her favorite sweater, and even with her somewhat vacant expression, it's clear she recognizes him. "Milya?" he sees her mouth.

He never actually *expected* to see her again. Despite being introduced to all the ghosts and supernatural and magic, Emil hadn't held onto any hope about this one.

"M-Mom!" He nearly falls out of the tree trying to move down the branch. *Oh my fucking god—she's going to kill me for being so stupid tonight.* He looks forward to a dressing down.

She pushes through the crowd, voice rising until he can hear it over the other noise. "Milya! *Milya!* Move, move out of the way, that's my *son!*"

He drops from the branch, almost landing on a wrinkly old man, and they fight through the crowd until they reach each other. Emil unabashedly bursts into tears as soon as her arms wrap around him.

The moment is instantly ruined, though, by someone reaching their hand through his stomach. He jerks in her arms and his mother snarls, tearing him away from the interloper. "That is my *son* you are trying to steal!"

He laughs through his tears at her anger, because she used her Mom Tone. Shit, he had *missed* that, more than he'd even realized.

"He's alive," the other ghost replies and swipes for him again. Others echo the phrase in agreement and more hands are seizing him, pulling at clothes and hair and trying to dig *inward*.

"You shouldn't be here," his mother whispers hurriedly, clutching at him tighter.

"But you—you're here, you're actually *here*. You weren't—anywhere else, you didn't come home." It stings as much as the tears sting his eyes. Christine had followed him. Christine had haunted him. Christine had *stayed*.

His mother hadn't.

She elbows another ghost before smoothing his hair back from his forehead. She had always been pestering him to keep it shorter. He missed that, too.

"Oh, *solnyshko*," and she hasn't called him that in *years* except in the hospital, "I passed on. It was my time. But you, look at you! You've grown! And why are you here, among all these ghosts? How do you know about this?"

"I, uh." How does he explain everything that has happened? How does he do it *quickly*? And how does he stop crying already?

Another ghost reaches through him, through his neck with an icy touch, then drags their arms up into his head. Emil chokes on a wet breath. He feels *frigid*.

Everything goes hazy, then black, then *nostalgic*. He recalls a flash of his child-hood—clutching at his mother's dress while she tries to goad him into socializing after church. The fabric had been yellow and patterned with flowers. He even remembers the perfume she used to wear.

It is the briefest flash, but laden with long-forgotten details, and when he focuses again, he's splayed on his back with his mother standing over him. She's not in that dress anymore, hasn't been for years, but still the same familiar old sweater.

Its sleeves have been shredded. Her fingers end in needlepoint claws and her skin is black as ink up to her elbows. She snarls at the other ghosts, baring sharp teeth.

"Mom?" Emil croaks. He sits up, holding his spinning head, and tries to blink away another afterimage. But this one stays.

She turns to him, all hostility gone, only wide eyes and parental concern left. "Milya? Oh, Milya, you're alright! Come, come, you have to get to safety! Back up into that tree!"

Emil doesn't think he can stand, much less climb a tree, but he does as he's told. His mother keeps other ghosts away like a lioness beating back hyenas. He can't stand to look at those *claws* of hers—he knows what those must be. He knows what that means.

She passed on. Isn't that supposed to fix everything for ghosts? He can't haul himself up like he had before, spurred on by adrenaline, but his mother laces her hands together and all but tosses him upward. He grabs the branch with a wheeze.

Emil scrambles and swings and flails until he is sitting on the branch once more. His feet dangle at least a foot over the highest reaching spirit. "Okay, now your turn."

"No, I'm fine down here," his mother replies with a tired smile. She looks at her new claws with an unreadable expression. Emil fears how long he was out. "Milya, how are you here?"

"I made a friend. She's, uh, a ghost, too. Sort of? It's a really long story, but I followed her here. You haven't seen a short Black girl who's glowing, have you?"

His mother looks at him like he's grown another head. "What? No. Ghosts don't glow."

"I know that."

"You've learned a lot since I passed."

Emil scowls at his hanging shoes. "I had to. But it's not all bad, just really weird. Christine is really cool, mom. And..." Maybe don't mention the cat monster right away. "And I've met a bunch of other people who've been teaching me stuff. Looking out for me."

"I'm so glad. I'm so glad you're taken care of."

"I can take care of myself, too, y'know," he grumbles. "I'm not five."

"I know, but you are so young—*ostav' yego v pokoye!*" she suddenly snarls at an advancing old lady. The old woman cows but does not back off more than two steps.

"...Think you can put those things away now? They can't reach me up here. I'm okay," Emil says. His mother looks back down at her claws. His eyes prickle and he tries to keep the pleading tone out of his voice. "Ghosts aren't supposed to do that. You don't have to—I'm fine, promise."

"I'm not sure, Milya. I don't even completely…" She turns her hands over, examining the backs, then the tips of the claws. His heart clenches in his chest.

Okay, so he's stranded in a tree, his mother might turn into a monster, Christine is lost and maybe semi-brainwashed by the magic ghost light, and Vivienne still hasn't texted back. No cavalry. No support. Just himself and what he's learned this past summer.

He can do this.

Probably.

· · · ● · ● · ● ● · · ·

Sam hadn't realized how hungry he had been until he feels *full* now. It's a wonderful feeling. No wonder humans ate so often! He wants this a *lot* more.

His full belly extends into his good mood. Isaac flails after ghosts, so unused to them, waving useless warded jars. He has yet to catch one, but Sam doesn't mind. He wouldn't mind *not* running away from Natalie and Vivienne, either, but he knows better than to voice that.

"Any luck?" Sam gleefully calls. Isaac glares at him, chest heaving for breath. He isn't wearing that tight tank top of his, but the cold air is enough to hurt any lungs. He wonders how he can ask Isaac to stop before he begins coughing.

A sudden *whoosh* overhead causes his hood to flop over his face. Isaac reacts instantly; he twists around and aims a *push* spell expertly at the streetlight their guest just landed on.

Mirai squawks in alarm, feathers ruffled, but talons firmly wrapped around the metal. "What was that for?! You are a very paranoid, hostile witch."

"An unknown spirit just swooped down on us," Isaac snaps back.

"Swooping is bad," Sam adds, peeking up at the tengu from beneath his hood, just to make sure they seem to be in a good mood.

For some reason, his remark makes Isaac snort a laugh.

Mirai's expression brightens at the sound, just as Sam's does. "Oh, good, cheer him up more. I have a… *favor* to ask of you two, so I'd rather you be in a good, gracious mood."

"How did you find us?" Isaac asks. Even Sam doesn't know where they are; they've been following pockets of ghosts from street to street all evening.

"I followed your scent," Mirai proudly replies.

Isaac turns to Sam in alarm, the same alarm shooting through him, but he pulls the amulet out from beneath his hoodie. It's still on, still active.

"Your clothes smell like lavender and human chemicals," Mirai adds. "That's how you wash them, right? With all those chemicals."

Sam sighs in relief. Isaac hides his better. "Alright, so, why are you out tonight? I didn't think many spirits other than ghosts went out on Halloween."

Mirai flusters, feathers fluffing, and they smooth them back down while avoiding eye contact. The streetlight beneath them casts odd shadows, but their body language is undeniable.

"I am... Strictly speaking, I *shouldn't* be here. I know. But none of you humans are acting with any haste!"

They hop down and land with a flurry of wind. Sam shoves his hood out of his eyes again.

Mirai looks between them, as if deciding who to address, shifting from foot to foot nervously. They aren't in human clothes, or at least not the usual fashion; they wear a tan sleeveless robe, low in the front, and high on their thick, feathered thighs. Their two-toned hair is not tied back, but held back with a woven headband. (It's a mess from their flight.)

"Friends do each other favors. It's okay," Sam points out, and Mirai nods, chewing on their lip.

"I *need* to return Hatsu's egg. They are trying to convince me to give it up, and I worry I will agree soon enough! But I already asked other humans to get it back from the thief, and they *haven't*. Mark Ito and Vivienne Sayre, their names were. You know them, right?"

They, of course, know Vivienne. (They know each other *because of* Vivienne.) Sam has heard the name Mark before as well.

"Are you assuming we know every other human in the city?" Isaac deadpans.

"Don't you?"

"Well, yes, these," Sam replies, despite Isaac's eye roll, "but what about them? I know they're looking for the egg. The egg of the barn owl, right?"

Mirai stills. "You... know them?"

"We met briefly while shopping in the market. Sam was quite friendly," Isaac dryly tells them.

Mirai covers their eyes with their claws with a long, embarrassed moan. "No, Hatsu *knows*? Oh, this is terrible! This is so humiliating!"

"That you gave away tengu friend status to someone who *asked*?" Isaac presses with a smirk.

"I just wanted someone to help you," Sam replies, indignant. He *still* doesn't understand why others find this so funny, or why it is so odd to be friends with a tengu. Mirai seems pleasant. "*Anyway*! That friend of yours doesn't want you looking for the egg. But you are. And you're going to ask us for help?"

"Not so directly," Mirai mumbles between their claws. "I wished to ask you to ask *Vivienne* to hurry. She and Mark are the ones I formally asked, and I've already dragged *so many* into this... Hatsu is going to eat me! That's why I'm not officially asking you two for help in this!"

"Well, if you get the egg back, then won't they be happy?" Sam returns.

"Yes, yes, exactly! That is what I'm aiming for!" Mirai exclaims with an excited hop. Their cheeks are still rosy and their feathers and hair are all manner of ruffled, but at least they aren't hiding anymore. "But I *need* that egg. To hell with the thief! I fear Mark and Vivienne are too taken with her, or too wrapped up in odd human punishment rituals, but I *really* don't care about her! I need the egg. I want you to relay that to Vivienne."

"I can talk to her for you," Sam replies. Is that all? He talks to Vivienne every other day.

"Thank you, thank you!" Mirai crows with another excited flutter.

"Why were you worried about asking a tengu friend for a favor?" Isaac asks.

Mirai scowls—no, *pouts*. "Human diplomacy is a mess, and I shouldn't... be doing any of this. I am not actually on official tengu business."

"We gathered that when you attacked those witches. Why *did* you attack them?"

"Oh, I thought they had another egg. Not Hatsu's, but one of my clan members', so I thought it polite to do what I could."

"And why did you think those two specifically had an egg?" Isaac presses in a hard voice.

"They smelled like crow? They had ill intentions and smelled like trouble, but I *definitely* smelled feathers on them. It was a guess, but since they were hostile, wasn't I right? And they were your enemies, too, so now they can remain my enemies."

Isaac nods, obviously thinking too much about that. Sam wishes he'd share half of his thoughts, but he is still so happy with being fed and having some answers about his summoning, he lets it lie without complaint.

"Oh, and... Could I ask you two to be guides for me? I understand most of the city layout from above, but being in around the buildings can get me lost. If I'm tracking humans, I need to think like them. If you won't, then I have to go do something annoying for a fox spirit, and I don't want to. The little luck spirit has a bakeneko with her and she's at the *Danse* all night."

"Luck spirit?" Sam asks with a confused frown. "Do you mean Christine?"

"I don't know her name. But I know a fox spirit named Lucien is trying to get a mane-ki-neko's collar from her. He's been asking other spirits to do it. Probably because he can't fight," Mirai scoffs.

"Did you say she's at the *Danse*?" Isaac asks with his own, darker frown.

"I saw *something* gold and lucky when I flew over. I was not going to get too close, not to *that*."

"She shouldn't be there," Isaac mutters, thumbing his lip, thinking hard again. "She's not enough—she can't pass on. Did you see a human boy with her?"

"It seems to me like you *do* know all the humans in the city," Mirai replies with an arched brow.

"They're kind of friends of ours. We're trying to do a business transaction—spellwork stuff. Witch stuff. But I don't think it's a good idea for them to be there. Sam, I think we should go check on them," Isaac pointedly says.

Sam doesn't understand his tone, but he agrees. Friends help each other out if there may be trouble, after all.

· · · • · • · · · ·

Brynja is built like a brick shithouse and somehow *twice as heavy*. They hardly drag her in the door before Vivienne has to dump her and retch into a vase. She has nothing left in her stomach; she's only throwing up acid and bile. Mark groans under the sudden shift in weight.

The flower nymph behind the counter gives them a squeak that is equal parts affronted and surprised.

"We need a healer," Mark gasps wetly. Blood pours from his nose (again).

"Not for us," Vivienne adds. She heaves into the vase again. She's going to pass out soon. She *hopes* she passes out soon. "Burned shapeshifter. Probable shock."

"What do you two humans think you're doing?!" the nymph cries but rushes over to them. She lifts Brynja with delicate, leaf-tipped fingers, effortless in her strength. Brynja flops like a dead fish. "What happened here?"

"Treat her," Mark stresses and ducks out from the heavy load. "Name your price. My name is Mark Ito and I—"

"I know who you are. You think I can run a shop in the human city without knowing who the rulers of the place are?"

"Don't feed his ego," Vivienne mutters. She wipes her mouth and drops onto the floor, unrepentant. "I'll be fine with water and sleep. But if you have any experience in treating post-possession mental trauma—"

"Viv, shut it," Mark snaps, "we are here to treat her. Any price. Any treatment that will *work*."

The nymph turns Brynja over, eyeing the severe burns on her arms, then places her on the sole cot. What Vivienne had assumed was a waiting room turns out to be most of the treatment room, too. "These are terrible, and these markings... These burns look old, but they've been untreated."

"They're not old. Just magic," Vivienne corrects.

"You said she's a shapeshifter?"

Mark and Vivienne exchange a look. "Selkie," they chorus.

Brynja lays there, pale as death, cold and burnt and still. The nymph smacks her cheek with no response. Vivienne has her doubts, but she's seen deader things come back, and who knows what rules a shapeshifting rage spirit from another dimension plays by.

"Do what you can. She'll survive. She *has* to," Mark says, a touch gentler, but the flower nymph shrugs off his hand.

"Of course I'll do what I can. But for a selkie, the important thing is to reunite her with her skin. She needs that most of all. These burns... They're deep, but if they *are* fresh like you say, I can probably fix most of the damage. But this comatose state isn't from some burnt tissue."

"She'll be fine. I'll bring her sealskin," Mark says, uneasy, and chews on his lip. He seems to notice his new nosebleed only then and shoves his sleeve up against his face.

"I need to get home," Vivienne groans. She scrambles back up onto her knees to retch again. Not even bile this time. "Sorry about your vase. Mark can—h-he can replace it for you."

"Need me to call you a car? You don't seem like you can stand, much less walk," Mark says. He, too, flops down, but beside the cot. His sleeve is still pressed against his nose.

Vivienne cannot handle another car ride tonight. She can barely handle *existing* right now. "If I heave any more, I think my entire diaphragm will come up. Let me walk of shame home. I can make it."

The flower nymph gives her a jar of spring water (with a disgusted look at her vase). Vivienne should have been home *hours* ago. She isn't entirely certain she *will* make it home, but if she passes out in an alleyway, it could be a mercy. She needs not to be conscious anymore.

Mark takes Brynja's limp hand in his own. He, too, appears ready to pass out. They deserve a rest.

Hopefully Brynja is only resting, not worse. But Vivienne isn't holding her breath.

Natalie is dozing on Hayley's shoulder during the movie when she drops into a vision.

It is not the gentle slide she is used to; she is dropped *in front of a thing that looms over her. It is crowned with branches and is impossible to gain any real details about its incandescent silhouette. It does not move so much as splinter into new parts of itself to reach toward her.*

"Hello, lloignyth,*" it tells her, tells* her, *and Natalie jolts back into the present with a scream caught in her throat.*

"Hey, hey, what's wrong? Babe, come on, breathe," Hayley says, snapping into aftercare mode, her arms coming to circle around Natalie's shaking shoulders. "You're okay. What's wrong? What was the vision like?"

Natalie pants into the crook of Hayley's neck. Blood smears onto her t-shirt. "It saw me," she confesses.

CHAPTER 30

IN WHICH THERE IS AN UNLIKELY RESCUE PARTY

Christine wades through the ghostly crowd like water in a dream. She pays zero attention to anyone she does not register as her brother. So many strangers, most of them happy, most of them also looking for others.

"Please, have you seen my brother? He's a—he's short, too, with short hair and a nice smile, not even dead a year!" she cries to anyone who looks as if they may listen.

Everyone is too focused on finding their own family to pay attention to each other. She ignores the plaintive call for parents, grandparents, siblings, children. This far into the *Danse* it's a writhing mass of people, a press of bodies that would have both enthralled and annoyed her just a few hours ago. Now, it's another thing to ignore. To fight through.

"His name is Logan—please, I'm looking for my brother!" Christine shouts. She wishes she had her old phone so she could show pictures. "He's a Black man, darker skin than me, but young, short hair, brown eyes, he was a witch! Are there any coven witches here who know Logan Davies?!"

They still ignore her.

Most of the surrounding ghosts are in white robes, but there are a few bright spots of other clothing here and there. She looks to those instinctively. She looks for deep brown skin against pale cloth. But it's easy to tune everything out, let it be a blur of pleasant, returned death.

Christine has the vague notion that she ought to look for someone else, too, someone not dead. Maybe somewhere else. Maybe she shouldn't be here at all.

But they are all tickles in the back of her mind. Her attention has tunneled down to finding someone in the middle of the *Danse Macabre*.

Instead, someone finds her.

A strong grip snags the back of her overalls and hoists her into the air. Christine kicks on reflex, surprised she is not still moving, still searching. She twists around to see tall and light-haired—she almost thinks *Emil*, she almost *remembers* Emil and that she should have stuck with him, but no, it's Sam. His hair is too light, skin too pale, expression too blank.

"Found you," Sam says. He smiles, but it doesn't reach his eyes.

He sets Christine down and she wobbles. It takes a moment for her to process that she is *standing*, not floating, and she stares down at her socked feet.

She turns to Sam again, blinking, like trying to wake up from a dream. The light of the *Danse* is beside them, bathing him in harsh, colorless light, but his clothes are colorful and there is a pallor to his cheeks that none of the ghosts have. He stands out. He's alive.

Demon, she remembers, just as she realizes the crowd has parted around them in a fearful, fidgeting ring.

But he is not her brother. He's not even Emil or Kirara. Her gaze slips sideways again to scan the crowd.

"Hey, what's wrong?" Sam asks. He snaps his fingers in front of her face and she jumps to attention.

"Have you seen my brother?" Christine asks, plaintive.

"Didn't you say your brother is dead?"

The tiniest thread of exasperation stings at her. "This is the *Danse*. It's for the dead. You... You're not..."

Her attention slides again.

"Are you *alright*?" Sam asks.

"I'm looking for my brother. Logan. Has anyone here seen him?"

"Well, I was looking for *you*. I was informed it's not the best idea for you to be out here in all of this, and seeing you now, I'm inclined to agree."

"My brother is shorter than him," she says to the crowd, waving an arm at Sam, "with short, curly hair and a really nice smile. He's a really nice guy. He was a coven witch. Has anyone seen him?"

"Hey, I'm talking to you?" Sam says with another snap of his fingers. She barely pays him any heed. "Okay, fine. I'm hauling you out of here. Maybe Isaac knows why you're so spacey."

Something niggles at the back of her brain again. "But Emil...?"

"Emil is here? At the *Danse*? Living humans *definitely* shouldn't be here. I had to leave Isaac two blocks away."

She recognizes the name. But still not her brother. She misses him terribly, more than she can explain to these strange ghosts. But aren't they also looking for loved ones? Can't someone understand her loneliness and pain? Her patience?

"Alright, stay with me here, Miss Luck. You're supposed to be a luck spirit, not a ghost or an icky demon, remember?"

Sam reaches over and *dings* the bell on her collar.

The sound carries unnaturally. It cuts through the singing like a knife, leaving a beat of silence, before the music uneasily resumes. Electricity shoots through her; Christine's spine snaps straight and it's like everything suddenly *focuses*.

She can't pinpoint the difference, but it's like having gauze removed from her eyes. The surrounding ghosts still watch cautiously. But now she can look at Sam, actually register him. She can remember that Emil followed her. She still wants to find Logan, but it is not the all-consuming longing she now remembers only in confusion.

Sam has backed up a step. He's no longer washed out by the cold light, but now warmed by a bright gold glow that she only then realizes is *her*.

"Uh," he says, intelligently.

Christine touches the bell collar again. It's warm, too.

Warm.

She *feels* warmth.

She looks down at her feet again and stomps her sock against the grassy path. She feels the cool, damp grass soaking into her socks. She can't believe she's happy about wet socks!

Christine sucks in a not-breath, the same quasi-breathing she has been doing on reflex for months, and that has not changed.

But what has is the stinging in her eyes.

She looks up at Sam, vision swimming with tears. Actual tears.

They feel hot on her cheeks.

Christine bursts into bawling tears and throws herself at him.

She doesn't know what she's feeling, only that she *is* feeling. Sam is warm and solid, his clothes are soft and thick, his hair is as fluffy as it has always looked, and he holds her like she is made of glass. For the first time in almost a year, Christine does *not* feel like she's glass anymore.

Sobbing while being unable to breathe—but not *needing* to—is as exhausting as it sounds. Her chest hurts with the force of it. She feels joy, unending joy, but somehow, sorrow, too. She crossed some threshold, hasn't she? She must have. She left *a lot* behind.

She still hasn't found her brother.

"Woah, alright, okay, um, breathe. Or. Um. I don't think you can, yet? O-Or are you?" Sam tentatively holds her with one arm beneath her thighs while she drapes herself over his shoulder and cries into his hood. (His hoodie is *so soft*. She shamelessly burrows her face into it.) "Oh no, are you *okay*?"

"I—" She interrupts herself with a hiccup and a sniffle. "I. Think I might be okay."

"You're still glowing. Uh, a *lot*," he replies with no small amount of fear.

Christine leans away from him, and he wobbles, adjusting for the movement, but she has largely forgotten that things like gravity means she can be dropped. Her skin is radiant, dark color shining with gold undertones, shedding luck like she has only seen Kirara do rarely.

She touches her cheeks. They are wet and warm and a little sticky. She puts her fingertip in her mouth, but no taste, even though she knows there ought to be salt.

"Your hair, too?" Sam says with a wince. "You're really bright, and you're attracting an awful lot of attention here. I hadn't counted on being this popular with the spiritual population tonight."

One hand checking one pigtail, the other on Sam's shoulder for balance, Christine only then registers the ghosts closing in. The ring presses inward, glassy eyes fixed on her, all of them reflecting her shining light. If there was any flicker to it, they'd look like they were bathed in firelight; as it is, it looks like headlights, complete with the wide-eyed stare of a rabbit about to get run down.

"Uh-oh," she says with another hiccup. "Um. Th-This was... not planned."

"I'll say," Sam mutters.

"Now what?" Even now, she cannot help but scan the advancing ghosts, looking for someone familiar. But the *Danse* is huge, and she hasn't had luck—ha—so far. She must put that on hold for the moment.

Sam backs up a step. The crowd parts behind them, but those in front advance further. They still have perhaps five feet no one dares cross, knowing instinctually of the demon's presence, but as Kirara had always warned her, luck spirits are popular for a lot of dangerous reasons.

After getting hunted as a ghost, she hadn't expected to be hunted *by* ghosts.

"Emil, I think, is still here? He followed me, but I'm not sure how far... I haven't seen him in a while." Christine abruptly realizes she doesn't know how much time has passed since this started.

"It couldn't be that hard to find a living human among all the ghosts, can it," Sam mutters, as if to himself, then, "Hold on."

"Huh?" she squeaks just before he tightens his grip and *jumps*.

His leap could have cleared a house. Christine hardly has time to scream, but she clutches at him, as awkward as it is—he's holding her too high, so she can't wrap her arms around his neck, and settles for his head.

He lands on a gravestone away from the crowd they'd drawn. "Ow," he says, flat as sin.

"S-Sorry, but putmedownputmedown!"

"Then you must let go, please."

She forces herself to uncurl from around his head. Neither comment on the hair-pulling or that she had shoved his face into her chest. Her cheeks feel warm, however, and she lets out a wild little laugh when she touches cold stone with her feet.

Standing, how novel. She's missed it.

"You're still, uh, literally a beacon," Sam tells her and points at the other ghosts, already noticing her new position. "They won't bother me. If you can't lead me to Emil, I think it would be wisest to drop you off outside of this area."

Christine chews her lip, thinking of a demon loose in the middle of the *Danse Macabre*. She doesn't think of herself as a chaperone, but neither does she like that idea. "I don't know where he is," she hedges, "but m-maybe we should stick together?"

Sam surveys her. Calculating. He probably sees right through her, and her shoulders edge up around her ears.

An arm slides around her shoulders, pushing them down, and she feels cool flesh against her exposed skin. "A ghost, a demon, and a friggin' nightlight walk into a *Danse*. Look, we're the start of a shitty joke."

Both Christine and Sam jump at the new arrival, but they're held in place with a firm grip. Between their surprise, Rory grins, smug as ever.

"Did Vivienne tell you about me?" Sam asks with a suspicious squint. It looks odd on him.

"I'm smarter than your average bear. I could put two and two together, especially based on how cagey Viv has been, *and* it was a wild guess. Thanks, sweetpea, for confirming that for me."

"Wh-Why are you here?" Christine asks.

"Uh. I'm a ghost?"

"But you're... I mean, with Hammond..."

"I'm still a ghost, no matter what Ham and Viv have to say about it. I don't go gaga over the pretty light like a lot of others, but it's nice to hang out here for a night. Catch up on all the dead gossip, see who's causing trouble, the usual."

"Let go of me now." Sam ducks out from under Rory's arm and Christine is quick to follow.

Rory maintains his shit-eating grin, rocking mid-air on his heels, hands clasped innocently in front of himself. He looks like he's dressed up for the occasion—he is the only ghost Christine has ever seen change clothes—with his brown hair jelled back and beard neatly trimmed. "So, let's see what trouble you two are in! I have to say, I disapprove of a demon haunting the *Danse Macabre*, if only on principle. But you look pretty well-fed already. Snack time before coming over to bother Vivienne's pet project?"

Sam colors and scowls. Christine chews harder on her lip. *He* was *eating people?*

"Don't look so judgy, princess. *You* look positively starved," Rory croons and tilts Christine's head back with a finger beneath her chin. She jerks away from him.

"I'm—what? No. I don't eat..." Ghosts, or anything.

"There's your first problem, Miss Ana. Between the shiny new look and your new nails, you're *gonna* have a hell of an appetite."

"What?"

Rory grabs her hand and holds it up for them both to look. "Girl, you got your nails did. And after the very nice warning I gave you," Rory says with cruel glee.

Christine's not-breath catches when she realizes her nails are *claws*. Her fingers—her *hands*—are fully black, and she can't distinguish where her skin ends and the claw begins. She rips her hand free and pulls it against herself, whimpering, but both hands are like that.

She whirls on Sam. "This was—just earlier, I was—when I grabbed you—!"

"I didn't do anything!" he exclaims with his own hands—white and human-looking—up in the air.

"That wouldn't have been him. Demons don't have their own magic," Rory drawls and grabs her chin. "Open up."

She wants to bite him.

"Your teeth are fine, very pretty, but also pretty damn glittery. Your gums are pale. Dehydrated, probably. Your blood is probably still red, if you have any, but you're shedding luck like it's going out of style," he surmises. Rory rubs his fingers together, both of them bright, glittery gold. "Congrats! I have no idea what the hell is going on with you."

"B-But these—!" Christine warbles and holds up her shaking, demonic hands.

"*And* you're literally glowing, girl. You wanted to give up the safe, static life of a ghost, so deal with it."

"Nonononono, it's supposed to be *luck spirit*," she says and shoves her hands into her armpits, out of sight. Her earlier joy has evaporated. "I'm a luck spirit... I can't do this, I'm *not* becoming a demon..."

"You're becoming a *something*."

"Demons aren't that bad," Sam stubbornly maintains. "Anyway, what of Emil? He's human. And here. *And* you're gaining attention again."

"Interesting that ghosts won't avoid a demon in the name of poking at something new," Rory wryly remarks, floating higher to peer around Sam at the advancing crowd. "Not that they can eat, but luck affects all manner of spirits. Maybe you could bring someone back from the dead tonight. Look on the bright side."

"What's that?" she demands with watery eyes. (Now from frustration.)

"You *are* the bright side," Rory gleefully replies.

Christine glares. Her eyes continue to sting.

Rory finger guns at her. "The nightlight look works for you, especially since you aren't in that friggin' white robe, at least. And you look good as a blonde."

"I'm *what*?!"

· · · · ● ● ● · · ·

"Found yoooou!"

A voice directly behind him almost startles Emil out of the tree.

Rory snickers behind his fist, ignoring Emil's glare, and swings down to loom over his mother. "Oh, and we have *another* wannabe demon this year! Seriously, what is in the air? Do you kids attract chaos? Not even Viv and Hayley were *this* bad, and that's saying something."

"Who are you?!" his mother demands and takes a swipe at him.

"Woah, mom, it's okay! I, uh, mostly know him. He's a jerk, but." Emil can't follow that up with much else. He hardly knows Rory. "You were looking for me?" he asks instead.

"Apparently I'm on babysitting duty tonight. And when I'm trying to get my *Danse* on. How fuckin' rude."

His mother's frown deepens at the profanity.

"Babysitter *and* messenger. I'm supposed to tell you we got Christine out of the graveyard in one piece. In arguably more of a piece than when she started this mess, in fact. And then I was sent for you, because she informed me that *some* dumbass living kid followed her here."

"It was a pretty poor idea," his mother agrees, to Emil's dismay. "Milya, sweetheart, you shouldn't be here."

"Especially not stuck in a tree like a cat. I wasn't a firefighter, you know. Do you need help down? Sam has offered his services," Rory adds with a leer.

Sam?! Emil thinks with ever-increasing dismay. With his mother already half-feral, he does *not* want her to meet a demon who he may or may not be on good terms with. Sam is nice, but his mother would *not approve*. Christine doesn't even approve.

"Oh, and you should know," Rory says, with a sidelong look down at Emil's mother, "Christine caught a case of those nasty hands, too. If you figure out something here, you may brighten her day by returning with a cure. That said, time is of the friggin' essence, because you are attracting even more of a crowd than she was, and that's saying something. She was actually goddamn glowing."

"She was... what?" His heart seizes with worry. Below, more spirits reach for him, despite his mother's warning growl.

A: Emil knows he needs to leave. B: He knows his mother will not leave the *Danse*.

He has never gotten to C. He has never processed that getting to safety would mean *leaving* his mother.

"Is this girl the friend of yours? You're worried for her?" his mother asks, shrewd as ever.

"Well, yeah, but..." Emil kicks his legs in frustration. His sneaker nearly catches an outstretched hand. "She's fine! Right? I should stay here."

"You should do no such thing! You need to leave this place and go back to safety. Back to your *life*, Milya."

"But mom..."

Rory watches the growing emotion with poorly suppressed snark. Emil wishes for *anyone else* as an audience to what feels like ripping his heart out of his chest. Even Sam.

"It's only until moonset," Emil croaks and clears his throat. He wipes at his eyes. "Mom, Rory can help you up here, and it's only a few more hours—"

"Someone will drag you down out of the tree before long," Rory points out.

"You are not risking your life! Not for this. Not for me, Milya."

"But mom!"

Rory grabs her around the waist and hauls her up. Emil helps her into the tree. A teenaged ghost, not older even than Emil, tries to follow them, using Rory like a ladder, and for a terrifying moment, he is dragged down into too many reaching limbs.

But he pops out before Emil can even shout, on the other side of the crowd, rumpled and sour-faced but whole.

"I'm going to go bring Sam here. It'll take twenty minutes, tops, so have all of your sappy, sad-eyed goodbyes then. Here's a tip, kid—it doesn't get any easier. Bite the bullet, be sad, then bounce back. It's the only way you'll come out of this sane," Rory dryly advises. He shoots one last nasty look at the other ghosts, as if they were beneath him, then floats off into the ghastly night.

"You've become a lot more social," his mother remarks, kicking her legs in time with his.

"I've made some weird friends while learning about ghosts and magic."

"It seems that way. Christine, was it?"

"*Mom*," Emil groans.

"I am free to ask about what my son has been up to! Especially with girls—"

"She's the one who died, mom! I told you, she's a ghost, too. And Rory—he died a while ago, I guess—and Sam, and Vivienne, and a lot of other *weird* people. But Christine is my friend, yes, and she's a girl, but she's a *dead* girl. And she doesn't like me, anyway."

He takes his mother's hand and smooths over her claws. Sam is supposed to be a demon, but he's never *seen* one. He only knows fringe details. Ghosts can become them. They're supposed to be scary. They eat things like wraiths and other spirits.

To his amazement, under his touch, her skin begins fading back to pale pink. Just an inch at a time, beginning at her wrists, but he can *see* the change. His mother seems as excited as he feels and clutches his hand with a squeal.

"See, see, it was temporary! I'm fine, Milya!"

"I know—I'm glad!" This proves it's reversible, to a greater degree than Rory had hinted at (the jerk). Emil throws an arm around his mother's shoulders. She's still a small woman, but her frame isn't as frail as it had last been in the hospital. That, too, warms him.

"I don't understand much of this," his mother admits, tone pleased, still-sharp fingers laced with his, "but I've heard things from other ghosts. You probably know so much more about this than me. But I've long accepted that I have such a smart son."

Emil smiles and rests his cheek against her hair. She's cool, the same temperature as the surrounding air, but solid. It's enough for him.

"Had," his mother softly corrects.

She squeezes his hand to keep him still. He loses the smile, however.

"I'm so glad I've gotten to see you again, *solnyshko*. But this is only tonight. It shouldn't have even been this, not like this, not in this way. I've passed on. You still have your life to live."

"Mom, I'm. Yeah, I mean, I *am* living my life," he says, though he pauses several times to fight the lump in his throat. "I'm still in school. Senior year, y-yeah? And I'm still working at the bookstore, and I've met a lot of new people."

"Don't surround yourself with death, Milya."

He can't force words past the lump.

His mother sighs. More of her hand, halfway through her palm, returns to its normal hue. "I always worried when you would spend every hour at the hospital. It's a sad place to grow up. You're free of that now—"

"I'm not free of *you*! Mom, I'm not just going to forget you and move on—!"

"I am not saying that! I do not want you to forget me, ever, Milya. But I am not here anymore. Death is an end, but life is continuing. You have to go on."

"I have been," he replies thickly. Resentment bubbles in his chest, warring with the lump of heartbreak in his throat. He fears vomiting either of them up. "I've stayed in school. I still have a job. I have been *going on.*"

More than the neighborhood *babushkas* have given him credit for, more than his sympathetic teachers have remarked upon, more than he himself feels like he could. It is *all* he has done.

"I am so sorry to have left you," his mother tells him, "but you don't need to live in the shadow of my death. And I don't want you seeking more."

"Christine is my *friend*, mom." Someone who *stayed* with him, unlike her.

"Look at these grasping hands. Death should not take you before your time. I want you to go out and live your life, *your* life, Milya—you don't have to worry about me anymore. Don't make me worry about you, either. You've spent so much of your life surrounded by sickness and death, and I *don't* want that for you anymore."

Emil doesn't know how to argue with her—no one can argue against their mother, and he hardly knows how to talk about death on a good day, much less with his dead mother about his dead friend.

But Christine deserves to be defended. She's been with him, navigating weird magic things, navigating living semi-alone as a teenager, navigating death as something that just *happened*, not the end of all things. He knows it's too late for his mother to try something risky like Christine is, and knowing she's passed on peacefully is a weight off his chest. But talking with Christine about the other parts is also therapeutic.

He's not giving that up.

Probably not Vivienne, either. He couldn't get rid of Kirara if he tried. (Maybe Rory, if he has to.)

"Mom, I'm going to be fine," Emil tells her. He won't lie and he can't argue. But he's a stubborn kid, through and through. "Yes, coming to this dance thing was a bad idea. But I'm getting through it. I'm getting through all of it. With my *friends.*"

"Milya, they're dead, too," his mother sadly replies.

"Christine's working on that! I'm helping her—so are others, and it's *working*! I don't know all the weird details, neither does she, but we're working on it together, and it's a wild ride but it's sort of fun—"

"Don't get further into these death and occult things than you must!" she scolds and squeezes his hand. Only her charcoal claws remain, pricking his skin.

"Of course, mom," he replies, cowed, but he privately adds, *I have to help Christine, anyway.* It isn't as if there's an oath made in blood, but they've weathered this much together.

The mass of ghosts beneath them part like a school of fish fleeing a shark. Sam strides up, hands in his hoodie pockets, casual as can be.

"Oh," he says, eyeing the crowd, "you're popular, too. Not wise for a living human to be out in the *Danse*, much less in the thick of it."

"Are you another of Milya's new friends?" his mother suspiciously demands. It's clear she can sense *something* off about him, as much as the other ghosts do, but Emil wonders if it's instinct rather than actual knowledge.

"My name is Sam," he says with a nod. "It's nice to meet you. You two look alike, so... I presume mother?"

"Yes," Emil replies. Sam nods again. "You can keep the others away, so I'll be fine here—"

"I have orders to grab you quickly," Sam interrupts. He shifts from foot to foot, like he's antsy about that order.

"You can't stay here any longer, Milya," his mother adds with a disapproving frown. "Even with these dangerous friends, it's not a good idea. It's not safe for you here."

"I've found I'm only dangerous when I want to be," Sam says, but she shoots him an annoyed Mother Look. He cows instantly, unused to such powerful weapons.

His mother cups Emil's cheeks, smoothing his hair behind his ears, checking over his face like she used to when he tripped. When he was a *child*. She looks like a version of her a few years past, fuller-figured and healthier and brighter, but he wonders if she's seeing a past version of him, too. If only through wishful thinking.

"You've grown, already, so much. You have so much more growing to do. I'm so proud of you, Milya," she says and kisses his forehead. "But it is time for you to go."

He puts his arms around her and pulls her, tight, against him. "Even if it was a bad idea, I'm glad I got to see you again, mom. I miss you. I love you."

"I love you too, *solnyshko*. Now and forever. But it's time for you to go without me."

Sam politely helps his mother out of the tree first. She touches him as little as possible, grimacing all the while, her own politeness warring with her reflexive need to get away from the demon. Emil wisely holds his tongue on Sam's true nature.

She shakes out her hands after touching him. They've returned to normal now.

Emil and his mother hug again. She's always been shorter than him, but he must have grown more; she barely touches his shoulder. Sam waits, patient but alert, and the ghosts of the *Danse* mill and murmur around them.

Emil says goodbye to his mother for a second time. It hurts less than the first, but at least Sam is kind enough not to comment on his tears.

• • • • • • • • • •

Christine sits with her knees drawn up to her chest, chin resting on them, still chewing on her lip. She *sort of* feels bits of pain from it. They are two blocks from the light, where the city is bathed in the reflection off the clouds, lending everything an eerie quality. Perfect for Halloween.

Isaac taps away on his phone beside her.

She's had worse company, but she doesn't think she likes present company all that much, either.

"Did Emil talk to you about my spell offer?" Isaac finally asks, without looking up from his phone.

"He mentioned it." On top of everything else—claws instead of fingers and *blonde hair* and shining like a nightlight—Christine doesn't want to think about dangerous magic, too. "You're a spellwriter, right? Is that why Sam is such a unique demon?"

"Yes and no. That was Vivienne," Isaac replies with a scowl.

"You said it's like... an anchoring spell," she says and hugs her knees tighter to herself. She buries her face against them. "So it's like Rory, right?"

Rory, who hides old resentment with fresh jerkiness. She sees the cracks in his prickly armor, having those same cracks herself, and she doesn't know how she could have *years* of being a ghost. She hasn't thought this out. What if becoming a luck spirit takes years?

What if she doesn't do it at all?

Her claws dig into her skin.

"Not exactly the same. I never saw the original spellwork. But, thankfully, or *luckily* maybe, all a spellwriter needs is an idea," Isaac replies.

"An anchor means there's something tethered," she says, muffled.

"Yeah. I don't think Emil has realized what all *that* entails yet."

"He's still new to this," she defends, peeking sideways at him, annoyed. "I only know bits and pieces. Vivienne has only taught him bits and pieces. Are you going to use that against him, too?"

"No, because *you* know what it means."

"I can guess," she reluctantly agrees. "You're going to use *him* to keep me in stasis. To keep magic from turning me into more of a... d-demon."

"Sam told me I should apologize for being a jerk about that," Isaac dryly remarks, which is not an apology at all. He continues scrolling. "But *you* were also a jerk about him, so."

"Demons *eat people*. They eat ghosts. The covens kill them on sight—for good reason! They're vicious, and cruel, and violent, and—"

"And good luck trying to reconcile all of that with Sam. It took me some getting used to, too, and I'm in the contract with him. But I'm not here to talk about what makes a person. I couldn't care less so long as no one actively hunts me down. Point is, I'm offering you a way out."

"By using Emil."

Isaac shrugs, remorseless. "It wouldn't hurt him. Shouldn't affect his lifespan, or health, or whatever. It's a matter of using a living, stable human life as a template."

"This magic... wouldn't it be dangerous?" Christine softly asks. "Even Emil's magic practice has been bad."

"You're just scared of everything."

She glares at him over her knees. Isaac spares her a cool look.

"Listen, use some logic. Yeah, we hardly know each other, but I'm offering you some impossible magic. Vivienne certainly did some impossible magic, didn't she? Seems like she's pretty judgmental for dabbling in dark arts herself. I can't be much worse than her."

Christine, oddly, never thought about *distrusting* Isaac before. She doesn't *like* him, and it's mostly because of his curt attitude and Sam's... Sam-ness. Which is also conflicting in her heart. Sam is friendlier and nicer. He's easier to like.

But she fears liking him.

But what about Isaac?

"What if this magic backfires? What if I fully become a demon?" Christine whispers.

Isaac finally rewards her by turning away from his phone. His hazel eyes seem to glow with the reflection of her golden light.

"Then consider this—if nothing else, you can trust *my* sense of self-preservation," he tells her. "Why would I want an uncontracted demon running around?"

Natalie cannot help but doze during the QPICC meeting. Her attendance has been sporadic since leaving the coven, as has Vivienne's, but it is still nice to show their faces once in a while. Deirdre leads tonight's discussion. The woman is skilled at many things, but public speaking is not one of them. (Megan is asleep, leaning on Alice's shoulder, in the front row. They're not the only one.)

The scene gives way to a dark night lit only by streetlights. Rory floats along, hands in his pockets, glaring at the ground. He appears truly angry, not his usual half-sarcastic surliness. His hair hangs lank around his ears, sticking out every which way, as if he had been running his hands through it repeatedly.

A pure black fox spirit appears behind him with a faint pop.

Rory does not have time to react to that, because something bursts through the concrete wall of the shop beside him. It is impossible to actually see, half invisible and half staticky afterimage, but it conveys the silhouette of some half-man beast with shaggy fur and large antlers.

Rory and the fox spirit both shout and backpedal in opposite directions, away from it. It lunges after Rory with a starved snarl.

Natalie jerks awake when Vivienne pokes her shoulder. She presses a hand to her mouth to stifle any loud breathing from the sudden adrenaline in her. Action-packed visions always make her heart rate skyrocket.

She only barely recognizes Rory, from their few meetings before his death and the few times she had spoke with him with spirit sight draught, but he is a troublesome one to see for twofold: she is not supposed to have visions of dead people, and since he doesn't age, she can never tell when that vision may come to pass.

CHAPTER 31

IN WHICH THERE IS A JACKALOPE

Most know not to bother Vivienne the day after Halloween. Her work phone is on silent for the day.

But Dana is new to her life and has her personal number.

And when Vivienne gets an alarming text asking for important help before her shift, it not only wakes Vivienne up, but it spurs her out of the apartment.

The silver lining is the follow-up text. *'I need help before my shift, but it's not super urgent!'* So Vivienne gets to take public transportation rather than vomit in a car (again). She hasn't eaten anything in almost a day, and her stomach cramps have not abated from last night.

She hardly processes that it is her first time seeing Dana's apartment until she knocks on her front door.

Vivienne's hair is a mess, unbrushed and not held back (so in her face already), she's still in yesterday's clothes, she is running on about two hours of sleep, and she thinks she may throw up again even without the extra nerves.

To be fair, Dana looks similarly poor when she opens the door.

Vivienne's mental alarm skitters like a skipping record.

Dana wears *glasses*, thick-rimmed things hanging low on her nose, and her brown hair is down. Not only is it the first time Vivienne has seen her with her hair down, but her hair is *long*. It's nearly to her *waist*, thick and wavy from yesterday's braid.

She's in an old band shirt from The Police and little pink shorts. Purple smudges beneath her eyes tell her she's as tired as Vivienne feels. (Well, charitably, Vivienne assumes they're similar.)

"Thanks for coming over so quickly, Vivienne. I'm sorry, it's... I'm such a mess, too, but my place is a little messy." She steps aside, hiding a yawn, and Vivienne takes a surreptitious peek around while she kicks off her flats.

"What's the emergency? Are you alright?" Vivienne asks. Dana is whole and uninjured, and for supposedly being messy, her apartment looks quite neat. She has decorated in warm tones, lots of beige and cream and brown, and, of course, there are multiple bookshelves in the surprisingly roomy place.

"Oh, jeez, I didn't—I didn't mean for it to come off so urgent," Dana grumbles. "I mean, I need help, but—sorry."

Vivienne blinks up at her. She is so tired she could *cry*, but she would swim across lava to help Dana. But if it *isn't* an actual emergency...

Or rather, Dana likely has a different definition of emergency than Vivienne's other friends.

Vivienne still kinda wants to cry, but Dana looks bad enough as it is, so she blinks the stinging out of her eyes. "What's wrong?" Despite the lack of urgency, Dana needs help in some form, and Vivienne is already here. Even though she may keel over within the hour.

"I'm... I don't know. I don't know where to start," Dana says. She shoves her glasses up to rub at her eyes. "I'm sorry, I'm hungover to hell and back. The party last night was rougher than I thought it'd be. But it's about that. I got really drunk, and I was playing cards, and apparently we were betting for stuff."

"Did you lose anything important?" *Please don't let her have lost anything to fae*, she privately adds. There's no getting that back.

"No, I actually won? A lot. Hold on, I need to get some more water before I puke. I'm sorry."

Dana sounds positively miserable. Her posture mirrors her voice as she shuffles over to her cozy kitchen. She downs half a glass of water before dragging herself back and blearily offering Vivienne a cup, too.

She sips at it. Her stomach both recoils and thanks her.

"Let me show you," Dana says and drags herself toward a hallway. She comes back with a large cardboard box.

With dread, Vivienne peers inside.

She's used to corpses, body parts, gore, and all manner of other gross things.

What's inside is *cute*.

A little bunny wiggles its nose, looking up at her with beady eyes. There's a bowl of water spilled in the box and a half-chewed carrot beside it. Vivienne coos and reaches in to pet it.

She then notices the antlers.

Supernatural Hunter Tip #53: Cute does not mean not dangerous.

"You have a jackalope?" she asks, looking to Dana for confirmation.

Dana nods gloomily. "I thought that's what it was..."

Vivienne scoops up the critter and plops down onto the couch. Dana sets the box down before joining her with a groan. The jackalope appears well-fed, coat shiny and *so* soft, and doesn't at all seem to mind being handled.

"Ugh," Dana says and gulps down more water.

"You doing okay?"

"The hangover to hell wasn't hyperbole. I feel like I want to melt into a puddle of goop."

"Here, hold on," Vivienne says and writes a *cold* rune against her pajama pants. She puts her now-cooler hand against Dana's forehead. Dana sags with a grateful groan.

"I never drank before I enlisted. And I'm glad Codi invited me, and that club night was fun, but this isn't for me. I don't want to drink so much just to fit in. I think I'm done with alcohol for a while. On a scale from one to ten, how bad is this?"

"Your hangover is worse than the cute jackalope, Dana." Vivienne can't maintain the simple spell for long and withdraws her numb hand. She pets the jackalope until she regains feeling.

"I ended up with a *live animal* I can't remember. We apparently kissed at the club and I don't remember. Hangovers suck, yeah, but I don't want to drink anymore! I was never religious, not really, but it's haram, and I just don't want to deal with this—"

"Dana, I get it, I'm not judging you. I'm sorry for any pressure I gave you, but you can drink what you want! Or not drink what you want! And I can help you with this," Vivienne interrupts, alarmed.

Dana pushes her glasses back to rub at her wet eyes. "Ugh, I'm *sorry*, I'm such a mess. I didn't want you to see me so pathetic, but I didn't know who else to ask about... that."

"Yes, I will accept being the go-to about cute animals." It beats everything else Vivienne has done in the past twelve hours.

"Still, I'm sorry. You look tired, too."

"Two hours of sleep, but a bit of panic wakes you right up."

"See, I didn't mean for you to come running—"

"It's fine. I'm here now. You're here now. So is this little guy." Vivienne picks up the jackalope's front paws and waves one at Dana.

"...Is it a boy?"

"No clue. But it's definitely a jackalope. And the good news is that they're pretty damn close to regular rabbits as far as diets and requirements go. What're you gonna name it? I'd *love* to hear about your naming scheme, given all the shit you've given me for mine, although it's not *my* naming scheme."

Dana frowns, thoughtful and weary, at the jackalope in Vivienne's lap.

"Or, are you not gonna keep it?" Vivienne asks.

"I just wanted to make sure it wasn't gonna eat me or explode or something. I think... I can't remember last night, sorry. I think I won some really strong booze in the first round, but Codi was giving me shit to drink, too, and..." Dana shudders. She empties her glass.

"They're harmless. The antler tips may need to be filed down to prevent stabbing, and they can kick like a hare, but otherwise pretty good pets, so I've heard. Quieter than a cat for sure."

"I'm glad. That it's harmless. Sorry, I just sort of... panicked. I saw it, and thought I was hallucinating, and you were the first person I could think of to ask—"

"Dana, *stop* apologizing," Vivienne gently commands. She sets the jackalope on Dana's lap and takes her hand to pet it. "You don't have to make any decisions about this thing right now. You go in at one, right? Let's nap until then. I don't mean to alarm you, but I'm about to pass out."

"What? Are you okay?" Dana sounds alarmed, anyway.

"I needed more sleep, that's all. Last night was rough. Friend got possessed, and another friend got fucked up, and Halloween is always rough for me, so it was... Yeah."

Dana's eyes go round and she stops her petting. The jackalope snuffles against her fingers. "I'm sorry."

"If you say that one more time, I'm putting a *mute* spell on you," Vivienne lies. She couldn't cast anything if she tried. "You look like you're ready to pitch over, too. This little guy will be fine without supervision for a few hours, and even if it's just loaning me your couch, I need a nap. Sorry, but I *do*."

"If I can't apologize, you can't either," Dana says with a wobbly smile.

"Deal. Naptime! Back into the box you go, little problem. Maybe at work you can look over rabbit pet care. I can ask around once I'm conscious again." Vivienne isn't sure how she will prematurely drag herself into consciousness a second time when Dana has to leave for work, but she'll burn that bridge when she gets there.

"...I'm not giving you the couch. Come on."

The jackalope goes back into its temporary holding pen and Dana leads her to the bedroom. Vivienne can't even be excited about getting into bed with Dana, she's so exhausted. She's asleep before she hits the pillow.

· · · · ● · ● · · ·

Emil shuffles into the living room, rubbing his eyes, utterly exhausted. Technically, he hadn't stayed up that late, barely past midnight. Still, he feels like he was run over by a steamroller.

Christine looks up from where she is *sitting* on the couch.

"Good morn—*ack!*" She falls through it a moment later with a flail, then climbs back up into the air with an offended frown. "G-Good morning. Um, I was on the couch for... a lot of last night. The sun's well up, but I'm still... I don't know. Semi-corporeal?"

Emil doesn't know how to process this, so he doesn't. Breakfast first.

He can't believe he spoke with his *mom* last night, can't believe he saw her again at all. Can't believe a thing like the *Danse Macabre* exists.

Can't believe that Christine is *still* tangible and *still* blonde and *still* clawed.

"How are you feeling? You still, um, look tired. I tried to get tired last night, but I don't think I'm close to sleep yet. Not like tired sleep. I'm sorry you lost that nice blanket last night, too. I, um, kinda miss it," she says with a nervous titter.

Emil glances sideways at her, drinking orange juice straight from the carton.

She wrings her claws in front of her, hovering half a foot off the ground, glittery like an art project. Not glowing anymore, though.

"Can you say something?" Christine pleads.

"I'm tired," he replies.

"Yes, um, I can see that..."

"Sorry, waiting for my brain to come back online." And trying, in vain, to collect his thoughts. He brings the juice and a pair of poptarts to the tiny dining room table and sits, expectant.

Christine's lamplight eyes track his meager breakfast and she chews on her bottom lip.

"You're still, uh... Blonde."

"I was worried about that. Mirrors don't work for me." She curls a claw around a lock of her hair, pulling it taut. Even stretched, it's *just* short enough she can't bring it out to look at properly. "I don't know if Logan ever mentioned it, but we actually bleached my hair once, before a longer hospital stay. It was a nightmare and really hard to do. He was convinced my hair was going to fall out anyway because of chemo, so he let me do what I wanted, but I barely lost any."

"He only showed me pictures of you really small. I didn't know you were a teenager until, like, three months after meeting him."

"He showed you *baby pictures*?!"

"A couple. Mostly toddler, grade school, that kinda thing. He acted more like a doting dad than anything else," Emil says. "In hindsight, I'm kind of glad, because I didn't have many pictures to show him of my mom. So it made me take more pictures of her. That's... It was nice, I mean. Now. It's nice to have those pictures now."

"Yeah, um, he did the same. We took a lot of pictures together. He became a selfie master. We'd go out on picnics, or on day trips to all kinds of things, or little road trips when I could go home."

Emil rubs his thumb over his phone. He still has a lot of pictures of his mother on there; prior, there was the odd picture, but many of them were physical and offline. These were different.

On a whim, he opens the camera app and points his phone at Christine.

Nothing on the screen. Vivienne said modern technology working with ghosts was a tossup, so he tells himself not to be too disappointed. Not like she suddenly lost the skill.

He accidentally taps the screen instead of closing the app. The taken photo reveals a short, blonde Black girl in overall shorts and knee-high socks, floating two feet off the ground in his living room.

"Holy crap—Christine, Chris, look! Look, it's you! Cameras work now!"

True, she's a little blurry, maybe a touch see-through, but nothing like a smudge of horror like in movies.

Christine rushes over so fast that they bonk heads. Emil rubs his forehead, holding his phone out indulgently, but she hardly seems to notice any pain. Can ghosts feel pain? Ghosts, luck spirits, whatever. He eyes her pitch black claws uneasily.

"That's... me," she says in wonder.

"Well, yeah. That's the exciting part."

"I haven't seen myself... I mean, no mirrors, no cameras, I haven't been able to look at myself since I... Since I-I..." Christine looks up at Emil and her golden doe eyes are overflowing with tears.

"You can cry now?!" he asks in sudden dismay. Every awkward teenaged instinct in him demands to be *away* from the crying person. Her dry-eyed weepiness had been bad enough, but possible to ignore. This is *not*.

"I know! Isn't it great?" Christine exclaims while rubbing her wet cheeks.

"Uh, if you *say* so..."

It isn't until the phone *clacks* to the floor that he realizes she'd been holding it on her own. She rubs at her eyes again, drooping apologetically, but that's what phone cases are for. Emil opens the camera again and grabs her wrist.

"C'mere, dry eyes now. Let's take a selfie together. I can send it to Vivienne."

"Um, I'll... keep my arms out of the frame."

Emil winces. "Right. Yeah, that's a good idea."

Christine wipes away all of her tears and smiles bravely for the camera. Emil presses closer, glad to be *pressing* now rather than phasing, and manages a grin too. They take their first picture together.

"First pic of a new life. What'll the caption be online? Hashtag zombie? Back from the dead?" Emil asks.

"What was that Evanescence song?"

"God, no, I'm vetoing it. You may have been off of social media for almost a year, but I'm not letting you jump immediately back into the emo pit."

"Oh, it was longer than that." Christine floats around to eagerly look over his shoulder, as if aiming for a photobomb. "My therapist recommended staying away from social media? Like, um, it'd be bad to compare to everyone else... What was it called, fear of missing out? But way worse."

"Guess you weren't one of those inspiration porn bloggers," he mutters.

"No, and I didn't like those movies, either."

"Good. Mom *loved* those things. I get that it gave you hope, or whatever, but they were *gross*," he says and scrunches his nose. "Hope is like... messed up, sometimes."

"That's defeatist," Christine scolds.

"Y'know, your brother said the same thing. But he thought those movies and books were crap, too."

"Hope isn't all bad. Even when you're facing the end, it's nice," she replies absently, and he shuts his mouth so fast he bites his tongue. "A-Anyway! I don't want to cry again. Could you take a picture of my hair for me? I want to see what it looks like from behind. So far, I haven't had to retie it or anything, but if I'm more physical now, what if I do? How will I know what point I have to take care of my hair again?"

"Are there ghost hair brushes?"

"It's a lot more work than a hair brush," Christine says with a frown. She pets her curly hair down defensively. "...But *do* you think there are things that work on spirits?"

"Rory always looks good, but I think he's a case of that ego representation thing Vivienne told you about. Like how you got that outfit. Wait, are we going to need to wash those clothes? Are they part of you, or...?" He reaches out and hooks a finger beneath an overall strap. It doesn't *seem* attached to her, but like hell he's going to strip her to figure it out.

Christine cocks her head in thought. "There's a lot to figure out. If I'm going to become a full luck spirit, there must be tipping points to these things..."

"Like sleep, and eating, and using the bathroom? Well, I guess pissing would come after eating... Wouldn't thirst come first? Humans die way faster without water than food. And what about sleep? I've read that Russian sleep experiment thing, I know what happens if you try to skip sleep for too long."

Christine falls out of the conversation, content to let Emil wonder aloud, but wraps her arms around her middle. She brings her knees up and floats, curled up.

She's still chewing on her lip when Emil notices and asks, "What's wrong?"

"Um..."

"You know where the bathroom is if you have to use it."

Even that doesn't stir her indignation. Christine avoids eye contact, long lashes dipped low, claws digging into the thick fabric of her overalls. "I've... Um, I mean, I think I might've slept. Once or twice. But I haven't felt tired."

That wasn't it; Emil knows her well enough to know her avoidance tactics—hell, he knows most avoidance tactics pretty damn well because of his own life. "Okay," he slowly replies. "What else?"

"What do you mean?" she murmurs, eyes still downcast.

"What else, Chris? Are you worried about the spell that Isaac offered?"

"It's not that... I mean, um, yes, I am. But I've been..."

She shrinks further into herself. She chews her lip so hard he's worried she'll bleed. *Can* she bleed (yet)?

"I've been hungry," she finally confesses in a whisper. "For a while."

Fear thrills through him, but looking at her shy, scared expression, it's easy to bat away. For the moment. He's certain it'll come back later that night when he's in bed with nothing but dark thoughts for company.

Emil slides a poptart across the table.

Christine blinks at him. She still looks afraid (and ashamed).

"Try it. Before either of us freak out, before *you* freak out, just try it. Don't think about bogles or demons or whatever Kirara says. Human food first."

Christine meekly takes the poptart, taking the tiniest nibble, as if it were a cockroach instead of a sugary breakfast treat. Then, a bigger bite, and another, and in no time flat, she inhales it all and licks the crumbs off her fingers.

"That didn't go so bad," he points out, hope bubbling in his chest.

"No," she allows, finger still in her mouth, "but I like cherry flavor better."

"I'll remember that—"

She suddenly dashes toward the bathroom before he can finish his sentence. Human or ghost, the sound of retching is universal. And miserable. Emil groans to his kitchen's ceiling.

· · · · ● · ● · · ·

Vivienne wakes slowly when she hears rustling. The room is dark—Dana must have *great* curtains—and when she rolls over, she sees Dana's dimly lit silhouette fighting with socks. As Vivienne comes back online, she feels a stab of guilt at sleeping through whatever alarm Dana had set for work; maybe they could have had a cute brunch.

"Did you do your hair with magic? That was fast," Vivienne drowsily tells her. She flops out an arm to touch her, but she's too far from the bed.

Dana looks at her over her shoulder, smile amused. Her hair is up in a crown braid, and Vivienne has no idea how long those take, but she's already dressed, too.

Then she takes her shirt *off*. She's getting *out* of her work clothes.

"Vivienne, it's ten thirty at night," Dana says with great amusement. "I'm back from work."

Dana pulls the old band shirt back on and shucks off her pants. Vivienne stares at her. She *does* feel unusually well-rested from what she had assumed was a nap.

"Sorry," she croaks and hides under a pillow.

Dana sits on the edge of the bed and tugs the pillow away. She tucks a stray curl behind Vivienne's ear for good measure. Vivienne's face flames. "I tried to wake you, but you looked pretty tired, and you lost sleep because of me. The least I could do was let you sleep it off. I was surprised I didn't get a text halfway into my shift, though. You really *were* tired, hm?"

"I need more sleep than the average person. It's one of my charm points," Vivienne mumbles through her embarrassment.

"You must be hungry."

"It's too late at night for you—"

"You think I'm responsible enough I don't eat full meals at eleven at night? For shame! It's not the proper date we've been planning, but I'd appreciate a bit of company to talk out *this*."

Vivienne peers over the bed at This: the jackalope, still in the box, wiggling its cute nose. She narrows her eyes at it for not acting like an alarm clock.

"I flipped through a couple of rabbit pet care books—the only two we had—and it doesn't look too bad? Assuming these things *are* like regular rabbits," Dana says and scoops up the offending critter. It nestles into her lap with an ear flick. "More importantly, I learned rabbits can be litter trained."

"Was cleaning up a giant hamster cage a dealbreaker for you?"

"It means *maybe* I've thought about this. Also, rabbits really need more space than a little cage. A large pen, or maybe free-roaming privileges around a room or two."

"You know, thinking about pets is the first step to admitting you're getting a pet," Vivienne points out, rolling onto her back, halfway curled around Dana. "How are you feeling?"

"Better. Getting out of the house actually helped, at least on the emotional side. Sunshine and fresh air and coffee, you know, all that fun stuff." Dana keeps the rabbit creature in her grip and stands. "C'mon, up. Living room for dinner and talking. Calmer talking now. What sorts of foods do you like? There's this Vietnamese place a few blocks away that I've been obsessed with lately."

They order delivery and cozy into the couch, albeit on opposite ends. There is a small fleecy throw blanket that Dana tosses over their feet; Vivienne supposes she's been spoiled by an unending amount of quilts at her disposal. The box and jackalope sit on the floor in front of them.

Vivienne fiddles with her phone. It's almost dead, but not so close she can't send a couple of feeler texts. "So, you're thinking about keeping the jackalope you won off of a drunk, illicit bet?" she asks.

"You make that sound so *bad*. How can something so cute be so bad? Or annoying?"

"I've done worse. No judgment, only teasing."

Dana huffs and crosses her arms.

Their food arrives blessedly quickly. Vivienne slurps down scalding pho broth while Dana unabashedly wolfs down the first of *several* banh mis she ordered. Hopefully, they can both remember a touch of decorum if they ever manage a public lunch date.

"These make for a really good lunch to bring in," Dana says defensively, though she's already unwrapping a second.

"No judgment," Vivienne repeats. Stomach temporarily sated with something warm and flavored in it, she holds the styrofoam bowl in her hands to warm them. "I was in high school before I realized I was pronouncing 'pho' wrong. With the long o and stuff."

"In eighth grade English class, I was *appalled* when I learned how epitome was pronounced. I'd read it a couple times before, and I thought it was how it was spelled, right? Like 'epic tome'. I led the class in a vote to try to change how it was pronounced," Dana replies in kind.

"That's even nerdier."

"I know."

"I guess it *should* be pronounced differently, huh?"

"Yep," Dana says with a satisfied grin. "I've been a bookworm for most of my life. So working at a cute little bookstore is pretty nice. I like it a lot more than the military, that's for sure. But now with the whole Magic Is Real revelation..."

"Books are still books," Vivienne points out. "It doesn't have to change your life if you don't want it to."

Dana inclines her head toward the jackalope.

"Okay, well, you *could* return it. I know some people who work with, let's say, magically-inclined animals." Not that Graham has texted her back, but at least Fiona had. "Oh, speak of the devil. My vet friend says to check a rabbit's sex, you... Okay, I don't get it, but it involves prodding around back there. She says you can bring it in to check it over, if you'd like."

She should probably tell Fiona about Mark's Halloween adventure, too, if he hasn't told her. It's always a toss-up to what he does and doesn't share.

"I'd rather not accidentally sodomize a jackalope, thanks. So your friend is like... a magical vet?"

Fiona Ramirez is *a lot* of things. Most of which Vivienne does not want to share with a newbie. "Vet tech, sort of, but also sort of runs the place? She helps with a lot of familiars and monsters and cute little cryptids like this guy."

"Sounds like another shady, back-alley thing."

"Hey, Meggy is a very good back-alley doctor!"

"Well, you can walk again, so... I suppose. How *did* that heal up?"

"No limp, little scar, no aches. Meggy's very good at their job," Vivienne primly replies. "Me and my back-alley friends are *good* at their jobs. I'm making you an appointment with Ramirez at her clinic for your new friend. Think of any names yet?"

"I'm not sure I'm keeping this thing. Yet. But it'd be nice to know if the little thing is healthy, or a boy or a girl, or—oh no, what if it's *pregnant*? Do they have horns coming out? Wouldn't that hurt the mom?"

"Those are antlers, not horns. And I doubt it. Deer don't have antlers coming out? Here, when are you free? For a vet appointment, *and* for a first date. I will *make* a day you're free work. And I have the perfect idea for our first Official Get Out Of The House And No Bleeding date! The zoo you haven't visited!" Vivienne holds out her phone's calendar.

"No one bled today," Dana points out.

Vivienne does the math, and she supposes Mark's situation happened before midnight last night. "You win this round."

"Get to know me. I'll win a lot more. What's this perfect idea of yours?" she asks while she pulls out her own phone. She opens her calendar, scrolling through it with a thoughtful frown.

Then, as a slow afterthought, she takes a picture of the jackalope.

"What if I post this on social media?" Dana asks, apprehensive.

"Okay, go search jackalope images."

Dana furrows her brow and types it in. Hundreds of images pop up. Most look obviously fake, but some are probably real.

Vivienne shrugs. "Go ahead. With stuff like that, there are so many fakes and conspiracy theories, no one will notice. You could get a few thousand followers on a pet Instagram before anyone who actually *knows* would notice it's real. Do you know how many familiars are Insta famous?"

"Aren't familiars... actual animals?"

"Yes. And that jackalope is an actual animal."

Dana frowns at the jackalope in the box. "Are there gryphon familiars? Do witches have pet dragons?"

"No, and no. Gryphons are just rare, so that's statistically unlikely, and dragon hide repels magic. I don't think you *could* bond with one. They also like to snack on people, so, that may put a damper on things. And no, no one's bonding with those unicorns, either, before you ask."

Dana sighs and tosses her phone to the cushion. "Are there *guides* to this sort of thing? It seems overwhelming. Need a *For Dummies* book on this."

"I have a list of some tips and tricks, but they're more specific than explaining magical fauna. But, speaking of—my zoo date idea!"

"That sounds nice."

Vivienne grins. Dana does not know what she's in for, and that's the best part of this date idea. "Perfect! So let's get a date hammered out. Come hell or high water, we *are* going out."

Dana gives her a tired smile. "Yeah. I'd like that. Finally."

A young man with an undercut and an eyebrow piercing, familiar and angry and wearing thick leather gloves, tries to shove the yowling bakeneko into the circle. The cat spirit is restrained with bands of metal that sizzle against her multicolored fur. "What kind of idiots are you?" The metal containing her begins to glow a dull red.

The young man trips and nearly drops the cat. He hooks one of his fingers in between fur and hot metal, and the glove begins sizzling, too. "Why are we doing this with a fucking luck spirit?"

Thomas stoops to pick the cat up. "We don't have time anymore," he angrily replies, and shoves his captive into the circle. The metal melts off, but the circle is already active.

She's trapped.

The temperature continues to rise. The young man sits back on his haunches and peels off his burnt gloves. "We have everything we need?"

"We should. Is the ghost still sealed? We'll need her, too, but quickly. They'll be here any moment."

When his younger compatriot returns, he's escorting a far tamer captive. The cat in the circle lets out a sad sound, and the ghost turns from her. She looks even younger than the surly witch shoving her forward.

Thomas gestures them both into the circle and helps pull the witch away before the cat spirit can pounce. Instead, the cat spirit jumps up into the ghost's arms, and her body language shifts away from rage and into sorrow. "Please," the cat says, quietly. "Not her."

The magic swallows them.

Natalie wakes with blood on her pillow and a migraine that prevents her from leaving her bed for another hour and a half. The only thing she accomplishes is halfhearted scribbling in her notebook. "Potential panic. Ghost and bakeneko this time. Acts with brashness."

CHAPTER 32

IN WHICH THEY MAKE GREAT PROGRESS

"I've done what I can. She is stable, physically. I can't help the scarring, but she's healing rapidly, and she shouldn't suffer any loss of mobility or strength. That said..." The flower nymph crosses her arms and frowns at the cot where Brynja lies prone. "I don't know if she's going to wake up. *Something* happened. The best I can advise is to get her somewhere dark and wet and let her rest."

"Dark and wet?" Mark asks with his own frown.

"You know. She's a selkie? A return to her habitat would be the best bet for her to overcome this. Give her time with her pelt."

Mark forces a rictus smile. "Right! Thank you for your help."

Except she's *not* a selkie. She is apparently a dreamwalking, shapeshifting *rage spirit* who is now comatose for vaguely traumatic reasons. Her biceps are heavily scarred nearer her shoulders, hair nominally tied to the side to keep it out of the way. Her expression is placid and her breathing is deep but very slow.

But there's a beating heart still in there. That's something.

Fiona and Benji arrive to help carry her home. The flower nymph squeals at Benji's proximity, but he stays by the door, tails wagging idly. Fiona glares at Brynja's body.

Mark's already called a (nice) car, but he's not strong enough to lift her by himself, he'd embarrassingly found out. And if there's any further risk to her, he'd rather not be alone to deal with it.

"You should hire a personal driver," Benji enthusiastically suggests as he pastes himself to the window. It is out of politeness that Mark suggested Fiona take the front; he and Benji sit on either side of the slumped Brynja, and in the backseat of a car with *two* rage spirits is not somewhere he'd ever thought he'd find himself.

Could Vivienne have been wrong? Mark wonders. She's prone to wild (educated) mass guessing, but she has an annoyingly high success rate with those guesses. She barely mentioned it, didn't *explain* it, but something must have tipped her off. More than Brynja's temper, at any rate.

"You have money, right? You act like you do. Don't rich people have personal drivers?" Benji presses.

"Be quiet back there," Fiona orders.

"Would it make you happy if I did?" Mark asks, absentminded, and nudges Brynja's head so it's not lolling so badly. She ends up with her cheek against Mark's shoulder.

"You don't have to keep him happy," Fiona grumbles.

"No, I think he should!"

"Benji," Mark says, and Benji's furry ears perk, "what do you know about other rage spirits?"

"Like onryou?"

"More like an erinys. A fury. Not ghosts."

Benji looks down to Brynja, expression unreadable. If she survived last night, she could probably survive Benji until Fiona ordered him off. So Mark tells himself.

"She knew you were a rage spirit after your first meeting," Mark adds.

"Easy to guess," Fiona mutters.

"She didn't know what *clairvoyants* were. I doubt she knows what an inugami is. She called you something else, something... I don't know, Nordic. But Vivienne told me she thinks—"

"Vivienne talks too much!" Benji interrupts.

"...Are you ever going to release her from that curse?" Mark asks archly.

"When she learns some respect, maybe."

It's a mild inconvenience at best, so Mark has never pushed the matter. Always bigger fish to fry. "It's possible, isn't it? About Brynja. She does have a temper."

"A temper does not a rage spirit make," Benji says like he's suddenly a great sage.

"And it doesn't answer whatever the fuck she is," Fiona adds from the front.

(Maybe he *should* get a personal driver, if only so he doesn't have to worry about supernatural supposition in front of strangers.)

There is also the fact that Brynja finally *told him* where the egg was. She did not expect to live. Perhaps she still wouldn't. Perhaps this is a kind of death unto itself, but Mark is not a pessimist.

And at any rate, he is a firm believer in silver linings.

She needs to have her pelt, he recalls, chin in hand, attention out the window. *Pelts, plural. The sealskin is at home. Does the dragon pelt count? And what of the one the tengu have...* Which is only semi-confirmed. The tengu have *something* on her; she had *something* to get in and around them without suspicion.

But wouldn't it be wiser to ask for information and further relations rather than the skin of a thief? If they must follow missing tengu First eggs to potential other gods, then having an in with them would be invaluable.

Mark glares sideways at Brynja.

So, it's either going to be his latest adoption, or getting ahead in life. He hates difficult decisions.

"Speaking of Vivienne," Fiona says, holding up her phone, "mind telling me why she has a jackalope?"

"She has a *what* now?"

"Hm. ...Have you met that friend of hers? You mentioned she was after someone."

"Oh, yes, I believe she still is. They're cute together. Tall woman, dark hair?"

Fiona narrows her eyes. "She fleeced us last night at cards. Ended up beating a faun, a siren, and Graham Yu. Almost made off with a Foxglove witch's familiar. Is Vivienne aware of who she's dating? I thought you said that bookshop was nonmagical."

"It *is*... Or was? Don't put more things on my plate right now. What does that matter?" Mark asks incredulously.

"Apparently I have an appointment to check over the jackalope on Monday," Fiona deadpans.

"I think you can handle that much, my dear."

"And *you* get to handle whatever this is," Benji says and *whaps* a tail against Brynja's thigh. His grin is sharp as a knife and Mark can only roll his eyes.

"Yes, I suppose that one falls to me. Gossip must wait. For now."

· · · · ● · ● · · ·

Christine has tried everything in Emil's house and she can't keep any of it down. She can't taste any of it, either, which is good, considering some of the weird Russian things he forced upon her. And at least it means she doesn't taste it on its way back up, either.

But it sharpens her hunger into something terrifying.

She *can't* do stomach pain or hunger pangs again. She just can't. Much of her time spent in the hospital was exhausted from medication, but she still remembers the pain. When it began, when treatments didn't work, and at the end.

Christine doesn't understand why her luck doesn't make Kirara appear sooner; it's been over a week of food test work, all of it unpleasant. She's going to go crazy soon.

But at last, their cat babysitter returns.

"Oh my," Kirara says, dragging the last bit into something too much like a meow. She appeared as a cat, but steps into her more human form as she approaches Christine. She takes her clawed hand in one of her own.

Those haven't disappeared, either.

"You smell more like luck, but these... *What* have you two been doing?!" Kirara demands.

"I went to the *Danse Macabre*," Christine says at once, because she does not like the slitted glare Kirara sends Emil. "And someone touched my collar, the bell, and everything... happened? I-I'm more physical now, too, and, um..."

"She's hungry. And tired, sometimes," Emil supplies.

"But I can't eat any food. I'm so *hungry*, Kirara, but I keep throwing it up! I-I don't even have stomach acid, it just comes up chewed, and I can't *taste* it, but—!" Christine bursts into hot tears and throws herself into Kirara's arms.

The bakeneko pets over her hair and starts a soothing purr. "Relax, kitten. If you can't eat human food, then you have to eat spirit food. That's an easy fix, see?"

"I... can't."

"It isn't like we've seen another ugly bogle thing. What should she be eating? We've been *waiting* on you for some advice," Emil pointedly adds.

Christine stays in Kirara's arms, enjoying the vibrations of her purr. She's so *warm* and her clothes are impossibly silky. Even before, as a ghost, she'd been able to touch her, but Christine doesn't recall so much sensation. This has to be progress, right?

Kirara's purr turns into a thoughtful hum. "Hm, let's see, what would be easy enough for you two to hunt..."

"I-I can't eat other spirits. I can't, Kirara," Christine miserably weeps into her shoulder. "I can't do that. I can't become a—a monster."

"We can fix your hands. I think. You're not a demon yet, hardly smell of it, so let's handle one thing at a time."

"But I can't eat..." Other things. Other people? What qualifies as a person is becoming a blurrier and blurrier line. And who is she to draw that sort of line to begin with?

"Aren't you hungry? You have to eat if you're hungry. Hunger can do bad things to spirits, and the last thing we need is you veering off into *that* territory," Kirara reasons. "This is something you must face. Maybe you'll be able to eat human food in the future. I certainly enjoy it. But maybe not."

"There's a chance I *won't*?" Christine squeaks. She sinks further into her despair.

"Who knows? This is unprecedented stuff. But most luck spirits—higher spirits in general—eat human food with no issue. Many prefer it. Humanity does some wonderful things with spices."

"What's a higher spirit?" Emil asks.

"Most luck spirits. Me."

"But what *are* they?"

Kirara sighs like she's stuck indulging a needy toddler. Emil's pout is practically audible. "Higher spirits are the better ones. Stronger and usually able to use some sort of magic. Human ghosts are lower spirits. So are demons, and house spirits, like that bogle. Poltergeists and ghouls are lower, too. So not only are we trying to change a ghost into something else, we're trying to break down barriers. Cheer up, Christine, isn't that exciting?"

Christine nods without meaning it. She can't be excited about another roadblock. She'd known, somewhat, about the difference between spirits, but she had never put much thought into what a luck spirit *is*. She won't become a maneki-neko—or any type of cat spirit—but she's going to become *something*.

What if that something can't eat all the food she's missed? What if she *does* have to eat other spirits? What if she has to hunt?

The future is a great unknown, unfolding before her, and it terrifies her.

But Isaac's spell is a waypoint.

He said I could stay like this. Would that get rid of the demon bits? she wonders. She can ask him more, but she's afraid of that, too. Safety from getting worse, but what if she's stuck like *this*? Sleeping only occasionally, hunger that cannot be sated by actual food, corporeal in some respects, but not others.

She'd be safe. She'd be stable.

But when is good enough *good enough*?

Christine laughs into Kirara's shoulder, a bitter little thing. Her tears have stopped, eyes still wet, but at least she'll go back to being a crybaby. Her own tears are soothing, somehow. Isn't crying supposed to be cathartic? Maybe it's that.

This isn't just a decision for her, either, which is another scary part. Emil is tied into the spell. Isaac said it won't harm him, but what if it does? What if other spirits come after him, too, because he smells like luck or ghost or something else?

But then he wouldn't have to be scared to use his own newfound magic.

Christine sees how it excites him. She's excited, too, on his behalf; magic *is* cool, when it's not trying to turn her into a monster. A bit of magic and a bit of luck would turn his life around. It already has in many respects, just as it has hers.

But can she tether their lives together? He is so frustratingly vague when discussing it, waiting on *her* decision, but she has to know *his* before she can come up with hers. How could she force him into that sort of thing based only on her own decision?

Christine was never meant for this sort of questionable magic. That had always been Logan's thing. He was supposed to be here to guide her through it all.

"You calmed down now?" Kirara gently asks.

Christine lets out another wild little laugh. *No*, she wants to say, but that would worry them both. And their worry can do nothing for her. "I'm still hungry. And scared," she says instead. Safer. Still true.

"I'll go find you a nice little sprite to snack on. That's a good starting point. And I'll cook it, alright?"

So it won't look like a sprite, Christine thinks miserably. She nods, because what else can she do? She would do too much to avoid this terrifying hunger.

Would Isaac's spell help with that? Or would it make her stuck like this? Can that be edited by him?

Kirara gently pushes her away and tilts her chin back to look at her. She wipes away a tear with her claw. "Have you been drinking? No matter what you are, if you eat, then you must drink, too. Water is good for everyone."

"No, not yet," Christine mumbles.

"Oh, maybe that can help the hunger issue a bit!" Emil excitedly adds, already rushing to the fridge. He tosses a water bottle over, and while she flinches, she's able to catch it. It's cold against her palms. "Maybe we can try smoothies?"

"Stick with water for now," Kirara deadpans. "I'll bring back dinner for you. Look forward to it!"

Christine nods miserably. She takes a sip of the water. It's cold and refreshing. Tears come all over again at the joyous feeling of *something* finally in her stomach.

· · · • · • · · · ·

"Weren't we supposed to be meeting up with Vivienne to tell her that Mirai wants her to hurry?" Sam asks with his usual unintentional holier-than-thou attitude.

Isaac sighs. Heavily. "No, it's halfway through November and you don't own a coat. We're going shopping. Haven't you gotten cold yet?"

"A little," he sheepishly admits. He tugs at the too-short sleeves on his borrowed hoodie.

Isaac does his best not to roll his eyes at him. "So, we're getting you a coat. And a hat and gloves, I guess. Do you need boots?"

"What would I need boots for?"

"Snow? Ice? To keep your toes warm?"

"It hasn't snowed yet," Sam points out, and Isaac resists the eye-rolling urge again. He's trying to be a *nicer person*, for some awful reason.

So he replies, as evenly as he can, "In the human world, winter means we'll get snow. And it's better to be prepared than need something later." Isaac could use some new clothes, too, but Sam takes priority. In this one case.

The Neiman Marcus Isaac has chosen is free-standing, not part of any annoying strip malls, and has no parking lot of its own because of its location downtown. But there is a quiet alley they duck into beforehand.

"Alright, this is going to be weird, but we're going to need to be *close*. And stay that way. This spell wasn't built for two people."

Isaac grabs Sam's hand and tugs him close before he can question anything. He loops their arms together and presses up against his side so hard his demon stumbles. Isaac doesn't actually know the range of this spell; the only time he had used it with another person was when he and Walker had broken into a hospital for supplies.

"We need to keep contact the entire time in the store. Don't use my name and I'm not going to use yours, but we can speak at normal volume. Don't do anything weird to attract attention," Isaac orders.

"What are we doing?" Sam asks curiously.

"Going shopping. Now hold still." Isaac grips his hand tight and with his free one, writes down their sleeves. "*Eyes veiled by cloth and ears by cotton, let all traces of me be forgotten.*"

"It tingles," Sam whispers with a half-aborted giggle.

"Magic does that." Isaac shakes the excess out of his fingers, then tugs him forward. "Come on, then."

"What was the spell for?"

"Ignore-me spell. It's not invisibility, and this is version two to avoid security cameras, but people will ignore us, provided they aren't looking specifically for us." Which is why Vivienne had broken through half his perimeter during the summoning; she had been looking for the summoner *specifically*. But Isaac knows that security guards half-assedly looking for shoplifters do *not* break it.

The electric doors slide open for them. Isaac allows enough space between them so they don't step on each other, and holding hands seems to be enough contact. It'd been enough with Walker, too, but Isaac's paranoia has saved his life more than once. Better safe than sorry.

The greeter glances over at them with an automatic smile, eyes sliding away without registering their presence. "Oh!" Sam exclaims and leans toward her, peering into her blank expression.

Isaac tugs on their connected hands. "Come on, shopping trip? Don't bother anyone. I don't want to test how far physical touch strains the spell."

While tempting to bulk up Sam's negligible wardrobe, they can only take what they can carry, and coats are big. (Thankfully, Oliver has more than enough out-of-season hand-me-downs for Sam.)

Sam oohs and ahhs over fur-lined hoods, free hand in everything he can reach. Isaac scans things disinterestedly. Sam's hand in his never loses grip, so despite his excitement, at least he isn't getting distracted.

As a nonhuman, he doesn't think to check price tags at first. He can only halfway try anything on, but Isaac is a firm believer in bigger clothes being better than tighter clothes, so he's erring *far* on the side of caution with sizing.

Sam picks out one he likes early on, which pleases Isaac. It looks good on him, too, a long army green one with a *very* fluffy fur-lined hood. Sam gets one arm through the sleeve, and with a near-hug and some shimmying, Isaac swaps around to hold that arm while he gets the other one through. Sam raises both arms in a silent ta-da once he's in it.

"Ow," he says when the price tag pokes his neck.

"Bend down and hold still." Isaac rips the tag off and hands it to him while he hunts down the security sensor.

"This is... really expensive, isn't it?" Sam has only a vague grasp of monetary value, since Natalie's shop has a wide range of prices and values.

"Yeah, that's why we aren't paying for it. Oh, here it is." He uses magic as a magnet to detach the security sensor.

"We're just taking them? That's stealing, isn't it?"

Isaac *gives in*. He rolls his eyes at last. "Yes, it is. They're expensive, and it's easier to do this in dedicated stores rather than the big, everything stores. The store won't miss these. Now come on, we need more."

Sam's excitement is dampened, but not extinguished. He finds great joy in browsing through scarves, for reasons Isaac can't comprehend. Isaac finds a thick maroon coat for himself and lets Sam spend the rest of his time eagerly touching every cashmere scarf he can.

Their time limit comes not as suspicious store clerks, but Sam pausing in his new coat, and commenting in a sad voice, "I'm getting hot in this."

"That means it's time to wrap things up."

Isaac uses his own new coat as a makeshift bag to shove *several* scarves into, putting the gloves and hat into the sleeve, and tugs Sam toward the shoe section. His demon sulks the entire way, pink-cheeked with his warm coat, but this bit goes even faster. Sam hasn't developed a taste in shoes yet, and Isaac values practicality over anything else. He balances the shoebox on top of his coat bundle and pulls Sam along.

They walk out the door with no one the wiser.

"See, wasn't that simple?" Isaac asks expectantly, trying to ease Sam's annoying sense of morals with a smile.

And it works. Sam smiles back, a little shy, a little flustered, still pink-faced. "Alright, yes. And look at this nice coat! It feels nicer outside in the air."

"That is the point of it," Isaac replies.

"Thanks," Sam says with a broader, warmer smile. It looks good on him.

Isaac ignores that part.

· · · ● ● ● ● ● · · ·

"You're unusually chipper," Mark mutters around the lip of the potion bottle.

"Well, *I'm* not the one about to jump into a freezing lake, but also, me and Dana are going to the zoo! We have a date scheduled. It's in her planner and everything."

"How cute," he deadpans.

Vivienne plants her fists on her wide hips and sticks her tongue out at him. Like an adult. So he sticks his tongue out right back at her. It's stained orangish from the potion.

"You're *sure* she's a rage spirit?"

"Is that really what you want to discuss right now?" Vivienne archly asks.

Mark strips off his jacket and tugs his sweater over his head. The warmth potion will work for an hour, but jumping into a lake in November will be unpleasant no matter what. "She said White Lake. All I have to do is find something that doesn't belong on the bottom."

Vivienne holds out a flashlight. "This will light up with more magic. No matter how good the container is, *nothing* could dampen that much magic and still be small enough to fit in this dinky little pond. Plus, if you're sure there's something else with it..."

"I told you, she has more skins."

"Yeah, and you want to trade the egg for one. Instead of, I don't know, asking for tengu friend status? Money? *Information?*" Vivienne points out.

Mark rolls his eyes. He takes the charmed flashlight and toes off his sneakers. Vivienne waits on the bank, prepared with a towel and another warmth potion should worst come to worst.

He wades into the frigid water with a displeased sound. But it feels more like a cold pool than the Arctic. He sucks in a breath and goes under.

Without his glasses, he couldn't see much, anyway. Add in the lake's murkiness, and Mark's stuck relying entirely on the flashlight. It creates a weak beam in the water, but noticeably stronger the further he goes down.

As an artificial lake, there aren't fish here, and hopefully anything *else* that may live here avoids the human. He can't sense anything. The flashlight is thankfully easier to follow than he'd feared. The closer he gets to the bottom and what he supposes is the center, the brighter it gets.

He finds a chest.

It doesn't *look* like a treasure chest, exactly, but what else can he think of it as? Huge runes are carved into its surface and its material is shiny, twinkling against the flashlight. He'd hoped it'd be smaller, something he could cart up to the shore with him.

Mark gives it an experimental tug. It doesn't budge.

It does, however, open when he lifts the lid.

His flashlight nearly blinds him when it lands on the egg.

It's in a cylinder, made of glass or something see-through, which is surprising. He'd expected to find just the egg, perhaps swaddled in a mystery pelt or warded cloth, but the cylinder is *definitely* more portable. Mark reaches in, worried about his hand melting off, but he trips no wards or traps. The cylinder floats gently into his grasp once pulled free.

Beside the cylinder is a wet bag made of animal hide. He knew it.

Egg under one arm, bag under the other, Mark heads for the surface.

• • • • • • • • • •

Mark sits cross-legged, tengu egg in his lap, drinking straight from a pot of coffee. Vivienne rips papers out of her notebook du jour until all of her research on Brynja is spread out on the low table between them. Most of it has runes they'd identified off her arms, and two pages are carefully censored notes on the Dreamlands.

Mark scowls at those.

"It's not relevant!" Vivienne preempts. "What *is* relevant is confirming whatever the hell she is, and whatever the hell her old boss thing is doing *now*. Halloween was probably its best bet at tearing through, and that didn't work. Some other things are trying, too, but supposedly don't have as much progress."

"But if there *is*?" Mark asks, eyes narrowed behind his glasses.

"We're going off of *her* knowledge. I trust that, to a certain degree. That's all we can give her without knowing more," she replies. "But her situation is also the one we know most about. Her thing is stuck in the Dreamlands—"

"It's not hers. Not anymore," Mark interrupts.

Vivienne sighs. "Yes, it looks like that was severed. How has she been doing, by the way?"

"Still hasn't woken up. Hasn't eaten, hasn't drank, hasn't done anything. It must be like hibernation, right?"

"Right," Vivienne uneasily replies. She doesn't like how attached Mark has gotten to this mess. He's stubborn about trouble, but this is a step too far. "Well, a beating heart is something, no matter how slow."

"Right," he echoes. He takes another long drink from the coffee pot.

"So! Dreamlands! It's the nearest threat, but it's still pretty separate from our realm. As the name implies, it used to be accessed through dreams, so that's probably the angle it's working."

"Brynja's list said nothing about sleep spirits as ingredients, and it isn't like she tried to eat that baku."

"It's the way *through*," Vivienne pointedly corrects, "not the *method*. The method seems to be overwhelming magic, based on the ingredient list she gave us. Brute forcing it. The good news is, the egg is going back to the tengu, and away from things that would use it as an ingredient to tear a whole in our dimension! *Riiiiight*, Markimoo?"

"She's not waking up. She has three skins on her. What if we need the other?" he shoots back, reproachful.

"We need information about who *else* may or may not have any other First eggs. We need information, if not tengu friend status. With how long we've been stringing Mirai along, that may be out of reach, but I think it's best to try. If only because there's apparently a future where I get mauled by one."

Mark snorts a laugh. "*Or* we could wake Brynja up and get information straight from the source."

"Only about hers! The tengu are the way to the others—"

"We have the method, a list of ingredients, and she is the one who mentioned the others! She has to know *something* else."

"She would have gotten that information from her boss that tried to eat your brain," Vivienne points out. "The one she's no longer speaking to? And if some other skin got burned, then she's not tethered there, either."

Except the Dreamlands don't function in that way. Once you go there, there will *always* be a tether, however minor. Usually during deep sleep. Vivienne bypasses that because of magical fuckery, but Brynja may still be haunted by that god. It's a terrible fucking notion and not one they can test until the god-thing proves it.

Vivienne's worried train of thought completely derails as she watches Brynja stagger out of the bedroom and shuffle down the hall.

Back to her, Mark doesn't notice. "But she still *knows* things! She only wanted freedom, why should we judge her for that? We should help her if we're able—are you paying attention to me? What is your thought process doing?"

Without a word, Vivienne points.

A thickly furred brown pelt is draped over Brynja's shoulders. That must be the one Mark fished out of the lake; he was coy in telling Vivienne what it was. (He probably doesn't know, the idiot.) Brynja rips the fridge door off its hinges and grabs an open package of bacon. She slurps up the raw meat like noodles.

Vivienne gets up to investigate, but Mark throws out an arm to halt her.

"There's nothing there," Mark whispers.

"Huh?"

"She has *nothing* in her brain right now. No instinct, no thoughts, no emotions. That's not Brynja."

"Goody." Vivienne digs around in her bag until she finds a packet of sleep soot. Anything that breathes and is capable of sleep is affected, so it can't hurt.

(Supernatural Hunter Tip #41: There are always exceptions to rules, and they usually pop up when least convenient.)

Vivienne, with Mark behind her, creeps toward the kitchen. Brynja finishes the bacon and shoves half a carton of raspberries into her mouth. Her teeth *crunch* on the plastic.

"Brynja? Dearest? Are you hungry?" Mark asks in a light tone.

Brynja doesn't respond.

But she turns when they get within arm's reach. Raspberry juice runs down her chin like blood. Her eyes are open but lidded, gaze completely unfocused.

"She's on autopilot," Vivienne realizes, waving her hand in front of her face. No eye tracking whatsoever. "You sure about that hibernation thing?"

"Educated guess," he dryly remarks.

Vivienne notices the pelt's clawed arms hanging off of Brynja's scarred ones. The dense brown fur, the thick paw pads, the long black nails—Vivienne stifles a gasp. "Is that a *bear* pelt?"

"Probably," Mark hums. Annoying jerk. "More importantly—"

"Bear, seal, and you said some kind of bird? Now dragon... These ones match up with many bird-related runes, and we'd seen the seal ones, but what about bears? And if these newer, bottom ones are for her new dragon—" Vivienne pokes around all over Brynja's exposed arm, but Mark yanks her back, narrowly avoiding a swipe of her hand. The bear paw sits atop her hand like a baggy sleeve, not quite on properly.

Ignoring all the Dreamlands stuff—and Vivienne feels comfortable doing that, at least for now—this is a puzzle piece she hadn't realized she needed. Brynja had only used selkie as a cover; the distraction was the sealskin, yes, but also the *shapeshifter*. They'd always been looking at *that* part to figure out what the hell she was.

But with the revelation that she's a rage spirit too...

They had been looking at it backwards.

Vivienne laughs, once, hollowly and without meaning to. A Nordic rage spirit who happened to shapeshift? "Mark," she croaks, feeling hysterics bubble within her, "you said she's old, right?"

"Yes, she's alluded to that multiple times. Centuries, at least."

"She's extinct!" Vivienne exclaims.

Mark drags her backward, because no matter how comatose Brynja may or may not be, she did not need to take another swipe at them. Heaven forbid she remembers the dragonskin in the bedroom. Heaven forbid she *actually* shapeshifts.

"Deep breaths before you freak out. What's the big deal now? Bigger deal than rage spirit, or dreamwalking, or the angry *gods* trying to eat our realm?" Mark flatly asks after parking her on the couch.

"You know the term berserk?"

"Uh, yeah, Benji has taught me several times over."

"It comes from an old Norwegian term. *Berserkr*. It literally means 'bear-shirt'. They were old Viking warriors famous for entering a rage state and ripping apart other soldiers. By the twelfth century, they were all gone, and Europe was turning against magic. In the *twelfth century*, Mark."

"So she's... nine hundred years old? How does this help us?"

"She's *old magic*, Mark! She's *making* herself shapeshift. That's how she learned dreamwalking. That's how she can just add a fucking dragon to her list of parlor tricks! And I bet that's how that god thing was going to use her to get here. Brute force and old magic." Vivienne gestures wildly, frustrated that he isn't as stunned as she feels.

"Okay, well, now she's here, and she's never going back there. Problem solved."

"Mark Ito, for once, *listen* to everything I'm saying and use that bright mind of yours to put the pieces together. She lived in the Dreamlands for centuries and *learned* how to live there. She adapted herself to it. Just like she adapts herself to different bodies."

"And? Vivienne, you're talking as fast as you're thinking, and neither are very helpful right now!" he exclaims.

But she can't help it. She can't help the euphoria when things just *click* together, when she *realizes*, when she suddenly finds herself neck-deep in knowledge. She had given up this kind of high when Hayley died. And Mark *isn't getting it*.

"Brynja was originally human. Humans are one of the few species capable of dreaming and lucid dreaming, and once we all shared this giant dreamscape called the Dreamlands. That got cut off from humanity ages ago, and that's where this nasty little thing is stuck. Brynja's magic adapts her body to what she's doing. She isn't a shapeshifter; she is a rage spirit who *happens* to shapeshift. And she just happens to dreamwalk. A human, able to connect to the Dreamlands, with the ability to dreamwalk, adapted to living there, and as a connection to this side—"

"Brynja *is* the bridge," Mark realizes aloud.

The vision is like looking through a prism; everything is disjointed, light every which way, scene broken up in refractions. Natalie doesn't understand what she's looking at, until the vision yanks her away from the too-bright, broken world and instead drops her into Mark Ito's living room.

Instead of him, however, it is a woman with long, black hair and a thick frame resting on his couch.

Her eyes open. There's no iris or pupil, only the black of one possessed, and she sits up as if jerked upright. She contemplates her hands in her lap a long, silent moment.

Then, she digs her fingers into her own chest.

She breaks ribs and rips through flesh, peeling open her ribcage, all without a whimper or hesitation. Something gleams beneath the blood and bone she bares.

An arm, deep as the night, thrusts itself out of her chest.

Another follows in a flash, and they finish the work she'd started of prying herself open. The woman splits into two as a monstrous form fights its way out of her body. Magic makes the air shimmer and boils off the blood. Flesh sizzles and the coffee table begins to char.

The figure, halfway out of the woman's chest, tilts back a huge head and laughs with no mouth.

CHAPTER 33

IN WHICH SOMEONE MAKES THE WRONG GUESS

Christine *really* wishes she could write. She can hold a pen more than half the time, but she can't exert enough pressure to write. And it usually ends up phasing through her fingers after a few tries. Definitely not worth the frustration.

Maybe she could talk to Rory. But he isn't corporeal, except to Vivienne and that Hammond man. But maybe he could help with other ghostly aspects? Except he's a little abrasive about his advice...

Maybe Vivienne would be a better choice. As a start.

Christine hovers over Emil's phone. She can't press buttons, either, though she got it to wake up exactly once. Taking pictures still works, too. They haven't tried phone calls again yet, so maybe a voice recorder app?

She *wants* to make a list of pros and cons about that spell and her uncertain future. Christine used to adore lists. (Well, she still does, just hasn't made any for a hot minute.) It helps her clarify her thoughts. She can't talk out lists, she has to see them, but even if she *could*, Emil is so skittish about giving concrete answers she wants to scream.

Maybe Vivienne could charm a pen for her. Didn't they used to sell gel pens with charms on them? She vaguely remembers her brother talking about that while waxing poetic about the nineties. She doesn't care if she has to write in sparkly neon orange, so long as she *could*.

She can still hear the shower running. Emil hasn't sung since he discovered her, and she oddly misses it. He has a pleasant voice when it isn't cracking on the high notes. And except for the poppy, mind-numbing stuff in stores, she hasn't been able to listen to music, either.

Maybe they could get one of those voice-activated things. Maybe she can trigger that to help her around the apartment. She still prefers visual lists and learning, but it would be better than *nothing*, and she wouldn't have to drag Emil into more things than he wants.

She worries about pressuring him.

What if he doesn't want to help her? What if he wants to help her *too much*? She doesn't know which is worse.

A *thud* comes from the bathroom direction, then the shrill scream of an unprepared teenaged boy. "Oh *shit*!" Emil shouts a moment later, and Christine is already in the air, panic zinging through her. "Chris! There's a—*ow*, goddamnit, help please!"

He sounds alarmed but not screaming for his life. Panic roars in her ears like a heartbeat she no longer has.

She pauses in front of the bathroom door, hand raised to knock. The sounds of a scuffle can still be heard inside.

She steels herself before floating through the door.

Halfway.

Christine stares down at herself, *stuck* in the door, halfway through and unable to move. She pushes against the door. She kicks the other side. It's all solid to her. "Uh, Emil?" she calls, scratching against the wood. Of all the times for tangibility! It has never turned *off* before. There have been accidental bumps here and there, but never getting *stuck* in something, being unable to phase through.

Emil slips and grabs the shower curtain. It rips on its way down. Hot water sprays the tiny bathroom, showerhead knocked askew by a little tailed *thing*. It doesn't look like a bogle, but about the same size. It has a bulbous nose and squat legs, almost paw-like hands, and a tufted tail. It swipes at Emil with short claws.

"Wh-What is that?!" Christine squeaks. She pounds her hands against the door.

"No clue, but a little help!" She sees that he's covered in shampoo, probably half-blind from it, and *thankfully* the fallen curtain covers his hips. Emil kicks upward, missing it entirely.

"I—I can't," she says and pulls again, in vain, against the solid door. "It can't reach you right now, it's still on the showerhead. But you're getting water all over your bathroom."

Emil swipes suds out of his eyes and slits one open, only to curse and shut it again. Christine pushes and kicks and scratches the door to no avail.

The little thing falls off the showerhead with a *plop*. Emil kicks it, vicious and quick, then pins it against the shower wall with a foot. He shuffles around, bending, until he can get a hand on it, now crouched and halfway under the crooked spray. He shakes suds and water out of his hair like a dog. Christine covers her eyes at the sight of his bare ass.

"Okay," Emil pants, squinting at his *Psycho* re-enactor wannabe. He swipes more shampoo out of his eyes. "Can you help stop the water from ruining my bathroom?"

"I can't," she repeats in a small, embarrassed voice.

Emil glances at her, then does a double-take. "Are you *stuck*?"

"Um, I think so."

"Ah, shit. Well. Hold on there, I guess." Emil shuffles and wiggles around until the curtain is nominally protecting his modesty. The thing against the wall wriggles ineffectually.

Then, it sucks one of his fingers into his mouth, and he releases it with a shout.

"Are you okay?! Did it bite you?" Christine exclaims.

"No, it... Its tongue was gross. Ugh. Wasn't expecting that."

Emil writes in the air, then aims a *push* spell up at his showerhead. It works, but, well, it's a straight push. Water sprays against the ceiling and rains over most of the tiny bathroom. He sighs in aggravation, then shoves his wet hair out of his face.

"Okay little guy, time to get the hell out of my shower. You have five seconds."

It wags its tail and tries to jump at him. He bats it out of the air and onto the wet rug.

"No! Gross. What *is* that? I don't think it can talk."

It's a tiny spirit, stupid, animal-like. Christine stares at it. Her stuck stomach rumbles. She reaches down for it with sharp claws. Its skin gives way like rotten fruit.

Emil makes another disgusted noise she hardly registers. Christine picks it up—it's already stopped struggling—and looks at the blue blood dripping onto her claws. It's definitely dead. It was definitely weak, and not intelligent, and definitely some sort of spirit. It had been trying to attack Emil.

So self-defense, right?

Hunger lances through her again.

Christine abruptly pops free from the door, unbalancing backward, falling onto her behind. The dead thing had scraped off her claws on the door, leaving only a smear of blood on her fingers.

Out of sight of Emil, she tentatively licks one finger clean.

It doesn't nauseate her.

"Ew," Emil's voice floats through the door. She rips her hand away from her mouth, though he couldn't have seen her.

Christine leans back through the door. It's an effort, like ripping through plastic wrap, but she does not get stuck this time. Emil has a towel wrapped around his waist and nudges the thing into the trash bin. The water is off, though most of the room is still dripping.

"At least those claws are good for something," he comments.

"Huh?"

Emil gestures vaguely at her. "You can protect yourself with them, right? A slap now carries more weight. Maybe that's why Kirara isn't worried. It's a silver lining."

"Oh, um, I guess so..." She looks down at her hands. Blue blood is smeared across a few claws, bright against the black skin. Maybe they aren't one hundred percent terrible; maybe just ninety-five.

· · · ● ● ● ● ● · · ·

They're finishing up at the gym when Oliver decides to be *stupid* again. For someone who only acts that way as a front, he's definitely acting it now and being nosy on top of it. Why does Isaac have so many goddamned nosy people in his life?

"So, like, what's this spell of yours that's so important?" Oliver asks with his arms extended over his head. He doesn't appear to care that he's covered in sweat *or* reeks from it.

Isaac squints at him. "*What* spell?"

Oliver stretches his arms out in front of him next. "The one you've been trying to hide? Sam says you been getting pestered about figuring something out for Natalie."

Sam ducks his head under the guise of pulling off his (sweat-free) t-shirt. The picture of kicked dog.

"Why do you care?" Isaac suspiciously demands. If Natalie roped Oliver in to try to be subtle, or hoping that he'll act as an intermediary, he'll set fire to the potion shop.

"Sam's worried? You're grumpy? Dude, you've been bitchy for forever, ever since I found out about all this magic shit. Is this a side effect *of* Sam? Did you just *love* being a law intern that much?"

Isaac grabs his clean shirt and stakes a claim in front of one of the private showers. Because of course Oliver drags them to a fancy-ass place that *has* private showers in their locker room. But he has to answer first, and with a forced casual air, he replies, "I have a lot on my plate right now. I don't need you adding to it by prying. Don't you have magic to practice or something?"

"Man, I still haven't gotten that to work! I even borrowed some of those notebooks Vivienne loaned you to browse through—"

"The ones full of illegal shit?" Isaac has to ask. He'd read over her so-called *research*. Most of it wouldn't fly with coven laws *or* anyone with a sense of morality about other sapient beings.

"Well, yeah, I guess. And demon shit. Which counts as that, I remember that much, but at least someone's trying to learn here. Is there some kinda magic symbol dictionary I should read instead of Vivienne's old stuff? Those did have couple rune lists I looked through. Look, I got 'em memorized, but they don't work for me, man!" Oliver draws a *fire* rune on his own bare chest with zero effect. (It would have been hilarious if he'd just set himself on fire with his first-ever magic use, though.) "Still, you and Natalie seem super chilly lately, and it's extra with her, not just this new and improved bitchiness of yours."

"It's because of the jar of blood," Sam offers, like he can't lie to Oliver, even though that's patently *bullshit*. He pouts at Isaac's ire. "Well, it's true, and Oliver is our friend. And he has a lot of money, doesn't he?"

"You need me to buy some... blood?" Oliver asks, pausing, obviously thinking over his life choices if it means offering to buy someone blood.

"I do *not*. It's a very rare magical ingredient, something I *could* use, but Natalie's being an asshole and dangling it in front of me. Except she hasn't actually spoken to me about it. *That's* why I've given up on playing nice at work," Isaac waspishly replies. He spares Sam one more glare, promising to carry his irritation over his forthrightness into the rest of the evening, then slams the shower door shut.

Isaac hears Sam and Oliver speak, in tones too low to hear, but what can he do? He's not their babysitters. Oliver can't even *use* magic, which is admittedly a relief, because guys like him without an ounce of self-preservation tend to be the ones who hurt themselves the most. Sam is... Well, he's Isaac's full-time roommate and life tether, but they've gotten along a little better recently—Sam's *annoying* hang-ups about friendship and niceness aside.

When Isaac is done showering, he finds Sam already sitting on a bench. Based on his dripping hair, he at least rinsed off, but as he also doesn't sweat during their gym sessions, Isaac doesn't overly mind.

He pounds on the door to Oliver's shower and shouts, over the water, "Oly, we're headed out!"

The door slams open a moment later. Isaac looks away, half-expecting it, but he does *not* need a reminder that Oliver is a jacked example of masculine physique (and Isaac is definitely *not*). "Wait, no, aren't we going out for food? I'm buying!"

Sam does his best hungry puppy dog look from the bench.

"No, I have to get home," Isaac tells them both. They droop with matching disappointment. "Sam, *you* go hang out with him if you want free food. You two get along better, anyway..."

"Yo, Isy, don't be like that, man!" Oliver exclaims and swipes for him.

Isaac ducks away, hackles raised, face hot. "Don't grab at me when you're naked! Go rinse the soap off before trying to be touchy-feely."

Oliver glances down, as if surprised he's naked. "Fine, whatever, dude. You owe me a dinner! I'll cash in later this week, 'kay?" He mercifully ducks back into the shower stall without putting on any more of a show.

Isaac looks, pointedly, to Sam. His demon shrugs. "So long as there's food at home, I'd rather be nearer you, Isaac. Even if we *can* stretch the distance between us, I don't like to. It's uncomfortable."

"Then come on." They grab their gym bags, Isaac ignores Oliver's exuberant goodbye, and head out into the frigid night. The icy air stings and Sam suppresses a shiver even within his big coat. "Need a warmth rune?" Isaac asks archly.

Sam shoves his face into the fur lining of his hood. "No," he replies, muffled, but sounds pleased that Isaac offers.

"Don't think you can freeze to death, if that's any consolation."

"I don't want to *try*!" Sam exclaims, wounded.

It's late enough at night that the gym had been empty—Isaac's favorite time—and the streets are nearly so. Thick clouds cut any moonlight, but streetlights dot the way, and Isaac buries his face in his phone and loses all nightvision, anyway. Walker has a stream tomorrow morning he wants to catch, but he wants to work on his spellwork a bit more tonight before crashing.

It's a short walk to the train station, a fairly short train ride, and a less-than-short walk to his apartment. Isaac scans over the mod chat on Walker's private server; there's been an uptick in transphobes getting banned. It probably goes hand in hand with her rising popularity, but he wonders if he can write a new filtering spell for her channel. It could be a fun distraction from his *other* spellwork. But technomancy isn't his strong suit, and he shouldn't *get* distracted if he can help it, considering he doesn't know what sort of timeline the apocalypse could come on. That's sort of a big problem. Isaac sighs to himself and pockets his phone.

They turn down a street, four blocks from his apartment, and find the two nearest street-lights broken. Isaac glares up at one and walks faster. He has little to fear from muggers—*they* should fear *him*, and that's not accounting for what's at his side.

But people look at him and see a short, skinny guy and think he's an easy mark. Isaac had used Oliver as a shield against such stupidity in the past, and he supposes Sam could function as that now, too, even if he's not as physically imposing.

"Why are you so tense?" Sam asks, utterly unaware of the risks of walking late at night in the city. "Is it because of the man following us?"

"*What*?!" Isaac whirls around with a snarl.

He spots the man—short, hood up, dog at his side—half a block behind them and is about to ruin the guy's day when he registers his outstretched arm. And the gun in it.

"So the rumors *are* true. You fucker really went and raised a demon," the man says, looking between Isaac's glower and Sam's bewildered expression.

He then shoots Sam.

He turns his gun on Isaac, but Isaac is already raising his hands and gathering magic into them. He doesn't even hear the second shot.

"*Wrong* guess!" Isaac snarls. He doesn't bother writing to cast. He layers *force-strength-down-gravity* and the man and dog both *crunch* into the suddenly cracked sidewalk beneath them. Adrenaline keeps him from noticing the drain on his magic, and panic overrides even that when Isaac turns to Sam.

Pain lances through him from the movement. Isaac glances down at the red spreading over his coat, then back down to Sam.

Black blood gushes from a hole in Sam's throat. He gurgles and reaches for Isaac, and terror eclipses the panic. He'd been shot through the jaw with a crossbow and had been fine, but this pours blood merrily.

Isaac is still standing and can shove the pain away. Sam obviously can't.

It's sheer dumb luck that the man had shot Sam supposedly fatally instead of Isaac. Probably thought Sam was the summoner, an easier target to kill. *That* is what Isaac has been so damn scared of—his *life* tied to another. And that dog with the man—that means he'd been a witch. Someone finally fucking tattled to a coven.

"*Oww*," Same whines wetly. His green eyes shimmer with tears and he clamps one hand over his neck. The other still reaches for Isaac.

Isaac drops to his knees, grabs his extended hand, and curses. "Shit."

"Don't you... have anything better to say?" Sam croaks.

"Not right now," Isaac all but snaps. His life doesn't flash before his eyes, and demons are *supposed* to be hardier than one gunshot wound, but what if it had been a warded bullet? What if it had been a blessed or cursed bullet?

Isaac's other hand hovers over Sam. After a beat of scared indecision, he pulls Sam up so he can lay his head on his lap. The movement makes the tears overflow, but he lets Isaac pull his hand away with another whine.

"Are you okay? You're scared," Sam says in a wrecked whisper.

"Of course I am! That man had been a witch, so it means someone finally told on us. I don't know if I can move you and someone's bound to have heard those gunshots." Also, Isaac had been shot, too. He is *not* doing great right now; pain throbs in his side at the belated reminder.

There's so much black blood and even the littlest touch makes his fingers burn. Isaac shoves his coat sleeve against Sam's neck.

Summoner's blood heals a contracted demon, and Isaac *is* bleeding himself, so is that considered lucky? Is it from his few run-ins with Christine, or karma for thinking of her as another pawn?

Isaac rips open his coat and shoves his fingers into his own wound. It hurts like hell, but he has little choice. A bullet wound is not something he'd collected thus far in his shitty life, but great, he has one of those now. He'll have to dig the bullet out before sealing the wound again.

"C'mere, up," Isaac says, and cups his hand beneath Sam's head. He hisses with the pain, more tears leaking down his cheeks, but Isaac's fingers come away stinging before he can even check. "Looks like the bullet went through. Good."

"Why's that *good*?" Sam cries in dismay.

"We don't have to dig it *out* of you." Isaac doesn't know how to check his own wound, but if he hasn't passed out yet, then he'll survive. Probably. Wait, why *is* he worrying about the very hard-to-kill demon instead of himself?

Because Sam's crying and covered in blood and looks absolutely miserable, whereas Isaac has never allowed himself to *show* vulnerability in his life. Right.

"Alright, hold still," Isaac orders and Sam freezes. There's no way around this part; his hands are going to hate him in a few moments. More than his side does. Isaac shoves his red-covered fingers against the black-soaked skin of Sam's ruined neck.

Sam exhales, *relieved*, and Isaac grits his teeth against the burning sensation. The hole visibly starts sealing itself. "It's working, right?" Sam asks with wide eyes, lashes still spiked with tears.

Isaac writes against the sidewalk. "*Pull*." It's disgusting to pull blood *out* of himself, but he guides it over to Sam's neck and drops it on. This would probably be easier or less painful if he knew blood magic. How does Thomas Novak manage this?

Is *he* the one who ratted them out? Why hadn't this happened sooner, then? It's obvious the man who'd shot them had only been working with physical description—and hadn't known *who* the demon had been. Why wouldn't Thomas (or his accomplice) have dumped everything they knew onto whatever private Eyebright message boards they had and washed their hands of it, content to lead it to overzealous coven guard dogs?

Within minutes, Sam is sitting up, color back in his face, expression filled only with concern. Not terror or panic or pain. Isaac grins at him, swaying. He's dizzy and his hands are shaking harder than ever, but Sam's not dying. *They're* not dying. And maybe he can research blood magic in the future.

Sam opens his mouth to speak but coughs up part of a bullet instead.

Isaac wheezes out a laugh, then promptly passes out.

Natalie peers into the scrying potion. Psychics can't scry, so she can't tell yet if it's active. How much longer does she have to stir this under the full moon? It's getting cold.

Despite her tension from shivering, Natalie finds herself struck with a vision of a roiling thunderstorm.

A witch with henbane in his ponytail angles his broom so the blond guy with him can leap off it. The blond one has claws, *fully black claws, and he lands end-first on a teenager with an undercut and a crossbow. They go down with a yelp of pain.*

The witch reels around on his broom when a gunshot, scarcely audible beneath the storm, rings out. There's a man standing on the far edge of the roof with a rifle pointed straight at him. The first shot must have missed, but the second doesn't, and the witch, already darting toward him, skids onto the concrete roof with a snarl and a smear of blood.

Even being shot doesn't keep him down, and he writes force-push-gravity *and the man with the rifle smacks onto the rooftop with a crunch.*

Before the fight could continue, the sky opens up overhead, and they all drop like puppets with their strings cut.

When Natalie comes back to herself, she is surprised to find blood dripping from her nose. That's never happened from a vision of a fight, no matter how graphic—it only happens when something stronger *is involved. Some sort of mental strain.*

The scrying potion, now ruined with a single drop of blood, turns murky green with a puff of noxious smoke.

CHAPTER 34

IN WHICH THERE IS (FINALLY) A DATE

Sam doesn't move an inch until he sees Isaac's eyes open. Then, it's all he can do not to throw himself at his witch.

Megan popping their head in between them also helps tamp down the instinct, as he doesn't want to get into a headbutting contest. "Good, you're conscious again!" they chirp.

Sam watches as Isaac comes to: awareness first, then recognition of who is crowded over him, and finally, realization of where he must be. Sam frets his ruined coat between his fingers, tearing the fabric further. He hadn't known where else to go but Natalie's.

Isaac's hard hazel eyes slide over to Sam. Sam tries his hardest to convey how little *choice* he had, with Isaac bleeding out on the sidewalk. *He* feels a lot better, but it had only hurt Isaac to heal him. Megan had even commented on that.

"Someone knew I had a demon," are the first words out of Isaac's mouth.

"Well, good, you remember who you are, your situation, all that jazz. Can you sit up?" Megan asks. Sam puts a hand on Isaac's back to help him. Isaac flops limply upward.

Isaac's glare locks onto Natalie, by the counter, watching them impassively.

"I don't know how it got out that you have summoned a demon, nor do I know who had come after you," Natalie coolly replies. "I personally checked the scene after Sam brought you here. There was not much left of the body to use for identification purposes."

"You pulped that guy!" Megan adds. "Probably a witch, probably a coven witch, but not Foxglove. Obviously."

"Why is that obvious?" Sam asks. He doesn't know the first thing about witch covens, given how staunchly Isaac avoids them.

"Foxglove Coven only allows women in their ranks," Megan replies. "Well, women and nonbinary people. It's an old tradition, but I got to draw attention to it when I came out, so mom changed that much for me. But still, no guys allowed type of club."

Natalie pushes off from the counter and puts a hand on Megan's shoulder. "I'll look into how this could have gotten out, but I personally have not heard anything about this. I hope you believe me. It could have been an isolated incident, or something someone else wishes to keep secret for the time being. I'll—"

"You *said* you'd keep us out of coven sight," Isaac interrupts.

"I'm doing my best. It's already been six months, hasn't it?" Natalie pinches the bridge of her nose with a deep sigh. "I know Thomas is the likeliest suspect, or whoever his accomplice had been. But this timeline doesn't make sense."

"Those two, plus your little mini-coven of a friend circle are the *only* people who know about me and Sam," Isaac growls. He leans toward her, expression fierce, but doubles over a moment later with a groan of pain.

Sam and Megan both rush forward. "You're *healed,* but that doesn't mean you're a hundred percent again! I had to triage a lot of the trauma, so I couldn't offer you any anesthetic magic—"

"I'm fine. Don't touch me," Isaac grits out.

Megan's hands snap back to their sides, but Sam keeps his hand lightly on Isaac's shoulder. The order hadn't affected *him.* (Not that Isaac can order anyone else around, as much as he'd like to.) "I just wanted to explain myself. I did what I could," Megan tells him in a smaller voice.

Natalie steps closer, expression colder than usual. Somehow. Sam can't actually *see* the difference, but unhappiness radiates from her. "Healers are exceptionally rare and are a *privilege* to ask favors of. I'd thank you not to snap at Megan again."

Isaac lets out a laugh at that, but it makes him clutch his side again. Sam doesn't understand why he finds that funny. "My issues with Megan are separate of my issues with *you,* Natalie. Isn't that right?"

Megan looks down at their feet.

"Isaac, they helped you," Sam whispers. He wishes they wouldn't fight.

"The help we were supposed to receive was hiding from the covens! Now there's a dead witch and who knows how many others out for our heads. Not everyone will be as stupid as thinking *I'm* the demon—what happens if *I* get shot in the neck next time? What happens if someone who isn't a complete moron tries to engage?" Isaac snaps at Natalie.

"You took care of yourself quite well tonight, I think," she thinly replies. "This is not the first body I've cleaned up for someone, Isaac."

"I don't care about your pristine image or what you've done. I care that there are now targets on our backs when you said there wouldn't be. It sounds like our little deal is over, isn't it?"

"Are you saying there is nothing else you want from me?" Natalie returns.

For a moment, Sam fears that Isaac may actually attack her. With the same ease that he killed that man earlier. But that tense moment passes, and instead Isaac jerks his chin at her. "Can you leave us for a moment? I want to talk to Megan. Alone."

Natalie regards him, then inclines her head. Isaac doesn't speak until her footsteps are audible upstairs, however.

And even then, Megan beats him to the punch. "I had to take off your shirt to treat your wound, but that's when Nat was out of the shop to go scrape that guy off the sidewalk! She doesn't know."

Further tension leaches out of Isaac. "Okay. Good. ...Thanks, for that, and for healing me, I guess."

"One of the worst examples of gratitude I've ever heard, but you're welcome!" Megan exclaims, beaming.

"Thank you," Sam adds, far more sincerely. Their grin widens even further.

"Do you even know what we're talking about?" Isaac flatly asks.

"You were healed," Sam says, nonplussed—he had been there for that part, and it is no mystery what Megan's magical specialty is.

"It's a really complicated human thing," Megan advises with a pat on his arm. "But it's secret, okay?"

"Okay?" Sam echoes. *What* is secret? He understands Megan and Isaac have *some* sort of weird relationship, but for as much as he's learned about humans in other ways, this one still eludes him.

"Solidarity!" Megan exclaims and holds up their fist toward Isaac. He stares at it, unmoving. "Come on, fist bump, Isaac! Give me this much. As *thanks*. You know, for saving your *life*?"

With a great roll of his eyes, he knocks his fist against theirs. Sam understands this part even less.

"Are you and Nat gonna be cool? I can give you my cell number so you can call me in this kind of emergency, too, but only if you and her are going to be okay together. I know you're kind of... Well, you're kind of a dick," Megan bluntly says, and Isaac spares her a highly unimpressed look, "but you're smart, and you know that it's not terrible sticking by her. Right? But she doesn't need this passive aggressive bullshit routine from you. She's done a lot to try to keep you safe, y'know?"

"*She* is the one being passive aggressive."

"Doesn't sound like her. And I think I know her better than you."

Isaac rolls his eyes again. "Can I go home, or do you need to keep me in observation or something?"

"Oh, no, you're fine to go! Well, don't get into any more fights on the way home—actually, we'll call you a ride!—and you should go right to sleep. Take some pain relievers. No magic use for a few hours. You'll have some nasty bruises for a while, but you're not bleeding anymore and nothing was broken, so deal with it, okay?" Megan sunnily informs him. "That's the best I could do, since I'm not a witch and all. But it's pretty damn impressive, if I do say so myself! Not everyone can be like Alice, and aren't you lucky I'm such good friends with Nat and Vivi that I can rush over to help you! Big point why you should stay here and keep working with us."

Isaac laughs. He doesn't actually sound all that amused, but it's not as mean as usual, and, glancing at Megan, it doesn't look like they're offended. "What choice do we have?" Isaac replies.

· · · ●·●·● · ·

Brynja has not gotten up, even to eat, since Mark returned the bear pelt. Not that she had a strict pattern, but every few days, she would eat.

Now, not even that.

At least she is a still sleeper, and at least he has a large bed. Fiona would take the floor if he claimed the couch, but sleeping next to a comatose shapeshifter is far from the weirdest—or most dangerous—thing he has done in his life. And she broadcasts no thoughts. Silence is nice to fall asleep to.

His dream is lucid enough that he initially wonders if Tsukiko has returned. He does not need regular baku maintenance like some psychics, but she always brings pleasant dreams. Wrought silver orchids burst into bloom as he wanders, crumbling to dust as soon as he passes. There is a large blue-green tree on the hill. Its black leaves droop and glimmer.

Grass breaks beneath his feet with the *crunch* of glass, but he feels no pain. Dreams aren't for pain. White orchids and purple belladonna flit through the air like birds.

Mark finds a figure seated beneath the tree's long boughs, but it is not the baku.

Brynja raises her head, red eyes sharp and clear. "You brought me my bear pelt. Did you return the egg to the tengu?" she asks.

"Oh... No, not yet. Is there anything else you're missing?" He vaguely recalls worry about it not being enough. Memories are hard in dreams.

Brynja rubs a thumb over the wide scar on one arm. "Not anymore, aside from my swan pelt. I have not felt this way in some time. ...Thank you."

"I'm glad to have helped you," he happily replies and plops to the crunchy grass beside her. Swan-like orchids land on her hair and sakura petals float by.

"I am healing, or trying to. You need not worry about me," Brynja tells him. He nods, even more pleased. "But my master—that thing. It is not dead and it is not stopped."

It's hard to think in dreams, but Mark tries his best. "Oh, I worried about that. You are... It has something to do with you, right?"

Brynja scowls. "Yes, it probably will. I don't understand most of the magic involved. Even without the First egg, knowing my betrayal, it will continue its plans."

"It is not your master anymore. It holds no sway. What did it call you? *Yhri—*?"

Brynja lunges forward to clamp her hands over his mouth. He does not know if it is the word or their contact, but abruptly, the dreamscape crumbles. Plant life withers to dust and the flowers in the air sprinkle into ash. Heat flares through the scene without visible flame.

"It will come yet for me," Brynja says, hands still over his mouth. She smells like smoke. "It will not stop. Thank you for your help, Mark Ito, but you and I do not win this one. You need to kill my body before it gets through—"

The earth erupts beneath them. The tree topples, roots melting, and a huge beastly form boils up from underground. It has no color to it, only far-off motes of light within its fur, and it raises many tails like axes ready to fall.

"*Yhri,*" the thing breathes, heat pouring from its mouth, and Brynja again lunges for Mark.

"You need to go!" She slices his throat open with claws the size of her hand. "Wake *up!*"

Mark jolts awake, clutching his neck, heaving for breath. His bedroom is cool and still. Brynja remains cool and still beneath her pile of pelts.

Benji, in dog form, lifts a sleepy head from the foot of the bed. "Bad dream?" he asks with a yawn.

Mark struggles to get his breathing back under control. They don't have as much time as he'd hoped. "You could say that."

· · · · ● · ● · · ·

It is finally time for D-Day. Date Day. Vivienne wears a thick cream sweater and a light blue maxi skirt, hair held back with a matching blue headband (with a cute rabbit-eared bow on it), and makes sure she pays special attention to her eyeliner and her favorite lip gloss. It tastes like strawberries. She hopes to share this with Dana.

No alcohol, no other people, no interruptions! A whole day together for a proper going-out date, Vivienne thinks with a private fist pump.

It's kind of an odd date. They've known each other for months now, have each seen each other's apartment, have grabbed quick meals and hung out at the bookstore and have navigated a few minor emergencies together. Vivienne thinks she knows Dana decently well within those constraints.

But this is a first major step toward something like a normal relationship.

"Sunny, papa has forgotten how to be normal!" Vivienne cries in dismay. Sunshine winds around her feet, politely adding fur to her skirt and leggings. "Dana knows about magic now, but…"

But even within the magical community, Vivienne is a freak. Dana doesn't have preconceptions about it, nor context, nor the entire picture.

How long before you would have told me? Dana had asked. There are more answers Vivienne will have to give her, eventually, but she doesn't know when or how to broach those topics.

Her heart beats, ever slow, in her chest. She presses a hand there and takes a few deep breaths.

They meet up at a cute cafe that proclaims delicious waffles. Pretty as ever, Dana wears maroon skinny jeans and a grey flannel underneath a *very* nice black leather jacket. (Vivienne wonders how she ever worried, however briefly, that Dana was straight.) Her hair is up in a mohawk braid, piled thick, trailing down her back.

Vivienne kisses her cheek in greeting. Dana flusters cutely.

"You've got two on me, then," Dana mutters with a hand to her cheek. "I'm going to ambush you with kisses later today."

"I look forward to it."

The waffles are amazing. The hot chocolate, less so, but Vivienne would sacrifice a lot in the name of a good waffle. Dana seems to be of the same opinion. Another way they mesh well. This is normal romance, right?

"So, zoo time? The weather is sunny, at least," Dana confirms, checking the ticket reservations Vivienne had texted. "I think I'm going to keep the… jackalope, too. I went to that vet you recommended."

"Oh?" Fiona is good at her job, but *not* the easiest to get along with.

"She seemed kind of familiar? Does she run a YouTube series or something?"

Fiona doesn't get along with technology any better than people. "No, I don't think so. Maybe she just has that kind of face?"

"Hm, well. Looks like you were right, it's a little guy. I've, uh, named him Pyewacket. I thought it was fitting. And now I'm acting like *you*—I've read all the rabbit care books we stock without buying any of them," Dana says with a chuckle. Her grin scrunches her nose a little. "I might send you more panicked texts if he starts shitting sparkles or something, but so far, it's nice to have a pet again. Kind of like toddler-proofing the apartment, though."

"We could have pet dates!" Vivienne exclaims, starry-eyed.

"Don't cats eat rabbits?"

"You've seen those antlers. And also, no, Sunny is a *very* polite gentleman. He used to have all kinds of pet dates with the other familiars at the coven," she says before she can think.

Dana tilts her head, cheek on her fist. "Coven, huh? Like witches?"

"Like I said, *I'm* not a witch, but... I sort of inherited him from my best friend. Who passed on."

"Oh, I'm so sorry."

"It's okay," Vivienne lies, "it was three years ago now! Anyway, he's actually her familiar, so he *is* smarter than the average cat. He knows how to behave. Just, like most cats, he *chooses* when to. But he likes you! I'm sure he'd like a pet date, and it's an excuse to hang out again. Pet enrichment and all that!"

"Fine, we can try it once. But if anyone gets eaten or gored, I'm holding you responsible."

"Fair enough. I usually carry that responsibility on my jobs."

Dana goes thoughtfully quiet again. Vivienne admits to testing her reaction, seeing what surprises her, what she seems to disapprove of, and what makes her the *really* cute excited and kind of curious Vivienne remembers most fondly about her own descent into magic. She's hoping for mostly that.

The zoo date will help.

Outside, full of waffles, Dana adjusts her jacket's collar. The wind is brisk, but the sunshine is nice. A really nice fall day. And chilly enough that Vivienne will *happily* invite her over for a cuddling warm-up session afterward.

Vivienne leans against Dana on the train ride under the guise of sharing warmth.

The zoo isn't terribly crowded in its off season. They are barely past the wolf enclosure before Dana grabs her hand. Elated, Vivienne twines their fingers together.

They coo over big cats, try to find exotic birds hiding in rainforest enclosures, share excitement over a gorilla being *right* by the glass, and take a scenic tram ride around the elephant and rhino section. It *is* a nice zoo.

But that isn't the reason Vivienne brought her here.

Having seen most of the enclosures, Vivienne surreptitiously tugs Dana down a service path. A wall of tall bushes and a lonely pretzel stand are the only things in the area. The attendant seems tired but pays them no heed.

"This is a dead end," Dana says, confused, but with a smirk, Vivienne tugs her through the greenery.

There aren't any plants. The path continues into another section of the zoo.

Dana stumbles to a stop, eyes wide, mouth agape. An oni father and daughter nearly bump into them. Vivienne, still beaming, tugs her off the middle of the path and near the first exhibit—a wyvern napping on a rocky outcrop.

Dana's eyes fix on the scales glinting in the sunlight.

"Why did you think this zoo was so expensive? Welcome to the other half," Vivienne says with glee.

"I thought it was just... You know, city prices..." Dana shuffles forward, watching the sleeping wyvern, and in the next exhibit, a pair of gryphon chicks tussle with each other. "Oh. Oh, my god... This is real, right? This is all real?"

"Yep. Might help put some stuff in perspective, right? All this magic stuff is real, including everything in this zoo. They don't have any jackalopes, but they do have a pair of Scottish unicorns. To bring it full circle."

Vivienne lets Dana lead. Area-wise, this part of the zoo isn't as large as the other, but they have enough to keep her awed. Child-like is the best way she can think of it; a person discovering brand new animals they've never seen before, just like schoolchildren on their first zoo field trip. It's a beautiful look on Dana.

She waves her hand back and forth in front of the nguruvilu exhibit, starry-eyed when it winds around and follows her movement like a playful otter. They wander through the aviary—Vivienne keeping a sharp, judgmental eye on the augury—and Dana feeds a pushy luan.

Dana and Vivienne share a glare for the unicorn exhibit. The unicorns don't care.

It is mostly a peaceful trip, aside from Dana's open staring at patron and creature alike, until they pass by the jabberwock and it snaps at her. Dana jumps a foot in the air, twisting so Vivienne is between them, and Vivienne cannot help but laugh at her fright.

"Wh-What is that thing?!" Dana squeaks.

The jabberwock bares its teeth, then roars again.

"Jabberwock, like the old poem? They're real, too. On the other side of the wall is the questing beast. There have been petitions to move them both to bigger enclosures for years, since they're large predators, but there're rumors they like them feisty to shock and awe zoo guests."

Dana warily studies the beast. "So there's stupid bureaucracy even in magic stuff?"

"I'd say there's even *more* of it."

"And that's just... allowed to be here? Its teeth are as long as my forearm!"

"Lions and tigers and bears can maul and eat a person, too. Hippos kill more people each year than jabberwocky ever will," Vivienne reasons.

The jabberwock hisses again as they edge around its area; Dana keeps up a guarded expression until they're out of sight. Vivienne not-so-subtly tugs her toward cuter things, like the hellhound pups and the peryton.

"Wait, what is *that*?" Dana gasps and seizes Vivienne's arm. At least it's toward more cuteness. At first glance, it looks like a jackalope in the small pen—a little hare with a matching little set of antlers.

But then it stretches a *wing* with a yawn.

Vivienne checks her map. "A... wolpertinger? Cute little thing. Now, imagine not only a jackalope, but one that could *fly*. Don't you feel lucky?"

"But it's so *cute*. It's snowy colored!" Dana coos. She shoots Vivienne a sly look. "I'm allowed to think zoo animals are cute without wanting one. Don't get any ideas."

"*I* haven't ended up with any exotic animals recently."

"You escorted some unicorns that seemed to want an adventure."

"Not *my* unicorns," Vivienne maintains. "I'm fine with a house panther, thanks. But yes, I will allow, cute exotic animals are cute. So long as they are not mine to take care of. But c'mon, next is the snipes! They're cute, too."

"Snipes, like... the little bird things you send newbies to hunt?"

Vivienne falters, but only briefly. "Yep!"

"They don't really exist, do they," Dana deadpans.

"You're too sharp for a newbie to the supernatural. No, they *probably* don't exist. Doesn't stop people from trying to find them. Myths had to have sprung up from somewhere, right?" And the zoo even has a cheeky declaration that they have a exhibit of them, too—if you can find it.

Her phone buzzes in her pocket. Vivienne checks it, frowning at *Mark* on the screen, but he's a texter. Supposed to be one, anyway. She leaves Dana watching the hellhound pups and steps aside to take the call. "This better be important, Mark. You're interrupting my long-awaited date with a babe."

"The Brynja bridge thing important to you?" he snarks back.

She groans. "Don't be a jerk. What's going on now?"

"It seems to be happening on a faster schedule than we expected. You said you were working on a method to help her, right? I need it. Now."

"*Now*?" Vivienne hisses with a glance over her shoulder at Dana. Dana gives her a confused smile. "Seriously. Honestly. Right *now*?"

"What do you need for your method?" Mark asks.

"Jesus, why can't the universe let me have *one date*?!" Alright, they've gotten through brunch and most of the zoo, and Vivienne has glutted herself on Dana's awed face. This still counts as a win.

And she supposes the apocalypse *should* come first.

"I'm gonna need... Ugh. Astral projection potion and Hammond. Space to write a big fuckin' circle. Brynja's, uh, body nearby, so long as she's not growing tentacles or trying to eat us."

"I have Fiona and Benji watching her. She's still out for the moment. They're Plan B. Please, Viv, I don't want Plan B if you have a working Plan A."

It is with a heavy heart and growing dread that Vivienne hangs up. It only now dawns on her that this could be an end of days scenario.

Despite hunting down the egg, despite the dragon migration fiasco, despite all the breadcrumbs they've been following, *now* it's all coming to a head? She somehow thought they'd have more warning.

"Hey, so, I'm *really* sorry to cut this short, but I gotta go," Vivienne sheepishly tells Dana. "Have to go help a friend with something."

"Can I come? I can help," Dana says.

Vivienne cringes. "That is... It's magic, right? A lot of magic."

"Oh."

Dana looks so crestfallen it wrenches her heart. What's the worst that could happen? It's astral projection, which doesn't affect the physical plane, and Dana could get a quick lesson in potions. And meet Fiona and Benji. And Mark, anew, as a psychic. She deserves that last one, at least, considering they'll be BFF-in-laws.

"Are you sure? It's gonna be... I don't know, actually. Either boring or messy. Probably both."

"If I won't be in the way, then sure, please. I'd love to see you on a job that isn't trying to eat me. And you know that whole 'when would you have told me' thing? I'd like to see firsthand what you do for a living," Dana gently adds. Vivienne grimaces, then nods.

She'll be safe, Vivienne tells herself. Astral projection is boring for nonparticipants. Dana can foist her questions onto Mark, who has no magical ability and only haphazard magical knowledge, which would be funny to see in other circumstances.

She'll be safe, because they're *preventing* the apocalypse.

And maybe it'll nice to go under while holding her hand.

Natalie is holding Hayley's red hair back while she heaves when the vision hits her. She's no longer in her bathroom, but a warehouse, and she has the feeling she's in her own skin. A potential future of her own.

But it's hot, tight, and wrong. Her arms glow, white-hot up to her elbows, and when she steps forward, her sneakers melt off her feet.

A witch with a ponytail and a terror-stricken sneer points a witch-bolt at her face. "This is why I couldn't let you have my spell!" he snarls at her.

Natalie watches as her molten fingertips drip off. Heat shimmers around her.

"Natalie?" comes a familiar voice behind her, and she whirls around, but the vision upends her with the movement.

Hayley coughs and sits back on her heels. Her hair is in her face, lank from sweat, several locks now coated in vomit, sticking to her chin.

"Thanks," she deadpans.

CHAPTER 35

IN WHICH VIVIENNE LOSES HER HEAD

Hammond has been waiting when Vivienne—and Dana—arrive at Mark's house. They've cleared the living room, couch and tables pushed aside, carpet rolled up. If Mark wants Vivienne to draw on his floor, so be it, it's not his place to judge.

The woman named Brynja lies beneath a *pile* of different animal skins on the table. Fiona leans beside her, shotgun resting in the crook of her elbow. Hammond respects her reputation and her relationship with Mark, but he does *not* like how Benji watches Rory.

To be fair, Rory started it by flipping off a rage spirit.

Hammond arches an eyebrow at Dana. "Viv mentioned you joined the club. Are you in on this job?"

"No, she's just watching, though she can go home at *any* time if this gets to be too much," Vivienne pointedly replies.

"I'm fine staying," Dana replies. She waves to the others, but does a double-take at Fiona. "Uh, wait, you're the vet, aren't you?"

Fiona jerks her head in a nod.

"Well, I'm glad you have apparently all met, since we get to make smalltalk while the adults are out," Mark says.

Vivienne rolls her eyes before thrusting her arm deep into her bag. Dana openly stares; Hammond supposes Vivienne hasn't shared *that* tidbit yet. "I told you, I'm *not* letting a psychic into the Dreamlands."

"I'm being excluded from my own job!"

"You usually are," Fiona deadpans. "Making us do your dirty work."

"I like her," Rory declares. Vivienne snorts. "I don't care that the dog cursed you, we need more people who can sass Mark Ito. The shapeshifting woman can do that, too, right? That's why he's so friggin' thirsty?"

"Brynja is a source of information. And a way to stop this today."

Vivienne starts with a big circle in magic marker on Mark's living room floor. Hammond stays back, letting her work, and wonders how this is going to go. He prefers more information, especially about unknown magics, but he trusts Vivienne.

"You going to behave yourself while I'm gone? Only the inugami can see you," Hammond asks Rory.

The ghost shrugs. "If you come back to a mangled twice-corpse, it'll be easy to finger the culprit."

"I'm serious. You don't have to stay. Anywhere in this realm works."

"Someone needs to keep an eye on things, including your body. You're the one not used to floating around dead," Rory points out. "I'll be fine, Ham. You can go save the world or whatever without me."

"It'll be easy. This is like a rescue mission—we're running in, grabbing Brynja, and hauling ass. Two hours tops," Vivienne says with a grin. She completes the first ring of the circle and wipes soot onto her brow when she tries to get her bangs out of her eyes. Hammond feels bad she's going to ruin such a pretty outfit.

It has to be important for her to ruin that date of hers, he thinks. He knows he can interrogate her to his heart's content as soon as they're alone. Because Mark hasn't told him shit.

While Mark and Benji distract Dana with feats of clairvoyance and the ability to turn into a monstrous dog, Vivienne goes over the broad strokes of the plan again.

She and Hammond will astral project themselves and wait for the nightgaunt to show up. Once it steps into the circle, they will sacrifice it, hypothetically opening a small portal to the Dreamlands, just big enough for two spirits to slip through. Rory will act as an anchor on this side so Hammond can find their way back.

As for navigating the Dreamlands themselves, Vivienne hedges. Fishily.

Vivienne paints runes on the insides of their wrists and uses her messenger bag as a pillow. "Okay, nap time! Welcome to the spiritual side of magic, Dana. You can't see shit. But neither can they, so you could, I don't know, play cards? Talk about your hobbies?"

Dana makes a face at the suggestion of playing cards. Interestingly, so does Fiona.

They drink the potions, and there is a sleepy lull in conversation. Hammond focuses on his breathing. He has only astral projected once before, and while it is uncomfortable, he knows what to expect.

A moment later, he sits up, out of his body.

He wriggles into the air and Rory snickers at his white robes. Vivienne pops up, too. Hammond floats without control, unable to remember how to aim, and Rory grabs him around the waist to keep him still.

"So, what's this going to be like?" Hammond asks. Only Benji watches them now; Dana accidentally leans through Vivienne when she checks on her body. Vivienne darts away with a squeal, covering her chest like a scandalized maiden. "Viv, the Dreamlands? What is it *like*? We've let you dodge a lot of questions so far."

"I've only been there once, okay? It's... different. Similar to lucid dreaming, and it'll be easier to navigate as spirits. Not that I could make a doorway, even temporary, big or strong enough for living humans. We're pretty lucky ghosts are the bottom rung of the spiritual ladder—"

"Bitch, focus!" Rory barks.

"Lucid dreaming!" Vivienne repeats with a huff. "We will have some level of control over our environment. We'll use that to our advantage. Hypothetically, we could create anything we need, but a word of warning—any nightgaunts we run into will *not* act like my stalker. That one has been starved and lost for three years."

"So more peppy, got it," Hammond says with a mock salute. "Avoid at all costs."

"That's the plan. And if worst comes to worst, our bodies are here, so while we could suffer some psychic damage, we should still be living. Technically. Can't do much worse to me, anyway."

It is *boring* waiting for the nightgaunt to show up. But as soon as it does, Vivienne freezes it in her circle, then slides around the magic like a shark circling prey. She taps various runes to activate them.

"I don't think Benji over there can see the nightgaunt. Can you?" Rory asks with a leer.

"I can still see and take a bite out of you," he replies, grinning sharply. Mark and Dana look uneasy at the sudden threat, but Fiona bops him over the head with the butt of her gun.

"So, Dana, hm? She's getting deeper into magic with you. How is that going? You took her to the zoo, right?" Hammond asks while Vivienne works.

"Actual question he means—when are you gonna *tell her*?" Rory translates.

Vivienne hardly pauses. "Listen, I don't know, and I need to concentrate on this right now. She's learning about magic and stuff at her own pace. Which apparently included watching today's nap session while we project."

"This is something you two are going to have to talk about eventually," Hammond says.

"Can't we talk about this *later*?"

"Are you going to talk to *her* later?"

Vivienne turns to them, hands on her circle, brow furrowed deep. "I *like* her! And she likes me. Why can't it be that simple until this is done? Right now, the priority is stopping Brynja from getting possessed. That's all I'm thinking about right now."

Hammond and Rory exchange a glance, then shrug in unison. "Fair enough. For now."

Like jaws closing, the circle snaps shut on the nightgaunt. The resulting portal is outlined in white so bright it hurts to look at, but the rest of it is a hole the color of embers on Mark's living room floor.

"This should remain open for at least an hour, but even if it closes, I'll figure out something on the other side." Vivienne grabs Hammond's hand and gives Rory a smile. "See you soon!"

She hops through the portal, dragging Hammond behind her. Gravity shifts, and they fall not downward, but flop out sideways onto solid ground.

Vivienne waves her hand over the hole, and it shimmers into a nearly invisible grey, blending in with their surroundings. Hammond isn't sure what he expected another realm to look like. Based on her descriptions, chaotic dream colors mixed with some Freddy Krueger for flavor.

This is far more *Silent Hill*.

The ringing in his ears isn't great, either.

"Let's keep holding hands," Vivienne says, rubbing at her eyes with her free one. She blinks like she can't focus.

"Worried about getting lost?" he jokes. There is nothing around them for what seems like forever.

"Space doesn't work the same here. Neither does time. What is an hour on their side will give us plenty of time to navigate... this." She rubs her eyes one last time. Quieter, she mutters, "It isn't supposed to look like this."

"So, you've been here before. What was that like?"

"It was three years ago. When I got my tail."

Hammond sighs at her. "You're going to have to tell me more about this, Viv. You already kept the nightgaunt secret for *far* too long. You owe me a little more for helping you with this."

"Can you make anything?" Vivienne asks, trying to change the subject.

Hammond raises his free hand and a neon blue and green, cartoonish version of a rifle drops into it. He keeps his face straight, even if it's not exactly what he wanted. Vivienne fights a grin and he smacks her in the ass with the butt of the rifle. "Let's see what you make, then, Ms. Expert."

Vivienne beams as she creates a rather good replica of Codi's crossbow.

"Mine's better," he says, and she nods. "So, how *exactly* does this place work?"

"The Dreamlands function almost entirely on thought and belief. We, on the other hand, are not from here, so though we're effectively spirits right now, this realm will treat us as living beings."

"So in case of emergency, dump dead blood on 'em, right?" Hammond asks archly.

"Yeah, that," Vivienne deadpans back.

"Is this place supposed to be so empty? You said nightgaunts are from here, and I have yet to see any. Or anything at all. It's *creepy*."

"I won't complain about the lack of trouble, but no, it's not *supposed* to be like this. There *is* supposed to be more color to the area, and honestly, we should be affecting the surrounding area with our subconscious thoughts. Something's oppressing the area around here..."

"You know it's going to be the god thing," Hammond says.

"Yes, I know," she sighs.

As if on cue, Hammond spots a blur of movement, and he shoves Vivienne to the ground just as giant claws swipe through where her head had been. Hammond lands on top, hastily rolls off, and they point their weapons up at the assailant.

Hammond had been expecting either a giant beast or a copy of the possessed-to-be woman. Instead, he finds a silhouette.

It's human sized and shaped, but completely black—and not even black *colored* like the nightgaunts. It's as if it's a simple void, save the two bright spots, roughly where its eyes should be. Its form is enormous, muscular, and imposing.

"*Ah, shuggoth-exorcist,*" the figure purrs, voice rumbling around them. "*How attached you are. How many friends naflyhri has.*"

Hammond rubs at his ear at the weird words, but keeps the gun level. "Viv? Do we shoot?"

"I honestly have no idea," she replies, crossbow also trained on the silhouette. They aren't supposed to engage. They need to find wherever the Brynja expy is.

Hammond has a sinking feeling that *that* is the Brynja expy.

"*I have no need of you here,*" it says and raises its arm. A sword appears in its grasp, curved and sharp. The figure staggers towards him, and he ducks out of the way, but he still doesn't pull the trigger. It's slow. That's good. But he needs to know if they're fighting or flighting here.

"Vivienne, yes or no!" Hammond barks.

"I don't know! We just have to slow it down!"

"It's swinging a sword at us! Let me know if I should switch or—*holy shit.*" So *that's* what a nightgaunt is supposed to be. In its homeland, it's fast and noisy, diving at Hammond with a garbled moan. He drops and rolls under it. It collides with the figure, who slices it without a care. "*Viv!* Tell me what I can and can't do here or else I'm shooting everything!"

"*Fine!*" she snaps back.

Despite being nearly bisected, the nightgaunt still thrashes, so he puts two bullets in its head. He puts another bullet in the back of the figure's knee, but it doesn't even seem to notice. Another two shots confirm that.

Swearing again, Hammond ditches the gun and spawns his own sword. The silhouette picks Vivienne up by the front of her sweater, and Hammond stabs it straight through the chest.

The figure *laughs*. "*How charming, shuggoth. You are new to these Dreamlands, yes? So very naïve.*"

"This isn't going to do anything to it!" Vivienne growls, wrestling with the hand holding her aloft. "It's too used to this area—headshots are what we need!"

"Got it!" With the figure still turned to laugh at him, Hammond respawns his gun and puts the barrel directly between its eyes.

He gets three shots off before it drops Vivienne, and, with a scream of rage (not pain, how annoying), it turns on him. He raises his sword to block the other blade, but to his horror, it cuts through his like butter. The sword slices down through his weapon, collarbone, and chest, and then it's his turn to stare down at the blade sticking out of him.

"It's okay, Ham!" Vivienne shouts, panic in her voice at odds with her words. Hammond staggers backward; he doesn't feel any pain, but his mind is telling him *this should hurt like a bitch*. "Pain doesn't work the same here, you're fine, just—!"

The blade abruptly starts to *burn*, and that much, he feels. With a yelp, he tugs it out, and the sword clatters to the ground.

Blood sprays out of his wound, splattering the grey ground scarlet.

Ghosts don't bleed.

The figure laughs again, and when it stoops to pick it back up, Hammond sees that *its* hand is burnt, too.

"What kind of sword is that?" Hammond wheezes, because his chest hurts like it's still stuck in him, and he is *bleeding*. This place is supposed to run on thought, right? He wants to believe it's *gone* already and he's *fine*. He is not bleeding. He is just a ghost. Ghosts don't bleed.

"*Naflyhri may not wield it well, but it is still a vorpal sword. Shuggoth's rules apply again,*" it replies in delight, and Hammond *does not* like the way Vivienne pales.

In dance, muting the song means a pause in movement. Where is that for fights? Hammond would also appreciate more equal weaponry. His chest hurts, his arm is growing heavier, and he's beginning to think that this means something more serious than a thought-injury.

Vivienne, using crossbow bolts to maintain a distance, circles the silhouette to reach Hammond's side. "You alright?" She gapes at the sight of blood seeping into his shirt. It does not improve his spiraling worry.

Hammond presses his free hand to his sternum. "This feels like it's still in me. I'm *bleeding*, Viv. Is my body alright?"

"A vorpal sword isn't from here, so it's real to us. ...So, uh, *maybe*," Vivienne answers, voice squeaky with panic. He swallows. This could have gone better. "Definitely need a new plan. I'm going to get close enough to let that thing get me, and then we're going with our emergency plan, alright? *Please* tell me you remember the marks I had you use on that nightgaunt."

"Of course I do!" Hammond retorts. Mostly. "But you—Viv, if that thing actually *hurts* us, as in our physical bodies a *realm away*, I don't think bleeding on it is going to help the situation."

"You're going to be fine! It's still mostly just a psychic injury!" she cries in alarm. Hammond rolls his eyes but smiles, anyway.

The figure charges at them, and they dodge in either direction, putting it between them again. Alternating between bullets and bolts, Hammond feels like they're merely annoying it further, but at least it lets them maintain their distance.

Vivienne tries to tiptoe closer, ducking more slowly and using larger arm movements, and while he can't blame her for being cautious, Hammond's getting worried. Time limit. Actual bodily harm. No clue if that thing is Brynja or not, and if not, where the hell she could be.

Vivienne creates a spear and shoves it through the figure's void of a chest.

"*Mnahn' shuggoth,*" it cackles, and Hammond shakes his head to get what he thinks is blood out of his ears. It turns and snaps the shaft of the spear, but puts its back to Vivienne in the process.

Too easy. Now when she attacks, it'll whirl back around, and its arc will be big enough for her to catch. And with dead man's blood, everything is easier.

Vivienne fires three bolts into its head, and there it's whirling back around with a snarl—and its elbow catches her stomach, winding her and sending her to her knees.

Laughing again, it grabs a fistful of Vivienne's hair and hauls her upright.

"*Kadishtu n'ghaog, lloignyth,*" it orders. It swings the vorpal sword down on Vivienne's neck, and with one blow, beheads her.

"I had to remind him that I don't know *ancient* Greek." Hayley twists in the mirror. The sleek fabric falls down her back in a flattering cascade. Her ruby hair is sloppily held up, but it works. She makes everything work, even the (objectively terrible) novelty t-shirts she usually lives in. "Neither does he. Right, right? Didn't stop him from—"

Natalie blinks and the scene becomes Hayley in combat wear, bleeding and crying and older.

"I-It ate h-her!" Hayley sobs into her hands. It looks as if several of her fingers are broken. "That thing—that *thing*—oh my god..." Her voice catches. It's unclear if there's anyone else in the shadowed, burned-out building she cowers in. The light that filters in through the broken windows is grim, grey, and could be from any time of day.

Hayley's crying has always been something private to her, but she weeps openly now, her grief too potent for her to notice the radiant figure outside.

The door on the far end of the room crashes open and Codi Clarkson bursts in. One arm hangs uselessly at her side, but she aims her shotgun at the window with one hand. "Hayley!"

Hayley breaks into a relieved smile just as a spear of *something* breaks through the wall to impale her.

Codi takes aim and fires twice out the window. Hayley slumps when the glowing spike is pulled from her. Outside, something hisses. Instead of fumbling to reload, Codi drops her shotgun and pulls out her 9mm. She fires until the ungodly thing outside crawls through the window with too many limbs and a great many antlers.

Natalie jars back into herself with her vision swimming. Her eyes burn, but not from tears. Something about whatever that was had been impossible to behold.

"Well, you know how he is," Hayley finishes and twists to check out her own butt. The green dress looks lovely on her. "Almost got his fingers bitten off for his trouble, but I think he made a friend with the cerastae."

Natalie wordlessly walks over and embraces her tightly. Hayley does not question her, but hugs her back.

CHAPTER 36

In Which Rory Finds Himself Happier With Less Information

Rory freaks the fuck out when Hammond starts *bleeding*. And it isn't weird nose-bleeding that mental strain causes, no, because that would be simple and maybe explainable. The fucker developed a *wound* from thin air, down the meat of his shoulder and into his chest.

"Oh my god," Dana gasps.

"You *fucker*! You told me you'd be safe!" Rory snarls and tries to shove his hands against Hammond to staunch the blood. His hands go *through*. Panic zips through him, but that has to be because he's astral projecting, right?

"What happened to him?" Mark asks in alarm. He rushes over to press against the injury, too, but frowns in confusion. He rips open Hammond's shirt—and there is no wound.

There is a *scar*.

It cuts across the juncture of his shoulder and neck, a jagged line breaking smooth brown skin, bisecting the tattoo curled over Hammond's chest. There is blood, but no wound. No *new* wound.

"What the hell?" Mark whispers.

"That's what I'd like to know!" Rory snaps, though Mark can't hear him.

Vivienne's body spasms.

Blood seeps out from a fresh scar on her throat, more blood than Hammond had let, and the scar winds all the way around her neck.

Dana's second gasp is wetter, tears audible. Vivienne doesn't appear to be breathing anymore.

"You friggin' *idiot* bitch!" Rory snarls. "I'm not letting you die, either!"

Mark puts his hand to her chest, ear to her mouth, but no one present has magic in any real quantity. No one here can *do anything*. So it falls to him, of fucking course.

Rory pushes through Mark, and, steeling himself for only a moment, dives into Vivienne's body.

...He's not even sure if you *can* possess a dead body.

She can't be dead, he tells himself, and when he rights himself out of the tumble into Vivienne's headspace, he finds himself surrounded by nothingness.

Rory looks around, feeling the hairs on the back of his neck rise at the lack of Vivienne.

"I know you're not dead, Viv!" he calls and forces his way in deeper. "This isn't gonna be the time that does you in!"

He's rewarded with a trickle of memories near his feet. Rory follows them, and soon, they grow stronger. Vivienne isn't gone yet. She *can't* be gone yet, because that's not how she works anymore. Neither of them can be gone, and that thought relaxes Rory as he trails along after the memories.

Hearing comes first to him, and in the worst possible way: there's a screech of car tires, then the shrieking of metal on metal. Glass breaking, a single shout, and then just simple, roaring *noise*. That's familiar. Rory swallows past the lump in his throat and is suddenly very grateful for the lack of anything else in here.

Well, it could always be worse. He could relive *his* memory of the crash.

"Viv, you have to be in here somewhere." *You have to be.* "Vivienne! Answer me, bitch!"

Everything about this oddly blank headspace makes him want to ditch, but he can't do that. More memories play their sounds at him (Natalie's soft laughter, Sunshine's meow, Codi's slurred Portuguese, Hayley's chirpy call of their names), but it keeps looping back to the car crash.

He's going to have to follow it. Fucker.

Smell comes to him, and thankfully, it's not that same memory. Sagebrush and someone's aftershave. It's not long then before Rory gains Vivienne's sense of sight, however, and that he *does not* want. He jerks back on instinct when he's in the car, except he can see *himself* sitting there, and Hammond on the other side, teasing him about being in the middle.

"What's it like to be the meat in our sandwich?" Hammond asks with a laugh.

Vivienne giggles and prods Rory, but he can't feel that, yet. She turns, dragging the memory along with her, to look out at the stormy weather.

Rory tries to fight his way out of this memory. *Not this one. Any fucking one but this one.* He'll do a lot for Vivienne, but he can't face the prospect of death again. He can't again—

There's the flare of headlights and the memory becomes both blurry and sharp. Disjointed. That screech of tires again, and then Vivienne whirls around, and Rory finds himself staring at his own scared features. None of them had time to brace, but from this view, he can see that Vivienne had been trying to cast before the other car hit them. He himself remembers that Hammond had grabbed his hand.

When the car crashes into their taxi, that's when Rory finds Vivienne's sense of touch again.

It's not pain he feels. Rory finds himself cold, not freezing, but entirely numb. It's frighteningly familiar.

The entire memory shudders when Vivienne *finally* sucks in a breath. It's like color rushing back into the world. Light pours in through the broken window and Rory can hear shouts as they try to drag the nearest—Vivienne—out. Vivienne reaches for him, just a twitch of one of her hands combined with a flood of *please help him first*, but Rory's memory self isn't looking at her, frozen with horror above his own body.

Rory is abruptly kicked out of the memory.

He staggers backward, heaving in lungfuls of breath that he doesn't need anymore. His heart rate—stolen from Vivienne's memories—is through the roof and he wants to vomit.

"Vivienne, please, stop thinking about death. I need to help you, but I can't friggin' work through this *again*." *I can't stand that again.* It's selfish to think, but he's always been a selfish prick. That's what got them into this mess.

Rory backs out, trading it for a dunk into what must be the Dreamlands.

Emotions seep more clearly into the memories, tainting his view of them, which means he has to be getting close. Hammond is beside Vivienne, joking about dead man's blood, holding an *ugly* rifle, and Rory sighs when he feels the discomfort the remark gives her. It's pleasantly normal, if he can ignore the unease permeating the memory. So this is recent. This one just happened.

The memory shatters under its own stress when *something* swipes at them.

"Viv, what happened? I need you to talk to me, I need to know what fucking *happened* to you! Is Ham still back there?!" he calls again, and no answer, save for the cacophony of other memories surging around him like surf.

It's getting more difficult to steer himself. Rory rubs his arms, bracing himself again, and tells himself that it'll be *fine*. He's been a spirit for long enough not to get lost in a few memories. (Even if they're familiar and painful and come close to triggering him—)

Rory trips into the next memory, startled by the loud sound of a dragon's roar, and finds himself back in the Dreamlands.

...Except not.

It takes him a few moments to align with Vivienne within the memory, but this place is nothing like that one he just saw. This is full of color and sensation, and Vivienne's presence echoes around him. He can feel things in the memories again, but what worries him is a distinct lack of feeling *here*, whenever here is—*this must be her first visit*, he realizes.

Her memory tugs him along, and Rory realizes she's crawling, unable to stand.

"H-Hay...! Hayley?" Vivienne sobs, looking around, and the sound brings a nightgaunt. Rory reacts on reflex, trying to pull Vivienne up, raising his arms to defend himself, but Vivienne just yelps and creates a fissure in the ground between them. They fall.

Rory tumbles out of the memory, losing his balance this time, and comes to a stop when his back hits something solid. He swipes his hair out of his eyes and twists around, finally finding Actual Vivienne.

...Or maybe not. Vivienne, sitting with her knees drawn up to her chest, mutely watching a memory from outside it, is hardly visible with all the *light* surrounding her. No, *coming* from her. She's the opposite of the thing they were fighting in the Dreamlands.

There are hints of color to her—her hair's light tips have a clearer shine than her cheeks, and there's the dark red of blood which stains her throat and chest—and areas without the light, too. Her eyes appear darker for the contrast, and runes line her fingers and wrists, with a large one over her heart.

Vivienne says nothing to him. Rory slowly leans away from her, cautious, but unable to help but smile at finding her. Everything else can be secondary. No more creepy memories, for the love of fuck.

"...Viv, you're still here," he finally says.

She nods and draws her knees tighter to her chest, concealing the mark there. The memory in front of them is indistinct, but Rory grasps flashes of it. The smell of pancakes, Sunshine getting flour in his fur, and Hayley's voice.

"This was two hours before she died. Before *we* died," Vivienne tells him. Her voice sounds far away, but at least it means it's actually Vivienne, here, and aware of herself. Rory falls to his knees and wraps his arms around her.

"You're alright, oh my friggin' god. I thought this wouldn't work—we don't have anyone magical with us," Rory grumbles into her cold skin. He lets out a shaky breath and tries to calm the panic buzzing through him, but a loud laugh from the memory breaks it and he lets out his own watery, tear-filled laugh, too. "You're alright, Vivienne. Thank god."

"I would have come back on my own without magic. Probably," Vivienne replies tonelessly. "You didn't have to come in here after me."

"How about a 'thanks'! You were *dead* and I came in here to friggin' save you!"

"The binding spell on you and Ham wouldn't break for another—"

Rory forces her out at arm's length and resists the urge to shake her, because *goddamn*, that is the last thing on his mind right now. "That's *not* what I'm worried about! And how *dare* you, Vivienne. How dare you think I'd only fucking come in here to *use* you!"

She looks away, but mumbles, "I'm sorry."

"Mark and Dana are worried, too. And is Ham still in the Dreamlands?"

For the first time since he found her, Vivienne's expression changes; she starts, eyes flying wide with alarm, and says, "He must be. He can't—he can't die there, it's using a vorpal sword to fight us. It injured him! I have to get back there!"

"*You're* injured!" Rory snaps back.

"You're his anchor, you can't go in after him. Just give me a moment, and I'll get back on my own. We have the blood there now, so that should work on it, and—!" she babbles. When she tries to stand, she sags against Rory, and they both topple over into the memory beside them.

"—did you even get it on you? Sunny, you know you shouldn't be on the counter, but especially when mama's cooking *actual* food," Hayley scolds the cat on her shoulder.

"He's light-colored, you can hardly see it from here," replies the Vivienne sitting at the small kitchen table. Rory isn't drawn to her role, and instead stands in the living room, one arm around the real Vivienne.

"If you want cat hair in your pancakes, fine, fine!" Hayley says, nose in the air. "Sunny, go shed on her plate, okay?"

The yellow cat jumps down from her shoulder and winds his way through the ingredients to Vivienne's plate. Memory-Vivienne scrunches up her nose, but she's laughing. Hayley scoops up her familiar before he can make it that far.

"We should be going back over the spells right now, not trying to cook."

"*Trying*? I'll have you know I'm a fantastic cook," Hayley declares, pointing her spatula at her. Memory-Vivienne scoffs. Rory feels actual-Vivienne tremble next to him. "Anyway," Hayley sings, "we need to have our strength up for this! That means lots and lots of carbs!"

"We need to leave," Vivienne murmurs, but doesn't move. Her too-dark eyes are stuck on Hayley, tracking her every movement. "We need to get out of this memory."

"We've been saving our strength and magic for a week solid, Hayley. I don't *want* a lot of carbs. I'll either throw it up or feel bloated during the entire process," memory-Vivienne drawls, flipping a page in her notebook.

"How can we leave this?" Rory asks, looking around the apartment. Moving is like fighting through water, but he makes it to the front door. It's not locked, but it won't open.

"You won't have my food baby?" Hayley exclaims in mock dismay.

"We need to get out of here," actual-Vivienne repeats, voice rising in panic. She finally moves, whirling around, eyes scanning the apartment for *any* way out. The memory warps with her emotional state, but they aren't kicked out.

Hayley wipes her hands on her apron and continues, "I'm so hurt! So you'll help me write and cast a spell to summon a Door, but you won't have my food baby. I think Sunshine wants a little sister, Vivi."

"Shouldn't you be asking Nat for that?" memory-Vivienne asks with a roll of her eyes, but Rory barely hears the words.

He'd stalled on *Door*.

The real Vivienne has her eyes squeezed shut, shoulders tense, and won't face him.

Rory turns from him to the memory continuing to play out (Hayley points out that two cis girls can't make babies, no matter how much magic they use, and Vivienne cackles over the idea of Mark and Natalie procreating) and tries to process *Door*.

She had definitely said that. She had definitely said that with the inflection that could only mean—

"*That's* what you were trying to do with her?" Rory croaks. His eyes burn, but no tears come, and instead he's forced to stand there and try not to hyperventilate or throw up or any of those things a ghost shouldn't do anymore. Too many of Vivienne's still-living emotions poison the memory.

"It wasn't just for you," Vivienne replies, tone pleading, "I promise, Rory, it wasn't just for you. We were already doing stupid shit like that—"

"You." He clenches his fists until they hurt. He relishes the pain. "You said you were trying to open a portal to another realm, Viv. You didn't tell me it was a *Door*."

Maybe he shouldn't have come in after her. Of all the things Rory has gone through in his life and non-life, he would have been perfectly content believing that lie (that *lie*, how can he ever look at her the same way again) for as long as he still existed. He has a thick skin for a lot of things, but this doesn't appear to be one of them.

Hayley died for this. Hayley died and Vivienne died and Vivienne is messed up and *it was all for a Door*. At this point in the timeline, Rory would have only been dead for a few months. He was already bonded to Hammond, but Vivienne had told them it was a temporary contract, just "until something better can be figured out".

"You were trying to bring me back to life," Rory forces out, although the words said aloud makes him want to die all over again. *How could they*. Not for him. They did this for *him* and he wants to kill both of them for it.

"It wasn't just for you! Remember, please remember, how into research we were. We wanted the academic fame, we just wanted to do something big!" Vivienne begs.

Hayley and memory-Vivienne pass through Rory, but he feels nothing. The smell of pancakes and syrup nauseate him. The memory fades, dripping off back into the blankness, and he and Vivienne are left staring at each other.

Rory doesn't know what to say. He's not sure he can believe anything she says now.

"I don't know what happened, that much *is* true. Hayley disappeared and I woke up in the Dreamlands," Vivienne says weakly, dark eyes welling up with tears, and Rory turns so he doesn't have to look at her. He's *disgusted*.

At *best*, he was a science experiment for a necromancer and a spellwriter. At worst, he caused the death of two friends and permanently fucked up one of them.

"None of it worked. I don't even know what happened to myself! I never told you because—how *could* I? Rory, please, I just didn't want to hurt you further. I didn't want to hurt *anyone* else—"

"Viv, I was *fine* with being dead. I came to terms with it once you and Ham could... Once I realized I wasn't forgotten or alone," Rory mutters. He's more bitter now than when he first died. He's disgusted at himself, too.

"It wasn't your fault. It was—"

The entire mindscape abruptly shakes and tosses them both into the air. Vivienne raises her arms, bracing as she seems to land in another memory, and Rory tries to catch himself in midair.

But then, he's even more suddenly thrown out of Vivienne's body. He scrambles for purchase, trying to maintain his hold, trying to keep up the possession—and then he realizes what he's doing. He gets one last glimpse of Vivienne (normal again, runes fading back to skin tone) and he knows she felt the way he tried to stay. Stay in control of *her* body.

So they're both disgusting. It's all fucking disgusting.

Rory falls through the table and lands in a heap next to Hammond's body. Though he doesn't need to breathe, he feels like he's winded, and he blearily looks up to find Mark performing CPR on Vivienne. Not a moment later, she jerks awake with violent coughing, which soon turns wet with a bloody nose.

"Ow, ow ow *owwww*," Vivienne whines, shoving weakly at Mark to get him off. The psychic responds by throwing his arms around her with a shaky sob of his own.

"Oh my god," Dana mutters, sagging against the back of the couch. She runs a hand over her face, further smearing tear tracks left from her makeup. "Y-You jerk, you said this was an easy job! You didn't say you'd *die*!"

Vivienne looks like a deer caught in the headlights when she notices Dana. Her gaze flicks to Rory, who instead looks at Hammond.

Who's still trapped in the Dreamlands, *alone*.

The portal remains open, but he doesn't know for how much longer, and he doesn't want him alone there with whatever killed Vivienne.

"Wait, Rory, you *can't*," Vivienne begs. Rory ignores her, because how fucking dare she try to order him around right now. "You're his anchor! You have to stay here so he doesn't get lost there. I'll just. Go back." She falters on the last bit, white-faced beneath the scarlet on her mouth and chin. It betrays her reluctance. Even Vivienne, reluctant to save someone?

"*You're* not going anywhere," Mark scolds as he pushes her back down.

"I need to—" Vivienne tries getting up again and ends up clapping a hand over her mouth when she bends at the waist to do so. Mark lets her go with fresh alarm and Vivienne hobbles to the bathroom. She slams the door shut behind her, but it doesn't drown out the retching noises.

"What happened to her?" Dana asks, stepping in the bathroom's direction, but keeping her eyes on Mark.

"I don't know much more than you do," he snaps.

"You definitely know more. She just—she nearly *died*, didn't she? And you revived her? I know what CPR is!" Dana snaps back.

"...I guess," Mark blatantly lies. "Why don't you go ask her for the details? I'm sure she needs someone to rub her back, too."

"I barely know you and I can tell what you're doing," Dana says with narrowed eyes. Rory looks up from Hammond in time to see Mark gulp down one of the potions, eyes defiantly on Dana.

Fiona steps forward with an even angrier expression. "They said you shouldn't go in wherever. You definitely shouldn't *alone*. I can't go in there with you, asshole, so I'm not letting *you*."

"Mark, don't you dare!" Rory starts, leaning into Mark's space. He flinches but doesn't respond. "I know you can sense enough of me to know I'm fucking pissed here! Viv said psychics shouldn't go into the Dreamlands!" *But Ham is there alone.*

"Why can't you go?" Dana asks Fiona.

"Bound to him by blood," she replies, jerking her chin toward Benji, "and I can't astral project."

Mark continues to ignore him, and of course Dana and Fiona can't see, hear, or sense him. But Dana frowns, looking between Mark and Fiona, then holds her hand out.

Mark spares her a disdainful look. "You're new to this, dear, and you'd do more good with Viv right now."

"Hammond is still stuck there, and you have orders not to go there."

"Ooh, 'orders'. I forgot you were military," Mark coos, coming close to venomous. Dana's glare hardens.

"Viv!" Rory yells.

"Vivienne knows binding spells. If you leave me here, I'm sure she can stop you by the time I can bring her back out here," Dana threatens. "I can fight one single magic monster if it means not having Vivienne or you or anyone else beaten up and bloody again."

"Why do you *care*? What if you'll just be a burden?" Mark demands.

"You don't know magic, either. Don't lie to me and say I can't help if you really want to save that woman," Dana responds and points to Brynja's body.

"*Vivienne*, they are going to go into the fucking Dreamlands!" Rory howls and dives for the bathroom. Of fucking course the woman Vivienne was wooing would have a self-sacrificial noble streak. Of fucking course Rory has to turn to Vivienne for help when he really wants to punt her off the roof.

But they *could* save Hammond. Hammond is injured and alone and fighting *something* that scared even Vivienne. Rory stills, turns, and watches the living room instead of heading for the bathroom.

Mark's body crumples against the couch and his spirit steps out of his body. He blinks at Rory. "And I suppose you'll be trying to stop me as well?" he asks coolly.

Dana fumbles for the potion bottle in Mark's hand. She frowns at it for a long moment, torn, but Fiona barks at her, "Don't let the idiot go there alone!"

"*I'm* not going to stop you. Either of you," Rory calmly replies as Dana downs the rest of the potion. "Bring Hammond back to me."

"I thought foxes were supposed to be clever," the calico cat sneers with her tail bottlebrushed behind her. Motes of cat fire dance overhead, casting the forest in flickering, unreliable light. The trees are thin and sparse, needles thick on the ground, and the rest of the scene is black.

The equally black fox is only visible for the gleaming eyes reflecting the firelight. "And you can't be very lucky, can you?" he replies in a silken voice.

"All the luck in the world won't help idiocy."

The fox advances, floating in the air, tail hanging limply beneath him. The cat backs up, fur rising higher, teeth bared. The cat fire coalesces above her in a bright arch.

"You're just so... giving, aren't you? What's wrong with asking for something you're giving away? It only makes others want to take it by force," the fox reasons, approaching again.

And again the cat spirit backs up. Shadows from the firelight dance around them. "Greedy bastard fox," she hisses. "I'll cook you if you don't back off now!"

The soft carpet of the evergreen needles hides both footsteps and the confinement circle beneath it. With a surge of magic, the trap slams shut, and the calico cat is left hurling fire ineffectually at the barrier. A black-haired witch steps out of the shadows, just out of range of the light, and smiles at the fox spirit.

Natalie jars awake when her alarm goes off. Visions don't slip away in the same way that dreams do, but they're hardly concrete memories, so she hastens to grab her notebook on her nightstand and record what she can.

CHAPTER 37

IN WHICH MARK TACKLES THE DREAMLANDS, AND THEY TACKLE RIGHT BACK

Semi-corporeal and in need of a good, soft thing to pet, Christine risks a daytime trip to see Sadie.

Except she doesn't.

She waffles across a dozen city blocks, back and forth too many times, weighing the pros and the cons. There are too many of each; she still can't write out any lists! She could use a good cuddle, especially since she had kind of slept and dreamt again, and she *misses* the nights she would spend curled up with Kirara purring on her lap. Ever since Christine had maybe moved in with Emil, Kirara seems content to let her be.

She *really* doesn't need to be *let be*. She needs support and answers and guidance.

And something soft to pet.

But it's the middle of the afternoon—who knows what Sadie's adoptive family does during the day? The kid is old enough to go to school, but what of the parents? What of anyone else in the apartment building?

Even walking along the sidewalk, occasionally people move out of her way, as if they can *see* her. Christine has yet to test this, and it appears to come and go as much as anything else in her life right now, but what if she can be seen? The last thing she needs is for someone to think she's breaking in to steal a pet ferret.

Christine turns and heads back. She is near enough to Emil's apartment that she isn't totally lost, despite her circular route. It isn't worth the risk of getting caught, especially if she couldn't get out through a wall. She hadn't gotten stuck again—yet—but she is feeling particularly risk-averse right now.

So she ends up in a small park. The trees are mostly bare, orange and yellow in patches, but the grass is still green. It's empty this time of day. She goes to sit on a bench to mope, but she phases through the wood and into the concrete beneath.

Christine groans into her black hands.

She's direly in need of a good cry, a good meal, and a good nap. She can only control one of those on her own, but all the crying she's been doing is exhausting. She wonders when she'll *feel* dehydrated.

She floats along the park path, face in her hands, willing the tears to come just so she can get them *over with*. But they don't. Like everything else in her life, it doesn't matter what she wants. She's too tired to even cry. Logan would laugh.

If he were still there.

But he isn't, so.

She nearly bumps into the man, unused to being tangible and uncaring of where she was going.

Christine hops back on reflex, peering up through her fingers to the all-too-familiar pointy nose and gleaming eyes of the fox spirit.

"You know, you must be *particularly* lucky. Not a single soul has agreed to pursue you on my dime," the fox spirit tells her jovially.

Christine slowly backs away. If Emil *had* broken his nose, it's healed perfectly. He is dressed as impeccably as always, in full black, smile charming and vile. She glances around for *anyone* else nearby.

He reaches for her, and she swats him away on reflex.

He hisses and draws back, sleeve shredded, tawny skin weeping red.

"Oh, is this a new look for you? I'd thought them decorative," he sneers, holding his bleeding hand. "If you are set on becoming a filthy demon, then why not give the collar to
. me? You won't be needing it."

"Demons aren't—filthy. But I'm not becoming one," Christine replies, faltering only briefly. She recalls Sam's help on Halloween. And she certainly doesn't want to agree with the jerk before her. "Leave me alone!" she adds.

"Not a witch, not a youkai, not a hunger spirit, nor any fae. You are singularly *annoying* to hunt alone, small spirit."

"M-Maybe you could take that as a sign. This isn't *ever* going to be yours," she snaps back. She keeps one hand around the bell at her throat, the other with claws extended. She doesn't know how to fight with *claws*—doesn't know how to fight at all—but they seem sharp enough to be a deterrent, regardless.

"You are new to the rules of the world, small spirit, but here is a very important one. I *always* get what I want." He leans in to punctuate this, baring sharp teeth, and she swings at him.

She slashes him across the face. Three bright red lines open up across his cheek, across his nose, cutting into his lip, and Christine watches in horror as he reels back with blood seeping through his fingers as he clutches his injuries. She had done it on reflex. She has slapped guys before.

She can fight back.

But Christine fearfully discovers only now that she doesn't *want* to.

He snarls at her, animalistic, but as before, he vanishes instead of retaliating. *He* is the noncombatant here. Christine sinks to her knees in the cold grass, staring down at the red streaked across one hand. The tears finally come.

· · · ● · ● · · · ·

Mark is absolutely not prepared for whatever the Dreamlands are supposed to be. He wasn't prepared to see his own body on the floor, either, or the portal Vivienne had opened. He is also not prepared to act as a tour guide to a mystery realm to someone *very* new to magic.

But, Mark must privately admit, he is glad that he's not doing this alone.

He ducks into the Dreamlands, Dana on his heels, and cannot help a gasp. His dreams have never looked like this. Everything is blinding, crystal or salt, white and reflective and crumbling with their first stumbling steps.

He feels too-solid and not real enough. Mark looks at his hands, expecting to see through them, but he looks as he always has. Dana, behind him, appears *very* queasy but at least as present as he is.

What was so wrong with bringing a psychic into the Dreamlands? So far, it doesn't seem terrible. He can do this.

Sensation smacks him like a brick wall.

His spine snaps straight and his mind clamps down on itself, shutting out all the information. A migraine screams in on the tail end of the oversensitivity. Mark screws his eyes shut and shoves his hands over his ears, but roaring white noise assaults him, punctuated by shrieks and groans and a single, clear note.

He turns on instinct toward its source.

He takes a step toward the ringing note. It could be a scream. It sounds like it needs someone. The salt-earth cracks beneath his foot, spiderwebbing into a deeper and grander fissure. He thinks he hears Dana shout, so far away, muffled by layers of wool and distance and dreams.

Mark takes another jerky step forward. The ground heaves beneath him, then melts into dust a moment later and whips up around him. The world becomes his treadmill; every staggered step forward brings the world rushing by. Colors and sensations and that ringing smear together in a cacophony his brain fights desperately to mute.

His next step takes him to a monochromatic sunset over a cliff, a waterfall of moss green to his right. A forest spreads out beneath him, a mix of tropical and cold-weather trees, none of them the right texture or size.

Mark groans and the waterfall freezes beside him. His knees buckle, and he falls, but the ground doesn't come up to meet him. There's another feeling of vertigo, longer this time—then finally, he faceplants into soft grass.

With incredible effort, he rolls himself onto his back. The grass above him sways in an unfelt breeze, ends furling and unfurling like tiny worms.

Everything is *too much.*

Mark regrets setting foot in this place and wonders if his mind will actually implode within his skull. As dimly as his mind can work on anything that isn't fighting for its life, he recognizes Vivienne had been right. He can't remember what she'd been right about. He can't even recall what she looks like.

A faceless, skeletal figure leans over into his vision. He can't summon the effort to react.

Nightgaunt! his mind screams when he belatedly recognizes it. It makes his migraine ring around his head like a bell. It smells strongly of rot as it reaches down, claws aiming for his wide-open eyes, but Mark remains pinned in place by the weight of an entire realm pressing on his brain.

Bad idea, bad idea, bad idea.

The nightgaunt's hand falls onto his face.

The nightgaunt pulls back, not-face turning quizzically to the stump where its arm had just been, and Mark jerks his head to throw the severed hand off. When his vision clears from the dizzying movement, the nightgaunt's head falls off of its shoulders, shattering the grass when it drops beside its body.

Mark doesn't feel relieved. He props himself up on his elbows, kicks away the melting carcass, and finds another figure standing in the chest-high grass—he can't look directly at it, though what he does see is that the grass is charred where it touches it. The figure is blinding, seemingly made of white fire, and even with his eyes squeezed shut the glow hurts.

"What...?" he begins, but the sound of his voice shatters the ground beneath them. Mark startles when he sinks, but he doesn't fall through.

So he can't talk here? Everything is too much, but he thought that, because of that, *he* wouldn't be too much.

But if he still has power here, he just has to use it.

"You're human, aren't you? *Shuggoth*?" the flaming figure asks. Something thrums beneath its voice. It makes the hairs on the back of his neck rise. "Ooh, ooh, your mind is—interesting, that is a good word for it. You're a..." It trails off thoughtfully, but comes back a moment later, as if recalling the term, "A psychic!"

Mark cracks open an eye to peek at the figure again. The grass between them has died away, crumbling into foul-smelling ash, and he is not reassured when he sees that it's fully humanoid. Maybe faintly feminine, but the brightness makes it difficult to see where its body ends.

Something about this specific pounding in his head rings familiar, but he's never seen such a creature before, in the Dreamlands or out of them.

"It's been a long time since I've seen anything other than nightgaunts. Oh, how long *has* it been...?" It trails off again, twisting away with a thoughtful cock of its head, and Mark can see that it *does* have eyes beneath the glow, two circles of comparative darkness. When it turns back to speak again, he sees it has a mouth, too, and he has to wonder just what else is concealed by its light. "Nightgaunts taste terrible!"

The bottom falls out of his stomach and Mark lunges to his feet. He overbalances and faceplants, and ends up falling through the long grass and into warm water. "Out!" he shouts. The water boils away, leaving him raw.

The figure lands lightly on its feet beside him, another hole in the grass above them showing where it followed.

"I've never gotten to eat a psychic before," it tells him conversationally.

"Get away!" he hoarsely barks and the darkness surrounding them blinks out in favor of a warm campfire glow, minus actual fire. The thing in front of him remains unmoved.

"I have been trapped here for a long, long time, *shuggoth*," it tells him, voice dipping lower. It advances.

The surrounding orange glow flares up in response to his panic, twisting toward the figure like claws, but it bats it all away. Mark backpedals, willing the environment to do what he wants, but he doesn't have a steep enough learning curve to put up a fight.

He turns to flee, concentrating on *Dana, please!* but the bright figure flickers into existence in front of him.

Vivienne had been right. He shouldn't have come here. He still remembers that much.

It takes one last step toward him, growing until it towers over him, and its jaws unhinge when it leans down toward his face.

••••••••••

"Mark!" Dana yells when the man disappears in front of her. She teeters on the ground he'd upheaved, then leaps to a flatter spot. The moment she leaves, the slab of crystal disintegrates into glittering bubbles.

She stares at the bubbles. They freeze and drop to the ground like lead. Long, billowing plants spring up around them, waving like flags, *reaching* for her.

Dana scrambles back. This had been a bad idea. Now she's alone, Hammond lost and injured, and Mark lost and... weird. Not to mention the weird-ass place *this* is. "*Mark!*" she shouts again, hands cupped around her mouth, but her voice only echoes.

It bounces back to her in a pink haze. She's in over her head.

Dreamlands, they had called it. So like dream logic? Dana grasps that it vaguely runs on reactive, *weird* logic, so she skitters away with caution. She only glimpsed the direction Mark had zipped off in, and she does not know where Hammond may be. She highly doubts a compass would work here.

She wishes she knew what direction Vivienne and Hammond had gone in.

To her amazement, she notices footprints—they must have been old, left by the pair in question. The soft indents fill up with a thick red liquid. Dana doesn't want to think of blood, but it stands out starkly against the crystalline ground. A path.

It's like a dream, she thinks, *so passive wish fulfillment?* She has never had lucid dreams, though she'd heard of them.

To test this, she thinks of a handgun.

To her shock, one drops out of the ground in front of her, landing in a pile of purple goo. She carefully picks it up, only to discover it's a water gun.

Beretta M9, Dana sourly corrects, and it melts off its plastic shell to reveal a neon orange cap gun.

Dana decides that this place is bullshit. She tosses it aside.

She creeps forward, following the footprints, ignoring how the red liquid fills her steps in turn. At least they can find their way back. She wishes Mark had left a similar trail, but nothing pops out of the ground to help her with that.

The crumbly ground gives way to something like ice. Slippery and hard, and when she falls on her ass, she finds it moist, too.

She hears a terrible *crunch* and sinks several inches.

Dana lunges to the side just as everything gives way beneath her. It falls in a shiny cascade and stops when it has created a perfect circle before her. Dana, clinging to the edge, kicks it to make sure it won't fall further, but her section is stable.

She finds the footprints again, and not a moment later, she finds Hammond.

Dana hadn't seen him in the distance, nor seen any movement, nor heard anything. She actually *jumps* when she finds him.

Contrary to everyone else's panic, there is no fight happening.

Hammond sits cross-legged, absolutely *covered* in blood, but otherwise looks quite bored. He's rebraiding his hair when he notices her.

Beside him is a long-haired woman in the middle of a glowing circle on the ground. She looks furious, but makes no move to attack. Brilliant teal scales cover most of her arms and back. She's going to assume that that's Brynja, somehow, but she does not remember getting the half-lizard memo.

"*Dana?*" Hammond asks with a suspicious squint.

"O-Oh, good, I found you," Dana croaks and collapses to her knees. The ground, luckily, does not disappear again.

"What are you doing here? You don't belong here! No offense intended."

"I don't think I belong here, either. But, uh, ta-da. I'm momentarily your rescue squad. Are you... okay?"

"This isn't my blood," Hammond dismisses with a wave of his hand.

"Friend of yours?" the woman in the circle growls.

"Yes, and unfortunately, not magic. You didn't happen to bring a dragonskin in with you, did you?" he asks.

"No, why would we? When Vivienne came back, we only knew that you were fighting, and injured, and there was a lot of panic," Dana says. Her gaze slides sideways to the Brynja woman, who she has just noticed has stubby *wings* jutting out from her back, plus a tail lashing angrily behind her. Definitely did *not* get the half-*dragon* memo.

"We?" Hammond and Brynja chorus.

"Mark came in with me, but he... disappeared? I don't know, it happened really fast."

Brynja growl-groans into her clawed, scaled hands. "The *idiot*! Now he will die, too! *Argh*, stupid, foolish human. You two, reinforce this circle, then retreat. I need someone magical."

"What, *exactly*, is going on here?" Dana asks of the bloodied man and the trapped half-dragon woman. She warily circles Brynja, noting the mix of scales and light human skin, but Dana's thought process completely derails when she finds the body.

A chubby woman's body, dressed in a soft cream sweater and a blue maxi skirt, missing its head.

The head lays about two feet away, black hair with grey tips strewn all over, cute blue headband still in place. The face mercifully is tilted away.

The body has been sliced open, *gutted*, like an animal, a large sword still stuck in its chest. It helps to think of it as *the body* and *it*, because while it looks like Vivienne, of course it can't *be* Vivienne. Vivienne was still alive.

Vivienne is alive. *Now.*

"She... actually died?" Dana asks breathlessly.

"She said it was psychic damage. But that sword..." Hammond glares at it, mouth a thin, grim line. "That changed things."

"It was from your realm," Brynja says, also eyeing the sword with great disdain.

Dana wants to feel sick, or shocked, or *anything* but the numb she feels when the realizations wash over her. Vivienne died. Hammond is sitting in *her* blood.

Vivienne was fine. Vivienne *is* fine.

Dana wants, more than anything else in any world, to not have to deal with this. It's too much. She really shouldn't have asked to come along. Is *this* what the world of magic entails?

She approaches the body, careful not to look at the head, and wraps her hand around the sword's hilt. "Wait, that will—" Brynja begins, just as Dana tugs it free with an awful *snick* sound.

"I didn't hurt Vivienne, did I?!" Dana asks in alarm. Can she put it back? What does the least harm in this otherworldly situation?

Brynja stares, hard, at her. "It's not hurting you?"

Dana notices that Brynja's scaled hands are blistered. She regards the sword with growing unease. "No?" She has *a lot* of thoughts about holding something that hurt Vivienne, but it doesn't feel any stranger than anything else in this realm.

Brynja lets out a sigh that sounds as if she's been holding in for *years*. "Alright then. We won't need magic or my pelt. We were lucky."

"Why *did* you need a dragonskin? Why do you have those lying around?" Dana asks.

"I'm still possessed," Brynja deadpans. Dana hastily steps away. "Good, you have sense. You are smarter than Mark and Vivienne."

"What about me?" Hammond huffs.

"I am still reserving judgment."

"I got us this far!" he indignantly exclaims.

"And we would both be stuck here, until your magic ran out, or another nightgaunt came to chew on you. But now we have a solution. To be honest, newcomer, this is panicked guesswork. But this is our best shot, you understand? Don't blame me if a very angry god comes back soon."

"That is *tremendously* reassuring. Thanks!" Dana creakily exclaims.

"Right now, I am still possessed, but the dragonhide and this confinement circle suppress it. You said you're not a witch?" she asks.

Dana shakes her head. "I learned about all of this magic shit *very* recently."

"Right. Original way it is. Here's the plan: the bloody one is going to dispel the confinement circle. I'm going to force a dragon transformation as far as I can, and that should buy you enough time to stab me in the heart—"

Dana throws the sword down at once. Its *clang* somehow sounds musical. "I'm not stabbing anyone with that thing, and this sounds like the *worst* rescue plan I have ever heard."

"That's a vorpal sword, and you are the only one who can touch the vorpium—"

"Why can't we do *literally* anything else? And why can I touch it?" She certainly doesn't want to touch that thing more than she has to.

"Genetic ability? Luck? Hell if I know." Brynja looks harassed, and she hunches her shoulders, flapping her partial wings to stretch them within the small circle. She takes a steeling breath and tells them, "Let's discuss that later and instead concentrate on escaping the very angry god, yes? If it reassures you, this will not kill me. Probably. I'm made of a sterner stuff than you humans. It's good that the blade still burns me—this plan will work. You won't kill me, and you won't kill my ex-master, but this is our best course of action for what we have now."

"Can't someone just... banish it, or something?" Dana pleads. Vivienne had said that was part of her job description. She knows it's a thing.

"No one in any world has that much magic," Brynja snorts. "This circle would not even come close to confining my ma—this thing if it weren't trying to take my body for itself."

"I still do *not* agree to this," Dana says.

"We have no other option. You want to stop an apocalypse in your realm, don't you? This is how. Strike during momentary weakness. Gods don't offer that often," she dryly advises. Her lashing tail betrays her agitation.

Dana is definitely going to have A Talk with Vivienne and Mark, because she hadn't signed up for any of this, and a *little* more preparation wouldn't have been such a terrible thing. *This is what Vivienne deals with regularly?* She doubts this is a regular job—right?

Dana must take Brynja's word for it.

She doesn't know what else she *can* do in this situation. She can't use magic, she hardly knows what's going on, and they still have to find Mark and get home. Dana grits her teeth as she picks the vorpal sword back up, and hopes that it's as easy as simply stabbing Brynja.

I want to go back to the zoo, she thinks dismally as she approaches Brynja. Brynja's expression has softened, and she doesn't look quite so intimidating when she's not scowling or snapping at them. *So. She's not human. There is an evil god. Vivienne can't die.* Oh yes, she vastly prefers getting overwhelmed by jackalopes and unicorns to this.

"Ready?" Brynja asks softly. Dana nods. "Alright. Break the circle. And aim for the heart," she says with a gesture to her bare chest, devoid of scales.

"It's in the same place as a human heart, right?"

"*Yes.* Don't be afraid of hurting me. The goal is to do enough abrupt damage that it forces it out of me."

"For the record, I'm still not happy about this," Dana says and raises her arm.

Hammond crouches by the other side of the circle, locking eyes with her from across it. Slowly, he nods, and the glow from the runes dies.

Brynja leans back, giving Dana a clean shot, and scales crawl up her shoulders, over her tattoos. She's growing a second set of wings when Dana plunges the sword into her chest.

Her body gives shockingly easily, and Dana briefly wonders just how sharp the blade is. Brynja's spine snaps rigid, body freezing up while the surrounding skin burns.

Dana goes to tug the blade out again, but Brynja asks her, "*Zhro? Uln naflyhri uh'e r'luh geb. Hrii? Ep nilgh'ri, nnny 'bthnk...?*"

The words pierce her ears like something physical. Dana lets go of the sword in favor of clamping her hands over her ears. She dimly hears Hammond shout and Brynja's raspy laughter. Dana looks back up and finds Brynja pulling the sword from her chest with a sharp-toothed grin.

That went about as well as Dana had figured.

She backpedals—only to trip over Vivienne's body.

Brynja stands over her, wound not even *bleeding*, teal scales dripping off like water as her body slowly darkens. "*Such a good attempt, shuggoth-grah'n. But not as good as the exorcist blood. You will not try again,*" the deity informs her.

Their positions are reversed now; the black silhouette of Brynja raises the vorpal sword over Dana. The sandpaper ground cracks and the figure staggers when a crossbow bolt finds itself lodged through its throat—and the arm holding the sword melts off of its body, the sword clattering to the ground.

Dana scrambles to her feet and dashes over to Hammond, with a crossbow, but they're *all* looking at the missing arm with the same level of confusion.

Mark strides up like he hasn't been missing the entire time.

"I was wondering what all of this noise was," he breezily remarks.

"You brought a psychic into the Dreamlands. And now the psychic is going to kick its ass for us. I can't believe this is happening," Hammond mutters, but he sounds relieved. Is Dana allowed to feel relieved yet?

Mark gives him a strange look over his shoulder. "Was I supposed to fare that badly? I thought I did pretty well," he replies. The ground trembles when he raises his hand. The night-sky figure, arm regrowing, stoops to pick up the blade with its other hand.

Its other arm falls off.

The possessed figure narrows its white, empty eyes and spits, "*Nalloignyth. Wgah'n 'bthnk ah?*"

Mark puts a finger to his lips and answers, "*Ya nafhtagn, Yaehathal. Yyar hai.*"

"*How foolish the shuggothh are,*" it says. It sounds *tired,* resigned.

"How foolish *you* are," he replies, and with a single step, he's in front of it. Mark smiles as he puts his arm through its chest, just as the sword had done moments earlier.

The darkness sloughs off and Brynja slumps against him, unmoving.

Mark gingerly pulls his arm back out, murmuring under his breath, and Dana has no idea what to make of that.

"Did Mark just take out a god," Hammond whispers, apparently sharing the sentiment.

Natalie flips through her vision notebooks, searching out patterns. Some, she has worked out. If there are others, they elude her. She doesn't dare voice her suspicions to anyone without hard evidence. She has had too many wild goose chases.

But isn't he planning something big? Something drastic, something dangerous?

All signs point to a screaming Yes.

As if brought on by recalling past visions, Natalie's head spins, then she slips into a new one.

Hayley grins, crinkling her emerald eyes. Her cheer is clearly forced. "Listen, listen, Vivi! This isn't all terrible, promise! I've been through it, too—okay, it was utter hell, and I never want to think of it again."

"Not helping!" Vivienne wails from beneath a blanket pile.

"But now we're prepared! Second time's the charm, right?" Hayley is quick to soothe. She sits on the edge of the bed and tries to tug the blankets away, but they don't budge in the least. "Viviiiii, c'mon! No one's better at rationalizing black magic bullshit than you!"

"This isn't black magic," comes the muffled response.

"Sunny wants you to come out. Sunny says he misses his papa," Hayley tries, though the cat is nowhere in sight.

"'m hungry," Vivienne grumbles.

"Okay, okay, we can order, like, five million pizzas! If you'll just come out of there and talk to me!"

The vision fades with Hayley laughingly pulling on the blanket pile. Natalie wakes with papers stuck to her cheek and her nose dripping blood onto her notebook.

It hurts to see Hayley again. She wishes it would stop.

CHAPTER 38

IN WHICH THERE IS SUPPOSEDLY A HAPPY ENDING

Everyone is really fucking lucky Vivienne likes them all too much to kill them the second they return through the portal.

(They're the second thing to come through; the first had been another nightgaunt she sacrificed on the spot to keep it open longer. Mark's kitchen is a disaster site from throwing together a restoration potion.)

Vivienne fidgets, watching Mark and Dana try to shove Brynja's spirit back into her body. It's an awkward affair—she's pretty sure that's not how they should do it at *all*—but it won't hurt things *further*.

Since those two are busy, Vivienne figures she's entitled to throwing herself at Hammond and Rory and sobbing into their shirts.

A beat too late, she remembers Rory's still mad, but to the ghost's credit, he doesn't shove her immediately off.

"I-I'm sorry, I'm sorry, I'm fine. I just—I'm really glad you all came back," Vivienne mumbles as she shifts to put both her arms around Hammond. Even as a temporary ghost, he is blessedly solid to her. "Just let me cry into your hair. Jesus, you reek of blood."

"Do *not* get me started on blood, Viv. I practically had to roll around in your organs to keep it off me long enough to—"

"I *will* throw up on you," she threatens, because the last thing she needs right now is hearing about her death. And leaving Hammond alone there. And everything about today. She had woken up excited to go on a *date*. "You smell and you're *back*. Let me look at that wound before you go back to your body."

Rory hovers beside them as Vivienne peels the blood-soaked robe away. She doesn't quite know what to make of the *scar* she sees there. It matches the one on his physical body. Vivienne clicks her tongue and runs her fingers over it, and Hammond flinches like the wound is still fresh. "Okay, that still hurts. And it ruined my tattoo."

Vivienne's eyes find the curling black lines of the anchor between their binding. "At least *you* don't have dead man's blood," she jokes to cover her worry. She'll just have to hope it doesn't interfere when she redoes it. *When I somehow redo it.* Because she doesn't have enough magic—

"Stop the sad look!" Hammond declares and pinches her cheeks, forcing her to smile. "We *made it*, Viv. Mark didn't explode in the Dreamlands, *I* got to confine a god, and your girlfriend got to stab a god. We all survived! Even you, in your own way. Oh, and Mark oneshotted the god thing so have fun talking *that* over with him."

"He... *what*?" Vivienne echoes.

She turns to find Brynja back in one piece, though her breathing is ragged. Mark has his hands on his hips, looking rather proud of himself, and Dana sinks onto the arm of the couch—and then through it with a squawk.

She went after them, Vivienne thinks, heart seizing painfully. *Dana went after my friends, into danger, and I didn't stop her.*

"Mark Ito, you owe us *so much fucking money!*" Rory shouts, cutting neatly across her thoughts. "I want hazard pay on top of double rates *and* a bonus."

Mark blinks over at them like he's noticing them for the first time. There's something in how his gaze lingers on Vivienne's face that makes her uncomfortable. She's going to spend the next two months getting Mark back to normal, she just *knows* it.

"Okay," Mark says simply.

"...Are *you* okay?" Vivienne suspiciously asks. She reaches up and grabs his face, peering up into his eyes. Aside from large pupils, his dark brown eyes don't give her much information. Mark smells like raw magic, but tainted into something sour and unpleasant, and she wrinkles her nose. "Ew, you smell, too. What happened in there?"

"Not much," he replies and averts his eyes.

"Don't make me tell Nat on you. Today was utter bullshit and if *anything* else happens, we need to tell others," Vivienne tells him. Mark's gaze snaps back to her at Natalie's name. He stares at her, mouth working on the syllables of her name, and then he looks up at her hair.

Mark pets her, *what the fuck.*

"What are you doing?!"

"Oh, nothing, nothing, your hair just looks fabulous today," Mark says cheerily and continues carding his fingers through the grey ends. "It almost reminds me of something. Like it's off, somehow. How weird, right?"

Fiona pries them apart with the butt of her shotgun. Vivienne skitters away, because the Proper Response to a shotgun anywhere near you is to back the fuck up. Mark, on the other hand, stares in confusion. "Alright, you clearly need a nap, asshole," Fiona growls.

How does one take care of an addled psychic post-Dreamlands? The adrenaline should lead to a crash soon enough. Vivienne chews on her lip. "Let Brynja sleep out here, and you go to bed. I don't want to hear a peep from you until tomorrow."

"You're spending the night?" Mark asks (though Fiona nods like she agrees with the decision).

Vivienne gestures to all the mess. The closing portal, the kitchen, the ash on the floor from the sacrifices, and all the unconscious people strewn about. (And she's going to steal Mark's bathtub for herself. She deserves a two-hour soak.)

Vivienne takes a deep breath when she turns to face Dana.

Dana meets her eyes—a good sign—but she doesn't seem keen on rushing forward for a relieved hug. ...Not that Vivienne wants her to or anything. Honestly, she can't bring himself to think about touching Dana in any sense right now; she *came back from the dead* in front of her. She's normally pretty good about keeping the z-word out of her mind, but right now, she just... doesn't want to deal with this.

Her eyes find the vorpal sword on the carpet and she nearly chokes on her breath. Vivienne understands why they brought it with them, since it's valuable, but *fuck* she doesn't want to deal with this at all.

But she has to, because she's a mature, responsible adult, and she has to make sure Dana is alright with what happened—

A shout of panic interrupts them. Vivienne whirls around—Brynja's unconscious, Fiona is pointing her shotgun at her still form, Mark's fine, and it turns out to be Hammond, back in his body and looking at Rory with open fear. From the way his shirt lays against his collarbone, Vivienne can see the reddish scar from his wound cutting through the ink.

Before she can ask what's wrong, Hammond reaches over and passes his hand *through* Rory.

Oh no.

No, no no no.

They were supposed to have *time*.

Vivienne nearly trips over herself and grabs onto Rory when she gets near. Still tangible to her.

She pulls Hammond's collar down and looks at the wound again, minus all the blood. It's a neat line that almost cuts the anchoring tattoo in half, mostly healed. So it's not the wound itself, but the mark. Rory makes a short, choked sound in the back of his throat.

It was a vorpal sword, but does that mean it can cut through spells? She doesn't have the magic or knowledge to rebuild the spell right now, and she doesn't know anyone else who would be willing or able to deal with that much necromancy.

She's going to look up vorpium and dig out her original notes, but none of that will be *fast*. She does not know how she can fix this as she is now. Vivienne can't bring herself to look up at Rory, and he moves, just a hair, to avoid touching her.

Vivienne rests her forehead against Hammond's shoulder. She focuses on taking deep breaths. *What am I going to do? What can I do?* She hadn't been prepared for today. She had been prepared for Date Day. She hurts all over and the drain on her magic sits heavily in her stomach. (She hopes it's her imagination that her neck hurts.) "I'll fix this, okay? Just give me a little time," Vivienne tells him in a voice hardly above a whisper. She just needs time to fix all of this. However she can.

"Yeah," Hammond croaks. He clears his throat, puts his hand on Vivienne's shoulder, and pushes her up. Vivienne is greatly surprised to find him grinning. "This only means I get to sleep in tomorrow since this guy can't drag me out of bed! So we'll be fine for a bit, okay? Don't kill yourself again trying to rush this."

Vivienne blinks at him, not quite able to articulate how much that reassurance means to her, even if she can still feel Rory's heavy presence behind her. Hammond doesn't know about *that*, yet, but she won't tell Rory not to tell him. They can both be mad at her, fine.

As long as she can still fix this.

Despite the awkward air (not that Mark seems to notice it), Vivienne manages to smile as she sees Hammond and Rory out. They insist on going home for the night, which she's grateful for, despite her worry. But they have to work out some of their stress on their own. *Right?* Vivienne just hopes she's not making another poor decision today.

Dana looks about as happy with the situation as Vivienne feels, but she doesn't press for answers right now.

"...Is tomorrow alright?" Dana asks, gaze downcast, and Vivienne's heart clenches. "I'd really like to talk about all of this stuff and sort of—unwind, I guess, but I get that tonight is... for sleeping. I'm fine with sleeping for about twenty hours."

"Yeah, uh, that seems to be the group plan. I'll definitely see you tomorrow." Vivienne can't look her in the eye, either, and instead she finds the vorpal sword on the carpet again. "Well, we'll have a lot to talk about, but if there's anything you need now—"

"Honestly, I'm just going to go home, try not to think about the later half of today, and then straight to bed. I'll probably even sleep in tomorrow." Dana lets out a humorless laugh. "For what it's worth, I don't regret getting into this, not if it helped. Even if I could live without all the stabbing and dismemberment. ...And apparently, so can you."

"We'll talk about it tomorrow," Vivienne firmly repeats. She can't even *think* about her mortality—or lack thereof—right now, much less try to explain it to someone who doesn't know the first thing about magic. "You'll be alright getting home?"

"I faced down a god of some sort, apparently, so I think I'll be fine."

Vivienne doesn't find that funny, but she nods, and waves goodbye at the door. Dana lingers for a moment, as if expecting something else, but Vivienne can't bring herself to touch her.

She risked her life because I failed. I died again because I failed. I can't touch her with this body. The z-word raises its ugly head again as Dana finally disappears from view.

"You have a pretty interesting thought process, Vivi," Mark remarks loudly once she's gone.

"Don't call me that," Vivienne growls on reflex. He should know better—only two people get to call her that.

Fiona points in the bedroom's direction, and with a high-pitched giggle, Mark follows Benji to bed. Weirdo.

Vivienne had expected him to be the most stressed, not to mention she'd expected to fight him to leave Brynja's side. But he hadn't argued it at all, had he? He doesn't (yet) seem as tired as the others and isn't even teasing Fiona for her slight expression of concern.

But that can be a problem for Tomorrow Vivienne. Or, better yet, not a problem at all, and just a result of an addled mind that can be slept off.

Vivienne sniffs at her clothes, then the air. That sour magic smell lingers, worsening her mood, and Vivienne can't help but cast a reproachful gaze in Brynja's direction. It's petty, but she can't help but think that a little of it is her fault. Her fault and Mark's. It is easier to blame others right now.

"I hope you were worth it," Vivienne mutters, before she goes to steal the bathtub.

· · • • • • • • · · ·

When Christine closes her eyes and focuses on breathing (that she doesn't need, but it's calming), she finally creates her list. She pictures it perfectly. Line paper, neatly cut into two columns, Pros and Cons of Isaac's Offered Spell.

Pros: she doesn't have to worry about becoming a (full?) demon, she can't fail in her luck spirit quest, and she and Emil will always be visible and tangible to one another.

Cons: she can't *win* in her luck spirit quest, Emil may get hurt, Emil is taking the brunt of a spell that is only to her advantage, and she will never know if good enough is *good enough*.

She will be safe.

But she will still not-sleep, and not-breathe, and hunger.

But she'll be hungry the further she gets toward becoming a luck spirit, won't she? Of course, it could get *worse*, and she particularly fears that. Bakeneko can eat humans. What if they become part of her diet? She may as well become a demon by that point.

Christine reopens her eyes to look down at her claws.

She can defend herself now. It had been *easy*. She is certain Kirara could teach her about using claws as self-defense. Maybe... Sam could help her, too. She keeps meaning to talk with him, but she is so scared of broaching the topic and how he may react, it leaves her paralyzed with her indecision.

Twice now they have bested that fox spirit. Maybe he will learn a lesson. Maybe other spirits won't see her as an easy target now. Once bitten, twice shy, right? Despite her revulsion at the claws she can't retract, Christine *is* glad for the security they offer. She feels safer than she has in *months*.

She can't rely on Kirara or Emil or Vivienne or anyone else forever. Perhaps she has already relied on others for too long.

I can't tie myself to Emil, Christine tells herself. She knows this. It would be unfair to him—he gets nothing out of it, except a roommate he can fight over blankets with. She can't ask him to literally bind his *life* just so she can stabilize herself.

But she is *terrified* of going further down this road. Violence has come too easily to her twice now. What if she must hunt? What if she has more dreams of *eating* Emil?

She needs some space. She needs time alone to herself.

Christine could laugh. She has been *alone* for so much time since her death, but always around others. First her brother, then only Sadie, then Kirara, then Emil, and now Vivienne and Rory and Sam can interact with her, too. But now, all of those options are *suffocating*.

"Hey, I'm back from school!" Emil calls as he kicks open the door. His hands are full of grocery bags. He grins when he sees her curled up on the couch. "Alright, so I was thinking cat stuff, and—no, I didn't get you *cat food*—but what about more meat and protein stuff? I've never actually cooked steak, but I splurged."

Christine's unbeating heart clenches with guilt. He is still trying to figure out a way for her to eat comfortably. Even with scratch cards, he cannot be making enough to support two people.

"You shouldn't have," she says, chewing her lip. "N-Not for me."

"It's okay to splurge once in a while, right?" he dismissively replies. "And I got things like bacon? Everyone likes bacon."

"How much did you spend?" she asks, floating through the couch and over his shoulder.

"What's it matter? I'm lucky enough to have hunted down a few forgotten sales, and you're worth it, Chris. I'm gonna help you figure out food things. And if worst comes to worst, oh no, I have all this delicious bacon and steak to eat *all* by myself!" he exclaims with fake horror.

She can't even muster a smile for it. She is too dependent on him. On others. She can't handle choosing Isaac's spell, and she can't handle the uncertain future *not* choosing it leaves.

"Hey, what's wrong?" Emil asks with a gentle hand on her shoulder. Even that makes her jump.

When she brushes him off, she accidentally catches his hand with a claw.

Emil isn't fazed; he inspects the tiny cut for a moment, then sticks it in his mouth. He doesn't appear to register pain or what she had just *done*.

This is the third time she has hurt someone else.

"I can't do this," Christine moans into her hands. She can't prick herself, but she *can* feel the hard press of nails against her face. "Emil—I'm sorry—I *can't*. I need to work on this on my own."

"Work on what? It's okay, I don't mind your weird eating schedule—"

"It isn't just about the food! It's about—these—" she thrusts out her hands, making him reel back, "—and this stupid collar the stupid fox wants, a-and Kirara never being *here* anymore, and you getting hurt because of me!"

"It's fine, it was just an accident!"

"I'm not taking the spell!" Christine declares, far more firmly than she means. She wraps her arms back around herself. She floats before him, curled into a ball.

"...Okay, that's fine. It was your decision, anyway," Emil replies after a beat.

"No! You said that too much—it was going to affect *both* of us! How can you say that about someone *using your life* like that?!"

"I wouldn't mind—"

Christine pushes him with the heel of her hand, only enough to make him back up. "You *would* mind! You'd come to resent me, and I'd come to resent you, because we're just *stuck* together! Kirara lumped us together for safety, but she's all but gone, a-and I'm... I'm...!"

She pauses, tears stinging her eyes, lip wobbling traitorously. She can't even be decisive without crying.

"I'm not going to stick around and hurt you or get hurt anymore. I need to figure out my *own* path forward," Christine forces past the lump in her throat.

Emil regards her with a wide-eyed, stunned expression. Somehow, that breaks her heart further, and she doesn't care right now to examine that. She lets out a weepy sigh with no real breath and forces the tension out of her shoulders.

"Goodbye, Emil. I've overstayed my welcome. Um, thanks for everything," she says, with an awkward pat on his shoulder, then sinks through the floor, leaving him.

· · · · · ● · · · · ·

Rory wishes he could brush Hammond's hair out of his eyes. The streetlights slant in through the blinds, painting his bed with tiger stripes, glinting off of his eyes when he looks up at Rory.

So they can't touch anymore. That's it, then.

"I can still see you," Hammond murmurs. He rolls onto his stomach, loose hair falling over his shoulders like water, but doesn't reach for Rory. Not anymore.

Rory has never felt so cold. "You almost died, too. In the car crash."

They've known that. They have also known that the spell was ending. It was always meant to be temporary; that's what Hayley had told them before tethering their lives together.

Of course they meant it to be temporary. She and Vivienne had been experimenting with how to bring him back. How to create a Door. For his stupid fucking sake.

He doesn't know how to tell Hammond.

Vivienne sure as hell doesn't deserve his secrecy, not after three goddamned years of her own, but he doesn't want to know how Hammond will react. Hammond had just lost the ability to touch the man he loves; should Rory pour salt on that wound? For once, he doesn't want to ruin something.

But he wants to ruin Vivienne and her fucking secrets.

"When Viv died," Rory starts, floating beside the bed like they're lying together, having years of practice at that much at least, "from the Dreamlands, I mean. She died for a hot minute. I possessed her to try to reboot her."

"Ah, shit. It must have worked, then?" Hammond murmurs.

"Think so. Didn't hurt things."

"How was it?"

"Saw a lot of her memories. Relived the crash, that was friggin' fun. But I also saw... when she and Hayley... I figured out what they were doing."

"Oh?" Hammond props himself up on one elbow, still sleep-lax, but as always, his attention is for Rory. It just hasn't felt so distant before.

"They were trying to create a Door."

Hammond stays quiet. Thinking. The pause stretches on like a torment, until finally he murmurs, "Did either of them say it was for you? Did you speak to Vivienne about this?"

"Judging from the guilty as hell reaction, she didn't *have* to say it. That's why Hayley's first spell was temporary."

"And how are you taking that?" Hammond asks neutrally.

Rory glares at him. "Me? What about *you*?"

"How does this concern me, Rory?"

"You gave up your life to be stuck with me! You agreed to unknown, dangerous magical shit just so you could—so *I* could—!" Fucking *hell*, now he's getting choked up with his own anger.

"We promised you wouldn't be alone," Hammond says. He puts his hand over Rory's and their fingers phase through each other. It makes Rory want to puke.

"I didn't want to ruin your life *and* hers," Rory croaks. He throws an arm over his eyes to hide his lack of tears. "You shouldn't have done that for me. They shouldn't have! I wasn't worth any of this pain—all this other fuckin' death, Hammond! How the fuck am I supposed to live with this now?! Oh, right, except I *can't* live! I'm stuck here in limbo!"

Hammond can't comfort him as he shakes with rage and grief, and Rory can't even cry to get the stupid catharsis afterward.

But as he calms, he realizes that it's not true.

With the spell gone, he *isn't* stuck here anymore. He's just a ghost again, now without the perks of a built-in bodyguard and cuddle buddy. Is this why Christine had always acted like a spooked deer?

Fear laps at him, rising, as he recalls the terror of his death. Being the bottom of the food chain, being new to the supernatural, being unable to talk to anyone except for Vivienne and Hammond in the hospital, being unable to *touch* anyone or anything. The ultimate isolation. He had always joked about being antisocial, but that had been torture.

Hammond and Vivienne will always be able to see him and any other ghosts. They'd nearly died, so that was the silver lining. Vivienne could still touch him from her own deadly mistake. That is its own brand of *unfair*, but he pushes it from his mind for now.

But now Rory was just another ghost. He wasn't special anymore.

What made him so fucking special in the first place? He never asked for any of them to throw their lives by the wayside for his sake.

He never asked for their fucking *promise*.

Hammond tries to lace their fingers together, but Rory tugs his hand away. He doesn't even want to *try*.

• • • • • • • • • •

"Hammond told me you could touch the vorpal sword without hurting yourself," Vivienne remarks as she slides into her seat.

"Hello to you, too," Dana replies, eyebrows raised at the smoothie already in her hand. "Why did you bring a drink from another restaurant?"

Vivienne sips at her drink for a long, thoughtful moment. Then, she says, "Pomegranate smoothie." Dana doesn't put it together, so Vivienne sighs, and taps the lid of the pink drink. "C'mon, Dana, I know you read enough to know what pomegranates are symbols for."

"Fertility?" Dana guesses with a straight face, and Vivienne snorts back a surprised laugh. The heavy mood lifts, just a little, and she can feel the tension ebb out of her shoulders. Dana gives her a smile and corrects, "Alright, so they're symbols for death and rebirth. *Symbols*."

"Symbols come from somewhere," Vivienne informs her, "and it's not like this is magical or anything. I've just found that eating and drinking certain foods helps me... I don't know, deal with things better. Less strain on my magic and fewer nightmares, things like that."

"I did wonder why you were always drinking smoothies at work. I thought you just had a very specific sweet tooth," she admits. "You can eat other foods, right?"

"My diet's still as unhealthily human as ever otherwise," Vivienne says with a small smile. Dana grins, and that banishes the rest of the heaviness.

The pair order a pizza to split—margherita, because Dana insists this is her favorite pizza place and Vivienne isn't picky—and Vivienne isn't sure where to begin for their Talk.

It's miraculously easy to get together for a not-date when there are emergency Talks to be had. She wishes they could get together under brighter circumstances.

Vivienne doesn't want to ruin the mood again, but there's really no way to ease into any of the topics she figures Dana will ask about. Truthfully, she doesn't want to be here *at all*. But Dana needs answers, and Vivienne promised to provide them.

It's the least she could do after the Dreamlands.

Outside of that?

Vivienne still likes Dana, a lot, but every time she thinks about a return to their teasing or attempts at dates, her stomach churns. She can't do that to her. Dana deserves someone who isn't a trouble magnet, who won't put her in dangerous situations, who is *still alive*.

Vivienne has enough on her plate without dating thrown into the mix, too. (She's had all night to find and memorize these reasons. Contrary to her exhaustion, she couldn't sleep, and spent most of the past sixteen hours tossing fitfully, trying to clean Mark's kitchen, or checking to see if he had any alcohol.)

So she'll do her duty and be Dana's teacher, but she won't let it be anything else. She's sure Dana won't mind; she can tell that yesterday freaked her out. Understandably.

"So, I brought a chart," Vivienne announces after their food arrives and Dana's already inhaled a slice. She digs in her messenger bag and Dana makes a questioning noise through her food. "A couple charts! For the timeline of things, and the hierarchy of spirits. I figured it'd be easier to talk about that way."

"You don't have to force yourself into anything," Dana says, frowning around her pizza, and the image is a little *too* endearing.

Vivienne triumphantly pulls out one of her old notebooks. It still had space in it, so she'd drawn up charts sometime around five in the morning. "What do you want to discuss first?"

"You," Dana says at once.

"We're, uh, still eating? I don't know how squeamish you are but—"

Dana rolls her eyes and finishes the slice. Vivienne still hasn't started hers. "Vivienne, I'm a big girl, promise. And I've been dying to know—oh my god, I'm so sorry."

Vivienne laughs, however, because Dana looks like she's just accidentally stepped on a kitten. "You'll have to try harder than that to offend me! I'm well aware of how colloquialisms work, and metaphors and sayings and all that jazz. I'm not technically dead, and even with Rory and other actual ghosts, they just shrug off things like that."

"So you're... alive. You came back from the dead," Dana haltingly prompts around another slice.

Vivienne figures she better stake a claim on their meal before she ends up with only a pomegranate smoothie for lunch. She grabs the pepper flakes and begins shaking it over her plate.

"I *am* alive," she says emphatically. That needs to be said, and thankfully she doesn't trip over the words. *I am alive*, she reminds herself. "I just... Maybe I'm not fully alive? Anymore? I average about forty heartbeats per minute, my body temp runs *way* lower than the average human, I require a ton more sleep than anyone else, and my magic reservoirs have been shot since then. But I still eat, and sleep, and breathe, and shit, and think, and all those other human things. Honestly, I don't know much past that myself."

Still shaking the shaker, she flips through the notebook with her free hand and arrives at Chart Number One. Dana has concern growing on her face at her pizza. "Is a side effect of your, um, condition a lack of taste buds?"

"I like spicy things, and I must assert my dominance on any and all social outings," Vivienne declares.

"Right. Fine. Take the lead, and I'll try not to pity your stomach."

Vivienne props the notebook against her drink and points with her fork. "Alright. Once upon a time, there was a very stupid necromancer named Vivienne. ...Okay, that's not gonna work," she sighs, then takes a bite of her pizza to stall. She's never actually *told* anyone about any of this; the only people who know were there at the time or psychic. "So, uh, three years and change ago, I was in a car accident. It was pretty bad. Ham and Rory were in it, too, and it hospitalized Ham and me. Rory died on the scene. So that's why Ham and I can see ghosts—you get that if you have a near-death experience."

Dana nods, eating more slowly, eyes remaining on her. Vivienne doesn't mind the focused attention. She picks at her food, nibbling at it between gestures to her chart. The first part of it shows a '3 YRS AGO' combined with a small list of 'car crash, binding, experiment'.

"Once Ham and I were out of the hospital—early, because we snuck in healers—and Rory actually admitted he was scared to leave us and pass on, a friend of mine, Hayley, helped me create a spell to bind them. You've seen Ham's tattoos?"

"Only yesterday."

"The one on his chest is the one I used to anchor the spell. Or part of it, since he's added more to it, but yeah, it's a magical tattoo. So Rory was safe from turning into a demon—"

"Wait, demon?.That happens?" Dana uneasily interrupts.

"I have a chart for that, too, but yeah. A demon is created when a human spirit tries to change itself over time, or when too much magic is used on one. They're... They *can* be nasty things, although usually they're bound to their summoners via contracts," Vivienne amends, thinking of Sam. She hasn't seen them lately, but all things considered, their situation could have turned out so much worse. "Anyway."

"Anyway," Dana allows.

"Rory was safe, and because we bound him to Ham, they were tangible to one another. Yesterday, they were upset because when he was injured, apparently it severed the spell, too. Or enough of it. The spell had a time limit, anyway, so maybe it was weakening. I don't know."

"And you'll fix it for them?"

"Yeah, I guess," she mutters and bites her lip, thinking, *Somehow.* Dana nods seriously. "A couple months after that, Hayley and I were messing around with more magic. We experimented a lot in college and after we graduated, we continued it. We—Yes?" Vivienne cuts off and blinks, because Dana raised her hand like a kid in class.

"Question, please. What did you go to college for? Was it a magic college?"

Vivienne cannot help but smile. Dana, while doing a surprising amount of interrupting, is doing a good job at keeping the (Vivienne's) mood light. "I wish. One of my professors was in Hayley's coven, but nah, I got a rather useless degree in psychology, minor in anthropology. I really wanted to learn about people, you know?"

"...Do magic colleges exist?" Dana asks after a beat.

Vivienne grins at that. Emil had asked the same thing, and she thinks Oliver had, too. She thinks *she* had, once upon a time.

"I think only a couple in the world, and no, they're not Hogwarts. As far as I know. I've never been to one so I can't tell you much about them, and while there is a whole magical-slash-supernatural underground world, mostly, it's still pretty well integrated with other worlds at large."

Dana groans and sets her head in her arms. At Vivienne's prodding, she just mutters, "Worlds. *Worlds.* Plural. Give me a moment, and don't you dare point out that we were in one yesterday."

"I wouldn't *dream* of it."

Dana levels a glare at her for her pun crimes. At least they can have this much levity between them.

Glare punishment enough, Dana sighs through her nose and pokes at another slice of pizza. "So, this... experiment. I notice I've never met this Hayley friend of yours."

"Yep! It all went to hell in a handbasket. Hayley died, and that was the first time I died. Sunshine was her cat, by the by, her familiar, so she was the friend that passed on. And he *was* yellow." Thank god she can finally get that off her chest. If nothing else comes from this, she can show Dana baby Sunshine pictures.

Vivienne rummages around in her bag and pulls out another book—not a notebook, but a photo album. (It is only partially brought out for Sunshine Picture Time.) She opens to the bookmarked page: her college years.

Dana's eyes land on a picture of Vivienne with her hair past her shoulders, most of it dyed soft grey, skin not so pale as she is now. Beside her is a striking woman with thick, ruby red hair actresses would die for. Hayley grins at the camera, green eyes crinkled, her obscene amount of freckles almost lost in the flush on her cheeks. Their arms are around each other's shoulders and Hayley is making a toast to the camera.

The next picture had been taken from the same party. Rory, squinting and fighting a smile, a little blurry from the movement of his laughter. His hair is up in a messy bun, and he'd been unshaven for days, grooming going out the window during finals. Half of Hammond can be seen on the couch beside him, one long arm reaching for his boyfriend.

"We were roommates in college, Rory and me. That's how we met. He knew nothing about magic until after he died. Ham... He has his own magic, but didn't really interact with the magical side of the city until we found out about each other's supernatural awareness," Vivienne says. "After we graduated, Hayley and I moved in. The apartment is still under her name."

"It's under the name of a, uh, dead woman? Doesn't someone notice?"

Vivienne gives her a grim look. "Dana... I spent two days in the morgue before I came back the first time. I am legally dead. My only bank account is under a fake identity bought from a fixer and a fairy queen. It's an easy way to get out of paying student loans, though!"

Dana, understandably, gapes at her. Processing, with equal parts confusion, fear, and concern. Vivienne can't ask anything more of her than to hear out some context.

"I've died... four times now, I guess. I don't know what it is, how I work, or when that's going to run out. If ever. I don't know what I *am* anymore. We ran enough tests on my memories and mental map that I know it's *me*, but... I know it's a lot, I-I'm glad you're not running out screaming—!" And fuck, *now* her eyes are stinging. Vivienne wipes her eyes with the back of her hand and buys time by cramming her super spicy pizza into her mouth.

"Vivienne," Dana gently says, and a guillotine could not sound more ominous. This is the part where they break up, even though they were never together, and even though there are *so many* bigger and worse things to worry about right now. The important thing is that Dana is alive and unhurt. Who cares if she's not going to be with Vivienne anymore?

Dana puts a hand over hers. Vivienne stares at her with watery eyes and cheeks stuffed round with pizza.

"Well, you know what they say, cold hands, warm heart," Dana says.

Vivienne laughs, surprised, and sprays the table and her not-date with pizza crumbs. Her face flames, tears trickle out her eyes, and she can't stop laughing because she might cry. She hurriedly chews and swallows while all but throwing napkins at Dana.

"This barely makes any sense. And the magic stuff isn't for me to figure out. What I *do* want to figure out is where we'll stand now. I still... I still really like you, Viv. Sure, you're a strange woman full of feminine mystique and apparently a tragic backstory, but you're still *you*. I don't see how you aren't still the Vivienne I met and came to care for. This is who you've been, for me."

Vivienne takes a greasy napkin to mop at her eyes. She looks like a raccoon from sleeping in yesterday's makeup, and this can't be making her look any better, but her heart feels full to bursting, regardless. Because Dana is still seeing *her*. She isn't seeing a zombie or a monster or an experiment.

"I can't promise not to freak out sometimes. I'm still freaked out about yesterday!" Dana admits with a half-wild laugh. "But it's *really* nice having a guide for this. If you say you're still you, then you are. I trust you."

Vivienne nods, finally swallowing her spicy concoction, tears still wetting her cheeks. She swipes them away quickly before retaking Dana's hand. "You can't know what those words mean to me," she admits. "It's still safer for you to keep your distance, but—"

"But that's a decision *I* get to make for myself," she firmly interrupts. "Like yesterday."

Vivienne nods again.

"And *I* have decided I'd like to plan another date with you, maybe with less crying and *definitely* with fewer emergencies. One day at a time. One date at a time, okay? If it gets overwhelming, I'll tell you. If I have questions, I'll *definitely* tell you. Believe me, you're not getting out of being my personal guide to all this just yet."

Vivienne nods again again, sniffling back the last of her tears, and manages a smile. "Together, then."

Dana smiles, soft and warm, then flusters unexpectedly. Her cheeks darken and she glances away, as if embarrassed, then mumbles, "Well, I meant to do this yesterday, before all of *that* happened, but better late than never, right?"

She leans across the table to kiss her.

Dana's lips are warm and a little greasy from pizza, and Vivienne can't be much better, but it's a damn good kiss. She smiles against her mouth until her cheeks ache. She would fight gods more often if it meant getting rewarded with a pretty girl's kiss afterward.

· · · · ● ● ● ● · ·

Vivienne stretches all four limbs at once, nearly smacking Natalie in the face, Sunshine wobbling on her stomach. He slits open an eye to glare his displeasure, but otherwise remains still.

Vivienne sets her head back onto Natalie's lap with a contented sound.

"So, your talk with Dana went well today?" she asks.

"Better than I could've hoped. I'm sure the freakout is still coming, and I'm not sold on *not* keeping her at a distance to keep her safer, but she's just *so* pretty and nice and I'm *so* whipped, Nat."

Natalie chuckles, low and soft, and runs her fingers through Vivienne's hair. Vivienne presses into her touch like a cat. "I'm glad it worked out for you two. Did you know, I believe I've seen a vision of a wedding?"

Vivienne's eyes fly open and her cheeks stain red. "What? *No*. Nat, you can't be mean to me right now, I'm fragile!"

"I am allowed one unit of teasing per week, as according to our friendship agreement. I also prefer to lighten the mood with happy thoughts. There is still work to be done. Have you heard anything from Mark today?"

"No, but Ramirez texted me. He's conscious and Brynja isn't. He's acting super peppy and absolutely ravenous, and she was pissed she had to go on a grocery run for him."

Natalie hums, thoughtful. She isn't yet sure what to make of the idea of Mark Ito, clairvoyant, in a realm like the Dreamlands. She hardly understands what the Dreamlands are or how they function, but psychics are delicate when it comes to other realms. Especially ones with so much mental stimuli.

But he survived. They all survived (in their own way). Natalie brushes more of Vivienne's bangs back, unconsciously lingering on the faint scar there.

"You're going to have to drink more of your potion," she reminds her, and Vivienne makes an *ick* face, nose scrunched. "But you did it. Even with your casualty."

"I wasn't there, so I can't be certain, but I doubt Yaehathal is completely dead. Maybe? It can't be that easy to kill a deity, no matter what bullshit Mark did. But at the very least, we stalled the hell out of its plans. If they forcefully broke a possession—that could've destroyed any chance it had at using Brynja like that again."

"That sounds like a sure victory. Even if it remains in some form, it cannot come back, not in the same way or with such ease," Natalie replies.

"So that leaves... others? Plural?"

"Others," Natalie echoes. She has seen too many visions of potential actions. A clear and present danger, isn't that the term? She needs to share them with Vivienne, but she's had too many cases of crying wolf in the past with futures that never came to be. Natalie needs further proof of who the other players could be before she mentions them to someone like Vivienne.

"You're thinking too hard," Vivienne says, poking her nose. Natalie blinks down at her. "I won't press you."

"Thank you, Vivienne. But it's alright. We can do it if we have each other. I've seen how," Natalie confides.

Vivienne grins, and Natalie returns it with her own smaller smile. Sunshine begins purring.

It is all okay, for the moment.

Supernatural Hunter Tip #2: If it sounds too good to be true, it is.

Connect With The Author

If you enjoyed the first entry in the Your Local Guides To The Supernatural series, consider giving it a review and telling your reader buddies! Every bit helps me get the next part out to you.
You can also connect with me on social media, with links to those plus my mailing list available on my website at www.bberrywrites.com.

ACKNOWLEDGMENTS

This book would not have been possible without the feedback I received during every step of this long journey. In particular, I would like to thank my beta readers and my sensitivity readers for allowing me to share the best possible version of this story, no matter how much of a brick the book is.

I would also like to thank everyone who has reviewed this book (and my others) online, and those who have enthusiastically foisted this upon their loved ones, and those who have requested it at their local libraries, as it helps tremendously in getting the word out and getting this book into the hands of more readers.

Thank you to everyone who's held my hand as I've screamed about writing.

CPSIA information can be obtained
at www.ICGtesting.com
Printed in the USA
LVHW111941070922
727695LV00003BA/544